CHHAAVA

Chhatrapati Sambhaji and His Fight for Swarajya

Maharashtra Government ‘Marathi Vangmaynirmiti Rajya Purskar’ (1980-81)

SHIVAJI SAWANT

CHHAAVA

Chhatrapati Sambhaji and His Fight for Swarajya

CHHAAVA / Fiction
by
SHIVAJI SAWANT

Translated from
Marathi to English by
KADAMBINI DHARAP

The Company Founder
SUNIL ANIL MEHTA

Publisher
Mehta Publishing House Pvt. Ltd.
1941, Sadashiv Peth,
Madiwale Colony, Pune 411030.
India

Printer
Manipal Technologies Limited, Manipal

Publishing Date
March, 2025

Cover Design Courtesy

Price
₹ 899

Layout
Falgun Graphics

P Book ISBN 9789357205634
E Book ISBN 9789357209526

E Books available on : amazonkindle Apple Books Google Play Books

This royal saga is
dedicated with
utmost reverence to
the sacred waters of
'Indrayani' and 'Bhima',
which witnessed
firsthand at Tulapur
how the Marathi
royal heart can,
if need be,
confront death—with
Time itself bearing
witness.

Bhandara Paradi

It was the Guru Dwadashi of 1972. On that glorious day, I had completed my morning ablutions and was performing puja, before commencing the writing of 'Chhaava'. I had recently visited Tuljapur with my family and taken the darshan of goddess Jagadamba. Hence, the form of Ashtabhuja (eight armed) Goddess Jagadamba gleamed before my closed eyes. While trying to grasp her all-embracing, universal essence, in my mind, I offered a symbolic flower to seek her blessings to embark on the story I was about to write. Just then, the loud chanting of Goddess Jagadamba's name echoed through the courtyard, merging with the resounding sambal drumbeats. A shiver ran down my spine! It had been three years since I came to live in this house in Kolhapur. Yet, not even once had a bhutya shown up at my door and sang the praises of the Goddess 'Ude ga Ambe, Ude'. But, of all days, he showed up today. I turned around and gazed at him for a while and invited him inside. I said, "Light up the Pota (a sacred torch) and sing as many sacred hymns of the Mother Goddess as you can." He asked my wife for some oil. Upon receiving it, he lit the Pota and started singing praises of the Goddess. The prayer room resonated with his divine singing for a long time. Before leaving, he placed Bhandara (sacred turmeric powder) and two cowries in my hands as the blessings from the Goddess.

To construct and frame the Shambhu saga, I traveled far and wide - from Salher-Mulher in Bagalana, Maharashtra to Shivoli in Goa, and visited numerous forts, historical places and museums related to the life of Shambhuraje. Only I know the countless pieces of historical texts I read to assess the Shiva-Shambhu era. After all, nothing haunts a writer like words do; especially while composing a historical tale. You don't even know when your mind gets tethered to the galloping hooves of history and loses track of time!

I've visited Raigad many times for this story. Nothing compares to the electrifying experience of walking across the entire fort in the eerie silence of night. At night Raigad whispers in a mysterious language that only the heart can comprehend.

Purandar - the birthplace of Sambhajiraje! Rajgad – where his childhood blossomed, and the most significant events in the life of Shivaji Maharaj took place! Raigad - the fort that crowned the father and son's legacy with glory! Aurangabad and Ahmednagar – the centers where Aurangzeb's major movements in the Deccan took place! Panhala – the fort that left indelible marks on Sambhajiraje's life, the Mandvi creek, Sajjangad, and Vadhu-Tulapur, where Sambhajiraje attained Shivaroop (his ultimate sacrifice). I visited many such grand and small places. What the ruins of those places whispered to me in a diving language unknown to me is beyond words.

Sambhaji – the protagonist of the story! The Controversial Hero! The one who drags anyone who tries to fathom him through turbulent tides. I remember the late Acharya Atre asking me after attending a function in Mumbai, "Shivajirao, are you going to portray Sambhaji as greater than Shivaji in your novel? " I humbly responded to him, "The title of my novel is' Chhaava, Acharya. Doesn't the name itself make it clear that his father was a lion? " While responding to him a thought lingered in my mind – The contemporary London durbar had referred to this 'Chhaava' of Maharashtra as a 'Warlike Prince'. Why then, was he presented to the Marathi people as an addictive, lecherous, reckless and temperamental king? However, one thought stirred me deeply - Sambhajiraje's biography should have been read by a great soul like Swami Vivekananda! He would have been able to give this son of Shivaji the justice he truly deserved. Had Sambhaji indeed been a depraved addict, he would have shattered in the moments of his final ordeal, because his punishment was brutal and inhumane in every sense. A true historical chronicle must be built on a foundation of factual historical references,

verified with an objective and impartial mind. When history falls silent, we should summon it with discretion. The customs, language, attire, and environment of that era must be revived with authenticity and vibrancy. The most complex of all are the historical characters, as delicate as the wings of butterflies. They need to be unfolded delicately and with caution.

That is why the Kanoji dialect of Kulesh in this story is distinct. Gagabhatta of Kashi Dharmpeeth speaks in a Sanskrit-laden tongue. Hambirrao, Yesaji, Kondaji, Mhaloji, Ganoji-Kanhoji etc. use the fiery Maval dialect. Shivajiraje-Sambhajiraje, the royal women, and ministers speak 'Daftari' (bureaucratic) language, a blend of Urdu, Persian, and Mawali as it must be used every day. Wise readers will easily realize this. A historical novel takes shape through a fusion of multiple elements. To ask how it happens is like asking a vine how a flower blooms!

For the past ten years, I have examined Sambhaji's life through every possible lens, and after filtering through every possible contrasting perspective I present this Shambhu-katha to the Marathi readers. As I present this intricate saga before the readers, I must put forth a couple of points I deeply felt as a writer - First of all, Sambhaji was not just a king. He was a poet at heart, a king who endured unfathomable trials, a warrior who faced a monstrous nemesis like Aurangzeb. He was a resilient force to be reckoned with. Yesubai, a woman of unique qualities – worthy of being called Jijabai's daughter, had come into his life as a companion. This radiant son of Shivaji was surrounded by gallant warriors such as Khandoji, Hambirrao, Nilopant, Yesaji Kanka, Harjiraje, Kondaji, Mhaloji, and Kulesh.

I have not penned this story with a motive to restore the tarnished reputation of the duo 'Kalusha kabji and Sambhaji' which has been depicted in the Marathi literature! The name 'Kulesh' in this story has been carefully chosen. It is derived from Kavi + Kul + Ish = 'Kavi Kulesh', meaning Lord of Poets, and not the derogatory name 'Kalusha Kabji'. Through this story, I have tried to capture a crucial period in the history of Maharashtra - from King Shivaji to Santaji-Dhanaji. Chhaava was published on Saturday, April 28, 1979, at Pratapgad, released by hon'ble Shri Yashwantrao Chavan. I'm forever indebted to him.

As this novel took shape, I was amazed by the love and encouragement I received from legends like late G.D. Madgulkar, Shiv-Shahir Babasaheb Purandare, G.N. Dandekar, Natvarya Chittaranjan Kolhatkar, and Dr. P.N.Kulkarni. I am grateful to them from the bottom of my heart.

With utmost devotion, I now place this story at the feet of Goddess Jagadamba, whose name inspired it, and this time I say, "Aai Raja Ude!" (Glory to the King!)

Date: September 1, 2000
Shivaji Sawant
Ganesh Chaturthi
Saka, 1922

Translator's Preface

It has been over 22 years since my father left this world, and yet his legacy continues to live on. It is truly incredible to witness the mark his works of art have left on the hearts of the people of Maharashtra and beyond.

When I see the young generation reading his novels Mrityunjaya, Yugandha and Chhaava, it fills my heart with genuine pride for my father's phenomenal writing style. I believe he was divinely gifted.

As a writer my father has presented the multifaceted personality of Chhatrapati Sambhaji Maharaj in this novel.

Chhatrapati Sambhaji Maharaj was a formidable warrior who combatted on five fronts – the British of Mumbai, the Siddis of Janjira, the Portuguese of Goa, the Mughal emperor Aurangzeb with his mammoth army and massive treasure. And the fifth front was that of his own greedy and treacherous kinsmen. Despite being a warrior, he had the tender heart of a poet and is renowned for his Sanskrit composition, 'Budhbhushanam'. His remarkable courage in the face of brutal, inhumane torture is beyond comparison.

On 14th February 2025, a Hindi movie produced by Maddock Films, directed by Lakshman Uttekar, with the same title was released worldwide and has taken the world by storm. The public has hailed the movie beyond our imagination and sales of the novel have escalated beyond expectations. Had he been here, my father would have certainly enjoyed the grand reception of the movie based on his novel. For me the success of the movie lies in the fact that it has raised awareness and garnered interest among the people in our history.

Translating this historical novel has been a great challenge linguistically and emotionally. It was agonizingly tough to translate the last part of the novel. Every time I opened the last few pages; it brought tears to my eyes. Finally, I feel relieved that this tale of bravery, courage, compassion, friendship and so much more, is reaching a wider audience. This is a tribute to the great warriors of freedom across the globe.

SriKrishnarpanmastu!

Chapter 1

At the crack of dawn, the priests performed the daily puja at the Kedareshwar temple. The glowing stone lamps, filled with Karanjel oil, illuminated the sanctum.

Usually by now the queens' apartments in the Balekilla on Fort Purandar would be bustling with the murmuring influx of palace maids, but the place was utterly quiet today. The door of the dimly lit maternity room was still closed.

An elderly, aristocratic lady was anxiously pacing back and forth in front of the closed door. She impatiently gazed at the door every now and then, imagining that it had been opened; then, staring at the floor in frustration, she kept mumbling to herself, 'Aai Jagadambe, Aai Jagadambe'.

She was Jijau Saheb! The queen of Shahajiraje Bhosale! The mother of Shriman Shivajiraje Bhosale - Aausaheb!

Since late last night Jijau had been pacing in front of that closed door. A few yards away from her, Netajirao Palkar, the custodian of Fort Purandar was squatting on a stone slab, his arms wrapped around his knees. He had been standing throughout the night. Finally, Aausaheb had told him to sit down in one place and relax. As the cool breeze caressed him, Netajirao dozed off before he knew it!

As the day progressed, the sun's rays, descending through the arches in the palace alighted leisurely on the carpet in the centre of the great hall. Jijau was quite concerned now.

All of a sudden, the door opened slightly with a creaking

sound. Aausaheb quickly rushed to the door.

The door opened fully and the baby's flattish first cry followed. Gojakka, the middle-aged, skilled midwife stood in the door. She bowed to Jijau, taking care to keep her soiled hands out of Jijau's sight.

A pure smile blossomed on her face like thick cream gathering on top of warmed milk. Before Jijau could ask her anything, she puckered her tattooed forehead and exclaimed excitedly. Her peasant words, full of affection sputtered like parched corn, "Let the cannons boom! It's a boy…a baby boy!! The baby and mother both are safe…"

"Aww, a baby boy…" Netajirao exclaimed and quickly hopped down from the stone slab. His slumber was long gone, but as he was aware of Jijabai's presence, he respectfully adjusted the turban over his head. He bowed down to Masaheb and said, "Aausaab, I will go and inform the cannoneers to fire the cannons on all bastions! Dhakale Dhani has arrived! Hail Goddess Jagadamba!"

Jijabai laughed heartily like a blooming Parijaat tree swaying in the breeze. Clever Netaji promptly picked up the cue and without showing his back to Aausaheb, he took a few steps back while making an obeisance to her. And then, Netajirao who otherwise went everywhere astride his horse, ran excitedly like a child to get hold of the cannoneers!

(observing his excitement.) Jijau smiled to herself She involuntarily touched the saffron border of her sari draped over her head and tidied it.

"A baby boy! Shivaba's son! First heir of the family!" Gojakka's ambrosial words left Jijau's forbearing mind in a euphoric state. She had become 'Thoralya aau', a grandmother now. Jijau's eyes filled with tears of satisfaction.

Jijau gathered herself together and asked Gojakka, "Who does the baby look like?"

"Just like Rajesaheb!"

"Rajesaheb!" Instantly, Shivajiraje's image flashed in front of Jijau's eyes. "Oh, who knows where he is travelling at this moment? Hmm – Jagadamb, Jagadamb!" Jijau let out a deep sigh.

Jijau thought, since Raje is not here, at least let me feast my eyes on his newborn son. She placed her foot on the stone threshold of the maternity room.

Inside, Saibai lay with the baby by her side on the wooden bedstead. The newborn baby's cry was giving even the stone walls goosebumps. Standing on the threshold, as she heard the baby wailing, Jijau quickly realised her impatience and smiled to herself. No one was expected to enter the maternity room until the fifth day after delivery! She realized her mistake and retracted her foot.

"Gojabai do the needful to ward off any ill effects of an evil eye on the newborn," she said, and bending down she placed a pouch of gold coins inside the threshold. With a peaceful gait and a contented heart, she began walking towards her private chamber. At the same time, over the four towering bastions on the four sides of Fort Purandar, the booming cannons were proclaiming to the blue skies of *Vaishakh*, "Saibaisaheb — the eldest queen of Shriman Shivajiraje Bhosale, has given birth to a son!"

Jijabai sat in the royal hall of Purandar, dictating official letters. Balkrishnapant Hanamante sat in front of her, noting down the content.

In the royal hall, the letters, sealed in red pouches, were ready for dispatch. A team of messengers was lined up by a wall of the royal hall. One by one each messenger approached Aausaheb, made an obeisance and left after collecting a pouch from Balkrishnapant. Those pouches were being dispatched to many places like Faltan, Talbeed, Sindakhed, Bengaluru and so on.

Jijabai held the last pouch in her hands. Vishwas – Nanaji

Musekhorekar, the most skilled informer in the Mavala region stood in front of her. Jijabai handed the last pouch to him and said, "Vishwasrau, deliver this pouch to Raje in person. Convey my message to him – "Come as soon as possible. Your son is born!"

"Ji." said Vishwasrao. He touched the pouch to his forehead, made an obeisance to Jijau and left the royal hall

Bahirji, the chief of intelligence, was galloping ahead of the cavalry to confirm that the road ahead was safe for Raje to travel. As they reached the outskirts of Supe, hawk-eyed Bahirji noticed a rider approaching him. Bahirji instantly held the palm of his right hand over his forehead and checked him out. As he saw the well-recognized Mavala saddle on the rider's horse, he sped up and quickly caught up with him.

When he saw Bahirji, Vishwas got off his horse.

"Any news Iswas?" Bahirji tried to dig deeper as Vishwas bowed to him.

"The most wonderful news, Naik! A son is born to our Dhani! I've got Masaheb's message from Purandar." Vishwas's shining eyes betrayed his excitement.

"O Ho, great! Our Raje's son! When did it happen? What great news!" said Bahirji and quickly leapt off his horse. He forgot that he was the chief of intelligence and Vishwas was an ordinary messenger; he stepped forward, patted Vishwas and embraced him with joy.

Heavy winds were blowing, indicating the onset of pre-monsoon showers. Bahirji promptly turned his horse around and dashed towards the cavalry squad in the back, with Vishwas, to present him to Raje.

As soon as the cavalry squad came in sight, both slowed their horses to a trot and approached Raje. They got off their horses and promptly made an obeisance to Raje.

Raje sat astride a gallant, brown Kummait stallion holding its reins with his lean, ring-studded fingers. He looked like a

'Rajayogi' with two horizontal stripes of sandalwood paste daubed across his forehead, a straight sharp nose, longish eyes; bright like the sun, tapering towards his temples, a radiant elongated face shaped like a conch shell, and the divine sixty-four-cowrie necklace of Goddess Bhavani resting on his chest, listening to his heartbeat.

As soon as Raje saw Bahirji, tender, golden words flew from his luscious, ruddy lips like pigeons taking flight, "Yes, what is it Naik? What brings you back in such a hurry? Is there any problem?" His right eyebrow curved into an arch.

"No, Dhani. Iswas has brought Masaheb's message from Purandar. It's very joyous news. Ranisaheb delivered a baby boy! Dhakale Dhani arrived last Thursday!"

"Ohh…! Jagadamb, Jagadamb!" For a moment the stripes of sandalwood paste on Raje's forehead creased with the memory of Saibai's dusky face. Unknowingly, his lean fingers ran over the cowrie necklace on his chest. Instantly, Raje pressed his palm on the saddle and dismounted. He quietly approached Vishwas; gave a gentle pat on his shoulder, quickly removed the golden bracelet from his left hand and handed it to Vishwas.

The leaders of the cavalry squad that followed – Manakoji, Murarbaji, Yesaji, Tanhaji — had already dismounted. The soldiers in their squad were asking them, 'What happened? What news?'. The news spread among the squad instantly like a flash of lightning illuminating an entire region. Hearing it a Mavala soldier spontaneously gave out a joyous cry, rising his head high – "Jai Bhavani! Har Har Mahadeo!" The entire squad joined him with excitement.

Raje glanced once at his gallant Mavala soldiers with a smile. He touched the pouch that Vishwas had delivered to his forehead and handed it to Nilopant Bahulkar standing next to him.

Nilopant began reading Jijabai's message, "Last Thursday, on the twelfth day of the bright fortnight of Jyeshtha, my eldest daughter-in-law delivered a son. By the grace of Goddess

Jagadamba, I became 'Thoralya aau'."

Raje's heart got drenched by those words. The fatigue of his arduous journey evaporated.

Raje left for Purandar as per Aausaheb's instruction. En route to Purandar he camped at the Lal Mahal in Pune, took the darshan of Shri Ganesh in the downtown and resumed his journey to Purandar.

Purandar came in sight. Netaji, custodian of the fort, had arrived at the foothills to receive Raje. Raje accepted his obeisance and sat in the palanquin. The palanquin-bearers picked it up on their shoulders while uttering, 'Jai Bhavani' and began climbing the fort.

As the palanquin passed through the entrance of the Balekilla, the sound of beating kettle drums echoed to announce Raje's arrival and directly reached the queens' apartments. The palanquin-bearers set the palanquin down. Raje climbed the steps of the Balekilla. He turned around and cast a watchful glance over Fort Purandar spreading the rugged hands of its ramparts. Then he started walking briskly, directly towards the queen's apartments, while graciously accepting obeisance from the people.

He removed his Jamadar sword tied around his waist and handed it to the guard standing at the door of the queens' apartments. He removed his mojaris near the threshold and stepped into the room lit up with gently burning lamps. As he saw Aausaheb standing next to Saibai's bedstead with a smile on her face, he promptly bowed down and made an obeisance. Jijau came forward with a smile on her face. Raje touched her feet with his right hand and touched it to his forehead. Jijabai handed him a pouch of gold coins.

"I wondered whether you would even remember the naming ceremony of the newborn, occupied as you were with military campaigns!" Jijabai said and smilingly she pulled Raje up. She approached Saibai's bedstead quietly and gently called out to her. Saibai opened her sleepy eyes. When she saw Jijabai, she tried to get up from her bed to offer her respects. "It's okay. Don't worry!" Jijabai comforted her and while picking up the frisky newborn wrapped in a blanket, and said to Saibai, "Your husband has arrived. Stay awake!"

Raje waved the pouch of gold coins around the baby's face to ward off any ill effects on him, and put it on a platter. Jijabai smiled and handed the baby to Raje. Raje leaned forward to pick up the baby and while holding him close to his chest, unwittingly he glanced at the bed …their eyes met momentarily, silently speaking with each other.

As Raje looked at the frisky newborn, his expression changed instantly. His tapering eyes that breathed fire while fiercely attacking his enemies, now started showering love on the tender newborn in his hands. He was captivated while gazing into the baby's bright, beady eyes. Saibai, and Jijabai were looking at Raje affectionately.

Inadvertently, Jijabai glanced at the entrance of the room. Raje's close friends stood cramped outside, eagerly waiting to see the newborn. As they saw Jijabai looking at them, all of them made an obeisance. They were all loyal, faithful friends of Raje including Manakoji, Subhanaji, Sambhaji Kavaji, Yesaji, Tanhaji and Noorkhan Beg. All of them just wanted to take a look at their 'Dhakale Dhani'. With that wish they had all gathered outside the room.

Jijabai turned her eyes to Raje and smilingly said, "The firstborn son is indeed very special, isn't it Raje?"

"Umm, what do you mean Masaheb? I don't get what you are implying…" Raje exclaimed, coming out of his trance.

"I meant that all your loyal friends who accompany you on your missions are still waiting at the door! They also wish to see Balraje!" Raje laughed heartily at Jijau's words. He handed the baby to Jijabai, turned around and signalled all his friends to come inside. Everyone entered the room.

After taking a look at Balraje everybody left. Jijabai had already left for her apartment to give some privacy to Raje and Saibai so they could chat openly.

Raje lay the baby down on the bed by Saibai's side and sat on the corner of the bedstead. Neither of them could break the ice. Just then, a maid entered the chamber holding an iron dhuni pot. In it Sizzling ajwain seeds were spread over live embers. She got startled to see Raje sitting in the room. Befuddled, she was about to go back, when Raje gestured her to come in.

She entered the room, hurriedly walked along the wall and pushed the dhuni pot under Saibai's bed. She promptly tidied the border of her sari over her head and left the room immediately. Raje and Saibai sniffed the pungent-sweet smell of ajwain seeds sizzling in the dhuni pot. While inhaling that scent their eyes met. Both smiled gently! Their eyes spoke abundantly in that moment.

"How's your health?" asked Raje.

Saibai didn't say anything; just closed her eyes and smiled. The baby inhaled the pungent smell of the ajwain seeds and started fidgeting.

"I should leave now," said Raje; pressed the baby's hands in his for a moment and started walking towards the door.

While looking at his back, Saibai's serene eyes were captivated by the strands of pearls studded on his Jiretop, swinging elegantly. Along with them, her mind was also fluttering like a bird. As if it was telling Raje – 'We have been blessed with a son after three daughters. After feasting your eyes upon him, you look so contented!'

From Saibai's chamber, Raje directly went to Jijabai's chamber. Jijabai gestured Raje to sit by her side and asked him, "Raje, did you get any spare time to find a suitable name for your son?"

Raje kept standing and answered respectfully, "No Masaheb, only one thing that you said in the letter kept coming to mind."

"What?"

"Your words – I have become 'Thoralya aau'!"

"I see that you are entrusting me with the responsibility of finding a good name for the baby. Aren't you? I have already decided on one. But still, the first son is indeed very special, isn't it Raje?" Jijabai repeated the question she had asked earlier. But this time that question left Raje completely baffled. What should I say? What should I do?

"Umm, what is it Masaheb? Did I make a mistake…?" Raje hesitated.

"Not a big mistake – but after climbing the fort you came directly to the queen's chamber, even without washing your feet before entering! How come?" Jijau asked smilingly. At those words, Raje's eyelashes fluttered momentarily. The next moment Raje made an obeisance to her and turned back. While looking at his back, Aausaheb's heart was telling her – 'He goes on so many missions, has fathered a son, but he is still a child at heart! And he should always remain so! What more could a mother ask for in her son!' Jijabai smiled to herself. Meanwhile, Raje was pouring water on his feet from a small pot placed outside the chamber.

The eighth day of the dark fortnight of Jyeshtha broke out on the eastern horizon. The saffron Jaripataka pennant was fluttering in the early morning wind against the vast skies.

Royal gifts kept arriving at the fort to the beats of tabors and lezim. The ladies of kith and kin who had received invitations, had already arrived at the fort. On the fifth day of the baby's birth, the palanquins of Raje's queens had landed on the fort. Soyarabai, Putalabai, Gunavantabai, Sakawarbai, Sagunabai, Lakshmibai, and Kashibai, the seven queens of Raje had already bathed and were clad in rich silk saris.

Saibai's chamber was glowing in the light of the burning lamps. Fragrant flower garlands enhanced the light of the lamps!

This was the day of the baby's naming ceremony!

Prabhakarbhat Rajopadhye placed a small time-measuring vessel in a big round metal pot to capture the exact mahurat. In Saibai's chamber, a few married women drew Rangoli designs around the baby's cradle decked with flower garlands. Five lamps made of wheat dough were lit and placed by the Rangoli designs.

Saibai wore a rich, brocaded sari. She held the baby dressed in a golden-bordered garment, wrapped in a hooded cloak bedecked with golden flowers, and sat on a sandalwood seat. Attractive Rangoli designs were drawn around the seat. With contented eyes, Jijabai beheld her daughter-in-law sitting on the east-facing seat, holding her son in her arms.

Five suvasinis of kith and kin like Soyarabai, Putalabai, Kashibai and others approached Saibai. They began performing her Aukshan by waving a platter of lighted lamps around her dusky face. Her forehead was adorned with kumkum. The women were offering a piece of bordered cloth and a coconut in the lap of her sari, and she barely got time to empty it, before accepting the next gift. The chamber was overflowing with gifts for the newborn baby and the mother.

Prabhakarbhat sent a message that the mahurat was approaching. The excitement in the palace increased. Putalabai and Soyarabai stood on either side of the cradle. A stoneroller 'Gopa' wrapped in baby clothes was placed on a platter near the cradle. Putalabai smiled demurely, picked up the 'Gopa' and handed it to Soyarabai three times over the cradle between them. Then she placed it back on the platter.

"What should we name the baby?" An elderly woman asked.

"Name him Sambhaji Raje! In the memory of his uncle!" Jijabai's eyes were moist at the memory of her eldest son while announcing the baby's name.

Putalabai gently picked up the baby from Saibai's lap, handed him to Soyarabai on the other side of the cradle three times and gave her a cheerful smile.

Putalabai carefully placed the baby from the rich bedspread

in the cradle and whispered his name – "Shambhooji!"— in his tiny ears. Then she cheerfully received the loving gentle pats of Kashibai and Gunawantabai on her back for enjoying such a sweet privilege. The gathered women began singing baby songs for Shambhoo. The time-indicating vessel sank in the big pot.

The thundering cannons fired by Netaji on the four bastion walls of Purandar announced the news to the skies overhead eagerly awaiting the rain– "The naming ceremony of the scion of the majestic and graceful, virtuous Shriman Shivajiraje Bhosale, born in the Kshatriya clan, has officially taken place! He has been named Sambhaji Raje!"

Jijabai sat eagerly on a carpet spread in the centre of the private chamber, leaning on a bolster. Shivaji Raje sat on her right, reclining on another bolster. Close friends like Manakoji, Tanhaji, Gomajibaba, Netajirao, Balkrishnapant and Prabhakarbhat sat on another carpet spread along a wall.

At the centre of the chamber, astrologer Harbhat from Saswad sat on a grass mat facing Jijabai. His eyes were fixed on the almanac placed on the wooden bookrest in front of him.

He picked up the quill from the stand in front of him. He dipped it in the ink bottle, prayed silently, to the family deity and quickly drew the horoscope in the notebook in his hand. All planets took their respective places.

"Yes Shastri, please fulfil everyone's wish to hear what's written in Balraje's horoscope." Jijabai's curious eyes were riveted on the horoscope that Harbhat had drawn.

"Ji! Aausaheb should pray to Goddess Jagadamba and listen to the horoscope." Harbhat began reading the horoscope.

"This baby boy is like the bright Sun of Vaishakh. Rudra himself has taken birth in his form! Just as Rudra lives in the Himalayas, he will also live in sky-high forts. He will carry the family legacy forward. He will fight ferociously just like Rudra. He will also be as gullible, hot-headed and candid as Rudra. Just like Rudra, he will have no fear of death! And …" Harbhat hesitated for a moment. He needlessly adjusted his shawl.

"What is it, Shastri? Please feel free." Jijabai sensed his hesitation.

"Forgive me, but it has been stated in the Puranas that Rudra was betrayed by his own people. This horoscope shows the same possibility!" Harbhat's words left Raje and everyone solemn.

"Oh, is that so? Even I was betrayed by my own people. Wasn't I?" Jijabai smiled and defused the stress.

Reassured, Harbhat rolled up the horoscope and put it in a pouch. He instructed Prabhakarbhat Rajopadhye to place it in front of the family deity and offer flowers and haldi-kumkum on it. He made an obeisance to Raje and Jijabai and left the chamber after accepting the pouch of gold coins that Jijabai offered him for his services. The meeting was over. Raje came to his private chamber. He could vaguely hear the distant sounds of ringing bells and cymbals being played for the evening arti near the tomb of Sopandeo in Saswad. His eyes fell upon the crystal Shivlinga placed on a platter on a wooden stool. He always carried it with him while travelling. He went near the Shivlinga, picked up some Bael leaves from the bamboo basket nearby, and offered them on top of it. He joined his palms in prayer and closed his eyes. The holy and tranquil Shivlinga stood in front of his closed eyes. Harbhat's, words echoed in his ears – "This horoscope depicts the same fate of betrayal from his own people that Rudra had to face during the Puranic times!" For a moment, Raje went into a trance. "You are born with all the virtues of Rudra – I hope you are also born with Rudra's courage, that gave him strength to digest any kind of poison! Jagadamb, Jagadamb!" He muttered and opened his eyes. His mind was at peace.

A maid informed Saibai that Putalabai was coming to visit her. She kept glancing at the entrance of her chamber frequently, with her weary eyes. The baby was craving for his mother's milk and was fidgeting in her lap. The moment Saibai took the baby to her bosom, he stopped fidgeting. This delivery had proved critical for Saibai's health. She had spells of dizziness while getting up from her bed, and cramps in her legs while walking. She resolutely put up with the stress of the naming ceremony so as to not spoil the joyous day for her baby boy.

Putalabai entered the chamber chatting with someone. Sakhoo, Ranoo and Amba, Saibai's three daughters accompanied her. Amongst them Sakhoobai, the eldest, was quite mature.

"Thoralya bai, how are you keeping now?" Putalabai approached the bed and asked Saibai with affection.

"Bai, nowadays I am getting bored of lying in the bed and staring at the ceiling. I would like to take a small walk, but my legs can't keep up." Putalabai was alarmed to see the dark circles under Saibai's eyes. She didn't know what to say. She quietly walked towards the wall and closed the window, from which the gusty wind was forcing its way onto Saibai's bed. The fluttering flames of the lamps steadied.

"Aau, can I hold the baby?" asked Sakhoobai.

"Hmm, sure you can." Saibai said and turning on her left she tried to sit up to pick up the baby. Putalabai promptly moved forward, picked up the baby from the bed and gently handed him to Sakhoobai. Then she assisted Saibai to lie down.

Sakhoobai held the baby and sat on the carpet by the bed. Ranoo and Amba wide-eyed, caressed the baby's cheeks. The three sisters were lost, watching their baby brother. The baby was watching the flames of the burning lamps, flailing his tiny arms and legs in Sakhoobai's lap. Looking at the four of them, Saibai was lost in thoughts of Raje and Putalabai was delighted to watch the joyous moment that they all shared.

Raje sat in the royal hall leaning against a decorative bolster. "Moropant has arrived from Pratapgad, Dhani. With your permission, he would like to present himself." Netaji delivered the news to him.

"Bring him in." Raje gave his consent.

Moropant entered the royal hall and made an obeisance. He was tall, like a banana leaf. His complexion and countenance were just as pleasant.

"Pant, I am eagerly awaiting the news of the completion of the ramparts around Pratapgad."

"Yes Maharaj, it is almost finished. Some work is pending due to shortage of funds, but that's nothing to worry about. I have come in person to deliver special news to you."

"What news, Pant?" Raje raised his eyebrows.

"Maharaj, something very auspicious happened during the construction of the ramparts. The labourers found a self-manifested Shivlinga while building the ramparts." Moropant's face lit up while delivering the news.

"Jagadamb! What a great coincidence, Pant. We recently named our son 'Shambhoo' and at the same time a self-manifested Shivlinga showed up during the construction of the fort! Let's see how auspicious Pratapgad proves to be for us in our great mission! Please have some food. I will travel to Pratapgad with you, to see the Shivlinga myself!"

Raje visited the Purandareshwar temple. He sent a message to Saibai that he was coming to visit her. He was going to leave Purandar today and travel to Pratapgad. That news had left Saibai nervous. For no reason, her hand kept caressing the baby again and again.

Saibai was lost in thought. "I am going to leave the fort today." Raje's words shook her out of her trance. She saw Raje standing in front of her and even in her disquietude, she thought, 'He is like the wild wind; he comes and goes without any intimation'. She inhaled the pungent smoke from the dhuni pot that a maid had kept under the bed and started coughing hard.

"Take care of yourself. The wind on this fort is quite strong and it will get turbulent during the monsoon. Don't go into the open without any reason. Take good care of Balraje. The astrologer says he is Rudra incarnate! It is indeed a very tough task to take care of Rudra!" Raje leaned forward and picked up Shambhoobal from Saibai's side. He fixed his eyes on the baby's face, smiled slightly and kissed the baby's forehead. He closed his eyes for a moment. With great effort Saibai suppressed the bouts of coughing and watched the contented face of Shivaji Raje gazing at Balraje. Her dusky face had lit up with joy.

Raje opened his eyes and put Balraje by Saibai's side. Saibai enveloped Balraje in her arms; the jingling bangles on her wrists brushed against Raje's lean fingers. Many melodious tunes resonated in their hearts.

"May I take your leave now?" Raje asked and started leaving the chamber. Saibai couldn't see anything at all. Was it due to the dense veil of smoke in the room, or due to the tears in her eyes induced by the pungent smoke? She couldn't tell…

After consuming the curds that Jijabai had put on his palm, Raje descended Fort Purandar with Moropant, Manakoji, Tanhaji, and Noor Khan.

Soon after Raje left for Pratapgad, his queens' retinue left for Rajgad. As a new mother, Saibai was stuck at Fort Purandar throughout the monsoon. She could not be taken anywhere for at least for three months. Only Putalabai stayed behind in Fort Purandar to keep her company.

Though Fort Kondhana, which was dear to him, had become a part of Swaraj, another soft spot for Raje was falling apart. On Fort Purandar, Saibai's health was on the decline. Jijabai summoned maven physician Gangadhar Vaidya from Mahad. For the last many days, he had been treating her with a discerning eye using his medical expertise. He had exhausted his medical resources, administering many herb extracts, various decoctions, pills, and poultices. He had already diagnosed her malady. He stood in Jijabai's private chamber, nervously looking at the floor, fiddling with assorted herbs.

"Vaidyabuva, my daughter-in-law is not improving at all,

and you are not telling me anything about her condition. Why so? I am losing hope now." Jijabai revealed her concern.

"Aausaheb, I have tried everything possible, but the herb extracts, decoctions, pills, poultices…nothing has worked. Ranisaheb gets gooseflesh all over her body at the slightest touch of breeze. With all the doors and windows closed her throat gets parched. Her dusky face is losing its lustre. I think these are the symptoms of…" The physician was hesitant to declare his verdict.

"Symptoms of what… Vaidyabuva?" Jijabai choked.

"Aausaheb, these are the symptoms of…postpartum consumption!" His voice cracked, and his neck drooped further. He unwittingly fiddled with the herbs.

"Postpartum consumption! Jijabai mumbled to herself in a daze as if she had been struck by lightning. Only two faces lingered in front of her still eyes, – the first was that of Raje, who had left his family behind and was travelling throughout the region, facing death constantly… and the other was that of Balraje who only knew to cry whenever he felt hungry and had no idea of what life or death meant! Outside, the ancient Fort Purandar was still engrossed in the game of light and rain of Shravana.

It now became necessary to transfer Saibai from Fort Purandar. Saibai's postpartum consumption left Balraje bereft of his mother's milk. Jijabai had desperately managed to stop his wailing by feeding him milk substitutes. She was awaiting the end of the monsoon to find a better option. Raje had already sent a message summoning his family over to Rajgad. On an auspicious day, Jijabai left Fort Purandar with Saibai and Putalabai. Their palanquins started the journey towards Rajgad. The palanquin-bearers carried Balraje on their shoulders and started tramping the ground! Shambhoobal left for Rajgad.

Rajgad came into sight. Raje himself had descended the fort and was present in person to receive his queens. He was accompanied by Shamrao Ranzekar, Vasudeopant Hanamante, Prataprao Silimkar and Sidoji Thopate.

Raje approached Aausaheb and made an obeisance. He held her hand and helped her to step out of the palanquin. Saibai had already stepped out of the palanquin at the rear, with the baby in her arms. Raje was appalled to see Saibai's emaciated frame and the loose bangles sliding down her arms.

"Let the queens' palanquins go ahead to Padmavati machi. I will walk with you, Raje. I want to speak to you in private." Jijabai said. Saibai and Putalabai sat in their palanquins again. Their palanquins went towards the fort. Raje walked behind Jijabai. She kept talking, Raje only listened quietly!

Jijabai sat in the private chamber on Rajgad. All the queens of Raje except Saibai stood in front of her.

After enquiring about the general affairs of Rajgad, Jijabai shared her concern with all.

"Alas, Thoralya soonbai is suffering from a terminal illness. She had to stop nursing Balraje. How can we solve this problem of providing milk for Shambhoobal?" Jijau spoke calmly. All queens stood still, silently gazing at the floor. A silence even sharper than Jijau's calm voice!

"Dhakalya soonbai, what do you suggest?" Jijabai asked Soyarabai, settling her gaze on her scarlet sari.

"What can I say? Who can solve problems the way Aausaheb does?" Soyarabai adjusted the border of her sari. The brocade design on her sari sparkled brightly.

"Indeed, I will certainly do that but just wanted to check if you have any ideas." Jijabai was as calm as before.

Only Putalabai looked up once. She possibly wanted to say something, but as her eyes fell upon the black soot on the lamp in front of her, she kept quiet and continued staring helplessly at the floor! A few moments passed by in utter silence.

"You may all leave now!" Jijabai dismissed all of them.

"Putalabai, send Raje to my chamber, and make sure to send

a coarse blanket to Saibai's room." Jijabai said looking at Putalabai who had turned around to leave the chamber.

"Ji!" said Putalabai, snapping out of her trance and following the other queens leaving the chamber.

After receiving Jijabai's message, Raje came to visit her.

"Come Raje, I have decided something for Balraje and I want to discuss it with you." Jijabai spoke to Raje decisively.

"As you wish Aausaheb."

"I think we should find a 'wet-nurse' for Shambhoobal."

"Ji!" Raje looked up startled, with eyes full of pain.

"Are you feeling hurt? There's no other way." Jijabai tried to comfort him.

"Masaheb knows better, but..." Raje wanted to say something.

"Tomorrow I am going to send for Dharau of the Gaade family from the hamlet of Kapoorhol."

"Ji!" Raje said and took a few steps back while making an obeisance. As he was leaving the chamber, a voice drenched in affection called him. It made him stop at the threshold.

"Raje...! You are leaving without saying what you wanted to say. I know it. Listen to me carefully. Unfortunately, none of your queens showed the willingness to be the wet-nurse for Shambhoobal. But Raje, one can't hide such pain in one's heart. I am your mother after all."

Raje couldn't bring himself to face Jijau. With a heavy heart, he stepped over the threshold.

The entire basin of Gunjanmaval had blossomed with lush green meadows. The gusts of wild winds produced gentle waves on the fresh, blooming grass blades. The lush green waves gradually merged at the foothills of the steep hills nearby.

While galloping through the surface of River Gunjavani, Zunjarrao Maral's horse left a trail of white foam. He was riding towards Kapoorhol to deliver Aausaheb's message.

Zunjaraba passed by Nasarapur and soon entered Kapoorhol.

Approaching the Gaade house built of stone, he dismounted, patted his horse and secured it to a tree. He wiped the trickles of sweat on his forehead. Then standing at the big gate of the huge house, he called in an affectionate Mavala style– "Dharakka ho ssss"

His call startled the goat kids secured near the veranda; they hurriedly tried to stand up tapping their hooves on the floor. The hens and roosters got spooked. Their din announced the arrival of the guest to Dharau who was occupied in kneading dough in the kitchen to make millet rotis. She dipped her tattooed hands in a pot of water and wiping them on the edge of her sari, approached the gate.

She wrinkled her forehead and asked, "Who is calling? Zunjaraba, is that you? And why are you standing outside? Come in."

"No, got no time to waste. I've come from Rajgad with an invitation from Aausaheb." Zunjaraba informed Dharau.

"But everyone's out in the field!"

"The invitation is only for you and nobody else!"

"For me? You must be mistaken. My sons serve in the king's army; it must be for 'em."

"Do you think I've gone deaf or what? Aausaheb herself said to bring you with me." Zunjaraba stamped his feet on the stone threshold to remove the dust gathered on his footwear.

"Really …" Dharau exclaimed and quickly went inside. She sent a neighbour's kid from her backyard to the field. Then she bundled as many of her clothes as she could in a big sheet.

Dharau's two brawny sons – Rayaji and Antoji – came back from the fields. Their mother shared the whole story with them. They both wondered why their mother might have got this invitation. Leaving the home in the care of their wives, they secured their shields on their backs and got ready to travel. After having some jaggery and water Zunjaraba felt refreshed. He untied his horse and started walking. Dharau followed him in her squeaking sandals, barely holding the slipping bundle of clothes under her arms. Rayaji and Antoji walked on either side of her. Dharau Gaade left for Rajgad.

Jijabai received the news of Dharau's arrival in Rajgad. She summoned her to her private chamber. Dharau leaned forward, touched Jijabai's feet three times and made an obeisance.

"Dharabai, I want to entrust you with a big responsibility. You are loyal at heart, and your sons are serving in Raje's army. That is why I considered your name for this responsibility."

"Your wish is my command. I am your humble servant." Said Dharau respectfully.

"No! Dharau, now you will become the 'wet-nurse' for Balraje. I would like you to nurse Shambhoobal, Shivaji Raje's son. What do you say?"

Dharau's innocent eyes got misty in memory of her six-month-old baby girl who had died recently. She couldn't even believe her ears. How could she?

"My milk, for Raje's son? I am just a peasant woman, are you making fun of a poor woman…?" said Dharau earnestly.

"I would never make fun of any person who is loyal at heart. My ears are eagerly awaiting to hear you say 'yes'."

"Ji!" Dharau nodded in affirmation.

Jijabai offered Dharau a piece of cloth and a coconut. She took her to Saibai's chamber and said to comfort her,

"Soonbai, this is Dharabai. From today onwards, Balraje will have no shortage of milk. Her milk and your vigilance will nourish his growth!"

Saibai picked up the baby from her lap with her emaciated, shaking hands. As she handed him to Dharau, she couldn't help but say, "From today onwards you are his mother. I am just the namesake." Her eyes welled up with tears.

"No Ranisaab, it's not so. Please don't cry. The Lord who creates the skies also gives the birds wings to fly. This heir of Raje is safe under my care. I will make sure that he is well taken care of!" Dharau spoke with pure affection.

Jijabai was not in the chamber to hear their conversation. The king had taken a vow in front of Lord Shabhoomahadeo to build a welfare state for his people and his budding scion was under the care of a peasant woman. Dharau had indeed become the 'wet-nurse' for Shambhoobal. Goddess Jagadamba had brought them together.

Dharau's milk proved very nourishing for Shambhoobal. He was growing chubby now. The feeling that the king's son was drinking her milk was so overwhelming for Dharau that at times milk flowing from her bosom wouldn't stop even after the baby was full. At such times, Dharau would sop up the extra milk in a piece of cloth without letting a single drop fall. Then she would hasten to Saibai's hammam khana and wash that cloth thoroughly under running water. One-time Saibai saw her hustle and asked her, "Dharabai, why do you hustle to the hammam khana?"

"Sarkar, ants should not touch a mother's milk! Otherwise, the flow lessens!" Dharau replied with a big smile.

Hearing her reply, Saibai smiled to herself dismally. She wanted to tell her 'Dharabai, a mother's milk can lessen even without an ant touching it!'... but she remained silent.

But Shambhooraje had no idea of what was going on around him; Dharau had dressed him up in a peasant-style hooded cloak, bracelets in his tiny hands and copper anklets around his tiny ankles. She had put a talisman around his neck and tied an amulet around his upper arm. Her pure heart naively wished 'No sinner's evil eye should ever fall on this growing son of the king!'

As the chilly weather of Rajgad became unbearable for Saibai, Jijabai brought her to the palace of Shivapattan located at the foothills of the fort and she herself left for Pratapgad to visit the temple of the self-manifested Shivalinga.

Shivajiraje, who had been proving to be a menace for Adil Shahi till Makarsankranti, had now arrived in Shivapattan.

Shivapattan housed the royal stable of Raje. All the horses captured during various expeditions, would be admitted here under the expert eye of Arabian equestrian connoisseur Mohammed Sais. His brawny horse groomers would mark them with branding irons to identify them as the property of Shivajiraje. When Raje arrived in Shivapattan the branding was in process in the stable. The horses being branded were neighing abnormally due to the pain caused by the branding irons.

Raje summoned Mohammed Sais to the royal hall and enquired about the overall maintenance of the royal stable, "How is it going with the horses, Sais?"

"Ji Huzur, almost everything is fine, but some 'defective' horses had been admitted to the stable. My advice is to sell them!" Mohammed replied.

During various expeditions Raje had collected many horses, and some of them had white spots on their hooves. Such horses were considered 'defective' or 'inauspicious' and Sais was advising Raje to put them up for sale. Raje was lost in thought for a moment. Then suddenly with a cheerful smile he said, "No Sais! I cannot sell the horses! First of all, any equestrian connoisseur would never knowingly buy 'defective' horses. Secondly, such 'defective' horses could come in handy to train the new recruits in our cavalry!" Raje offered the solution.

"Ji Huzur!" said Sais and took a few steps backwards. The moment he lifted his head up, Raje said to him, "And Sais, keep in mind that I don't consider anything created by the Lord as 'defective'."

After wrapping up official matters in the royal hall, Raje came to Saibai's chamber. Sakhoo, Ranoo, Amba were there engrossed in playing with Shambhoobal. Raje felt elated looking at them and moved forward with a big smile. He picked up Shambhoobal from the circle of his sisters and held him close to his chest.

Shambhoobal got confused looking at Raje. For a moment,

he glanced at Raje's swaying golden earrings. The next moment, he grabbed a few strands of Raje's beard in his fist and tugged at it couple of times. That jerking motion made Raje feel a shooting pain running from his chin through his entire body. He felt that he had wanted to feel such pain since a long time. He looked at Shambhoobal as if he was looking into a mirror. Shambhoobal let go of the beard and while grabbing one of the cowries in Raje's necklace he giggled loudly, babbling 'taa, taa'. He was trying to put the cowrie in his mouth.

"Ah, very well! It's fine if you don't recognize me but never forget the cowries of Mother Bhavani!" Raje mumbled.

Raje gingerly handed Shambhoobal to Sakhoo. He glanced at Saibai standing near the sanctum holding a platter of arti. She had a faint smile on her face. Raje was surprised to see Saibai's smile like the gently burning flame of a lamp. Approaching her Raje asked, "Why are you smiling?"

Saibai smiled slightly again. She had found it funny that Shambhoobal had tugged at Raje's beard with his tiny hands. Until today she had never seen anyone dare touch Raje's beard. But she didn't know how to say this to Raje.

"Just your presence here brings a smile to my face!" Saibai replied tactfully. She applied tilak on Raje's forehead, and with her trembling hands she circled the arti platter around Raje's face. Looking at her, Raje immediately realized that just as Shambhoobal had been gaining weight Saibai had been losing it.

"The ceremony to start solid foods for Balraje is going to take place soon. My elder brother from Faltan should be…" Raje interrupted her.

"That will be done, but you should prepare yourself to go to Pratapgad. The change in weather will improve your health." Raje revealed the deepest woe in his heart.

Saibai became solemn at once. Her eyes became moist. She leaned forward and put the arti platter on a small wooden stool in front of the sanctum, so that Raje would not see her tears in the light of the lamps.

Raje noticed her distress. Unwittingly, he said with affection, "Sai, don't lose heart!"

His tender words touched her soul, and her suppressed emotions broke out. No matter how hard she tried to suppress her sobs she could not hold herself back. In a hoarse voice she said, "Don't know…how much time…I have! You should allocate monthly wages for the baby's nursing mother Dharau!"

Her words left Raje benumbed. He was speechless.

"I have to go." Said Raje and left the chamber. The children were still engrossed in their play.

Raje left the chamber, but Saibai's words kept rushing through his mind. 'Don't know how much time I have! Don't know…!'

And he heard an unknown voice as if it was coming deep down from a valley, "The most 'defective creation' of the Devil is 'Death', Sais!"

Raje began ascending Rajgad with Netajirao, Aabaji Mahadeo, and Yesaji Kank. For the past eight days, new guests had been arriving at the fort via the Padmavati, Sanjivani and Suvela machis. Raje had dispatched messengers and summoned all noblemen to Rajgad.

Everyone including Kanhoji Jedhe, Moropant Pingale, Manaji Bhosale, Sonopant Dabeer, Tanhaji Malusare, Raghunath Ballal Atre, Baji Sarjerao, Nilopant and Ramchandrapant Bahulkar, Sambhaji Kavaji, and Subhanaji Ingale had arrived on the fort and were wondering why Raje had invited them all at once.

Raje's palanquin arrived in front of the royal hall on Padmavati machi. Everybody made an obeisance to Raje.

While walking towards the royal hall with all of them, Raje shared his plans about the proceedings of the honour assembly with chief tatasarnoubat Sidoji Thopate. He also instructed

Vasudeopant Hanamante to prepare gift platters for the honour assembly.

After visiting the temples of Lord Shri Samba and Goddess Padmavati, Raje came to the royal hall and took his seat. He instructed all to be seated and everyone took their seats. The assembly began. Raje expressed his motive behind summoning the assembly —

"Twelve years ago, I took the vow to establish Swaraj. Though I was of a very tender age and had only a few faithful people at my disposal I set my sights on a highly unattainable goal. So far, I have achieved success with the blessings of Lord Shree Samba. One cannot build one's house on one's own! Then how could I build a kingdom with only my two hands! Gradually, I garnered a lot of support from thousands of people. The advice of many veterans ushered me onto the right path. Aausaheb offered me courage with her loving hands and blessings with her loving eyes. I remember Dadoji and Baji Pasalkar on this occasion!" Raje's voice became heavy with emotion for a moment.

"It is because all of you stuck it out that this kingdom has turned the corner. Today, forty forts are hoisting our Jaripataka pennant with pride. We have gathered ten thousand soldiers in the infantry as well as cavalry. I have called this assembly as I want to honour all of you today. I will do so to the best of my ability. May the Lord give me the wisdom for the same. If any mistake is committed at this time, consider me like your own child and please forgive me for the sake of God. All of you should support me as your own child!!"

This was the other side of the same Shivajiraje who would fall fiercely upon his enemy on the battlefield while shouting the slogans of 'Har Har Mahadeo' at the top of his lungs. The rough and tough hearts of the assembled men were deeply moved, seeing him like this.

Raje stood up. His sharp, florid nose protruding like the blade of a dagger demanded everyone's attention. With pride, he announced the name of Netaji Palkar who was sitting in the royal hall – "Netajirao, come in front of me."

Netajirao approached Raje and stood in front of him. He made an obeisance to Raje. An attendant stood nearby holding a platter. He removed the cloth covering the platter. It contained a sheathed sword with a diamond-studded hilt, a crested orange turban, a pure white barabandi vest and churidar. Raje picked up the sword from the platter. He tied it around Netaji's waist and declared – "From today onwards Subhedar Netaji has become the Sarnoubat of this kingdom."

Overwhelmed, Netajirao leaned forward to touch Raje's feet. Raje promptly stopped him and pulled him up. With eyes shining brightly like the sun, he stared at Netajirao for a moment and held him in a loving embrace.

Likewise, Raje also appointed Nilo Sonadeo as Mujumdar and Aabaji Mahadeo as Surnis. Yesaji Kank was appointed as the Sarnoubat of the infantry and offered a sword with a diamond-studded hilt. Raje honoured all for their loyal services to the kingdom; some were bestowed with silver anklets, some with bracelets, a few with daggers and others with swords.

An administrator of Rajgad presented the recently designed royal seal to Raje. Raje looked at the mirror image of the letters that were inscribed on the octagonal seal that read – 'Like the brilliance of the moon keeps waxing and is worshipped by the whole world, the glory of this Mudra of Shahaji's son, Shivaji will always keep expanding.'

The royal seal reminded Raje of Saibai. He summoned the newly appointed Mujumdar Nilo Sonadeo and said to him in a weary voice, "Mujumdar, Dharau of the Gaade family from the hamlet of Kapoorhol is serving in my queens' retinue. Grant her a yearly stipend of twenty-six hons! And you personally make sure that it is delivered to her."

Shambhoobal had now started taking baby steps. Jijabai sent a messenger to Faltan to invite Bajaji Nimbalkar for the ceremony to start solid foods for Shambhoobal.

Bajaji arrived in Shivapattan. He was Shambhooraje's mama. He had been forcefully converted to Islam, but Raje got him reconverted into Hinduism with proper religious rituals. Raje had also got Saibai's eldest daughter Sakhoo married to Nimbalkar's son, Mahadaji, and thus accorded them status in society. As Sakhoo was still quite young she was living with her parents. Bajaji came to Shivapattan for two purposes – to attend his nephew's first feeding ceremony and to visit his daughter-in-law.

Jijabai consulted the astrologer and chose an auspicious day for the ceremony. On that day, Bajaji sat on a rectangular sandalwood seat and held Shambhoobal in his lap. Jijabai, Saibai, Dharau and all the queens sat around him.

Bajaji took off his ring and dipped it in the sweet porridge in a silver bowl. Then he touched the ring to his nephew's tongue and made him taste it. He handed Shambhoobal to Saibai, got up from the seat and placed the sweet porridge-covered ring on the seat as a gift to his nephew. Shambhoobal could eat solid foods now.

Saibai's health showed no improvement, therefore, after consulting Jijabai, Raje decided to move her to Pratapgad. Jijabai was going to accompany her.

Shambhoobal had now turned one and a half years old. He had started babbling and running all over the place. He was emotionally attached to Dharau. He had picked up bits of her peasant dialect. He started calling Raje 'Aaba' and would cling to Saibai while calling her 'Maa' and 'Aau'. Shambhoobal became a source of relaxation for Raje. Raje wanted to keep him in front of his eyes and never let go of him, but Shambhoobal had to go with Saibai.

One day the queens' palanquins got ready for departure. From Rajgad Raje came to the palace of Shivapattan. After finishing the daily worship, Jijabai got ready to leave the chamber with Saibai, Dharau, Shambhoobal, and the girls. Raje approached Jijau and touched her feet. "Don't worry, I am with her." Jijabai reassured Raje.

Shambhoobal was holding Dharau's hand. Raje picked him up and kissed his bright forehead adorned with sandalwood paste. Raje peeked into his tiny but fearless eyes and asked him with a smile, "Shambhoo, will you climb Pratapgad on foot?"

"Yes Aaba, I will race to the top of the fort!" Shambhoobal widened his eyes and replied in his babbling tongue. Raje patted his back gently and placed him down.

Jijabai pulled him close and picking his chin up she said to him, like the grand tranquil bed of River Ganga would say to a tiny rippling spring clinging to her! "Shambhoo, my dear, aren't you going to touch Aaba's feet?"

Balraje nodded in affirmation. He let go of Jijabai and approached Raje. He put his tiny knees and hands on the floor, looked at his Aaba who looked as grand as the skies above and said, "Aaba, I bow to you. Jai Bhavani!" Then he put his forehead on Raje's feet. As he felt that touch Raje instantly closed his eyes.

All family members sat in their palanquins. The palanquin bearers picked up the palanquins. Raje walked a few steps alongside the palanquins. Then, standing in one place, he kept staring at the palanquins going away from him.

Pratapgad, in the Javali basin, came into view. The palanquin bearers were taking frequent short breaks while climbing the steps of the fort.

The location of the self- manifested Shivlinga that was recovered during the construction of the ramparts, came into sight. Moropant had erected a small elegant dome over the Shivlinga on that place. A jasmine creeper enveloped the dome from all sides. Jijabai and Saibai stepped out of their palanquins. Dharau stepped out with Shambhoobal in her arms. All of them went inside the dome to worship the deity. Saibai instructed

Shambhoo to kneel in front of the self- manifested Shivashambhoo.

While praying to the Shivlinga Saibai's eyes closed for a moment. She spoke to Lord Shiva in a silent language of an aristocratic Hindu woman, "Oh God, bless my husband with great success and take good care of my son!"

Peshwa Moropant and Arjoji Yadav had come to receive them. They made an obeisance to Jijabai and Saibai.

Shambhoobal, dubbed as 'valiant Rudra' by astrologer Harbhat, had arrived at Pratapgad!

Sometimes, for a breath of fresh air, Saibai and Dharau would take Shambhoobal on the rampart wall and take a stroll there. Saibai would watch the thick, lush green forests around the fort and think to herself, 'So many medicinal herbs must be hidden among all these trees! But not even one is proving effective for my sickness! It is just like being in the ocean but unable to drink a single drop of water when thirsty. Isn't it?'

Nowadays, Saibai's mind could not focus on any thing. It was acting like a swallow hovering in the skies atop the fort summit, suddenly changing its direction for no reason. It was trying to suggest that something was close upon her; it was desperately trying to hold onto something, something that was going far away from her

But Dharau and Shambhoobal had got well acquainted with each other now. It had become Dharau's daily duty to take Shambhoobal to the temples on the fort and toll the bells for him. Sometimes Balraje would raise his hands and insist upon tolling the bells himself. Then, for quite some time he would be happily occupied in tolling the bells.

Winter over, colourful bunches of wildflowers started appearing. With the help of the physician, Jijau was trying every kind of medicine on Saibai. The medicinal herbs were shrinking bit by bit and so was Saibai. She couldn't even hold Shambhoobal in her arms for a minute.

The dry weather of summer made Saibai feel a bit better, but her health did not improve. Moropant, Arjoji, the physician and Jijabai – everyone was worried for Saibai's sinking health. Jijabai started conducting religious rituals and observing fasts. Summer was almost over.

Monsoon was approaching. The skies were overcast. The first deluge of the monsoon showered upon Pratapgad. Chilly winds started blowing over the fort. As soon as the icy, biting wind touched her body, goosebumps rose on Saibai's emaciated frame. She fell ill. A message was sent to Raje on Rajgad.

Calamities have the innate tendency of walking hand in hand! Raje received the news that Saibai's health was failing. Right after that, he also received another news– Adil Shah's general Khankhana Afzal Mohammed Shahi had taken a vow to capture Raje alive or dead and present him to the Sultan. He had already left Bijapur with his army.

One Friday, Badi Begum had convened a special assembly to discuss a critical matter. Her faithful combatants like Siddi Hilal, Rustam-i-zaman, Ankush Khan, Muse Khan, Rajashree Mambaji Bhosale, Baji Ghorpade, Zunzarrao Ghatage, Pahilwan Khan, and Abdul Sayyad were present in the assembly with their hands folded and their heads lowered. The Begum berated them, and they listened to her silently in embarrassment. Not a single valiant warrior dared to come forward to reassure the Begum. Her royal wrath erupted like scorching fire and she roared in fury – "Is there no one man enough in this assembly who can confront and challenge that backstabber of Deccan? Isn't there a single pillar of strength in this empire who will stand up to that fiendish insurgent? Have all men in this assembly become effeminate and feeble? Shame… shame on you!"

The Begum's scorching words ignited a fire in the heart of Khankhana Afzal Khan, he tightened the grip on the hilt of his sword and stepped forward. He tramped on the exquisite carpet and approached the platter on which the betel leaf had been placed. He threw a contemptuous glance at the silent crowd, made a devout obeisance to the Begum and promptly picked up the betel leaf to take up the challenge.

"Huzur, I will present that wretched infidel in this assembly – alive or dead! I will not rest till it is done. He raised his hand holding the betel leaf and took a vow in his raspy voice.

"Bravo! Hail Allah! Glory to Allah! Grace of Allah! The entire assembly cheered in ecstatic frenzy. Everyone felt as if they themselves were Afzal Khan and they themselves had taken up the challenge. But neither the Begum and Afzal, nor a single warrior in the assembly had a clue as to whose downfall Destiny had inked on that betel leaf.

Khan's entourage consisted of twenty thousand staunch armed men, eighty to ninety bombard cannons, three hundred mortar cannons, one thousand camels, and sixty to seventy spirited elephants. Afzal Khan Mohammed Shahi hoisted the royal flag with the symbol of the moon and the star, on a designated elephant and left on the mission to eclipse the Sun! To demolish the idols! To shatter Shivaji's faith!

'Afzal' means 'the most Beautiful', 'the Great'! Indeed, he was 'the Great'! He had handcuffed Shahajiraje Bhosale and had him paraded disgracefully on the streets of Bijapur! He had betrayed Shivajiraje's elder brother – Sambhajiraje – and left him to die during the siege of Kanakgiri! It was he who had convinced Kasuturi Ranga to attend a meeting for an alliance and had him killed treacherously! He had also concocted the plot to assassinate Commander Khan-Mohammed at the Mecca gate for letting Prince Aurangzeb escape unscathed during the siege of Kalyani. Such a 'Great' Khan had now set out on 'the great mission' to thrust his hand in the mountainous caves of Sahyadri to pull out a lion named 'Seva' by his mane!

Raje had speculated that Khan was going to camp at Wai no matter from what direction he came. Now, it was dangerous to keep Saibai at Pratapgad. Raje sent a message to Jijabai conveying his plan to move the queens' retinue from Pratapgad to Shivapattan at the foothills of Rajgad.

The palanquin bearers carried the palanquins of Jijabai and Saibai to the base of Pratapgad, braving the end of the season monsoon showers. Two-year-old Shambhoobal and Dharau sat in one of the palanquins. Shambhoobal had now begun speaking fluently. He was always badgering Dharau with his curious queries. 'Why are the sandalwood stripes applied on the forehead, always horizontal?' 'Why do the soldiers always tie their sword on their left?' 'Why does only one edge of the spear have a blade?' Why is the horseshoe always attached to the hooves of a horse? Poor Dharau was so baffled, she couldn't answer even a single question. Neither of her own sons had ever badgered her like this.

Shivapattan was around the corner. The palanquins stopped in front of the Mahadeo temple on the outskirts of the town. Raje received the news of their arrival in the palace of Shivapattan. After the scattered rain showers stopped, Raje mounted the horse and rode with Firangoji Narasala, Netaji Palkar and Sambhaji Kavaji to the Shiva temple to receive Jijabai.

After paying respects to Jijabai, Raje visited the temple. Jijau didn't speak to Raje as usual with a smile on her face. She only pointed to Saibai's palanquin. Raje trudged towards the palanquin and pulled the curtain open. On a soft blanket lay the dusky skeleton of a myriad of his reminiscences! Looking at the emaciated Saibai, lying with her eyes closed, Raje's fiery eyes went frigid. The memory of a childish, innocent Saibai entering the palace of Lal Mahal after knocking down the container full of grains, lingered in front of his eyes. So many years have come to pass! So many twists and turns life has taken! Sai kept glowing like a lamp in the sanctum! If ever Masaheb spoke to me sarcastically anytime, it was to support this daughter of hers. A loving wife, a forbearing daughter-in-law, a conscientious queen, a doting mother, a patient woman – Sai has played so many roles! 'Sai' is the most beautiful dream I have ever seen. A beautiful dream never withers away – then how did it come to this? How?

Countless thoughts filled Raje's mind. His eyes became wet and the palanquin in front of him became a blur. He instantly took a step away from the palanquin and signalled the palanquin bearers. They picked up Saibai's palanquin and began trotting towards the palace of Shivapattan.

Dharau stood next to Jijabai with Shambhoobal. Raje approached them and picked up Shambhoobal. Ranoo and Amba, Raje's young daughters called him 'Aaba' and clung to him.

"Raje, everything is up to Lord Shree Samba now. All efforts have proved futile." Jijabai couldn't help telling Raje.

"Indeed Aausaheb, everything is up to Lord Shree Samba. But we should not give up. Adil Shah's general, Afzal, is on his way here with twenty thousand armed forces. He has taken a pledge to present me 'alive or dead' in front of the Sultan..." Raje's voice became hoarse.

"Afzal! Twenty thousand armed men!" Jijau exclaimed and fell silent momentarily.

"Aaba, so much water spills onto Pratapgad whenever it rains!" Shambhoobal said spreading his arms wide.

"Yes Balraje, but the ocean takes all that water in! Raje replied with a smile.

"Where is that ocean?"

"It is far far away; farther away than the distance you travelled here from Pratapgad." Raje's mind was preoccupied with the thoughts of Pratapgad!

Afzal Khan wreaked havoc in the precincts of the temple of Raje's family deity, Jagadamba at Tuljapur; battered the murti in the Pandharpur temple – the folk deity of the Marathi region and then encamped at Shirval. On his way, he captured Bajaji

Nimbalkar in Malwadi; accused him of being 'an accomplice of Shivaji, a traitor'; had him tied to the barrel of a cannon and paraded him throughout the campsite.

Raje negotiated with Naikji Pandhare from Khan's side and got Bajaji freed in exchange for sixty thousand hons. Raje extricated himself from the entanglement of familial relations.

Khan had implemented all these strategies to upset Shivaji and make him leave the basins of Bara Maval to attack Khan's army in the open, but all his efforts were futile. To alienate Shivaji, Khan ultimately implemented the cunning strategy of bribing his allies. He started taking people under his wing by hook or crook.

The Deshmukh of Gunjanmaval – Vithoji Silimkar, the Deshmukh of Utroli – Khandoji and Kedarji Khopade, the Manes of Mhasawad, Jagadales of Masoor, Pandhare from Malwadi, Tanhaji Kokare, Ravirao Dhone, Dhuloji Shedge, Kate, Dhayagude and many more Mavala chieftains had surrendered at Khan's feet. With increasing support Khan left Shirval and arrived at Wai.

Kashirao, a loyal supporter of Adil Shah came to the outskirts to welcome Khan in person. Kaliya infiltrated the depths of River Krishna.

Kashirao presented Gomaji Helavaakakar of Sangameshwar in front of Khan. Gomaji was the diwan of the Deshkulkarni of Sangameshwar. The only survivor of the Kulkarni family was an old woman. Gomaji had travelled to Wai with the plan of usurping her hereditary estate with the help of Khan's decree.

Khan approved his bid on one condition. Gomaji was to keep three hundred boats at the ready on the banks of the rivers that Khan was going to pass by on his return journey. In return, Khan was going to appoint him as the Deshkulkarni of Sangameshwar.

The Deshmukhs and sardars had already assisted in Khan's advent. Gomaji promised to assist in his return journey. Now nothing could save the cursed infidel 'Seva'. But neither Gomaji nor Khan himself had any inkling that Khan's fate had a very different 'return journey' in store.

Now only two elements were working in Raje's favour like his longstanding, stalwart generals – first, the inaccessible, safeguarded region of the Javali basin, and the other was the tempestuous monsoon of Bara Maval that could not be contained by anyone!

Raje had to leave Rajgad in the rainy weather, to block the torrent of Khan. Raje took the blessings of Killeshwari and Bhavani and began climbing down the Padmavati machi. Firangoji Narasala, Gomaji Panasambal, and Sidoji Thopate were to stay back to defend the fort. Kanhoji Jedhe – who had relinquished his rights over his family estate, Babaji Bhosale – a family relative, Balaji Silimkar, Netajirao Palkar, Yesaji, Moropant, Tanhaji, Sambhaji Kavaji, Subhanaji Ingale and others were going to accompany Raje.

They all descended the fort and reached Shivapattan. Raje went to Jijabai's palace to pay obeisance to her. Jijabai was explaining something to Shambhoobal. As soon as she saw Raje, she stopped speaking and came forward walking composedly. Raje touched her feet and said, "Masaheb, I am leaving on the mission. Khan has settled in Wai. I should go to Pratapgad."

"Okay, don't worry about us now. Don't let go of your allies. Had Saibai not fallen ill, I would have come in person to see Khan. I still bear one grudge against him. Do visit Soonbai before leaving." Jijau stopped for a moment.

"Shambhoobal, touch your Aaba's feet." Jijabai instructed Balraje, patting his shoulder.

Shambhoobal put his head on Raje's feet. Raje pulled him up and holding him close, patted his back.

"Who is a 'Khan', Aabasaheb?" Balraje asked furrowing his forehead. Raje couldn't answer that unexpected question. "One who is keen on devouring others, but whom no one can devour is called a 'Khan' Shambhoo!" Jijabai glanced at Raje and pulled Balraje close to her while replying.

"May I take your leave?" Raje said in a hoarse voice.

"Yes. May you live long!" Jijau raised her right hand in blessing.

"Jai Bhavani!" Shambhoobal completed the obeisance.

Raje entered Saibai's chamber to bid farewell. The lamps in the chamber were burning, but her bed was enveloped in shadow. Raje gingerly approached her bed and looked at her. She lay with closed eyes. Her dusky face appeared dull and gloomy in the dim light of the lamps.

"Listen, I am about to leave." Raje said to wake up Saibai.

Saibai heard his words and woke up as if she was awaking from a deep slumber. She tried to smile. "Did Balraje meet you?" She asked Raje in a feeble voice.

"Yes, he did. He is in Aausaheb's chamber." Raje leaned on the edge of the bed. He gently held her scrawny hand in his own. The golden bangles in Saibai's hand slid towards her elbow making a jingling sound. While holding her frail hand in his own, Raje's heart weighed heavy. Both of them were tongue-tied. What to say? How to say it? So much to say but both of them were at a loss for words. An awkward silence surrounded them.

"Sai..." Raje called her in a hoarse voice and patted her hand. The silence broke and waves of words started flowing.

"Umm hum, don't be so heartbroken. My path is set now! I never asked for anything. Whenever you were in front of me, I could not think of asking for anything else. Now, I don't have much time. That is why, I would like to ask for one thing." Saibai had a bout of coughing while speaking.

Raje let her coughing abate and said, "Now, don't lose heart. Just speak your mind. You will get better!"

"I gave birth to Balraje but failed to satiate his need for mother's milk. Dharau came to take my place despite being a peasant woman. That is why I must speak." Saibai stopped speaking. She closed her eyes momentarily. The dark circles under her eyes pierced Raje's heart deeply.

"Go ahead Sai, speak up. Don't stop." Raje's voice was husky.

"My baby – dear Shambhoo…is alone. Today, I am entrusting him into your care! You are his mother and father now! That…that is all I ask for." Saibai turned her head to hide the tears in her eyes. Her tears trickled from her closed eyes and slid onto the bedsheet!

"Sai, I give you my word; I am bound to Balraje for your sake. Don't worry. May I take your leave now?" Said Raje and gingerly put Saibai's hand on the bed. The cowries in the necklace on his chest weighed heavy on his heart. Raje left Saibai's chamber.

After leaving Shivapattan Raje visited Purandar, Torana, Mohangad, Vardhangad and Tunga-Tikona forts and garrisoned their defence. In pouring rain, after tightening the security of the Javali basin by erecting multiple surveillance posts, Raje arrived at Pratapgad with a select crew.

The end of monsoon was approaching. At the end of the rainy season, the land of Gunjanmaval, Kananda and Velkhand basins had come to blossom like the beauty of a married woman. Her forehead was adorned with the crimson stripes of the inundated Gunjavani and Kanandi rivers. This stretch of land was very proud of her fertility. As long as her forehead was adorned with the stripes, she was ready to embrace death with a smile!

In the queens' apartments of Rajgad, Saibai was embracing a similar death. Her bed was surrounded by Jijau Saheb, all the queens of Raje, Dharau, her daughters – Sakhoo, Ranoo, Amba and toddler Shambhoobal. Saibai had held Shambhoobal's tiny hand in hers and lay on her bed with closed eyes. Her forehead was adorned with kumkum stripes. In her mouth, Dharau had kept a Tulasi leaf dipped in the waters of Ganga. The wicks of the lamps in the chamber had gathered soot. Everyone's face looked distraught in the melancholy, dim light. The skies atop the summit of Rajgad were overcast. Saibai was in a trance, completely unaware of her surroundings. Her forbearing mind was playing an altogether different game today. It was trying to capture the innumerable facets of 'Sai'. The game was in full swing. Countless shapes were dancing. Saibai was slipping into a coma.

A zillion shadows! Young Sai dressed in a skirt in Mudhojibaba's house in Faltan. Demure Sai, entering Lal Mahal in Pune as the daughter-in-law of the Bhosale family, who easily became Jijabai's daughter when she called her 'Aau' and clung to her. Sai, who became 'Saibai' unbeknownst to herself. Sai, who became 'Thoralya Akka' or elder sister as the number of Raje's queens kept increasing, who became mother-in-law in Sakhoo's wedding ceremony. Sai, who was treated with due respect by Raje's ministers and generals as 'Ranisarkar'. Contented Sai, who was delighted to become the mother of Raje's first son Shambhoo. So many shadows were manifesting in front of Saibai's closed eyes, but she could not even get hold of one, no matter how hard she tried! She could lay her hands on only one shadow. But… it was not her own; it was the shadow of Raje – her better half! A shadow that did not stay in one place even for a moment; that would speak everything through only the eyes! A shadow that would keep whispering 'Jagadamb, Jagadamb'!

She couldn't find 'Sai' anywhere amidst the hubbub of so many shadows and memories. All she could see was the magnificent expanse of the horizontal crimson kumkum stripes spread all over her forehead. A symbol of a 'Suvasinee. A symbol of marriage divine! Gradually, the kumkum on her forehead kept expanding! It continued expanding and became as colossal as the sky! It spread beyond her forehead now!

Saibai could only see Raje's radiant, vibrant, crimson

silhouette completely drenched in the crimson-kumkum on her forehead! Saibai started walking with a suvasinee's splendour to catch hold of that silhouette. The Tulsi leaf in her mouth shook momentarily trying to stop her, but Saibaisaheb left anyway! Forever! Way way beyond! Raje's beautiful, dusky dream was shattered!

Saibai's lifeless hand slipped out of Shambhoobal's hand! Her loving, feeble hand collapsed on the bed and lay askew. The forlorn Tulasi leaf on her lips slid over her throat and fell upon her Mangalsutra. The palace drowned in lamentations. The blackened flames of the lamps in the chamber flickered in profound pain. The stone walls shivered.

"Aau, Aau ..." frightened Shambhoobal called Saibai and shook her lifeless hand vigorously. All the queens were wailing loudly, standing around the bed. Shambhoobal was puzzled to see everyone crying loudly. He rushed to Jijabai calling her 'Thoralya Aau' and clung to her instantly. Dharau picked up Shambhoobal and took him out of the chamber.

By the end of monsoon, the fortress of Shivajiraje's heart was shattered. One of his beautiful dreams was crushed! Saibai had gone on a long voyage, never to return.

When Raje received the news that Saibai had breathed her last in Rajgad, he closed his eyes inadvertently and exclaimed 'Jagadamb, Jagadamb' putting his hand on his chest in immense agony. He immediately travelled from Pratapgad to Rajgad. His dusky, tender dream was burning along with the flaring funeral pyre of his eldest queen. The flames of a myriad memories of Saibai were fluttering, and Shivajiraje Bhosale was getting singed in that fire.

Raje had other queens too, but he was most attached to Saibai. A warrior can never forget the first sword tied around his waist and the first lady that stands in front of him on the marriage altar! Minimal use of words and greater communication with their eyes—Raje and Saibai were such a dignified royal couple.

Saibai's demise had turned the joyous occasion of Dussehra into a grieving one.

Bajajimama who had shaved Shambhoobal's head during his tonsure ceremony, now shaved his head completely for the mourning of Saibai. Now his innocent face looked like an orphan's face. Jijau felt devastated to see his face and pulled him close with emphatic affection. She had now decided to be his 'Aau'. Jijau had come into the Bhosale family only to mend all the cracked walls of strained familial relationships.

Raje sat on the bed in his chamber with bare-headed Shambhoobal. With one hand he was stroking Shambhoo's back and with the other he was caressing the cowries in his necklace. His heart was besieged by Saibai's memory on one hand and by the thoughts of Afzal Khan's encampment in Wai on the other.

"Aaba, where did Aau go?" Shambhoobal asked Raje.

The question left Raje rattled. He had no answer to that question. With immense affection he kept patting his son's shoulder. The words of astrologer Harbhat sprang up in his mind, "This horoscope depicts the possibility of being betrayed by his own people just like the Puranas portray the betrayal of Rudra by his own people!"

Raje felt agitated looking at Shambhoo. A bizarre thought passed through his mind, "As soon as you were born, you had to be nurtured on Dharau's milk! But… even the astrologer couldn't have presumed that you would be betrayed in such a way by your own kin at the very beginning of your life!" Raje simply kept patting Shambhoobal's shoulder.

The terror of Afzal Khan's attack on the Marathi Empire was lurking in Wai. Khan had devised a cunning plan of confining Raje to one place by posting Pandhare in Shirval, Kharate in the basin of River Karha, Jadhav in the Supe district, Siddi Hilal in the Pune district and Saif Khan in Tal Konkan.

It was not wise to stay at Rajgad in such confining circumstances. For that purpose, Raje had long back assessed the inaccessible Javali basin located on the border of Khan's encampment in Wai. Perchance, he could safely and securely travel to the coastal region of Konkan from the West via Pratapgad located in the basin. Raje devised a plan to travel to Pratapgad near Wai.

Only Masaheb could have made him change his plan now. After the recent demise of her daughter-in-law, would Jijabai be able to bid farewell to Raje, who was her only surviving son? How much turmoil her heart would have to go through! What if she tries to stop me with a sentimental appeal…?

To avoid all this, Raje himself instructed Jijau's personal assistant to make sure that Aausaheb would not come to bid farewell to him when he left Rajgad. While giving such an instruction his trembling hand ran over the cowrie necklace. Many cowries of thoughts scattered through his mind… 'And what if I do not come back alive from this mission of Khan? In that case, Sai's departing footprints will guide me further. And Masaheb will daub Shambhoobal's forehead with Goddess Jagadamba's haldi in my name, and take a vow to defend the kingdom! Goddess Bhavani has indeed blessed her with such resolve!'

'But would Shambhoobal be able to handle such responsibility?' My father had to take up arms at a very young age. I also set foot on the barren land of Pune at a very tender age. If need be, Shambhoo will have to walk on a similar path. Raje prepared his heart. It was essential to forsake the very wings of affection that had nurtured him with warmth of love. Otherwise, one cannot soar high in the blue skies! One must sacrifice personal relationships in the line of duty. A king does not have the luxury of nourishing personal relationships!

The day of departure from Rajgad dawned. Raje took a bath and performed Shivalinga puja. He left his chamber and started walking towards the royal hall. All his queens waited behind the arches in the passage, in anticipation of his departure. They quickly came forward one by one, touched his feet and stood aside modestly. As he passed by Saibai's private chamber Raje's feet lingered in front of it momentarily. He glanced at the empty chamber and with a heavy heart he walked briskly into the royal hall. Netaji, Yesaji, Sambhaji Kavaji and Sidoji Thopate paid obeisance to Raje.

"Sidojirao, go and check where Shambhoobal is." Raje commanded.

"Ji" said Sidojirao and left for Dharau's room.

Dharau followed Sidojirao and ushered Balraje to the royal hall. As Raje was present in the royal hall, she hesitated, wondering whether it was alright for a woman to go inside. So, she let go of Shambhoobal's hand and waited outside. But he was quite adamant! He grabbed Dharau's hand again and started pulling her inside the royal hall. Raje saw the tattooed hand and the bangles and said, "Come Dharabai, Balraje won't listen!"

"Ji" said Dharau and entered the royal hall. Shambhoobal knelt and put his head on Raje's feet. The tiny Jiretop fitted tight on his bare head. Raje put one hand on the Jiretop and gently pulled him up with the other. Raje put his forefinger under Shambhoobal's chin, leaned forward and briefly kissed his forehead. Raje patted his tiny shoulders and asked in a hoarse voice, "Shambhoobal, did you pay obeisance to Masaheb before coming?"

"Ji. Aaba, once you climb down the fort I am going to take off into the sky!" Shambhoobal exclaimed pointing towards the sky.

"What for?"

"To pay obeisance to my Aausaheb! Thoralya Aausaheb says she has gone way up in the sky!"

Shambhoobal's words left everyone in the royal hall stunned. Raje fixed his eyes on Jijau's chamber, next to the royal hall. His heart was in turmoil.

"Dharau, hold Shambhoobal now." Raje resolutely handed

Balraje to Dharau.

"Come everyone, it's time to leave," said Raje and started walking through the passage. He had barely walked halfway, when he heard a strong voice drenched in affection, vibrating like the thundering war horn, coming from one side of the royal hall, "Shivaba…! You are leaving without meeting me! Are you turning your back on me?"

At that very moment, Raje turned around swiftly just as a pure-bred Arabian stallion responds to the voice of its groomer. He walked briskly and went past the stairs of the royal hall. He couldn't dare to look at Jijau. He directly approached his Masaheb and rested his head on her fair, sacred feet.

Jijau held his shoulders lovingly, pulled him up and said, "Arise! Who says I am going to stop you? The queens of the Bhosale family have never been so faint-hearted and never will be. Rest assured! Avenge the death of Shambhoo, my son and your elder brother. Destroy Khan and remember that I am looking forward to your return. Here, have this" Jijabai said and looked at Dharau. She gave a bowl of curds to Jijabai. Jijabai put a thick blob of curds on Raje's rosy palm. Raje consumed it and looked at Jijabai for a moment. He felt as if Goddess Bhavani herself was standing in front of him!

"Fare well. May you live long! May Mother Amba shower her blessings on you!" Jijau held Raje in an embrace. Raje felt as if the quiver of his heart was being imbued with an unknown flash of lightning.

"I need to leave now!" said Raje, loosening the embrace.

"Masaheb, please take care of Shambhoobal. I have appointed Gomajibaba, Firangoji-baba and Sidojirao to assist you. Jai Bhavani!"

Raje calmly walked out of the royal hall with select people. He approached the tunnel that set out from the Balekilla and opened on the Padmavati machi.

Raje walked through the tunnel and reached the Padmavati

machi. He gave detailed instructions to the people who were going to stay behind. He visited the Padmavati temple on the machi. Then, with select people he left the machi and came to the foothills by way of Pali Darwaja. He glanced at Rajgad; mounted his horse and prodded it.

Raje's cavalry troop began galloping towards Pratapgad. Jijabai stood with Shambhoobal near the ramparts. To her, the horses looked like spots galloping away in clouds of dust.

Jijabai lay on her bed and kept staring at the stone ceiling throughout the night. Dreadful thoughts kept hounding her. Whenever the thoughts became unbearable, she stroked Shambhoobal's back, who slept peacefully next to her. As she looked at Shambhoo, who was the only son of Raje, her only son, she thought, 'The wives of the Bhosale men have to enter the Bhosale household with complete awareness that their lives are tethered to fire. But what kind of curse is this that befalls the Bhosale children? Shivaba faced calamities as a child. Now similar calamities are befalling his innocent son.

He asks, who is Khan? Who can answer him convincingly and how? He directly wants to fly in the sky to pay obeisance to his deceased mother! How can anyone hold the reins of his mind racing like a horse and bring it to a halt? Dharau offered her milk for him, I will give him my love, but who is going to understand the loneliness of his heart and stand strongly by his side? Shivabaraje was deprived of his father's love. Shambhoo is bereft of his mother's affections. And now his father's life is at stake. Afzal's intentions are treacherous. What if something bad happens to Shivaba…'

The mere thought left Jijabai trembling. She became a bundle of nerves. She couldn't think straight. Her trembling hand unconsciously kept stroking Shambhoo's back, who was sound asleep.

After bathing Shambhoobal, Dharau dressed him and brought him to Jijau's chamber. Every day, after his bath, Jijau applied stripes of sandalwood paste on Shambhoo's forehead.

Shambhoo touched Jijau's feet. Dharau held the platter of sandalwood paste at a convenient distance from Jijabai. Jijau applied horizontal stripes of sandalwood paste on Shambhoobal's forehead. Those stripes of sandalwood paste further enhanced the already charismatic face of Balraje. It reminded Jijabai of Raje's longish face. She kept gazing at Shambhoo's forehead adorned with sandalwood paste. She used to adorn Shivabaraje's forehead just like this when he was a child. As she gazed at Shambhoo's smooth forehead, a thought came to her mind – 'Shivabaraje and Shambhoobal's faces look like the Shivalinga after applying the stripes of sandalwood paste on their forehead! But...but the Shivalinga needs a constant stream of water on its head. Oh, Mother Amba, keep these Shivalingas of mine perennially drenched under the stream of your gracious blessings. Let it not cease even for a moment. Oh Mother, please save all of us from this disastrous catastrophe!'

An urgent messenger dispatched by Raje came to Rajgad to deliver his message. Jijau's personal assistant started reading the message ... "My deepest obeisance to revered Aausaheb, the news is, Khan is camping in the village of Paar in the Koyana basin with his army. Our meeting is scheduled for tomorrow. Give me your blessings. Take care of Shambhoobal."

Jijabai muttered, 'Jagadamb, Jagadamb'. She held Shambhoobal's hand in hers and came to the ramparts. She kept staring in the direction of Pratapgad desperately. She was unnerved.

Balraje noticed her silence and asked her, "Aaba has gone to visit Khan. Then why doesn't he bring him here?"

Jijabai gave Shambhoo a startled look. "May your words come true." said Jijabai and returned to her chamber.

Annaji Malkare erected a grand pavilion at the foothills of Pratapgad for the rendezvous with Khan. On the night before the rendezvous, Raje convened a secret counsel to discuss the particulars of the meeting with Khan. Netaji Palkar, Kanhoji Jedhe, Moropant Pingale, Yesaji Kank, Babaji Bhosale, Balaji Silimkar and Pantaji Gopinath sat in a circle around Raje. Everyone's forehead was daubed with haldi.

Raje commenced the counsel in a resolute, vigilant, hoarse voice – "Tomorrow, in the late afternoon, I am going to descend the fort to visit Khan. Khan is harbouring a treacherous plan to assassinate me.

At such a time, if all of you courageously face the situation together, then Khan will certainly be destroyed along with his entire army. Each one of you should carefully listen to the duties that I assign you. Don't be negligent in the execution of your duties.

Moropant, your infantry troops should lie in wait in Paarghat and keep a vigilant eye on the Kineshwar basin.

Kanhojibaba, along with Annaji Dutto, you should cover the path that Khan is coming from, with your troops of Bandal fighters and Pasalkar's swordsmen.

Balaji and Haibatrao, you should take your armed troops to Khan's encampment near the village of Paar during the night and keep them camouflaged in the woods nearby.

Babajiraje, your infantry troops should be posted on watch, in the vicinity of Wai-Javali to block the return route of Khan's troops.

Netajirao, keep your nimble cavalry ready on the plains of Kudsar village. You are going to wipe out the rear-guard of Khan's forces located at Wai.

Tanhajirao, Krishnaji Kank, with select swordsmen, you should hide in the trenches dug by the cliff near the pavilion erected for the meeting.

Sambhaji Kavaji, Jiu Mahala, Kondaji and uncle Yesaji, Sambhaji Karwar, Kataji Ingale, Visaji Murumbakar, Suraji Katke, Siddi Ibrahim and Krishnaji Gaikwad – these ten swordsmen will accompany me.

By the grace of Goddess Jagadamba, if I succeed in executing Khan, three cannon shots will be fired on the bastion walls as intimation. Unfortunately, if Khan stabs me in the back, five cannon shots will be fired as a warning signal.

Whether I come back alive or not, all of you must come together and wipe out Khan and his entire army stranded in the basins of Koyana. Always remember, that if anyone avoids their duties in this regard, or harbours any doubts in their mind, such conduct will not befit Jagdamba's devotees.

Don't lose heart at my death. We must establish a holy and sacred kingdom of the Lord. For that purpose, we may have to sacrifice many more Sivajirajes if needed.

In case I don't come back alive, make Shambhoobal your leader. Consider him in my place and all of you stand up together for the Swaraj under the guidance of Netajirao's mature expertise. Masaheb's blessings are already with all of you."

As Raje remembered Jijau and Shambhoobal his voice got heavy. He was overcome with emotion. The counsel on Pratapgad was over. Raje embraced everyone. Netajirao stepped forward and knocked the hilt of his sword three times on the huge boulder at the mouth of the secret chamber. The big boulder was pushed aside. Everyone made an obeisance to Raje and began climbing down the fort while pondering over the responsibilities assigned to them.

Raje entered his private chamber. He removed his Jiretop, placed it on a platter and lay on the bed. His mind was filled with doubt. 'Indeed, what if Khan betrays me in this meeting? … What will happen to this newly built kingdom? How will Masaheb handle it? And Shambhoobal? That boy wants to fly in the sky to pay obeisance to his mother. He will badger Masaheb with questions about me! He will climb down the fort all alone just to find me. Oh, dear Shambhoobal, have you indeed… indeed been born to be deceived by your own people?'

The memories of Balraje brought Saibai's dusky face in front of Raje's eyes. He recalled her heart-wrenching final words – "My baby will be alone now! I leave him in your care!"

Raje became utterly restless. He could not think straight. Tossing and turning did not dispel his apprehensions.

'Swaraj! The patriotic lives lost for the sake of Swaraj! Masaheb, who had been forbearingly enduring a calamitous life with a smile on her face! Shambhoobal, who had been crowned with embers at the very beginning of his life!

Raje was ill at ease. Out of the blue, a thought occurred in his mind, and he sat up at once. He approached the door of his chamber and called out for an attendant – "Anybody there?"

"Ji" an attendant entered the chamber and made an obeisance.

"Summon Hiroji now." Raje dismissed him.

Hiroji Farzand presented himself in front of Raje and made an obeisance to him.

"Hiroji, I cannot sleep. I want to visit the Kedareshwar temple. Come with me."

"Ji," exclaimed Hiroji and left the chamber. He went ahead and woke up the priest of the Kedareshwar temple.

Raje wrapped a shawl around himself and left for the Kedareshwar temple along with two swordsmen carrying torches, the priest of Kedareshwar temple carrying a platter of Bael leaves, and Hiroji Farzand.

They came in front of the Kedareshwar temple. The Shivalinga was glistening in the sanctum, in the vigil of the serene light of stone lamps. Raje removed his mojaris and leaned forward to touch the threshold before entering the temple. A captivating face of a roaring tiger was carved on that stone threshold centred between images of two Dharma Chakras. Raje kept staring intensely at the tiger's face. He felt like something was gushing through his spine and his chest was bulging.

A tiger's face! Warrior Goddess Jagadamba astride a tiger! The tiger taking one step forward at a time, with a challenging look in his eyes. Fiery, red-eyed, armed Bhavani – the Goddess of War, riding on its back! The Chakra whirring alongside the tiger's raised paw! The tiger's face, his raised paw, Goddess Bhavani wielding her weapons, the rapidly whirring Chakra and – ferociously storming ahead to block it, gnashing his teeth and biting his lips, was Khan! Khan! Khan!

Instantly, Raje raised his head, much like a cobra raising its hood. His wide, bright eyes were breathing fire! The tiger's raised paw was dancing in front of his eyes.

Raje walked briskly and entered the sanctum. The temple priest presented a platter of Bael leaves in front of him. Raje picked up a palm full of Bael leaves and offered them over the Shivalinga like the sky scattering the stars around. He brought his palms together, closed his eyes and exclaimed – "Jai Shambho! Jai Bhavani!" His voice echoed in the sanctum. Raje had received an assurance! The water from the Abhishek vessel over the Shivalinga kept trickling in a narrow stream!

The seventh day of the bright fortnight of Margashirsha broke out over the summits of the Bara Maval region. Jijau's heart was overcast with anxiety. She was sitting in the temple on Rajgad and kept offering one Bael leaf at a time on the Shivapindi in front of her. Shambhoobal sat next to her on a flat wooden seat.

As the day progressed, Jijau got utterly exhausted, planting her apprehensions on each Bael leaf and offering it on the Shivapindi. Almost all the Bael leaves had been offered, but the lake of her heart was still overcast with anxiety! As the sun came up overhead, Jijau rested her weary head in front of the Shivapindi. Tears started rolling down her tranquil eyes. Her body started shaking. All her superficial relationships had been washed away with the tears trickling from her eyes. All that remained was the maternal instinct! Only one strangulating thought filled her mind. It was smothering her– 'Maybe Shivabaraje has descended the fort by now and got caught in some trap! Why were the cannons fired during the night?

Shambhoobal was frightened to see that Jijabai was not raising her head, her whole body was shaking, and muffled cries were surrounding the pindi. He approached Jijau, shook her vigorously and called out to her – "Thoralya Aau! Thoralya Aau!"

Thoralya Aau was oblivious to her surroundings. She stood up and with tearful eyes walked briskly towards her chamber, the edge of her sari dragged along the floor.

Shambhoobal spread his arms and ran after her. Dharau came forward and held him back. She took him to her chamber.

Jijau locked herself in her chamber. She was feeling utterly lonely. Shambhoobal was utterly baffled in Dharau's chamber.

The early hours of the night passed. A fakir approached the closed Pali Darwaja. He tapped the gate three times and said the code in a thick, hoarse voice loud enough for the gatekeeper to hear.

The gatekeeper heard the code attentively and opened the wicket. The fakir promptly came in and rushed to the Padmavati machi. Sidoji Thopate recognized him. He was Vishwas Nanaji Musekhorekar – the ace informer! Sidoji and Vishwas came to the Balekilla on Rajgad. Sidoji sent intimation to Jijau that he was coming to visit her.

Jijau sat in her chamber with Shambhoobal. Her face looked drawn due to the anguish she had gone through the day. Sidoji and Vishwas entered Jijau's chamber.

Jijau got anxious when she saw a fakir with Sidoji. She got up at once. Sidoji and Vishwas made an obeisance to her. Jijau got confused for a moment. The next moment she recognized Vishwas. She trembled with fear and barely spoke in a strained voice – "Vishwas..."

Vishwas, who was making an obeisance to her stood erect. He had travelled a long distance. He spoke spiritedly – "Masaheb, time to distribute sweets! Goddess Jagadamba has saved us all. Raje cleverly destroyed Khan. Raje pulled Khan's guts out with tiger nails! Sambhaji Kavaji chopped Khan's head off with a single strike of his sword! Khan's head is in the royal hall of Pratapgad! And his headless body is rotting at the bottom of the fort. Jedhe–Silimkar, Bhosale– Pasalkar have surrounded Khan's army of twelve thousand in the town of Paar! A fierce battle has broken out in the valley of Javali. The Sarlashkar is riding towards Wai with his cavalry. Khan has been completely wiped out with his army. We have succeeded!"

Tears of joy rolled down Jijabai's eyes as she heard Vishwas. She turned around, stroked Shambhoo's temples and cracked her knuckles over her own temples. She picked up Shambhoo in her arms and said to Vishwas, "Vishwas, come to the royal hall. I must reward you for delivering this good news."

Jijabai was holding Balraje in her arms and couldn't resist the urge to say to him – "You keep asking who Khan is! The person who craves to devour all but ends up getting devoured by somebody else – is called 'Khan' Balraje!" Shambhoobal didn't understand what she said.

Jiva Mahala came from Pratapgad to Rajgad. He had carried a bamboo sling pot with Khan's head smeared in curdled, blackish streams of blood. To show it to Jijau, Jiva had placed it on a platter and covered it with a piece of cloth. The platter was placed on a wooden stool in the royal hall. All local inhabitants of the fort had assembled in the royal hall of the Balekilla to see Khan.

Jijabai entered the royal hall with Shambhoo on her left. Everyone made an obeisance to her. Jijabai took her seat in the royal hall along with Shambhoo and said, "Jiva, you have travelled a long way. Have you eaten anything?"

"No Maasaab, I am already full!" Said Jiva and removed the cloth covering the platter on the wooden stool. Jiva made an obeisance and said, "Dhani has sent this gift to Masaheb.

As she saw Khan's head soaked in curdled blood, with his eyes half open and mouth agape, she stood up at once. Her nostrils flared and her breathing intensified. Her lips trembled for a moment.

"Afzal Khan, you reap what you sow!" Trembling words slipped from her lips. This was the same Khan who had been the cause of endless worries for Jijau for the last many years.

Jijau immediately controlled her anger. She took her seat again and commanded, "Sidojirao, keep this head in a cage and place it in a corner of Pali Darwaja. Everyone on the fort will get a chance to see it. Perform the final rituals and bury it with full military honours. The enemy is dead – the enmity is over!"

Shambhoobal sat next to Jijabai and stared at Khan's head with wide eyes for quite a while. Many burning questions arose in his mind. 'Aba had gone to meet this Khan. How could he meet him when he has no hands and legs?' Thoralyaa Aau said – "The one who is eager to devour others, but whom no one can devour is Khan!" Then why didn't she simply tell me that Khan means just a head without hands or legs! Khan is the one who doesn't ride a horse but just sits on a platter!'

Finally, he couldn't contain his curiosity and asked Jijabai, "Dharau was saying that Khan is very big, then how come he is so small?" All courtiers in the royal hall laughed at his unexpected question. Balraje was confused. Jijau calmly patted his shoulders and said, "Your father brought as much Khan as he could. You can bring an even bigger Khan than this!"

Shambhoobal liked her suggestion very much.

Jijabai was awaiting Raje's return now. She wanted to feast her eyes upon Shivabaraje who had destroyed Afzal completely. Shambhoobal had many doubts and questions to ask his father. But Raje did not return to Rajgad.

A true commander exploits the terror compounded by one victory to his advantage and plans his future strategy accordingly. Raje did the same. He left Pratapgad and with his expeditious cavalry attacked the Adil Shahi sultanate with vengeance. Raje kept riding all over the region and notched up many victories.

Raje conquered places like Khatav, Mayani, Rampoor, Kaledhon, Valva, Ashti, Karhad via Nerle, Kameri, Battis-shirala, Paargaon, Kodoli, and after occupying Panhalgad he made an incursion into Kolhapur.

The entire Rajgad got drenched in the ocean of joy. Every day, the news of Raje's victories kept arriving at the fort. All the queens of Raje showered their affection on Shambhoobal, who seemed to make up for Raje's absence.

One day Shambhoobal was sitting in the private chamber surrounded by all the queens. Soyarabai asked him, "Balraje, would you give me the necklace you are wearing?"

"Sure, I will give you any necklace except the cowrie necklace!" Balraje replied.

"Why?" asked Soyarabai.

"Thoralya Aau says, 'the cowrie necklace is the real ornament of the Bhosale clan! When one is wearing the cowrie necklace, it keeps the mind in control. There is no chance of going astray!"

His answer left Soyarabai solemn, but Putalabai felt proud of him.

The last days of Chaitra arrived. It had been six months since Raje had left Rajgad. Jijabai was anticipating Raje's return before the advent of the monsoon. And one day her personal assistant informed her, "Bahirji, the leader of the espionage team has arrived."

Jijabai approached the royal hall with Shambhoobal, to meet Bahirji. Bahirji made an obeisance to her and stood in front of her with his head bent low. He could not lift his head. He didn't know how to speak in front of her. Finally, Jijau asked him in an intimidating voice, "Naik, why are you quiet? What's the news? Speak up. Don't try my patience."

Bahirji covered his face with his palms and in a heavy, hoarse voice he barely managed to say, "Terrible news Maasaab! Maharaj is trapped on Panhalgad, besieged by Siddi Jauhar. The enemy has surrounded the fort tightly!"

"Naik…!" Jijabai screamed in a strained voice. Her entire body went rigid. Her motherly heart was instantly surrounded by many apprehensions. Unwittingly, she pulled Balraje close. Her wandering mind fluttered around Panhalgad. Her heart was heavy. "How many times will Shivabaraje have to dodge death? How many calamities will continue to mar his happiness?"

Without uttering a word, Jijabai got up and holding Shambhoobal's hand, with a heavy heart, she trudged towards her private chamber.

She was the one who reassured others at tough times. But except for the omniscient Goddess Jagadamba, who else was there to reassure her?

Jijau's urgent firmans were immediately dispatched from Rajgad throughout the Bara Maval region. Chakan, Purandar, Sinhagad, Vardhangad, Pratapgad – from all sides Marathi troops began assembling at Rajgad. Everyone was wondering how to break the siege that Raje was stuck in. Sarnoubat Netaji was in the Gadag district in the Karnataka region.

Two months had passed since Jauhar had laid a tight siege to Panhalgad. Even a tiny gust of wind could not move in or out without his permission. Mighty sardars like Siddi Masood, Bhai Khan, Saadat Khan, Baji Ghorpade on the western side, and Fazal Khan, Rustam-i-Zaman, Bade Khan and Sarjerao Ghatage surrounded Panhala on the eastern side. Pudgy-lipped Salabat Khan Siddi Jauhar kept a keen eye on all of them and made daily rounds around the fort. The lion of Sahyadri was trapped in the siege of the Siddi hyenas and the local wolves.

Jijabai got tired of waiting for Netaji. She decided to break the siege of Panhala herself. The horses were saddled amidst rain showers. Jijau fastened the sheathed sword around her waist band. The infantry and cavalry were instructed to be ready to commence the journey.

Nobody dared to go to the royal hall to face Jijau. Shambhoobal, who lingered around her, didn't understand all the hustle. He had seen Thoralya Aau with a sword in her hand for the first time. He couldn't comprehend why. Finally, he asked Jijabai, "What is a siege, Thoralya Aau? I want to accompany you in breaking the siege!" Even in that condition, Jijau was moved by his innocence. Shivabaraje was her only surviving son and Shambhoo was his only son. Raje had told her to take care of Shambhoobal while leaving on the mission of Afzal Khan. He had not yet returned to Rajgad. Raje himself was trapped on Panhalgad. His innocent son is asking me, "What is a siege, Thoralya Aau?"

Jijau wanted to hold Shambhoobal in her embrace and tell him, 'A siege is something that stops life in its tracks and pulls at the hearts of women like me, who are left behind!' But she did not tell her grandson anything at all. Now, Jijau could not tell anything to anybody. It was not the time to tell but to do something; not the time to sit quietly but to act. Masaheb got ready to prove that 'the queens of the Bhosale clan will never be faint-hearted'. She had lived many deaths worrying for Raje's welfare. Now she was ready to die a conscious death for him.

All of a sudden, the kettle drums at Pali Darwaja reverberated. Immediately after that a message arrived, "Sarnoubat Netaji Palkar is climbing up the fort with Siddi Hilal!"

Netaji approached Jijau and made an obeisance to her. The raindrops were trickling down his barabandee vest and his twisted turban. He could not raise his head.

"Welcome Sarnoubat, I am climbing down the fort to break the siege around Raje. I am taking Shambhoobal with me. I had hoped to see you before leaving. Just remove your sword and give it to me! I have heard that the sword of the Maratha Sarnoubat bears the power of an elephant. That power will be useful for me to free Shivabaraje!" Devastated Jijabai rebuked Netaji with afflicting words.

All wet and teary-eyed, Netaji was shaken by her words. In

a hoarse voice, he said, "Masaheb, throw me down a cliff, but don't break my heart like this!

"I am not so weak hearted as to give up my sword. A mere siege cannot crush my loyalty. I will free Raje and only then come to seek your blessings. Farewell." Netaji made an obeisance to Jijau and Balraje and turned around.

Jijau looked at him and realized that she had spoken too harshly to him. In her usual motherly tone, she said, "Sarnoubat, rest for a couple of days, get refreshed first, and then do the needful!"

Netaji left no stone unturned in his efforts. He took Siddi Hilal with him and in the rainy season he fell upon Panhalgad to break the siege. But the alert Siddis defeated them. Siddi Hilal was captured. Netaji had to retreat from the foothills of Panhalgad.

Jijabai could do only one thing, make sure that Shasta Khan did not unite with Siddi Jauhar. She had summoned Firangoji Narasala, the senior, experienced custodian of Chakan fort for that mission. Firangoji arrived at Rajgad.

Masaheb said to him with quiet determination, "Firangojibaba, yet another dreadful calamity has befallen my son. There is no telling when some excruciating news will burn my ears. You are a veteran custodian of the fort. You remain in Chakan and take Shasta Khan upon yourself. If you do that, he will not come after Rajgad and Panhalgad. What do you think?"

"Masaheb, you are giving me such an easy task. I thought the siege of Panhala needs to be broken; you are waging a war on Panhalgad." Firangoji spoke his heart out.

"No, waging war on Panhala at this stage would unnecessarily put our people in the jaws of death. I am not ready to do that." Jijau convinced Firangoji.

Firangoji bade farewell to Masaheb and got ready to leave for Chakan. He was very fond of Shambhoobal. Since Raje was not there Firangoji bowed down in front of Shambhoobal and said, "My obeisance to you Dhakale raje". Balraje rushed to Firangoji; wrapped his arms around his legs and looking up he said, "I am going to besiege you Firangojibaba; or else you take me to Chakan with you!"

Gently removing Shambhoobal's arms wrapped around his legs, Firangoji, who had become solemn, said to himself, "Dhakale Dhani, how wonderful it would have been if everyone had a childhood like yours!"

Jijabai was losing heart now. It had been more than four months since Jauhar had laid his siege. More than eleven months had passed since Raje had left Rajgad. The entire fort was going through a nerve-racking ordeal. Jijau stopped talking to anyone.

Dharau prepared a Puja platter and placed it in front of the sanctum in Jijabai's chamber. Balraje stood by her side. He had seen his father come many times in the same chamber to take Jijau's blessings. He thought, 'it's been many days, Aabasaheb is not to be seen anywhere'. He was baffled and asked Dharau, "Dharau, what is a siege? Where does it live?"

Taken aback, Dharau glanced at Balraje. "I know nothing. Please don't ask me such questions." She said earnestly.

She checked the Puja platter to make sure everything needed for the Puja was in place. She saw that black ants had enveloped the chunk of jaggery in the bowl of Prasad. Dharau felt uneasy, looking at the chunk of jaggery covered by ants. She moved forward, removed all the ants with her hands and put the jaggery in another bowl.

She ushered Shambhoobal to Jijabai's chamber to meet her. Just then, she saw messenger Vishwas Nanaji coming there. His face had lit up. He made an obeisance and puffing his chest he said, "Masaheb, last night – the full moon night, Raje escaped from Jauhar's siege safely!"

"Vishwas...Raje escaped safely? Tell me everything quickly. How did Raje escape? Where is he? When will he come to meet me?" Jijabai got up and approached Vishwas. Her eyes were teary.

Vishwas recounted with pride, "Yesterday, during the full moon night, Raje climbed down Panhalgad with six hundred Bandal men. In the darkness of the night, the Bandals seated Raje in a palanquin and hastened towards Vishalgad. But the enemy got wind of his escape. Jauhar's son-in-law, Siddi Masood chased the Bandals with one thousand five hundred cavalries. The Bandals took turns carrying Raje's palanquin; running through the mud and slush; moving through the woods during the night and brought it near the Ghodkhind of Gajapoor. Baji Prabhu Deshpande of Hiradasmaval, saw that Masood's Siddis were approaching the gorge rapidly, so he split the troops in two. One unit left towards Vishalgad with Raje. Baji and his young brother Fulaji stayed behind with three hundred Bandal men to block the gorge of Ghodkhind. For about twenty-one hours Baji and the Bandals fought against the Siddis charging at the gorge. When Raje approached the foothills of Vishalgad the fort was surrounded by Surve and Palvankar. With the chant of 'Har Har Mahadeo' Raje broke the siege. Raje has broken through two circles of siege and is now at Vishalgad. He will come here tomorrow. But..."

"What happened Vishwas? Speak up." Jijabai noticed the change in his tone.

"But Masaheb, all three hundred Bandal men, Baji and his younger brother Fulaji, were slain while fighting against the Siddis in the gorge of Ghodkhind. The heartless Siddis trampled their dead bodies under the heels of their horses and crossed the gorge!"

As Masaheb heard the news that Vishwas had delivered, Baji's face lingered in front of her eyes.

In the Ghodkhind of Gajapoor the Bandals had sacrificed their lives in the service of their king. The lion of Sahyadri had thrown dust in the eyes of the Siddi hyenas and escaped.

The Ghodkhind of Gajapoor reverberated with the sounds of Baji's fighting sword and thus became the 'Bajipoorkhind'.

In the memory of the pure, faithful souls of the Bandals it came to be called 'Pavankhind'.

The kettle drums near the Pali Darwaja on Rajgad began booming rhythmically. Raje, who had arrived from Vishalgad was climbing up Rajgad, after eleven months!

Sidojirao came to receive Raje. Raje came up the Balekilla with him. While walking towards the royal hall, Raje was thinking about only Jijau and Shambhoobal. His eyes were eagerly searching for her. He approached the threshold of the royal hall. Shambhoobal came running, put his tiny arms around Raje's legs and affectionately called him, "Aabasaheb!"

Raje lingered at the threshold, glanced at Sidojirao and exclaimed, "I could break the armed siege of Jauhar, but… this siege is very difficult to break, Sidojirao!" Raje smiled and picked up Shambhoobal in his arms. He kissed Shambhoo's forehead, patted his back gently and put him back on the ground.

Jijabai stood in front of him. Raje approached her and put his head on her pure, holy feet. Jijau's eyes were brimming with motherly affection as she pulled him up and held him in an embrace. Shambhoobal was clinging to them. The trio could not break the siege of their kinship!

True to its name, Sangram Durg of Chakan besieged by Shasta Khan resisted him for fifty-four days. On the fifty-fifth day, Firangoji, the custodian of the fort put down his arms, surrendered Sangram Durg, and left for Rajgad.

Around the same time, realizing that his sardars could not deal with the tribulations caused by Raje, Adil Shah had proceeded from Bijapur in person towards the Maratha kingdom with a strong army.

But Raje could not leave Rajgad. The death anniversary of Saibai was approaching. Perturbed by Saibai's memories, Raje had summoned Shambhoobal to his chamber. As Saibai's dusky face lingered in his mind, Shambhoobal stood in front of him. Raje held his shoulders with affection and said to him,

"Shambhoobal, you asked Aausaheb what a 'siege' is! Let me tell you Balraje that a siege is something that cannot be broken when it is in front of you and doesn't let go of you when it is out of your sight. Raje's voice was heavy with the memory of Saibai. His eyes were searching for the 'dusky reflection' in Balraje's dark pupils.

Balraje stared directly at Aabasaheb and resolutely said, "No Aabasaheb! I know very well now what a 'siege' is! A siege is, when soldiers wielding naked swords want to kill the king who is trying to escape from the fort!"

Raje was moved to hear his words. He promptly picked up Shambhoobal and placed him in his lap. While stroking his back gently Raje thought, 'Balraje, it is not enough to understand the meaning of a siege. One should know the trick to break it effectively. You should never get caught in a siege.'

By now, Dharau's sons Rayaji and Antoji Gaade had formed a strong bond of affection with Shambhooraje. Growing up, Balraje was involuntarily getting trained in line with the legacy of the Bhosale family. Except for the time spent in Jijau's palace, Shambhoobal had been spending most of his time with Antoji and Rayaji. During his daily rounds around the fort, Shambhoobal had been closely observing how Raje had established the administrative systems of the eighteen departments. He had also been noting the customs of the seasoned staff employed in the Bara Mahal. While sitting in the royal hall by Jijau's side, he had been listening to the verdict given by the family council during various trials. He had been politely accepting the obeisance made by people to their 'Dhakale Raje'.

A young child learns more by observing others around him than under the tutelage of a guru. Children deprived of the loving care of a parent at a very young age learn a great deal from their circumstances. And a child born as the son of a king who faced death at every step of his kingship, learns substantially from the blood flowing through his veins!

Diwali lamps lit up Rajgad. Raje received the news that Shasta Khan's sardar Kahartalab Khan was travelling to Konkan by way of Umberkhind, along with the royal treasure. He bade farewell to Jijau, Shambhoobal and left Rajgad.

At the same time, Raje's subedar Tanhaji Malusare had been camping at Sangameshwar. His encampment was attacked in the middle of the night, by the combined armies of Suryarao Surve of Shringarpur and Jasawantrao of Palvan. Raje received the news of the attack in Rajapur. Raje returned from Rajapur to Shringarpur with his personal cavalry to settle the score with Surve. During the return journey, a skilled penman was recruited into the army. His name was Balaji Aavaji.

Raje travelled via Sangameshwar-Pali and reached Shringarpur. Raje's informers openly entered Shringarpur astride their horses. They brought news that Suryarao Surve had abandoned his fortress like a coward. But his diwan Pilajirao Shirke, a proficient swordsman, fiercely committed to his master was getting ready to defend the fortress.

Raje's personal cavalry fell upon Shringarpur, hollering the war slogan of 'Har Har Mahadeo'. Surve's fortress was surrounded within moments. Raje brandished his Bhavani sword and entered the fortress. The Mavala soldiers had already captured Surve's men and tied them up.

Raje forcefully kicked the bare throne of the Surves and roared, "A traitor's throne is only worth dust!"

The chest of a brawny man was heaving up and down while watching that scene. He was the diwan of the Surves – Pilajirao Shirke!

Tanhaji Malusare presented Pilajirao, tied in ropes, in front of Raje and exclaimed, "Here is the loyal servant of the deceitful master".

Raje walked towards Pilajirao composedly and untied his ropes. Raje said to Tanhaji, "You are wrong Tanhajirao, a loyal servant always overlooks his master's blunders."

Pilajirao stood in front of Raje, and staring into his eyes fearlessly he said, "Why did you release me? You kicked the throne that I used to make an obeisance to, and now you are praising me. Why? Instead, why don't you tie me to a horse and parade me in my own town!"

Raje patted Pilajirao's shoulder with his left hand and said, "Pilajirao! You are making a mistake! I did not raise these stables to crush loyal men under the hooves of horses! If required, they will bear the weight of the king's loyal men!"

Pilajirao who had made up his mind to face utter humiliation at his enemy's hands, had certainly not expected to hear such moving words worth sacrificing one's life for!

Astounded, Pilajirao looked at Raje in wonder. Raje understood the turmoil in his mind. Raje patted his shoulder and said, "Don't worry Pilajirao, I am not going to persuade you to join my army! I am quite impressed by your loyalty. But I would definitely give you a piece of advice – to be in the service of an insolent, traitorous master, is akin to a weapon that has lost its edge. It's better to cultivate crops than to serve the Surves!"

"Tanhajirao, please release Pilajirao honourably." Raje commanded and placed his Bhavani sword back in the scabbard.

Pilajirao's sideburns shook. He promptly leaned forward, touched Raje's feet and said, "Raje, I had heard a lot about you, but today I experienced it myself. I surrender myself to you. Now it is up to you whether to accept or reject my services."

Raje pulled him up, embraced him and said, "Pilajirao, I am not for breaking a friendship. All my life, I have been building new relationships with people. It is easy to break relationships, but quite difficult to build them!"

Pilaji implored Raje to visit his house. Raje went to Pilajirao's house with select men. Two children were playing in the courtyard. They were startled to see so many people.

Raje asked, "Whose children are they, Pilajirao?"

"Ji, my children. He is my elder son, Ganojirao and she is

my daughter, Rajasbai. Everyone calls her 'Rajau'. We call her 'Jiu'." Pilajirao informed Raje.

Ganoji looked very sharp, and he stood up with swagger. Rajau looked lovely and smart. There was no fear in her eyes. Furthermore, the moment Raje saw her, he felt that her facial features resembled those of Jijau's!

Raje stepped forward and patted both children. He said to Pilajirao, "Your children reminded me of my children!"

Pilajirao gave Raje a warm welcome. Raje assigned the subah of Shringarpur and Prabhanvalli to Tryambak Bhaskar and appointed Pilajirao as his assistant. Raje left Shringarpur and came to the outskirts. There was a temple in a corner.

"Whose temple is this?" Raje asked Pilajirao who had come to bid farewell to him.

"It is our family deity – Bhaveshwari." Pilajirao replied.

"Then, let's go and visit the temple." Raje said, and dismounted. He went inside the temple and prayed to Goddess Bhaveshwari. As he stepped out of the temple, he said to Pilajirao, "This family deity of yours may be related to our Goddess Jagadamba! This murti resembles our Goddess Jagadamba!"

After leaving Shringarpur, Raje's cavalry troops were trotting slowly. Two images lingered in Raje's mind –'Rajau' or 'Jiu' and Bhaveshwari!

As soon as Raje reached Rajgad, incessant monsoon showers began. The flora on the fort got drenched in streams of water. Raje took Shambhooraje with him and started reviewing the registers of the record office. The sword blades were being forged in the smithy by heating the metal on live coal and shaping it with sledgehammers. Raje visited the smithy and started assessing the sword blades. The rain waters kept plummeting. In Raje's mind, only one torrent kept surging – the thought of the green serpent that had infiltrated the Lalmahal – Shasta Khan!

Aashadh was over. The end of Shravan was approaching. Sunlight and rainfall kept playing a game of hide and seek! As scattered rain showers continued to fall from the foothills of Rajgad, the sounds of lively, ecstatic roars of "*Ude ga Ambe – Ude*!" were rising towards the sky.

Mambaji Naik had placed the stone murti of Bhavani Jagadamba in a palanquin and carried it towards the Pali Darwaja. Mambaji had succeeded in securely bringing the murti of Bhagavati Jagadamba to the Marathi kingdom from the green empire of Aurangzeb who was notorious for destruction of idols.

Raje came to the foothills with Shambhoobal and approached the palanquin. Mambaji applied haldi on the foreheads of Raje and Balraje. Both the sons of Goddess Jagadamba walked towards the palanquin placed on the floor. As soon as Raje saw the tall standing murti of the dark-coloured, weapons-wielding goddess, crushing the demon Mahishasura under her feet, he brought his palms together in prayer and closed his eyes while chanting 'Jagadamb-Jagadamb'. Raje and Shambhoobal stepped forward and touched Jagadamba's feet.

Raje signalled the palanquin bearers and gave the customary touch of his shoulder to the palanquin. When all the mavalas around them saw it, their hearts were filled with devotion and they hollered, '*Ude ga Ambe Ude*! Har Har Mahadeo!'

The palanquin arrived at Rajgad. Jijabai and all queens including Putalabai, Soyarabai, and Kashibai offered a piece of cloth and a coconut to Goddess Jagadamba.

On an auspicious mahurat, the palanquin descended Rajgad with splendour to travel further to Pratapgad.

Raje accompanied the palanquin along with Shambhoobal to the plains of the machi to bid farewell. While watching the palanquin climbing down the fort, Raje strongly felt, 'Saibai should have been here to take darshan of this murti!"

Raje arrived on Pratapgad with his entire family, for the installation ceremony of the murti. On an auspicious mahurat, Raje touched the murti of the goddess exclaiming, 'Jai Jagadamb'.

Amidst the chants of 'Ude ga Ambe Ude' the murti of

Goddess Jagadamba was installed upon the platform in the sanctum. Pratapgad was illuminated in the spirit of exuberance. All natives from the Javali and Koyana basins gathered on the fort to take the darshan of Goddess Jagadamba.

At night a huge crowd packed into the courtyard of Pratapgad, eager to watch the Gondhal of the goddess. In the courtyard, the bhutyas of Goddess Jagadamba had spread some rice grains in a square and kept a coconut on it.

Dressed in flared kurtas and churidars, and twisted turbans, the Gondhalis applied haldi on their foreheads and got ready. Some of them carried the Sambal drums and some were holding the single-string instrument, Tuntuna. Everyone was eagerly waiting for Raje's arrival.

Jijabai entered the courtyard, followed by Raje and Shambhoobal. The crowd was astonished to see both Raje and Balraje dressed up as bhutyas. They looked quite striking. There was no sign of any royal air, only passionate devotion!

Raje and Shambhoobal took their seats on the platform in the courtyard.

The chief Gondhali approached Raje, made an obeisance to him and said, "Dhani, I request you to begin the Gondhal by holding the sacred torch and doing the customary dance of honour in front of the goddess."

"As Mother Jagadamba wishes," Raje said and climbing down the stairs he came into the courtyard. The chief Gondhali handed the sacred torch to Raje. Raje held it in his hands and touched it to his forehead. The Gondhali poured Karanjel oil on the torch. Raje held the torch over a lamp that the Gondhali carried and ignited it. The Gondhali handed the stick he carried to Raje.

While chanting "Aai – Raja – ude ude!" Raje started dancing to the beat of the stick, holding the sacred torch of the goddess in the other hand.

While looking at the burning flame, Raje's eyes shone with

an unknown divine light! His body warmed up. In the fluttering flame of the sacred torch, he saw Afzal Khan with his hands spread wide! Drops of sweat gathered on the tip of Raje's sharp nose. For a moment, he felt as though white horses were running wild through his spine. 'I felt something just like this, when I killed Khan!' Raje's eyes glowed with intense splendour. He was lost in dancing.

While incanting "Aai – Raja – ude ude!" with his eyes closed Raje started dancing the torch frenziedly to the beat of the stick.

Shambhoobal's back inadvertently straightened while watching the shimmering flame of the torch from his seat. He had never seen his Aaba like this.

As Raje got tired of dancing the torch, he stopped. His dress was drenched in sweat. His hand holding the torch was shaking. In the reddish yellow light of the torch, Raje's perspiring frame looked like a Shivlinga that had been freshly bathed. Raje wiped his sweat with his forefinger and looked at the torch. Then he looked at the platform where Shambhoobal was sitting and said, "Shambhoobal, come into the yard."

Shambhoobal got up from his seat, came and stood in front of Raje.

Raje handed the torch to Shambhoo and gently patting his shoulder he said, "Here, take this Balraje, and you also dance the torch; better than me!" The entire crowd was surprised.

The Gondhali poured Karanjel oil on the torch flame and brightened it again. Raje gave the stick to Balraje, climbed up onto the platform and took his seat next to Jijau.

Shambhoo threw a glance at the burning flame of the torch with fearless eyes. Then, pounding the stick on the floor he roared "Bhavani – Raja – ude ude!" And the shimmering flame of the sacred torch in the hands of the Bal Rudra began dancing. Balraje started dancing with the torch spiritedly, to his heart's content.

The turban on his head kept bouncing and finally tumbled

onto the floor; his hair came loose. With his open hair, Shambhoo kept dancing the torch all over. His ruddy lips kept chanting, "Bhavani – Raja – ude ude!" The shimmering flame of the torch kept dancing around Balraje rapidly.

As she watched Balraje dance passionately, Jijau unwittingly took her palms near her temples and cracked her knuckles!

From the crowd, a mavala hollered in excitement, "Har Har Mahadeo!" Everyone around shouted in unison.

The loud sound made Balraje stop his dance. His hand holding the torch was trembling! His dress was drenched in sweat. He felt like he was going to faint. He threw a silent glance at Jijau. Jijau rushed into the courtyard. She took the torch from Balraje's hands and handed it to the Gondhali. Jijau held Shambhoobal and gently ushered him to the platform. Fatigued, Shambhooraje sat on Raje's right. His face had lit up with intense splendour. Unknowingly, Raje's hand started stroking the wet dress stuck to his back.

The chief of the gondhalis, carrying a wicker basket, approached Raje. There was a mixture of haldi-kumkum in it. A necklace made of sixty-four cowries lay in there, daubed in the haldi-kumkum. The Gondhali chief leaned forward and holding the basket in front of Raje, he said, "Dhani, this is the Vaan of the goddess. When you become the Bhutya of the goddess, you must keep this basket in the sanctum of your family deity and perform a puja for it. During the Navaratri festival, as the Bhutya, you have to seek alms from five homes." "We would be happy to seek alms in the name of the goddess." Raje said and accepted the Vaan of Goddess Jagadamba.

The gondhali came back to the courtyard. He sang prayers of Lord Ganesha and began describing the glory of Adishakti Jagadamba. The night continued to ascend on the fort and the Gondhal of Goddess Bhavani continued in the courtyard.

A sorrowful incident happened at the time, that broke the hearts of the Marathi people – the courageous and ingenious

Sarnoubat, aged Mankoji Dahatonde passed away in Shivapur. Swaraj lost one of its valiant, patriotic gems.

Raje made some changes in his administrative system. He removed the fraudulent Shamrao Ranzekar from the post of Peshwa, allocated that responsibility to Narahari Anandrao and appointed Annaji Dutto as Waqia Navis.

One more member was added to Raje's family. Sakwarbai ranisaheb gave birth to a daughter. She was named Kamalabai.

The festival of Navaratri arrived. On the ninth day, Shastra puja was performed, and goats were sacrificed. The dawn of Vijayadashami broke out on the eastern horizon.

Raje and Shambhoobal took a bath. Both wore the dresses of Jagadamba's Bhutyas and donned graceful turbans. The father and son came to visit Jijabai. Both touched her feet and made an obeisance to her. Raje cheerfully said, "Aausaheb, we are going to visit five households on the fort today and seek alms from them in the name of Mother Jagadamba. Give us your blessings and advise us as to whom we should visit today."

Jijabai replied, "Raje, as Jagadamba's Bhutya you should hold out your hands in front of the senior people. The darshan of seniors early in the morning is always fruitful!"

Raje took Jijabai's blessings and left the palace with Shambhoo.

Raje and Shambhoobal sought alms from the houses of five elders – Sonopant Dabir, Netajirao Palkar, Moropant, Yesaji Kank and Annaji Dutto, and went back to their chamber. The machi surrounding the fort looked at their figures and wished wistfully, "Saibai should have been alive to see this!"

The sizzling days of summer arrived. Raje was going to travel to Vardhangad. He bade farewell to Masaheb and Shambhoobal and left Rajgad.

Shambhoobal was now taking more interest in horses. Rayaji and Antoji Gaade would carry Balraje on their horses and practise horse riding with him. Mohammad Sais would train and teach him the habits of the horses.

The horse became Balraje's favourite animal.

Various images of the horses got engraved on Shambhoobal's royal heart like the seal engraved on gold coins in the mint.

Gomajibaba Pansambal started training 'Dhakale raje' to balance the hilt of a sword, to wield the Patta sword, to throw a spear accurately while running, to protect himself using the shield while fighting with the Patta, and to throw and retract the blade of a Vita sword quickly.

Jijau began telling Balraje the stories of mighty and valiant characters from Ramayana and Mahabharata. She affectionately answered all inquisitive queries of Balraje and satiated his curiosity. Abhimanyu, fighting all alone at the centre of the Chakravyuha formation; Srikrishna, sitting on the chest of mighty Kansa at a tender age; elephantine, powerful Bheema defeating Bakasura; skilled archer Arjuna, shooting an arrow into the eye of the fish; Karna, desperately trying to pull out the wheel of his chariot trapped in the mire; loyal Jatayoo, fighting ferociously till Ravana slashed his wings; Bharata, who came back only after receiving the prasad of Ramachandra's wooden clogs; Rama, Lakshmana, Sita, who were banished from Ayodhya, due to Kaikeyee's diabolical plan – all these characters made a deep impact on Shambhoobal's mind.

Autumn was coming to an end. Rajgad received the news that Raje was coming back after finishing a mission. In the Pen region, Raje had collided with Namdar Khan, a sardar of Shasta Khan. During the skirmish, Raje lost his subedar Krishnaji Babaji. Vaghoji Tupe was injured. Raje arrived on Rajgad with their thoughts in mind.

Meanwhile, in Delhi, Aurangzeb had fulfilled an old wish that he had harboured for a long time. He got his brother Murad, who was imprisoned in Gwalior, accused of murder by the Muslim priests and jurists, and sentenced him to death by the decree of the holy Quran.

As coldly as a goat is sacrificed publicly for 'Bakari Id' Aurangzeb's executioners beheaded Murad in the central square of Gwalior!

Dara had already been disposed of. Now Murad was executed too; but such trivial events barely affected Aurangzeb's personal life. Within three months of executing Murad, he hosted a grand feast in Aurangabad to perform the circumcision ceremony of his son Mohammed Akbar!

'Aurang' means the royal throne. 'Zeb' means the one who enhances its power. Only a monarch of elite aristocratic descent such as Aurangzeb could interpret the meaning of his own name in such a distorted way. 'Kafirs' like Shivaji considered the royal throne as a 'Gadi' and believed that loyalty was the virtue that sustains the 'Gadi'. Aurangzeb utterly disapproved of such nonsense.

Moropant, Annaji Dutto, Nilo Sonadeo, Netajirao, Yesaji and others had gathered at Rajgad for the honour assembly. Raje, Jijau and Shambhoo took their seats in the royal hall.

Raje signalled the courtiers to sit down and commenced the honour assembly, "I have called this honour assembly to propose some modifications in the rules and regulations of the administrative system. As Shasta Khan is encamped in Pune and determined to destroy our kingdom, it is imperative that we make our administrative system infallible.

"This is Swaraj, the kingdom of God. I have raised this Swaraj on the strength of the support I got from all of you. Now, all of us need to think collectively about how to expand the borders of this kingdom.

"It is an arduous process to raise a new kingdom from the ground up; it is even more difficult to maintain it, and expanding its borders is the most laborious task! Everyone should give their best to sustain Swaraj! We should remember all the men who sacrificed their lives for Swaraj and put our best efforts in this mission.

"Power corrupts man. The Greater the power, the more the corruption. The rights that power brings along should work like restraining reins. They should not be used for whipping innocent people!

"I appraise your qualities. You should appraise the qualities of our Mavalas! The elders – the youngsters – by taking everyone along, the ones who are sitting should be made to stand up; the ones who are standing, should be made to walk; and those who are walking, should be made to run! We should delegate responsibilities to everyone to keep the kingdom running smoothly!"

Shambhooraje was listening to Abasaheb attentively and holding the words close to his heart. Raje stood up while speaking and gestured to his personal assistant. The personal assistant approached Raje with a servant who was holding a big platter.

Raje looked at Moropant and said, "Moropant, please come forward!"

Moropant got up promptly and approached Raje. He made an obeisance to Raje and while keeping his head bowed, he stood in front of Raje respectfully.

Raje picked up a golden-bordered white shawl from the platter, placed it on Moropant's shoulder and addressed the assembly,

"From today, Moreshwar Nilkanth Pingale is entrusted with the post of the Peshwa of this kingdom! I will assess the enemy attacking this kingdom with my own eyes and treat him accordingly. And I will evaluate the administration of the kingdom through Moropant's vigilant eyes!"

Moropant was overwhelmed. He leaned forward and touched Raje's feet. Raje pulled him up and held him in a deep embrace. Moropant made an obeisance to Jijau and Shambhoobal.

Raje assigned Moropant's Mujumdari to Nilo Sonadeo. Annaji Dutto Prabhunikar was appointed as Surnis. A new position of 'Panditrao' was created. This was assigned to Raghunath Bhat, a scholar of religious matters.

Before concluding the honour assembly Raje delegated the responsibility of curbing the hostile activities of Namdar Khan in the Supe region, to Netaji Palkar.

The assembly was over. Raje went towards his palace while pondering about how to overpower Shasta Khan. But Shambhoobal, walking with Jijau, was still musing about one thing – 'Abasaheb speaks so splendidly! The ones who are sitting should be made to stand up; the ones who are standing, should be made to walk; and those who are walking, should be made to run!'

As per the command, Netajirao attacked the army of Namdar Khan near Supe. As Khan was more powerful, Netaji's troops could not sustain the battle. Netaji himself was gravely injured and hence had to retreat. Namdar Khan and Sarfaraz Khan chased Netaji, but Netaji eluded them successfully and proceeded towards Rajgad.

Injured Netaji arrived at Rajgad. Raje inspected his wounds in person, instructed the physician to administer medication and advised Netaji to take a break.

As the Sarnoubat himself was injured, Raje's hands were tied. To make matters worse the monsoon started. Wild clouds began pouring water on the Maval region. The eaves of the palaces on Rajgad began trickling. Red streams started cascading down the fort.

During this monsoon Raje entrusted the post of Waqia Navis to Gangaji-Mangaji. The tumultuous rains lasted for five months. News arrived from the Bara Maval region that Namdar Khan had returned with a vengeance. He was destroying all the villages in his path. From the Rohida basin, Baji Jedhe, Kanhoji Jedhe's son, wrote a letter detailing Khan's atrocities.

Raje sat in the royal hall to send a reply to his letter. Jijau and Shambhoo sat next to him. Raje began dictating the contents of the letter to Chitnis Balaji Avaji.

"To Sarjarau Jedhe–Deshmukh, Rohida basin, from Shivaji Raje – Our informers have brought news that the Mughals have recently been attacking your region. Therefore, I advise you to evacuate the ryots in your region and move them to a safe and secure place, where the enemy won't be able to reach. As soon as you see the enemy at a distance, you change your path and flee!"

Balaji Avaji completed the letter, took Raje's signature on it and sealed it with the official seal. Then he put the letter in a pouch and secured its mouth.

While hearing the contents of the letter, one line uttered by Raje, was imprinted on Shambhoobal's mind, "As soon as you see the enemy at a distance you change your path and flee!"

Though Raje advised Sarjerao Jedhe to flee for the safety of his ryots, for himself he had chosen the mission to infiltrate Shastakhan's fiendish encampment at Pune which consisted of one lakh twenty-five thousand soldiers. It was imperative to infiltrate the camp now, but not easy. Raje had been contemplating it for many days and nights.

The night of Hutashani Purnima descended on Rajgad with a shining, platter-sized full moon. The players of Holi found a tall Aina tree in the Kananda basin and carried it to the fort. They cut it into pieces and erected a pile for the Holi fire in the centre of the chowk. The Mavalas devoured many Puranpolis and began gathering in the Holi chowk afterwards. The booming sounds of tabors reverberated all around.

Raje donned an exclusive attire and came to Jijau's chamber with Shambhoo. He sought Jijau's blessings and proceeded to the Holi chowk on the Balekilla. Balaji and Chimanji Narhekar, Moropant, Netaji, Firangoji, Yesaji, Kedarji Jedhe, and Sidoji Thopate joined him. Raje held Shambhoobal's hand in his left hand.

Raje came to the Holi chowk with his retinue. The booming sounds of the tabors subsided and the commotion of the Mavalas abated. Raje held the lighted torch in his hand and gazed at it for a moment. He uttered, 'Jai Jagadamb!' and touched the lighted torch to the pile of wooden logs arranged in the Holi to set it afire.

The assembled Mavalas hollered, "Har Har Mahadeo!" The Holi fire started burning.

Raje sat down with Shambhoo on the raised platform meant for the royals.

As per the custom, a few coconuts were tossed into the flaming Holi. Young, audacious Mavalas encircled the Holi to extract the coconuts briskly from the burning fire, before they were completely burnt.

A robust Mavala succeeded in grabbing a coconut from the fire! "Well done, way to go, my man!" the Mavalas around him cheered and lifted him onto their shoulders.

Sidojirao proudly presented that Mavala in front of Raje. Raje got up from his seat, patted his shoulder and put a golden bracelet around his wrist. When the winner received a golden bracelet from Raje's noble hands, that young Mavala felt as if his whole life was blessed!

The moon of the Hutashani Purnima was ascending in the sky while watching the flaming Holi. Raje was returning from the Holi chowk to his chamber with Shambhoo, but a Holi of thoughts had inflamed his mind.

'If I want to ignite the Holi of my enemy and smoothly pull out the coconut of success through the scorching embers...I must get in the field now. I must stick my hand in the scorching flame!'

Shambhoobal was walking with him. He asked Raje, "Aba, will you too pull out a coconut from the flaming fire of Holi?"

Raje smiled, nodded, and whispered to himself, "I will try!"

The day of Ramanavami dawned. Balraje took a bath early in the morning. After getting Jijabai's blessings, Balraje left to pay obeisance to all Masahebs in the queens' apartments.

He arrived in Soyarabai's chamber with Dharau. He leaned

forward and touched Soyarabai's feet. Soyarabai pulled him up and looking at Dharau she said, "He is so well-mannered! I wish Balraje was named 'Ramraje'!"

Balraje sat on the bed. While taking the glass of saffron milk from Soyarabai, Balraje noticed her bright complexion, like a Kewra flower. He tried to imagine his mother's face but couldn't do it to his satisfaction. All he could visualize was a vague, dusky face. He put the glass of milk to his ruddy lips while questioning himself, 'I really wonder what my masaheb looked like!'

Shambhoobal drank the milk and placed the glass on the wooden stool. He bade farewell to Soyarabai and left the chamber. As she looked at him, Soyarabai's royal heart felt, 'I don't have a son like you, otherwise I would have named him 'Ramraje' for sure!'

From Soyarabai's chamber, Shambhooraje came to Putalabai's chamber with Dharau. Putalabai sat in front of the sanctum with her eyes closed, after offering the flowers to Rama's murti. Balraje didn't want to break her reverie, so he stood gazing at her intently. Putalabai opened her eyes after some time. She joined her palms in prayer, touched them to her forehead and whispered something. Balraje stepped forward to touch her feet and said, "Masaheb, I would like to seek your blessings!"

"Arise Balraje." Putalabai said and quickly getting up from her seat, she pulled up Balraje up before he could touch her feet. She put her hand on his shoulder, took him to the bed and made him sit there. She picked up the prasad of dry ginger powder mixed with sugar as well as a flower placed in front of the sanctum and approaching Balraje she said, "Here, take the prasad of Lord Rama's birth!" Shambhoobal placed his right palm over his left palm and accepted the prasad and the flower. Then he lifted both his hands and touched them to his forehead; he held the flower in his left hand and consumed the prasad.

Balraje sat in the chamber for some time. He looked around the chamber and thought, 'Whenever I come to this chamber, it feels like I am in a temple!'

"Aausaheb, may I take your leave now?" Balraje asked and got down from the bed.

"Yes of course." Putalabai said with a smile. Balraje left the chamber with Dharau. As she looked at his back, Putalabai's loving heart felt, 'Balraje, whether you are in my presence or not, you remind me of your father! I feel you are like my own son!'

Chimnaji and Balaji Narhekar were climbing Rajgad. Raje's palanquin was at a distance behind them, surrounded by Sarjerao Jedhe, Netaji, Moropant and Tanhaji. The kettle drums at Pali Darwaja resounded to announce Raje's arrival. Along with Balraje, Jijabai went to the gate of the Balekilla to receive Raje. It had been five days since the festival of Ramanavami.

Raje had employed an exclusive strategy to uproot Shasta Khan's barrier from the encampment of Pune, one single move that no one could have ever imagined.

Raje left Kondhana and went into the woods of Katraj. He stationed Netajirao with one cavalry unit to the east of Pune and Moropant with another unit to the west of Pune. He selected about a hundred and fifty skilled swordsmen. Raje and his swordsmen entered Shasta Khan's base at Pune, disguised as guests of a wedding party, playing lezim to the beats of drums in the wedding procession.

Raje, who knew every nook and corner of Lal Mahal, was accompanied by his childhood playmates Chimnaji and Balaji. Raje had already surmised that Shasta Khan and his attendants were going to be in slumber due to the fasting of Ramzan. After midnight, along with Chimnaji, Balaji and a few Mavalas wielding swords, Raje broke through a window and infiltrated Lal Mahal. A skirmish broke out. Furious Raje passed by many chambers and entered Shasta Khan's sleeping chamber. Khan was within his reach now. To finish Khan with a single strike of his sword, Raje struck promptly. But Khan jumped through a window in desperation. The blade of Raje's sword struck Khan's fingers holding the window frame for support. It sank in the wooden frame, after slicing the tips of Khan's three fingers! Khan's fingertips fell on the floor, smudging the window frame red!

"Ya Allah!" Khan screeched, shaking his bleeding hand. Khan hid behind a wall and fled from the chamber. Khan's son Abdul Fatteh was killed instantly during the skirmish. In the darkness of the night the Mavalas mistakenly slashed many women in the harem. A few Mavala swordsmen were also killed. When Raje realized that the camp was becoming aware of the attack, he signalled all to withdraw from the palace.

"The enemy is escaping! Follow the devils!" The Mavala swordsmen shouted and left from the back door of Lal Mahal. They started galloping rapidly towards Kondhana.

To mislead the enemy's horse riders who were following them, Raje instructed his men to tie lighted torches to the horns of some bullocks and drive them towards the Katraj ghat. Raje reached Kondhana safely by a detour.

This raid on Lal Mahal served its purpose of terrorizing Shasta Khan. On the third day, Shasta Khan entrusted the responsibility of the Pune encampment to Jasawant Singh and left Pune in fear. After camping in Pune for three years, capturing two forts of Raje and losing three fingers, within three days of the raid, Khan left Pune.

Raje climbed the Balekilla and touched the feet of Jijabai who had come to receive him. Shambhoobal stepped forward and grabbed Raje's finger. Raje held his tiny palm and said with a smile, "Balraje, I couldn't take the whole coconut out of the Holi! I could grab only its tail!"

As Shambhoobal's forehead puckered, Raje smiled and affectionately stroked his small fingers. Then he recounted how he sliced Shasta Khan's three fingers in Lal Mahal.

The sizzling days of Vaishakh arrived. One morning, Gomajibaba was practising the Dashrang with Balraje, on the open ground of the Balekilla, on the black, Mallakhamb pillar made of stone. Shambhoobal was wearing only an orange loin cloth. His bare body was shining like a ripe lemon.

Gomajibaba helped Balraje climb up the Mallakhamb. Like a bright yellow Dhaman snake slithering swiftly along a bamboo shoot, Shambhoobal rustled along the pillar in the upward Dashrang move and reached the top in no time. He tightly held the tip of the pillar in a scissor fold of his legs and carefully looked up. He saw Raje coming out of the royal hall of the Balekilla! Behind him were Doroji, Netaji, Yesaji, Tanhaji and others.

At once, Shambhoobal swiftly rustled down the pillar with a downward Dashrang move and leapt onto the ground. The moment his feet touched the ground, he sprinted towards Raje. He was oblivious to Gomajibaba who was calling after him, "Dhakale Raje, O Dhakale Raje…wait a minute!"

Breathless Balraje caught up with Raje who had reached the entrance of the Balekilla.

Balraje embraced Raje's legs and urged him with loving implorations, "Abasaheb, can I come to the battle with you?"

Raje hesitated for a moment. He was descending the fort for the Konkan campaign. Raje affectionately ruffled Shambhoobal's thick, black, curly hair and said to him, "I will definitely take you to a battle, but for that you have to grow up a little bit. Now, go to Gomajibaba, he is waiting for you. Go back to your training."

Shambhoobal leaned forward to touch Raje's feet and seek his blessings.

Jijabai saw both father and son from the window of her chamber and said to herself, "Aai Ambe, may no evil eye ever be cast on this treasure of mine!"

And while observing the same scene from her chamber, Soyarabai mumbled to herself, "Balraje is so ill-mannered! He approached Maharaj in bare minimum clothes, but that sweet imp looks very charming. He reminds me of my intimate moments with Maharaj!", Lost in this thought, she kept gazing at Raje who left from the main gate of the fort.

Immediately after the Dussehra celebrations, Raje secretly delegated his skilled informers like Karmaji, Bahirji, Vishwas, and Mahadeo to Aurangzeb's subah of Gujarath. They thoroughly inspected the harbour of Surat, located near the western ocean, with their sharp eyes and delivered every minute detail to Raje.

The harbour of Surat rested near the ocean like Lakshmi, the goddess of prosperity. Raje devised an ambitious plot, that of ransacking Surat!

For that purpose, Raje had to coerce Jaswant Singh out of Pune. From Fort Kondhana, Raje's Mavala soldiers audaciously began attacking Jaswant Singh's encampment in Pune by day and night. Offended, Jaswant Singh left Pune with his army and laid siege to Fort Kondhana. The path for the Surat campaign was now wide open!

The raid on Shasta Khan had led to the rise of a rumour everywhere that Shivaji practised sorcery! He can vanish from a place suddenly and appear anywhere, anytime he wants!

Indeed, Raje had cast a spell of enchantment on the black boulders of Sahyadri and the loyal hearts of the faithful Mavalas! On that strength, Raje was not going to 'vanish' at all, but only going to 'appear', wherever he wanted to!

The day of marching towards Surat dawned. Soyarabai gazed in the mirror that her maid Chandra held in front of her and drew two horizontal lines of kumkum on her forehead. She kept staring at her own ravishing reflection. Those kumkum stripes perfectly complemented her fair complexion and straight, rosy nose. Her reflection in the mirror was telling her, 'These two stripes of the kumkum represent myself and Maharaj!' Soyarabai felt delighted at her own idea.

"Maharaj is on his way." A palace maid announced the arrival of Raje and left the chamber promptly. Chandra, who was holding the mirror, put it on a wooden stool and was about to leave the chamber. Just then, Raje entered the chamber with a smile on his face. He had come there after taking Jiajabai's blessings and taking leave of all others. He had donned a blue Jama decorated with gold-threaded design. The saffron Jiretop enhanced its grace.

As soon as Raje entered the chamber, Chandra gingerly walked along the wall and left promptly.

Raje sat on the bed. Soyarabai offered him a glass of saffron milk. Raje took a sip of the milk and looking at the statuesque figure of Soyarabai he asked, "Where is Balibai?" Balibai, Soyarabai's daughter had gone to Jijabai's chamber.

"She doesn't like it here. She must have gone to Masaheb's chamber!" Soyarabai gave Raje a pointed look. Raje understood what she was implying. He emptied the glass of milk and got up with a smile. Going towards the window, he said, "If engaged properly, anyone would stay back."

From the window, Raje could see the horse-riding arena. He could see two stable boys, Mohammed Sais riding a tall, elegant stallion and Shambhoobal standing aside, holding the reins of a pony.

A ripe lemon was placed on a stone plinth in the field. Sais guided his horse to one edge of the field. Then he turned his horse to the opposite side, facing the stone plinth. He took a moment and prodded the horse with his heel. The horse sprinted towards the stone plinth. Raje watched with curiosity.

As soon as Sais came close to the plinth, he pulled the reins of his horse and prodded it to change its gait. The horse picked up its front hooves and rose up in the air. While leaping over the plinth it unerringly tossed the lemon in the air with its rear hooves!

Raje exclaimed unwittingly, "Well done Sais." Soyarabai heard Raje's words and came close to him out of curiosity.

Mohammed Sais repeated the same feat a couple of times as accurately as before. Then, he dismounted and approached Shambhoobal. He made an obeisance and said, "Chhote Raja Saab, your turn now!"

Balraje held the reins of his pony and placed his left foot in the stirrup, but he couldn't lift his right leg and mount the pony. Sais interlocked both his hands and created a brace for him. With the support of that brace, Balraje lifted his right leg and mounted the pony. Raje and Soyarabai watched curiously.

Balraje took the pony to one end of the field. Then he turned it around and prodded it. The pony sprinted towards the plinth. As Balraje came near the plinth he pulled the reins of his pony and prodded it to change its gait. The pony took a leap over the plinth... but the lemon remained there, shining in the sun. Raje frowned, watching it and became solemn. Soyarabai covered her mouth with the edge of her sari and sniggered.

Two-three times Balraje took a leap with his pony over the plinth, but that lemon did not move at all. Raje felt agitated and restless.

Balraje got ready to take the leap again when Mohammed Sais grabbed the reins of his pony and said, "Chhote Malik, the leap is good. Now keep your eyes on the lemon, and not on the pony! Try it again."

Balraje focused his eyes on the lemon and rode the pony again. As he came near the plinth, he gave enough pressure with his heal to lead the pony. While leaping over the plinth the pony tossed the lemon with its rear hooves!

Raje applauded unknowingly and exclaimed, "Bravo, well done!" His face lit up, but Soyarabai was unmoved.

Balraje's pony took a leap over the plinth, but while landing, it lost its footing and collapsed on the ground along with Balraje.

"Ya Allah! Sais exclaimed in fear and promptly rushed to release Balraje's feet from the stirrups. He shook off the dust on Balraje's jama and said, "Chhote Malik, whenever your horse trips, don't forget to release your feet from the stirrups without delay! Or else, the frightened animal stands up and drags the rider along recklessly! Quite terrifying!"

"I see Balraje tumbling down like this every day!" Soyarabai said to Raje in a dull voice.

"He falls, but he gets up again! He rides his pony effortlessly! I must leave now. I must bid farewell to Balraje," Raje said and hastily walked out of Soyarabai's chamber.

A month and a half had passed since Raje left for Surat with Netaji, Tanhaji, Yesaji, Kudatoji and the cavalry. As usual, Jijabai took a bath in the morning and after performing the puja, she went to the royal hall with Balraje. She wore a white sari. Her forehead was daubed with thick, horizontal stripes of kumkum.

Jijabai entered the royal hall with the usual smile on her face. She signalled to the courtiers to take their seats and took her seat with Balraje.

Though she told everyone to 'sit' nobody sat down. No one raised his head as usual with shining eyes to deliver news of Raje's valiant feat. Everyone stood with their hands folded. Jijabai was alarmed. Instantly, countless dry leaves of suspicion scattered on the lake of her mind. She rose from her seat, and said in a trembling voice, "Why are you all so quiet? Tell me, is there any bad news about Raje?" She couldn't say anything further.

The courtiers were agonized by her words. Sidoji Thopate barely raised his head and said, "No masaheb, Raje is doing fine. He is on his way back after a successful attack on Surat, but..." Rough and tough Sidoji couldn't understand what to say next. He lowered his head again. Tears streamed down his eyes.

Balraje left his seat, came close to Jijabai and held her hand.

"Then tell me whatever it is." Jijabai said with relief, but the dreadful silence in the royal hall did not break. No one raised their head. In the end, Mujumdar Nilopant barely managed to utter, "Masaheb, a bareheaded messenger has arrived from Bengaluru!"

"And…?" Jijau frowned at once.

"Thorale Maharaj was on a campaign in the Bednur region. He went hunting in the woods of Hodigeri. He was following a wild animal on his horse and..." Pant hesitated.

"And...and what Pant?" Jijabai exclaimed in agitation.

"And his galloping horse tripped in a hollow. With his feet caught in the stirrups, Maharaj was dragged along the ground. Masaheb, Thorale Maharaj...has left all of us!" Nilopant covered his mouth with his shawl and tried to suppress his sobs. Tears began rolling down the eyes of all present in the royal hall.

Jijabai kept staring with vacant eyes, as if she had been struck by lightning. Her body was trembling intensely like the staff of the royal pennant trembling in stormy winds. Her senses were completely benumbed. She felt as if the royal hall was revolving around her. "How could he go like this, without meeting me or talking to me?" She burst out. At once, she yanked her hand out of Shambhoobal's hand and as she wiped off the kumkum from her forehead, her forbearing heart was completely shattered. Dressed in a white sari, with a bare forehead, sobbing Jijau left, her body trembling, and her face covered with her hands.

Balraje stood alone. The words of Mohammed Sais echoed in his ears, 'Whenever your horse trips, don't forget to release your feet from the stirrups without delay! Or else...' With tears streaming down his eyes, distressed Shambhoobal sprinted towards Jijau's chamber.

Jijabai decided to follow in the footsteps which had always remained out of her sight. Aausaheb decided to commit Sati! Rajgad was devastated. Jijabai ordered her personal assistant to make arrangements for the ritual of Sati. There was turmoil in the queens' apartments. Not a single queen dared to try and make Jijabai change her decision. Jijabai sat on the floor, behind the closed doors of her chamber, dressed in a green sari, wearing green bangles, horizontal lines of kumkum drawn on her forehead. She felt like an empty earthen pot! She had a blank look on her face. Raje was on his way back from the Surat campaign.

In Rajgad, only one woman was utterly disturbed – Putalabai. She took Shambhooraje with her, stood near the closed door of Jijabai's chamber, and gestured to Balraje.

"Thoralya Aausaheb …" Balraje stepped forward, knocked gently on the door and called Jijau.

"It's me – Shambhoobal. Could you please open the door?" Shambhoobal took his mouth close to the door and asked Jijau in a tender voice. He waited for some time, but there was no response from inside.

"Thoralya Aau, please open the door, or else I will start banging my head on the door! Open the door, Aau." Balraje started thumping the door loudly.

Jijabai was shaken and her resolve weakened, 'Indeed, Balraje will not hesitate to bang his head on the door!' She somehow managed to get up and open the door. Her condition was like that of a worn-out cow who, trying to find her way out of a thick green forest had unknowingly reached the edge of a giant cliff!

Balraje quickly moved forward, clasped her legs and looked up. With tears rolling down his eyes he said, like a young Bhutya imploring Goddess Jagadamba, "Are you… are you going to leave me alone Aausaheb? I – I will also come with you!"

When Jijabai heard these words, her suppressed grief burst out. She took Balraje in an embrace and began crying freely.

"Aausaheb, please don't go anywhere till Aabasaheb comes back!" Balraje implored her. Jijabai nodded in affirmation while controlling her sobs.

Putalabai wiped her tears and looked affectionately at Balraje who had succeeded in preventing Aausaheb from committing Sati till Raje returned from his campaign.

After successfully completing the campaign of Surat, Raje arrived at the foothills of Rajgad. The victorious cavalry followed him along with sacks full of gold, silver, gems pearls, and so on. But no one had come from the fort to receive him as usual. Raje frowned; his right eyebrow arched with royal wrath.

He threw a glance at the top of Rajgad. The moment he saw the flagstaff standing bare on Padmavati machi his anger vanished instantly. The triumphant horse of his mind was instantaneously reined in by countless apprehensions.

Raje dismounted with a frown. He began ascending Rajgad, seated in a palanquin. As the palanquin passed through the Pali Darwaja, he immediately felt the absence of the drum beats that usually announced his arrival. His mind was filled with doubts.

Raje passed by all chambers and finally stood in front of Jijabai's chamber. Raje, who had defiantly broken through the doors of many mansions of oppressive, insolent, and wealthy traders of Surat, opened the closed door of Jijau's chamber with trembling hands!

Jijabai, dressed in the garb of Sati, was sitting on a carpet. Putalabai and Balraje were sitting on either side of her.

As she heard the door creak, Jijabai raised her head, and the moment she saw Raje standing in front of her she screamed profusely. Her lamenting left Rajgad's heart in tatters, "Shivaba … my fate is sealed! Maharaj Saheb is no more!" Jijabai was shaking like the forbearing earth trembling during an earthquake.

Raje felt as if molten lead had been poured all over his body. He froze. He closed his eyes and held the tip of his sharp nose with his right hand. The image of Shahajiraje flashed in front of his eyes. Raje glanced at Jijau with tearful eyes. Through the whitish veil of tears, he saw an obscure green vertical line. His entire body trembled.

'Why is Aausaheb wearing a green sari today? She hasn't done this before.' As the doubt arose in his mind, Raje felt as tormented as a mighty elephant that feels the pain of serrated hooks digging into its feet. Raje immediately wiped his tears and stepped forward. He pointed towards the platters prepared for the ritual of Sati and asked in a tremulous voice, "Masaheb, what are you doing?"

"I am going where my husband has gone Raje! I am going to follow your Maharaj Saheb in the blazing palanquin of the pyre! With my widowed hands I am going to give away the Vaans of Sati!" Jijau had never spoken with such grief in her entire life. But today, she spoke with great determination.

Raje, who was always astride a horse with his head held high, stepped forward with lowered head and sunken heart. He knelt in front of Jijau and placed his head on her lap. With his body trembling in grief, in a shaken voice he said to her, "No Masaheb, please don't leave me alone! Don't leave Shambhoobal alone! I am going to fulfil my vow of raising Swaraj. Who is going to watch it happen? Who is going to watch Balraje growing up into Shambhooraje? Until today, I always touched your feet to seek your blessings. Today, I am spreading my hands in front of you to seek the alms of your life. Please don't leave me empty-handed.

Jijabai did not expect Raje to react in such a manner. Her resolve weakened, and she hesitated. She closed Raje's palms with her hands adorned with green bangles and said earnestly, "No Raje, don't spread your hands for alms! Mother Amba Herself has bestowed you with bountiful blessings –what more can I give you? I – I will learn to live with my widowhood. For the sake of this kingdom! For you! For the sake of Balraje! You are already facing many problems. I will not make life more difficult for you by committing Sati."

Raje's spirit rose like a flag flying at full mast on a conquered fort. And yet, his heart ached in the memory of Shahajiraje!

Putalabai listened to everything with a heavy heart, her gaze fixed on the floor. Only one thought nagged her, 'It must have been incredibly painful for Masaheb to change her mind.'

Balraje who was observing all this with an overwhelmed

heart, understood two things clearly, 'Aabasaheb gets teary eyed too! And Thoralya Aausaheb is far greater than I can comprehend her!

As the news of Shahajiraje's demise spread in the Maval region, Raje's kith and kin arrived on Rajgad. Shambhoobal's mama Bajajiraje Nimbalkar also came from Faltan. Raje's head was shaved in the presence of all the relatives. Raje performed the obsequies of Shahajiraje with a bare head and a heavy heart.

While watching the rituals, Shambhoobal was trying hard to picture the image of Thorale Maharaj Saheb whom he had never seen. But no matter how hard he tried, the image of his Aabasaheb kept appearing in front of his eyes!

Finally, one day, when he came to Jijau's chamber to seek her blessings, he asked her, "Thoralya Aau, what did Thorale Maharaj Saheb look like?"

As misty-eyed Jijabai looked at Balraje, she felt for the first time that, 'Shambhoobal's face resembled his grandfather's! The nose and eyebrows, broad forehead and keen eyes like a clean mirror; he looks just like his grandfather!'

Jijau wanted to pull Balraje close with affection and tell him, 'Shambhoobal, you look just like Thorale Maharaj Saheb.' But she didn't say anything.

Bajaji mama came to visit Raje in his chamber to express a wish before going back to Faltan. He made an obeisance to Raje and said, "Raje, I would like to go back to Faltan. With your permission I would like to take Balraje with me. It will be a good change for him. What do you think?"

Raje remembered Saibai while looking at Bajaji and realized that Shambhoobal had never got a chance to visit his maternal grandparents' home. I could never visit Sindakhed – my maternal grandparents' home. Shambhoobal should not have to suffer the same fate. Raje thought for a moment and said to Bajaji, "Sure Bajaji, you can take Balraje with you! But seek Masaheb's permission too. Take Dharau and Antoji-Rayaji, and a troop of armed guards with you. You are family. I understand your feelings. But make sure that you accompany Balraje during the return journey."

Bajaji felt jubilant as he received Raje's permission. He left Raje's chamber while imagining how joyous the family would be to see Shambhoobal in person.

After seeking Jijabai's permission, preparations were made for Balraje's travel. On an auspicious day, on Padmavati machi, a palanquin was kept ready for the travel. Balraje took the blessings of Jijau, Raje and all his Masahebs and left from the royal hall of Rajgad. Dharau and her two sons, Antoji and Rayaji walked with him. Raje held Balraje's hand and came up to Padmavati machi, to bid farewell to him.

Balraje touched Raje's feet and looked at him. "Take care of yourself." Raje said and patted Balraje's shoulders.

Shambhoobal and Dharau sat in the palanquin. The palanquin started descending Rajgad. Young Rayaji and Antoji walked on both sides of the palanquin, wielding their swords. A troop of armed guards walked behind the palanquin. Bajajimama, who had donned an elegant Adil Shahi kimosh on his head, embraced Raje with affection. He gave Raje a reassuring look and he too started walking behind the palanquin. Raje kept looking in the direction of the palanquin till it disappeared.

At twilight, Faltan came into sight. At the periphery of the town, Bajajiraje instructed the palanquin bearers to set the palanquin down. Then, he sent a horse rider to give intimation to his family that Shambhoobal was coming to visit their home. The dormant Nimbalkar residence came alive with fervour after hearing that news.

Bajajiraje's sons Mahadaji, Tuloji, Kanhoji and Gorkhoji came to receive Balraje on the outskirts of the town. Shambhooraje hugged his four cousins.

Balraje entered the town of Faltan, the birthplace of his Aausaheb, along with his mama, Bajajiraje and cousins.

As their residence, built of stone, came into view, Bajaji pointed towards it and said, "Balraje, look there, that is your Masaheb's home!" While listening to his mama's words, Balraje didn't realize when and how his right hand touched the cowrie necklace on his chest.

Shambhooraje came to the nail-spiked entrance and feasted his eyes on the house in front of him. Married women performed aukshan for him. Gold coins were waved around and showered upon him. Shambhoobal entered the home of his Masaheb. His eyes were moving around rapidly, observing every nook and corner of the house.

"Come Balraje, let's pay obeisance to the family deity first." Bajaji pointed to the sanctum in the house. Shambhooraje followed his mama to the sanctum and prayed to God. Bajaji summoned all the ladies of his family to the sanctum.

In his heart of hearts, Balraje was looking for something that he had lost. After dinner, he came to the sleeping chamber. Dharau was with him. Balraje removed his Jiretop; she placed it on a platter on a stool. Balraje lay down on the bed. Dharau sat near his feet and started pressing his legs gently. As soon as Dharau felt that he was fast asleep, she spread a shawl over him and lay down on a carpet.

Dharau slept on her side, folding her tattooed arm under her head like a pillow; her breathing was rhythmic; but Balraje had become restless on the bed. He could not sleep in the new place. He was tossing and turning frequently. The shawl over his body had already fallen aside. Only one thought kept nagging him. 'What did my Masaheb look like? Why can't I remember her face?' Shambhoobal felt suffocated like a fish out of water. Suddenly, he heard a thudding sound coming from the adjacent chamber. The windows in that chamber were banging. The gusty wind coming from River Banganga had wildly swept into the Nimbalkar residence!

The sounds of the swishing air and the banging window,

coming from the adjacent chamber, continued. Shambhoobal was tossing and turning. The bedsheet under him was crumpled.

'Masaheb!' He felt like screaming at the top of his lungs and calling out to his Masaheb. Suddenly, a hand touched his back, which startled him, and he sat up. It was Dharau! Though she had a fair complexion, she looked 'dusky' due to her tattooed hands, forehead and neck. As Shambhoobal saw her, unwittingly he uttered in a tremulous voice, "Dharau …, aausaheb!" Dharau affectionately stroked his thick, curly hair with her peasant fingers and said, "Don't be scared, I'm here for you!" And she held Balraje's head to her bosom.

By now, the banging of the windows in the adjacent chamber had died down. The swishing winds had disappeared. The adjacent chamber in the Nimbalkar residence was the 'maternity room'! Many years ago, Saibai had been born in that chamber! Dharau and Shambhoobal knew nothing about it. Dharau wiped the sweat on Balraje's forehead with the edge of her sari.

Shambhooraje spent a few days at Faltan and returned to Rajgad with Bajaji mama. Meanwhile, Jasawant Singh who had laid siege to Kondhana got frustrated due to the constant firing of cannons from Kondhana, and after ending the siege of Kondhana had left for Aurangabad in despair.

Raje himself had returned to Rajgad after conquering the Mughal territory from Ahmednagar to Aurangabad. Things were heating up in the Delhi durbar of Aurangzeb. thanks to the ransacking of Surat, the retreat of Jasawant Singh, and the Mavalas attacking Mughal territory. Raje was standing near a window in his chamber, with his hands clasped at the back, thinking about Aurangzeb's next move in retaliation. His eyes were fixed on the meandering bed of River Gunjavani. He was repeatedly fidgeting his lean fingers. He had already forgotten the intimation that Bajaji was coming to visit him.

Bajaji entered Raje's chamber and hesitated as Raje was standing with his back to him. To make Raje aware of his presence he politely said, "I would like to go back Raje."

Raje's chain of thoughts broke. He turned around and said to Bajaji, "Why are you leaving so soon, Bajaji?"

"I must go, Raje. The Monsoon is approaching. I wanted to discuss something before leaving, that is why I am troubling you."

"What trouble? Tell me." Raje calmly came close to Bajaji.

"Thorale Maharaj is no more..." For a moment Bajaji fell silent in memory of Shahajiraje.

"What is meant to happen will surely take place. One's life is not in one's hands. When I saw Balraje up-close in Faltan, it reminded me of Maharaj many times and I strongly felt one thing. We should get Balraje married! It should be done within a year of a family member's demise. Otherwise, as per the Shastras, for the next three years we cannot get him married!"

While hearing Bajaji's words Raje felt a deep turmoil in his heart. It was not Bajaji speaking. It was his love for Saibai; his gratitude for Raje, recalling Raje's gracious support during his hard times.

Raje stared at Bajaji for a moment. 'Shambhoobal's wedding!' Just the idea made Raje forget all politics – Aurangzeb, his schemes, and retaliation...for a moment, he was only Shambhoobals's overjoyed father. The image of Shambhoobal as a bridegroom appeared before his eyes. With a peaceful smile Raje said to Bajaji, "It's good that you broached this topic. At least, such an occasion will alleviate Masaheb's pain a little bit. Please broach this topic with her before you leave."

Bajaji mama's face glowed with joy when he heard Raje's words. He bade farewell to Raje with content and left the chamber. While looking at him, Raje's lean fingers tenderly kept stroking the cowrie necklace on his chest. Raje was lost in thought; in front of his watchful, tapering eyes stood Shringarpur, a town surrounded by luscious mango orchards. Only two images flashed in front of his eyes – the family deity of the Shirkes of Shringarpur – Bhaveshwari, and Pilaji Shirke's lovely daughter who had a divine countenance – Rajau – Jiu!

Raje dispatched a messenger to Shringarpur and summoned Pilaji Shirke immediately with Ganoji and Rajau. Pilajirao arrived at Rajgad with his retinue and both children.

Raje summoned a council in the presence of elders and veterans. On one side of the royal hall, Raje's queens and other ladies of the family sat behind a curtain. Raje sat by Jijabai in the royal hall and presented a marriage proposal to Pilajirao, "Our Maharaj Saheb passed away... as per the custom, we must get Balraje married within a year of his demise. I would like to have your daughter Rajau as the daughter-in-law in our family. That is why, I have summoned this council. Please express your opinion about this candidly."

Raje's gracious words touched Pilaji's simple heart. He realized now, why Raje had summoned them so urgently. Pilaji looked at Jijabai and Raje with misty eyes and said, "Raje, we are no match for your family! If you had simply ordered me to get my daughter here to tie the knot with Balraje, I would have surrendered her at your feet. What more could she ask for from life?" Pilaji spoke earnestly, from the bottom of his heart, acknowledging Raje's higher status.

"No Pilajirao, yours or mine, a daughter is the 'treasure' of a family. She must be received ceremoniously. I haven't asked for the hand of your daughter just for the sake of my son's marriage, but to respectfully welcome her as the daughter-in-law of our family. Your loyalty to Swaraj matters more than your social status. We value this alliance as we hold your loyalty precious. Therefore, at this time, I would also like to offer my daughter Nanibai's hand in marriage to your son Ganojirao. What do you think of this mutual relationship between our families?" Raje asked Pilajirao with a smile.

The veterans in the royal hall were impressed and looked at the wise king with admiration.

Pilaji, who received another shock that was least expected, nodded in affirmation, and just barely uttered "Ji".

Shambhooraje, Ganoji, Rajau, and Nanibai were summoned to the royal hall. All four of them made an obeisance to everyone in the royal hall.

Raje got up and gently approached young Rajau. An attendant held a platter of sugar in front of him. Raje picked up a fistful of sugar from the platter, raised Rajau's lowered head with his left index finger and glanced into her eyes. Rajau could not completely take in Raje standing in front of her! Raje glanced at everyone in the royal hall and said, "In the presence of the people in this royal hall and with Masaheb's blessings, I have chosen Rajau, the daughter of Pilajiraje Shirke of Shringarpur, to be wedded to my son, Shambhooraje." Raje poured the fistful of sugar in Rajau's mouth. The family priest presented a platter of kumkum to him. Raje picked it up and drew a horizontal line of kumkum over Rajau's forehead. Then he threw a quick glance at the curtain behind which the queens were sitting. Rajau leaned forward and touched Raje's feet.

There was a murmur among the queens to decide who should go and feed sugar to Rajau. The royal hall was waiting. Golden-hued and gold-hearted Putalabai pushed the curtain aside and came forward. She touched Masaheb's feet and then fed sugar to Rajau. Rajau leaned forward to seek her blessings. Putalabai blessed her wholeheartedly, 'May you be blessed with a long life!'

Pilaji and his wife fed sugar to Nanibai and applied the kumkum on her forehead. The Bhosale-Shirke marriage alliance was thus formalized.

Both girls paid respects to Jiaju and everyone in the royal hall and went inside. Shambhooraje and Ganoji sat next to Jijau respectfully.

Balaji Aavaji prepared the guest lists for the ceremony in his neat handwriting. A collective decision was taken to solemnize the wedding on an auspicious mahurat in Margashirsha. Dried dates and pieces of coconut were distributed in the royal hall. The betrothal ceremony took place. At night, delectable food was served to celebrate the betrothal between the Bhoasle and Shirke families.

Pilaji Shirke returned to Shringarpur with Rajau. The Mriga constellation showered blessings over the Maval region! Inundated, reddish rivers rushed to unite with the ocean. Now, for at least four-five months Raje was going to stay at Rajgad. Raje took upon himself the responsibility of the preparations for Shambhoobal's wedding. Putalabai's enthusiasm knew no bounds. Dharau's tattooed hands got busy in making sure that everything went smoothly. Jijau visited every department in the fort and checked everything in person.

After the wedding ceremony, Shambhooraje and Rajau leaned forward to seek Aabasaheb's blessings. Shambhooraje touched Raje's ruddy, fair, lean toes with his hand and stroked it over his Jiretop. He put his forehead on Aabasaheb's feet. That touch gave Raje goosebumps. Raje put his hands on Balraje and Soonbai's head who were making an obeisance to him and blessed them in a gentle voice, "May you be blessed with good life! May you achieve success in your life!"

Raje leaned forward and gently pulled up both. Shambhooraje was dressed in wedding attire and a few grains of rice were stuck in the folds of his Jiretop. Raje looked at Shambhooraje as if he was looking at his own reflection. The image of Saibai's dusky face arose from the deepest recesses of his heart. Her last words echoed in his ears, 'My Shambhoobal... a lonely baby... leaving him in your care...!' Raje got lost in thought and kept gazing at Shambhoobal dressed as a bridegroom. As Raje looked at Rajau who had lowered her head, a thought flashed in his mind, 'Sai, when you left Balraje in my care as a lonely baby, neither you nor I realized that this child would eventually bring new people into our lives, forging new bonds of familial relationships! Give them your blessings now.' Raje patted Shambhooraje and Rajau's shoulders as gently as he used to caress the cowries on his chest.

At night, both bridegrooms were made to sit on embellished horses, and a big procession was taken out. Skilled swordsmen displayed various feats in front of the procession to the rhythm of resounding tabors. Troops of lezim players kept dancing in various formations. Gold coins were showered on the brides and bridegrooms. The Ukhali cannons kept booming.

After midnight, the couples paid a visit to the temple, and the processions came back. As Shambhooraje was entering the house, Sakhoobai spread her arms and stopped him at the door. She reminded her brother of their blood bond and asked him, "Will you give your daughter in our family?"

Shambhooraje was baffled. Netaji whispered in his ears and told him the answer to the question.

Shambhooraje told Sakhoobai with a smile, "If a daughter is born to us, then we will give her in your family!"

Sakhoobai made way for him. Shambhooraje crossed the threshold. Rajau followed him with lowered head, and she pushed the cylindrical container filled with rice grains, placed at the threshold. The rice grains dispersed near the threshold of the Bhosale household. Rajau entered the house as the daughter-in-law, like the auspicious Goddess Lakshmi.

The bride and groom took darshan of the family deity and performed Ganapati puja. A golden platter full of rice grains was presented in front of Shambhooraje. A discussion took place about what name should be given to the new daughter-in-law. An order was issued from Jijabai's chamber, 'My grand daughter-in-law should be named 'Yashoda".

Prabhakarbhat Rajopadhye took off Shambhooraje's ring and gave it to him to hold. Then he held Shambhooraje's hand in his own and on rice grains spread on a platter, wrote the name 'Yashoda' with the ring.

After concluding all wedding rituals, Shambhooraje took Rajau with him to Jijabai's chamber. Dharau stood behind Jijabai.

With misty eyes, Jijau kept gazing at Balraje decked up in wedding attire. Shambhoobal stepped forward and put his head on Thoralya Aausaheb's feet. Rajau touched her forehead daubed with horizontal kumkum stripes to Aausaheb's feet. As Jijau pulled up Balraje and Rajau and held them in an affectionate embrace, she remembered her husband. Jijau lifted Rajau's chin and said with love, "Yesu ss". Rajau raised her head and gazed into Aausaheb's eyes. She saw an abundance of love in Jijau's tranquil eyes.

Jijabai stroked Balraje's back and said to him, "Shambhoobal, touch Dharabai's feet."

Dharau was moved to hear those words and unwittingly uttered, "No! Please! Not my feet!"

Yet, Balraje and Rajau stepped forward and touched her feet to seek her blessings. Dharau pulled them up, and blessed them, "Be happy, my children!"

Rajau of the Shirke family had now become 'Yashoda', the harbinger of victory for the Bhosale family. When Jijau lovingly called her 'Yesu', 'Yashoda' became 'Yesubai'!

As Shambhooraje was leaving her chamber, Jijabai remembered Shahajiraje and thought, 'Balraje, you look just like Thorale Maharaj Saheb. But you should never turn your back on your family like he did! You should never abandon my granddaughter-in-law Yesubai!'

Chapter 2

After the wedding, the Gondhalis performed the customary Gondhal dance of Goddess Bhavani. The hustle and bustle of the wedding calmed down, and all the guests left. Pilajirao Shirke took Yesubai, now the treasure of the Bhosale family, back to Shringarpur.

Pausha Amavasya was approaching. The Maval region was abuzz that 'the sun was going to be eclipsed' on this Amavasya. Prabhakarbhat consulted the almanac and confirmed the occurrence of the eclipse. He advised Raje to go to a holy place and offer clothing, food and gold as charity to offset the effects of the eclipse.

Raje chose the holy place of Mahabaleshwar to offer charities. Raje was going to fulfil a wish on this occasion that he had held for quite some time. He was going to conduct a 'Suvarntula' of aausaheb and aged Sonopant Dabir, who had dedicated his life to the service of Swaraj selflessly. He was going to offer gold, equal to their weight, in charities.

Raje left Rajgad on an auspicious day, along with Jijau Saheb, Shambhooraje, Putalabai, Sonopant Dabir and select troopers. Raje had not given any intimation of the Suvarntula to Jijau and Sonopant.

The palanquins reached the holy place of Mahabaleshwar. Basking in the glow of fading winter, the town was camouflaged by dense woods.

Raje helped Masaheb to alight from her palanquin. Putalabai

and Shambhooraje also stepped out of their palanquins. The surroundings looked mesmerizing in the slanting rays of the setting sun. Shambhooraje was delighted by the beauty of the landscape. An unknown excitement stirred his heart. He looked all around and tried to feast his eyes on everything he could.

The cowrie necklace on Balraje's chest rose and fell in a rhythmic beat, but with an increasing tempo. His golden earrings swayed. He couldn't comprehend the tumult in his heart and kept gazing around intently. He felt something but couldn't quite grasp it.

A hand touched his shoulder, and someone called out his name 'Shambhoobal'; he came to his senses. It was Aabasaheb. He said with a smile, "Balraje, what are you staring at so intently? I called you twice, but you didn't hear me!"

Shambhooraje smiled. He pointed at the surroundings and said, "Maharaj Saheb, I was observing all this. It felt like these mountains, the sky, the birds, the trees – everything was saying something to me!"

Raje became solemn as he heard these words. He patted Balraje's shoulder and said, "You are so blessed! One needs to possess the heart of a Yogi or a poet to understand the language of the trees and the birds! Very few people have such a heart!"

Shambhooraje gazed at the horizontal stripes of sandalwood paste on Aabasaheb's forehead. Raje began walking with Balraje towards the place where preparations for the Suvarntula were in progress.

The ominous day of the solar eclipse was about to dawn. Raje took a bath, and with Putalabai, Aausaheb, Sonopant Dabir and Balraje, he came to the place where the Suvarnatula was going to be held.

On the early morning mahurat, the priests began performing the puja of the large-sized, silver pans. The surroundings resonated with the chanting of mantras.

Raje touched Jijabai's revered feet and said politely,

"Masaheb, come. Take a seat on the weighing scale."

Jijabai looked into Raje's eyes and in a voice choked with emotion she said, "Raje, why are you doing my Suvarntula?"

Raje kept gazing at her feet and said, "The Sun God is going to be over-shadowed soon. Who else is worth weighing, to ward off the ill effects of the solar eclipse? Masaheb, this is what I wish. Come."

Raje supported Jijabai and ushered her to the pans. Aausaheb offered haldi-kumkum to the pans. While muttering 'Jagadamb' Masaheb put her right foot on one of the silver pans. It hit the floor. Masaheb took a seat on it like she would do in the royal hall.

The ritual of Tuladan began with the chanting of mantras. Raje and Putalabai started pouring shining gold coins onto the empty scale.

The pan onto which golden coins were being poured began descending slowly. The pan on which Masaheb was sitting, lifted and began rising slowly. Raje felt content while watching it happen and didn't even realize that tears of joy were trickling down his eyes onto his beard. The Suvarntula of Aausaheb took place in the true sense.

After that Raje performed the Suvarntula of venerable Sonopant Dabir who had withered with age. Raje gave the customary touch of his hand to the platters full of gold coins from the Suvarntula. The gold coins were distributed as charity. After accepting the charities, the happy crowd hailed Raje.

The Suvarntula and charity offering was over. The palanquins of the royal family left Mahabaleshwar. The Bhosale family returned to Rajgad from Mahabaleshwar. A message had arrived from Malvan that the construction of the sea fort had been completed. Raje was planning to launch a naval attack on the region of Karnataka, but he could not leave Rajgad. Shahajiraje's first death anniversary was approaching. Raje instructed Prabhakarbhat to plan for the annual Shraddha ritual.

Prabhakarbhat made all the preparations for the ceremony.

Raje took a bath and got dressed. He came to Jijabai's chamber with Shambhoobal while reminiscing about Shahajiraje. Jijau Saheb was sitting on a carpet, melancholy and still. She was lost in thought. Her heart was brimming with memories of dashing Shahajiraje.

Raje stepped forward and touched Aausaheb's feet. Jijau Saheb raised her head. Her eyes were tearful. Her words choked in her throat. As she saw Shambhooraje standing in front, her aching heart was stirred.

Shambhooraje came forward and bent down to touch Thoralya Aausaheb's feet. Jijau got up at once; holding his shoulders she pushed him aside, and as if she was talking to herself, she said to him, "No Balraje, not today!"

Raje got confused and with his head held low he said, "I am climbing down the fort to perform the ritual of pind daan, Masaheb... we are going to the banks of River Kanand...."

"Farewell." Jijabai said while turning her back and started walking slowly towards a window in her chamber.

Raje left her chamber with Shambhoobal, wondering, why Masaheb did not allow Balraje to pay obeisance to her today. Did Balraje commit a mistake? Raje couldn't find the answer.

There, Jijau was standing at the window in her chamber. While looking at the meandering bed of River Kanand, she remembered her late husband and said to herself, 'Shambhoobal, you – you look exactly like your Thorale Maharaj Saheb! Just like my better half!'

Raje and Shambhooraje perfomed the pind daan ritual on the banks of River Kanand, and offered cows in charity to the assembled Brahmins. Then, the father and son left the banks of River Kanand and started walking barefoot towards Rajgad.

The palanquin arrived at Padmavati machi. Just as Raje was stepping out of his palanquin, Tatasarnoubat Sidojirao said to him, "The Chief of surveillance, Bahirji Naik has reached the fort and seeks permission to present himself." Raje's forehead furrowed in concern. In a grave voice he said, "Present Bahirji in the royal hall on the machi."

Raje came to the royal hall on the machi with Balraje. Courtiers present in the royal hall made an obeisance to them; Raje and Shambhooraje accepted their obeisance and took their seats. They sat down and immediately dismissed all courtiers. Everyone made an obeisance and left the royal hall. It was now completely empty. Sidoji Thopate presented Bahirji in the royal hall and went outside. Bahirji Naik, the chief of surveillance, stood in front of Raje with his head lowered.

"Yes Naik, what is it?" Raje reassured Bahirji. Bahirji kept gazing at Shambhoobal's feet and gave the news in a trembling voice –

"Dhani, a mammoth army of Mirza Raja Jai Singh with Diler Khan, thirty thousand cavalry, and five thousand Pathan soldiers is coming to charge upon us. The enemy is encamped at Burhanpur. Jai Singh's army is getting reinforcements from various places!" Bahirji's heart weighed heavy.

Raje got up at once after hearing the news. His fingers moved faster than usual over the cowries resting on his chest. Many thoughts rushed through his mind.

Aurangzeb dreamed of Shivaji's death by his birthday, and had appointed Mirza Raja Jai Singh, a Rajput sardar, to attack Shivaji. He had played a diplomatic move of using one thorn to remove another, by pitting one Rajput against another. To make sure that his strategy worked out well, he had imposed the company of Pathan Diler Khan on Mirza Raja.

Raje was momentarily shocked on hearing the news, but he recovered quickly and said, "Bahirji, you have travelled quite far. Please have something to eat. You may leave now!" Bahirji made an obeisance and left.

Raje was lost in thought. He took Shambhooraje with him and came near the tunnel behind the royal hall on Padmavati machi that opened on to the Balekilla. The guards stationed at the tunnel made an obeisance to Raje and pushed aside the huge boulder covering its mouth.

Two Mavalas went inside the tunnel to show Raje the way. Raje entered the tunnel after them. Shambhooraje stood at the mouth of the tunnel. Raje held Shambhooraje's hand and took him inside. In the dim light of the torches, they started climbing down the stone steps

Raje was very quiet. Balraje followed him. He thought, 'when is this tunnel going to end?'. He asked Raje while walking behind him, "Maharaj Saheb, when is this tunnel going to end?" Balraje's voice echoed in the tunnel.

That echo made Raje stop in his tracks for a moment. Without looking back, he said, "Shambhoobal, keep walking behind me! Tunnels are endless. One should never stop walking!" Raje's solemn voice echoed in the tunnel again…" And Raje kept walking ahead. His son Shambho followed his orders and kept walking behind him.

Raje left on the Karnataka campaign. To impart the daily training of Fari-gadakaa, the shield and the club, to Balraje, Gomajibaba had girded up his loins and taken his stance. The veins in his legs had protruded and his churidar had tightened on his calves. He was wielding a platter-sized shield stuffed with felt and covered in leather, in his left hand. He wielded a club in his right hand and said to Shambhooraje, "Yes, Dhakale Raje, take your stance. Keep your eyes on my legs and on the club in my hands." Gomaji's feet were rooted to the ground as he got ready to attack.

Shambhooraje squeezed his left fist on the handle of the shield and brandished the club in his right hand. He stepped forward with his left foot and held the Fari, in front of him. Then arching his back carefully, he took a stance. He touched his club to Gomajibaba's club and exchanged salutations gracefully.

"Jai Bhavani!" Gomaji roared and pulled his club back to attack. The eyes of the old veteran were shining.

"Jai Bhavani!" Shambhooraje shouted and tightened his body to gauge Gomajibaba's attack. The practice of the 'Ghai' manoeuvre began. Gomaji kept moving swiftly around the ground. He attacked with pre planned blows after giving intimation each time. Shambhooraje started blocking his blows with the thick shield. His nimble body swayed like a cobra's hood. Their bodies, hot from exertion, began sweating. As the Gadakaa touched the Fari the sounds of 'Dhuup, dhuup...' resounded.

While practising the 'Ghai' manoeuvre, Shambhooraje had successfully managed to keep the club away from his body. Gomaji was impressed by his alertness. The first round of practice ended. Gomaji made a gesture to stop. He wiped the sweat on his forehead and said, "Dhakale Raje, I am getting old now. I start sweating very quickly! Okay now, let's practise the 'Chhoot' manoeuvre!"

Gomaji took the stance of the 'Chhoot' manoeuvre! His body was now going to be as swift as the wild wind! It was not going to be easy to throw a punch at him. The opponent could not be sure from which side he would attack. The 'Chhoot' manoeuvre was a kind of free fighting; with an attitude of 'kill or die' while fighting against the enemy. In this manoeuvre one was supposed to deceive the enemy and strike him freely, from any angle one wanted. One was not supposed to spare the enemy for his laxity. Shambhooraje held the shield and wielded the club in his hand. Gomaji kept waving his club left-right and started moving about freely. To divert Balraje's eyes fixed on the club he kept tricking Balraje. Shambhooraje did not take his eyes off the club. He started gauging the moves and kept moving about vigilantly.

"Balraje, be ready, I am going to strike any time now. Be watchful!" Gomaji spoke slowly.

"No, it won't touch me!" Shambhooraje said resolutely while staring at Gomaji's club.

Suddenly, Gomaji raised his club high and to confuse Balraje he hollered at the top of his lungs, 'Har Har Mahadeo'. His scream startled Shambhooraje! He thought the strike was going to land on his head and therefore, he raised his shield over his head! Before he knew what was happening a heavy strike of Gomaji's club struck right below his chest! Balraje writhed in agony.

Gomaji promptly threw away his club, rushed towards Shambhooraje and pressed his palm on the spot where his club had struck. Words flew from his mouth, "How can I tell you how I feel when I have to attack you like this? But you shouldn't be careless. One needs to be strong hearted to wield a weapon. In a real battle, there will be a bigger commotion. Balraje, you shouldn't lose heart so easily!" Gomaji's loyal eyes got misty. Shambhooraje pushed his hand aside and said determinedly, "I am not going to lose heart! Gomajibaba, take your stance!"

They took their stance again. Shambhooraje forgot the pain in his chest. He was planning different strategies of attack.

Shambhooraje kept moving around cautiously and waving his club left-right, while dodging Gomajibaba. He realized that it was difficult to attack him from the front. Shambhooraje swayed his body loosely, hollered 'Jai Bhavani' and swiftly went behind Gomajibaba. He bit his lip and struck Gomajibaba hard on his bare calf. An acute pain shot from Gomaji's calf to his head, and unknowingly he exclaimed, "Well done!" A shooting pain had spread in Gomaji's leg, but his eyes were filled with tears of joy. He dropped his club, came close to Balraje and said, "Baldhani, my bones are old now, but I have endured countless strikes. My skin has become thick. It's not going to break so easily! Ten strikes of your weapon are like ten jewels for me, Balraje!" Gomaji was looking at his Dhakale Raje with misty eyes.

"Gomajibaba …!" Suddenly, a voice came from the side gate of the ground. Antoji Gade came panting. Gomajibaba had a premonition. He felt worried. Antoji's voice was shaky.

He asked Antoji, "What happened Anta?"

"Masaheb sent me to get Balraje. Our… our Pant kaka is no more!"

"Aww, who?" Gomajibaba exclaimed. His thick moustache trembled. He kept staring at Antoji in shock.

"Dabir kaka!" With his head held low, Antoji answered in a low voice.

Shambhooraje forgot all about the training as he heard the news. He didn't even realize when the club slipped from his hand. The scene of the Tula ceremony at Mahabaleshwar flashed in front of his eyes. He could see well-built Sonopant Dabir sitting in the silver pan with his neck trembling!

It had been a month since Raje had gone on the Basnoor campaign. The night of Holi Pournima dawned on Rajgad.

The platter-sized moon rose, climbing above the mountains of Bara maval. In the middle of the chowk, wooden logs were stacked up to erect the Holi. A special platform had been erected for the royal guests.

Shambhooraje, dressed in a blue jama and saffron Jiretop came to Jijau's chamber. A message had arrived from the Holi chowk – "The Holi was not going to be ignited without the customary touch of a royal family member. The players of Holi were waiting!"

Shambhooraje leaned forward to touch Jijabai's feet. Jijabai pulled him up and said, "Balraje, go and light the Holi. The players of Holi are waiting."

"Thoralya Aausaheb…", Shambhooraje wanted to say something, but he hesitated and stopped.

"What happened?" Jijabai asked him lovingly.

"…!" Shambhooraje was still quiet.

"You should speak your mind. Tell me what it is." Jijau

reassured him.

Shambhooraje looked at Jijabai with respect and said, "Will you...come with me? The Holi will be ignited, and the Holi players will try to grab coconuts from the burning fire. It's fun to watch! Will you come?"

Jijabai was touched by his words. A fountain of thoughts erupted in her mind. 'Nobody ever implored me to 'come with' them! I could never go to any place I wished!'

Shambhooraje saw that Jijabai was silent and felt awkward. He said "Sorry, I made a mistake...". He made an obeisance to her and started walking backwards.

Jijabai exclaimed, "Wait, I am coming!" The starlit night of Pournima shone brightly in Shambhooraje's eyes when he heard her words.

Masaheb wrapped a shawl around herself and began walking towards the Holi chowk with Shambhooraje. It seemed as if Goddess Jagadamba was walking with her devotee.

'Aausaheb is coming with Balraje to honour the Holi'; the news had already reached the Holi chowk. The assembled Mavalas felt exuberant. The tabors started resounding loudly.

Jijau and Shambhoobal arrived in the Holi chowk accompanied by Nilo Sonadeo, Prataprao Silimkar, Zunjararao Maral, Gomajibaba, Sidoji Thopate, Antoji and Rayaji. The clamour of the Mavalas subsided. The sound of the tabors dwindled. Even the stars shining in the sky paused for a moment!

Jijau took her seat with Shambhooraje, on the platform erected for the royal family. A designated player of Holi, holding a torch in his hand, approached Masaheb and made an obeisance to her. He humbly said, "Masaheb, Dhakale Raje should ignite the Holi as per the custom."

Jijau turned her head and glanced at Shambhooraje. Shambhooraje got up from his seat. He touched Thoralya Aausaheb's feet and went near the Holi. The designated player of Holi handed the torch to Shambhooraje.

Shambhooraje roared 'Jai Bhavani' and ignited the Holi. The flames of fire soared in the sky. The Holi was alight! The Holi festival was in full swing.

Shambhooraje came back to the platform and took his seat. Many coconuts were rapidly thrown into the burning fire. Daring, audacious Mavalas circled the Holi to extract the coconuts from the fire. Fearless hands were confidently piercing the burning fire and were withdrawn quickly after getting scorched

Jijabai stared at the red-yellow flames of the flaming fire. She was thinking about Shivajiraje – 'Where could Raje be? What must he be doing?'

"Thoralya Aausaheb..." Shambhooraje's voice broke her reverie.

"What is it Balraje?"

"Once, in the Holi festival, I had asked Aabasaheb..."

"What?"

"Aaba, will you pull out a coconut from the burning fire?"

"Then what did he say?" Jijabai asked curiously.

"He said – I will try!" Shambhooraje replied.

Jijabai tidied the edge of her sari over her head and let out a deep sigh. She looked at Balraje and said, "Shambhoobal, if needed, even you and I will have to try it!"

The moonlight had dispersed all around; the night of Holi Purnima kept advancing on the fort. The Mavalas kept pulling out coconuts from the flaming fire. Shambhooraje kept honouring them with the golden bracelet in front of Thoralya Aausaheb. Neither he nor Jijau Saheb knew that Raje had ransacked Basnur, visited the Shivalinga of Gokarna Mahabaleshwar, and arrived at Karvar harbour today.

Raje wanted to ransack the British warehouse in Karvar, but Adil Shah's sardar Sherkhan reached Karvar on the day of the Holi festival. He paid five thousand hons in settlement to Raje and saved Karvar. Raje accepted the settlement from him and while leaving Karvar, Raje said to Sarlashkar Netajirao, "Sherkhan deprived me today, of the pleasure of hunting on the day of the Holi festival!"

Raje returned to Rajgad via Karvar and Bhimgad after finishing the Karnataka campaign successfully. As soon as he arrived at the fort, he received news that Mirza Raja Jai Singh and Pathan Diler Khan had met with the Mughal prince Muazzam in Aurangabad and were now on the way to Pune. Mirza Raja's army was swelling like a river in full spate. A green cyclone of eighty thousand soldiers was coming to strike. It had befriended and taken along the armies of Raje's adversaries such as the king of Javhar, Afzalkhan's son Fazalkhan, the Mores, Desais and Dalavis of Javali.

It was imperative to tighten the security at the major forts of Bara Maval. In the royal hall of the Balekilla, Raje was dictating letters to Chitnis Balaji Aavaji.

"At present, our informers have brought news that Rajput Mirza Raja Jai Singh and Pathan Diler Khan are coming to attack us with an army of eighty thousand soldiers. Therefore, all of you, wise veterans should be vigilant and stay where you are. All sentinels and night guards should be armed and should stay alert throughout days and nights. Food grains, fodder and explosives should be safeguarded. I will soon visit all the forts in person...."

Balaji sealed the letters and kept them ready. Raje gave the requisite instructions to each sardar. He spoke with everyone composedly; but everyone could feel the concern in his eyes. Sambhajiraje was listening with astonishment, to the prudent instructions that Raje was giving the sardars.

Raje left the royal hall with Sambhajiraje and came to his private chamber. He was preoccupied about Mirza Raja's next move. The slanting twilight rays were still lingering on the Balekilla. Balraje sat on the bed and kept staring at Raje, who was pacing back and forth restlessly. Finally, he could not resist asking Raje, "Maharaj Saheb, who is a Rajput?"

As Raje heard the question, he stopped pacing. That question tore Raje's heart apart. For a moment he gazed at Balraje. Then, he approached the bed slowly. He peered into Shambhooraje's eyes and said in a hoarse voice, "Rajput means the son of a Raja! The scion of a Raja! The rulers. But that was a very long time ago. Now the Rajputs have become loyal servants of the Raja!" You are a Rajput; I am a Rajput and Mirza Raja is a Rajput too!" And after that Raje continued, recounting to Shambhooraje many things about Rajputs, Rajputana, Mirza Raja, Aurangzeb, and the Mughal sultanate.

Shambhooraje got down from the bed and stood behind Raje. Shambhooraje wondered, 'We are Rajputs. Mirza Raja is a Rajput too! What kind of a person could he be? Could he be like Aabasaheb? No, then Maharaj Saheb would not have been so worried about him!"

It was scorching hot outside. The entire Rajgad was burning from inside. In Shambhooraje's chamber, Dharau gave him a glass of cold water and said, "This heat is killing me!" And she wiped the sweat on her forehead with the edge of her sari. Just then, Jijabai entered the chamber.

Dharau hastily tidied her sari. Shambhooraje transferred the glass to his left hand and made an obeisance to Thoralya Aausaheb.

"Here, finish it," Jijau said and touched the glass to his lips. Balraje's eyes closed for a moment while drinking water. Jijau's eyes fell upon the two horizontal stripes of sandalwood paste on his forehead. She herself had applied them in the morning. There were many maids on the fort, Raje's seven queens were there too, but so far, Jijabai had not let anyone apply the horizontal lines of sandalwood paste on Balraje's forehead. Doing it herself gave her immense satisfaction.

Balraje put the empty glass on a wooden stool. Jijabai was about to say something to him, when they heard the kettle drums announcing Raje's arrival. Instantly, Jijau's troubled face lit up. "Come Shambhoobal, Raje is climbing up the fort. Let's go to the royal hall."

Jijabai held Balraje's hand and started walking towards the royal hall.

Raje was returning after inspecting the security arrangements of all the forts in the Bara Maval region such as Torana, Pratapgad, Chandan-Vandan, Rohida and Purandar.

Raje's palanquin arrived at Padmavati machi. He climbed up the Balekilla via the tunnel located behind the machi. His forehead was sweaty, and the horizontal stripes of sandalwood on his forehead were trickling from all sides! Jijabai's heart broke to see such a sight!

Barely eight days after Raje arrived at Rajgad, Diler Khan and Mirza Raja's mammoth imperial army entered Pune, stirring the waters of the Mula and Mutha rivers. The reflections of the orange tents of Rajput clans such as Gour, Hada, Bundela, Rathod, Kachhawah, Chandravat, began swaying on the waters of Mula and Mutha. Under the leadership of Diler Khan all 'Khans' camped in Pune. Pune was benumbed by the commotion of elephants, horses, and camels.

Diler Khan's Pathan and Bahaliya soldiers dressed in their kimosh and glittering vests over their Jama and churidar, started raiding Pune astride their horses. Mirza Raja's Rajput informants sporting thick beards, and clad in orange turbans, dispersed in the Bara Maval region to collect information about Raje.

Finally, the most powerful assault of the Delhi durbar befell the Maratha kingdom. Mirza Raja, who was a descendant of Lord Ramchandra, the scion of the Raghu clan, fell upon Raje's Swaraj. He had ignited the yajna of Goddess Ranachandi before coming. To keep it aflame, he was now going to ignite the Holi of the Maratha kingdom. The radiant Sun was, very soon, going to be eclipsed by the descendants of the Suryavansha.

As soon as Mirza Raja arrived in Pune, he took charge of the encampment and relieved Raja Jasawant Singh of duty. Jasawant Singh went back to Delhi.

In his pavilion, smoking the hookah, Diler Khan was pondering over which fort of Shivaji to attack first. Mohammed Tar Khan, Rasoolbeg Rozamani, Kuwat Khan, Saiyyad Bukharee, Turkataz Khan, Zabardast Khan, Ghairat and Mujaffar, and Meer Atish Khan stood in front of him.

Mirza Raja was planning moves against Shivaji while sipping sherbet in his lavish shamiana. 'Seva', who had killed Afzal Khan, cut Shasta Khan's fingers, and stripped 'Surat' of its dignity, lingered in front of his eyes.

Raje offered Bael leaves on the crystal Shivalinga in the sanctum. Shambhooraje stood next to Raje. Raje signalled to him with his eyes, to offer Bael leaves on the Shivlinga. Shambhooraje offered a couple of Bael leaves on the crystal Shivlinga. Just like Raje, he joined his palms in prayer and closed his eyes.

"Let's go now." Raje said to him, putting his hand on Shambhooraje's shoulder and walking towards Jijabai's chamber.

They made an obeisance to Jijabai, and with her, they came to the royal hall of the Balekilla. Sarlashkar Netajirao, Anandrao, Kudatoji, Yesaji, Moropant, Niraji, Ravaji, Karmaji, Annaji Dutto, Sidoji, and Raghunathpant Korade stood in the royal hall with their heads bent. As Raje gestured, everyone sat down. A dreadful silence prevailed.

Raje spoke in a solemn voice like never before, "My worst fear has come true. Our kingdom is a thorn in Aurangzeb's flesh. He has appointed Diler and Mirza to destroy our kingdom, and accordingly they have assaulted Pune. Mirza Raja hasn't revealed his strategy yet, but I know it beforehand. Now, his army will move either in the direction of Kondhana or Purandar. Mirza Raja will leave no stone unturned to please Aurangzeb. What do all of you think about this? Please state your honest opinions." Raje stopped talking. Sambhajiraje noticed how his voice trembled and his eyes breathed fire while uttering the name of 'Aurangzeb'.

Kudatoji Gujar raised his head and said, "We should launch an open attack on the Rajput encampment."

"Your words suit your fearless attitude Kudatoji, but that Rajput is not so negligent. He is not going to repeat the mistakes of the previous sardars. He has served two generations of emperors." Raje said calmly.

"What if we penetrate the Mughal territory and divert his attention...?" Netaji put forth his plan.

"You took the words right out of my mouth, Netaji. That is exactly what I want you to do. You strike the pargana of Parinda with your troops. But I am still doubtful about how effective this strategy will prove. Mirza Raja is an astute statesman. He takes his time."

Raje spoke for quite some time. He acquainted everyone with Mirza Raja and Pathan Diler Khan. He unravelled Aurangzeb's crafty political plan to all. In the end, he said, "I don't feel bad about Aurangzeb's cunning, but I pity Mirza Raja. He has the calibre of becoming the emperor of Delhi, but today, he is falling upon our hilly region as a loyal servant of the Mughal emperor. Now, everything is up to God. I surrender to Him." Raje got up from his seat.

Sambhajiraje walked with Jijabai, behind Raje. He stared at the brocade design on the back of Raje's jama and was lost in some thought. As soon as they entered Raje's chamber, he asked Raje, "Who is this Aurangzeb and why do you talk so much about him?"

Startled by his question, Jijabai and Raje stared at each other. Raje approached Balraje, put his hands on Balraje's shoulders and said, "Shambhooraje, he is the emperor of Delhi! I have never seen him. In fact, no one can see him, except for a few of his loyal sardars. But his deeds can be seen by the whole world! His own brothers and even his father suffered due to his deeds!"

Raje paused.

"I want to meet Aurangzeb and ask him…" Shambhooraje could not complete his sentence. Raje put his forefinger on his lips and stopped him from speaking further. "No Shambhoobal, by the grace of Lord Samba, may you never face such a situation." Raje said while looking at the crystal Shivlinga on the platter.

Finally, Mirza Raja disclosed his strategy. He and Diler Khan proceeded to Fort Purandar with the frontline troops. The artillery of Mirza Raja marched towards Fort Purandar, in the custody of Meer Atish Khan and the white overseer, Niccolao Manucci.

Finally, the Holi of the Bara Maval region ignited in the middle of summer. The hamlets, villages and towns located at the foothills of the mountains were getting crushed under the hooves of the horses. Young peasant girls and women who went outside to collect firewood were abducted because they were 'Kafir', as they screamed and struggled to break free. Their heart-rending screams dispersed and got lost in the valleys of the Maval region. The Mughal soldiers seized the cattle by cutting their tethers and forced them to move in flocks towards the Mughal camps. Those innocent animals with their tails erect and their muzzles foaming, ran towards the unknown territory, mooing haplessly. In broad daylight, the Pathan, Turkish, Mughal and Bahaliya soldiers started setting houses afire. The poor peasants were captured for slavery and were lashed. Town after town was being plundered, burnt, and crushed.

Diler Khan and his army travelled via Rajewadi–Saswad and reached the foothills of Purandar. At the same time, Mirza Raja travelled via the Bhuleshwar pass and reached Karhepathar. Fort Purandar was besieged by the mammoth imperial army!

On the side of Sadar Darwaja, the armed soldiers of Diler Khan, Kirat Singh, Meer Atish Khan, Indraman Bundela, Udaybhaan Gaur, Rasoolbeg, and Zabardast Khan were lined up. Facing the fort, the cannons started breathing fire on the fort continuously.

Fort Purandar was a twin fort. A small fort called 'Rudramal' or 'Vajragad' was located on the east side of Purandar. The machis of Purandar had spread alongside Vajragad. A narrow pass called 'Bhairav Khind' connected them. Purandar depended heavily on Vajragad for its defence. That fort was like a step on the threshold of a temple. As one directly enters the temple, after crossing the step on the threshold, similarly, if Vajragad fell, the enemy could directly enter Fort Purandar.

Fifteen hundred Ramoshi, Mahar, Koli and Kahar swordsmen were stationed on the fort. The fort relied on their loyalty and the ferocious, skilled swordsman Murarbaji, whom Raje had appointed to the fort.

The palanquins for the queens were ready at the Padmavati machi on Rajgad. Jijabai, Soyarabai and Raje climbed down Balekilla and arrived at Padmavati machi. Raje was accompanied by his family which included Sambhajiraje, Sakhoobai, Ranoobai, Ambabai and Nanibai. Dharau, who had become a family member by now, was also present. As per Raje's plea, Jijabai was going from Rajgad to Kondhana with Soyarabai. The enemy forces were stationed around Fort Purandar, which was close to Rajgad. In such a situation, it wasn't wise to keep the entire family in one place. Jijabai was not ready to leave the fort, leaving Raje and Balraje alone to face the enemy. But Raje succeeded in convincing her to do so. Raje stepped forward and touched Masaheb's feet.

Sambhajiraje touched Thoralya Aausaheb's feet. Jijabai pulled him up and said, "Balraje, I am leaving now. You should sleep in Raje's chamber."

Raje was touched to hear her words. Sambhajiraje touched Soyarabai's feet, but Soyarabai didn't notice it. She was engrossed in feasting her eyes upon Raje, before leaving the fort. Raje's eyes were focused on the high-flying Jaripataka fluttering on the flagpole.

Everyone made an obeisance to Jijau who was leaving the fort.

Fifteen days had passed since Purandar was besieged. Purandar kept fighting tenaciously. The Mavalas on the fort ferociously attacked Diler's encampment in the middle of night. Vigilant Diler Khan determinedly crushed their strikes. The Karhepathar region echoed with booming cannons. The skies were overcast with smoke. The Mahars, Kahars, Kolis and Ramoshis were falling dead, but kept fighting till their last breath.

Diler, Meer Atish Khan and Niccolao Manucci kept lashing their hefty Pathan soldiers, and led the mammoth cannons, 'Fattelashkar', 'Abdulla Khan' and 'Maheli' onto mounds tall enough to launch fireballs at the heart of Vajragad. The three booming, cannons breached the ramparts of Vajragad.

The Pathan, Bahliya and Mughal soldiers wielding their bare swords, attacked Vajragad ferociously. Vajragad fell. Pathan Diler Khan's feet touched the threshold of Purandar. Now, he was determinedly going to break into the temple, Fort Purandar!

"Dhani, we fought to the best of our ability, but we were overpowered. I am ashamed to show my face to you. Now, behead us or have us thrown over the cliff. At least death will save our reputation!" The custodian of Vajragad was pouring his heart out in front of Raje, with his head bent.

Raje got up from his seat as after hearing the custodian's heart-rending plea. He plodded towards the custodian, put his hand on the custodian's shoulder and said, "Oh how can you say this? Winning or losing is not important to me! You fought the enemy's mammoth, ocean-like army with meagre forces at your disposal! My hands are tied today, otherwise, I would have rewarded all of you with gold coins!"

"Mujumdar...!" Raje summoned Nilo Sonadeo.

"Ji" Nilo Sonadeo rushed towards Raje.

"Please check how many men are here. I want to honour my soldiers in whatever way I can. Bring scarves and turbans for all of them here."

Nilo Sonadeo counted the number of Mavalas and brought the scarves and turbans to the royal hall. Raje offered a scarf and a turban to each Mavala who had fought hard. Sambhajiraje got up from his seat and came close to Raje. He courteously began handing over the turbans to Raje to reduce his burden.

Sambhajiraje had realized a deep truth of life, 'Winning or losing is not important! What is important is to fight determinedly, till the last breath!'

Raje visited Goddess Jagadamba's temple on Pratapgad and came back. Every day, defenceless, homeless people who were looted and devastated, thronged Rajgad in large numbers. Raje personally inquired about their condition with sympathy; he opened his granaries to distribute food to his destitute ryots.

As usual, Raje descended the Balekilla with Sambhajiraje and arrived at Padmavati machi to meet his ryots.

Raje was walking with a heavy heart. People were prostrating themselves at his feet. Eighty-year-old Haibatabaa Pandhare was among the crowd. He saw Shambhooraje walking behind Raje and was overcome with emotion. He pushed aside the crowd with his shaking hands and came forward. He held Shambhooraje's hand in his wrinkled hand and said in a breaking voice, "Please wait for a moment, my child! Let me look at you to my heart's content!"

Raje stopped in his tracks as he heard these words. He turned around and looked back. Aged Haibatabaa was stroking Sambhajiraje's flushed cheeks with his rough, trembling hands. Tears trickled through his aged eyes into his white beard.

"What happened baba? Why are you crying?" Raje asked him.

Old Haibatabaa promptly wiped his eyes and replied, "Dhani, sometimes I get emotional due to old age. That's all, nothing else!" Haibatabaa was not ready to share his pain with Raje.

"Baba, I am like a son to you. You should share your pain with me." Old Haibatabaa's was touched by Raje's words.

Haibatabaa's withered body began shaking. The pain that he had resolutely buried deep in his heart, broke into tears and burst out, "How should I tell you Raje? I am destroyed. My only son has lost his mind. Those brutes tied him to a tree and molested his young wife in front of him. She didn't even have the strength to get up. In that condition, those bastards put her on a horse and took her away. Since then, my son has gone berserk. His only son lay dead outside our hut. I came back from the fields and saw all this destruction. I buried that child with my own hands Raje! When I saw your son, I remembered him. He was about the same age! Raje, why are you giving me food to keep me alive? Just cut my head and toss it over the ramparts!... I can't bear this hell any more, Raje!" The old man covered his face and started crying like a child.

As Raje heard Haibatabaa's story his body stiffened. His eyes breathed fire. But – but Raje was lost for words to console that old man. He felt like the cowries on his chest were transforming into a big boulder and he was getting crushed beneath it. As he put his hand on Haibatabaa's shoulder to console him, tears trickled down his eyes.

When he saw it, hunchbacked Haibatabaa stood erect and with fiery eyes he said to Raje, "No Raje, I implore you not to bring tears to your eyes! We farmers are like the plant of Ghaypaat, if one dies ten more will spring up from the ashes. But you... you are the amulet tied around Goddess Jagadamba's arm. I have faith that you are the one who will save all these people. I bow down to you Raje." Haibatabaa bowed down to Raje and disappeared in the crowd.

Raje was benumbed; instead of going forward to Sanjivani machi he went back to the fort.

Raje had sent a message to Mirza Raja at the hands of Karmaji. He was ready to surrender two forts to Mirza Raja and had proposed a peace accord. He also showed willingness to provide Mirza Raja with his army to attack the Adil Shahi sultanate of Bijapur. Raje was trying every strategy to convince the Rajput. In the meantime, Kudatoji Gujar had tried to infiltrate Mirza Raja's encampment and attack him with a naked sword, but he was captured. Mirza Raja had purposefully presented him with a horse and a sword and released him with honour. Cunning Mirza Raja was not wasting a single opportunity to provoke Raje.

Balaji Aavaji presented Karmaji who had returned from Mirza Raja's encampment, in front of Raje. Karmaji's face was drawn. He made an obeisance to Raje and handed Raje the pouch containing Mirza Raja's letter. Raje gave it to Balaji. Chitnis Balaji began reading the letter aloud –

"Our imperial army is infinite like the stars in the sky. Your region of mountains and valleys is not unconquerable for it. Any territory will be destroyed under the heels of our horses. If you care for your own life, you had better surrender to the emperor and serve under him! If you don't do what I say, then you will be inviting ruin for yourself and your ryots!"

Mirza Raja wanted complete surrender. Raje was stunned by the letter.

"Sarkar, I heard two very bad pieces of news in the Rajput camp." Karmaji said.

"Tell me...now there is no hope of hearing any good news." Raje said.

"Diler Khan has erected wooden platforms in front of the Safed Buruj of Purandar and has continued the cannon fire. One cannon ball shot from one of the wooden platforms directly fell over the artillery store on the Safed Buruj. The store room blew up and the Safed Buruj, made of stone, exploded. The eighty swordsmen on the buruj were instantly blown to pieces. Their broken limbs showered all over the machi. The custodian of the fort collected all the body parts and put them on one funeral pyre! And…

"And what Karmaji? Did the fort fall?"

"No, not the fort but one fearless soldier fell in the battle! Yesterday, Diler Khan launched a vehement attack on the fort with five thousand Pathan soldiers. Murarbaji opened the main gate to counter his attack and fell upon his army with seven hundred Ramoshi and Mahar swordsmen. A skirmish broke out. While shouting loudly 'Attack them - Har Har Mahadeo!' Murarararau was brandishing Pattas in both hands. He was cutting the Pathan soldiers like a farmer cuts the ripe crop in his field. It was a ferocious battle indeed.

"Pathan Diler Khan was standing on a mound and while watching Murarararau fight ferociously he exclaimed, "Ya Allah, what an extraordinary soldier you are! Join the service of Alijah and we will shower you with riches!"

"Murarararau stopped fighting for a moment, threw a fiery glance at Diler Khan, and spat with contempt. He shouted 'I am a loyal soldier of Shivaji Raje! Why would I come to your side?' And he dashed towards Diler Khan to kill him.

"Someone shot an arrow towards him; it pierced his throat and got stuck there; blood spurted out from his throat. Murarararau screamed 'Aai Ambe' in agony and with the arrow stuck in his throat he rushed into the enemy's army. He could not shout 'Har Har Mahadeo' due to the arrow stuck in his throat.

"Murarbaji killed as many Pathans as he could, and finally he collapsed." While delivering that heart-breaking news Karmaji's eyes got teary.

Raghunathpant Korde's palanquin left from the Pali Darwaja of Rajgad. He held the pouch containing Raje's letter of 'complete surrender' to Mirza Raja. Ten swordsmen were guarding the palanquin. As a royal envoy, Pant was going to deliver Raje's letter to the Rajputs. The news that Raje was making an accord of complete surrender with the Rajput, spread over the fort like wildfire.

Sambhajiraje didn't understand the meaning of 'accord'. From his chamber, he came to Raje's chamber. He tried to open the closed door. It was locked.

"Maharaj Saheb" Sambhajiraje called, but there was no response. Shambhooraje lingered in front of the closed door for some time and then his feet turned towards Masaheb Putalabai's chamber.

Putalabai had drawn two thick horizontal lines of kumkum on her forehead. She wiped her fingers on the rag that a maid held in front of her. After entering the chamber, Sambhajiraje made an obeisance to Putalabai and approached her. He looked at her freshly drawn, wet kumkum stripes and asked, "Masaheb, what is an 'accord'? Why do we do it, and with whom do we do it? Have you ever made an 'accord' with anyone?" After hearing his questions, even in that tense situation on the fort, Putalabai's face flushed. She wanted to say, "I have made an 'accord' with the kumkum on my forehead, for many lives! May Goddess Amba give me the courage to honour it."

But she couldn't say it. She said, "An accord is the surrender of a person who is trapped in a political deal or a treaty!"

Soyarabai who had accompanied Jijau Saheb to Kondhana had returned to Rajgad and was in her chamber. She had not yet heard anything about all this.

Raje was going to descend the fort today, to meet Mirza Raja at his encampment, for an unarmed and unconditional surrender! To stop further destruction of his people and his territory!

This life was akin to that of a lion bereft of his mane, and a royal elephant whose trunk has been slashed. Alas, the agony of surrendering to the enemy! Only a noble king would know how painful it was! To endure such pain, one must wear the deeply cherished cowrie necklace.

Raje was not speaking to anybody. His heart had gone numb like a fort brutally beaten by torrential rains.

Obeisances were made, and goodbyes were said. As Raje approached Sambhajiraje, he put his forehead on Raje's feet and got up.

Without uttering a word, Raje put his hand on Shambhooraje's shoulder and slightly patted his shoulder.

Raje sat in his palanquin. Anandrao, Raghunathpant, Niraji Ravaji, Nagoji-Bahirji Farzand, Vishwasrao and Krishnaji Joshi surrounded the palanquin. The swordsmen walked with the palanquin, holding shining, bare swords. The radiant Sun who had taken the oath of raising Swaraj was going to make an accord with darkness.

Sambhajiraje's eyes were rivetted on Raje's palanquin. Something that had never happened before, had happened today. Maharaj Saheb had not talked to him at all while leaving the fort.

The palanquin was going away. Sambhajiraje remembered Raje's words in Mahabaleshwar, near the banks of River Krishna, on the day of the solar eclipse. "Rahu-ketu, the malefic planets from the Sun's own family block his path and eclipse him; Balraje, even the Sun gets eclipsed!"

Raje went to meet Mirza Raja. Now, Jijau Saheb and Raje, both were not at Rajgad. Unknowingly, Sambhajiraje was spending more time in Putalabai's chamber.

The way Putalabai performed her puja with full concentration, her affectionate treatment of the palace maids, her respectful attitude towards other queens, the way she looked after Sakhoo, Ranoo, Amba and Balibai like they were her own daughters, her minimal speech in a tinkling voice that one would remember for a long time, and her radiant complexion, like a petal of the Kewra flower glistening in the sun—everything unknowingly made a deep impact on Shambhooraje's mind. Indeed, an affectionate woman doesn't have to go around publicizing her affectionate nature!

Sambhajiraje stood behind Putalabai, looking at the eight-armed Goddess Jagadamba, whom she had just worshipped. He kept glancing out of the window and looking at the meandering curves of River Gunjavani.

"Sarkar, Thoralya ranisaheb has summoned you to her chamber." Soyarabai's chambermaid Chandra announced politely.

Putalabai heard her and turned around. She glanced at Shambhooraje and tidied her sari. Chandra, the maid, left the chamber immediately.

"Balraje, let's go, we have been summoned by Thoralya ranisaheb." Putalabai said and unwittingly glanced at Goddess Jagadamba's murti. She put her hand on Shambhooraje's shoulder and started walking towards Thoralya ranisaheb's chamber.

Ravishing Soyarabai, dressed in a blue sari, was chatting with her daughter Balibai, in her chamber.

As soon as Shambhooraje entered the chamber, he touched Soyarabai's feet. Soyarabai pulled him up.

Soyarabai's daughter Balibai saw Putalabai and rushed towards her. Putalabai held both her shoulders lovingly and asked Soyarabai, "Any news of Swari...?"

"Bahirji and Nagoji have just arrived on the fort from the Rajput encampment. That is why I summoned you."

"What happened...?" Putalabai's heart was pounding.

"Swari has made an accord! He has agreed to surrender twenty-three forts including Purandar, Kondhana, Rohida, Mahuli, Lohgad and territory worth four lakh hons, to the Rajput! Now Swari will possess only twelve forts and a territory worth of one lakh hons!"

Putalabai looked at her sharp rosy nose and asked calmly, "How is he doing?"

"He is okay. He is going to surrender Kondhana to the Rajputs tomorrow and will be coming to Rajgad with Masaheb." Soyarabai spoke curtly. Her black eyes were filled with worry, but it was difficult to figure out if she was worried about the forts or about Raje!

Sambhajiraje's face lit up when he heard the news that Jijabai and Raje were coming. For quite some time, he kept looking at Putalabai and Soyarabai and wondered, 'Both of them are fair, but why do they seem so different from each other?'

Shambhooraje noticed that they had stopped talking, and he asked Soyarabai, "Masaheb, have you ever made an accord with anyone?"

Soyarabai's dark black eyes lit up with a strange spark, her rosy nose flushed a bit more and she instantly responded, "No! I never approved of any accord! But what can be done now that Swari has accepted it?"

Soyarabai pulled Shambhooraje close and said to him, "But everything has worked in your favour. Without making any kind of 'accord', the Rajput has offered you a mansab of five thousand soldiers! The only sad part is that you will have to go to the Rajput's camp to accept it. I am worried for you. How are you going to bear this responsibility?"

Shambhooraje did not say anything, because he was confused – he wondered why Aabasaheb accepted the mansab even after surrendering so many forts.

Putalabai did not understand Soyarabai's words. She had spoken like she cared. She always spoke like she cared. Whenever Soyarabai spoke, Putalabai always felt uneasy. Without responding to Soyarabai, Putalabai said to Shambhooraje, "Balraje, come, let's visit Goddess Kaleshwari's temple."

Putalabai and Shambhooraje returned to their chambers after visiting Goddess Kaleshwari's temple.

Mirza Raja's luxurious orange shamiana stood on Karhepathar, at the foothills of Purandar. Fort Purandar, battered by the firing of the cannons, stood in front.

Exquisite, designer Hindustani carpets were spread in Mirza

Raja's shamiana. Recliner pillows wrapped in brocaded pillow covers had been placed. A tall hookah, with golden tracery design stood on a wooden stool. Mirza Raja was reclining on a pillow, holding the black hookah pipe in his left hand.

Raje sat with his head held low, in front of Mirza Raja, staring at the black and white squares of the chess board spread in front of them. The black and white squares were observing his agony.

Niccolao Manucci, the white officer, sat close by deferentially, holding a big, feathered hat on his lap. He was Mirza Raja's artillery chief. He was quite interested in the intellectual game of chess.

Raje's eyes were red around the corners. He had negotiated the terms of the accord with Mirza Raja's munshi Udayraj and Ugrasingh Kachhawah, throughout the night. Late at night, he had accepted the terms of the five-point accord and signed it. Then, with his hands tied and head bent, he had met with Mirza Raja.

As per the accord, Raje was going to surrender twenty-three forts to Aurangzeb and cede his territory worth four lakh hons. He had agreed to join Aurangzeb's subedar in Deccan on any military campaigns with his army, whenever he received such orders. He had accepted the condition to keep Shambhooraje as hostage in Mirza Raja's camp.

In these circumstances the game of chess had been laid out. Mirza Raja presented a platter to Raje. Raje picked up the white pieces from the platter and started placing them on the chessboard. The rooks, the knights, and the bishops took their places on the board.

Mirza Raja placed the black pieces, made from the black horns of the wild cows. The board was ready for the game.

A few moments passed by. In his northern Hindustani dialect Mirza Raja slowly said, "Please open the game, Raja Saab."

Without looking at him, keeping his eyes on the game board, Raje said, "Rajaji, you should open the game, as you hold the right and the rank too."

"No. That's not how it works." Mirza Raja puffed on his hookah and said, "The official rule of chess is that the player with the white pieces always makes the first move. The white pieces are considered feminine, and the ladies make the first move in the game of chess. The black pieces are considered masculine, and the men make their moves in response." Mirza Raja felt happy with himself. He thumped his thigh and looking at Manucci he laughed loudly.

Raje gave Mirza Raja a startled look. The cowrie necklace on his chest trembled. His eyes breathed fire, but he couldn't say anything.

Mirza Raja was taken aback by that look. He put aside the pipe and quickly said, "Raja Saab, please don't take it otherwise. I just told you the official rule of the game. If you wish, I can open the game." Mirza extended his hand to move the white pieces on the board to his side.

Raje stopped him and moved a pawn forward. The game began. It continued for a long time. Raje's heart was not in the game. On the board, he kept seeing the twenty-three forts that Mirza Raja had seized from him. He kept visualizing Shambhooraje tethered to the squares on the board.

Many feminine and masculine pieces were now removed from the game board. They were lying in a platter, clinging to each other, watching the game leisurely. The game was now in the last phase.

Suddenly, Mirza Raja astutely moved his Wazir forward and checked the white king. Raje put a pawn between them and saved his king. The game was now getting exciting. Each piece had to be moved with careful consideration.

With the support of his Wazir that he had moved forward, Mirza Raja moved his bishop diagonally. Raje's white king was in check again. Raje took some time to think about the next move and saved his king by moving his knight two and a half squares, putting him in front of the king. That knight put Mirza Raja's black king in check.

Manucci was watching the game intently. He liked Raje's move very much. He kept stroking the feathers on his hat and tried to guess how Raje would move his knight in the next few steps. He could clearly see that Mirza's black king was completely trapped with Raje's single move of the knight.

Mirza Raja put his fingers on his Wazir to kill Raje's knight. He thought that was the only move he could make. Raje also thought that Mirza was going to make that move. He felt bad that he had sacrificed his knight in vain.

Mirza Raja took a deep puff of the hookah and said, "Your knight made the mistake of attacking my king and got killed needlessly." He picked up the white knight from the board and placed his black Wazir in its place. He dropped the knight in the platter.

Niccolao Manucci, who was quietly watching the game so far, couldn't resist and exclaimed, "Oh…no…it can't! It can't kill the knight!" Manucci picked up the white knight from the platter and placed it back on the same square it was before, and placed Mirza Raja's black Wazir in the square it was before.

Manucci pointed to Raje's white bishop placed in a corner and convinced Mirza Raja that if the black Wazir left his place, the white bishop would put the black king in check. Unknowingly, Raje had placed his knight in such a way that his bishop placed in a corner became free to put the black king in check. The bishop, with his diagonal move, had automatically confined Mirza Raja's Wazir to one place!

Mirza Raja raised his curved eyebrows and kept staring at Raje's white bishop! Then he looked helplessly at Manucci and Raje and thumping both his hands on his thighs he muttered to himself, "You are right, it can't be killed!"

Mirza Raja had no way of saving his king from the check given by Raje's knight. To accept his defeat Mirza Raja flipped over the platter of black pieces and said, "You have won Raja Saab. I accept my defeat." As a custom, Mirza Raja removed his diamond-studded ring and placed it in front of Raje. It was the customary royal reward to the winner of the game.

Raje quickly picked up the ring, handed it back to Mirza Raja and said, "Rajaji, I consider winning or losing a game insignificant! With your permission, I would like to say something at this time!"

"Yes, you may!" Mirza Raja couldn't imagine what Raje wanted to say. Unknowingly, he puckered the orange tilak on his forehead.

Raje briefly glanced at the white pieces on the board and in the platter. While looking at the fair pieces, he remembered his Masaheb.

The next moment, he looked into Mirza Raja's eyes with his keen eyes and holding his head high he calmly said, "No matter how great a man is, he takes birth from a woman's womb!" On hearing his words, Mirza Raja choked on the smoke in his throat and the hookah pipe slipped from his hand!

As Mirza Raja insisted, Raje met with Pathan Diler Khan. He sent a message to the custodian of Fort Purandar to vacate and surrender the fort. Then, Raje made arrangements for his return journey.

Mirza Raja had already selected his men to accompany Raje on his way back. Two special people were among them – one was his own son, Kirat Singh and the other was Ugrasen Kachhawah. Kirat Singh was going to accompany Raje till Kondhana and get the possession of the fort. Ugrasen Kachhawah was going to accompany Raje till Rajgad and bring Sambhajiraje back with him. Till the conditions of the accord were fulfilled, that is, till Mirza Raja officially received possession of the twenty-three forts, Sambhajiraje was going to remain hostage with the Rajput on behalf of the Maratha kingdom.

Mirza Raja wanted to make sure that this plan was

implemented flawlessly. Therefore, he summoned Kirat Singh and Ugrasen Kachhawah to his shamiana at midnight and gave them two very important instructions. He warned his own son, Kirat Singh, "Kunwar, be alert! He is Sevaji; the lion of the mountains!"

He instructed Ugrasen to be vigilant, "Ugrasen, make sure that Sevaji sends his own son with you. Don't be careless. It is possible that Sevaji might hand somebody else's son to you!"

In his shamiana, Mirza Raja picked up a betel leaf from a platter and offered it to Raje. Young Kirat and Ugrasen, wearing orange turbans, stood by the curtained walls of the shamiana.

Before bidding farewell to Raje, Mirza Raja once again broached the primary topic artfully, "Raja Saab, here I am to bid farewell to you, but it's not in my nature to say goodbyes. I like to welcome people. Please send Kunwar Shambhoo; I will give him a royal welcome."

Raje held the betel leaf of farewell and kept gazing at Mirza Raja's fair face. He was feeling sympathetic towards Mirza Raja, but more than that he was feeling sorry for himself. His expressionless look baffled Mirza Raja. He promptly put his hand on Raje's shoulder and said, "Don't be afraid Raja Saab, send your son without any hesitation. No harm will fall upon him here. Trust me. I will vouch for his safety." Mirza looked at the entrance of the shamiana and clapped. He called for Munshi Udayraj and instructed him to get a platter of Bael leaves offered to the Shivlinga that he worshipped daily. Mirza Raja picked up a couple of Bael leaves from the platter, put them over the betel leaf in Raje's hand and said resolutely, "I take an oath in the name of Lord Shiva that, as long as I am alive, no harm will fall upon your son here."

Raje left Mirza's shamiana and sat in the palanquin that was kept ready for him. The select cavalry of Kirat Singh and Ugrasen, along with a few armed Rajput swordsmen began the journey with Raje's palanquin.

Raje gave possession of Fort Kondhana to Kirat Singh and returned to Rajgad with Masaheb. He was restlessly pacing back and forth in his chamber. The lamps in the chamber were burning brightly.

He had received a message from Jijabai's chamber that it was mealtime, but he had sent a message that he was not hungry. He had no courage to face Jijau and tell her that he had to send Sambhajiraje to the Rajput camp as a hostage!

Politics doesn't care about relationships. It keeps a man blindfolded and makes him walk on soft grass and scorching sands at the same time. A king is not supposed to have any familial attachments, and even if he has such attachments, he must keep them sealed in his heart.

Raje had taken a decision, but he was facing a big challenge – how to make Shambhooraje understand this decision? How to convince Aausaheb about it? Again and again, he felt like going directly to Jiaju's chamber and pouring his heart out to her. But he could not bring himself to even step out of his chamber. His fingers kept stroking the cowries on his chest. His feet dragged along with his worried mind.

"Aausaheb is coming here with Balraje." An attendant guarding Raje's chamber came in, made an obeisance to Raje and informed him. Raje stopped in his tracks.

"Why didn't you join us at mealtime? Are you worried about the forts?" Jijau said as soon as she entered Raje's chamber with Shambhooraje. Shambhooraje touched Raje's feet. Raje pulled him up and stared momentarily at the two horizontal stripes of sandalwood paste on his forehead. He remembered the words of Harbhat, the astrologer, "Rudra himself has taken birth in his form! He will live in sky-high forts...He will fight ferociously like Rudra, but he will be betrayed by his own people just like Rudra." That memory left Raje distressed. Many undesirable thoughts filled his royal mind.

'Rudra – Shankara had to consume venom for the benefit

of gods. His throat had turned blackish blue due to that, but all the gods and goddesses were saved. You and I may have to consume such venom for the sake of this kingdom and its people. Rudra did it once in his life, you and I may have to do it many times if needed.'

Raje was determined now. He stepped forward and calmly touched Masaheb's feet.

"Raje, I have been watching you since the surrender of Kondhana. You have been avoiding me. You are distressed because of the accord you had to make with the Rajputs. Raje, you cannot hide anything from me. You should not lose courage because you lost your kingdom." Jijabai said in a very affectionate and reassuring voice.

As Raje heard her words, he unwittingly raised his head. He put his rosy hand on the shoulder of Sambhajiraje, who was standing next to him and relying on the reassurance in Jijabai's tranquil eyes he said, "Yes Masaheb, it's true that I cannot hide anything from you. In the Rajput camp, I felt like an elephant that has serrated hooks tied to its feet. To top that, the Rajput pierced the goad of the last condition of the accord in my heart. I don't know how to share that with you." For a moment, Raje gazed at Sambhajiraje. His hand moved from Sambhajiraje's shoulder to his back and kept stroking it as if it wanted to tell him something.

"What condition are you talking about Raje? Tell me clearly what it is." Jijabai's mind was filled with doubts.

Sambhajiraje was sitting next to Raje. Raje pulled him between himself and Masaheb. He held him close and said in a solemn voice, "Until the accord is fulfilled, that is, until the possession of twenty-three forts is transferred to the Rajput, I have to send Balraje to live in his camp...as a hostage!" Raje's eyes slid from Jijau's face to her feet.

"Raje ..." Jijau trembled and almost screamed while looking at Raje's sharp nose. "What – what are you saying? You – you accepted this condition! You forgot that he is your only son? If that Rajput wanted to hold somebody hostage for his accord...then wasn't I enough for it? As it is, I was about to go Sati with your father; I would have sat in the palanquin as the Rajput's hostage!"

Raje was hurt to hear her words. Baffled, he looked at Masaheb with pained eyes and promptly said, "Masaheb, Mirza Raja imposed this condition on me. I had no option but to accept it..."

"That is what I am saying – you should have proposed my name instead. The new generation takes a kingdom forward. If need be, the old generation should be sacrificed for it. God forbid, if something bad happens to Balraje in Mirza's camp who should I turn to? If I die tomorrow, what will I say to my Soonbai in heaven?" Jijabai was not ready to move her eyes from Raje's face at all.

"Masaheb, don't lose courage. Mirza Raja held Bael leaves in his hand and promised that no harm will befall Balraje in his camp. Mirza is true to his word. If he wanted to betray me, he would have done it when I went to meet him unarmed. Not everyone is a traitor, Masaheb."

Raje was trying to explain his diplomatic manoeuvre to Masaheb respectfully. But Sambhajiraje was the most tender spot of Jijau's forbearing heart. With her own hands, she had thrust Raje in the mountainous region of Maval to fight the battles and raise Swaraj. Her aristocratic heart was trying to protect 'Shambhooraje', the heir of the Bhosale family. That is why, whatever she had done determinedly in case of Raje, she was hesitant to do the same with Sambhajiraje. A grandson is dearer to a woman's heart than her own son.

"Raje, you are vouching for the enemy! But I can't bear it. Balraje, let's go!" Jijabai said and turned to leave the chamber. Raje made an obeisance to her and said, "Let Balraje stay here."

Without looking back Jijabai said, "As you wish." And she

directly started walking towards her chamber.

Raje kept talking to Shambhooraje in his chamber till midnight. He was giving him instructions about how to behave in the Rajput camp.

"Call Mirza Raja 'Dadaji'. Consider him in my place. Speak as little as possible. Don't remove your Jiretop in front of him." Raje gave many instructions to Sambhajiraje.

Sambhajiraje attentively listened to every word of Raje. Raje's diplomatic words were filling Sambhajiraje with hope. Raje was getting him ready for the first race of life; preparing his mind for it.

Raje came close to Sambhajiraje. He held Sambhajiraje's face in his hands and peeked into his eyes briefly. Then he held his shoulders tightly with his strong hands and asked him determinedly, "Tell me the truth, are you scared to go to the Rajput camp?"

"No!" A voice as clear and loud as a golden coin falling on the floor, responded.

"Then what are you thinking about? Shambhoobal, you are not saying anything at all?" Raje shook his shoulders gently.

"Aabasaheb, I am going to face one problem there!" Sambhajiraje said while looking into Raje's eyes.

"What problem? Tell me." Raje's eyebrows arched, trying to guess.

"Here, on the fort, after I take my bath and get dressed, Thoralya Aausaheb applies the horizontal lines of sandalwood paste on my forehead. Who is going to do that in the Rajput camp?"

That unexpected question left Raje rattled. Unknowingly, he pulled Shambhooraje close and held his head close to his chest.

It seemed like the day of Jyeshtha Purnima had dawned! Though the day had dawned, it didn't seem like it. As the sky was overcast. Today Sambhajiraje was going to descend the fort with Netajirao Palkar. Ugrasen was going to take Shambhooraje with him. The entire fort was overcast with stifling air.

Sambhajiraje took a bath and donned a special attire. Like Raje, he was dressed in a blue jama with tracery design and orange Jiretop. A small jamadar was tied around his waist.

Sambhajiraje came to Jijau's chamber to seek her blessings. Putalabai and Dharau were also there. Sambhajiraje touched their feet and sought their blessings.

Dharau politely held a platter of sandalwood paste in her hand. Jijau Saheb applied two horizontal lines of the sandalwood paste on Sambhajiraje's forehead. Jijau's heart was filled with affection as she looked at his face that looked like a Shivlinga. She held him close with love and said," Shambhoobal, don't eat anything anywhere without getting it checked. Pay attention to Netaji's instructions and follow them." Jijau couldn't say anything further. She looked at Dharau and said, "Dharau, get some breakfast for Balraje."

"Ji!" Dharau said and left the chamber.

Jijau and Putalabai ushered Sambhajiraje to the inner sanctum. The murti of the eight-armed Goddess Jagadamba, wielding her weapons with enlarged eyes, trampling the demon Mahishasura under her feet, stood in the sanctum. Shambhooraje offered her Bael leaves, haldi-kumkum and prostrated in front of her. Jijau applied haldi on Sambhajiraje's forehead and ushered him to Raje's chamber. Putalabai went to prepare breakfast for Balraje.

Raje was giving instructions to Sarlashkar, Netaji Palkar in his chamber. Netaji was listening to his instructions attentively while nodding his head and saying "Ji". He held the hilt of his sword tightly in his fist.

Raje received intimation of Masaheb's arrival. Raje and Netaji stopped their conversation and came near the threshold of the chamber.

Jijau entered Raje's chamber with Sambhajiraje. Raje and

Netaji made an obeisance to her. Sambhajiraje touched Raje's feet. Raje pulled him up, held him close and said, "Balraje, Netajikaka is coming with you. If you need anything, tell him. Address Mirza Raja as 'Dadaji'."

"Ji," Sambhajiraje affirmed.

"Netajirao, send us news about Balraje's well-being daily. You be with him like his shadow." Jijau expressed her heart's desire to Netaji.

"Masaheb, if anyone even touches his hair, then as many severed heads will rain on Karhepathar as the hair on their heads. You can rest assured." Netaji reassured Jijabai with his head held high.

Meanwhile, Moropant entered the chamber. He made an obeisance to Raje and Jijabai and said, "Swami, the Rajput envoy, Ugrasen Kachhawah, is seeking permission to offer royal presents to Balraje."

Raje got lost in thought when he heard it. The royal presents should be bestowed upon Balraje in Mirza Raja's encampment! Why is it being done in advance? Or is this Mirza Raja's move to shower his affections on Balraje to make him feel comfortable? Raje couldn't guess what it was. To exercise caution, he instructed Moropant, "Pant, as the Peshwa, you accept the royal presents on behalf of Balraje! And offer him appropriate presents in return on my behalf."

"As you wish, Swami," Moropant said, and left the chamber.

The plan of Ugrasen Kachhawah, who had arrived at Rajgad, was unsuccessful. He was astutely trying to fulfil the task that 'Ranaji' had assigned him. He wanted to see Sambhajiraje in person! He had not forgotten Mirza Raja's warning, "Beware! Shivajiraje might send somebody else's son disguised as his own with you." But since arriving at the fort, he had not got the chance to see Sambhajiraje in person even once. He was anxious.

A palanquin was ready for Shambhooraje at Padmavati

machi, to descend the fort. It was surrounded by hefty, armed swordsmen chosen by Netaji. Ugrasen Kachhawah stood among them in a corner, along with his Rajput men. With their orange turbans and twisted beards, they looked different and stood out in the crowd.

Shambhooraje left the Balekilla with Raje, Netaji, Moropant, Gangadharpant, Anandrao, Yesaji and Prataprao.

All of them approached the mouth of the tunnel that led to Padmavati machi. At Netaji's signal, the guards pushed aside the boulder at the mouth of the tunnel.

Netaji stepped forward and entered the tunnel. He gave his hand to Sambhajiraje and took him in. Raje and all others followed them. As everyone came inside, Netaji moved back. Sambhajiraje started climbing down the steps with Raje. Others who had come to see them off followed them.

All of them arrived at Padmavati machi. Netaji scrutinized his swordsmen with a keen eye. Raje and Sambhajiraje started walking towards the palanquin. The entire machi was thronged with people.

"Maharaj Saheb, will you take me on a campaign with you?" Raje remembered Sambhajiraje's desire that he had expressed many times. That opportunity had presented itself today, but in such a strange way! Shambhooraje had to undertake the first mission of his life, on his own.

Raje, who had convinced Jijau, 'No one will even touch Balraje's hair in the Rajput camp', immediately touched the cowrie necklace on his chest. He gingerly removed it, twisted it into double strands and put it around Sambhajiraje's neck!

"Take care." he said in a heavy voice and stroked his son's back. Ugrasen Kachhawah stood in the crowd and watched everything. He looked at Shambhooraje with suspicion. When Raje put the cowrie necklace around Shambhooraje's neck, he asked a Mavala standing next to him, "What is it? What did Raja Saab put around the kunwar's neck?"

The Mavala gave him a strange look and exclaimed, "You don't know such a simple thing? It is a symbol of Goddess Bhavani!" To explain it to him properly, the Mavala touched his ears like he was performing the Namaz and said, "Like your Allah! See, nobody else is wearing such a necklace." The Mavala tried to explain, knowing that the person who had posed the question was a Rajput. Ugrasen probably understood it.

As he was convinced that it was Goddess Bhavani's symbol and nobody else was wearing such a necklace, his handsome Rajput face lit up. He stepped forward and saying 'Jai Eklingji!' he made an obeisance to Sambhajiraje who was getting into the palanquin.

Sambhajiraje sat in the palanquin. Netaji held his bare sword in one hand and began walking along with it.

Raje stood in his place with a heavy heart and kept watching the palanquin going away. In his mind, many thoughts clashed against each other like weapons clashing against each other - 'Though it was barren, my father handed me a separate jagir of Pune and sent me here from Bengaluru. And here I am sending you to the enemy's camp to accept his mansab!'

'As soon as you were born, you had to be nursed on Dharau's milk. Today, you are taking your first step in politics, and you have to accept the fake mansab of Aurangzeb! I should put my life on the line for you, but you are going into the enemy camp as a hostage for me! Indeed, Shambhooraje, how many times are you going to be deceived by your own kin? Sai, you left him in my care saying that he was alone, but at that time, I didn't realize that a king is never alone!'

Raje remembered Sambhajiraje holding the torch of Goddess Bhavani and his dance on Pratapgad, while looking at the palanquin descending the fort. The song of the Gondhali describing Goddess Jagadamba's glory echoed in his ears.

Raje muttered, "Shambhooraje, we are the Bhutays of the Goddess. Whatever she offers us in life; we must accept it. Her wish is final!" Raje turned back from the machi.

The cub of Sahyadri's lion had left his cave to descend to the plateau, to undertake his first political mission.

Chapter 3

Sambhajiraje's palanquin left Rajgad and reached near Mirza Raja's encampment at the end of the day. The land of Karhepathar was swamped with orange tents and shamianas, like a big lake swamped with blooming red lotuses.

Kirat Singh set down Sambhajiraje's palanquin at a close distance from the encampment and sent advance intimation to Ranaji.

Mirza Raja's huge encampment, the screeching elephants and camels, the booming cannons—Sambhajiraje did not notice anything around him. He was staring at Fort Purandar in front of him, enveloped in the black smoke of cannon-shots. It was his birthplace. An unknown turmoil filled his heart.

Mirza Raja's munshi Udayraj, Indraman Bundela and a few Rajput swordsmen came to receive Sambhajiraje. The camp echoed with sounds of various musical instruments.

Sambhajiraje left with Netaji to visit Mirza Raja in his lofty shamiana.

The Rajput, Pathan and Bahaliya soldiers in Mirza's camp rushed to see 'Seva's son'. Sambhajiraje entered Mirza's shamiana after Netaji.

As Mirza saw Sambhajiraje, he mumbled, "Oh Goddess Chandi! What a handsome young man!" Mesmerized, he kept gazing in front of him. He saw a fresh, raw, sprouting bud of brilliant lightning flash in the sky, standing at the door of his shamiana!

He completely forgot to verify with Ugrasen Kachhawah that he was indeed the 'real Kunwar' of Shivajiraje.

"Welcome Kunwar Shambhooraje!" Mirza Raja came forward to receive him with a smile. Sambhajiraje approached him and said, "Dadaji, please accept my obeisance, give me your blessings." He touched Mirza Raja's feet.

Mirza didn't understand what Sambhajiraje was doing. He took a few steps back and exclaimed, "What are you doing, Kunwar?"

Sambhajiraje looked at him with fearless eyes and said in a clear, loud voice, "Maharaj Saheb has asked me to address you as 'Dadaji' and consider you in his place. I should obey his instructions." Gangadharpant interpreted his words for Mirza Raja.

Sambhajiraje's words made Mirza Raja realize the huge responsibility Shivajiraje had put on his shoulders. At the very first meeting of Sambhajiraje and Mirza Raja, Raje's strategy of binding a man by putting faith in him, had done the trick.

Mirza Raja held Sambhajiraje's hand and ushered him to a lavish seat. Ugrasen was present in the shamiana. He approached Mirza Raja, made an obeisance to him and said, "Ranaji, one thing..."

"Yes, Ugrasen, what is it?" Mirza asked.

Ugrasen quickly whispered in his ears, "He is Kunwar Sambhu indeed! Raja Saab himself put the necklace of their family deity around his neck!" He began explaining everything to Mirza Raja by moving his hands around his neck.

Mirza Raja heard everything, and laughing out loudly, he said, "Oh Ugrasen, you are such a fool! Just go to your shamiana!"

Ugrasen's actions alarmed Sambhajiraje and Netaji. They glanced at each other with caution.

Netaji's fingers sunk into the hilt of his sword unknowingly. He stared at the entrance of the shamiana, suspecting betrayal. All this had happened because of Ugrasen's suspicious actions.

Mirza Raja's hawk eyes quickly noticed that Netaji and Sambhajiraje had some misapprehensions. He promptly said, "Please, don't misunderstand, Kunwar! Ugrasen was telling me with gestures about the necklace you are wearing, that you are Raja Saab's real Kunwar and nobody else!"

Netaji exhaled a sigh of relief as he heard it. He loosened the grip on his sword and said, "You can't tell the difference between a live ember and a dead coal until you hold it in your hands!" Mirza Raja did not understand his Mavali tongue.

A cloudy evening loomed over the encampment. The flocks of birds had returned to their nests and were resting. Sambhajiraje stood at the entrance of Mirza Raja's shamiana. He was lost in watching the hazy summit of Fort Purandar veiled in the rainy clouds. Netaji's select soldiers kept a vigilant watch along the wall of the shamiana, holding bare swords. Netaji himself stood among them, keeping a keen eye on Sambhajiraje.

As a precaution and a special privilege, Mirza Raja had made arrangements for Sambhajiraje's stay in his own shamiana. He had appointed Kirat Singh and his personal Rajput guards as sentries. Mirza Raja was engaged in the evening worship of Goddess Ranachandi in the inner section of the shamiana. Sambhajiraje kept watching the smoke-covered summit of Fort Purandar for a long time. It was getting dark now.

Netaji got restless and approached Sambhajiraje. He made an obeisance to Sambhajiraje and said, "It's getting dark now; Balraje should go inside! He should not stay outside anymore."

Sambhajiraje's chain of thoughts broke, and he came out of his reverie. He looked at Netaji's big turban and said, "Netajikaka, this fort is calling out to me. I don't feel like taking my eyes off it. My heart is in turmoil."

Netaji shook his head and said, "Yes Baldhani. A man's birthplace always calls out to him. You were born on this fort. I was the custodian of the fort at that time. Masaheb was quite excited to hear your first cry! This fort is now in possession of the Pathan, otherwise I would have shown you Thoralya Ranisaheb's chamber! His rough heart felt heavy while saying it.

Sambhajiraje felt like he had solved all the puzzles posed by his mind. But such puzzles can never be solved! One can't find an open thread in an entangled mesh. Sambhajiraje started thinking about his 'Aausaheb'. He wondered what Fort Purandar looked like from the summit. He turned around and slowly walked over the soft carpet.

After having dinner with Sambhajiraje, Mirza Raja lay on his soft bed in the sleeping apartment of his shamiana. Sambhajiraje lay on a wooden bed, on the western side of the shamiana. He had tossed aside the shawl over his body; it lay crumpled at his feet. The lamps in the shamiana were burning gently.

Sambhajiraje kept tossing and turning restlessly on his bed. He frequently changed sides. Thoralya Aausaheb used to stroke his back at night; he was used to her affectionate touch while he fell asleep.

Mirza Raja noticed his uneasiness. He got up from his bed and kept his kimosh aside. His silver hair shone in the light of the lamps. He approached Sambhajiraje's bed and put his hand on Sambhajiraje's back. Shambhooraje got startled with that touch and got up at once. He kept looking at Mirza Raja's silver hair.

"Kunwar, looks like you are finding it difficult to sleep! A new place leaves one sleepless. Here, come and lie down on my bed! Don't be scared." Mirza Raja held his hand and ushered him to his bed.

Sambhajiraje sat on Mirza Raja's bed. He looked at the hefty but calm-faced Mirza Raja standing in front of him. An emerald-studded pendant that Aalampanha Aurangzeb had bestowed upon him was shining in a pearl necklace on his chest. Sambhajiraje looked at that pendant and fell silent for a moment. Then he asked Mirza, "Dadaji, can I ask you something?"

"Sure, you can Kunwar Sambhoo!" Mirza said in a calm voice.

"Aabasaheb told me that you are a Rajput, and we are also Rajputs. Then, why don't you wear the cowrie necklace of Goddess Bhawani?"

That question left Mirza Raja, the veteran politician of the Delhi Durbar, baffled. A tinge of melancholy flashed in his eyes and disappeared. He caressed the green pendant on his chest in a strange manner and said, "It's late night now. Go to sleep, Kunwar!"

Mirza Raja laid Sambhajiraje on the bed and spread a shawl over him. He himself lay down beside Smabhajiraje, and while muttering "Chandi... Chandi ..." he reminisced about the blunders and fallacies of his life.

After some time, Mirza Raja turned on his side and looked at Sambhajiraje; he was sound asleep.

A platform embellished with royal décor had been raised on the open ground, in front of the shamiana. It was covered with soft Rajput tapestry, and brocaded bolster pillows were arranged on the seats.

Mirza Raja had got the platform erected in one night to offer royal gifts to Shambhooraje and impress him. A few attendants stood near the platform, with covered platters of royal gifts. Royal attendants holding embellished umbrellas stood at the back. A band of war horns, trumpets and drums was standing on a side. All soldiers in the encampment had gathered to see the sight.

It was mid-morning, but the overcast skies made the atmosphere gloomy. Mirza Raja Jai Singh came out of his shamiana with Sambhajiraje and started walking towards the platform with Sambhajiraje. The war horns resounded; the musical instruments echoed.

Behind them, Netaji, Gangadharpant, Karmaji, Kirat Singh, Rai Singh Rathod, Chaturbhuj Chauhan, Ram Singh Hada,

Mohammed Tar Khan, and Turk Taz Khan walked courteously. Mirza Raja led Sambhajirae to his seat. Then he took his own seat and signalled Kirat Singh and Munshi Udayraj with his eyes.

The attendants holding the platters of royal gifts kept approaching them, one by one. They paid obeisance to Mirza and kept presenting the gift platters to him. Mirza then gave them the customary touch of the hand. The platters were then presented to Sambhajiraje. Sambhajiraje gave them the customary touch of acceptance.

All of a sudden, everyone heard the sound of galloping horses coming from the foothills of Fort Purandar. All eyes turned in that direction. Many hearts started pounding. Mirza Raja got up from his seat at once. He looked at his son and said in a daunting but low voice – "Kirat...!"

"Ji" said Kirat Singh and held the hilt of his sword tightly. He quickly mounted a horse and began galloping towards the approaching cavalry troop.

A few moments passed. Sambhajiraje and Netaji had already signalled each other! Before anyone realized it, Netaji's expert swordsmen had surrounded Sambhajiraje from all sides.

Everyone looked in the direction Kirat Singh had gone. The galloping sounds came closer. A cavalry troop of about thirty soldiers was galloping through thick bushes. Two gallant riders were leading it– Kirat Singh and Diler Khan, the commander of the Pathans!

The cavalry troop approached the platform. Mirza Raja frowned at seeing Diler Khan. Diler Khan dismounted and threw a quick glance over the encampment. He appeared huge due to the puffed-up robe of honour draped over his shoulders.

He came in front of Mirza Raja and made an obeisance. Then he pointed towards Fort Purandar, and before Mirza could ask him anything, he promptly said, "We must deliver provisions to the fort! Kafir Marahattas haven't left a single grain behind!"

Mirza Raja couldn't argue with that excuse. He put on a fake smile and said, "Welcome Khan Saab!"

Sambhajiraje observed Diler from his seat. He had thick eyebrows. His neck sat tightly between his shoulders. He had piercing eyes. His Pathan face looked tough and rough due to the constant travelling for various war campaigns. He had tied a knot of the robe of honour he was wearing, on his left shoulder. A green emerald was studded in his kimosh.

Mirza Raja introduced Diler Khan to Sambhajiraje and offered him a seat on the platform.

The remaining gift platters were presented. Sambhajiraje glanced at Netaji. Netaji summoned the attendants with the platters of return gifts. Sambhajiraje gave the customary touch of his hand to the platters to be presented to Mirza Raja and Diler Khan.

The scene looked quite odd. Two veteran commanders of the Delhi durbar and a young bhutya of Goddess Jagadamba were sharing the same platform.

Mirza Raja gestured at Kirat Singh and with a smile on his face, said to Sambhajiraje, "And I will present one more gift to you that you will like very much, Kunwar!"

Sambhajiraje's eyebrows arched as he heard it. Even Diler Khan couldn't guess what gift Mirza was going to give. A mammoth elephant was embellished with a rich brocaded fabric on his back and an open silver howdah was placed on top of it. As Kirat Singh signalled the mahout on the elephant's back, he brought it in front of the platform.

Mirza Raja pointed towards the decorated elephant and said, "Kunwar Sambhu, the Shahen Shah has gifted you this elephant called 'Anwar' from the royal feelkhana! You are the youngest mansabdar of the Delhi durbar to be gifted a five-thousand cavalry!"

Sambhabjiraje unwittingly got up from his seat when he saw the magnificent animal. He signalled Netaji to come close to him and whispered something in his ears.

"Ji" said Netaji and nodded. Netaji went to the feelkhana in the camp and brought a stack of hay. He handed it to Sambhajiraje.

Sambhajiraje took the haystack and approached Anwar who kept swaying in his place. He raised his hand and held the haystack in front of the elephant. Anwar extended his trunk like a hand and grabbed the haystack. The mahout on his back kept gazing at Sambhajiraje.

The elephant held the haystack in his trunk, shook it thoroughly and swallowed it whole.

Everyone around the platform watched the scene in astonishment. Pathan Diler Khan was delighted to watch it. Sambhajiraje smiled at Netaji and went back to his seat. Mirza Raja, who was impressed by Sambhajiraje's personality and his polite behaviour, asked him with pride, "Do you like the elephant, Kunwar Sambhooraje?"

Sambhajiraje looked at him and Diler Khan alternately and said, "It is a poor, voiceless animal! Anybody would like it. It will obey the hand that feeds it."

So far, Diler Khan had been silently watching the boldness of kafir Seva's son. He felt like teasing Sambhajiraje. He puckered his thick eyebrows, pointed towards Anwar and asked, "Sambhooraje, how will you carry this mammoth elephant?" Pathan Diler's eyes twinkled.

As he heard the unexpected question, Sambhajiraje unwittingly took his hand towards his chest and stroked the double-stranded cowrie necklace. Maharaj Saheb's face with a sharp nose, looking like the Shivlinga, bright like the flame of a torch, flashed in front of his eyes. He threw a fearless glance at Diler Khan and raising his head like a serpent's hood, Sambhajiraje spoke in clear, loud words, like a hammer striking on metal, "Your elephant walks slowly. It is easy to take it along, but the forts that our Maharaj Saheb has surrendered to you, don't walk! It is impossible to carry them!" Mirza and Diler were taken aback by that answer.

"Farewell, Dadaji," said Sambhajiraje. He got up from his seat and threw a pouch of gold coins to the mahout sitting on Anwar's back. He started walking towards the shamiana with Netajirao in front of him.

Diler Khan kept staring at him agape. To him, Sambhajiraje seemed like a scorching ember dressed in a royal robe of fiery flames. Words slipped from his thick lips, "Mashalla, what a sharp tongue he has! And at such a young age!"

Mirza Raja Jai Singh and the white officer, Niccolao Manucci were playing chess in Mirza's shamiana. Netaji stood at the entrance. Mirza and the white officer were engrossed in the game. Everyone was quiet. Mirza Raja was occasionally smoking his hookah. Outside, it continued to pour.

Sambhajiraje was watching the black and white pieces on the board.

Mirza Raja looked at him and asked with a smile, "What are you thinking, Kunwar? Would you like to play a game or two?"

Sambhajiraje responded while gazing at the chessboard, "No, I don't want to."

"But why? Raja Saab is quite good at the game of chess! Didn't he teach you the game?" Mirza teased him.

"I don't like this game. It is incomplete." Sambhajiraje was looking at Mirza Raja calmly.

"How so?" Mirza Raja frowned.

"This game has a bishop, a rook, a knight, the pawns, a wazir and a king. But – but it has no prince, and no queen. This game is incomplete."

Mirza Raja pulled down the hookah pipe that he had taken to his lips to smoke and while looking at Sambhajiraje he muttered to himself, "Oh, what an exceptional brain!"

What Sambhajiraje had thought of, had never occurred to

Mirza Raja though he had played chess all his life.

The festival of Krishnashtami was around the corner. Jijau Saheb desired to see her 'BalKrishna' in Rajgad. She compelled Raje to write a letter to the Rajput. As per the accord, Raje had given the possession of almost all forts to Mirza Raja. Mirza Raja received Raje's letter in his encampment. He gave orders accordingly. Anwar, the elephant gifted to Sambhajiraje, was embellished with a brocaded fabric and a howdah. Kirat Singh was going to accompany Sambhajiraje in person.

Netaji prepared his Mavala troops and the palanquin for the journey. Hefty Netaji had tied a shield on his back and accompanied Sambhajiraje like a shadow.

Mirza Raja had observed Netaji with hawk eyes. He had taken note of his vigilance and loyalty, unbeknownst to Netaji.

Sambhajiraje, dressed in a special attire, put his left hand on his sword and leaned forward to make an obeisance to Mirza Raja. While touching his feet he said, "My obeisance to you, Dadaji. If at all any mistake was committed, it was my fault and had nothing to do with Maharaj Saheb! Farewell."

Mirza Raja's heart got heavy as he pulled Sambhajiraje up and held him close. In his entire life, he had never seen a young child with such courage, such touching speech, and such courteous behaviour. Mirza Raja was a Rajput after all. He was a seasoned man.

He patted Sambhajiraje's shoulders and said as if talking to himself, "Only Goddess Chandi knows who is right and who is wrong. But now that I am bidding farewell to you, I remember Mount Aravalli of my homeland, Rajasthan! It stands tall with the scorching dessert at its feet, Kunwar...!" Sambhajiraje did not understand what exactly Mirza was trying to tell him, but he realized that Mirza's hands stroking his shoulders had gotten heavy with affection.

Mirza Raja picked up a betel leaf from the platter and offered it to Sambhajiraje as a custom to bid farewell. Sambhajiraje gazed at the betel leaf. It was the first betel leaf that he had received from a valiant statesman, connoisseur Rajput, who had lost his way. Sambhjiraje held the betel leaf in his fist!

Sambhajiraje stood at the entrance of Mirza Raja's shamiana momentarily and glanced at the summit of Purandar in front of him. He had been born on this fort. Now it was in Diler Khan's possession. Netaji's words echoed in his ears, "The place where one is born, calls out to him!" Unknowingly, he squeezed the betel leaf in his fist.

Sambhajiraje walked briskly and sat in the palanquin. Netaji and Kirat Singh walked on both sides of the palanquin. Anwar, the elephant, started walking slowly in front of the palanquin, swinging its trunk and flapping its ears.

The resounding kettle drums on the Pali Darwaja of Rajgad, announced Sambhajiraje's arrival. His palanquin ascended the fort and arrived at the Padmavati machi. His eyes were looking for Maharaj Saheb, but Raje had not come to the machi. Netaji ushered Sambhajiraje to the chowk in front of the royal hall of Padmavati machi. Jijau stood in the porch of the royal hall. She had descended the Balekilla and come to receive Balraje at the machi.

He was seeing Thoralya Aausaheb after a long time! Sambhajiraje's feet turned into a whirling top. He walked rapidly, passed through the chowk, and jumping over the steps of the porch he clung to Jijau Saheb. He was at a complete loss for words. Jijau was trying to lift his chin and look at his face, but she couldn't see his face clearly through the veil of tears in her eyes!

They spoke through their silence. Sambhajiraje gathered himself and touched Jijau's feet. Jijau leaned forward and pulled him up.

"Thoralya Aausaheb, didn't Maharaj Saheb come with you?" Sambhajiraje asked Jijau.

"No, he didn't come. He doesn't leave his chamber and tries

to avoid me. He doesn't speak to anyone. Come, let's go and see him."

Jijau left the royal hall on the Padmavati machi, with Sambhajiraje. Netaji and Sidojirao made an obeisance to them and walked in front of them.

All of them came to the mouth of the tunnel on the Padmavati machi. The boulder over the tunnel's mouth was pushed aside. Four men with torches got in the tunnel. Netaji and Sidoji followed them.

Netaji conducted Masaheb and Sambhajiraje into the tunnel.

Sambhajiraje was thinking about Maharaj Saheb. He occasionally kept stroking the cowrie necklace that Maharaj Saheb had put around his neck when he left for the Rajput encampment. Suddenly, he remembered Aabasaheb's words, which had echoed while passing through the same tunnel before – "Tunnels have no ending. One should never stop walking!" That memory made Sambhajiraje suddenly stop in his tracks. No one understood why he had stopped so suddenly.

"Shambhubal, what happened?" Jijau asked him affectionately. Jijau's words echoed in the tunnel.

Sambhajiraje got goose bumps when he heard that echo – this is how Aabasaheb's voice had echoed too. He looked at Jijau and replied, "Nothing Aausaheb, I was just checking how far ahead we had come."

Jijau stared at him for a moment. Then she patted his shoulder and said, "There is no point in looking back when you are walking forward! It makes you feel tired. You should focus on the distance you have to cover further and keep your eyes in front; it gives you the strength to continue the journey." Sambhajiraje listened to Jijau's divine words attentively. He felt that Aabasaheb's earlier words and what Aausaheb had said just now, was quite similar— just like a sword has the same sharpness on both sides.

As soon as they arrived at the Balekilla, Jijau, Sambhajiraje and Netaji started walking towards Raje's chamber. Raje had already been informed of their arrival.

Raje had put aside all his agony for Jijau's sake and had come up to the entrance of his chamber to receive them. As soon as Maharaj Saheb came into sight, Sambhajiraje started running like a horse that has been prodded hard by its rider. His hands engulfed Raje's waist within no time.

Raje was unable to speak. His lean fingers kept stroking Sambhajiraje's back. Suddenly, Sambhajiraje took a few steps back and stared at Raje's mojaris. He gently removed the cowrie necklace and held it in his palms. He raised his palms and said, "Maharaj Saheb, I spoke very little, and only when needed!"

Raje picked up the necklace and put it around his own neck. Raje's stress had vanished. Sambhajiraje touched his feet.

"Go and seek the blessings of the goddess." Raje said, pointing towards the temple.

Jijau Saheb and Sambhajiraje started walking towards the temple. All the employees of the eighteen departments on the fort kept coming there under some pretext or the other to see Sambhajiraje to their heart's content.

The queens' apartments came closer. From Putalabai's chamber, Dharau came forward. As she saw Jijau, she hesitated for a moment. Then, she approached Sambhajiraje determinedly. She waved some black thing from Sambhajiraje's head to toe three times. Sambhajiraje smiled at her and touched her feet. Dharau quickly moved aside and walking along the wall she disappeared.

Sambhajiraje entered the temple. He prostrated in front of Goddess Jagadamba. He plucked out the sprouts of eight grains from the bed of grains. He removed the soil attached to the roots and thrust the tender sprouts, the symbol of prosperity, into his Jiretop.

In front of Goddess Jagadamba, various weapons were placed in a line and worshipped. Sambhajiraje leaned forward and from the line of weapons, picked up his Jamadar sword sheathed in the scabbard and touched it to his forehead briefly. Then he put his hand on the hilt of the sword and swiftly pulled it out. He looked at Jijau Saheb who stood behind him. Jijau gave him a delightful smile.

Inadvertently, the sword shifted from his right hand to his left hand and his head rose like a serpent's hood. He quickly moved his right thumb along the sharp edge of the sword. Drops of blood sprouted on his thumb. Sambhajiraje took his bleeding thumb near Goddess Jagadamba's feet. Two drops of his warm blood spilled on the head of demon Mahishasura, who was getting trampled under Jagadamba's feet. Then he applied the blood from his thumb to his forehead. Jijau's eyes lit up with pride looking at his fierce yet divine Kshatriya form.

"Let's go." Jijau put her hand on his back and said to him contentedly.

Today was the festival of Vijayadashami. In the Dussehra chowk, branches of Sonpatta were arranged in a pile. A member of the royal family was supposed to break the pile with a sword. It was a tradition that had been followed for generations. It was a festive occasion – and this occasion was special. Till today, Raje had broken the pile with his own hands. But this time, Raje felt that all his golden dreams had been shrouded by the rough green leaves of the Mughal onslaught. That is why he had instructed Sambhajiraje to break the pile this year.

The evening was approaching, dispersing the golden rays of the sun. Sambhajiraje and Jijau Saheb came to Raje's chamber.

Raje made an obeisance to Masaheb, as he saw her entering the chamber. Raje's face was calm, but his eyes were full of pain. Jijau was heartbroken to see the pain in his eyes. Raje stood silently in front of her.

Jijau composed herself and said in a gentle voice, "Balraje is here to see you." She always hid the burning pain in her heart, and spoke with only cool, soothing words on her lips.

Raje looked deep into Sambhajiraje's eyes and to check if he was ready Raje asked him in a raspy voice, "Have you understood the whole ritual clearly?"

"Ji." Sambhajiraje responded.

"How will you break the pile?"

Sambhajiraje's eyes changed colour. He visualized the Dussehra chowk thronged with a crowd. Sambhajiraje gazed at his Aabasaheb's aquiline nose and said, "In the Dussehra chowk on Sanjivani machi a platform has been erected. Branches of Sonpatta have been arranged on that platform. A Sonpatta tree is located on the border of the machi. A bundle of weapons that were worshipped during the nine days of Navaratri festival has been placed near its trunk. The Tatasarnoubat of the machi will bring the weapons to the Dussehra chowk and place them in front of me. I will give the customary touch to that bundle. The bundle will be placed on top of the pile of Sonpatta branches. Then, the Tatasarnoubat will request me to break the pile. I will offer Bael leaves and haldi-kumkum on the pile. Then, chanting the name of Goddess Bhavani, I will break the pile with a single strike of my sword. I will not retract my sword but will push it forward and touch it to the Sonpatta branches and taste the symbolic gold. Then, the gathered crowd will fall upon the platform and the gold will be looted!"

Raje looked at Jijau. Masaheb herself had explained the process in detail to Balraje.

"Whoever succeeds in grabbing a weapon that was worshipped during the Navaratri festival, after breaking the pile, you should meet them personally and reward them with bracelets of honour and gold coins. Farewell now." Raje told Sambhajiraje the last and most important practice to follow.

Sambhajiraje made an obeisance to Raje, sought his blessings and left the chamber.

A Pathan messenger, dressed in a brocaded vest, had arrived at the fort with two soldiers. He had got a letter for Raje, and he dispatched it to the Balekilla while looking contemptuously at the ongoing Dussehra celebrations on the fort. Chitnis Balaji accepted the letter on behalf of Raje and presented it to him for the customary touch of his hand. As per custom, Raje touched the letter and ordered it to be read.

Balaji started reading the letter –

"... I am happy to announce to you that Badshah has generously accepted your loyal services. Additionally, the Badshah has kind-heartedly released orders to offer the mansab of five thousand soldiers, the gift of two lakh rupees, and the permission to carry the Nishan-Naubat in the name of your son, Sambhajiraje. Therefore, as soon as you receive this letter, send Sambhajiraje back immediately, so that as per the royal firman, he can be bestowed with these honours..."

Balaji finished reading the letter. Pathan Diler Khan had sent the letter from Fort Purandar. He had sent a special messenger on the auspicious day of Dussehra.

Raje was lost in thought looking at the pouch in which Balaji had placed the letter. He let out a deep sigh. Just then, Sambhajiraje entered Raje's chamber to offer the Sonpatta leaves to Raje that he had collected after breaking the pile. Sambhajire touched Raje's feet, put the Sonpatta leaves in Raje's palms and said, "Maharaj Saheb, I broke the pile accurately, and in a single strike."

The Sonpatta leaves were sitting on top of Diler's letter in Raje's palm. Raje glanced at his palms and then at his son. He was still lost in thought.

"You broke the Sonpatta pile and pulled out the gold from it, but you are my gold leaf which I have thrust into the pile of treacherous politics! Sometimes, a person must cross unknown borders, and swim against the tide. Resentful Diler Khan has grabbed an opportune moment. Balraje, just as adeptly as you broke the pile of Sonpatta leaves, you should now handle this political situation with a great deal of tact. May Goddess

Jagadamba bestow strength upon you, to face this difficult time!"

The celebrations of Dussehra were barely over when Sambhajiraje had to leave Rajgad again, to accept the royal firman.

After seeking blessings from Raje and Thoralya Aausaheb, Sambhajiraje reached the Rajput encampment. He was accompanied by Davalji Ghatage, Netajirao, Gangadharpant and others.

Kirat Singh came forward to receive him. Mirza Raja approached him, held his hand and greeted him saying, "Welcome, Sambhooraje".

Mirza Raja let Sambhajiraje sit on his own seat, and introduced him to Bakshi Jani Beg and Tej Singh Kachhawah, who were present in the shamiana. As a courtesy, he enquired about Raje's health. With great satisfaction, Mirza held the hookah pipe in his hand and smoked it momentarily. Then, he looked at Jani Beg and said, "Bakshi, explain the customary process of accepting the firman to Kunwar Sambhuji; make no mistake."

Bakshi Beg promptly leaned forward and made an obeisance to Mirza. "As you wish, Ranaji!" he said and observed Sambhajiraje. He realized that no sardar of the Delhi durbar was so young.

The weather outside was cold; a menial brought bowls of hot wheat porridge with almonds and pistachios spread over it. He kept the platter on a wooden stool in front of Mirza Raja and left. Mirza picked up two bowls; steaming vapours arose from the bowls. Mirza handed one bowl to Sambhajiraje and said, "Here, have some porridge, Chhote Raja Saab!" Sambhajiraje held the bowl in his hands. Mirza Raja took a sip of the hot porridge and said, "Chhote Raja Saab, you will have to go to Bakshi's shamiana, listen carefully to the instructions he gives you and accept the firman with honour. You are mature enough to understand it. Everything will be alright."

Sambhajiraje had touched the bowl to his lips to take a sip of the porridge, but as it burned his tongue, he quickly pulled it down. He looked at the bowl and remembered his Aabasaheb. He had also explained the procedure – of how to break the pile of Sonpatta leaves, how to offer the gold coins and bracelets of honour. Mirza was also explaining the procedure – of how to show deference to the royal firman.

"Let it cool down." Mirza said looking at Sambhajiraje's bowl. Sambhajiraje raised his head and glanced into his eyes for a moment; he remembered the Mavalas thrusting their hands into the burning Holi fearlessly, and falling upon the pile of Sonpatta leaves at the time of Dussehra. He took the bowl to his lips and gulped the entire bowl of hot porridge, without blinking.

Mirza raised his eyebrows and while gazing at Sambhajiraje, he put his own bowl down. A bizarre thought crossed his mind. To him, Shivajiraje seemed like a glowing ember. His son also seemed to be like that ember, but Mirza couldn't figure out exactly how.

The answer was simple, but Mirza had not realised it. Raje was indeed like a scorching ember that always kept burning and could never be quenched. His son, Sambhajiraje was like a flame emanating from the ember, that unmistakably sears the hand that touches it!

Mirza composed himself and instructed Jani Beg, "Bakshi, take Chhote Raja Saab to your shamiana respectfully."

"Ji Huzur!" Jani Beg nodded.

"Sambhooraje, please go with him!" Mirza told Sambhajiraje.

Sambahajiraje left Mirza's shamiana with Netaji, behind Bakshi Jani Beg and Kirat Singh.

Bakshi Beg's small tent with the crescent moon and star pennant came into sight. Sambhajiraje and Netaji entered the tent behind Bakshi Beg and Kirat Singh. Fate is indeed unpredictable. One can never tell when it will lead one to the unknown door of ominous misfortune! Kirat Singh offered his seat to Sambhajiraje. Netajirao stood close to him vigilantly.

Like a trained parrot, Bakshi Beg started recounting the customary process of accepting the firman.

Sambhajiraje had never heard anything like that. Aurangzeb Alamgir, the Mughal emperor, had dispatched the royal firman from Delhi, granting him the mansab of five thousand cavalries. The imprint of Aurangzeb's hand, dipped in henna paste, was imprinted on the firman as the royal seal. The camel rider with the firman had arrived and was waiting at some distance from Mirza's encampment. Mirza had raised a 'firmanbadi' on the north of his encampment, where a lofty shamiana had been raised, into which a camel could easily enter.

The camel rider carrying the firman was going to bring the camel into the lofty shamiana and make it stand there. The loyal servant of the durbar was supposed to approach the camel without showing his back. Then, the camel rider was going to make the royal camel sit down. The loyal servant was supposed to kneel and sit beside the camel, with his head bent. Then, while sitting on the camel, the camel rider was going to put the pouch of the firman, on the loyal servant's head. The loyal servant was then going to hold the firman with his hands and take ten steps backwards, without showing his back to the camel. The loyal servant was supposed to act as if the Emperor of Hindustan was present in person and finish the procedure accordingly. Till today, many valiant warriors had accepted the royal firman in the same way.

Every single word of Bakshi Beg was making Sambhajiraje increasingly uneasy. Till today, he had knelt only in front of Masaheb, Raje, Goddess Jagadamba, loving elders and no one else! He kept staring at Netaji frequently. His chest was heaving. Suddenly, he exclaimed, "Okay, I have understood the procedure of accepting the firman. Farewell."

Before Kirat Singh and Bakshi Beg could say anything, he signalled Netaji and instantly left Bakshi Beg's tent. Netaji promptly rushed after him.

"Netajikaka, just tell Dadaji – I cannot follow this procedure! Somebody else will accept the firman on my behalf."

"But...Dhakale Sarkar, Raje has agreed to this condition in the accord. This will be like breaking his word. The Rajput will not accept it." Netaji was trying to convince him as he walked with him.

"No, Netajikaka, I cannot kneel in front of an animal, and hold the pouch of the firman over my head."

"Please listen to me Baldhani. This is a trick. Raje and all of us are waiting for the Rajput to leave our land. Please understand it, Balraje. Otherwise, Raje will blame me for your actions! It will damage my reputation. Just accept the firman and as far as the three obeisances are concerned, do one to Goddess Amba, one to Masaheb, and one to Raje; kneel while keeping your eyes on Purandar and making an obeisance to the eldest Ranisaheb!" Netaji was speaking earnestly.

Sambhajiraje stopped as he heard Netaji's words. He stared at Netaji with keen eyes and threw him a question like a stone shot from a slingshot, "...Will you do all this Netajikaka?"

Netaji instantly lowered his head. He did not know how to convince Balraje.

Sambhajiraje walked further and entered Mirza Raja's shamiana. He looked into his eyes and said, "Somebody else will accept your firman on my behalf. I will not do it Ranaji!" For the first time, unwittingly the word 'Ranaji' slipped from his mouth. "Why? What happened Kunwar?" Mirza became anxious and got up from his seat at once.

"I cannot follow the procedure prescribed by your protocol. I will not kneel." Sambhajiraje said resolutely. Mirza could feel the determination in his voice.

"No...! You should not do that. Dishonouring the firman could create major problems for me and Raja Saab." Mirza approached Sambhajiraje. As he put his hand on Sambhajiraje's shoulder, he fell silent briefly. While gazing at him intensely, he let out a deep sigh. "Who do you respect? Raja Saab, right?" He asked in a low voice as if he was smoking his hookah in a slow rhythm.

"Ji" Sambhajiraje nodded his head gingerly.

"Didn't Raja Saab tell you to call me 'Dadaji' and keep my word? So, Kunwar, don't you consider me as 'Dadaji'?" Mirza spoke in his diplomatic sweet tongue.

Sambhajiraje hesitated. This was the man who had offered Sambhajiraje space in his own shamiana, let him sleep in his own bed, who had shared his shawl with Sambhajiraje, gifted him a big elephant, and treated him with a lot of respect and politeness. He was an outsider, but he possessed a skill that endeared him to others.

Sambhajiraje was observing him, trying to assess him.

Suddenly, the musical instruments in the camp began resounding. The royal firman was being greeted with music. The Ukhali cannons started booming.

"Come Sambhooraje, leave your mojaris right here." Mirza Raja gently put his hand on Sambhajiraje's shoulder and opened a fragrant vial of sweet words.

Sambhajiraje removed his mojaris. Mirza Raja left with Sambhajiraje. People from both sides – Raja Raisingh, Kirat Singh, Tej Singh Kachhawah, Indraman Bundela, Niccolao Manucci, Badal-Bakhtyaar, Netaji, Davalji, Gangadharpant – followed them.

Finally, Sambhajiraje left barefoot, to the 'firmanbadi', to accept the royal firman. This was the darkest day in his life.

He could see Fort Purandar, veiled in smoke, in front of him. Raje's solemn words kept echoing in his ears – "Aurangzeb is the emperor of Delhi. No one can see him, except for his sardars – but the consequences of his actions can be seen by the entire world! His brothers saw it and so did his own father…"

Sambhajiraje dragged himself with great difficulty into the

firmanbadi with Mirza Raja. The firmanbadi was open from all sides. The entire camp had gathered to watch the scene. The camel rider arrived at the firmanbadi in a grand parade.

Sambhajiraje made an obeisance and knelt on the wet ground by the camel's side and bent his head low.

The camel rider prodded the dust-covered camel carrying the royal firman, to sit down. He picked up the fastened pouch of the firman. In a grandiose manner, the camel rider put the pouch on top of Sambhajiraje's orange Jiretop! Then, in a loud voice he proclaimed the titles - "Abul Muzaffar Moiuddin Mohammed Aurangzeb Bahadur Alamgir Padashah Gazi, Malik-e-takhte taus, Shahenshah-e-Hindustan bestows the honour of royal firman upon Sambhooji, the son of Sevaji Bhosala of the Deccan subah...!

Formal words of the royal decree were popping like corn from the camel rider's mouth. The cannons in the camp began booming.

Sambhajiraje bent his head; tears streamed from his bright eyes, rolling down the cowrie necklace, merging into the ground below. He felt suffocated! Fate was playing a merciless game with his tender emotions! He wanted to spring up like a horse, toss the pouch of the firman in the dust and sprint away hastily.

"Arise Kunwar." Mirza leaned forward and put his hand on Sambhajiraje's back. He made Sambhajiraje take ten steps backwards along with the firman. Sambhajiraje raised his head and handed the firman to Netaji. Balraje's eyes were filled with immense pain. As Netaji looked into his eyes, his head dropped low, and his eyes that used to breathe fire while shouting 'Har Har Mahadeo', got teary. He could see the stains of dirt on the white jama that his Dhakale Raje was wearing! These stains were never going to fade!

As Raje believed that Mirza Raja's pestering demands had reduced, he had gone on a campaign in the Tal Konkan region. It had been five days since he left.

Jijau was about to finish dictating some letters of formal correspondence. Her mind was not at rest nowadays.

"Balaji let's stop now. I am done." Jijau said to the Chitnis while getting up from her seat. It was almost time for lighting the lamps.

"As you wish," Balaji said, and gently placed the white quill in its stand. He quickly stood up.

Lakshmibai, Putalabai, Sakawarbai, Gunavantabai, Kashibai and other queens had gathered in Jijau's chamber to make the evening obeisance to her. Sambhajiraje stood next to Putalabai. His sisters, Sakhoobai, Ranoobai, Ambabai and others stood next to him. Everyone waited for Jijau. Just then, fair complexioned Soyarabai in a brocaded black sari, casually entered the chamber with her daughter, Balibai.

Sambhajiraje leaned forward and bowed to her three times.

Soyarabai went near Putalabai. She gazed at Sambhajiraje with her dark black eyes, put her hand on his shoulder, and without looking at Putalabai she said, "Dhakalya bai, it was good that Balraje had to accept the firman! If Swari had to accept the firman in person, it would have been quite embarrassing for all of us! Balraje is very clever, he did not commit any mistake!"

Putalabai raised her head and glanced at Soyarabai. She felt as if Soyarabai's eyes reflected the intricate henna designs on her feet.

"Balraje, what are you discussing with Thoralya bai?" Jijabai said with a smile as she entered the chamber. The entire chamber was filled with fragrance at her entry. Before anybody could say anything, Soyarabai tidied her sari and responded, "Nothing, I was just saying to Balraje...' The tip of Soyarabai's reddish nose got flushed.

Jijau calmly sat on the bed and asked her, "What were you saying?"

"That he had to accept the firman at such a tender age! Only he could deal with the situation successfully!" At her words, all the queens kept looking at each other in shock. Soyarabai had completely twisted her own words in an instant!

Jijabai, Sambhajiraje and the queens had no inkling that Raje was not in Tal Konkan. He was in Mirza Raja's encampment, in a shamiana provided for him, like a tiger trapped in a cage restlessly pacing back and forth.

Mirza Raja had dispatched an urgent message to Raje in Tal Konkan and had summoned him to the encampment in Karhepathar. Without informing Raje, Mirza Raja had sent a letter on Raje's behalf to Aurangzeb, claiming his loyalty to Aurangzeb. Aurangzeb had immediately sent a firman in Raje's name. Raje urgently travelled from Tal Konkan to Mirza's encampment. Today, Raje had accepted the firman with a heavy heart, as per the royal procedure described by Bakshi Jani Beg.

Raje had returned after accepting the firman; he was agitatedly pacing back and forth in his shamiana. Suddenly, he stopped in his tracks. A thought crossed his mind, 'Shambhooraje, you came to meet me after accepting the firman. I held you in my embrace without saying anything. Today, I have also accepted the firman, but no one is here to embrace me!'

Raje and Sambhajiraje had surrendered their nobility in Mirza's camp and thus provided their people the courage to survive. True kingship is about protecting the rights of the defenceless people! Raje had paid a huge price to fulfil his duty as a king!

As far as Mirza Raja was concerned, Shivajiraje's Swaraj was finished. Now his sultry, Rajasthani eyes were gazing in the direction of Bijapur's Adil Shahi sultanate. He had come to trample the entire Deccan under his feet.

Mirza Raja sent a special messenger to Rajgad and summoned Raje with his army, to the encampment near Fort Purandar. He wanted Raje to attack Bijapur and serve the Mughal sultanate. For that purpose, he had trapped Raje in the accord.

Two months had passed since Raje had left with the Rajputs towards Bijapur.

Jijau was concluding official correspondence as usual. Balaji Aavaji was taking down the dictation with full concentration.

Jijau finished dictating the last letter. Peshwa Moropant who was waiting outside for her to finish her work, came into the royal hall. He made an obeisance to Masaheb.

"What is it Pant?" Jijau asked him.

"A shastri, well versed in the Vedas has come from Shringarpur. His name is Keshav Pandit. He is seeking permission to see you. If you wish..." Moropant stopped courteously.

"Please bring him here, Pant."

Moropant looked at the entrance of the royal hall. Keshav Pandit, who was waiting outside for his signal, came inside.

Keshav Pandit leaned forward, brought both his palms together and made an obeisance to Jijau. It had been his desire for many days, to see Aausaheb in person, and so, he observed Jijau intently with his radiant eyes.

"Shastribuva, what brings you here?" Jijau looked at Keshav Pandit and asked calmly.

Keshavbhat bowed again as he heard the question and said, "I have some knowledge of the Shastras, Ramayana, Mahabharata, Vedas-Upanishads... If I can be of any service to you..."

"Good! I have been looking for such a person. Moropant, please conduct him to my chamber. Jagadamb!" Jijau looked delighted. She got up from her seat and started walking towards her chamber.

One glance at her, and anybody would have known that she was thinking about someone. But those thoughts were neither about Raje, nor Sambhajiraje; not the queens of Raje, and not even about the kingdom. Jijau was thinking about her granddaughter-in-law! Yesubai!

After Sambhajiraje's wedding, Yesubai had gone to Shringarpur with Pilajirao.

Jijau said to herself, "It's been a long time since I saw her. I should send for her now!"

Bahirji Naik, who had travelled from Panhala, arrived on Rajgad at twilight. He reached the Balekilla and sent intimation of his arrival to Jijau. At that time Jijau was in her chamber with Moropant and Keshavbhat. Jijau was sitting on the bed with Sambhajiraje.

After cordially enquiring about Keshavbhat, Jijau had assigned him the task of imparting the stories of Ramayana and Mahabharata to Sambhajiraje.

As Jijau received the intimation of Bahirji's arrival she dismissed Moropant and Keshav Pandit.

Bahirji, disguised as a Ramoshi, entered the chamber. He looked weary due to the arduous journey. He made an obeisance to Masaheb and looked at her.

"What's the news, Naik? Tell me." Jijau reassured Bahirji, who was visibly hesitant about sharing the news he had brought.

"A fierce fight took place at Bijapur. Dhani and the Rajput had to accept defeat against Sarja Khan."

"I already know that. Bijapur's Sarlashkar, Sarja Khan displayed the strength of a mountain. I have heard that Raje left from Bijapur and was travelling towards Panhala. What happened at Panhala?"

"Ji Aaisaheb, something very bad that shouldn't have happened, took place on Panhala...we lost about a thousand foot-soldiers in the raid on Panhala! But we couldn't win the fort." Bahirji dropped his head low.

"What?" Sambhajiraje frowned, his body stiffened. One thousand soldiers had been killed in a single raid!

"Dhani divided the army into two troops when he left Bijapur. One troop was under Sarlashkar's command. Raje himself had led the second troop to Panhala a few days before and hid near the foothills. He had instructed Netaji to join him on the same night. But Netaji did not show up there on time! Raje got agitated waiting for him. As the night was passing by, he began climbing up the fort with his troop, but the custodian of the fort had already got intimation of the attack. He was hiding with his swordsmen behind the ramparts covered in fog. As soon as Raje came within range, he attacked directly. A fierce skirmish took place! About a thousand of our men fell on the incline of the fort. Raje hastily moved towards Vishalgad with the remaining soldiers."

"So..., Raje is at Vishalgad now, and where is our Sarlashkar?" Jijabai could not condone Netaji's behaviour.

"No Masaheb, Raje has reached Konkan via Fonda, and..." Bahirji's voice broke.

"And what Naik?" Jijau suspected that someone had got killed in the battle.

"How can I say this, Masaheb? It would have been better if I had no tongue at all to deliver such horrible news!"

"Naik, even if you don't tell the truth, truth will not stay hidden for long. Tell me what happened." Jijau chided Bahirji.

"Raje sent a letter to the Sarlashkar from Vishalgad. 'Why did you not show up on time, despite being the Sarlashkar? How could you come so late? You are hereby relieved of your responsibility as Sarlashkar,' After reading that letter, Netaji flew into a rage, deserted Raje and defected to the Bijapur sultanate with his troop!" Bahirji shook his head in shock and spoke in a choked voice.

Jijabai stared blankly at Bahirji with strained eyes.

There, in Agra, the Taj Mahal was suffocating in the same manner. The seven-year imprisonment of Shahajahan in the Red Fort was finally over!

Shahajahan had breathed his last in the Red Fort, while pleading to Khuda, "Oh Allahtala, let me die in peace. Save me from the wrath of hell." This news had travelled like the wind from the North to the South. People were surprised to hear it.

Aurangzeb had bribed Shahajahan's loyal masseur and had him massaged with poisonous oil under the pretext of applying medicinal oil!

Shahajahan was pleading to Khuda to save him from the wrath of hell, but Aurangzeb had left no such opportunity for him. Shahajahan had already suffered the torture of hell during his imprisonment.

Aurangzeb had left his father in the custody of Mutamad, his personal Khoja, who was as loyal to him as a dog.

When Khwaja Mamur, the supervisor of Shahajahan's wardrobe, died, Mutamad sealed the wardrobe for good. Shahajahan who was used to changing his imperial garb frequently during the day, was forced to wear the same jama for many days! He breathed his last in the Red Fort one evening after suffering such humiliation.

Be it an emperor or a mere servant, in the end, life fades into nothingness!

Shivajiraje who had retreated from Fonda, met with Mirza Raja in the camp near Bijapur and arrived at Rajgad. During this visit, Mirza Raja had advised Raje to present himself in the Agra durbar with Sambhajiraje, to participate in the celebrations of Aurangzeb's fiftieth birthday!

This was just a pretext. Mirza had his apprehensions. The Qutub Shahi sultanate had provided fifty thousand cavalry to the Bijapur sultanate. Raje's right hand, Netaji, had defected to the Bijapur sultanate. Moreover, if Raje would have defected to Bijapur, it would have proved disastrous for Mirza. Due to this apprehension, Mirza corresponded with Aurangzeb and had planned Shivajiraje and Shambhooraje's visit to Agra beforehand.

Mirza presumed that if Aurangzeb concurred, he might offer Raje the rank of Deccan's subedar. Raje had no option left but to accept the title of the subedar for the time being.

Before going to Agra, it was essential to appoint the right

person for the position of Sarlashkar. Raje convened a meeting for that.

Raje entered the royal hall with Sambhajiraje; the courtiers were already present.

Mujumdar Nilopant stood to Raje's right; the platters containing the attire of the Sarlashkar, red twisted turban, and a sword placed in its scabbard, were placed on a platform Raje's heart was momentarily stung by the bitter memories of Netaji. Grave silence had spread in the royal hall.

"I am going to the North to visit the emperor!" Raje's voice got heavy while speaking. He composed himself and said, "I have decided to appoint Kudatoji Gujar as the new Sarlashkar. Kudatoji, please present yourself."

Kudatoji approached Raje's seat. He made an obeisance and stood politely in front of Raje. Raje got up from his seat. Nilopant presented the platter of Sarlashkar's attire to him. Raje placed the attire on Kudatoji's shoulder and tied the sword around his waist. Kudatoji removed his turban and held it in his hands. Raje picked up the red twisted turban and placed it on Kudatoji's head. Raje looked at the courtiers and said, "I declare Kudatoji Gujar as our army's Sarlashkar from today." I bestow the title of 'Prataprao' upon him." Raje embraced Kudatoji. While doing that, neither Kudatoji nor a single courtier realized the immense pain in Raje's heart. Raje had called Kudatoji 'Our army's Sarlashkar' and not 'The Sarlashkar of Swaraj'.

But Sambhjiraje who always listened attentively to Raje, noticed it. A thought crept into his mind – 'You should not abandon my Maharaj Saheb like Netajikaka did! Don't do anything against his wish!'

The meeting was over. The courtiers left the royal hall. None of them knew this at the time, that Aurangzeb had come from Delhi to Agra, to visit his late father's tomb.

Chapter 4

The news of Raje's impending travel to the North with Sambhajiraje spread throughout the region.

The cunning statesmen of Adil Shahi, Qutub Shahi, Siddi, British, and Firangi durbars were convinced that Shivaji was finished now! A new 'Mirza Raja' would be born in Shivaji's form!

Raje travelled throughout the Maval region with select people and surveyed the measures of security for all forts in his possession.

Jijau Saheb dispatched Keshav Pandit with a message to Pialijirao in Shringarpur, "Please bring my grand-daughter-in-law to Rajgad at the earliest."

Raje's loyal advisors guided him in every way possible. Masaheb encouraged him to gather his courage. But Raje was trapped in such a dilemma that he had begun doubting himself.

At Rayareshwar, Raje had taken the vow of raising Swaraj, with great vigour. But now he was benumbed to see all his dreams turning to dust.

Raje went to Pratapgad with Sambhajiraje, to visit the temple of Goddess Jagadamba. Prataprao, Prabhakarbhat, Moropant, Anandrao and others accompanied them.

Raje took the darshan of Kedareshwar and came to the temple of Goddess Jagadamba. Raje and Sambhajiraje washed their hands and feet and entered the temple. As Raje saw the idol of the eight-armed Goddess Durga in the ready-to-strike pose, he knelt, joined his palms in prayer, closed his eyes and touched his head to the floor. Countless flaming torches kept dancing in front of his eyes, and his mind kept dancing to their rhythm.

'Oh mother, my hands are tied. What a predicament you have put me in! Your child is getting trampled in your dance of destruction! Oh, Goddess Amba, open your eyes! Darkness is consuming us from all sides, light the torches!' Raje kept pleading in desperation. He did not want to raise his head.

Sambhajiraje sat on his knees to Raje's left. He was glancing alternately at the ferocious Goddess Jagadamba and at Raje.

After a while Raje raised his head. His eyes were misty. He got up, went inside the sanctum and put his head on Goddess Jagadamba's feet. Raje and Sambhajiraje took darshan and left the temple.

After inspecting the ramparts and patrolling units of Pratapgad, Raje's palanquin descended the fort.

At Rajgad, an aristocratic, young girl sat on the bed in Sambhajiraje's chamber. Putalabai's personal maid had ushered her there.

Her eyes kept moving around the chamber, curiously examining the weapons hung on the walls and the white and orange Jiretops placed on separate platters on the wooden table. From time to time, she looked at the Shivlinga in the sanctum. She asked herself, "Why have I been ushered to a man's chamber?" Suddenly, she heard the beating of the kettle drums.

Raje and Sambhajiraje's palanquin ascended Rajgad and arrived at the Balekilla. Sambhajiraje visited Jijau Saheb and came to his chamber, completely exhausted. There was no maid in his chamber.

Sambhajiraje approached the table to place his Jiretop on a platter. He put his hands on his Jiretop to remove it and looked at the bed at the same time. He saw shining, silver toe rings!

Someone was there! He instantly brought his hands down

and observed the girl sitting on his bed. He couldn't recognize her. He held his head high and glancing at the bed asked, "Who…who is sitting on my bed?"

The young girl gave Sambhajiraje a startled look. Sambhajiraje was baffled to see her round face and her beady eyes shining like stars in the light of the lamps!

He looked at the Jiretops on the table again to make sure he was in his own chamber.

"You?" Sambhajiraje exclaimed, immediately turned his back on her and left the chamber. With her heart beating loudly, the young girl, too, left the chamber hastily. She was wondering, "Where to go now?" She was Yesubai! She had arrived at Rajgad with her father, Pilaji.

The ninth day of the bright fortnight of Falgun broke out. Sambhajiraje took a bath and donned a blue, brocaded jama, a golden-bordered white Jiretop, golden red churidars, and a white scarf around the waist. He left for Jijau's chamber with Rayaji and Antoji Gaade; she was going to apply horizontal stripes of sandalwood paste on his forehead. Jijau was giving quick instructions to the maids in her chamber.

Sambhajiraje's sisters stood next to her. Putalabai stood along a wall; Dharau held a platter and stood next to her humbly. Yesubai stood between them, keeping out of sight!

"Yesu, come forward and stand here." Jijabai told Yesubai.

Yesubai was baffled for a moment and lingered. Then, she recognized the affectionate tone and moved forward. She mingled with her sisters-in-law, and stood with them, keeping her head low. Sambhajiraje entered the chamber. Rayaji and Antoji followed him. All of them made an obeisance to Jijau and Putalabai. Jijau came forward slowly. As she looked at Sambhajiraje, a big turmoil arose in her heart –'Alas, he has suffered so much at such a young age!'

Sambhajiraje put his head on Jijau's feet and held it there for some time. He felt the huge difference between accepting a firman holding one's head low and putting one's head on Thoralya Aausaheb's feet!

"Arise." Jijau's voice got heavy. She leaned forward and pulled him up delicately.

Without looking back, she called out, "Dharau..."

"Ji" Dharau said as she composed herself and promptly came forward. She held the platter in front of Jijau. Jiaju checked the vials of haldi-kumkum and sandalwood paste in the platter. She dipped a brass needle in the vials and drew two horizontal lines of the sandalwood paste on Shambhajiraje's forehead! As she looked at the stripes she had drawn, Jijau thought,

"Shambhooraje, you are Lord Shiva's devotee. Lord Shiva himself has drawn the two stripes of joys and sorrows on your forehead! Everything is in his hands now. He is your saviour!"

Jijau pulled Sambhajiraje close and said, "I have received intimation that Raje will be arriving here soon. Go with him to the temple of Goddess Jagadamba and other temples on the fort."

"Ji" Sambhajiraje nodded in affirmation.

"Meet Gomajibaba, Sidoji, Mohammed Sais and Keshav Pandit before leaving. Visit the queens' apartments too." Sambhajiraje listened to her attentively.

"Go and seek her blessings now." Jijabai told Sambhajiraje, pointing to Putalabai.

Sambhajiraje approached Putalabai. He leaned forward and touched her feet. With that touch, goosebumps arose on Putalabai's body. Her eyes got misty.

"Arise!" Putalabai pulled up Sambhajiraje lovingly. She lifted his chin with her forefinger and said, "After visiting all, come to my chamber. I am going to tie an amulet around your arm!"

"Ji" Said Sambhajiraje and stepped forward to touch Dharau's feet but retreated quickly as he saw Yesubai standing behind Putalabai.

"Now Shambhoobal, don't stop from seeking Dharau's

blessing!" Jijau did not let him turn around.

Sambhajiraje moved forward and touched Dharau's feet. The platter in her hands shook, her voice choked. She wiped her running nose, touched the border of her sari to her eyes, and faced the wall. Her peasant heart was crying out loud and her bosom was heaving. Her heart was in utter turmoil.

"Aau, I will come back soon, safe and sound." Sambhajiraje said to her. Just then, Raje entered the chamber. Antoji and Rayaji made an obeisance to him.

"Masaheb, I am going to visit all the temples on the fort." Raje said in a calm voice and made an obeisance to Jijau.

Jijau left everyone behind and walked towards Raje serenely. Raje knelt in front of her and put his broad forehead on her pure feet.

"Arise..." Aausaheb said in a low voice as she pulled Raje up. She was looking at Raje but was unable to see anything through the veil of tears. She effusively embraced Raje.

Raje left the chamber with Sambhajiraje and visited all temples in the fort. Then he went to his chamber to perform the Shivlinga puja.

Sambhajiraje visited a few close people on the fort such as Gomaji, Sidoji and Nilopant and came to Soyarabai's chamber to seek her blessings. Soyarabai said to him, "Summer is here, and you have a long way to travel. Take care of yourself. After this visit, Swari will be appointed the subedar of Deccan. You will become a prominent sardar! I am worried – how are you going to handle the big responsibility?" Her words could be interpreted either as genuine concern or as derision.

"Let me take your leave now. Masaheb, take care of my sister, Balibai." Sambhajiraje said looking at Soyarabai's daughter Balibai and left the chamber.

He ate a few morsels in Putalabai's chamber. Putalabai tied an amulet around his arm.

Raghunathpant Korade, Tryambakpant Dabir, Nirajipant,

Sarjerao Jedhe, Madari Mehatar, Hiroji Farzand, Davalji Ghatge, Duttajipant, Ragho-Mitra, Ramaji Manakoji, the people Raje had selected to accompany him, had gathered in the royal hall of the Balekilla. Moropant, Annaji Dutto, Nilopant, Yesaji, Tanaji, Anandrao and others who were going to stay behind had come to bid farewell.

In Raje's chamber, Raje and Sambhajiraje got ready to go to the royal hall.

Jijabai came to Raje's chamber with all his daughters – Sakhoo, Ranoo, Amba and Balibai. All the daughters touched Raje's feet.

Pilaji came to the chamber with Yesubai. He pointed to Raje and Masaheb and signalled Yesubai to touch their feet. Yesubai came forward. She courteously touched Raje and Masaheb's feet. Raje pulled her up and lifted her chin with his forefinger. Raje forgot his own problems for a moment, as he looked at the polite young girl. He gently said to Yesubai, "Soonbai, don't go back to Shringarpur in a hurry!"

"Masaheb, let her stay here for a few days." Raje looked at Jijau and said to her. Bashful Yesubai gingerly pulled her chin off Raje's forefinger and quickly stood near Pilajirao.

Pilaji gently put his hand on her shoulder and whispered in her ear, "How could you forget? You haven't touched your husband's feet yet?"

Yesubai widened her beady eyes and frowned.

"Go now..." Pilaji said to her in a low but stern voice.

Yesubai moved forward reluctantly. Without looking at anyone, she stood in front of Sambhajiraje, leaned forward and hastily touched the carpet three times.

Sambhajiraje purposely looked elsewhere! He acted like he had not seen her. Raje noticed that Sambhajiraje was avoiding her. Raje put one hand on his shoulder and pointing the other to Yesubai he said, "Say farewell to her."

Sambhajiraje felt baffled. He kept looking at Raje and said

to Yesubai, "Farewell."

Raje, Sambhajiraje touched Jijabai's feet. Jijau, who had prepared her heart for the impending danger, blessed them "May you have a long life!"

Sambhajiraje paid respects to Pilajirao and other elders. Jijau offered him a blob of curds. He took it on his right palm and consumed it.

Antoji Gaade stood at a side with a platter covered with a cloth. Jijau pointed to him and said, "That is the crystal Shivlinga that you worship daily. Keep it with you in the palanquin."

"Ji Masaheb. Take care of yourself. Many a rumour will fall upon your ears, just ignore them. Farewell." Raje left the chamber with Sambhajiraje.

Raje and Sambhajiraje came to the crowded royal hall of the Balekilla. Goddess Jagadamba's priest came forward and applied haldi on their foreheads.

Raje and Sambhajiraje left from the chowk in front of the royal hall. The crowd that had gathered there followed them.

Raje arrived in Shivapattan with Sambhajiraje, where Prataprao had made all arrangements for the journey. The royal elephant embellished with rich brocaded fabric and carrying a howdah on its back, saddled horses selected by Sais, that would last for the long journey during the hot summer days, the camels and bullocks, everything was ready. A big palanquin for Raje and a small one for Sambhajiraje were kept ready.

A troop of three hundred and fifty staunch Mavala soldiers, who could wield various weapons, stood in line. Bahirji's special informants, Vishwas, Karmaji and Mahadeo stood around them along with ten more informants.

Raje bade farewell to all who had come to meet him. Pilajirao was among them. He remembered something as he said goodbye to Raje.

"Please wait for a moment Raje. I forgot something." Pilajirao said and pulled out a pouch of sacred ash enclosed in the scarf wrapped around his waist.

"Bhaveshwari's prasad, Raje," said Pilajirao and applied the sacred ash on Raje and Sambhajiraje's forehead.

Sambhajiraje sat in his palanquin. Antoji kept the Shivlinga in Raje's palanquin. The kettle drums resounded for the last time, announcing the time of departure. The palanquin-bearers hoisted the palanquins onto their shoulders. Bahirji took the troop of his informants, quite some way ahead, to lead the expedition. He was going to travel with a troop of Ramoshis to mark select places with flags for their sojourns.

Finally, the 'Mavala King' of Deccan was on his way with his entourage, to meet the emperor of the North; with his only radiant scion, his son, Sambhajiraje! The royal of father and son pair would be forced to walk on arduous paths such as they never imagined; that would test their mettle thoroughly.

The entourage, travelling at leisure, came to Verul via Nagar-Aurangabad. On their way, they took sojourns at places such as Nevasa located on the banks of River Pravara, and at Gangapur near the banks of River Godavari. The Ghrishneshwara temple where Raje's grandfather, Malojirao, used to worship devoutly was situated nearby.

Tents were raised in front of the temple. Raje performed Abhishek on Ghrishneshwara's murti. Raje and Sambhajiraje took darshan and left the temple. Raje was reminiscing about his grandfather, Malojiraje, who he could never meet.

From the temple, Raje and Sambhajiraje started walking towards their shamiana. They were looking at the beautiful region of Verul. It was the motherland of their ancestors.

Raje stopped in his tracks while walking. He saw his informant, Karmaji, approaching from the direction of Aurangabad. As Karmaji saw Raje, he made his horse gallop faster. He pulled the reins of his fatigued, foaming horse and dismounted. Meanwhile, Raje had reached his shamiana. He was surrounded by Tej Singh Kachhwah, Bakshi Beg,

Raghunathpant and Tryambakpant.

Karmaji came forward, he was sweating profusely. He made an obeisance to Raje and stood quietly in front of him.

"What is it Karmaji?" Raje saw Karmaji's hesitance and asked him.

Karmaji glanced at the people standing around Raje and said, "Nothing that important, but..."

Raje glanced around. Everyone around him made an obeisance to him and left. "Tell me now." Karmaji had aroused Raje's curiosity.

"Maharaj, Adil Shahi sardar, Sarja Khan is brutally tormenting Mirza Raja. The Rajput has constantly been moving his camp. He moved from Tulajapur to Naldurga to Gunjoti and has now encamped at Nilanga in the basin of River Bhima. There Netaji deserted Bijapur and joined hands with Mirza!"

Raje was stunned to hear Karmaji's news. Netaji's life was going astray. Only Ghrishneshwara knew where he was headed.

When Sambhajiraje heard Karmaji's news, he remembered Netaji with his puffed chest, telling Mirza Raja in his own encampment, "You can't tell the difference between a live ember and a dead coal until you hold it!". A bizarre scene flashed in front of his eyes – Mirza Raja was reclining against a pillow, holding the pipe of a hookah! Netaji was placed in the flat bowl of the hookah. He was looking like a live ember. As Mirza Raja kept smoking the hookah, the live ember was losing its heat and turning black. It was turning into ashes!

That night was spent near the Ghrishneshwara temple. The next day Tej Singh Kachhawah suggested that Raje visit the caves of Verul. As per his suggestion Raje and Sambjajiraje went to see the caves of Verul.

Raje and Sambhajiraje passed through the caves one by one and came to the sixteenth cave, 'Kailas'. Many generations of sculptors had spontaneously exhibited their artistic talents here. They had made the stones speak through the strokes of their chisels. These sculptures were indeed marvellous!

Raje came to the centre of the cave with Sambhajiraje. A magnificent sculpture of Lord Shiva sitting on Mount Kailas and Goddess Parvati sitting on his lap, was carved there. Ravana was struggling to lift the entire mountain to carry it over for his mother. The exquisitely carved sculpture clearly showed the strain on his face.

Sambhajiraje was intently observing Ravana's face. Many thoughts crowded his mind, 'Who did Ravana look like?' Like Afzal Khan? Or Mirza Raja? No... No... No matter who he looked like, he was unable to pick up Lord Shiva's Mount Kailas!

Sambhajiraje saw a sculpture of a couple lost in each other's embrace on a pillar, as he was getting out of the cave. He could not decipher the emotions in the sculpture. The woman in the sculpture was wearing an ankle and as he watched her, he remembered a girl sitting on the bed in his chamber. He quickly moved away from the pillar.

After passing through cities such as Burhanpur, Indore, Gwalior, and crossing rivers like Girana, Tapi, Narmada, and Chambala, the entourage came closer to River Yamuna.

They waited at a distance from Agra. Bakshi Beg and Tej Singh Kachhawah made an obeisance to Raje and left in the direction of Agra astride their horses to apprise Kunwar Ram Singh, Mirza Raja's eldest son.

Mirza had corresponded with Ram Singh from time to time and given him detailed instructions to welcome Raje. Despite that, Ram Singh could not come to give Raje a warm welcome.

Raje could see Tej Singh and Bakshi approaching his shamiana with a few people. Raje was trying to identify Ram Singh among them.

The cavalry troop approaching the camp stopped at a distance. A middle-aged man, wearing an orange turban, with a tilak on his forehead, approached Raje and Sambhajiraje. He made an obeisance to them. "I am delighted to welcome you on behalf of Kunwarji," he said courteously.

"Introduce yourself, please!" Raje accepted his obeisance and questioned him with a frown. Raje was baffled. Ram Singh was not present in the group that had come to receive them.

"I am Girdharlal! I serve as a munshi at Kunwarji's haveli. Girdharlal responded, looking at Raje's orange mojaris.

A Munshi! Raje felt a pin prick his heart. A mere clerk had come to welcome him.

"Where is Kunwar Ram Singh?" Everyone felt the sternness in his voice.

"Please forgive me. Kunwarji has been assigned patrolling duty at the emperor's palace. He won't be able to leave from there. Please come with me!"

Raje sighed loud enough for everyone to hear.

The city of Agra woke up to the festivities of Aurangzeb's fiftieth birthday.

In Mulukhchand's serai, Raje and Sambhajiraje took a bath and donned special attire. Raje performed the puja of the crystal Shivlinga in his chamber.

On the Red Fort, Aurangzeb had performed his morning namaz. Though it was way past morning, he was still reciting verses from the Quran.

Sambhajiraje was gazing at the River Yamuna that could be seen from the serai. Ram Singh continued patrolling outside Aurangzeb's palace.

Raje's entourage was ready. Raje and Sambhajiraje had donned brocaded white jamas, orange turbans, with two horizontal stripes of sandalwood paste on their foreheads, pearl and cowrie necklaces, and golden earrings. They stood near their embellished horses. They were surrounded by Tryambakpant Dabir, Raghunathpant Korade, Sarjerao Jedhe, Hiroji Farzand, Madari Mehatar, Ragho Mitra, and Davalji Ghatage, dressed in festive attire.

Raje was waiting for Ram Singh. He was going to escort

him to the durbar. But Ram Singh had still not arrived. He had not met Raje yet.

In the end, munshi Girdharlal came to the serai. He made an obeisance to Raje, trying to hide his embarrassment and said, "Ranaji has not yet come from the Red Fort. Please come to the haveli with me. I have sent a messenger to the Red Fort. Ranaji will be coming soon." The Rajput clerk had heard many stories about the 'Mavala of Deccan'. He kept bowing, tidying the shawl over his shoulder and kept uttering, 'Ji'.

Raje frowned but didn't say anything. Girdharlal guided Raje, Sambhajiraje and their entourage to Mirza Raja's haveli in Agra. It was built like a Rajput haveli, with many balconies. Ram Singh had made thorough preparations for Raje's stay. Many tents and shamianas had been raised in front of the haveli for Raje's entourage.

It was late morning now. Fakirs, holding pots of burning incense in the left hand and bunched peacock feathers in the right, had collected alms from the alleys and lanes of Agra and were flocking near the ramparts of the Red Fort. Aurangzeb's sardars, generals and subedars, who had camped at various places, were heading towards the Red Fort with pomp and splendour.

An agitated Raje was waiting for Ram Singh at the entrance of his shamiana, with Sambhajiraje.

It was almost noon. The kettle drums at the main entrance of the Red Fort kept resounding frequently. Honourable sardars were entering the Red Fort one after the other.

Aurangzeb left from his dressing room. He had donned a brocaded green jama, and feather-crested elegant kimosh. Menials kept unfolding soft rugs under his feet, with each step he took.

The honorifics were announced in a loud voice – "Here comes Abul Mujaffar Muiuddin Mohammed, Aurangzeb, Bahadur, Alamgir Badshah Gazi Malik-e-takht-e-taus! Arise! Ram Singh's Rajput heart got smothered as he listened to the honorifics, as if someone had shoved something down his throat.

As soon as Aurangzeb stepped into the durbar of Diwan-e-Aam the courtiers bowed down to make an obeisance to him, like the grass blades in a meadow bend when a strong breeze of wind gushes in.

Ram Singh dispatched messengers to his haveli with a message for munshi Girdharlal – "The durbar has commenced. Bring Raja Saab with you. I will come to receive him!"

Now, Raje didn't even have any time to convey his displeasure to Girdharlal. Raje and Sambhajiraje came out of the shamiana. Raje assisted Sambhajiraje to mount his horse, and he mounted an embellished Kummait horse.

Raje headed towards the Red Fort with Kunwar Singh, Tej Singh, Girdhar and Bakshi Beg. His entourage followed him. Raje and Sambhajiraje kept giving alms to the fakirs they met on their way. As no other sardar of Aurangzeb was going to ride on the streets of Agra now, the news that 'Seva from Deccan' is passing through the city, spread like wildfire throughout Agra. As all the men had already assembled in the Red Fort, the women, the aged and children had gathered in the balconies.

Aurangzeb had purposely neglected them and though he wished to, Ram Singh could not welcome them. However, the city of Agra and the subjects of Shahjahan welcomed the two Mavalas with pomp and splendour like never before!

Raje's entourage was so small that it would have gone unnoticed. But just the name 'Seva' was enough to attract everyone's attention.

Raje was going with Sambhajiraje to the 'Dahar Ara' garden. As he passed by every haveli, the women in the havelis raised their black burkas with their henna-adorned fair hands. They paused in awe momentarily.

Raje and Sambhajiraje were distributing alms in the streets of Agra and in the Red Fort, Aurangzeb was accepting the platters of royal gifts in the durbar of Diwan-e-Aam. Suddenly, two

Rajput riders came out of an alley and approached Raje's entourage. They were sweating profusely; drops of sweat were trickling from their grey beards. They were Ram Singh's employees, Dungarmal Choudhary and Ramdas. They made an obeisance to Raje and took their horses near Girdharlal's horse. They were talking to Girdharlal in low voices, in the Rajput tongue. Raje could hear some words like, "Ranaji... durbar... rasta... Noorgunj...".

"What is it munshi?" Raje asked Girdharlal.

"Nothing Sarkar. Ranaji lost his way and has reached the haveli by another route. He has sent a message to bring you near the Noorgunj garden." Girdhar replied.

Ram Singh had left the fort with Mukhlis Khan to meet Raje. He had lost his way and reached his haveli by another route to meet Raje.

Girdhar and Kunwar Singh escorted Raje's entourage towards Noorgunj garden. As they passed by the Firoz Garden, the durbar of Diwan-e-Aam concluded in the Red Fort.

Raje and Sambhajiraje waited near the Noorgunj garden. Ram Singh rushed there with a herd of seven-eight elephants to gift them to Raje.

Kunwar Singh introduced Raje to Ram Singh. Fair-complexioned Ram Singh, astride a horse, was sweating profusely. First, he wiped his forehead with the shawl on his shoulder, and in that moment thought of how to approach Raje to seek forgiveness for the mistakes he had committed so far.

Ram Singh pulled the reins of his horse and slowly brought it close to Raje's horse.

He barely managed to say, "Raja Saab..." and simply opened his arms to take Raje in an embrace. Raje embraced Ram Singh from his horse. Raje had never met anyone in such a way before. Sambhajiraje realised its significance. He thought, 'Ram Singh is a very special person.'

Ram Singh brought his horse close to Sambhajiraje's horse.

He put his hand on Sambhajiraje's shoulder and said, "Kunwar Sambhoo Raja!"

Ram Singh dispatched the elephants towards Raje's camp and proceeded to present the two Mavala sardars in Aurangzeb's durbar.

The main entrance of the Red Fort came into sight. The drummers who had been sitting silently for a long time, started beating the kettle drums to announce the arrival of the guests, giving strange looks to Raje and Sambhajiraje. At that time, in the Red Fort, the second durbar of Diwan-e-Aam had concluded.

Raje and Sambhajiraje were observing the Red Fort intently. Ram Singh's grooms had taken charge of their horses. Raje and Sambhajiraje walked towards the durbar of Ghusal Khana, followed by Mavalas carrying platters of gifts.

As they arrived at the gate of Ghusal Khana, Ram Singh stopped. He bowed down and implored Raje, "Raja Saab, please remove your footwear here!"

Raje puckered his forehead and removed his orange mojaris. Sambhajiraje placed his mojaris next to them.

Ram Singh sent a message inside, to Wazir Jafar Khan.

Jafar Khan approached Aurangzeb in the courtyard enclosed with imposing walls. Aurangzeb sat on his seat, leaning against a pillow. Jafar Khan bowed down, put his hand across his chest, and delivered the message to Aurangzeb, "Aala Hazrat, Seva Bhosale has arrived from Deccan, with his son. Ram Singh seeks your permission to present them in the durbar."

On hearing that message, the rosary moving on his fingers stopped for a moment. A few moments passed in silence.

Then, in an extremely calm voice, Aurangzeb said to Wazir Jafar Khan, "Permission...granted...!" Aurangzeb glanced at the gate of Ghusal Khana and... the rosary started moving again!

Raje followed Ram Singh into the durbar. Ram Singh stopped again. He pulled out an embroidered handkerchief from the scarf tied around his waist, gave it to Raje courteously and said, "Please take this."

Raje arched his eyebrow, looked at the handkerchief and asked Ram Singh, "Why, what is this?"

"Raja Saab, we follow a custom in our durbar. When presenting gifts to the emperor, if he asks you anything, you should cover your mouth with this handkerchief and answer him. This is a regular custom in the durbar."

Raje and Sambhajiraje entered Ghusal Khana with Ram Singh. Many of Aurangzeb's staunch supporters such as Shasta Khan, Bahadur Khan, Ameen Khan, Sheikh Meer, Zulfikar Khan, Najaabat Khan and Jaswant Singh had assembled in the durbar.

Raje approached Aurangzeb's throne with Ram Singh and offered one thousand golden coins, two thousand rupees as 'Nazar' and five thousand rupees as 'Nisaar' to Aurangzeb. Both father and son offered a courteous obeisance.

In the entire durbar, Sambhajiraje was the youngest, nine-year-old sardar. He was intently watching Aurangzeb, about whom his Aabasaheb always said, 'The consequences of his actions can be seen by the entire world.

Sambhajiraje thought Aurangzeb will say something, but he did not.

Bakshi Aasad Khan approached Raje and Sambhajiraje and offered them betel leaves as they were honourable guests. Ram Singh had already taken a few steps back, without showing his back to the emperor and stood in the rank of sardars who held the mansab of two thousand and five hundred cavalries. Bakshi Aasad Khan conducted Raje and Sambhajiraje to the rank of sardars who held the mansab of five thousand cavalries. This rank was further away from the emperor's throne. The ceremony of distributing the Khilats began. Khilats were offered to Aurangzeb's princes, Jafar Khan, and Jasawant Singh.

Jasawant Singh accepted his Khilat, took a few steps back, without showing his back to the emperor and stood in front of

Raje. The royal durbar was about to conclude now.

'Why did I travel thousands of miles in the scorching heat to come here? Is this a royal durbar or a farce? Is this how I am going to be treated? A lightning-like wave of rage surged in Raje's heart!

A munshi came to welcome me! Aurangzeb sat smugly on his throne and did not bother to talk to me! Those who were driven away by our Mavalas are bestowed with Khilat!' Raje could not bear the humiliation, his chest heaved. Raje's entire body became a sizzling, burning, flaming torch!

Clear, loud words spilled from Raje's mouth, raising goosebumps on the marble walls of the Ghusal Khana - "Ra..m... Sin...gh!" They seared the silence of the durbar. Raje's right eyebrow had arched like a horseshoe.

Raje turned around and stared at the row where Ram Singh was standing. He roared again, "Ra..m… Sin...gh!"

Sambhajiraje felt that Aabasaheb's hand, which he held, had suddenly warmed up and was shaking intensely. With that touch, an unknown wave surged through his body. Their hands were shaking together. Ram Singh somehow managed to make his way around the sardars and approached Raje with fear.

Raje pointed to the sardar who stood in front of him with fiery eyes and questioned him, "Who is standing in front of me, Ram Singh?"

"Ji, he is Maharaja Jaswant Singh." Ram Singh couldn't figure out the cause of Raje's agitation. His mouth was parched.

"Jaswant Singh? The one who fled from our kingdom! You made me stand in the rank after him? No! I cannot bear such ignominy!"

Unknowingly, Raje's hand slipped from Sambhajiraje's hand! He completely lost sense of who he was and where he was standing. His earlobes were flushed. Drops of sweat had gathered on the tip of his sharp nose.

Raje dashed out of his row without thinking. The moment he stepped on the soft carpet, he turned his back to Aurangzeb!

A trembling Sambhajiraje exclaimed, "Maharaj Saheb!" and sprinted towards Raje. Raje's ears were numb. He walked briskly towards the exit, throwing angry glances around the hall and breathing heavily. Ram Singh started running backwards to catch up with them.

Ram Singh's tongue got stuck in his parched mouth and stifled him. He took a few steps back, without turning his back to the emperor, and somehow managed to catch up with Raje. Ram Singh held Raje's hand and shaking it intensely he said in a low voice, "Please listen to me Raja Saab!"

"No, never!" Raje exclaimed and shook his hand off! The handkerchief that Ram Singh had handed him before, slipped from Raje's hand and fell on the soft carpet.

A fearful Sambhajiraje ran behind Raje exclaiming, "Maharaj Saheb! Maharaj Saheb!" The handkerchief got trampled under his feet and lay askew. Sambhajiraje held Raje's hand. Both father and son came to the courtyard outside the durbar and stopped for a moment.

Raje saw a staircase near the courtyard and went towards it. He let go of Sambhajiraje's hand and sat on a step, holding his head tightly. The betel leaf offered in the durbar was still in his fist.

A big commotion had broken out in the durbar. Aurangzeb came to know from Jafar Khan that 'Seva is upset because he did not receive Khilat.' He ordered Mulatip Khan, Mukhalis Khan and Aakhil Khan, "Offer Khilat to Seva, calm him down and bring him back to the durbar.

The three Khans approached Raje and implored him to accept the Khilat, which infuriated Raje further. He declined their offer and told them, "Your emperor can kill me if he wants to, but I am certainly not coming back to the durbar now!"

Aurangzeb summoned Ram Singh and inquired, "What happened Ram Singh? Why is Seva upset?"

"Aala Hazrat, he has taken ill due to the heat in our city!"

Ram Singh answered diplomatically.

Aurangzeb smiled and said, "Send him back to the camp."

"Ji Huzur," Ram Singh responded and came outside.

Raje tossed the green betel leaf that he had squeezed in his sweaty fist, on the floor. Sambhajiraje had already thrown his away.

After some time, Raje calmed down and his trembling abated. Ram Singh walked with them to guide them to their camp.

"Maharaj Saheb, your mojaris." Sambhajiraje reminded Raje. Sambhajiraje did not wait for anyone, he picked up Raje's mojaris himself and placed them in front of Raje. Raje wore them.

Raje and Sambhajiraje mounted their horses. Ram Singh escorted the entire entourage back to the camp. No one spoke anything at all.

Raje and Sambhajiraje exited from the main gate of the Red Fort.

Aurangzeb's fiftieth birthday had come to an end!

Raje and Sambhajiraje sat in Ram Singh's haveli. A visibly worried Ram Singh stood in front of them. He was trying to convince Raje that he had been placed in the right row in the durbar. It was the same row where Mirza Raja himself and Tahir Khan used to stand. But now the arrow had been shot.

"Bhai, you don't worry!" Raje consoled Ram Singh. He had deliberately used the word 'Bhai' for Ram Singh.

Raje spent half an hour at the haveli and returned to his shamiana. Ram Singh sent some dry fruits and sweetmeats for Raje at the hands of his personal assistant, Gopiram Mehta. Raje presented him a crest of feathers. Ram Singh's trusted aides, Ballu Shah and Girdharlal came to visit Raje.

Ballu Shah had heard many tales of Raje's valour and was mesmerized by his charisma. He had come to advise Raje to make amends with the emperor. He earnestly wanted Raje's safe and secure return to Deccan. Ballu Shah and Girdhar left after meeting Raje. It was twilight, the time of lighting the lamps. As per his daily routine, Raje sat down to worship the crystal Shivlinga.

There, in the Red Fort, Aurangzeb concluded the council in his private chamber and went to perform the evening namaz.

During this council, Aurangzeb's sardars, Jafar Khan, Jaswant Singh, Murtuza Khan, Shasta Khan and his sister Jahanara had insisted that he should execute 'discourteous Seva'.

As he performed the Namaz, he decided two things –compel Seva to present himself in the durbar and accept the Khilat. Once he accepted it, send him on a campaign to Kabul. He would never return alive from that campaign. And if this plan did not materialize, then to file a case of defamation against Seva in the court of religious leaders. And Aurangzeb was confident about what their sentence would be.

Aurangzeb summoned Faulad Khan, the kotwal of Agra and commanded him, "Tell Ram Singh to reassure Seva and present him in the durbar tomorrow."

From the Red Fort, Faulad Khan directly came to Ram Singh's haveli and delivered the emperor's message.

At night, Ram Singh went to Raje's shamiana and brought him to his haveli. For quite a while, he tried convincing Raje about the significance of meeting the emperor. Raje bade farewell to him and returned to his shamiana.

After waiting for a long time for Raje to return, Sambhajiraje had gone to bed. He had not eaten anything. Raje also did not feel hungry.

Raje removed his Jiretop and placed it on a platter. He glanced at Sambhajiraje, sleeping soundly and felt, 'I should not have brought him here with me!'

Raje muttered, "Jagadamb! Jagadamb!" and lay down next to Sambhajiraje. The father and son were on an empty stomach, in their shamiana, by the banks of the Yamuna. Raje could not sleep.

In the Red Fort and throughout the city of Agra, feasts were being organized. The people of Agra were discussing the incident at the durbar and telling each other, "Seva of Deccan will meet the same fate as Prince Dara, Murad and Shuja".

The next day, Raje got up very late. He summoned Tryambakpant, Raghunathpant, Niraji Ravaji and told them, "I have contracted fever!"

The news reached Ram Singh. He knew that 'Raja Saab had contracted fake fever' but he didn't dare ask Raje, 'How did you contract fever so suddenly?' He understood that 'Shivaji was not going to present himself in the durbar under any circumstances.'

Raje sent a message to Ram Singh at the hands of Raghunathpant Korade, "I cannot come due to my illness. Please take my son Sambhajiraje to the durbar."

Raje could not get out of Agra without devising some cunning strategy and using his men as a bait to fulfil his purpose.

Ram Singh was trapped in a terrible situation. He had to protect Raje and not lose Aurangzeb's trust at the same time. Sambhajiraje was facing the toughest test of his life. He was the youngest in Raje's retinue, was in enemy territory at present, and all of them were in grave danger currently.

Raje gave Sambhajiraje many instructions, in his shamina. "Observe and remember the route you take to the durbar. On your way back, implore Ram Singh chacha to take another route. If the emperor questions you, answer him fearlessly. Speak the Hindustani language as much as possible. Get introduced to as many people as you can."

It was late afternoon. Raje lay on his bed. Ram Singh came to take Sambhajiraje to the durbar. Sambhajiraje touched sleeping Raje's feet to seek his blessings and said, "So long Maharaj Saheb."

"Umm..." Raje moaned as planned.

Ram Singh left with Sambhajiraje to attend the durbar. Raje's entourage followed Sambhajiraje. Sambhajiraje mounted an embellished pure white horse. Nine-year-old Sambhajiraje was going to visit the emperor of Delhi, astride a horse, riding along with Ram Singh. Alone! Countless durbars had been held from the time of Babur to Aurangzeb, but such an event had taken place for the first time.

Ram Singh and Sambhajiraje entered the Red Fort with the entourage. The evening durbar of Diwan-e-Khas was in session. Ram Singh stood in the durbar with Sambhajiraje.

The honorifics were called out. Aurangzeb entered the durbar immediately after that. The courtiers made an obeisance. Sambhajiraje stood looking at Aurangzeb, who was at a distance. As everyone had bowed down, no one noticed that he was standing.

First, Wazir Jafar Khan enquired about Ram Singh. Ram Singh presented himself in front of the throne, with Sambhajiraje. As Ram Singh made an obeisance, Aurangzeb questioned him, "What is this Ram Singh? Where is 'Seva'?"

"Ji Huzur, he has taken ill. He has high fever!" Ram Singh replied. Aurangzeb nodded knowingly.

"He has sent his son, Alijah!" Ram Singh tried to soothe Aurangzeb before his feelings got ruffled.

Aurangzeb's beady eyes gazed at Sambhajiraje. Sambhajiraje stood looking fearlessly in his eyes, in the durbar full of courtiers. The four eyes were in stark contrast. Aurangzeb's eyes were like a mirror covered in the dust of his own karmas, and Sambhajiraje's eyes were crystal clean inside out.

Aurangzeb sarcastically asked Sambhajiraje, "How come you didn't contract any fever?"

Sambhajiraje was not used to such sarcasm. He responded with shining eyes, "No! I never get fever! Others contract fever because of me!"

"What did he say?" Aurangzeb puckered his eyebrow and asked Ram Singh.

Even Ram Singh did not know what exactly Sambhajiraje had said, but he had to say something. He bowed down and said, "Ji Huzur, he said, he doesn't have fever!"

"Oh, such innocence! Jafar, offer Sambha his gift." Aurangzeb commanded his Wazir. Sambhajiraje was gifted with a crest of feathers, a pearl necklace and a decorative dagger.

The day after Sambhajiraje attended the durbar, Aurangzeb commanded Siddi Faulad Khan, "Transfer 'Seva' from his camp to Ranandaz Khan's haveli".

The plan was to transfer Raje to Ranandaz Khan's haveli and assassinate him without raising a hue and cry! It was not possible to do it in front of Ram Singh's haveli in the open camp. However, somehow, Ram Singh got wind of the plan. He immediately went to meet Meer Bakshi Mohammed Amin Khan. He was Ram Singh's friend who held a high position in the durbar. Through him Ram Singh sent a resolute message to Aurangzeb, 'Before assassinating Shivaji, finish me off with my family!"

After receiving this message, sly Aurangzeb quickly realized that his plan to assassinate Shivaji had leaked out. Aurangzeb decided to entrap Ram Singh by using Amin Khan who had approached him as a mediator on Ram Singh's behalf.

Aurangzeb sent a message to Ram Singh, 'Can you be the guarantor and vouch on Shivaji's behalf that he will not leave Agra?'

Ram Singh heaved a sigh of relief that Raje's life would be spared by his guarantee. He signed the official papers of guarantee and sent them through Bakshi Amin Khan. Aurangzeb approved the contract. Ram Singh became the official guarantor for Raje.

Raje became pensive as he came to know that Ram Singh had averted the attack on Raje by putting his own life at risk. He reassured Ram Singh, "I will vouch in front of God that your promise will not get broken. Have no fear."

Raje embraced Ram Singh. Ram Singh became the guarantor to Aurangzeb. Raje became a guarantor to Ram Singh by his promise. Raje was trapped in a dual imprisonment–that of Aurangzeb's politics and of Ram Singh's affection!

Sambhajiraje and Ram Singh were returning from a stroll in Agra city. A few Rajput horse riders were behind them. It was twilight. The troop entered the potters' colony. The potters had arranged small and big clay pots in front of their shacks. As he saw them, Ram Singh raised his hand and signalled his troop to stop. Without looking back, he called out, "Dungar...!"

"Ji" said Dungarmal and came forward.

"Buy a few small clay pots for Raja Saab's people." Ram Singh pointed to a potter's shack and commanded him.

The potter saw the royal riders and stopped his potter's wheel with a stick. He approached Ram Singh and Sambhajiraje, made an obeisance to them and politely said, "Sarkar, what do you want? How can I serve you?" He had tied a northern turban on his head. He brought his soiled hands together in the style of a Mavala greeting.

"Give us your best clay pots. We want to gift them to our guests." Ram Singh said, pointing to Sambhajiraje.

The potter observed Sambhajiraje keenly and casually mumbled, "Looks like these riders are from the Maval region!" The potter glanced at the cowrie necklace around Sambhajiraje's neck.

Sambhajiraje's right eyebrow arched unwittingly as he heard the potter. 'Seems like this potter is from our homeland. He speaks the Maval dialect.' The potter's words triggered a thought; as Sambahjiraje pondered over it, an idea began taking shape.

The potter picked up a round stone and striking it on the clay pots he made clear knocking sounds to show Dungarmal the quality of the pots.

Dungar held the pots in his hands, checked them thoroughly,

and bought four pots. Ram Singh pulled out the pouch of Dinars tied around his waist and tossed it to Dungar.

Dungar paid the potter's money from the pouch and returned it to Ram Singh. The potter and Dungar picked up the pots and handed them to four riders. Dungar mounted his horse.

The potter bowed down again and made an obeisance to Ram Singh who was pulling the reins of his horse.

"Let's go, Kunwar." Ram Singh signalled Sambhajiraje.

Ram Singh and the Rajput riders with him, prodded their horses and left. Sambhajiraje pulled the reins of his horse and pretended to prod it. The horse got confused, wondering whether to go ahead or back. It danced on its hooves and stopped in its place. Sambhajiraje made sure that Ram Singh and his troop had gone ahead. He removed the pearl necklace he was wearing.

The potter was watching Sambhajiraje's horse and waited there holding the Dinars. Sambhajiraje tossed his pearl necklace to the potter. "I am a Mavala, remember me. So long!" Sambhajiraje prodded his horse hard.

The potter was delighted to receive the pearl necklace. He looked at it and thought, 'He looks like the son of a Mavala sardar'. The potter was originally from the Maval region. He had travelled to Agra in search of work.

To reassure Ram Singh, Raje permitted his Rajput swordsmen to stand guard at his camp.

The bond of affection between Sambhajiraje and Ram Singh was getting stronger. Ram Singh was exercising extreme caution to protect Raje and Sambhajiraje. He was concerned about his guests' safe return to their homeland for two reasons – first, it was in the blood of the Rajputs to keep their promise at any cost. Secondly, if Raje and Sambhajiraje were hurt in any way, he was worried that his father, who was posted in the Deccan, would not be able to escape from the clutches of the Mavalas.

Aurangzeb discussed the plan of sending Raje on the Kabul campaign, with Ram Singh. Eventually, for some reason, that plan fizzled out.

Raje visited Aurangzeb's Wazir, Jafar Khan, in his haveli and offered him expensive gifts. It was an effort to make amends with the emperor, but that also did not succeed.

Aurangzeb was receiving letters from Mirza Raja who was in the Deccan. Ultimately, he got frustrated and sent a letter to Mirza Raja –'Give me a detailed list of the promises you have made to Seva!'

Raje had no choice now but to keep sending imploring petitions to Aurangzeb.

Raje submitted a petition to Aurangzeb through Amin Khan –"If you yield all my forts currently in your possession, as per the Purandar accord, I will deliver two crore rupees to the durbar. Permit me to go back to the Deccan. I will leave my son, Sambhajiraje in Agra. If the emperor so wishes, I am ready to vouch for the same. Currently, the emperor is organizing a campaign to attack Adil shah of Bijapur. Send me on that campaign. I will make the campaign successful. If needed, I will sacrifice my life in the service of the emperor!"

Amin Khan handed Raje's petition to Wazir Jafar Khan in the durbar, and he read it out to Aurangzeb. Sambhajiraje was present in that durbar with Ram Singh.

Aurangzeb stopped counting the beads in his rosary and listened intently to every word of the petition intently.

Aurangzeb looked at the roll of Raje's petition in Jafar Khan's hands and said calmly, "Jafar, see how shrewd 'Seva' is! He looted three crore rupees from our royal treasury in Surat and is offering us two crore rupees in gift." Then, he muttered something to himself and rose from his throne. The durbar was concluded.

Ram Singh came to Raje's camp with Sambhajiraje. Raje was waiting for Ram Singh in his shamiana. Tryambakpant, Raghunathpant and Niraji were also present in the shamiana.

Ram Singh and Sambhajiraje entered the shamiana.

"Ram Singh, has the emperor responded to my petition?" Raje asked Ram Singh.

"Raja Saab, Alijah did not express his thoughts about your petition. He will ponder over it and take a decision, rest assured."

After some time, Ram Singh left for his haveli with his people. Raje tied his hands at the back and lost in thought, began pacing back and forth. Sambhajiraje felt uneasy watching an agitated Raje.

"Raghunathpant, what decision will the emperor take about my petition?" Raje stopped pacing and asked Korade.

"Swami, I feel the only clause that would make some impact is that of leaving Sambhajiraje behind!" Raghunathpant said. As Raje heard his words, he looked at Sambhajiraje.

Raje turned towards Sambhajiraje, with the intention of convincing him.

Suddenly, everyone heard galloping horses. Raje was taken aback. Sambhajiraje sat up at once.

Ram Singh's soldier, guarding the entrance of the shamiana came in with a naked sword. He was frightened. Raghuanthpant, Tryambakpant and Niraji also came in after him, wielding their swords. They were also terrified and out of their fear, began to speak all at once. Their terrified voices fell on Raje and Sambhajiraje's ears at the same time. "Dhani, we have been betrayed! The Siddis are coming to attack us. Run! Run for your life!"

The words pierced Raje's ears like an arrow. He got confused and stepped forward to pick up the Bhavani sword placed on the platter, but just then he remembered Sambhajiraje and retreated. He pulled Sambhajiraje close and embraced him tightly! In that fleeting moment, many thoughts clashed in Raje's mind like weapons clashing against each other. After leaving Rajgad he had suppressed many of his feelings – feelings of humiliation, concern and pain. All his suppressed emotions erupted now.

Raje got terrified at the thought that countless brutal strikes of the Siddi soldiers were going to fall upon himself and Sambhajiraje. All his plans were coming undone, and he was about to be pathetically slaughtered along with his son, in a foreign land! His entire life was going to turn into ashes! It was a lost game of chess! Humiliating defeat!

Raje embraced Sambhajiraje tightly; words full of affection trickled out of his trembling lips, "Oh my dear son, we are undone! We have been betrayed!"

Sambhajiraje put both his arms around Aaba Saheb and clung to him tightly.

"Maharaj Saheb!" He exclaimed and rubbed his head against Raje's jama.

Within moments, the shamiana was besieged by rapidly galloping horses. The horses raised their front hooves in the air, neighed loudly and came to a stop. Their neighing echoed in the air. At once, a brawny and hairy hand, rashly flung aside the thin curtain at the entrance. Dark-complexioned, thick-lipped, stout, kotwal of Agra city, Siddi Faulad Khan, entered the shamiana.

He stopped right near the entrance, holding the hilt of his wide-bladed Jamadar sword in his thick fist. He stared at Raje with big, beady eyes and said, "My armed soldiers are going to keep a close watch on you. You are prohibited from meeting anyone. Keep in mind that this is Alijah's order." His thick eyebrows puckered momentarily.

Raje's camp was surrounded by the tents of five thousand stout Siddi soldiers. They lined up cannons, with their muzzles pointing towards Raje's camp.

Just like the siege of Panhalgad another siege was laid by 'Siddi'. The Lion of Maval was trapped in the green meadows of Agra! Raje was incarcerated!

Though Raje was confined, Sambhajiraje was free. He could

visit Ram Singh's haveli, the Agra city and the Red Fort. Aurangzeb was unaware that he had committed the biggest blunder. He had forgotten that even a baby snake is venomous. And these two were the snakes of Maval after all. They were going to raise their hoods as soon as they got a chance!

Outwardly, Raje looked very calm now, but inwardly, he was having an intense conversation with himself. His cautious mind yearned for only one thing, safe escape for himself and his entire entourage along with Sambhajiraje. How should I use my skill? What kind of move should I make? Finally, Raje chanted the name of Goddess Bhavani in his mind and made the first move of the game.

One evening when the Mavala soldiers of his entourage came to make an obeisance to the royals, Raje raised his eyebrows and asked in an intimidating voice, "Why have you come here? Just go back! Leave Balraje and me alone, whatever is destined will happen!" Sambhajiraje was standing next to Raje. Raje pulled him close.

The Mavalas were startled. Faulad Khan heard the commotion and approached the shamiana. As soon as Faulad Khan came into sight, Raje roared loudly, pacing back and forth, "I plead you to leave us alone. I don't have time to think about all of you. So just leave!"

Raje saw the confusion on the faces of the Mavalas. He picked up the cowrie necklace on his chest and touched it to his forehead, to give them a hint. The clever Mavalas understood the 'plan'.

"But where should we go?" Davalaji Ghatage asked, keeping his head low.

"Anywhere! Go back to your homes. Just go." Raje continued pacing back and forth.

"What happened?" Siddi Faulad Khan entered the shamiana and asked Raje.

"They are serving a prisoner! Khan, why should I bear the

expenses of these people? Let them go. I will send a petition to Alijah. Sanction them a permit to leave."

Raje submitted his petition to Aurangzeb through Faulad Khan, to sanction permit to his entourage to return to their home.

Bahirji had spread his messengers in various disguises throughout Agra city.

Raje submitted one more petition to Aurangzeb, "Transfer me somewhere else from Ram Singh's camp."

"Ram Singh is my loyal servant; you must stay with him." Aurangzeb sent his response.

"I am bored of this life. With Ala Hazrat's permission I would like to go to Kashi and spend the rest of my life there as a sanyasi." Raje sent another petition to Aurangzeb.

"'Seva' wants to be a sanyasi. Fine, tell him to go to the Allahabad fort and live there as a sanyasi. My Subedar, Bahadur Khan will take good care of him there." Aurangzeb responded.

Raje and Aurangzeb were playing a game of chess by anticipating each other's move and spoiling it. Unbeknownst to him, Sambhajiraje was becoming more mature due to what was happening and what was about to happen. He had become aware of the danger they were in. He started treating Ram Singh more courteously and continued meeting the potter in the potter's colony whenever he could. One day, as usual, he came to the Red Fort with Ram Singh. Ram Singh came to know that the emperor was watching wrestling matches.

Ram Singh ushered Sambhajiraje towards the wrestling pit. It was located on a capacious, circular ground. It was prepared with red sand kneaded in buttermilk and oil. The pit was surrounded by a sturdy wooden fence.

Aurangzeb sat on a seat placed near the wooden fence. The royal umbrellas were shielding his head. A few sardars stood behind him. The red sand glistened in the blazing sunlight of Agra. Aurangzeb glanced at it and thought 'Khudatala has produced sand of many colours–red, black, white, but how come he did not produce green-coloured sand?' He felt restless and sniffed the rose in his hand. Just then he saw Ram Singh and Sambhajiraje.

Pathan, Siddi, Uzbek, Turk – burly wrestlers entered the wrestling pit. They bowed down to Aurangzeb and shouting "Ya Moulali..." they danced on one foot around the edge of the wrestling pit. They offered their rivals some sand to commence the match; they thumped their thighs loudly and clashed against each other. Their shining bodies perspired profusely.

Sambhajiraje stood with Ram Singh, near the wooden fence. Intently he watched their hefty bodies that looked like the loaded ears of corn. Ram Singh too waited there thinking, 'how can I approach Jile Subahani directly?' Both were engrossed in watching the matches.

"Ram Singh!" Bakshi Asad Khan approached them and broke their trance.

"What is it?" Ram Singh had got the chance to watch a wrestling match leisurely after so many days, but that moment got ruined.

"Ala Hazarat wants to know if Seva's son would play a wrestling match." Asad Khan directly posed a sharp question to Ram Singh.

Ram Singh promptly grabbed Sambhajiraje's hand and exclaimed, "Bakshi, at least consider his age".

To Bakshi Asad Khan's surprise, Sambhajiraje said, "Yes, certainly, I will play a wrestling match, but not with these hired wrestlers. Such wrestlers bow down to me every day. If a prince of my age is ready to play a match, I will also get into the wrestling pit."

Asad Khan conveyed Sambhajiraje's response to Aurangzeb. Aurangzeb keenly observed Sambhajiraje from his seat.

"Asad, give him the drink that the wrestlers consume." Aurangzeb said and left to perform his Namaz, wondering, 'How will my own son turn out?'.

At Rajgad, Jijau sat in the sanctum, on a flat sandalwood seat. She was offering Bael leaves one by one on the Shivlinga, with trembling hands. She had vowed to offer one lakh Bael leaves.

Jijau sat facing the Shivlinga and the murti of wrathful Jagadamba. Through closed lips and open eyes, she was protesting in front of them.

'Oh mother, how long are you going to give me grief? You snatched my elder son Sambhajiraje from me at Kanakgiri. You trampled upon the kumkum on my forehead in the forests of Hodigeri. I barely opened my mouth to express joy when Raje's son was born, and you took away my eldest Soonbai! And...and today...

'Everything I liked from the bottom of my heart, you cast your eyes on it! Then how come you never cast your eyes on me? Or do you dislike me because of my widowhood? Tell me, oh mother, for how long are you going to point your trident at my throat? Why should I even worship you?

'No, this must stop! If Raje-Balraje get hurt in any way, I will not spare you too! So, you better beware!'

The torrid region of Agra got inundated with rain showers of the Mriga constellation. The deluge drenched the Red Fort, Taj Mahal, the havelis, and mansions.

Faulad Khan transferred Raje to a stone haveli, next to Ram Singh's haveli, so it would be easier to keep an eye on them. Raje, who had been living in a shamiana on an open ground, felt even more confined.

And suddenly, healthy Raje fell ill intentionally, surprising even his own men.

'The Marhatta has taken ill', the Siddi guards delivered the joyful news to Faulad Khan. He came to Raje's room to enquire about his health.

"I heard that you have been taken ill!" Faulad's beady eyes shone. Faulad observed Raje like a Siddi equine expert observes a horse that keeps limping.

Raje first whimpered just like a horse and then his chest heaved as he coughed hard.

"Khan..., I am unsure about my health. I am feeling restless. Please do me a favour. Let me seek redemption for my sinful acts. I would like to give away alms of sweetmeats, dinars and much more...!" Raje stopped, as if he was gasping. He held the edges of his bed tightly. Khan kept staring at him, wide-eyed.

Sambhajiraje who was sitting on the next bed, observed Raje with concerned eyes!

"Khan, please obtain Alijah's permission for me, to offer alms. Please do me this one favour!" Raje acted like he was in tremendous pain. He sighed heavily, mumbled, 'Jagadamb, Jagadamb' and sank slowly on the bed.

"Yes, definitely...I will try!" Khan's thick, rough lips spoke gently for the first time in his life. Khan left the chamber.

Sambhajiraje kept looking at Raje's forehead. Raje's eyes were closed; his forehead was getting puckered from time to time.

Aurangzeb gladly granted permission to distribute alms. Tryambakpant and Nirajipant began buying sweetmeats from the 'Mewamandi' of Agra, filled them in the containers, and sent them to the stone haveli for the customary touch of Raje's hand.

Faulad's hefty Siddi soldiers on guard never realized that unbeknownst to them, the size of the containers was getting bigger day by day.

The containers of sweetmeats, touched by Raje, moved freely throughout Agra city. The fakirs from every serai and the people of Agra consumed the delicious sweets, raised their hands and chanted – "May Khuda cure his disease!"

Outside, the skies of Agra were overcast. Inside the chamber, Raje's mind was overcast with dark clouds of unbearable thoughts. His mind raced to the top of Rajgad. It saw Masaheb sitting in front of Jagadamba with a darkened face and retreated hastily.

Sambhajiraje sat at his feet and looked at Raje with concern. 'Is Maharaj Saheb really sick?' One moment he had one doubt, the next moment he had another. His mind was torn by countless doubts.

Raje noticed the concern in his eyes...he got up gingerly and whispered reassuring words into Sambhajiraje's ears, "Don't worry! My sickness is fake. You and I, both must escape from here. You should attentively listen to every guest that visits Ram Singh chacha. Continue visiting the potters' colony. Be vigilant!"

"Jagdamb, Jagadamb," Raje mumbled and lay whimpering on his bed again. Sambhajiraje's hands moved forward unwittingly. He started pressing Raje's legs gently.

A strange atmosphere prevailed in the room. Sambhajiraje feigned concern that Raje was indeed quite sick.

"Two pandits are here to visit you. Alijah has granted them permission." Nathavat, Ram Singh's swordsman who was guarding the entrance of the haveli informed Raje.

"Send them in." Raje said, lying on the bed. Nathavat ushered two north Hindustani men in Brahmin attire. One of them was, Kavindra Parmananda, and the other was Kavi Kulesh from Allahabad.

As Raje saw them, he tried to get up from the bed. Paramanand made an obeisance to Raje and promptly moving forward he said, "Swami, please lie down."

After hearing Raje's acclaim, both the poets had travelled to Agra to meet him. They had submitted a petition to Aurangzeb, seeking permission to visit Raje. Aurangzeb had granted them permission with only one agenda in his mind. He felt that these two pandits would be better able to convince the 'sick Seva' that life is indeed ephemeral.

Parmananda introduced himself to Raje. Raje sat up. "He is a poet from Kanoj, Kavi Kulesh." Parmanand pointed to Kulesh and introduced him to Raje, and said, "We are indeed very fortunate to meet you in person."

Raje put his hand on Sambhajiraje's back and stressing each word, said, "My son – Sambhajiraje". Sambhajiraje folded his hands and greeted them.

Raje had a peaceful discussion with both the poets. Both were about to leave. They made an obeisance to Raje and Sambhajiraje in the northern style.

"Hiroji, inform Ram Singh of my wish to gift all my elephants to both the poets." Raje commanded Hiroji.

"Ji, Sarkar." Hiroji bowed down.

Parmanand and Kavi Kulesh kept staring at Raje in amazement. Parmanand couldn't help it, and courteously said, "Swami, of what use are the elephants to us?"

"Kaviraj, I have become detached. I want to leave this serai. You should show me the path. You should take the elephants to the right place and reduce my burden." Raje said every word equivocally. Parmanand understood what he wanted to say.

Raje lay down on his bed. Sambhajiraje spread the shawl lying at his feet, over his body.

Sambhajiraje gently pressed Maharaj Saheb's feet. Raje's 'illness' was gradually 'worsening' in the haveli.

Aurangzeb always ensured that the plans he made were put into action. He devised a plan to assassinate Raje! The construction of Vitthaldas' haveli in Agra, was about to be completed. He wanted Faulad Khan to transfer Raje there, and the very next day Siddi soldiers would infiltrate the haveli with naked swords. The 'Kafir Marhatta of Deccan' was going to meet the same fate as kafir Dara Shikoh.

Aurangzeb had devised this detailed 'royal scheme'.

Aurangzeb granted Raje's entourage the permits to leave Agra. He wanted the least number of people around Shivaji, to capture Shivaji in his clutches. Raje's entourage left Agra.

Raje kept imploring Ram Singh to get his guarantee revoked, and not stake his life for the sake of Raje.

After many attempts, Ram Singh managed to get his guarantee revoked. Aurangzeb revoked it thinking that it wasn't required any more. Ram Singh was officially released from the contract.

Every day, the containers carrying the sweetmeats for distribution among the people, to seek 'blessings' for the 'ill' person kept arriving at the scheduled time in the haveli. Raje kept sending Madari Mehtar and Hiroji Farzand from time to time, with the containers.

The day of 'Krishnashtami' passed. This was the day when Yadava leader Vasudev successfully escaped from Kansa's prison, during heavy rain showers, carrying baby Krishna with him, hidden in a basket. Raje was Krishna's devotee. Vasudev's action led Raje's mind to an extraordinary idea. 'But how should I make this work? By hiding in the containers?' Countless burning torches of Goddess Bhavani started dancing in front of Raje's alert, open eyes. The bulls at Katraj! The burning torches! The ruse! 'Deceiving the enemy by using the sweetmeat containers!' At that thought Raje sat up at once. "Hiroji, my throat is dry! Water please!" Raje ordered Hiroji.

Hiroji approached Raje with a pot of water. As Raje took the pot from him he glanced at Hiroji, and kept staring at him, as if he was staring at his own reflection! Hiroji was Raje's half-brother. He looked like Raje. He wore a tapering beard just like Raje.

Raje decided one thing for sure – 'Hiroji will wear my attire and lie on the bed in my place, as the sick prisoner of Aurangzeb! I will dress up as Hiroji. And then? Then, the goddess will show me the way!'

"Maharaj, water!" Hiroji tried to bring back Raje, who was lost in thought.

Raje gulped the water. He returned the pot to Hiroji, and calmly told him, "Hiroji, observe all my words, actions and mannerisms thoroughly! We have to execute a big plan."

"Ji" Hiroji whispered.

Raje took of the shawl tied around his waist and said to Hiroji, "The containers will arrive now. Hide this in one of the containers and keep its edge peeping out of the lid. You go with that container and tell me what happens."

"Ji" Hiroji couldn't understand what Raje had in mind.

As usual the northern attendants carrying the containers arrived. Raje gave the customary touch of his hand to the sweetmeats in open containers.

Hiroji hid Raje's shawl peeking out of a container. He made an obeisance to Raje, took five steps back, and went out with the containers. He kept walking by the side of the containers.

They passed the first post of guards. Just when they passed the second post, a Siddi guard noticed the tip of the shawl peeking out. He widened his eyes and shouted at the carriers, "Wait! Open this box!" He pointed his sword towards the container.

The carriers placed down the container. Hiroji moved forward promptly and opened its lid. The Siddi guard held the tip of the shawl and pulled it out swiftly... "Empty this box completely." He made them take out everything from the container and made sure that 'Seva' was not hiding among the sweets!

Everything had happened just as Raje had anticipated! The Siddis had been checking the containers any time and were going to continue to do so.

The eleventh day of the dark fortnight of Shravan was about to set on Agra. Ram Singh left the durbar; his cavalry troop left from the main gate of the Red Fort. Ram Singh looked concerned. Sambhajiraje, astride his horse, holding the reins, was trotting slowly by his side. Everyone was quiet. The Rajput horsemen followed them.

Aurangzeb had shrewdly planned Raje's assassination, but somehow the treacherous walls of the Red Fort had conveyed the news to Ram Singh today.

Raje was going to be transferred the next day. The day after that, on 'holy Friday', 'infidel' Raje was going to be dispatched to the durbar of 'Jahannam' to accept the Khilat of death. The horses kept trotting forward. Honourable Ram Singh felt suffocated, as if his neck was caught in a noose.

He wanted to deliver the message to Raje, "Tomorrow you are going to be transferred. Be vigilant." And he had to do it today with great precaution. But how to do it? Ram Singh was prohibited from meeting Raje. He could not go to the haveli. If there was a delay in delivering the message, it would lead to only one consequence. His reputation as a Rajput was going to be tainted for the rest of his life.

Ram Singh reached his haveli. The grooms promptly came forward and took charge of the horses.

Ram Singh ushered Sambhajiraje to a seat in the centre of the hall and made him sit on it. He was restlessly pacing back and forth in the chamber.

Sambhajiraje saw Ram Singh chacha's agitation and got up from his seat. He went close to Ram Singh and said, "Chacha, what is the problem?"

As Ram Singh looked at Sambhajiraje he was moved. He put his hands on Sambhajiraje's shoulders and kept staring into his eyes. As he looked at the two horizontal stripes of sandalwood paste on his forehead, an idea flashed in Ram Singh's mind. He inadvertently mumbled, "Oh Chandi...Chandi..."

He pressed Sambhajiraje's shoulders hard and said, "Kunwar, come with me." He came directly to the sanctum in the haveli with Sambhajiraje, knelt in front of Goddess Ranachandi's murti and touched his forehead to its feet. He got up and quickly closed the door of the sanctum.

He picked up a trifoliate Bael leaf placed at Ranachandi's feet and plucked two of its leaves. As he gave them to Sambhajiraje his eyes moistened.

"Kunwar, listen to me carefully. Meet Raja Saab tonight in

his chamber and tell him that tomorrow you will be transferred to another haveli. Give this Bael leaf to him and tell him that only one leaf is left!" Ram Singh choked and could not speak anything more. He affectionately embraced Sambhajiraje.

As Ram Singh was stroking him, words coming from the deep recesses of his heart, echoed in Sambhajiraje's mind, 'Rajput means the sons of a Raja! I am a Rajput, and Ram Singh is also a Rajput!'

Sambhajiraje freed himself from Ram Singh's embrace and looked at his chest. There was no green pendant on his chest like the one Mirza Raja had.

After having dinner at Ram Singh's haveli, Sambhajiraje came to Raje's chamber. He touched Maharaj Saheb's feet and glanced around the chamber vigilantly. Madari and Hiroji were standing against a wall. The torches were burning, chasing the darkness away.

"Come, have a seat!" Raje said.

Sambhajiraje politely sat on Raje's bed.

"Ji!"

Again, silence prevailed in the light of the burning torches. The Rajput and Siddi soldiers guarding the chamber, were as usual pacing back and forth, holding their weapons.

"Have you eaten something?" Raje asked affectionately.

"Ji!" Sambhajiraje affirmed.

"Maharaj Saheb...." Sambhajiraje whispered, "Ram Singh chacha has sent a message. The emperor is going to transfer you from here tomorrow! Chacha told me to give you this Bael leaf and said with misty eyes, 'Only one leaflet is remaining!" Sambhajiraje put the single Bael leaf on Raje's palm.

In that moment, all the terrifying thoughts that Raje had restrained so far, burst out instantly. Transfer from one haveli to another meant slaughter! Pitiful death!

Raje instantly pressed his elbow and got up halfway. He anxiously held Sambhajiraje's upper arm tightly.

Raje made a firm decision in him mind. A decisive plan! 'If I can get out of this chamber safely, it is good. But if that doesn't happen – at least Balraje should escape from the enemy's clutches! To live on high forts and fight ferociously! Raje, who looked calm outwardly, said to Sambhajiraje, "You sleep here tonight."

Raje lay himself on the bed slowly. He coughed so hard for a long time that an onlooker would have felt suffocated himself. Hiroji came forward and held a spittoon in front of Raje.

Raje spat in it and said, "Hiroji, send a message to Khansaheb that Balraje is insisting on sleeping in my chamber tonight. Please let him sleep here."

"Ji!" Hiroji placed the spittoon near the bed and went outside. Madari began grinding a medicinal herb.

Hiroji came back with Faulad Khan's message, "Maharaj, Khansaheb said – Sure, sure, let the child sleep with his father!"

The night descended. The drama that was about to unfold was going to determine the future of the coming generations of Swaraj! A drama that required courage and skill.

Raje, Sambhajiraje, Hiroji, and Madari, all were set to play their roles. One small mistake, and it would be curtains!

Raje lay on his bed, his left hand resting on his forehead. Hiroji sat on the floor by his side. Sambhajiraje sat on the bed near his feet. Under the pretext of massaging oil in Raje's feet, Madari sat near his feet. The torches burning in the corners were warming up the room with light. Raje started speaking in a low voice, keeping his eyes closed, "Balraje, come a bit close." Sambhajiraje moved forward.

"Listen to me very carefully. Don't forget a single thing." Raje waited for a moment, then started talking steadily, "Tomorrow morning you go to chacha's haveli. Go to the durbar with him as usual. Take Sarjerao with you while going there. As soon as the first durbar concludes, tell Ram Singh chacha that you are not feeling well and would like to leave. Then get out of the Red Fort with Sarjerao and wait in the potters' colony near the shack of the potter, who is from our region. Tell Sarjerao to be ready with two horses near the Noorganj garden. I will meet you tomorrow in the potters' colony. In case, I don't come by late afternoon, you leave Agra with Sarjerao. He has the permits; use the permits and go to Mathura. Do what he tells you to do. Speak less, and don't wait for me." Raje stopped speaking. The faces of Masaheb, Putalabai, Dharau, Yesubai and late Saibai flashed in front of his closed eyes.

Raje made Sambhajiraje repeat everything twice and made sure he had understood everything.

"Now, you can go to sleep." Raje told Sambhajiraje. Madari came forward and took Sambhajiraje's Jiretop and placed it on the platter next to Raje's Jiretop. Sambhajiraje lay on the bed. Raje looked at Sambhajiraje's open hair; it broke his heart. He placed Balraje's head on his lap. God alone knew whether this would be their last meeting!

Sambhajiraje had experienced such a loving moment after a long time. He fell asleep quickly.

As Raje looked at Sambhajiraje's sleeping face in the light of the torches, he thought, 'You are fortunate indeed. I don't remember if I ever got to sleep on my father's lap like this!'

Raje gingerly put Sambhajiraje's head on the bed and lay by his side. Hiroji lay on a coarse blanket on the floor, near the bed. Madari kept walking around the chamber, keeping a watch.

"Hiroji" Raje called in low voice.

"Ji!" Hiroji responded from the floor.

Raje kept looking at the ceiling and talked to Hiroji in a soft voice. Hiroji was listening to him attentively.

"Have you observed all my habits?" Raje asked.

"Ji" Hiroji responded.

"Stay awake until the kettle drums on the Red Fort start beating in the early morning. The emperor performs his Namaz of dawn at that time. The patrolling soldiers' shift changes at that time. That is when you are going to take my place as the patient! Your facial features match mine. So, from tomorrow morning you are going to be Raje and I am going to be Hiroji. Keep your back to the entrance of the chamber and sleep in my place. Tomorrow, I will leave as Hiroji with the containers of sweetmeats. In the evening, you change into your own attire again. Arrange the pillows available on the bed in the shape of a person and spread a shawl over it. Press the legs of the fake Dhani. When the shift of the patrolling soldiers changes again at the time of the evening Namaz, you get out of the chamber cleverly. Travel as fast as you can and go back to our land. Don't be negligent. When you sleep here, in my place, don't stroke your moustache with the back of your palm!"

"Go to sleep now." Raje instructed Hiroji. The drama had begun. In the Red Fort, Aurangzeb who was sleeping in a rich, soft bed, pulled the warm blanket over his body, raised both his hands towards the sky and murmured–"Oh Khuda Amen! Amen!"

The twelfth day of the dark fortnight of Shravan was trying to break out through the overcast skies.

"Dud...dud...dhumm..." the kettle drums began beating in the Nagar Khana of the Red Fort. The sound travelled to Raje's chamber.

Raje was alert and awake. He heard the kettle drums and whispered his most favourite and trustworthy mantra – "Jagadamb, Jagadamb!"

Lying in the bed, Raje touched the cowrie necklace. Raje's fingers and the cowries conversed with each other silently.

Aurangzeb removed his soft blanket and left his sleeping chamber. He performed his ablutions, turned in the direction of Mecca, sat down on his knees and began his Namaz – "Alhamdulillaha..."

"Hiroji!" Raje called.

"Ji!" Hiroji, who had been awake through the night, responded in a soft voice.

"Madari!" Raje called Madari in whom he had put his faith.

"Ji, I am awake!" Madari responded.

For a moment silence spread its dark blanket in the chamber again.

"Madari, stand guard at the door. Give us a signal if anyone comes this side!"

"Ji!" Madari got up and kept a watch on the door and the netted window of the chamber. The torches had dimmed as the oil had gone down.

"Hiroji, remove your dress lying on the floor." The Gondhal that Raje had planned, began.

Raje removed his jama, innerwear, and churidar, lying on his bed. One by one, he removed his necklaces, the cowrie necklace, golden earrings, and rings, and handed them to Hiroji. Raje tried to remove the golden bracelet from his right wrist, but it was very tight. Hiroji placed his barabandi and churidar on the bed. Raje wore Hiroji's dress lying on the bed and scrubbed off the sandalwood paste on his forehead. Then, he affectionately stroked Sambhajiraje, who was fast asleep.

Hiroji was ready in Raje's attire. "Hiroji, I will get up, you take my place quickly. I will hold the mirror in front of you to draw the stripes of sandalwood paste on your forehead."

Raje gingerly pushed his blanket aside and got off the bed. Hiroji resolutely got into the bed. During all this hustle, Sambhajiraje let out a sigh in his sleep and turned on a side. Hiroji stroked his back with affection.

Raje tied Hiroji's white shawl around his waist. Then, facing the wall, biting his lower lip under his teeth, he pulled out the golden bracelet from his right hand. He went close to the bed and told Hiroji to remove his silver bracelet. Raje himself put the golden bracelet on Hiroji's hand and put Hiroji's silver bracelet on his own hand. Raje wore the big, twisted turban over his head.

An overwhelmed Hiroji said, "Maharaj..." Raje assured him,

"You are Raje now. Don't be shy. Say 'Jagadamb' once just like me."

Hiroji hesitated for a moment, then, he resolutely put his hand on the cowrie necklace around his neck and whispered, "Jagadamb, Jagadamb!" Indeed, it felt as if Raje himself was sleeping in the bed!

As he heard that, Raje bowed down, and just like Hiroji he said, "Maharaj, my obeisance to you." He straightened up and with his left hand, he pulled up his right sleeve up. Then, he pulled up the left sleeve too, like Hiroji and rubbed the back of his palm over his moustache.

Outside, the shift of the patrolling soldiers had changed. Inside, Raje had changed places. Sambhajiraje who was sleeping by Hiroji's side had no idea of what had happened!

Raje held the mirror in front of Hiroji. Madari held the platter of sandalwood paste. Hiroji drew two horizontal lines of sandalwood paste on his forehead.

Lord Shiva had applied two stripes of joy and sorrow on their foreheads. Now, he was going to take care of everything.

The day broke out. Sambhajiraje woke up. Madari handed him a pot of water. Sambhajiraje began washing his hands and face in a platter. As Raje dressed as Hiroji, watched him, he found a solution to a problem he had been thinking about for a while.

Raje wanted to check if the guards outside would recognize him in disguise. Shambhooraje was not paying attention to the fake Hiroji. Raje quickly came forward and picked up the platter. He held his head high, took the platter outside, emptied it and came back inside.

Raje stood along a wall courteously. Madari presented the Jiretop to Sambhajiraje.

Hiroji was still sleeping.

"Maharaj Saheb," Sambhajiraje said, approaching the bed.

"Hmm..." Hiroji responded and faked a bout of coughing.

"I am leaving!" Sambhajiraje said, and to touch his feet. (moved towards the foot of the bed.)

Hiroji promptly pulled his legs up while coughing and hastily said, "Remember, what I told you. Go now and wait for me in the potters' colony, late in the afternoon. May you live long!"

"Ji" Sambhajiraje said. He made an obeisance to the bed three times and left the chamber.

At that moment, Raje, dressed in the Mavala attire, couldn't resist himself and moved forward. As he looked at the young bhutya's back, who was walking forward, thoughts erupted in his mind, 'It is God's wish that this kingdom be established. All of us are bound by that vow. May you be successful!' Raje kept staring at Sambhajiraje's back.

With a heavy heart Madari kept gazing at Raje, because Raje had completely forgotten that he did not have the cowrie necklace around his neck anymore. He was lost in thought, stroking the barabandi on his chest.

The afternoon was almost over. In the potters' colony, Sambhajiraje, Tryambakpant and Nirajipant were waiting at the potter's shack. Sambhajiraje sat on a coarse blanket, he was quite agitated by troublesome thoughts. He got up frequently, looked at the path coming from the Noorganj garden and kept checking it. Then, he came back inside again, and sat on the blanket.

Sambhajiraje's agitation increased, '... and... what if Maharaj Saheb doesn't come at all! In that case... I am supposed to leave Agra today with Jedhe kaka and go to Mathura. Mathura! Where is it located? What does it look like? From there, I am supposed to go back to our homeland. And what if Thoralya Aausaheb asks, where is your Aabasaheb, what am I going to tell her?' - His royal heart drifted away.

'Clip clop clip clop' Sambhajiraje heard the faint sound of horses' hooves. His thoughts vanished in the air. He rose at once, holding the hilt of his sword. He glanced once at Nirajipant and hastily walked out. It was drizzling outside. Through the silver mesh of the drizzle, Sambhajiraje saw two horse riders trotting towards them. Both had twisted turbans on their heads.

One of them was Sarjerao Jedhe. He came forward and approached Sambhajiraje. He made an obeisance to Sambhajiraje and said in a husky voice, "Let's go. We must leave immediately."

"Leave? Without Maharaj Saheb? Why? Where?" For a moment Sambhajiraje felt overwhelmed.

The rider behind Sarjerao dismounted. He had held his head low under the pretext of avoiding the drizzling rain. His steps were falling in a rhythm and his Mavali footwear was creaking under his feet.

As Sambhajiraje watched his gait, he felt delighted. 'He is Maharaj Saheb for sure!' As their eyes met and his hunch was confirmed, Sambhajiraje moved forward in haste.

Raje was bewildered for a moment. With his eyes, he signalled Sambhajiraje to be cautious and not say anything! Sambhajiraje understood his signal.

"Niraji, you go to Balaji's serai. There you will meet two poets of Mathura. Tell them – 'The elephants are arriving at Mathura's ghats. Keep the ship ready!'" Raje instructed Niraji.

Niraji mounted his horse and left, but he did not make an obeisance to Raje!

"Tryambakpant, is everything ready as I had instructed?" Raje asked Tryambakpant. Tryambakpant raised the bundle in his hand and nodded in affirmation.

"I will bid farewell to the potter." Sambhajiraje addressed Raje while looking at Sarjerao.

"Come, I would also like to meet him." Raje came to the potter's shack with everyone.

The potter was completely unaware of what was happening in his shack. He was busy with his work.

"Baba, I am leaving." Sambhajiraje said to him.

"But it's raining outside!" He came forward and said in a half Maval half northern dialect.

Shambhooraje removed his pearl necklace. Raje grabbed the opportunity and whispered in Sambhajiraje's ears – "Give him the necklace but tell him one more thing. The sentries will come looking for us after we leave. Ask him to tell them that we went south, towards Aurangabad!"

"Baba, take this and do me a favour!" Sambhajiraje gave the necklace to the potter and said to him.

"What is it, Sarkar?"

"We are going to Aurangabad. If anyone comes asking for us tell them so. Farewell!"

"Ji" the potter said, looking at the necklace.

Raje, Sarjerao, and Tryambakpant came to the southern border of Agra, keeping Sambhajiraje in the lead. As Raje had presumed, the sentries at the gate stopped them. Sarjerao took his horse forward and approached them. He showed them the permits tied around his waist.

Still, one sentry questioned them, "Whose guests?"

Raje moved forward and pointing in the direction of Ram Singh's haveli he said, "Rana Ram Singh's guest! Seva's son!"

The sentries checked their permits and remembering Mirza Raja's high position in the durbar they allowed the troop to leave the border. Now, the news that Raje had gone south would spread everywhere.

Everyone left the southern border. All of them were utterly silent. The evening of Shravan was descending on Agra. Raje pointed to the north, towards the Yamuna. The horses started galloping towards the Yamuna. As the shores of the Yamuna came in sight, the horses stopped. All of them dismounted. Tryambakpant opened the bundle he carried. Raje and Sambhajiraje changed into the saffron clothes of sanyasis.

Tryambakpant tied the discarded clothes into a bundle and placed it on his horse. He and Sarjerao held the reins of their own and of Raje and Sambhajiraje's horses and started walking towards the north, along the bank of Yamuna. Raje and

Sambhajiraje walked behind them at a distance; the wet sand on the bank of the Yamuna squished under their feet. They reached the pier from where they were going to take a boat to Mathura. Raje embraced Tryambakpant and Sarjerao.

Niraji was ready at the pier, with Kavindra Paramanand and Kavi Kulesh. Raje and Sambhajiraje folded their hand, prayed to the unseen waters of the Yamuna and boarded the boat. Niraji boarded the boat after them. The boatmen wielded their oars. The boat sailed, cutting through the darkness.

Meanwhile, in the Red Fort, Aurangzeb had concluded the Namaz at sunset! He prayed to Khudatala, raising his hands towards the sky, "Arrhamma...nirrhimm" - 'Indeed you are the most merciful one!'

Taking advantage of that mercy, Hiroji had arranged the pillows on the bed, replaced Raje's Jiretop on the platter with a water goblet, covered it with a cloth and left the haveli. Madari had already escaped from the haveli under the pretext of getting medicines. All the birds had flown away! Only the feathers were left behind!

A noble Rajput had put his head on Goddess Ranachandi's feet, in his haveli and implored her – "Please keep our guests safe!" He was Ram Singh.

The boat was approaching the shore, generating ripples on Yamuna's surface.

Raje gently voiced the doubt he had had in his heart for a while. He asked Sambhajiraje, "How did you recognize me in Hiroji's dress in front of the potter's shack?" Even the rising waves of Yamuna remained calm to listen to the answer.

Sambhajiraje looked at Raje's feet and replied politely, "By your gait, Aabasaheb, you walked as if you still had the Jiretop on your head!"

An older sanyasi and a young sanyasi, dressed in saffron robes entered a tiled house in the Brahmin colony in Mathura. Niraji followed them. The house belonged to Moropant Pingale's brother-in-law, Krishnajipant Trimal. Niraji had located him and brought Raje to his house as it was a safe place to hide.

Krishnaji and his brothers Kashirao and Visajipant welcomed their honourable guests in the cordial northern style. Their mother Lakshmibai started cooking for the guests. The aroma of Mathura's delicious cuisine filled the kitchen.

Raje and Sambhajiraje, clad in saffron robes, sat on the clean carpet spread in the courtyard. You can never tell where your destiny may lead you. In fact, it was Raje who was supposed to welcome sanyasis and yogis, but today he was dressed as a sanyasi accepting the hospitality of a Brahmin in a holy place like Mathura!

After having dinner at the Trimal house, Raje held a council, and they planned the strategy for the remaining journey. Raje and Sambhajiraje lay down. The young sanyasi snuggled up to the elder sanyasi and fell asleep.

In Agra, all hell had broken loose. The news that 'Seva has disappeared' spread like wildfire all over the city. A paranoid Aurangzeb tightened his own security first.

"You incompetent fool, get lost from here!" Aurangzeb reprimanded Faulad Khan and threw him out of his chamber.

"Wazir-e-Azam, how many rupees did Seva gift us in Nazar and Nisar?" Aurangzeb asked a strange bitter question to Jafar Khan.

"Huzur, the father and the son, together gifted us about fifteen hundred gold coins and fifteen thousand rupees!" Jafar Khan replied.

"How much allowance was granted to him for his journey to Agra?" Aurangzeb frowned.

"One lakh rupees, Alijah!" Jafar Khan replied in a soft voice as he understood the intent of the question.

"Oh, what a traitor and a fraud!" Aurangzeb muttered, angrily moving the beads of his rosary. He became restless as he realized that Shivaji had depleted his treasury.

Meanwhile, Raje had crossed the borders of Mathura with Sambhajiraje, carrying precious jewels and diamonds in the bag on his shoulder. Raje's men were also disguised as northern ascetics and monks. They were travelling to Banaras in different groups but kept in touch with each other. Krishnaji Trimal and Kavi Kulesh were navigating them. Krishnaji's brothers Kashipant and Visaji also accompanied them.

The group of ascetics was travelling from Mathura to Banaras. Everyone was walking fast. Inadvertently, Sambhajiraje would fall behind. Then Raje, who would have gone ahead would stop for him. All of them would then stop and after coming together again, would resume walking.

"Are you tired?" Raje asked Sambhajiraje, breaking his trance.

"Ji, no."

Raje decided something to himself and stopped at once. He frowned. His face was determined.

He glanced at Sambhajiraje who was sweating and flushed. Raje approached him and put his 'sanyasi' hand on his shoulder!

"Can you please come with me?" Raje spoke in a heavy voice, pointing to a sprawling tree by the roadside.

Sambhajiraje nodded. The father and son came under the sprawling tree. The others stood by the side of the road. No one could guess what was going on in Raje's mind.

"Will you do me a favour?" Raje didn't sound his usual self.

"Ji!"

A few moments passed. Till today, Raje had never struggled for words while sharing something with Sambhajiraje, but today was different.

"We have a long way to go..." Raje stopped for a moment.

"Ji,"

"You...can you stay back?" Raje held Sambhajiraje's shoulders tightly in his hands. His touch conveyed way more to Sambhajiraje than his words.

"Ji, as you wish!" Sambhajiraje spoke resolutely.

Raje's eyes moistened on hearing his words.

"Let's go!" Raje put his hand on Sambhajiraje's shoulder and walked towards their group.

"Krishnajipant, listen to me very carefully." As soon as they approached the group, Raje took Krishnajipant aside and spoke to him determinedly.

"Yes, Swami!"

"I will go ahead. My son will stay behind and go back to Mathura with Kesopant and Kaviji. After reaching my kingdom I will send my people with a letter bearing my official seal. Till then, Kunwar will stay with your brother. From this moment he is your son, not mine." Raje spoke calmly.

Krishnaji Trimal felt like his chest was weighed down with the weight of a heavy boulder.

"Say something!" Raje urged him.

"I'm a poor brahmin. He is a prince. What if something unforeseen happens? How will I face you, Swami?" Krishnaji spoke his mind.

"Krishnajipant, anything unforeseen can happen even now! I will never blame you for the things that are not in your hands." Raje reassured Krishnajipant. Krishnaji agreed to do it, and convinced Kesopant.

"You go back with Kesopant. Do what he says. Do not go outside without company." Raje gave instructions to Sambhajiraje in a heavy voice. Sambhajiraje etched Raje's precious words in his memory.

"Kesopant, who all are there in your family?" Raje asked Trimal to assess the situation in his family.

"My mother, brother and sisters." Trimal responded.

"Then, from today, he is your nephew. Keep that in mind." Raje spoke with courage.

And the moment of bidding farewell to each other arrived! Raje patted his dear son's shoulders with trembling hands. The father and son looked like the two eyes of Goddess Bhavani!

They appeared separate, but they were one in their experience of joys and pain. Their hearts throbbed as one.

Raje pulled out a tiny golden Shivlinga from his bag. He had left behind his crystal Shivlinga with Hiroji. Therefore, he had bought this to perform the daily puja. Raje placed it in Sambhajiraje's palms and said, "Offer your daily morning and evening obeisance to this now. Speak less and have faith in Lord Shiva."

Sambhajiraje held the Shivlinga of ascetic Shiva given to him by his ascetic Aabasaheb and stared at Raje. His eyes instantly welled up.

Sambhajiraje held the Shivlinga close to his chest and knelt. He put his ascetic forehead on the peregrinating sanyasi's feet!

"Arise Shambhoobal." Raje hastily pulled him up.

"Maharaj Saheb, convey my obeisance to Thoralya Aausaheb, Masaheb and Dharau..."

Raje felt suffocated when he heard those words. He became quite agitated like an elephant with all his legs shackled with sharp fetters, 'And...and what if Shambhoobal doesn't return home safely...then... Masaheb will never see my face again! I won't be able to console her like I did when she was going to commit Sati!' Raje felt a hole in the pit of his stomach. He hastily pulled Shambhooraje into a tight embrace.

Raje let go of Shambhooraje determinedly. He gave a few jewels and diamonds to Kesopant to safeguard his most precious diamond.

Raje put his hand over Shambhooraje's head and said, "I wish you a long life! I will send messengers with a letter bearing my official seal. As soon as you receive it leave immediately with caution. Do as Trimal kaka tells you. Be careful. Jai Bhavani!" Raje's eyes were tranquil.

"Jai Bhavani!" Sambhajiraje responded with the same tranquillity.

Chapter 5

For the first time ever, the Bhosale family was scattered in four different directions – Sambhajiraje in Mathura, Raje travelling through many holy places, weary Jijau Saheb at Rajgad and Yesubai in Shringarpur!

With his head shaved and just a tuft of hair on it, Sambhajiraje was completely unrecognizable now. He had tied the edges of the garment he wore behind his neck, donned the holy thread across his chest, and applied a kumkum tilak on his forehead. Even without having performed the thread ceremony he looked like a young Brahmin boy.

Kashipant had taught him the daily rituals that a Brahmin boy was supposed to perform. Shambhooraje heard the Sanskrit language for the first time in Kashipant's cultured home. He was mesmerized by it.

This language is like the one that I hear daily, but exactly how, Sambhajiraje could not figure out.

Once, while visiting the Harihareshwar temple with Visajipant, he heard some people singing a bhajan. It made him realize, 'This language is like the local dialect of the Gondhalis in our kingdom, singing the praises of Goddess Bhavani!'

At the same time, Raje had taken a bath at the confluence of three rivers near Prayag. As he was climbing the ghat after the bath, a hunter had stopped Raje. He held a bunch of feathers in front of Raje and said, "Buvaji, these are eagle feathers from Mount Mainak. They give you success in everything you do.

Take five for yourself!"

Raje looked at the hunter and arched his eyebrow, "Eagle feathers that give success in everything you do!" Raje remembered Sambhajiraje as he looked at the feathers in the hunter's hand. 'Now, I need success in only one thing, to bring Shambhoobal back safely!'

Raje held five eagle feathers in his hands. Sarjerao paid dinars to the hunter. Raje glanced at the feathers for a moment and put them in his bag.

One and a half months passed. Raje eventually reached the Marathi kingdom safely, dressed as a sanyasi!

Rajgad was ebullient. Moropant delivered the news of Raje's arrival at the foothills of the fort to Jijau, "Aaisaheb, Raje has reached the kingdom safely. They will be reaching the foothills soon – in the attire of sanyasis. I am going to receive them with the palanquins. All the people on the fort are climbing down to see Raje!" Moropant was overwhelmed and he let his tears flow freely, releasing the tension in his heart.

Jijau's heart fluttered with joy. "Jagdamb! Jagadamb!" she muttered in a feeble voice. With teary eyes, she tried to look at Goddess Jagadamba, standing in front of her. She could not see her. Jijau got startled for a moment. 'Oh mother, in my moments of suffering, I said many things to you that I should not have said. Please don't get upset with me. I am your child!' Jijau wiped her eyes and placed her forbearing forehead in front of the sanctum.

Jijau forgot that Moropant was waiting for her orders.

Moropant was eager to rush to the foothills of the fort, and said, "May I take your leave, Masaheb?"

Jijau signalled him to come close and uttered very slowly, "Pant, carry his royal attire with you! A son should not face his mother in the attire of a sanyasi. You may go now!"

Moropant was not aware that Sambhajiraje had not come, so he carried the royal attires of both Raje and Sambhajiraje with him and descended the fort with the palanquin.

Raje sat on a coarse blanket, with his troop, in a colony at the foothills. Crowds had gathered outside. The excited clamour of the crowd could be heard. The sanyasi was moved by their excitement.

Moropant arrived with the palanquin. He entered the chief's house, where Raje was sitting, with a few attendants who carried platters. As soon as he saw Raje, Moropant moved forward. He was about to touch Raje's sanyasi feet when Raje got up from his seat and stopped him. Raje embraced him. Both felt overwhelmed.

"Raje should come with me immediately. Masaheb..." Moropant choked on his words. "Please wear the royal attire before leaving. Our Shastras say that a son should not face his mother in the attire of a sanyasi." Pant conveyed Jijau's wish to Raje.

The attendants placed the platters inside the room. Raje touched his saffron robe to take it for it and paused for a moment. A thought flashed in his mind, 'Here I am, removing my sanyasi robe...but Shambhoobal must be still wearing his! Such thoughts and such moments make me feel that I should never remove these clothes! The son donning a sanyasi's robe and the father donning royal attire! What kind of a game is this? What does the mother goddess have in mind?'

"Jagadamb! Jagadamb!" Raje removed his attire. He picked up a jama from the platter to wear it and thorny goosebumps arose on his entire body! With widened eyes he kept staring at the short-sleeved jama in his hands. It was Shambhooraje's jama.

Raje's heart stirred; his 'royalty' as well as his 'asceticism' vanished instantly. An unwanted thought crept into his heart, the heart of a father – 'What if Shambhoobal never returns...?'

Raje got dressed and walked out of the chief's house with his ministers. The crowd assembled outside became clamorous.

Many people were falling at Raje's feet. Their faithful eyes were filled with tears.

In all that commotion, no one except Moropant noticed the absence of Sambhajiraje.

Moropant was shocked to see that one platter of the royal attire was untouched.

After meeting the ryots Raje sat in the palanquin. He became very uneasy with the thought – 'Masaheb will definitely ask me – where is my Shambhoobal?'

How should I comfort her weary mind? Raje's mind was lurching with every swing of the palanquin. His heart was numb...

After a long period, the kettle drums at the Pali Darwaja resounded. Raje arrived at the Balekilla. His face looked resolute. His eyes were running like a wild deer, in search of Masaheb. Jijau stood at the entrance of the royal hall. Dharau stood behind her, barely able to control herself, desperately looking for Balraje.

Raje entered the courtyard with his close associates. Jiaju stood in front of him.

For a moment, Raje felt as if his feet were stuck to the floor. The next moment, with a heart overwhelmed by emotions, he rushed forward.

Raje prostrated at Jijau's feet. With the touch of his forehead to her feet; goosebumps arose all over Jijau and her entire body trembled. Jijau's pure, forbearing soul trickled through her tears. She leaned forward and pulled up Raje with trembling hands, and Raje rested in Jijau's embrace; like a whitt of fragrance blending in the morning breeze, like the ball of the Sun resting on the back of Yamuna's waters.

A son felt contented and delighted. A mother had no words to express her joy! Every person witnessing that moment in the courtyard felt as if they themselves were 'Aausaheb' and were holding 'Raje' in their embrace. Only Dharau's mind was full of apprehension. She wondered, 'where is my baby?' and her eyes moved rapidly, scanning the group of people who had accompanied Raje. She felt as if her heart was getting crushed under the thick ramparts.

One – only one word escaped Jijau's choking throat! It was completely drenched in affection –

"Shivaba...!"

Jijau herself felt the drenching affection wrapped around that word! Hearing the echo of her own voice, her ears went numb. And in that instant, the serpent of a wrenching apprehension slithered through Jijau's mind, like the serpent of a bolt of lightning instantly slithering through the cerulean sky – 'Where is Shambhoobal?'

Jijau immediately loosened her embrace. She held Raje's shoulders tightly and asked in a trembling voice, "Raje, where is Shambhoobal?"

Raje was stunned, to her stern words full of affection. His eyes fell at Jijau's feet, like the Jaripataka pennant sliding swiftly down the flagpole!

Jijau could not bear his silence. She fiercely shook his shoulders again and demanded an answer – "Tell me Raje, tell me something!" Her trembling words echoed her apprehensions.

Raje held his nose, closed his eyes, and said in a heavy voice, "Masaheb… Masaheb – our Shambhoobal is no more! He has left us!"

Jiaju closed her ears with shaking hands and let out a heart-rending scream – "Shambhoobal!" All the courtiers were shocked.

Jijau collapsed like Jagadamba's murti collapsing after being uprooted from its pedestal. "Oh dear Lord!" Dharau cried in shock and collapsed on the floor. Her entire body shook violently.

Raje promptly moved forward to console Jijau. All the people gathered in the courtyard shook their heads in disbelief.

Their heads dropped, and tears flowed from their loyal eyes. The mood of the entire courtyard changed drastically in a trice. Nobody could understand whether they should feel joyous about Raje's safe return or mourn the demise of Shambhooraje.

"Masaheb...please listen to me!" Raje tried to console Jijau, ushering her to the sanctum in the palace. Jijau could not hear anything.

"Pant, please send Dharau too." Raje pointed towards the sanctum in the palace and instructed Moropant as he left the courtyard.

Raje took Jijau to the sanctum and seated her properly.

Dharau entered the sanctum, shoving the edge of her sari in her mouth, desperately trying to control her sobs. As she entered the sanctum, Raje locked the door from inside. He picked up a Bael leaf lying at Bhavani's feet. He calmly approached Jijau who had put her head on Bhavani's feet.

"Masaheb!" Raje put his hand on Jijau's shoulder and called her calmly.

"I urge you, please lift your head and listen to me carefully."

Jijau lifted her head with tearful eyes. Raje placed the Bael leaf in Masaheb's palm, and said in a resolute voice, "Masaheb, don't lose heart! Shambhoobal is safe in Mathura! I have purposefully played this game, so he can safely escape from Aurangzeb's tight security. This is the only way to bring Shambhooraje back home safely!" Raje stopped for a moment. He looked at Bhavani's murti with serene eyes and said in a sad voice, "That is why I put you through a hell of pain, but please understand the situation, and forgive me with a big heart!"

Jijau's heart was swamped with tumultuous emotions; she had no words. She nodded her head and barely managed to speak, "Shivaba, your solutions are beyond the limits of my endurance. Do whatever you have to and bring Shambhoobal in front of me as soon as possible!"

Dharau was looking at Raje with widened eyes. She wanted to say, "How could you do this?" But she couldn't speak at all. Her mind had already reached Mathura, a place that she had never seen in her life!

Raje pushed aside his grief, and performed the obsequies for Shambhooraje at

Rajgad. The news of Sambhajiraje's demise spread throughout the region of Bara Maval. The entire kingdom was grieving.

A messenger sent by Raje from Rajgad, entered Shringarpur. He removed his turban and entered Pilaji Shirke's residence.

Raje had written a very short message for Pilaji, "Leave immediately. I need to talk to you in person."

Mathura was now engulfed by the northern wintry weather. The bed of the Yamuna wore a thick misty blanket. Even at midday, the dome of the Radha-Krishna temple was not visible. It had been two months since Raje left Mathura. Sambhajiraje was eagerly waiting for the messengers.

Every day, he would take a bath, visit the temple and after coming back, he would ask Krishnajipant's mother, Lakshmibai, "Did anyone come today?" As the days passed, the Trimal family started getting worried.

One day, two men dressed as northern traders, carrying bags on their shoulders, entered the Trimal household. The swordsmen accompanying them, waited at the borders of Mathura.

Shambhooraje had gone to the city with Kashipant. Only Visaji and Lakshmibai were at home. The traders recognized them.

One of the traders pulled out a sealed pouch from his bag and handed it to Visaji. Then, he gave a jewel-studded ring to Visaji and said, "You are to show this to your nephew!" The traders rested on a carpet spread in the courtyard.

Shambooraje returned from the city, and asked Visaji as

usual, "Did anyone come today?" He did not notice the traders sitting in the courtyard.

Without saying a word, Visaji placed the jewel-studded ring in Sambhajiraje's palm. The shining jewels of the ring ignited a radiant fire in his eyes. 'Maharaj Saheb's ring!' He got lost in thought and kept staring at the ring.

At once, he glanced at the traders sitting in the courtyard. Both immediately bowed down and made an obeisance to him. They uttered the code words to disclose their identity. They were Raje's messengers.

Shambhooraje approached them. He had heard the Mavali tongue after a long time and it stirred his heart. He promptly responded to their code words.

Kashipant hung a bundle of clothes on his shoulder and left Mathura on a holy pilgrimage! Shambhooraje was with him as his nephew, dressed as a Brahmin boy. His mother Lakshmibai also accompanied them to avoid any suspicions. Indeed, they were going on a pilgrimage! The entire Trimal family wanted to see 'Maji Jijau' in person, who had shaped Raje and Sambhajiraje's characters.

They kept moving from the north towards the Maval region. From time to time, Sambhajiraje's legs would ache due to the constant walking. Then at night, Lakshmibai would massage his legs with oil to alleviate his pain. She would put up a stone stove, cook rice on it and serve it to all.

The city of Ujjain was now approaching near. The pilgrims camped at a serai in a town called Haveli.

Kashipant fetched a pot full of water from the river. Lakshmibai put up a stone stove and placed a pot on it to cook some rice. Kashipant began massaging Sambhajiraje's legs to reduce his pain. No one was speaking. Everyone was performing their chores as decided.

Suddenly, the galloping of horses was heard, approaching the serai. The pilgrims glanced at each other to be vigilant.

Before long, four Mughal riders came right in front of the serai. The soldiers dismounted and tossed the reins on the backs of the horses. All four of them walked rapidly. The pilgrims were terrified, but they continued their chores as if nothing had happened.

"O kafir, where have you come from?" the leader of the troop looked at Kashipant and asked him aggressively.

"Ji, from Mathura!" Kashipant Trimal implored him.

"Where are you going?"

"On a pilgrimage. We are going to Rameshwar, Huzur!"

"Who is he?" The troop leader stood in front of Sambhajiraje. His name was Harhikmat Khan.

"He is my nephew, Sarkar!" Kashipant replied.

"Liar! You swine, he is 'Sambha', the son of Seva from Deccan!"

Shambhooraje's ears flushed as he heard the words. He felt like someone had kept a burning ember on his chest. He had thought it was going to be over soon! The pain in his legs returned.

"Seva? Who is Seva? I don't know any Seva. This is my nephew!"

Kashipant spoke in a high voice, pretending he did not know who 'Shivaji' was and was not going to let go of his nephew. He quickly pulled Shambhooraje close.

"This is your nephew! What is his name? Where is his mother?" The troop leader lashed a whip of questions.

"His name is Madhav! His mother is no more!" Kashipant said in a heavy voice, remembering his sister.

"You liar! You will not open your mouth so easily." The troop leader lashed his whip on Kashipant.

"We are poor brahmins. We are going on a pilgrimage. Sarkar, have mercy on us." Kashipant forgot his pain and showing the sacred thread on his chest, he started fighting against his ebbing fate, with all his skill. He started pleading with them.

"Harhikmat Khan, if he is a Brahmin, we will know soon enough! Just tell him to eat food with his nephew, in one plate." One rider suggested to the leader.

"Marhabba...you are right!" said the leader and arrogantly ordered Kashipant, "You, idol worshipper, if he is your nephew, then why don't you eat food with him in the same plate? You, old woman, get a plate ready for them." Harhikmat Khan commanded.

All the pilgrims were shocked, and wondered, how was this possible?

"In our Shastras this is not..." Kashipant tried to explain.

"To hell with your Shastras! Bring the plate now!" Harhikmat Khan did not give him a chance to speak.

Kashipant glanced at Sambhajiraje, and wondered whether his royal blood would rebel at this time. Shambhooraje will misbehave, and then everyone will be sent to the dungeon of Ujjain. Our reputation will be ruined. Lakshmibai astutely served a plate full of rice with a piece of sweetmeat from Mathura.

Kashipant spread two coarse blankets on opposite sides of the plate and sat on one side.

"Have a seat, my child!" He said and signalled Sambhajiraje to sit on the other blanket. Some incidents in a man's life take place only to teach him invaluable lessons!

Shambhooraje sat on the blanket. He and Kashipant placed a few morsels of food around the plate as an offering to the gods. Their eyes met for a moment. Both braced their hearts. Eyes can be very communicative. Often, they convey much more than words!

They said their prayers and put their hands in the plate. One hand was that of a Brahmin who offered the oblations of Yamuna's waters to the sun. The other hand was that of a Bhosala, who had the legacy of offering oblations of blood to the earth.

This was destiny's game. Kashipant and Shambhooraje started eating from the same plate. Harhikmat Khan and his soldiers were quite peeved to see that.

"Those imbeciles! They gave me the wrong news!" Harhikmat Khan cursed the people who had given him the information.

"This rice-eater, chubby boy cannot be Seva's son! Let's go!" The riders left the serai as quickly as they had come. All the pilgrims let out a sigh of relief. Silence prevailed in the serai.

Kashipant looked at Shambhooraje with pride and admiration and felt in his heart, 'I should have had a real nephew who had such presence of mind and maturity!'

But Sambhajiraje's fingers were just mashing food in the plate. He had never felt like this before. He was thinking, 'I never got a chance to sit in front of Aabasaheb and eat with him from the same plate!'

A virtuous Brahmin, who was born in the north, and the only scion of the founder of Swaraj were lost in quite different thoughts while eating the meal.

Sometimes, destiny deals a very strange hand indeed!

After an arduous journey, the pilgrims of the Trimal family came near Rajgad. Messengers had already delivered the news of their arrival on the Balekilla.

Raje took Jijau's blessings and descended the fort, to receive Sambhajiraje in person. He was accompanied by Moropant, Annaji, Prataprao,

Anandrao, Keshav Pandit, Krishnaji, Sais, and Gomajibaba. Some attendants carrying platters of Sambhajiraje's royal attire were with them. An exquisitely decorated palanquin was kept at the ready to ascend the fort.

Sambhajiraje walked between Kashipant and Lakshmibai. From a distance, he saw the saffron dot on the Sanjivani machi of Rajgad. He touched his hand to his chest and made an obeisance to the saffron pennant. The moment he saw Rajgad, all his suppressed thoughts gushed like clean, white streams of water gushing from the hooves of horses galloping across a stream. Many memories, faces and places flashed through his mind.

Like the sun rising on the water of the ocean, Sambhajiraje saw something sparkling at the other end of the road that merged in the meadows around. He momentarily stopped in his tracks and narrowed his eyes to check out what was sparkling. Unwittingly, he extracted his hand from Kashipant's hand.

Sambhajiraje suddenly raised his hands and shouted "Maharaj Saheb!". Lakshmibai and Kashipant who were with him got confused. The next moment he realized that his words were sprinting ahead of him, and so he dashed forward immediately. The loose clogs on his feet flew away.

Raje saw a golden bud sprouting up from the meadows around, dashing forward in his direction. He puckered his forehead and narrowed his eyes.

'Shambhoobal! He is running so fast – what if he stumbles?' Raje rushed forward as if an unknown force was pushing him. Raje's companions did not understand at first why Raje was rushing forward, but the moment they realized it, all of them rushed after Raje.

With his face flushed and drenched in sweat, Shambhooraje dashed forward, raising his hands in the air. The bag on his shoulder was slipping down, and he tried to keep it from falling while running wildly. If possible, he would have simply tossed it aside.

Raje was moved to see the sight of Shambhooraje trying to hold his bag while running.

Sambhajiraje came running and embraced Raje like wild winds wrapping the ramparts of the fort; like a cascading stream uniting with the free-flowing, foamy river. The sword got its edge back. Wise, mature Aabasaheb met clever, forbearing Balraje!

Shambhooraje wrapped his arms around Raje's waist tightly. His face was covered in Raje's jama. He swayed his head left to right; it smudged the sandalwood paste on his forehead.

"Maha..." Shambhooraje tried to say something, but he was so overwhelmed with emotions that he choked.

Raje gently stroked Shambhooraje's back. Was it affection? Pride? Or Satisfaction? Only the stroking hands and the back being stroked knew what it was!

Raje's gentle touch slowly brought Shambhooraje's rapid breathing back to normal. He lifted his head and looked at Raje. Then he knelt and put his forehead on Raje's feet! He stood up, pulled the bag on his shoulder in front of his stomach, and pulled out the gold Shivlinga that Raje had handed him when he departed from the North. It sparkled in the rays of the sun.

"He quickly glanced at Raje, placed the Shivlinga in Raje's palm and courteously said, "I – I spoke very little!"

Raje looked at the Shivlinga in his palms, sparkling in the sun, and strongly felt, "He – He should speak more!'

Raje remembered the hunter he had met in Prayag at the ghats near the confluence of the three rivers! "The eagle feathers that give success in everything you do." Raje let out a sigh of relief.

Sambhajiraje took of the Brahmin attire and donned the royal attire. Raje and Sambhajiraje sat in the palanquin. The palanquin-bearers gave out the slogan, 'Jai Bhavani' and picked up the palanquin. The palanquin began ascending Rajgad. Moropant followed the palanquin with his brother-in law, Krishnaji and Kashipant. Lakshmibai sat in another palanquin.

The palanquin arrived at Sanjivani machi. Raje and Shambhooraje got out of the palanquin and started walking together. Their loyal supporters followed them. The ryots assembled on the machi started touching their feet in flocks.

They arrived at the Balekilla. When they came near the

threshold of the royal court, Dharau suddenly came forward, holding a black rooster tightly in her hands. As soon as she saw Shambhooraje, her peasant heart was filled with joy. She inadvertently uttered, "Oh my child, where were you all this time?"

"She circled the rooster around Shambhooraje three times. The scared rooster made a weird sound. Dharau threw him away. It made a fluttering sound as it flew off.

"Aau!" Sambhajiraje put his royal forehead on her feet, in front of everyone. Dharau leaned forward and hugged him tightly.

Shambhooraje freed himself from Dharau's embrace, and clinging to Raje, he stood at the stone threshold of the courtyard. Married women poured water over his feet and did aukshan to welcome him. The water seeped through Shambhooraje's cracked soles, stinging his bare feet. Sambhajiraje's eyes were moving around rapidly, eagerly looking for Thoralya Aausaheb! He crossed over the threshold and came into the courtyard. Jijau had hardly ever done it before, but today she was standing in the courtyard. Aged Jijau's weary legs gained strength. She didn't even realize that her sari drapped over her head had slipped. She approached Shambhooraje.

Shambhooraje let go of Raje and rushed forward. Instantly, he embraced Jijau tightly. Everyone assembled in the courtyard was moved.

"Thoralya Aausaheb! Aausaheb!" with every single utterance, Shambhooraje's heart felt overwhelmed. His chest puffed up with one thought – 'Even the sari that Thoralya Aausaheb is wearing emits a holy fragrance. It just overwhelms me!' And Shambhooraje eagerly kept rubbing his face in the folds of her sari.

In that moment, Jijau realized 'why Goddess Bhavani has eight hands!' Even those might seem inadequate at such a moment. Jijau tried to make up for the inadequacy of her arms with the words from her mouth – "Shambhoobal...! Shambhoobal...!"

Even in that effusive embrace, a terrifying thought jabbed at Jijau's heart – 'Shambhoobal...is no more!' Jijau shivered.

"When people you love the most die, life becomes desolate for people who are left behind. Jijau herself had endured it. At once, Jijau tightly clasped Shambhooraje in her embrace. Her love for him trickled through her eyes, over his head.

As they watched the moving scene, every person in the royal court felt like they themselves were 'Dhakale Raje' getting drenched in the love pouring out of Jijau's eyes.

Jijau calmed down and wiped her eyes. She circled a pouch full of gold coins around Shambhooraje's face, put her hand over his shoulder, and calmly said – "Let's go!"

Jijau walked towards the sanctum! To surrender Shambhooraje at the divine feet of Goddess Jagadamba!

After visiting the temple, Shambhooraje came to Putalabai's chamber. She kept gazing at Shambhooraje, forgetting the lamp platter she held to do aukshan.

Shambhooraje approached her, touched her feet and said, "Masaheb, please do the aukshan!" The same words, cascading like a stream; the same eyes, as clear as a mirror. Putalabai did the aukshan with shaking hands.

Sambhajiraje pulled out the amulet wrapped in the scarf around his waist. He placed it on the platter and said, "I came back safe and sound. During the journey, I kept this amulet in the bag on my shoulder. As long as I carried the bag with me, I feared nothing."

"It's very effective indeed!" Putalabai thought, looking at the amulet in the platter. Putalabai placed the platter on a wooden stool. Then, for some reason, she picked up the amulet from the platter again. She approached Shambhooraje and without saying anything, she tied it around his upper arm, and embraced him.

From there, Shambhooraje came to see Soyarabai in her chamber. He put his head on Masaheb's feet. Soyarabai pulled him up and said, "How could Swari even say that you were no more? Arise. May you have a long life! We performed your funeral in the fort! I should tell Masaheb that we should perform the rituals to remove this blemish!"

"Sambhajiraje frowned. He looked at Soyarabai's feet and tried to unravel the puzzle of the intricate henna designs her feet! He couldn't find a single clue. He was never going to find it!

That night, in Jijau's chamber, Shambhooraje lay in bed with his eyes closed. He should have fallen asleep due to exhaustion, but he was still awake. Many questions arose in his mind, 'Why did Maharaj Saheb tell everyone that I was no more? Even my funeral rites were performed on the fort! Why? Why did Aabasaheb do it? Maybe, he had some plan behind it too! Otherwise, why would he have climbed down the fort and come to receive me in person?' Shambhooraje drifted off to sleep.

Dharau, who was massaging his feet with oil, kept gazing at him. Devoted affection knows only one thing, to serve silently!

The foggy day of Margashirsha Purnima broke out in Gunjanmaval. Shambhooraje took a bath, got dressed and came to Jijau's chamber.

Jijau applied two horizontal stripes of sandalwood paste to his forehead. Jijau left for the royal court with him. Behind her walked a few attendants holding platters of gold coins. Jijau had used those coins to count the Bael leaves she had offered Lord Shiva, for Raje and Shambhooraje's safety, when they were trapped in Agra. Today these gold coins were going to be distributed as alms.

The royal court of Rajgad was full of courtiers. This was an honour assembly. Raje was going to honour Krishnaji, Kashipant and Lakshmibai Trimal in front of the royal court, for safely bringing Sambhajiraje back home from Mathura.

Jijau and Shambhooraje entered the royal court. As Raje saw Jijau, he promptly arose from his seat and made an obeisance to her. The honour assembly commenced. The attendants lined up the platters of gold coins by a wall of the royal court.

Raje glanced at Mujumdar Nilopant. Nilopant commenced the assembly and shared the agenda – "In the north, Sarkarswari was caught in a life-threatening situation. Raje and Sambhaji Raje deftly escaped from the enemy's clutches. They disguised themselves as ascetics to reach the kingdom safely. But a major problem arose during their journey. It became increasingly difficult to travel with Dhakal Raje. Therefore, Sarkarswari left Dhakate Raje in the care of the Trimal family in Mathura. The Trimal family endured lot of hardships on their way here and brought the jewel of the family back home safely. That is why, Raje has organized this assembly to honour the three members of the Trimal family."

"In this honour assembly, Kashi Trimal of Mathura is being offered twenty- five thousand rupees..." Nilopant stopped.

Kashi Trimal was sitting next to Moropant. He got up from his seat and approached the throne courteously.

Raje and Sambhajiraje gave the customary touch of their hands to the platter full of silver coins. Kashipant bowed down and accepted the platter. He was overwhelmed by the appreciation. He placed the platter aside and prostrated himself in front of the royal trio– Raje, Sambhajiraje and Jijau. Kashipant, Krishnaji and Visaji were bestowed with a palanquin, elephant and fief each.

Nilopant tidied the shawl over his shoulder and announced further – "Lakshmibai, the mother of the Trimal brothers is hereby offered twenty-five thousand rupees."

Lakshmibai was sitting in the royal ladies' section, with Raje's queens. Nilopant glanced at the curtain and signalled Laskhmibai to come outside. She came out and accepted a platter of silver coins touched by Jijau. With tears in her eyes, she observed Jijau from up close.

Lakshmibai put the platter aside and bowed to touch Jijau's feet. Jijau held her hands and said "Bai, you have done me the biggest favour of my life! Please don't touch my feet. Had it been possible, I would have offered you an Oti as a suvasinee in front of the royal court." At this moment Jijau regretted that she was a widow.

The platters of charities kept coming in front of Shambhooraje. He kept giving the customary touch of his hand to the platters as the names of the beneficiaries were announced.

Jijau, who had broken her fast, was feeling contented. As the platters were about to finish, a frown arose on Sambhajiraje's face. He leaned towards Raje and whispered, "Maharaj Saheb…"

"Yes, what is it…" Raje said with a contented heart.

"One platter of alms should be sent to Agra!"

"….." Raje raised his eyebrows, and without saying anything he questioned with his eyes, 'For what?'

"Sambhajiraje looked at the cowrie necklace resting on Raje's chest and said, "The potter from the potters' colony helped us in our hour of need, for him!"

Unknowingly, Raje put his hand on Sambhajiraje's back. A platter full of silver coins was set aside for the potter in Agra. From his seat Raje glanced at his personal secretary. He approached Raje with an attendant holding a platter covered with a cloth. They made an obeisance to Raje. The attendant removed the cover over the platter and held it in front of Raje. Sambhajiraje saw a pendant set in a golden socket! It was made of some kind of feathers!

"What is this?" he asked Raje.

"These are eagle feathers that give success in every endeavour you undertake!" Raje replied, gazing at the pendant in the platter. He signalled the attendant to hold the platter in front of Jijau. "Masaheb, please give the customary touch of your hand to the platter!" Raje looked at Jijau. Jijau gave the customary touch of her hand to the pendant of eagle feathers. Now, the pendant was truly blessed, it would certainly make every endeavour a success.

Jijau was about to ask Raje something, when the beating sound of the kettle drums coming from the Pali Darwaja, entered the hall of the royal court!

Raje and Jijau gave each other a smile as they heard it. No one in the royal court understood why they smiled.

The assembly was about to conclude. The torchbearer of the fort promptly approached the throne. He made an obeisance to Raje and said, "Sarkar, it is Purnima today. May I have your permission to present a Gondhal today? Please honour the Gondhal dance with your presence tonight."

"Certainly!" Raje offered a betel leaf and a coconut to the torchbearer. The assembly concluded.

The Gondhalis prepared a square of raw rice grains in the chowk in front of the courtyard. After dinner, Raje sat in the courtyard with Sambhajiraje and Jijau, to watch the Gondhal dance. The courtyard was packed with people.

As soon as the preparations for the Gondhal dance were completed, the chief of the Gondhalis came forward. He bowed down and said, "Sarkar, may I have your permission to begin the Gondhal?"

Raje raised his palm and gestured to him to stop for some time. Raje gazed at the door of the inner apartments. All eyes turned in the same direction.

Behind that door, the sound of two hands tidying a sari was heard. The delicate jingle of bangles was audible. A few moments passed, Yesubai came in, walking between Pilajirao and Dharau. She bent her head low, her heart was beating fast!

Pilajirao had believed the rumour that Sambhajiraje had passed away and had come to Rajgad to carry Sambhajiraje's mojaris with him for Yesubai who was going to commit Sati.

At that time, Raje had managed to convince him and sent him back to Shringarpur.

After Sambhajiraje reached home safely, Raje immediately sent a messenger to Shringarpur with his letter. He had told Pilajirao – "Reach here by the night of Purnima with Soonbai. Bring the holy ashes of Goddess Bhaveshwari with you when you come. Shambhooraje has reached the fort safely!"

Sambhajiraje saw Pilajirao coming to the courtyard and arose to receive him, but the moment he saw the sparkling toe-rings by Pilajirao's side, he inadvertently sat down again.

But Raje went ahead to receive her and said, "Come Soonbai..." He held Yesubai's hand and ushered her to the seat next to Masaheb. Pilajirao also took a seat. Raje signalled the Gondhalis to begin the dance. The chief Gondhali put his hand over his ear and began singing the praises of Goddess Jagadamba to the rhythm of the dancing torches.

Sambhajiraje's maturity had increased considerably because of the journey to Agra and the unexpected calamities he had faced during this journey.

Raje visited the custodians of all the forts in his possession and inspected the forts. With the assistance of Annaji Dutto he got sufficient supplies stocked in each fort. He implemented a new disciplinary system for his army with strict rules to be followed.

'During the monsoon, the soldiers should spend time with their family and till their farmlands. After Dussehra celebrations, all soldiers should resume their duties. For eight months, they should participate in the military campaigns. During such campaigns they should not violate the honour of women. All soldiers should pay their taxes at the authorized offices when going on military campaigns and coming back home. No soldier should behave in an improper manner. A soldier who breaks the rules will have his hands severed.' Raje had implemented a very rigorous disciplinary system.

Raje formulated a system of land assessment and revenue collection that surpassed the system designed by Malik Amber. 'The Deshmukh, Deshpande, Patil and four wise elders, a total of seven people from a village, should collectively examine the land to be assessed and determine its quality. Then they should classify the arable land into monoculture and polyculture grades and collect revenue accordingly. They should accept raw grains in revenue from people who cannot pay taxes in cash. The farmers should be provided with ploughs, bulls and seeds for sowing as per their needs.' This was the strategy for further development. It was all being keenly observed by Sambhaji Raje.

Shambhooraje observed at first hand, how Raje's heart was filled with compassion when he spoke about the farmers and soldiers in the royal court.

The royal court of Rajgad brimmed with courtiers. Peshwe Moropant held an open letter in his hands like a mirror. Raje, Jijau and Sambhajiraje took their seats. Raje's queens, Putalabai, Soyarabai and the others sat behind a curtain, in the royal ladies' section. Yesubai held her head low and sat next to Putalabai. A humorous thought instantly popped into her mind. 'Will I be able to see the Jiretops sitting in the court, from behind this curtain?' But instead of raising her head, she continued holding it bent and kept listening. Pilaji had returned to Shringarpur. As per Raje's wish, Yesubai was now going to live on Rajgad. Moropant's words cut through the silence in the royal court. Raje gestured to Moropant to read the letter. Moropant started reading. Yesubai could hear a soft voice speaking rhythmically.

"To His Royal Highness Prince Muazzam, Subah Deccan – Greetings from Sivajiraje -

"The intent of this letter is to inform you that I left Agra as I feared for my life. My son, Shambhooraje has also reached here safely. We could not meet Ala Hazrat before leaving the city. As you know very well, life is precious for every living being.

"Though I left in a hurry, without meeting the emperor, I still consider myself his humble servant. I am always ready to serve him in any way I can. Please do me a favour and convey the same to the emperor. My son, Sambhajiraje is still in the military service of the emperor. We have surrendered all our forts and wealth at the feet of the emperor. Please give my son a second chance, to prove his loyalty to the emperor. What more can I say? Thank you."

Aurangzeb had dismissed Jaswant Singh from the post of the Subedar of Deccan and had instated his son Muazzam in Jaswant Singh's place. Muazzam wanted no conflict with Shivajiraje, not as a political move, but as a security! He felt that his conniving father had purposely sent him to deal with Shivaji. Raje also did not want any discord with the Mughals till he got his kingdom back on track. He wanted to make a treaty with Muazzam, the subedar of Deccan.

After listening to the letter, Jijau, all the ministers and courtiers kept staring at Raje in wonder. The life-threatening episode of Agra was barely over and Raje was trying to make another move using Sambhajiraje as a pawn. But Raje was calm. He glanced at Balaji Aavaji. Balaji presented himself in front of the royal court and made obeisance to Raje. Balaji was going to Aurangabad as Raje's emissary.

Moropant placed the letter back in its pouch. He bowed down and held the pouch in front of Raje. Raje gave it a touch of his hand.

"Balaji, please handle everything carefully. This treaty must materialize." Raje instructed Balaji.

"As you wish Swami!" Balaji accepted the letter from Moropant. He took a few steps back, made an obeisance and left the royal court to begin his journey towards Aurangabad.

"Shambhooraje, if this treaty materializes...you may have to go to Aurangabad, to have an audience with the prince, alone. Will you go?" Raje questioned calmly.

"Yes, for sure, I will go. During my return journey from the North, I did not take the same path. I bypassed the Verul caves. Given an opportunity, I would like to visit them." Sambhajiraje replied. Raje had not expected such an answer. He glanced at Jijau. Jijau's face was solemn.

Sambhajiraje didn't realize why his eyes inadvertently turned towards the curtain in front of the royal ladies' section, at the recollection of the Verul caves.

"Maharaj, Naik is here!" the attendant informed Raje.

"Let him in." Raje stopped pacing in the chamber. Shambhooraje also came close to Raje and stood next to him. Bahirji Naik presented himself in the chamber and made an obeisance.

"Dhani, Raghunathpant and Tryambakpant who were stranded in the Mughal region have escaped safely. They have arrived at the foothills, but they are in a really bad condition." Bahirji caught his breath.

Raje remembered –

'We escaped from Agra, but Raghunathpant and Tryambakpant were left behind and were captured by Aurangzeb's sentries. I heard that Faulad Khan tortured them brutally. In fact, they would have died in the dungeons, but the negotiations I started through Muazzam proved effective and Aurangzeb let them go alive...this means the negotiations are going to materialize for sure...'

"Dhani, we should send some clothes for them to wear. They are in a very bad shape. And..." Bahirji hesitated.

"Tell me Naik, and what...?"

Bahirji shook his head, his throat choked with emotion –

"No Dhani, I can't bring myself to deliver the news."

Raje walked calmly towards Bahirji and said in a firm voice, "Naik, had something terrible happened to me in the prison, you would have had to deliver the news to Masaheb! An informer and an astrologer must tell the truth. So, tell me, what's the news?"

"Maharaj, Netaji was circumcised in the Jumma masjid of Delhi! His name has been changed to Mohammed Kuli Khan now. Netaji converted to Islam. Nisar Khan captured his wife and sent her to Delhi. She was also converted to Islam and the Maulanas performed their nikah again." Bahirji's heart was stirred by the memory of valiant Netaji. His eyes filled with tears.

Raje's hand on Bahirji's shoulder trembled. His eyes became misty. Netaji! A walking inferno astride a horse! The blazing ember has turned into dead coal.

As he looked at Bahirji and Raje, Shambhooraje's fist on his Jamadar tightened unwittingly. His ears flushed, as if molten lead had been poured into them. His eyes breathed fire.

He remembered Aurangzeb's hand which held a rosary! And every moment his grip on the Jamadar kept tightening, unknowingly!

Raje was in the process of rejuvenating his kingdom. Aurangzeb had accepted Raje's accord. He had sent Raje an imperial order through the subedar of Deccan, Muazzam alias Shahalam. It was for Shambhooraje!

Pursuant to the accord, Shambhooraje was offered a royal Mansab as Raje's representative. A mansab of four thousand cavalry! He was also going to be bestowed with the Mokasa of Varhad and Khandesh regions, worth fifteen lakh hons!

Shrewd Aurangzeb had calmly pretended to make the move of a rook – in reality he made the crooked move of a rook!

The Mokasa was of the Varhad-Khandesh region. It meant that Sambhajiraje would have to stay in Aurangabad. As a 'Mansabdar', Shivaji's son would again be a hostage to Aurangzeb. Otherwise, he would have given Sambhajiraje the Mokasa of the Maval region that he had obtained in the treaty of Purandar. But he didn't do it. Raje sent a forthright message to the Delhi durbar, "My son Sambhaji will accept the charge of the Mokasa at a convenient time. Till then, Prataprao Gujar and Niraji Ravaji will maintain the jagir as his deputy ministers. My son will not stay in the region of his Mokasa!"

All conditions of Raje were accepted. Muazzam dispatched a letter from Aurangabad, "Please send Shambhooraje to Aurangabad for the ceremonial acceptance of the jahagir and the firman!"

Raje dispatched his best informers Bahirji, Karmaji, and Vishwas towards Aurangabad, to collect information about Muazzam. Only Raje could make such bold moves. He had always been one for taking such risks. He would break one siege to get out of it and then enter another willingly with audacity. He had got Sambhajiraje released from one tricky situation and was now ready to send him into another one. The success of this move depended upon Muazzam's temperament as well as Sambhajiraje's mettle.

The informers picked up detailed information about Muazzam and delivered it to Rajgad. "Muazzam is a self-indulgent man. He leads a life of luxury. He is in awe of Raje, and not loyal to ever his own father!"

Raje took the thoughtful decision of sending Sambhajiraje to Aurangabad. He was confident that Shambhooraje would handle the formalities of the durbar efficiently. If he went there in person, Aurangzeb would be convinced at least for a brief period.

This diplomatic move was going to take place right at the time of Diwali.

The chilly day of Naraka Chaturdashi broke out on Rajgad. Today was the day to march towards Aurangabad.

Sambhajirajiraje took the blessings of Jijau, Dharau, Putalabai, Soyarabai and other masahebs. He also bade farewell to Yesubai.

Prataprao, Niraji Ravaji, Ravaji Somnath, Pralhad Niraji, and Anandrao had assembled in the courtyard of the Balekilla to descend the fort.

Jijau and Raje came to the courtyard with Sambhajiraje. Shambhooraje put his head on Jijau's feet. "May you live long! Come home as soon as your work is done." Jijau blessed him.

Sambhajiraje started walking towards the Sanjeevani machi with Raje and the team that was going to accompany him. The palanquin in which he was going to descend the fort was ready on the machi.

They arrived at tunnel leading to the machi. The boulder over the face of the tunnel was pushed aside. Raje and Shambhooraje entered the tunnel. Prataprao, Nirajipant, Ravaji, Anandrao, Pralhadpant followed them. They all started walking.

They arrived at Sanjivani machi. Sambhajiraje put his head on Raje's saffron mojaris. Raje pulled him up, took him in an embrace and firmly said, "Take care! Though I am not there, Prataprao is there for you. Take his advice and behave accordingly. May you be successful! I will be waiting for you!"

Shambhooraje sat in the embellished palanquin. The mission of Agra was over. Now, he was on the way to Aurangabad!

Sambhajiraje reached Aurangabad with the army. On behalf of the prince, Jaswant Singh, a prominent sardar of the Delhi durbar, came to receive him. In front of Jaswant Singh, Sambhajiraje accepted the robes of a Mansabdar and offered him some presents in return.

In the imperial palace of Aurangabad, Sambhajiraje had an audience with Prince Shah Alam, along with Prataprao, Nirajipant and Ravaji. Ruddy, fair complexioned Shah Alam was very pleased to see Shambhooraje. He muttered to himself, "Oh Allah, what a handsome boy!" He presented an embellished elephant and a jewel-studded sword to Shambhooraje with royal pomp. Sambhajiraje offered him presents in return. Shah Alam ushered Sambhajiraje to a lavish seat in the palace and seated him by his side. Even Jaswant Singh had never been honoured in this manner. He stood in front of them, with his hands folded.

The prince politely inquired about Sambhajiraje's journey and Raje's health.

It was time to leave now.

Sambhajiraje visited the Ghrishneshwar temple with Prataprao, Pralhad Niraji, and Ravaji Somnath. He also viewed the engraved sculptures in the mountain caves of Verul that had fascinated him.

The Maratha army had encamped on the southern border of Aurangabad. Numerous tents and shamianas had been erected. Every day, Sambhajiraje would take a stroll in the city with Prataprao. Aurangabad was the Mughal capital in the Deccan. The city was surrounded by ramparts and looked quite splendid.

Raje had instructed Shambhooraje when he left, "Survey as much area of the city as you can!" Shambhooraje returned after taking a stroll in the city. Prataprao was with him.

As soon as they returned to the camp, Nirajipant informed him, "The Mughal prince is asking for an audience with you. We can't tell for sure why he wants to meet."

After hearing the news, Sambhajiraje glanced at Prataprao to seek his advice. Prataprao frowned, but still he said, "When in water, obey the fish. Dhakale Raje should go and visit the prince."

Accompanied by Prataprao, Nirajipant, Ravaji Somnath, Sambhajiraje went to the imperial palace with his retinue, to meet the prince.

The Prince's Wazir received Sambhajiraje and ushered him respectfully to the meeting hall.

"Welcome!" said the handsome prince, Shah Alam. With a broad smile on his face, he rose from his seat and ushered Sambhajiraje to a seat by his side. His loyal sardars had folded their hands and stood aside courteously.

Prataparao and the Maratha sardars stood at a distance from where they could easily keep an eye on Sambhajiraje. After having a general conversation, the prince broached the subject he had on his mind. "Have you ever gone hunting Shambhooraje?"

"No." Sambhajiraje responded calmly.

"Really?! It is rare to meet a prince who doesn't fancy hunting!" The prince raised his shapely eyebrows.

"If I ask Maharaj Saheb, he will allow me to go hunting."

"Then, come and join us today on our hunting expedition. We are going to the forests of Ramtek."

"Sorry, but I won't be able to come." Sambhajiraje said vigilantly.

"Why? Are you scared of going with me?" The prince provoked him. Sambhajiraje looked at Prataprao. Prataprao had not anticipated this. He didn't know what to advise Shambhooraje in this matter.

"I am not afraid. I will come with you on the hunting trip." Sambhajiraje held his head high and instantly responded to Prince Shah Alam.

"Wah! Great! I expected just such as response from you! Everything will be kept ready for you. Just bring your loyal people with you." The prince said, glancing at Prataprao.

The plan was to cross the city borders in the late afternoon. An attendant applied fragrant perfume on Sambhajiraje's hand, and a rose was offered to him. Sambhajiraje bade farewell to the prince and returned to his camp.

With the assistance of Prataprao, Sambhajiraje chose expert swordsmen, archers, spearmen and riders to join him on the hunting expedition. Anandrao, Prataprao, Niraji, Ravaji wielded their arms and mounted their horses. Sambhajiraje put on an iron armour and headgear under his Jiretop and got ready. As promised, he waited for the prince in his shamiana.

When he got the intimation from the prince, Sambhajiraje left the camp with his retinue. The prince mounted an elephant and sat in a canopied howdah. He had brought along another elephant with a howdah for Sambhajiraje.

A ladder was put up by the elephant's side. Armed Sambhajiraje climbed up the ladder and sat in the howdah. The mahout made the elephant stand up and brought it near the prince's elephant. Prataprao, Ravaji, Niraji, Anandrao and select soldiers surrounded Sambhajiraje's elephant. The prince raised his hand and greeted Sambhajiraje with a smile. Sambhajiraje reciprocated the gesture.

The sounds of musical instruments erupted at once. The hunting expedition with the entourage of elephants, horses, expert hunters, and the callers, left from the southern border of the city.

When they reached the forests of Ramtek, the elephants stopped. The horse riders, callers and hunters dispersed. Sambhajiraje's troops stood around his elephant.

When they reached the forests of Ramtek both elephants climbed up a big hill and stopped there. From here, the hunters were going to shoot their arrows. In front of the hill, there was a plateau.

Sitting in the howdah, the prince picked up a tall bow and an arrow. He stretched the bow string and checked its tension. His sardars brandished their bow-arrows and spears. Maratha spearmen followed them and brandished their spears; hunters wielded their bows and arrows.

The callers started hollering from all sides. Immense commotion ensued. Within moments flocks of frightened black, white and grey cows with their tails erect, rushed onto the plateau. Wild cows! The Maratha hunters were stunned to see the sight. The terrified, mooing cows dashed against each other in confusion, crashing their horns. The swift arrows and spears shot from the hill, pierced their bodies and many wild cows collapsed on the plateau, whimpering in pain. The wounded cows kept twitching and flailing their hooves in the air and finally lay dead.

As soon as Sambhajiraje saw the wild cows mooing in fright, in a flash, he stood up in his howdah. The bow and arrow slipped from his hands. His hand restlessly stroked the cowrie necklace around his neck, watching the carcasses of the wild cows dispersed on the plateau. For a moment, he closed his eyes tightly. The whimpering moos of the cows echoed in his ears.

"Sarlashkar..." he shouted, addressing Prataprao. Prataprao brough his horse close to the elephant.

"Tell the prince that I don't like this hunting game. I am leaving now." And he commanded his mahout, "Go back!" The mahout immediately made the elephant turn around.

Prataprao conveyed Shambhooraje's message to the prince.

The riders, hunters and spearmen surrounded Shambhooraje's elephant that was going back. Everyone was completely silent.

Not a single Maratha hunter had shot an arrow after seeing wild cows in front of them! Even in that situation, Sambhajiraje's eyes lit up with contentment. He asked Prataprao who was riding by his side, "Gujarkaka, if I really want to hunt, which animal should I hunt?"

"Ji Dhani, wild predators! Wild boars!" Prataprao replied, looking towards the howdah. The royal mahout controlling the elephant did not know that a lion of Maval was sitting on his elephant's back! Now he was also going to hunt, but only wild boars!'

Sambhajiraje left Ravaji Somnath and Pralhad Niraji as his representatives in Aurangabad and returned to Rajgad after successfully completing the task that Raje had assigned him.

At the same time, Raje entered an accord with Adil Shahi. The Bijapur durbar had agreed to pay Raje three lakh hons per year as tribute. Swaraj was now secured on two fronts – the Mughal and Adil Shahi sultanate.

The destitute people in Goa were fed up with their lives. The Portuguese there, were forcibly converting people to Christianity. Everyone who resisted conversion was burnt alive in the town square. The defenceless people, who had no saviour coming to their rescue, were desperately abandoning their ancestral lands and migrating to Karvar and coastal Konkan regions. Raje descended into the Konkan region with his army to crush the arrogance of the Deshmukhs and the Portuguese.

Jijau and Sambhajiraje sat in their private chamber. Keshav Pandit sat in front of them. In front of him, the holy book of Ramayana was placed on a wooden bookrest. Keshav Pandit was rhythmically reciting each page in his clear voice and expounded the meaning of the Sanskrit verses in the Prakrit language.

Just then, Gomajibaba entered the chamber. He bowed down and said, "Aausaheb, a young man from the village of Punal in the Kolhapur region has come here. He is from the clan of Kesarkars. His name is Jotyaji. Quite a skilled man. He wants to meet Aausaheb and appeal for employment."

"Bring him in." Jijau said calmly. A young, brawny Jotyaji came in and made an obeisance.

"Where are you from?" Jijau questioned him, observing him carefully.

"Ji, Punal." Jotyaji responded politely.

"Which weapons can you wield?"

"Patta, Bhala, Bothati, Gadaka – everything Sarkar."

"Where do your loyalties lie?"

Jotyaji hesitated for a moment. "Like those of a son to his mother!"

Jijau's face lit up with Jotyaji's reply, and Sambhajiraje was ecstatic to hear it.

"Gomaji, take him to the office of business and introduce him to Balaji. Get him employed in our service." Jijau instructed Gomaji.

Gomaji and Jotyaji made an obeisance and took a few steps back. As they were about to leave, Jijau stopped Jotyaji and said to him, "Punalkar, don't harbour any doubts in your mind because I asked you where your loyalties lie. It may be easy to win a kingdom, but it's quite difficult to find a loyal employee. This is what Ramayana teaches us."

In the presence of the ministers and Sambhajiraje, Raje called for an assembly. In this assembly, Sambhajiraje honourably offered clothing, coconut and a betel leaf to Prataprao, Niraji and Anandrao, who were going to the Varad, Khandesh region as his representatives. The three valiant Mavalas made an obeisance to Raje and Sambhajiraje.

Prataprao's Maratha contingent descended Rajgad. To bid farewell to them, the kettle drums at Pali Darwaja resounded. As he heard the drums Sambhajiraje felt, 'When am I going to lead my own contingent?'

Now, on Rajgad, in every place – the queens' apartments, the ministry, the eighteen workshops – Sambhajiraje was being regarded as the spitting image of Raje.

By now, Dharau and Yesubai had formed a strong loving bond. Yesubai called Dharau 'Mamisaheb' and treated her with due respect. Dharau called her 'Soonbai' and treated her like a daughter. Every morning and evening she conducted Yesubai to Jijau's chamber to pay respects.

Initially, Yesubai was bemused, but Jijau, Dharau, Putalabai and Raje's nurturing, affectionate behaviour helped her to settle down in the fort. Though in one place she continued to feel tongue-tied – in Soyarabai's chamber. Yesubai was not afraid of Aausaheb, Aabasaheb, not even her husband but she was in awe of Soyarabai! Due to her remarkably radiant, fair complexion, she seemed to Yesubai like a blazing sword shining in the sun!

As usual, in the evening, Dharau conducted Yesubai to Jijau's chamber to pay respects. The entire family had gathered there, to seek the blessings of Aausaheb. Sambhajiraje and all queens were present there too.

Raje had marched towards Mahad-Raigad. The lamp-lighter lit all lamps in the chamber. Jijau who had visited the sanctum to pray to Goddess Amba, entered with her maids. She was quite old now. The queens approached Jijau one by one and touched her feet. Jijau blessed them from her heart.

Sambhajiraje stepped forward and touched Jijau's feet.

"Shambhooraje, you should not follow this custom alone anymore! Yesu, come forward and join your husband!" Jijau glanced at Dharau with a smile and called Yesubai.

Yesubai came forward with Dharau and stood on Sambhajiraje's left. Both touched Jijau's feet together.

A smile flashed on Jijau's face. With a contented heart she said, "May you both live long!"

Jijau pulled up Yesubai's chin and looked at her silently. And, for the first time she realized, 'My granddaughter-in-law's eyes are like that of Goddess Jagadamba! Beady, and far-sighted!'

One by one, all family members left Jijau's chamber. But Soyarabai lingered behind with her maid, Chandra. As Yesubai was leaving the chamber, she approached her and gently said to her, "Could you please come to my chamber?"

Yesubai nodded in affirmation and started walking courteously behind Soyarabai. Dharau frowned and followed her 'daughter'.

Putalabai saw Yesubai walking behind Soyarabai, and felt, 'I should join Soonbai…' but when she saw Dharau with Yesubai, she relaxed.

As soon as they entered Soyarabai's chamber, she gestured Yesubai to take a seat on the bed and signalled Chandra with her eyes.

Chandra went inside and brought a decorative wooden casket with her. She handed the casket to Soyarabai Saheb.

Soyarabai took the casket and approached Yesubai. She

opened the casket, held it in front of Yesubai and said, "These are my personal ornaments. I have received them from my parents. Place your hand on the one you want." The casket had armlets, pearl necklaces, anklets, Rajput style Bindis and other ornaments in it. Soyarabai's parental family, the Mohite family, was originally from Rajputana. As she was a Rajput, her complexion was quite fair. She had a penchant for ornaments and her feet were decorated with designs of red dye.

Yesubai was bewildered and simply kept gazing at her. Then, unwittingly, her head turned towards Dharau, to ask her 'What should I do?'

Soyarabai noticed it and said to Dharau, "Dharabai, tell Soonbai to choose an ornament. She is feeling shy."

"Yes, Soonbai, feel free to choose. Consider this chamber as your own." Dharau told Yesubai. Yesubai examined the ornaments in the container and placed her hand on a necklace with a typical Konkani design.

Soyarabai laughed to see that. Her laugh had maybe a tinge of adoration in it or a hint of something else that was beyond one's comprehension.

Soyarabai instantly picked up the necklace and handed the casket to Chandra. With her own hands she put the necklace around Yesubai's neck. Then she leaned forward and fastened it properly around Yesubai's neck.

Thereafter, for quite some time, Soyarabai kept talking about Raje, Aausaheb and her parental home. Yesubai and Dharau listened to her quietly.

"Soonbai, I am the only one speaking here. You are not talking at all!" Suddenly Soyrabai stopped talking and changed the subject. Yesuabai raised her head and simply looked at her but did not say anything.

"So silly of me! I didn't realize that you feel shy! You speak the Shringarpuri tongue of Konkan, the country dialect! You are not yet used to the sophisticated language that is used at the fort. That is why you feel shy. But don't be so shy, feel free to speak." Soyarabai sugar-coated what she wanted to convey to Yesubai.

After hearing her words Yesuabai realized a flaw in herself that she had not even consedered. And, in that moment, she decided – 'I must listen to the official language spoken at the fort attentively and get accustomed to it!'

Dharau quickly realized that Soyarabai might continue with her jibes. She also noticed the change in Yesubai's facial expressions and promptly said, "Don't you have to break your fast? Let's go, Soonbai!"

Yesuabai got up after listening to Dharau's words. "Let me take your leave." She said and touched Soyarabai's feet. As she was leaving the chamber, Soyarabai looked at her and saw the orange tuft of the necklace resting on her back and laughed again. Just like before! She was amused by Yesubai's choice. 'There are so many exclusive Rajput ornaments, pearl and diamond necklaces but still Yesubai chose a necklace from Konkan!'

Dharau thought of turning back and telling her, 'Ranisarkar, the tender bond of affection between two people is much stronger than the language they speak.' But she did not say anything. She looked at the tuft resting on Yesubai's back and muttered, "She should have at least put haldi-kumkum on the necklace before putting it on Soonbai!"

Yesubai heard gunshots fired in succession, coming from the ground in front of the courtyard of the Balekilla. She went to the window of her chamber to see what was happening. Dharau walked gingerly and stood behind her. It was late afternoon. Both saw a body of a stuffed wild animal in the field. It was in a running stance and was fixed on a wheeled wooden stump. A long rope was tied to the rear hooves of the wild animal.

Sambhajiraje had knelt and taken a stance at a distance from the stuffed animal. Gomajibaba, Jotyaji, Mohammed Sais, and Balaji stood around him.

Mohammed Sais loaded some gunpowder and shot in the barrel of the rifle. Then, with his fingers he stuffed some wads through the barrel.

Gomajibaba pushed a ramrod in the barrel and secured the charge of the gun. Then he checked the balance of the rifle with both his hands and handed it to Sambhajiraje.

Sambhajiraje secured the rifle stock against his right shoulder and touched his cheek to the stock. He closed one eye and looking through the eyepiece, he took the shooting stance.

Jotyaji held a scarf in his hand. He made sure that Dhakale Raje has taken a proper stance and was ready to fire a shot. Then, he held the scarf high and dropped it to give the signal.

As soon as the scarf fell, the attendants on the ground pulled the wooden stump and kept it wheeling. The stuffed animal began 'running.' Sambhajiraje moved the barrel of his rifle swiftly, along with the moving animal and fired a shot. The rifle recoiled, and his shoulder jerked with the backword movement. Wisps of smoke rose near his ear. There, as the shot pierced through the stuffed animal, the rice straws were flung all over the ground.

Jotyaji kept dropping the scarf as a cue, and the shots kept tearing off the moving stuffed animal. After firing shots for a while, Sambhajiraje's shoulder throbbed with pain. The sun was about to set.

Everyone heard the kettle drums resounding at the Pali Darwaja. The peals of the horn mingled with it. Sambhajiraje broke his stance, stood up straight holding the rifle in his hands, and he glanced at Balaji Chitnis standing next to him.

Raje, who had marched upon the Janjira fort of Siddi Fatteh Khan in Dandarajpuri, was ascending the fort with the army. Sambhajiraje handed the rifle to Mohammed Sais and began walking towards Jijau's chamber. By now, he knew that whenever Maharaj Saheb returned from a campaign, he directly went to Masaheb's chamber to seek her blessings.

In her chamber, Sambhajiraje and Jijau kept waiting for Raje. The night fell. The lamps and torches were lit, but still Raje did not come. There was no intimation either from his chamber. Jijau became restless. She came to Raje's chamber with Sambhajireaje. Raje sat bare headed, his hair dishevelled, and his face looked weary. He touched Jijau's feet, put his hand over Sambhajiraje's shoulder, and pulled him close. With that touch, the throbbing pain in Sambhajiraje's shoulder returned. A wave of pain shot from his shoulder and spread all over his body.

"What happened, Raje? I waited for you for a long time, and finally came to see you myself." Jijau gazed at Raje.

"I had to concede defeat against the Siddis of Janjira. I was about to acquire it but lost the opportunity. Siddi Fatteh Khan had consented to surrender the sea fort to us. But his own sardars, Siddi Sambool, Kasam and Khairat Khan shackled him in chains and incarcerated him. Our plan failed." Raje paused while speaking.

"Is that why you avoided meeting me today? Raje, who hasn't faced failures? Even the gods could not escape failures."

Raje was startled to hear Jijau's words, he raised his head and read Jijau's eyes like he was reading a letter.

"So, Masaheb has already heard about all that, it seems!" Raje said in a hoarse voice.

"What are you talking about?" Jijau sensed the pain on Raje's face.

"About the gods?" Raje's voice got heavy.

"Tell me Raje. What happened?" Jijau stood behind him along with Sambhajiraje.

"Masaheb, my kingship is futile. I am ashamed to call myself your son. The terrible news that I heard when I had besieged

Janjira, has filled me with anxiety. I fear that our dream of swaraj might sink in a dark abyss. I cannot dare to share the news with you." Raje paused

"Raje," Jijau put her hand on Raje's back.

"Tell me, what news did you hear in Rajpuri?" Jijau gently nudged Raje to open up.

"Masaheb...Masaheb, Aurangzeb has waged war against all Hindus in the north. Holy temples of Hindus are being desecrated. The imperial army is wreaking havoc in the temples. The Mughal army demolished the Kashi Vishweshwar temple and raised a masjid in its place. The gods may take defeat in their stride, but human beings cannot bear the desecration of their deities. I am utterly ashamed to even face you." Raje's eyes welled up.

What Sambhajiraje heard from Raje's mouth, stopped the throbbing pain in his shoulder! It moved from his shoulder to his heart.

Chitnis Balaji Aavaji came hurriedly and delivered some news to Raje, "Swami, Prataprao and Ravaji have returned with the army from the Mughal territory, without any intimation! They are ascending the fort right now."

Raje was performing his daily puja in the sanctum. When he heard the news, he got up from his seat. He looked at Prabhakarbhat and Keshav Pandit and said, 'Jagadamb'.

Jotyaji Kesarkar reported the same news to Jijau in her chamber. Jijau was in the middle of a discussion about the decorative frame of flowers needed for Soyarabai's baby shower ceremony.

As soon as she heard the news, she stopped the discussion and left her chamber. Soyarabai's maid, Chandra had come to Jijau's chamber to check the materials needed for the frame of flowers. She waited till Jijau left the chamber. Then, she promptly came to Soyarabai's chamber, but seeing Dharau and

Sambhajiraje in the chamber, she hesitated.

Soyarabai lay on her bed. She momentarily gazed at the dome of the Kaleshwari temple that was visible from a window.

Sambhajiraje, who was sitting on the side of her bed, was lost in thought. For quite a few days, he had been noticing a change in Masaheb's behaviour and attitude.

During her pregnancy, Soyarabai had been treating Sambhajiraje with an inexplicable affection. In Sambhajiraje, she was picturing Raje whom she could not see frequently. Her heart was trying to capture something from Sambhajiraje's vivacious presence.

Soyarabai saw Chandra coming in and asked her, "Come Chandra, for whom did the kettle drums beat at the break of the day today?"

Chandra looked at Sambhajiraje and kept mum.

"Feel free to speak. He is my own!" Soyarabai said with a smile.

Baffled Chandra blurted out, "Sarlashkar has come back from the Mughal territory!" Sambhajiraje heard Chandra's words and got up from the bedside.

"Please let me take your leave Masaheb. Farewell."

"Okay." Soyarabai raised her hand, lying in bed.

Sambhajiraje came to the royal court. Prataprao and Ravaji stood in front of Raje and Jijau. As they saw Sambhajiraje coming towards them, both made an obeisance to him. A few moments passed. Then, Prataprao began recounting the developments in the Mughal territory to Raje.

".... We moved the entire camp in one night. Ravaji was in the Varad region. I sent him a message to withdraw his troops and return to our kingdom as quickly as possible. Dhani, the emperor had devised a very diabolical plan. Our entire army was going to be captured. But the prince came to our rescue. He sent his Wazir to inform us about leaving the camp during the night. Otherwise..." Prataprao paused.

Aurangzeb had dispatched a decree to Shah Alam in Aurangabad to incarcerate the Marathi forces. Prince Shah Alam who had got an inkling of that, had himself warned Prataprao before the decree fell into his hands.

After hearing Prataprao's report, Raje kept gazing at Sambhajiraje, who was sitting next to him. He let out a deep sigh with only one thought in mind – 'Be it a firman, a visit, or anything else, Sambhajiraje will never go to the Mughal camp again! I will not send him there!'

"Soyarabai Saheb, the majestic and noble eldest queen of Shriman Shivajiraje

Bhosale, was blessed with a son!"

Riders galloped in all directions to deliver the auspicious news of a son's birth. Sweetmeats were distributed over all the forts. The kettle drums resounded, and cannons boomed.

Raje's extended family had gathered in front of Soyarabai's chamber in the royal palace, to see the baby for the first time. Sambhajiraje was also among them. Yesubai stood with Dharau. The priest had fixed an auspicious time for everyone to see the baby.

Raje came and joined his family members who had assembled.

The time-indicating vessel in the big water containers sank in the water. The door of the chamber creaked. The entire Bhosale clan led by Jijau entered the chamber.

The midwife picked up the baby wrapped in a blanket, from Soyarabai's side. She smiled and held the baby in front of Jijau. Jijau waved a pouch of coins around the baby. She tenderly picked up the baby and held him in her hands. She looked at him affectionately and as she handed him to Raje she said, "He looks like his mother, but...but I heard that he was born face down! ..." Jijau's voice trembled.

Raje raised his eyebrows and gazing at the beautiful baby in his arms he exclaimed, "Masaheb, don't worry. As he was born face down, he will make the Mughal empire fall on its face!" Sambhajiraje liked Raje's words from the bottom of his heart.

"Here, you hold him." Raje held the baby in front of Sambhajiraje. Sambhajiraje waved a pouch of coins over the baby.

He tenderly held the baby and kept gazing at it, as if he was gazing at the statues in the Verul caves. It seemed as if Soyarabai had plucked out the moon from the skies and brought him to the earth.

As he looked at Balraje, Sambhajiraje felt, 'Surely...he will make the Mughal empire fall on its face.'

As a strategy, Raje started keeping Sambhajiraje with him round the clock. He started training Sambahjiraje in administrative matters such as stamping and sealing an official letter, handling a legal case, reaching a vigilant verdict by consulting the ministers, honouring soldiers for their feats, reinvigorating the ryots be reassuring them, extracting information from a foreign envoy and forming an alliance with an opponent by treating him respectfully.

Now, Sambhajiraje was getting acquainted with the ministers who handled administrative duties. Among them were Chitnis, Balaji Aavaji, Peshwe, Moropant Pingale, Surnis, Annaji Dutto, and Mujumdar, Nilo Sonadeo.

All these men treated Sambhajiraje with due respect. He would have touched their feet and sought their blessings if needed. All these men were Raje's trustworthy associates. They had earned their status due to their calibre, honesty, and loyalty.

All the ministers and administrative officers had witnessed the events of the Purandar treaty and Sambhajiraje's stay in the enemy camp as a hostage, the capture in Agra and the clever escape from there, Sambhajiraje's visit to Shah Alam in Aurangabad, Raje and Jijau Saheb's genuine affection for him.

That is why, all the ministers and administrative officers were well aware that 'Sambhajiraje is the successor of the expanding Swaraj. Sambhajiraje is the scion who is going to oversee the future Maratha kingdom!'

The cannons on the fort boomed in welcome. The kettle drums and horns resounded intensely. After looting Surat again, after completely crushing the army of Mughal sardar Ikhlas and Daud Khan Qureshi in the woods of Vani-Dindori, and raiding the affluent trading market, 'in the Varad region, after prevailing in the open combat of Salheri, and marauding the Mughal territories of Baglan, Varhad and Khandesh, triumphant Raje had returned. The horses were drained after carrying the heavy sacks full of booty. This was a feat much greater than the previous one.

Raje ascended the fort with Prataprao Silimkar, custodian Subhanji Balaji, Annaji, and Nilopant who had descended Fort Rajgad to receive him with a palanquin, along with Rupaji, Prataprao Gujar, Moropant and Yesaji, who had accompanied him on the campaign.

A fortnight passed since Raje had arrived on Rajgad. The booty was assorted and was organized accordingly. The physicians took custody of the wounded soldiers and horses and treated them.

The eleventh day of the bright fortnight of Magha dawned on the Maval region. An honour assembly was organized on Rajgad. A durbar was arranged to honour the war heroes.

Raje, Jijau Saheb and Sambhajiraje took their seats in the royal hall. Moropant, Annaji, Balaji, Yesaji, Prataprao, Nilopant, Niraji, Ravaji, Raghunathbhat, and Duttaji Trimal stood around them courteously.

Soyarabai, Putalabai, Kashibai and other queens, Raje's daughters, Sakhoobai, Ambabai and others, and Yesubai, and Dharau had assembled in the royal ladies' section.

As per custom, Raje tossed haldi in the air. Then he glanced at the soldiers to be honoured, with pride and signalled Chitnis Balaji Aavaji.

Balaji commenced the honour assembly for the war heroes, "By the blessings of Matushri Aausaheb, Sarkar Swami organized a campaign in the faraway Mughal regions of Baglan, Varhad, Khandesh and Surat. He took a limited number of infantry and cavalry with him and carried out the campaign successfully.

"Today's assembly has been called to award the soldiers who displayed valour during this campaign, the ones who got injured while fighting, and the heirs of the ones who gave their lives.

To honour in this assembly, I call upon..."

Balaji announced the names of the recipients one by one. Raje offered bracelets, coins, robes of honour, and so on to the recipients.

The honour assembly in appreciation of the war heroes ended. Balaji bowed and took a few steps back.

Raje glanced at Jijau. A fleeting smile lingered on Jijau's face and blended with the wrinkles on her face.

Raje rose from his seat and began addressing the durbar – "The honour assembly for the war heroes is over. I personally have to share something with all of you." Raje took a pause. He glanced at Sambhajiraje once and resumed his speech, "Rajput Mirza Raja came from the north, presented robes of honour and an elephant to my son Sambhajiraje and awarded him a Mansab.

In Agra, the Mughal Emperor Aurangzeb gifted him a gem-studded dagger. Prince Shah Alam offered him an elephant and robes of honour in Aurangabad.

Only I could not give him anything or do anything for him till today. That is why I am going to express my thoughts in front of Masaheb and all of you.

Today, I am going to assign independent responsibility to my son Sambhajiraje! I hereby bestow upon him the royal seal and dagger with robes of honour. Raje paused and signalled his personal secretary.

"From today onwards, Sambhajiraje will seal the official documents with his own name and endorse firmans, verdicts, treaties and documents with his own signature.

I appoint Mahadeo Yamaji as his personal secretary and clerical secretary Parashuram as his Chitnis. The office assistant Dhararao Nimbalkar should assist him in every way he can. From today, Sambhajiraje has assumed independent office!"

Raje's personal secretary held in front of him the platter containing the official seal, dagger, apparel and a sheathed sword. Raje picked up the sword from the platter and told Sambhajiraje, "Come in front of the assembly".

Sambhajiraje rose and approached Raje courteously. Yesubai watched from behind the curtain of the royal ladies' section. She saw Raje tying the saffron cords of the sword around Sambhajiraje's waist.

Raje placed the apparel on Sambhajiraje's shoulder.

Sambhajiraje made an obeisance to him and Jijau.

Raje held Sambhajiraje's arm in one hand and with the other he assisted Jijau to get up from her seat. Sambhajiraje started walking between them.

But Soyarabai, who sat in the royal ladies' section got up immediately. She did not bother looking at the other queens and said to her maid Chandra who stood behind her, "Chandra, let's go. Balraje is alone in my chamber!"

And without even checking whether Chandra was following her, she started walking briskly towards her chamber.

Aabajipant, the head of the construction department, sent a message from Raigad – "The fort has been constructed exactly as per your plan. I would like to request your presence to examine the construction built in stone. Please let me know if you find any flaws. I am always at your service."

Raje went to Raigad with Sambhajiraje and select men. The

craftsmen had done their job for beyond Raje's expectations. As if the sculptors of heaven had gently descended on the summit of the fort, drawn a captivating rangoli with assorted boulders, and vanished in the starlit night!

After watching the splendidly constructed fort, Raje returned to Rajgad with a contented heart. He consulted the royal astrologer and family priest, Prabhakarbhat to fix an auspicious moment to shift to Raigad. The news spread across Gunjanmaval. The simple, unpretentious ryots thronged Rajgad in flocks to see the Bhosale family in person. The people on the fort got emotional.

First, the treasury was moved in the custody of armed soldiers.

The Mavalas carried over their heads, packs of official documents from the fort's Daftar Khana to the foothills.

The maids on the fort packed the royal costumes from the Asababkhana.

Bundles of weapons such as spears, swords, daggers and shields from the armoury were loaded onto the horses. The muzzles of the weighty cannons were loaded on the backs of the elephants.

The day of departure broke. Sambhajiraje took a bath for the last time in the Hammam Khana here. He felt as if the bath water was washing out a lot with it.

He got dressed in the royal attire and came to Jijau's chamber to seek her blessings.

In Jijau's chamber, a sobbing Dharau was saying to her, "Masaheb, let me go to Kapurhol now. How can I come with you? I could stay here because it is closer to my village. Whenever needed, I could easily visit my village from here. Who knows how far away the other fort is?"

Jijau was not ready to let go of Dharau. She was trying her best to convince Dharau to stay back. Dharau could hear her words, but they were only entered her ears, and did not reach her heart. Finally, Sambhajiraje came forward and said only one thing to Dharau, "I will also come to Kapurhol with you!"

His words left Dharau stunned. "Oh, my dear child! I will come anywhere you tell me to! You mean the world to me, my child!" Dharau said and finally she agreed to go to Raigad with all of them.

Jijau was going towards the royal hall with Sambhajiraje. Raje also joined them from his chamber.

The Bhosale trio came to the royal hall. The courtyard was thronged with people. Though it was crowded, there was no sound at all, only a grave silence prevailed.

Raje, Jijau and Sambhajiraje took their seats and offered alms for the last time on this fort.

After the session in the royal hall concluded, an intimation was sent to the royal ladies. All the women in Raje's family wrapped shawls around themselves and left the queens' apartments. The royal family members sat in the palanquins kept ready for them. The palanquins started descending the fort.

Jijau sat in her palanquin at the very end. Her heart was heavy like the overcast skies. She did not show the pain on her face and just whispered – "Jagadamb, Jagadamb." Her palanquin began going down the fort. Dharau, who was walking with Jijau's palanquin, picked up a pinch of sand and tied it in a knot of her sari.

Raje and Sambhajiraje left towards the tunnel leading out to Sanjivani machi, with the ministers and the custodian of the fort, Subhanji Silimkar. He had been recently appointed as the custodian of the fort in place of Sidoji Thopate.

Raje stopped as he saw the edge of the Suvela machi in front of him, at a distance. No one understood why he stopped there. It was on this machi that Saibai's funeral pyre had been ignited. The memory brought tears to Raje's eyes, he put his hand on Sambhajiraje's shoulder.

The father and son arrived on Sanjivani machi. The entire

machi was packed with people. Sidoji Thopate had ensured that the palanquins were ready to descend the fort.

Raje and Sambhajiraje approached the flagstaff on the machi. They raised their heads and glanced at the Jaripataka flag.

Raje said to Sidoji Thopate, "Sidoji, I am not taking the palanquin today to descend the fort. I will walk down with everyone."

"Ji." Sidoji nodded in affirmation.

Raje and Sambhajiraje visited the temple and started walking towards the Pali Darwaja. The people on the fort followed Raje, like tiny fish getting pulled along by a whale.

They arrived at the Pali Darwaja. In the Nagar Khana near the Pali Darwaja, the kettle drums began resounding to bid farewell. Raje and Sambhajiraje heard the kettle drums while standing at the threshold of the Pali Darwaja. The rhythm of the sticks beating the drums was not in tune as usual! It was going offbeat occasionally. As soon as Raje crossed the Pali Darwaja, the drummers put their sticks down and followed them.

Surrounded by the Mavalas, Raje and Sambhajiraje came to the foothills of Rajgad. Raje handed a coconut and a betel leaf to Subhanji. He gazed at the fort and said, "Subhanji, take care of the fort like a gardener takes care of the garden. Farewell." Raje removed his pearl necklace and placed it in Subhanji's hands.

Subhanji put his head on Raje's feet and started sobbing like a child. Raje pulled him up, embraced him and said, "Subhanji, get hold of yourself. One must let go of everything one loves, someday."

Not when Raje marched on Surat, not when Raje went to meet Mirza-Afzal, or when Raje left for Agra, but today –people got emotional! They started crying. They rushed to touch Raje's feet.

Prataprao had saddled two white horses and kept them ready. Raje and Sambhjiraje approached the horses. Raje assisted Sambhajiraje to mount, and then mounted himself.

Finally, he was leaving! The imperial ascetic and the Balbhutya set forth from Rajgad, leaving behind footprints of many memories!

Raigad came into view. Aabajipant had built a grand palace for Jijau in the village of Pachad at the foothills.

Before moving to Raigad on an auspicious mahurat, the entire royal family stayed in the palace of Pachad. Pachad was a military station. It had a marketplace to supply provisions to the fort.

The next day dawned. From the courtyard of the palace, Raigad was visible, like a lotus rising out of a lake. Jijau narrowed her eyes and gazed at Raigad; it was calling out to her. While she was engaged in watching the fort, the edge of her sari wrapped over her head had receded. Raje noticed a white strand of her hair that peeked out.

"Masaheb, in front of us is the 'Khoobladha' Buruj!' Directly above it is the western machi." Raje pointed with his forefinger.

Sambhajiraje, who stood close by, watched the bastion wall and the machi.

"Raje, why did you build an independent palace for me?" Jijau said, gazing in front.

Raje became solemn. His voice became heavy as he watched her bare head. "Masaheb, what can I do for you? No matter what I do, I will always feel that more should be done. You never told me, but I have heard you coughing hard due to your asthma. Masaheb, the cold weather on the fort won't suit you. That is why I have built this palace." Raje paused.

Sambhajiraje kept gazing at Raje.

"Masaheb, didn't you realize why I showed you the bastion wall and the machi in front of us?" Raje pointed his finger to the bastion wall again and asked.

"Why? Anything special about it?" Jijau glanced at the sandalwood stripes on Raje's forehead.

"Masaheb, you will be living in this palace, and I have to live at the fort. I can't even partake a sip of water without taking your blessings. Therefore, I instructed Indalkar to construct the palace at an angle. By standing on the machi above the 'Khoobladha' Buruj I will be able to at least see your silhouette in this courtyard from a distance! The world sees the sun rise in the east; I will see it rise in the west!"

Raje kept gazing at the machi intently. Jijau kept gazing at Raje, with moist eyes.

At the fixed mahurat, the palanquins left the palace of Pachad. In the cool morning breeze, the palanquin-bearers started climbing the fort.

On their way up, they reached a flower garden hidden among thickets. After viewing the garden, the retinue resumed their ascent. The first phase of the ascent was over, and the second began.

The granaries passed by; the stone threshold of the first post passed by. The 'Maha Darwaja' came into view. It felt as if 'Raigad' was welcoming them with open arms.

Raje performed a puja of the 'Maha Darwaja'. This gate adjoined lofty bastion walls with engraved designs on both sides. The Nagar Khana was located on the upper deck.

As the Bhosale family crossed the gate, the kettle drums resounded for the first time! Golden coins were showered over Raje, Jijau and Sambhajiraje.

Now, the steep ascent of the fort began. Raje and Sambhajiraje got out of their palanquins and started walking on either side of Jijau's palanquin. The Hatti reservoir passed by; lofty five-level towers came into view.

The retinue arrived at the main gate of the Balekilla.

Raje performed the puja of the gate of Balekilla and showered coins over it. Then Raje and Sambhajiraje stood on either side of Jijau, and crossed the stone threshold of the main gate of Balekilla.

As they entered through the Palakhi Darwaja, they saw seven adjoining palaces built in stone, in front of them.

Sambhajiraje observed the seven palaces and asked Raje, "Who are these palaces for?"

"These palaces are for the queens and the royal ladies, Sambhajiraje." Raje's voice got heavy as he responded. He remembered Saibai. There were seven palaces. There should have been an 'eighth' or rather the 'first' palace here – for Saibai! But it was not there, it couldn't be there. Still, it was there! In Raje's heart, in the form of her memories! No one else could ever see it.

Raje viewed the 'royal palace' which had been built for Jijau. Raje and Sambhajiraje, and came to the royal court where the royal throne was located. This was the place for the royal durbar. From the royal throne to the grand Nagar Khana in front of it, there was a broad path covered with carpets. In the middle of this path, there was a pond with an elegant water fountain. Everyone viewed the magnificent throne intently.

Raje, Sambhajiraje and Jijau viewed the magnificent design of the lofty Nagar Khana and came to the open courtyard in front of the durbar.

A palanquin was arranged for Jijau. Moropant, Annaji, Balaji, Duttaji, Prataprao, Indalkar, Aabajipant, Mudhoji Sarakawas, Changoji Katkar, Raje and Sambhajiraje

surrounded the palanquin. All queens, Yesubai, Dharau and other women followed the palanquin. Jijau left to visit the temple of Lord Jagadishwar!

The marketplace came into sight. On both sides of the road, shops were built in a row, with a raised platform to make shopping easier for the riders astride their horses. The market was not yet inhabited. Nagappa Shetti had come to the fort to seek Raje's sanction to make the marketplace operational. He showered Jijau's palanquin with gold coins and sought her blessings.

The golden dome of the Jagadishwar temple, glistening in the sun, came into sight. Jijau's palanquin stopped in front of the temple.

Raje assisted Jijau out of the palanquin. Raje and Sambhajiraje stood on both sides of Jijau.

The three of them leaned forward and touched the first step of the temple and entered the first square of the temple. The queens and the royal ladies, and the ministers followed them.

Raje stepped forward, viewing the Shivlinga, half-covered with flowers, getting drenched in the water streaming from the vessel of Abhishek, in the dim light of the lamps in the inner sanctum.

After visiting the Jagadishwar temple, Lake Kushavarta, and Shirkai temple, Raje climbed up the stairs to the Nagar Khana with Sambhajiraje.

It was the summit of Raigad! The sound of the saffron Jaripataka pennant fluttering on the flagstaff was clearly audible to everyone.

"That is Fort Torana..." Raje faced the east and pointed towards it. "That is Rajgad there."

"Ji." Sambhajiraje responded.

Raje started showing Sambhajiraje the forts merged in the black mountain range of Sahyadri.

"That's Songad, that's Chambhargad, there's Ghosala, here's Lingana, this is 'Kangora', this one's 'Kokandiva', that's 'Talegad'. Shambhooraje, this Raigad is the greatest Bhutya of Goddess Jagadamba. He has donned the cowrie garland of all these surrounding forts around his neck." Raje touched his fingers to his chest to honour the Bhutya with respect.

On an auspicious mahurat, as per the wishes of Raje, an Abhishek was done by Jijau on the idol of Lord Jagdishwara.

Within a month, the administrative offices on Raigad started operating. Raigad was now inhabited.

The cold weather on the fort triggered Jijau's asthma. On Raje's advice, she left the fort and went to live in the palace at Pachad. Putalabai accompanied her to look after her. Raje summoned Gangadharpant, the expert physician of Mahad.

Raje gave strict instructions to the chief custodian of the palace in Pachad, "Install a big bell at the front porch of the palace and appoint an attendant for it. Every day, after finishing her morning rituals, Aausaheb will come to the courtyard to worship the Tulsi plant. At that time, the attendant should keep tolling the bell continuously. On that signal, Prince Sambhajiraje and I will come to the western machi. Though from a very long distance, we will at least get a chance to view Masaheb. This should be done daily, without fail!"

One day, Raje came to the western machi with Sambhajiraje. The tolling of the bell from the palace of Pachad travelled on the wind and reached the machi. It was late morning. Raje and Sambhajiraje stood on the stone-built bastion walls, gazing intently in the direction of the courtyard in Pachad.

Like a thin white line, Jijau appeared in the courtyard, at a faraway distance. As both saw her, they bowed down to her. The white line stood straight in the courtyard. The father and son had already touched the feet of the line in their heart.

Ganoji Shirke came to bid farewell to Sambhajiraje. Sambhajiraje embraced him. While doing it, he felt deep down in his heart that, during his stay for the last fifteen days here, Ganoji did not speak freely with Aabasaheb, with his sister, or even with me. He barely speaks a word, and then keeps staring at the golden bracelets that Aabasaheb and I wear.

Pilaji went back with his son and daughter-in-law.

Sambhajiraje's daily routine began. One morning, on an open

ground, he was practising the Dasharang move on an iron Mallakhamb.

The iron Mallakhamb got drenched in the sweat dripping from Sambhajiraje's body. He could not get a firm grip on it, and like an arrow, he came sliding down from the top of the Mallakhamb. As he came closer to the ground, he skilfully jumped into a standing stance, in front of Gomaji. He was perspiring profusely, but still smiling!

Gomaji promptly came forward and wrapped a shawl around Sambhajiraje. "Dhakale Dhani, one should not expose one's sweaty body to the cold wind, after such heavy exercise." Gomaji said.

After the practice, Sambhajiraje got dressed, drank the milk that Dharau gave him, and came to the royal hall. Raje had already marched towards Mahad. Balaji Chitnis saw Yuvaraj and rose from his seat courteously. Annaji, who was standing there, promptly made an obeisance.

A few peasants and the chief revenue collector of a village from the foothills were present in the royal hall.

"Who are these people?" Sambhajiraje took his seat and asked Balaji.

"They are hunters from the village at the foothills. The revenue collector has a complaint against them." Balaji replied while standing.

"What complaint?" Sambhajiraje asked while looking at the revenue collector.

Everyone kept quiet.

"Why are all of you so quiet? Am I not mature enough to deal with his complaint?"

"No Yuvaraj, it's not like that! But this case is a bit complicated. I will deal with it myself." Annaji, who had been reticent so far, said politely.

"As you wish!" Sambhajiraje said with a smile.

But the hunters got anxious. Their leader, Gunjote, made

an obeisance and said, "Sarkar is not present on the fort, so Dhakale Dhani, you should hear out our case."

"What case? What happened? Don't be afraid, tell me everything freely!" Sambhajiraje assured Gunjote.

"Dhani, they have committed an offence. I am the one who you should listen to and not them." The revenue collector said cautiously.

"What offence?" Sambhajiraje stared at the revenue collector.

"They went into the forest near the village and hunted many animals. But they did not hand me my lawful share! They fled the forest secretly to avoid paying charges for hunting in the forest." The revenue collector presented the case. It was amusing. The hunters had not paid their share to the revenue collector after hunting!

"Annajipant, what is the law regarding hunting?" Sambhajiraje asked.

"The revenue collector is right, Yuvaraj. He has been granted the rights to collect revenue, by the administrative office. Gunjote and his hunters are the culprits." Annaji stated the law.

"What is the punishment for this offence?" Sambhajiraje remembered the hunting expedition in Aurangabad.

"Penalty! The hunters should deposit the penalty in the administrative office. The collector will be remunerated his share from that amount. For every animal the hunters have killed, they should pay a penalty of four Shivrai coins!"

The hunters got anxious when they heard about the penalty. The revenue collector's face lit up.

"Do you ever go hunting?" Sambhajiraje asked an unexpected question to the revenue collector.

"Ji. I do!"

"Then do you pay the revenue on that to the Subedar of the village?"

"No Dhani." The revenue collector's voice dropped.

"As a hunter, you must be knowing that the kind of animal that a hunter might encounter can't be anticipated. In this risky game, if a hunter encounters a deadly beast like a tiger and gets wounded, do you ever investigate the matter?"

"No Dhani." The revenue collector was perplexed.

"If a hunter kills a tiger, do you give him a pat of approval on his back or only demand your share in it?"

"...." The revenue collector had no answer to that question.

"Yuvaraj, this law does not apply in case of deadly beasts like the tiger." Annaji tried to defend the revenue collector by stating the law politely.

"Exactly my point, Annajipant. Such laws should not be applied rigorously in cases of hunting. If a hunter gets attacked by a deadly beast, this officer will stay at home and do nothing about it, but if a beast is killed for food, then he won't fail to ask for his share! I – These hunters will not be charged any penalty!"

"But – but Yuvaraj, as per the law..."

"Annaji, there will be no penalty! This is an order!" Sambhajiraje's voice became sharp, and his neck straightened.

"Ji." Annaji promptly bowed down.

Sambhajiraje addressed the revenue collector, "Khot, remember that a true hunter never consumes the game received as a share. Gunjote, don't forget that a true hunter never flees the forest secretly, without sharing the game with those who know about the hunting expedition."

He turned to Annajipant and said, "I commanded you, but please don't take it to heart and forgive me. I have witnessed first-hand how wild cows were hunted in the forest of Aurangabad. None of us had the authority to punish those hunters! At that time, I felt very proud of my hunters who did not raise their weapons when they saw wild cows!"

Sambhajiraje said to the revenue collector "Khot, I will come in person for a hunting expedition in your forest! To hunt the wild boars! Join me at that time. Carry the whole carcass to the village. You can eat the meat and share it with the villagers too!"

"Jagadamb – Jagadamb!" Sambhajiraje uttered just like Raje. He rose from his seat, caressing the cowrie necklace on his chest and walked towards the inner apartments to prepare for the visit to the Jagadishwar temple. Everyone bowed down to him. Annajipant had tightly squeezed the edge of his shawl. He was dazzled by the display of nobility on the part of the Yuvaraj but was also hurt deep down by the way he had been ordered in front of the plaintiff and the defendants!

The bell in the courtyard of Pachad kept tolling whenever the constant rain showers abated. From wherever they were, when Raje and Sambhajiraje heard the bell, both of them rushed to the western machi.

Raje and Sambhajiraje would bow in the direction of that sound. For quite some time, both would simply keep gazing at the fog-covered foothills, without speaking. If the rain showers began, the attendants would hold umbrellas over their heads.

Eight to ten days passed like this. They had not seen Jijau. As they stood on the western machi, anxious Sambhajiraje said to Raje, "Aabasaheb, I can't bear to hear the tolls of the bell anymore. I want to go to Pachad."

Raje knew the deep bond that Masaheb and Sambhajiraje shared. He looked at the fog-covered foothills and said, "Sometimes I envy you. You freely speak whatever comes to your mind. I cannot do that. Sure, you should go to Pachad. Stay there with Masaheb for a couple of days and come back to the fort. You must understand the particulars of a campaign. It is easy to pass a judgement in the case of the hunters, but it is much more difficult to solve complicated cases!" Raje said, staring in the direction of invisible Pachad.

"Maharaj Saheb, did I make a mistake in the case of the hunters?" Sambhajiraje glanced at Raje.

"No, not in the case of the hunters, but you failed to follow the protocol of the royal court. You should not have commanded Annaji in front of the plaintiff and the defendants!"

Raje pointed towards Pachad and poured his heart out, "We can't see anything in that courtyard, but both of us know that at this moment Masaheb is standing there. Why? Because we have faith. Masaheb must also be looking at us from there in spite of her poor eyesight. Why? Because she loves us. Always remember, that because of faith and love, people form a strong bond with each other, and at times they even sacrifice their lives for each other."

"I was wrong. After leaving from here, I will go and meet Annaji, and ask for his forgiveness." Sambhajiraje's heart was full of respect for Raje.

"Don't do that. It will be another mistake! You are a Yuvaraj!" Raje said hastily.

"Remember that a king is not allowed to make a mistake! And he can't justify his mistake once it is committed! Let's go now. You have to prepare for your journey to Pachad." Raje put his hand on Sambhajiraje's shoulder.

After visiting the Jagadishwar temple, Sambhajiraje returned to his chamber with Jotyaji Kesarkar. An attendant informed him, "Deputy minister Mahadeo Yamaji wants to meet you."

"Let him in." Yuvaraj gave his consent.

Elderly Mahadeo Yamaji entered the chamber. He made an obeisance and said, "Thorale Swami has summoned Yuvaraj to his personal chamber."

Sambhajiraje immediately left his chamber with Jotyaji. Mahadeo Yamaji conducted them to Raje's personal chamber.

Moropant, Annaji, Duttaji Trimal and Balaji stood courteously on both sides of the chamber. Raje's faithful personal attendant, Khadoji Dabhade stood behind Raje, holding the hilt of his sword. As they saw Yuvaraj, all of them made an obeisance.

"Come." Raje said to Sambhajiraje.

Sambhajiraje approached Raje's seat and made an obeisance three times.

"Let me introduce you to him." Raje pointed towards a radiant ascetic who had donned an orange cloak.

Sambhajiraje took a seat one level below Raje's seat.

"He is Divakar Gosavi, the disciple of Samartha." Raje introduced the ascetic.

Divakar Gosavi had a glowing face, and a beard, and wore armlets and wristlets of Rudraksh beads. He leaned forward to pay respect, while holding his staff.

"And this is my son, Sambhajiraje." Raje put his hand on Sambhajiraje's shoulder and introduced him to Divakar Gosavi. Sambhajiraje paid respects to him.

"Yes, Divakarpant, tell us what brings you here." Raje glanced at the horizontal stripes of ash on his forehead.

"Gurudeo is currently residing at Kodoli Parasgaon. He wants to meet you. He has sent a letter for you." Divakarpant's voice was like the sound of a bell tolling in the Hanuman temple. He pulled out a rolled parchment from the bag on his shoulder. Then he approached Raje and handed it to him with a bow.

Raje closed his eyes and touched the rolled parchment to his forehead. He thought of handing it to Balaji to read. But suddenly he changed his mind, and gave the rolled parchment to Divakarpant and said, "I would like to hear what Samartha has written, from his own disciple."

Divakar Gosavi took the rolled parchment from Raje's hands. Even he had no idea what was written in the letter.

Fourteen years ago, Raje had met another disciple of Samartha, Bhaskar Gosavi. At that time, Raje had asked him, "Who is your Guru? Where is he from and where does he live?" Bhaskar Gosavi had provided all the information about his Guru at that time, but due to political engagements, Raje could not meet Samartha. Today, Samartha had sent him a letter on his own. He had fluently expressed his feelings about the triumphant feats of Raje.

"Jai Jai Raghuveer Samartha!" Divakarpant chanted the name of Lord Rama before reading the letter. Samartha's words began falling upon everyone's ears.

They earnestly took in the ambrosial words.

Every word that Divakar Gosavi pronounced helped Sambhajiraje paint a clear picture of the multi-faceted personality of Maharaj Saheb – 'As determined as Mount Meru!'

'The guardian of the masses!' The one who said, 'Take everyone along, the ones who are sitting, make them stand up; those who are standing, make them walk; and those who are walking, make them run!'

'The possessor of success, glory, might, grace, virtues and victory' – like the bell tolling in the courtyard of Pachad, the words echoed in Sambhajiraje's ears.

Sambhhajiraje closed his eyes inadvertently. He was engrossed in the words he had just heard and was visualizing the many facets of his Aabasaheb in his mind.

Moropant's army had conquered Bagalan and had camped at Mahad. Raje summoned Peshwe Moropant on Raigad.

Raje devised an infallible plan of attacking the kingdoms of fishermen of Javhar-Ramanagar on the borders of Gujarat, with Moropant's triumphant forces under the leadership of Yuvaraj Sambhajiraje.

This was going to be Sambhajiraje's first military campaign! At the advent of monsoon! A Bhosale must always pass the severe tests of weather and time to prove his mettle as a king.

Raje shared his plan with Moropant, who presented himself in the royal hall, "Pant, support Yuvaraj with your forces and attack Javhar-Ramanagar. Treat Yuvaraj like you would treat me in a campaign. Take boats and ships to cross rivers on your way, and keep expert fishermen, attendants at your disposal too. Continue the campaign dauntlessly despite the rainy weather. This is the first military campaign for Yuvaraj, make sure he succeeds in it."

Raje offered robes of honour to Yuvaraj Sambhajiraje and Moropant and formally assigned them the charge of the campaign.

In the inner sanctum of Raigad, Sambhajiraje offered a fistful of Bael leaves to Goddess Jagadamba and offered haldi at her feet. He gazed at her fiery eyes for a moment and observed the flame in her eyes. Unwittingly, Sambhajiraje knelt on the floor and touched his forehead in front of Goddess Jagadamba.

"Ude-Ude" He whispered in earnest.

He lifted his head and placed the feet of Raje, who was standing behind him.

"Arise. May you bring success home! Send us news from every sojourn you take. Follow Pant's advice." Raje held his shoulders tightly. Today Sambhajiraje was to descend the fort to start the campaign. Raje himself was going to accompany him till Mahad.

Yuvaraj sought blessings of all the queens. Yesubai stood in front of Dharau and performed Aukshan for him. He gazed at the wick of the burning lamp in the platter that Yesubai held and said goodbye to all of them.

When she heard his words of farewell, Yesubai wanted to lift her head and throw a fleeting glance at him if possible! But she was unable to do it.

Dharau, who stood behind her, prayed to the Mahadeo of Kapurhol – 'Sambu Mahadeva, my child is going on a mission for the first time. Give him success!'

Sambhajiraje touched Dharau's feet and sought her blessings. Moropant, Rupaji Bhosale, and Khandoji Jagatap were waiting in the courtyard of the Balekilla.

Sambhajiraje joined them with Raje, Rayaji, Antoji, and Jotyaji.

All of them visited the Jagadishwar temple, offered Bael leaves and descended the fort.

They went through the Lahana Darwaja and the garden and reached the palace at Pachad. Raje and Moropant waited in the courtyard. Sambhajiraje went to the private chamber of the palace with Antoji and Rayaji. Jijau and Putalabai were waiting there for him. Yuvaraj touched their feet and sought their blessings. Jijau and Putalabai ushered him to the inner sanctum of the palace. All of them prayed to the goddess.

Jijau, who was lost in thought, said, "When he was about your age, your Maharaj Saheb had attacked Fort Torana and conquered it successfully. I believe that you will do the same!"

All of them left the palace at Pachad. Outside, the grooms had saddled their horses and kept them ready. Raje-Sambhajiraje started galloping in the direction of Mahad.

They reached Mahad, where the military stable was located. The troops of ten thousand pugnacious soldiers, prepared by Pant's men, were ready to march forward. An elephant carrying a howdah on its back was kept ready, to lead the cavalry troops.

They took a break in the palace that Raje had erected in Mahad, till evening approached. In the evening, the kettle drums began resounding.

Raje left the palace in Mahad with Sambhajiraje. Both approached the elephant. The mahout goaded the elephant to sit down.

Sambhajiraje knelt in front of Raje and placed his head on Raje's feet. At that moment, he realized the stark difference between kneeling down in front of the dirt-covered camel, carrying the royal firman and kneeling in front of Maharaj Saheb amid the troops ready to embark on a campaign!

Raje pulled him up and holding him close Raje said, "Take

care. Once, during the festival of Holi you had asked me – 'Aabasaheb, will you also pull out a coconut from the burning Holi?' Today, I ask you the same question – will you do it?"

"Ji. I will do my best." Sambhajiraje responded spontaneously.

"Farewell. Jai Bhavani!" Raje's eyes lit up.

"Jai Bhavani." Sambhajiraje responded voluntarily to the light shining in Raje's eyes.

A ladder was placed against the elephant. Sambhajiraje climbed up the ladder to enter his howdah. Moropant followed him in the howdah to keep a watch over the army. Rupaji Bhosale, Rayaji, Antoji Gade, Khandoji Jagatap, and Moreshwar Naganath astride their horses, surrounded the elephant.

The flag-bearers raised the flags in their hands. The horn-bearers blew the horns.

And so left Shambho, with the blessings of Shiva, surrounded by a pugnacious troop of ten thousand soldiers!

Raje kept gazing at Yuvaraj and his army till it disappeared from view. He could not clearly remember when and from whom he had heard it, but he recalled the words – 'He will live in sky-high forts, he will fight ferociously like Rudra!'

Chapter 6

After a long journey, Javhar came into view, camouflaged by trees. Moropant sat in the howdah, behind Sambhajiraje. He pointed towards the dome of Vikram Shah's fortress, and courteously whispered in Sambhajiraje's ears, "Javhar – the fisher king Vikram Shah's capital!"

Sambhajiraje heard his words and rose at once. He gazed at the dome of the palace. The next moment, he pulled out his sword, pointed it towards Javhar and gave the battle cry – "Har Har Mahadeo!" Thousands of soldiers joined him.

Moropant immediately called out the names of cavalry leaders in a loud voice and commanded them - "Surround the city on all sides. Keep the horns resounding and the drums beating. Two cavalrymen with one infantryman. Har Har Mahadeo!"

About fifty miles away from Surat, Sambhajiraje's spirited army fell upon Javhar.

During the skirmish, Maratha soldiers captured the dark-skinned fishermen and forcibly mounted them on the horses. One unit of the Maratha cavalry kept them at the front and infiltrated Javhar.

The frontline troops of fishermen started shouting in their Koli tongue – "The Marathas are here! Shivaji's son, Shambhooraje has attacked us with his fierce army! Run for your lives!"

The Maratha forces fell upon them like the sea in high tide.

The bewildered fishermen did not know what hit them. Complete mayhem ensued. The Mavala infantry took advantage of the commotion and infiltrated Javhar from all sides, wielding their spears, swords and shields, shouting 'Jai Bhavani'. Weapons clashed against one another.

Vikram Shah, the terrified fisher king, abandoned his palace with select fishermen. He left his people behind, in the jaws of death, in the clutches of the Maratha army. He fled towards Nashik; to seek shelter under the wings of the Mughal sultanate, in Gulashanabad!

Sambhajiraje's elephant broke into Javhar with the bell around its neck tolling loudly. The Mavalas, thrilled to see Sambhajiraje, promptly started moving the booty out of the city.

Sambhajiraje took a stroll around the city and came to the western border. Tents and shamianas were raised to set up a camp.

Sambhajiraje sat on a raised platform. Raje had previously plundered Surat not once, but twice. In this region of Khambayat,. Only fifty miles away from there, his son was ransacking Javhar!

Heaps of gold, silver, pearls were arranged in front of Sambhajiraje. The riches were worth seventeen lakh rupees.

The burly fishermen who had resisted the attack resolutely, were shackled and presented in front of Sambhajiraje. Though captured, they were haughtily ready to accept any punishment meted out to them.

Moropant presented Sambhajiraje the letter of triumph to be dispatched to Raje. Sambhajiraje signed and stamped it with his seal. The letter was sealed in a pouch and given to a messenger.

"Yuvaraj should announce the sentence for the prisoners of war." Moropant pointed to the prisoners and said courteously.

Sambhajiraje threw a glance at them. After all, they had

fought resolutely for their kingdom. He said in a calm and grave voice, "Pant, whoever is ready to join our forces, enlist them in our army. Release those who don't accept this proposal and send them back with honour."

"Ji. As you wish." Moropant bowed in surprise. He did not expect such a mature decision from the Yuvaraj.

The Maratha army left Javhar. The booty collected during the raid was dispatched to Raigad with due security. Yuvaraj started marching towards Ramanagar with his army.

The Maratha army set up a camp at a short distance from Ramanagar. Ramanagar was located about thirty miles, to the south of Surat.

Moropant entered the shamiana of Yuvaraj to discuss war strategy. Rayaji, Antoji, the faithful men of Yuvaraj were present there.

"Yuvaraj, if we attack Ramanagar, the Mughal forces at Surat will surely come to their aid." Pant said and made an obeisance.

"That is why we should do something that will keep Surat in check." Sambhajiraje responded.

"In my opinion, before attacking Ramanagar, our cavalry should surround Surat once, to pressurize them." Moropant advised. Khandoji Jagatap and Rupaji Bhosale seconded him.

Sambhajiraje got lost in thought after hearing the plan. "I think, we should directly demand a tribute from the subedar of Surat. Make him believe that Aabasaheb is present in person. We should send our spies to Surat and spread rumours about Aabasaheb's presence. The people of Surat will be forced to stay where they are in order to protect themselves." Pant and all others kept staring at Yuvaraj in amazement. This was a perfect strategy. Everyone approved of it.

Pant dispatched an intimidating letter with a messenger, to the subedar of Surat, "Pay the tribute of four lakh rupees, or be prepared for Shivajiraje's armed attack on Surat." Along with the messenger, astute spies infiltrated Surat. A great commotion ensued in Surat.

This was the perfect time to charge upon Ramanagar, but news arrived from Nashik-Bagalan that Vikram Shah and Diler Khan were gathering a massive army. Meanwhile heavy rains started.

Sambhajiraje's army retreated at a safe distance from Ramanagar. The walls of the Mavala tents were drenched in the downpour of Gujarath.

The rain lasted for a fortnight. The cold showers cooled off the sweltering horses. Moropant dispatched two more letters to Surat's subedar to warn him that they were still camping in the Khambayat region.

As soon as the rain stopped, the Maratha army marched towards Ramanagar again. Som Shah, the king of Ramanagar had already fled the city after hearing the news, "The Marathas have arrived!" He had taken shelter with his family in the Surat area, near Ganadevi, in Chikhali.

The bags of booty collected in Ramanagar were sealed. Sambhajiraje summoned an honour assembly in the camp. The soldiers who had displayed valour in both campaigns were rewarded with anklets, bracelets, gold coins, and apparel. The hearts of the Mavala soldiers swelled with pride on seeing the handsome Sambhajiraje in person.

The Maratha army departed from Ramanagar, with uncertainty hanging over Surat. It ascended the western ghat and arrived near Nashik-Tryambak.

Sambhajiraje's triumphant army was divided into two flanks near Nashik. One flank marched towards Tryambak and the other charged upon Nashik.

The combined army of Vikram Shah of Javhar and Diler Khan had attacked the Maratha forces fighting in the northern region of Thane. A fierce battle had taken place there. Many Mavalas had lost their lives, but the Marathas had succeeded in capturing Dhararao Koli and the son of Vikram Shah and had beheaded them.

Nashik (also known as Gulashanabad), the powerful Mughal post, was under the control of Jadahavrao, serving in the Mughal sultanate. Jadhavrao was Raje's maternal cousin.

The Maratha army conquered Tryambak and Nashik. Rupaji Bhosale presented shackled Jadhavrao, in front of Yuvaraj in the Nashik encampment.

Sambhajiraje observed Jadhavrao Sindakhedkar with a keen eye. His heart was agitated to see Thoralya Aausaheb's nephew dressed in Mughal attire. He remembered Jijau and put his hand on his chest, to pay respect to her. Jadhavrao mistook his gesture; he thought, Yuvaraj has remembered our familial relations and is therefore paying respect to me.

"Rupaji, remove Kakasaheb's shackles."

Sambhajiraje said coldly. Rupaji was baffled, he hesitated for a moment.

"Rupaji..." an admonishing voice echoed from the seat, like the sound of a whiplash.

Rupaji hastily removed Jadhavrao's shackles.

Sambhajiraje glanced at Moropant and said to him, "Pant, please warn Kakasaheb that I am the Yuvaraj. He hasn't yet offered customary obeisance to me. His chains have been removed so that he can offer obeisance appropriately."

"Ji." Moropant bowed down. He approached Jadhavrao and warned him – "Rao, you are a prisoner. You must offer customary obeisance to Yuvaraj."

Jadhavrao was startled. He held his head high and glaring at Yuvaraj with fiery eyes, he exclaimed, "A tiger remains a tiger, even in captivity! The Jadhav family doesn't follow the custom of bowing down to the youngsters in the family!"

"Tiger? What tiger?" Sambahiraje rose from his seat at once, his eyes breathed fire. His roaring voice startled Rupaji, Pant, Rayaji, and everyone around.

Sambhajiraje walked defiantly and stood in front

of Jadhavrao. His sharp eyes pierced his uncle's eyes like a spearhead; his nostrils flared, and his words fell on his uncle's ears like a whiplash, "A tiger remains a tiger, but a tamed cat shouldn't pretend to be a tiger! Your status is so high that I should touch your feet and seek your blessings, but I feel ashamed to call you my uncle! You are Thoralya Aausaheb's nephew, that is why you must bow down! Not to me, but to her! You did not remember her even after seeing me, but I remembered her the moment I saw you! You better bow down to that seat! It is Thoralya Aausaheb's seat! Or else...!"

"Or else! What will you do?" Jadhavrao raised his eyebrow and exclaimed haughtily.

"What will I do? I will order your arrogant tongue to be slashed from your mouth. Pant..." Sambhajiraje's chest heaved.

Moropant was stunned to hear the vicious words of Yuvaraj. He shook Jadhavrao's shoulders and said to him, "Rao, you better make an obeisance to the seat and the Yuvaraj!"

A moment passed– then, his wretched life spent in the service of the Mughal sultanate flashed in front of Jadhavrao's eyes. He realised the worthlessness of it all. His heart felt heavy, his eyes got moist, and his breathing intensified. Jadhavrao stepped forward and directly touched Yuvaraj's feet. He nodded and said in a heavy voice, "I am not worthy of aatyabai's mercy! In fact, I don't deserve your mercy either!"

Instantaneously, the Yuvaraj's attitude changed. He hastily pulled Jadhavrao up.

Jadhavrao, the Mughal thanedar of Nashik-Tryambak got ready to serve Swaraj.

During the return journey, after conquering the post at Vani-Dindori, and getting its thanadar, Siddi Hilal enlisted into the service of Swaraj, Sambhajiraje's army entered the Marathi region to proceed to Raigad.

Pant dispatched messengers to Raigad with the intimation, "Yuvaraj is returning after successfully executing Swami's plan."

Yuvaraj and Pant reached near Pachad with their victorious army. Advance intimation had been sent. Raje had arrived, in Pachad, to receive Yuvaraj.

Yuvaraj, Pant, Jadhavkaka, everyone walked to the palace of Pachad. At the threshold of the courtyard, Putalabai waved a fistful of cooked rice around Yuvaraj and tossed it away. Sambhajiraje came to Jijau's chamber with Raje.

Jijau came forward. As Yuvaraj tried to bow down, she stopped him, kissed his forehead with her wrinkled lips and blessed him, "May you always be successful!" She stroked Yuvaraj's back with affection.

"Thoralya Aausaheb, I would like to present a special person in front of you. Please allow me." Yuvaraj said smilingly.

"I have settled in this palace for the same purpose – to meet everyone. Please call him in." Jijau said.

Yuvaraj signalled Jotyaji. Jotyaji came forward, and Jadhavrao followed. The moment Jijau saw him, a web of wrinkles formed on her already creased forehead. Her mind was dragged into the past.

"Kakasaheb is repentant for his mistakes. Masaheb, please accept his obeisance!" Sambhajiraje noticed Jijau's unrest.

Jadhavrao stepped forward and clasped Jijau's feet. Jijau vividly remembered how her parental family had been ruined by the family feud and the helplessness brought about by serving various sultanates. Her legs gave way, she held the side of the bed and sat down silently. Raje and Sambhajiraje promptly stood on either side.

"Raje, let him go." Jijau said in a dull voice while nodding her head. Jadhavrao felt ashamed and left with his head bent. Now he realized why Sambhajiraje had been so eager to defend Jijau's honour.

Raje and Sambhajiraje had their meals in the palace of Pachad and ascended Raigad with Pant. Yuvraj ascended the fort after his first victorious campaign.

With the advent of Shravan, the sun and the rain started playing hide-and-seek with each other. Preparations were made for Raje's journey. Khandoji Dabhade delicately packed the crystal Shivlinga that Raje worshipped daily, in a wooden casket.

"I will take darshan of Samartha and come back right away. Until then, Raigad is your responsibility. Take good care of everyone." Raje advised Yuvaraj and was about to leave the royal hall to go to the fortress of Chaphal to visit Samartha.

"Ji." Sambhajiraje wanted to say something but stopped.

"Anything more?"

"Please convey my obeisance to Samartha."

"Certainly."

"And..." Yuvaraj hesitated again.

"What is it? Feel free to tell me."

"It is my humble wish – can Samartha depict Thoralya Aausaheb in his ambrosial verse, just as he has depicted you?"

Raje smiled, and suddenly became solemn. He put his hand on Sambhajiraje's shoulder and waited for a moment. He wanted to say, "I felt exactly the same when I heard that letter of Samartha!"

But Raje outwardly said, "Yuvaraj, Samartha may have contemplated that capturing her personality in verse would not be an easy task to accomplish. I am leaving now. You keep a watchful eye on the palace of Pachad. Whenever your heart desires, descend the fort and visit her in person. Farewell."

Raje started walking with Moropant, Annaji and Prataprao. Yuvaraj accompanied them to the main gate.

The festival of Naga Panchami was two days away. Soyarabai instructed her personal assistant and made a list of ornaments and attire to be worn during the festival. An attendant delivered the list to the chief of Treasury, Nilo Sonadeo.

Nilopant sent a reply, "This list needs to be approved by Yuvaraj with his seal! The treasury cannot be opened without his official approval!" The moment the attendant delivered the news to her, Soyarabai's nose and ears flushed, her eyes turned red. For no reason, she reprimanded the attendant.

"How could the Mujumdar send me such a message? Did he forget that I recognise only Swari's authority?"

Dharau, who was helping Ramraje get dressed, was shaken by her raging words. She applied the horizontal stripes of sandalwood on his forehead and left the chamber with him. As she left the chamber vague words fell on her ears, "Go and summon the Mujumdar here." Soyarabai dismissed the attendant abruptly.

Dharau entered the chamber of Yuvaraj, with Ramraje. Ramraje was calling him "Dada… dada…" and trying to leap towards him. Sambhajiraje stepped forward and held him in his arms. Ramraje giggled in excitement. To calm him down, Yuvaraj smiled and said, "Okay… okay… take it easy now. Are you going to topple your own Dadamaharaj instead of the Mughal Empire?"

Dharau was startled to hear his words and checked around to see if anybody else had heard them. She could not restrain herself and said, "Please don't say such things to him! People are already making a mountain out of a molehill, please don't add fuel to the fire."

"Why?... What happened, Dharau?" Yuvaraj was confused.

Dharau told him what she had heard. For a moment, Yuvaraj's hand, stroking Ramraje's back, stopped. He looked at the door and called out – anybody there?"

An attendant came in. Yuvaraj ordered him, "Go and give my message to Mahadeo Yamaji that I have summoned the Mujumdar."

Yuvaraj continued pacing back and forth, holding Ramraje in his arms. Dharau anxiously looked at both of them, and wondered, "What is going to happen now?" She kept quiet.

Nilopant entered the chamber with Mahadeo Yamaji.

Soyarabai had already reprimanded him scornfully. He bowed down and couldn't resist asking, "Yuvaraj, what should we employees do? Maharaj has commanded us that no one should open the treasury without your approval."

"Pant, give me the list please." Sambhajiraje said calmly. He gently handed Ramraje to Dharau.

Nilopant gave the list of ornaments and apparel to Yuvaraj. Sambhajiraje glanced through it and said, "Come with me."

Dharau wanted to say, "Don't go" but words didn't come out of her mouth. Sambhajiraje came to the treasury with Nilopant. The armed guards made obeisance to him and made way for him. Yuvaraj resolutely said, "Pant, open the door."

Pant took the keys from the attendant and opened the door of the treasury.

"I will read each item on the list, and you place it on the platter." Sambhajiraje started reading one item at a time. Nilopant moved swiftly and fiddling with the keys, he started placing each item on the platter. The list was over. Yuvaraj stepped forward, grabbed as many golden ornaments as he could in his fist and placed them on the platter.

"Please collect each item on the list of apparel and present it to Masaheb in person." Yuvaraj handed Nilopant the other list of apparel.

A sentinel of the treasury came forward to carry the platter of ornaments. Yuvaraj gestured him to stop and picked up the platter himself!

Sambhajiraje determinedly came to Soyara masaheb's chamber. A guard saw him coming and gave intimation to Soyarabai. When Soyarabai heard the news, she decided something, and turned her back to the door. Yuvaraj entered her chamber with the platter in his hands. He placed the platter on a wooden table and made an obeisance to Soyara masaheb. A few stifling moments passed in silence.

"Masaheb, I have personally come to give you the ornaments

and attire for the upcoming festival. Please accept them."

"One more request to you. All the servants on the fort are at your disposal. I am also your humble servant. Please let me know whatever you need." His demeanour was courteous.

Soyarabai was seething inside. Yuvaraj had left her with no chance to make a counter move. But still, she was Soyarabai! Without looking at him she asked him sarcastically, "Will you do the same for Soonbai, if she needed them?"

"No!" Sambhajiraje responded calmly.

"Why?"

"She is from a peasant family! The peasants are not used to such ornaments! Farewell."

Soyarabai had not expected that her earlier sarcastic comment about Yesubai coming from a 'peasant family' would backfire in this manner. She fretted and fumed.

As he was leaving her chamber, Sambhajiraje remembered Ramraje and wanted to say to her, "You are fond of the golden ornaments in the treasury, but if you ask me, I am fond of Ramraje, who is your best ornament!" But he didn't say anything.

Rayaji and Antoji planted the red, blue and white lotus buds brought from a lake in Mahad, in the wetland on the banks of Lake Kushavarta. Sambhajiraje stood near the lake, in the shadow of a tree. He himself had brought the lotus buds.

"Rayaji, let's see how lucky you prove to be. Let's see how many of these buds bloom into flowers!" Sambhajiraje said.

"Dhakale dhani, these types of lotuses grow very fast. They will cover the whole lake in no time!" Antoji said with a smile.

"Please forgive me Dhakale dhani, Sarkar has summoned you. Two guests from Hindustan have come to the fort. Their foreheads are smeared with long stripes of sandalwood paste." Jotyaji Kesarkar approached the tree and delivered the news.

Raje had come back from Chaphal. Already one and a half hour had passed since his arrival.

"Let's go." Sambhajiraje said and came out of the shadow.

'Who could be the guests from Hindustan?' Lost in thought, he entered Raje's meeting room, and made an obeisance. He placed his hand on the hilt of his sword and approached the two guests standing in front of Raje.

"Come here, do you recognize them?" Raje asked him with a smile, pointing to the guests.

Both the men from the north brought their palms together and bowed down to the Yuvaraj. Many memories unfurled in Sambhajiraje's mind.

"Oh he… he is the poet!" Sambhajiraje puckered his forehead, trying to recollect his name and said, "Kavi Kalash, who accompanied me from Varanasi to Mathura!"

"Please forgive me Yuvaraj, for correcting you, but my name is not Kalash, it is Kulesh!" The poet corrected him with a smile.

"And he is Kavi Paramanand who met us in the haveli." Raje reminded him about the man clad in the saffron cloak.

"Yuvaraj, they say, 'We have come here to visit you. We will stay here for a few days and go back.' Tell them how much you cherish poetry. I am thinking of keeping them here forever." Raje said with a smile.

"Ji. What you say is right. I would also like the same." Yuvaraj said. Everyone laughed.

Sambhajiraje was astride a black horse, taking a ride along the Bhavanitok. He could see Lingana on the left, Potla on the right and the blackish summits of Torana and Rajgad in front of him, at a distance.

'Rajgad! Standing tall like the king of birds, an eagle, spreading the wings of his machis, ready to soar!'

He heard the beating of the drums coming from the Nagar Khana of Raigad. The cannons boomed right after that. He pulled the reins and prodded his horse. The dark horse wiggled its tail and sprinted forward. They passed the Kala houd and the Jagadishwar temple.

The Holi chowk went by. As Sambhajiraje entered the Nagar

Khana, he faintly saw a tiger raising his paw, carved on the stone arch.

As soon as he entered, he pressed the left stirrup and dismounted. He tossed the reins in his hands to the groom who had approached him. He walked briskly and rushed past the Hajari fountain in the royal courtyard.

Raje stood amid people in the royal courtyard. As soon as he saw Sambhajiraje, he picked up a fistful of sugar from a platter on a Mavala's shoulder.

As Sambhajiraje saw Raje climbing down the stone steps, he rushed forward. He was about to bow down to make obeisance to Raje, but Raje stopped him.

"Shambhooraje, have some sugar. Panhala has been conquered! My wish has been fulfilled after twelve years." Raje smiled and fed Sambhjiraje a fistful of sugar.

In the evening, a content Raje came to Soyarabai's chamber. Soyarabai had instructed a palace maid to place a platter of sugar on a wooden stool.

She stood near the stool with Ramraje in her arms. When Raje approached them, she said to Ramraje, "Here, Aabasaheb is going to give you something. See what it is!"

Raje held Ramraje in his arms, kissed him on the cheek and said, "What can I give him? God is the giver after all."

Soyarabai stared at the cowrie necklace on Raje's chest, and a nasty thought occurred in her mind, 'only the elder ones get the privilege of eating sugar!'

From Raje's arms, Soyarabai took Ramraje in her arms. Soyarabai's informer Bayaji had seen Raje feeding sugar to Sambhajiraje smilingly in the courtyard, and he had not forgotten to report it to Soyarabai.

The month of Chaitra arrived. It was the time to celebrate Gudhi Padwa. Poles striped with haldi-kumkum paste, embellished with fresh green mango leaves were raised in front of each house on the fort. The shining goblets hung on top of the poles sparkled in the sun. Pieces of colourful cloth, and garlands of white Champa flowers swayed on the wind. Raje was going to leave Raigad today for a visit to Fort Panhala which had been audaciously conquered by Kondaji Farjand, Annaji, Motyaji Khalekar and Ganoji Kavala. Prataprao was going to accompany him with the army. Yuvaraj Sambhajiraje was going to take charge of Raigad.

Feasts were organized on the festive occasion. The afternoon siesta was over. At twilight Raje, went with Sambhajiraje and Prataprao, to take the darshan of Jagadishwar. After the darshan everyone came out of the temple. Sambhajiraje gazed at the mountain range of Lingana visible at a faraway distance.

Due to the trees brushing against each other or from the embers of the fire lit by the peasants, a wildfire had broken out on the inclines of Lingana. It was grabbing one's attention in the rays of the setting sun.

Yuvaraj rested his hands on the stone parapet of the temple and kept gazing at the dancing fire intently.

When a lean-fingered, rosy hand patted his shoulder his reverie broke and he turned around.

Raje was looking at the fire on Lingana. His eyes were solemn.

"Dhani, such sudden and unexpected wildfires are very dangerous. Many birds get swayed by such fires and get burnt to death needlessly." Prataprao Gujar said while looking at the fire.

"Neither the birds nor the fire is at fault, Sarlashkar. The fault lies in the moment when two branches brush against each other and ignite the inferno. And no one ever has any control over such moments."

Yesubai had come to Pachad with Dharau. She spent a week with Jijau and was now climbing the fort to go back. Chilly winds were blowing, and she was trying to block them by covering her face with the edge of her sari.

Yesubai came out of the Mena Darwaja and arrived on an open plateau adjacent to the queens' palaces. Aabajipant had purposely kept this area open so that the royal ladies of Raje's family could spend some free time here.

Sambhajiraje had gone on a hunting expedition with other hunters, in the forests near Pachad. Raje was on Fort Panhala.

Yesubai walked around freely, watching the blossoms of Chaitra. She talked to Dharau now and then. The cliffs around were covered with sprawling Palash trees laden with fiery red flowers and Bahava trees laden with yellow flowers. Yesubai tightly held on to the edge of her sari around her face, and it was fluttering with the wild wind.

As she watched the setting sun, she had a vision. The orb wore a red turban of the Palash flowers! The shield-like orb was melting and dispersing on the horizon! She felt like the orb was melting inside her! On her bosom! What is happening to me?"

"Dharau" Yesubai uttered in a tremulous voice, bit the edge of her sari and sat down at once.

For a moment, Dharau was baffled. Then her eyes sparkled. She affectionately stroked Yesubai's back. Knowing, affectionate peasant words rushed from her lips, "Don't be afraid. It's okay. Let's go from here. You should not stay out in this chilly wind." Yesubai was shaking.

Dharau helped her stand up and ushered her to the queens' palaces.

Eight swordsmen, gasping for breath, carried the carcass of the tiger hunted by Sambhajiraje, on Raigad. The populace on the fort from all departments thronged the courtyard to see it. Duttaji Trimal, Balaji Aavaji and Raje himself left to see the carcass.

The crowd whispered in soft voices, lauding the valour of Yuvaraj. Countless flies buzzed around the open jaws of the dead animal. The black stripes on the dark yellow skin of the large animal, were shining. His bushy tail which used to wiggle ceaselessly lay lifeless. The crowd was watching in awe, the slain 'wild wonder'. Balaji's now grown-up sons, Khandoji and Aavaji, and Nirajipant's son, Prahlad, were also among them.

Raje arrived. The crowd made way and made an obeisance. Yuvaraj Sambhajiraje held the gun in his left hand and made an obeisance to Raje. His chest swelled with pride as he looked at the carcass of the tiger.

"How the loud sounds of drums reverberated the forest and woke it up, and the wild animal attacked them with loud roars; how the rabble surrounded the animal; how he shot the animal sitting on his horse." Sambhajiraje was proudly recounting everything.

After hearing his account, Raje only said, "Come and see me in my chamber immediately!" Raje left soon after.

Sambhajiraje started walking towards the palace through Palakhi Darwaja. He came to the courtyard of the Balekilla. Yesubai sat with Dharau, in the balcony of Putalabai's palace. Dharau was running her fingers through her wet hair, fixing her dishevelled hair. As soon as Yesubai saw her Swari with a gun hanging over his shoulder, she got up immediately and went inside the palace. Dharau didn't understand what happened.

"Soonbai, your hair is still wet…" Dharau said and went after her. Dharau held a mirror in front of Yesubai so that she could see her own expression, but Yesubai didn't dare look at it.

As instructed, Sambhajiraje came to Raje's chamber. Raje stood near a window, lost in thought.

"Yuvaraj, hunting is the privilege of valiant men. Even I go hunting at times." Raje's voice was resolute.

"But…but we are Bhosales first and foremost, and then hunters! I had committed the same mistake that you committed today, that of killing a tiger! Masaheb opened my eyes. We are Goddess Jagadamba's devotees. Henceforth, don't forget that the tiger is Jagadamba's mount!"

"Ji. I… I did not realize it." Yuvaraj lowered his head in shame.

"Well, now you should realize it." Raje did not let go of the point he was making.

"Ji."

Raje sensed his regret. He turned around and approached Sambhajiraje. He pulled him close and held his shoulders tightly.

"Lift your head."

Yuvaraj raised his head. His crystal-clear eyes met with Raje's tapering, divine eyes. Raje felt the fearlessness in his eyes. He admired it and said, "I want your prowess – not the one that kills a tiger – but the one that displays the audacity of a tiger!"

"You may go now." Raje patted his shoulders.

Yuvaraj took a few steps back, made an obeisance to him and was about to leave. Raje noticed his courteous behaviour and said with a smile, "Get that animal's skin stuffed by a cobbler and get it installed on a sturdy platform in the courtyard, as an icon of your courage and also as a reminder of your blunder!"

"Ji."

As he left the chamber, Sambhajiraje's mind was consumed by the thought, 'Aabasaheb is indeed very difficult to comprehend'.

"I am going to visit the temple and will be back in a couple of days." Raje told Sambhajiraje and went to his palace.

The next day, Pilaji Sundar, the Maratha vakeel in the Mumbai durbar of the British, ascended the fort. He had brought news that on behalf of the British, one Officer Thomas was ready for discussions with Raje. Since Raje is not here, he is asking for permission to visit Yuvaraj.

"Let the officer come on the fort." Sambhajiraje granted permission to Pilaji.

Thomas Nichols, the white officer of the British durbar had left from Mumbai and had arrived at Raigad via Nagothane, Pai, and Sarasgad. He had a group of thirty-seven people and an interpreter named Shamaji Shenavi with him.

Officer Thomas had come to make two business deals for his durbar. Recently, during Prataprao's cavalry attack on Hubli, the British warehouse had been plundered. He had come to seek compensation for the loot in Hubli as well as for the previous attack on the British warehouse in Rajapur. He also wanted to obtain authorized permit to import salt and timber from the Marathi kingdom to Mumbai.

Pilaji descended the fort and delivered Yuvaraj's message to the officer. Thomas, who was eager to see Fort Raigad and the Yuvaraj, wore his uniform and got ready to ascend the fort. But suddenly, stormy dust-laden winds encircled Pachad and in no time the monsoon showers began beating down on Raigad and Pachad. Thomas got stranded in Pachad.

The next day, Officer Thomas climbed up the fort with Shamaji and Pilaji, gasping for breath. He sent intimation to Chitnis Balaji. Balaji received the officer and ushered him to the royal hall.

"Yuvaraj, the British officer has presented himself in the royal court." Balaji came to the Yuvaraj's chamber, made an obeisance to him and delivered the news.

Balaji was a bit sceptical. He thought, this officer is a representative of a foreign country. He might trick Yuvaraj into getting what he wants, during the negotiations.

Yuvaraj was about to leave his palace. Balaji politely advised him, "Yuvaraj, Swami is not present on the fort. This is a British officer. Hence my humble request to you, please be careful when you talk to him."

"Chitnis, I've heard that this officer has climbed up the fort to see me in person. Let him see me to his heart's content." Sambhajiraje said with a smile.

Sambhajiraje came to the royal hall with Balaji. Pilaji and Shamaji made an obeisance to him. Officer Thomas took off his white feather-crested, big red hat. He held it close to his chest, bowed, and made a courteous obeisance to Sambhajiraje in the British manner. Yuvaraj took his seat in the royal hall, observed the officer keenly and asked Shamaji, "How is your officer doing?"

"Ji, he is doing fine. He wants to submit the petition of the Mumbai durbar to Yuvaraj." Shamaji began the mediation. The officer's face was flushed with the exertion of climbing up the fort. With his blue eyes, he was observing the audacious prince in front of him.

"Permission granted." Sambhajiraje picked up a rose bud from a platter and sniffed it. He thrust his elbows in the bolster behind him and leaned against it.

"Your Sarlashkar mistakenly plundered the British warehouse in Hubli. Since there is no enmity between this durbar and the British, they have requested compensation for the loot." Shamaji used sweet words to convince Yuvaraj. Balaji, Shamaji, Pilaji – everyone pricked up their ears to hear what Yuvaraj was going to say.

"Shenavi, as far as I know our Sarlashkar is in the Panhala region. Are you sure you have the right information? Did he really plunder Hubli? Yuvaraj evaded Shamji's request. "Do you have any other appeal to make?"

"Ji. If the British durbar is granted permission to import salt and timber from the Marathi region to Mumbai, it will help establish trade relations between the two durbars." Shamaji played his next move.

"Salt and timber are daily essentials! Shenavi, you must wait for Maharajsaheb to make a final decision on both your appeals. I will convey your appeals to him. He is not at the fort presently; he will be back in couple of days." Sambhajiraje placed the rose bud in the platter and said to Balaji, "Chitnis, please offer the betel leaf to the officer to conclude this meeting."

"Ji." Said Balaji and presented the platter of betel leaves to Officer Thomas.

Sambhajiraje arose from his seat, looked at his vakeel, Pilaji Sundar and said, "Pilaji, make sure the officer reaches Pachad safely. He won't be able to sustain the weather at the fort!"

"Ji." Pilaji nodded in affirmation. Sambhajiraje looked at Balaji and gave him a smile.

Thomas bowed down to make an obeisance to him; Sambhajiraje turned around and left the royal hall, whispering 'Jagadamb… Jagadamb'.

After two days, when Raje returned to Pachad, Shamaji directly met him and arranged a meeting with the white officer. At the fixed time, Thomas Nichols came with Shamaji to meet Raje in the royal hall of Pachad.

Shamaji stated the purpose of their visit – "Two days ago, we ascended the fort and presented our appeal to Yuvaraj." Shamaji paused to gauge Raje's response. As soon as Raje heard Shamaji's words he rose from his seat and said in a cold voice, "Shenavi, it looks like today is not a good day for my meeting with the white officer! I will see him tomorrow!"

Raje had given an excuse to Shenavi. He did not know what Shamaji and Thomas had spoken to Yuvaraj at their meeting. To avoid any discrepancies in making a decision, it was necessary to know what they had talked about.

Just as the meeting with Sambhajiraje was unproductive, the meeting with Raje also proved unfruitful for Officer Thomas. Officer Thomas, who had come to meet 'Shiva' and 'Shambho' in pursuit of salt, returned to Mumbai emptyhanded.

Monsoon arrived; the skies of Maval started thundering with pouring rain. Roaring red streams started cascading down the cliffs of Raigad. A messenger from Pachad came to the fort in the pouring rain. He had brought news, "Due to the cold weather Masaheb has developed joint pains. She is also suffering from asthma."

Sambhajiraje went to Pachad with a special oil made from the fat of the tiger that he had slain recently. Jijau was bedridden.

She was surround by palace maids who were looking after her. Putalabai remained by her side all the time, to keep a watchful eye on her treatment. Even so, Jijabai was glad to see Yuvaraj.

The eleventh day of Aashadh passed. Sambhajiraje was still in Pachad. As usual, he began massaging Jijau's knees with oil, tenderly. Jijau said to him in a calm voice, "I wanted to speak to you about something for quite a while now. Will you listen to me?"

"Ji."

"I have heard rumours of frequent clashes between Thoralya Soonbai and you." Jijau stopped. Her weary eyes stared at the burning wicks of the lamp at her bedside.

Sambhajiraje moved his hands from her knees to her feet and said in a hoarse voice, "Thoralya Aausaheb, I swear that I honour her and treat her with due respect."

"Deference is a feminine trait. Men should practise tolerance. Even if she deviates from deference, you should not lose your patience. You have been facing this since your mother's demise, and such problems are going to increase with your age. I looked after you as far as possible, but now I have become weary with age. Jijau gazed at the ceiling as if she was gazing at a faraway distance and said, "The five fingers of our hands are not the same, but we cannot just remove one of them because of that. Don't forget that we must take along people of different abilities and keep moving forward."

"Ji." Sambhajiraje was touched by her affection.

"Go outside and check if the downpour has eased." Jijau astutely changed the topic to relieve the tension in the chamber. Sambhajiraje left the chamber and came to the courtyard.

He went back into the chamber and assisted Jijau to get out of bed. He supported and took her near the bell in the courtyard. The timekeeper came forward and made an obeisance. The bell started tolling.

Within a short time, a small dot of the saffron Jaripataka

pennant was visible on the western machi of Raigad. It was the signal that Raje had arrived on the hazy machi faraway. Jijau could not see it with her weary eyes. Therefore, Sambhajiraje said, "Thoralya Aausaheb, Maharajsaheb has arrived on the machi."

As soon as she heard it, Raje's oblong face flashed in front of Jijau's eyes and words slipped out of her lips spontaneously, "May you live long!"

The monsoon showers ceased. Raigad blossomed with greenery. Sambhajiraje bade farewell to Jijau and came to Raigad.

Meanwhile, two events had taken place. Prataprao had committed the grave mistake of releasing Abdul Karim Bahalol Khan, the commander of Vijapur, who was captured in the battle of Umarani. And a regiment of the Maratha army had attempted to capture Fort Pandavgad in the Wai region.

After the Dussehra celebrations, Raje went to the Satara region. Within four days, Raigad received news that his army had conquered Pandavgad. After hearing that news, Sambhajiraje distributed sugar on Raigad.

Sambhajiraje consumed the porridge that Dharau gave him and left his chamber. Yadav Namaji stood guard outside. Yuvaraj accepted his obeisance and said, "Yadavrao, come with me."

Yuvaraj visited the temple of Jagadishwar with Yadav Namaji and came to Lake Kushavarta. Bountiful multicoloured lotuses had blossomed on the surface of the lake, capturing the beholder's attention, gently swaying on the breeze.

Mesmerized, Sambhajiraje kept gazing at Lake Kushavarta. A thought came to his mind – 'Thoralya Aausaheb is fond of flowers. I should bring her to the fort sometime and show her the lotuses here.'

"Yadavrao, get in the water and pluck some lotuses of different colours." Yuvaraj commanded. Yadav Namaji removed his footwear and entered the lake. He plucked some blue, red and white lotuses and came out.

Yuvaraj returned to the Balekilla, gazing at the flowers in his hand. He reached the fountain in the main chowk of the courtyard. Sambhajiraje entered his chamber, gazing at the hundreds of springing jets of water.

He did not know that Dharau and Yesubai were in his chamber. Yesubai was holding Ramraje in her arms. As soon as Dharau saw Yuvaraj she said as if to herself, "Oh, I have become so forgetful lately! I completely forgot to give the puja material to the priest!" And she left the chamber immediately.

"Come here." Sambhajiraje spread his arms to take Ramraje in his arms. As he took Ramraje from Yesubai's arms, his fingers touched Yesubai's arm slightly. His touch gave her goosebumps all over. Her eyelashes fluttered. She boldly looked into the bright eyes in front of her, and immediately looked at the floor. She was about to leave the chamber in haste, when somebody stopped her,

"Wait!"

Sambhajiraje stepped forward with Ramraje. He stretched out his hand holding the lotuses, looked at Yesubai's lotus face and said, "Here, take these. I was either going to offer them to Lord Jagadishwar or give them to you!"

Yesubai's heart pounded. Her hand trembled as she took the flowers from him. Again, her fingers touched his fingers, her eyes fluttered, her ears flushed. Her eyes met his.

Baffled, Yesubai instantly left the chamber, dragging the edge of her sari along the floor.

After some time Dharau entered the chamber. She smiled when she saw the two brothers together. She saw that there were no lotuses in Yuvaraj's hand now, and said, "All puja material is ready except for the lotus flowers for the goddess. Who is going to bring those for this poor lady now?" And holding Ramraje in her arms Dharau left the chamber smiling.

After plundering Bankapur, ravaging Karvar, and stationing

Anandrao Makaji in the Panhala region, Raje returned to Raigad after two months. As soon as he arrived at the fort, one good and one bad news followed him.

The bad news was the sad demise of Mujumdar, Nilo Sonadeo, a veteran officer of the kingdom. And the good news was the arrival of Pandit Gaga Bhatt of Kashi to meet Raje. Raje's family priest, Anantbhat Kavale of Nashik, had dispatched a special envoy to Kashi and had invited Vishweshwar Bhatt, alias Gaga Bhatt, who was a Vedic scholar, to Nashik.

Raje dispatched Annaji to Nashik, with the palanquin and royal retinue, to receive Gaga Bhatt with royal protocol and bring him to the fort. And Raje assigned Sambhajiraje the responsibility to go to Pachad and bring Jijau to Raigad so she could meet Gaga Bhatt.

As per Raje's command, Sambhajiraje came to Pachad. He held weary Jijau's hand and helped her get in the palanquin. Putalabai sat in the other palanquin. The retinue arrived at Raigad, but ailing Kashibai remained in Pachad.

Anantbhat sent advanced notice from Mahad – "Acharya is coming the fort with select disciples."

Raje and Sambhajiraje sought Jijau's blessings and descended the fort. Their palanquins were accompanied by select people such as Moropant, Annaji, Duttaji, Yesaji, Nishchalpuri, Kavi Parmanand, Kavi Kulesh, Prabhakarbhat, and Keshav Pandit.

They reached the shamiana erected for the welcome. The palanquins were set down. Raje and Sambhajiraje walked on the carpets laid out on the ground and entered the shamiana. Raje checked the seating arrangement. The mattress, the bolsters, the carpets… everything was in place. An attendant stood near the seat, holding a golden platter on his shoulder. It was covered with a cloth.

As Raje looked at Moropant, Annaji, Yesaji, Parmanand, Kulesh and others, he was lost in deep thought.

'What an auspicious moment this is! It wouldn't have been

possible for me to invite him here, as he would have to cross through enemy territory due to the rival kingdoms around us, but today the Acharya of Kashi's religious establishment is coming to visit me on his own.

Raje's reverie was broken by the resonating conches. The sound was coming from the direction of Mahad. Prabhakarbhat came in and announced Gaga Bhatt's arrival.

Raje and Sambhajiraje came out together. Acharya's disciples blew conches at the top of their lungs and raised their heads high. The loud beating of drums mingled with that holy sound.

Raje approached the palanquin promptly and helped Acharya Gaga Bhatt out of the saffron-veiled palanquin.

With Raje and Sambhajiraje on either side, Gaga Bhatt walked on the carpet and entered the shamiana. Raje courteously ushered Acharya to his seat and seated him with respect. Raje honoured him with a betel leaf, a coconut and a shawl placed on a golden platter.

Raje and Sambhajiraje touched Acharya's feet. Acharya leaned forward to accept their obeisance, raised his hands, closed his eyes and blessed them, "May you be victorious!"

Acharya climbed Raigad with Raje and Sambhjiraje. He took the darshan of Lord Jagadishwar and after visiting the marketplace, the Nagar Khana and the courtyard, he came to Raje's personal chamber. A grand seating platform had been arranged there for Raje, Jijau, Sambhajiraje and Ramraje. In front of it, a seat covered with deerskin had been placed for Acharya.

Jijau received intimation of Acharya's arrival. Clad in a white sari, she came to Raje's personal chamber accompanied by Raje's queens, daughters, Yesubai and Ramraje. When Acharya Gaga Bhatt saw her, he rose from his seat and approached her.

Without blinking his eyes, he leaned forward and touched Jijau's feet saying, "Maaji, my obeisance to you!"

Jijau did not expect such a thing; she quickly retreated her step and exclaimed, "Acharya, please! You are a great and distinguished person."

Gaga Bhatt recognized her sentiment and clarified his actions, "Maa ji, your feet are holier than the holy River Ganga! I am a mere pandit of the religious scriptures. You are a living embodiment of dharma!"

His words sounded like the gushing waters of the Ganga. Raje's eyes became misty on hearing his words. Sambhajiraje's chest swelled with pride.

Acharya requested Jijau to take her seat. Jijau walked steadily and sat on the seat.

Raje requested Acharya to take his seat. Acharya sat on the seat covered with deerskin. Prabhakarbhat placed a salver on a stool, at his feet.

Raje, Sambhajiraje, Ramraje, all queens – everyone performed the ritual of washing Acharya's feet. As Gaga Bhatt saw Jijau rising from her seat, coming forward to wash his feet he said to Raje, "Oh Raja, please take her back to her seat. A mother washing her son's feet reduces the son's lifespan, and I want to live – at least until I perform a religious duty I am destined to carry out."

Raje conveyed Acharya's wish to Jijau and made her sit. Raje sat near her feet, with Sambhajiraje and Ramraje on both sides. All the queens and family members stood at the back. All the ministers and select guests stood around courteously. Everyone was eager to hear the discourse between Gaga Bhatt, the religious authority and Maharaj, the regal authority.

Gaga Bhatt, the master of the Vedas, chanted the name of God; eloquent Banarasi language started streaming from his virtuous lips. "Oh, noble Shivajiraje, I came to Deccan from the holy place of Kashi, with a purpose in mind. It gave me intense pleasure to come here and visit this fort of yours. There is everything in this fort except a royal throne! Oh Raja, religious authority is ineffective without the support of imperial power. The Hindus of the entire Aaryavarta today, don't hold authority over a single royal throne that will cause them to hold their heads high with pride that will inspire them to fight for their lives. That is why, today, Hindus feel insecure and defeated. Unprotected dharma does not remain dharma.

"Oh, Raja Shivaji, my instinct tells me that you have the mettle to shoulder the responsibility of the entire Aaryavarta...

In the north, our holy temples are being desecrated; our gods and goddess are being disgraced. The Muslims have wreaked havoc. The feeble Hindu ryots are being forcibly converted to Islam." Acharya's solemn voice became heavy.

"If this continues this holy land of Lord Rama and Lord Krishna will turn into hell. That is why, here I stand in front of you, imploring you on behalf of the populace of the North. Oh, protector of Dharma, oh great luminary, enthrone yourself and become a Chhatrapati. Give us shelter." Overcome with emotion, Acharya spread both his arms wide. The North was calling out to the Deccan.

Tears filled Jijau' eyes, and she could not see anything.

Raje responded to with Gaga Bhatt's earnest appeal. The birds of Raigad soared in the sky, spreading the news all over Maval.

"Raje is going to sit on the throne! He is going to be a big king and form a grand durbar! Every hearth and home in Bara Maval was euphoric.

To ensure that no objections arose during the coronation ceremony Anantbhat Kavale went to Nashik again. He organized an assembly of the Brahmins. Two objections were raised in the assembly – Kshatriyas have become extinct in the Kaliyuga and Raje's thread ceremony has not been performed, but the marriages have taken place.

Gaga Bhatt presented evidence from the Shastras and Puranas and convinced the Brahmin assembly that Kshatriya dharma can be reinstated by atonement.

Raje dispatched Balaji Chitnis to Rajputana, to obtain the

record of his ancestry. Balaji visited many places such as Mewar, Udaipur, Jaipur and obtained the records. Raje was a Rajput Kshatriya, a descendant of the 'Shisodiya' family of Suryavansha; the scion of valiant rulers such as Rana Bhim Singh, Sajjan Singh, Dilip Singh, Devarajaji and others.

All the issues were resolved. Elaborate preparations for the coronation ceremony began under the guidance of Gaga Bhatt. Acharya Gaga Bhatt instructed that Soyarabai should be inducted as the Maharani, as she was the eldest queen, and Sambhajiraje as the Yuvaraj to inherit the privileges and responsibilities of Raje.

Raigad was bedecked as the future capital of the Mavalas. Hiroji Indalkar, Aabaji and Arjoji Girjoji Yadava undertook the mission of decorating the courtyard of the durbar and the palaces on the Balekilla.

The sculptors began pounding their chisels. Every stroke of the chisels was singing the tune of "Raja Shiv Chhatrapati!" The carpenters, goldsmiths, ironsmiths… all kinds of skilled artisans commenced work.

Jewellers, perfumers and moneylenders gathered at Raigad in anticipation of good business. The horses were taken out of the royal stable to get the horseshoes fixed. The huffing and puffing beasts of burden carried sacks of provisions and salt from various parts of the kingdom to the fort, filling up the granaries.

The idols of all deities on the fort were burnished. Messengers started descending the fort with letters sealed in red pouches, wrapped in the scarves around their waists. The surveillance troops of Bahirji, Karmaji and Vishwas girded their loins and started picking up the news from all over. The eighteen departments were hustling and bustling. Brave men, sporting silver bracelets and delicate women, bedecked in dozens of green bangles – everyone contributed to creating a grand design.

Ramaji Dutto, an expert in casting, undertook the task of

creating the royal throne. Ramaji knew that he was creating the royal throne for Lord Ramchandra of the Mavalas! It was going to weigh thirty-two mounds; made in pure gold!

Sambhajiraje stood near the 'Hatti' lake. Many years back, an elephant cub, Trishul, had been brought to Raigad via Chor Darwaja. Trishul had now grown up and was being adamant today. The mahout was exhausted, trying to get Trishul out of the lake. Trishul was adamant and not ready to get out of the water. Sambhajiraje was lost in thought, watching the distressed mahout. Mahadeo Yamaji and Yadav Namaji stood near him.

The evening drums began beating, and stopped at once, as if someone had stopped it on purpose.

Sambhajiraje walked towards the Balekilla; the mahout's frustrated words fell upon his ears, "Trishul…can you stop being stubborn?! Do you want to keep sitting in the lake forever?!""

Sambhajiraje walked briskly and entered the Balekilla through the Palakhi Darwaja. Mahadeo Yamaji and Yadav followed him. As he climbed up the steps of Raje's private chamber, he felt that something was amiss.

Raje stood in the chamber, his head bowed. Anandrao's messenger Karmaji stood in front of him. Annaji, Balaji, Moropant, and Yesaji stood around. Everyone had lowered their heads.

As Sambhajiraje bowed down to make an obeisance, Raje stopped him and said, "Shambhooraje, make an obeisance to your late deputy minister!"

Raje dragged his feet and approached Sambhajiraje. He put his hand on Sambhajiraje's shoulder and said, "Sambhajiraje, Prataprao thrust himself into the inferno of Pathan Bahlol's army of ten thousand and sacrificed himself! Adamant as he was, he was upset with me; and took six other valiant soldiers along!"

Sambhajiraje remembered the letter of reproach that Raje had written to Prataprao for releasing Bahalol Khan from his custody – "Why did you make a truce with the Pathan? Show me your face only after you have finished the enemy!"

Ungrateful Bahalol wreaked havoc in the Marathi region after his release. For one whole year, Prataprao kept chasing him, waiting for an opportunity to fix his mistake. But Bahalol had secured himself.

Prataprao came to know that Raje was going to be enthroned. He wanted to come back to Raigad for the coronation ceremony. But how could he show his face to Raje if Bahalol was still alive?

Prataprao got the information that Bahalol Khan's army of ten thousand Pathan soldiers had encamped in the gorge of Kupe near Nesari. A direct attack on him with their small army would have proved futile. Therefore, Prataprao summoned a few select swordsmen in his tent. Out of the blue, he announced at the meeting, "I am going to charge headlong at the enemy! Alone! Convey my regards to Raje!"

The six swordsmen wielded their swords and upheld his decision resolutely, "Sarlashkar, we will go wherever you go!" And on the day of Mahashivaratri, Prataprao astride his horse, accompanied by the six swordsmen, brandished his sword and attacked the enemy hollering war cries of "Har Har Mahadeo".

The seven fierce soldiers attacked the army of ten thousand, never to return. Seven roaring thunderbolts plummeted in the ocean of the Pathan army and were snuffed out.

As Sambhajiraje heard Karmaji's account from Raje's mouth, Prataprao's bold face stood in front of his eyes.

For no apparent reason, the words of the mahout echoed in Sambhajiraje's ears, "Trishul…can you stop being stubborn?!"

Embellished Raigad went into mourning for the sacrifice of Prataprao. With a heavy heart, Raje performed the obsequies. Hansaji Mohite was offered the robes of honour and inducted as the new Sarlashkar. He was bestowed with the appellation of 'Hambirarao'.

Gagabhatt referred to all ancient scriptures and inscribed a comprehensive list of rituals for the coronation ceremony.

Raigad received news from Pachad that Kashibai's health was on the decline.

Raje, Sambhajiraje, Jijau, all the queens, Yesubai, Dharau, the entire royal family came to Pachad. Kashibai departed with a contented heart, looking blissfully at Raje and Sambhajiraje, who were about to be enthroned soon. She left silently, with many things unsaid, buried deep in her heart. The palace of Pachad drowned in lamentations.

Sambhajiraje gazed dolorously at the sandalwood funeral pyre burning on the plains of Pachad.

Within one month of Prataprao's death, Kashibai also passed away. As a Yuvaraj, Sambhajiraje was supposed to wear the royal crown on his head, but instead, as the eldest son, his head was shaved as part of the funeral rites. Raigad went into mourning again.

Kashibai's last rites were performed. Raje was going to Pratapgad with Sambhajiraje; to seek the blessings of his family deity, Bhavani; to present her with the golden parasol created by Ramaji Dutto; to go to the cavern of Shivathar Ghal and meet Samartha in person.

The father and son bade farewell to Jijau and left Raigad with a select retinue.

The golden parasol was placed in a palanquin bedecked with flower garlands. The palanquin-bearers chanted the name of Goddess Bhavani and picked up the palanquin.

The journey continued in the hot summer weather. The retinue ascended the mountain ghat and entered the Javali basin. It passed by Afzal Khan's tomb and arrived at Pratapgad.

The placement of the parasol was going to take place the next day. After having their meal, in the evening, Raje left with Sambhajiraje to inspect the fort.

After checking the important places on the fort, they came to the 'Afzal-buruj'. Afzal Khan's tomb was visible at a faraway distance. Raje looked at it and became solemn.

"Maharaj Saheb, Khan had taken a solemn vow and came to kill you, but you gave him a proper ceremonial burial after his death. Why did you do it?" Sambhajiraje looked at Afzal's tomb and asked Raje.

Raje looked at the sandalwood stripes on Sambhajiraje's forehead, and his black moustache curling on his cheeks and exclaimed, "I fight against the deeds of a person and not the doer. I believe that enmity should end with the enemy's death."

"But the enemy doesn't think the same! We could not obtain Gujarkaka's remains and perform his cremation. The enemy still throws and will continue to throw the bodies of our dead soldiers to the wild animals. Why is it so?"

What he said was right. For a moment, that thought left Raje benumbed. But then, he calmly said, "That is where our Swaraj differs from the Mughal Empire. I erected the demolished temples again and will continue to do it. But I just cannot bring myself to destroy the holy places of other faiths. Earlier, I used to feel just like you, but Masaheb corrected my mistaken beliefs and taught me to think nobly."

They both remembered Jijau and fell silent. They could hear the beating sound of the Sambal drums, coming from the Bhavani temple.

Annaji Dutto tidied his shawl and came to Soyarabai's chamber on Raigad.

He made an obeisance to Ranisaheb.

"Surnis, I have heard that the comprehensive list of rituals for the coronation ceremony is ready." Soyarabai broached the subject directly.

As Raje and Yuvaraj were not at Raigad, Soyarabai had summoned Annaji through Chandra, to dispel a doubt she had.

"Ji..." Annaji responded holding his head bent. Just then, Ramraje entered the chamber with the maid Chandra. Annaji made an obeisance to him.

Soyarabai pulled Ramraje close to her, and while casually arranging his pearl necklace neatly, she decided how she would broach the topic she wanted to discuss. "What rituals is Balraje going to perform during the ceremony?" Soyarabai's intimidating gaze moved from Annaji's big turban to the horizontal stripes on his forehead.

Annaji had no answer to that question; he remained silent.

"Why? Surnis, isn't Balraje going to take part in any ritual during the ceremony? Why are you quiet?" Soyarabai said in a disgruntled tone.

"Ji. There is no specific mention of Balraje's name in the comprehensive list of rituals that Acharya has prepared!" Annaji said cautiously.

"How can it be? Isn't he part of this family? Then why make an obeisance to him at all?"

"Rani Saheb, please don't misunderstand me. I am not at fault here. Swami has conferred complete authority upon the Acharya to make the decisions about the rituals of the coronation ceremony."

"That is what I am saying. Acharya doesn't know the protocol on the fort. Who is going to tell him, if things are overlooked? Shouldn't you bring it to his notice?" Soyarabai spoke in a roundabout way and brought Annaji to the point where she wanted him to be.

"Ji. I will suggest this to acharya but cannot guarantee that acharya will accept it."

"You should at least give it a try."

"Ji." Annaji nodded. He made an obeisance to Soyarabai and Ramraje and left the chamber.

After some time, Soyarabai's maid Chandra went to Annaji's residence and invited his wife to Soyarabai's chamber for the Haldi-Kumkum ceremony.

In the evening, Annaji's wife came to Soyarabai's chamber. Soyarabai gifted her a brocaded sari with a pearl-studded nose ring and said, "It feels good when family members come to visit."

Raje and Sambhajiraje were on the way to Shivthar Ghal with the entourage.

They reached Shivthar Ghal. It was covered with veils and creepers. The peals of conches permeated the entire forest.

As Samartha had received the intimation of Raje's arrival, he was coming with his disciples, to receive Raje.

"Jai Jai Raghuveer Samartha!" As Raje heard the distinct voice of Samartha, he said, "Shambhoo, Samartha himself is coming to receive us. There he is, in the front. Let's get down."

Raje dismounted and removed his mojaris. He walked briskly towards Samartha and put his head on Samartha's feet. Samartha gently put his hand on Raje's jiretop and blessed him.

Raje moved aside. Sambhajiraje came forward and put his head on Samartha's feet. Samartha blessed him.

Sambhajiraje stood up and gazed into the tranquil, radiant eyes of Samartha. His visage looked determined, pure, tranquil, having complete control over the senses and dispassionate eyes of a sanyasi!

Samartha gazed at Sambhajiraje, with pure eyes that brought a sense of calm to him. He puckered his forehead and said, "You are… Yuvaraj… Sambhajiraje. Hmm!"

"Ji." Sambhajiraje's golden earrings swayed gently.

"Swamiji, you need not have come personally to receive us." Raje said affectionately.

"Raje, those who lead the subjects onto the right path, deserve this honour! Come with me." Samartha pointed to the cavern.

The devotee of Lord Rama walked into the cavern with the devotees of Goddess Jagadamba. Raje's voice echoed in the stone-walled cavern, "I have come to invite you to Raigad."

Samartha sat on a tiger skin mat spread on a stone platform. A tall idol of Lord Hanuman, posed to soar high, stood behind him. A sturdy bow was placed near it, and a quiver full of arrows was placed next to it.

Raje and Sambhajiraje sat on a woollen blanket spread in front of Samartha. The soft spirals of smoke emanating from the dhuni pot permeated the cavern.

Samartha closed his eyes and kept pulling the beads of his rosary for some time. Then, his eyes opened slowly, and earnest words started trickling from his mouth.

"Raje, I have come to know of the auspicious news of your coronation ceremony. I feel honoured that you came in person to invite me. Sivabaraje, long for a time, I have bestowed my blessings upon you. We hermits spend our lives in hilly regions. We are not bound by the rules of society. We dress ourselves in loin cloths only for the sake of social modesty and seek alms only for survival. Even that is a burden for us. Therefore, please don't get me involved in any social celebrations."

"I consider you as the incarnation of Lord Ramchandra. Please listen carefully to the advice that I am going to offer now. Do not hesitate and let the coronation ceremony be conducted as per the prescribed rituals. You still have a lot more to do than what you have done so far."

Samartha closed his eyes again and went into a meditative stance.

Samartha concluded his meditation chanting the name of Lord Rama and opened his eyes. He rose from his seat and went near the Hanuman idol behind him. The shoulder-high bow was his own that he used for practice.

Raje and Yuvaraj stood up on the woollen blanket.

Samartha approached Raje and said in a dispassionate voice, "I have already given you my blessings, now accept my bow as a gift to you on your coronation. This is the only thing I can give you, and it is appropriate for the occasion. Please take this. May you always be triumphant!"

Samartha held the bow in front of Raje. Raje's eyes got misty. He bowed down and accepted that prasad of Lord Rama respectfully. He closed his eyes and touched the bow to his forehead and handed it to Sambhajiraje.

As Yuvaraj closed his eyes and touched the bow to his forehead, one thought put forth by Samartha pierced his heart like an arrow – "One who is afraid of death should not call himself a Kshatriya."

Sambhajiraje held the bow and the quiver in his hand and wanted to say something to Samartha but stopped. He glanced at Raje.

"Yuvaraj, feel free to speak." Samartha noticed his hesitation.

"Nothing…I just wanted to say…" Sambhajiraje hesitated.

"Yes, tell me what it is." Samarth smiled.

"You have rendered Maharaj Saheb's personality in a verse. I would be grateful if you could do the same for Thoralya Aausaheb.

As Samartha pictured Jijau, whom he had never met, he remembered his own mother whom he had seen in his childhood. He determinedly pushed her memories aside.

"Yuvaraj, you and Raje are fortunate to be in her company every day. I have not met her, only heard about her. And even if I had met her, I would probably not be able to depict her personality in words. I composed Dasbodh using words, but she has moulded this living 'Shivabodh' who inspires people!" Samartha pointed to Raje. "Maharishi Valmiki composed the 'Ramayana' but even he could not capture Mother Kousalya in entirety. How can I forget it?"

Raje and Sambhajiraje touched Samartha's feet.

They spent the night at Shivthar Ghal and left for Raigad at the crack of dawn. Samartha accompanied them to the entrance of the cavern to bid farewell.

As Raje joined his palms to say goodbye, Samartha put his hand on Raje's shoulder and said in a tremulous voice, "Raje, don't forget to convey my respects to Aaisaheb. Farewell. May Lord Rama bless you! Jai…Jai…Raghuveer Samartha!"

Samartha closed his eyes. Sambhajiraje was looking at his back, with a wandering mind that wondered, "Samarth is such a great man! What does his mother look like? Where could she be now? Is it possible that she might have heard the Dasbodh?

Sambhajiraje observed the crystal clean water of 'Bara-take'. Samartha's face and his words lingered in his mind.

Suddenly, there was a rustling sound of dry leaves from a bush nearby. A speckled serpent was sliding on the ground as fast as an arrow. Suddenly, that speckled, spirited animal stopped, raised its shining hood high and flicked its tongue a couple of times.

Rayaji, who stood behind Sambhajiraje, wielded his spear and aimed it at the serpent. Antoji promptly pressed his hand down and said, "It's an ornament of Lord Shambhoo. Just let it go its way."

Rayaji frowned and stopped. The serpent slithered away and disappeared among the bushes. Sambhajiraje was about to say something to Rayaji, when Mahadeo Yamaji came with Kavi Kulesh, made an obeisance to him and announced, "A bard from the North has come to stay in the Jagadishwar temple. Swami wants Yuvaraj to meet him."

"Sure, let's go." Yuvaraje left Bara-take wondering who the poet could be. He came to the courtyard of the Jagadishwar temple with Kulesh and Mahadeo Yamaji.

A white mare was pegged under a tree and a man was humming a tune while grooming it.

Sambhajiraje came to the first chowk of the temple. He walked around the stone tortoise on the ground and tolled a bell. Then, he entered the inner shrine of the temple and knelt in front of the Shivlinga enveloped by Bael leaves and flowers, soaking in the water of Abhishek. The temple priest offered him tirtha. Sambhajiraje held the tirtha in his palm, touched it to his eyes and sipped it.

Outside, Kavi Kulesh and Mahadeo Yamaji were searching

for the poet in the rooms around the courtyard. The rooms were occupied by ascetics and monks who had arrived in anticipation of alms and charities. Raje's disguised informants had already mingled among the monks. One of them recognized Mahadeopant and approached him.

He came out of the chowk and whispered in Mahadeopant's ears, "That's him, the poet. Dhani just heard his poems in the inner chowk and left. He was very happy to hear the poems, but the poet did not recognize Dhani at all! I also heard his poems but did not understand his language." The informant disguised in the cloak of a monk pointed his finger to the dwarfish man grooming the mare.

"Greetings to you Kaviraj!" Kavi Kulesh stepped forward and stopped the man from grooming the horse.

"Jai Jayanti, greetings to you too!" The groom stood straight and glanced at Kavi Kulesh in surprise at hearing the Hindustani language.

His complexion was like a ripe mango. He wore a Kanauji turban, a white northern style jama, and red-bordered dhoti. He had applied horizonal stripes of ash on his forehead.

He asked, "Pardon me, but who are you?"

"I am Kavi Kulesh, from Prayag. And may I know your name please?"

"Yes. I am Bhushan Tripathi from Trivikrampur,"

"Oh Chandi…Chandi…my greetings to you Kaviraj Bhushan. I have heard a lot about you; glad to meet you in person." Kulesh paid respects to the brilliant poet from Kanauj once again.

As Kulesh saw Sambhajiraje coming towards the tree, he whispered to Bhushan, "Yuvaraj Sambhajiraje!"

Bhushan leaned forward, made obeisance to the radiant Kshatriya coming towards him in the Kanauj style and whispered, "Jai Jayanti! Raja Sivaji's son."

"Kaviraj, it is by Aabasaheb's order that I am here to meet

you. Where are you from? What is your name?" Sambhajiraje noticed the similarity between the turbans Bhushan and Kulesh were wearing.

Bhushan introduced himself to Yuvaraj and implored him, "Yuvaraj, I have come from a faraway country. Please let me visit Raja Sivaji in person."

"Certainly. You should indeed meet him. But first, you should move from here and come to my chamber." Yuvaraj said with a smile.

"Yes, sure." Bhushan courteously accepted his offer.

Rayaji untied Bhushan's mare and took her in custody. Bhushan went inside with Antoji and brought his belongings.

Sambhajiraje started walking towards the Balekilla with the two poets. Rayaji and Antoji held the reins of Bhushan's mare, 'Kesar' and followed them. As they entered the market, people began making obeisance to Sambhajiraje. Kavi Bhushan was taking in the royal riches of Raigad.

As Sambhajiraje entered his chamber, he held Bhushan's hand with respect and signalled his attendant Yadav Namaji to bring something.

He ushered Bhushan to the seat in the centre and seated him by his side. Kulesh and Mahadeopant stood along a wall courteously.

Yadav brought in a silver platter with silver glasses full of saffron milk. Sambhajiraje picked up a glass from the platter, offered it to Bhushan and said, "Here, have some milk please."

"Ji!" Bhushan responded, touched by the hospitality.

Sambhajiraje took a sip of the milk and said, "Poetry appeals to me. Whenever I meet a poet, I feel like I have bathed in the pure waters of River Bana Ganga."

"Ji!" Bhushan kept wondering in his mind about only one thing, "If Shivaji's son is so handsome, how handsome would Shivaji be?"

"Kaviraj, which language do you speak?"

"Ji! Brajbhasha! With your permission, I would like to present a glimpse of my language in front of you."

"Yes, certainly! I would be happy to hear it." Yuvaraj said with a smile.

Bhushan got up from his seat and pulled out the tambourine and a scarf from his bag.

He stood in the centre of the chamber and wrapped the scarf around his waist. He made an obeisance to Sambhajiraje, closed his eyes and beat his tambourine a couple of times. And suddenly, Bhushan's voice transformed into a bard's voice.

For a long time, Bhushan presented his select compositions to Sambhajiraje, to the beat of his tambourine.

Sambhajiraje was ecstatic to hear Bhushan's spirited lyrics. He rose from his seat and went to Bhushan. He removed one of his pearl necklaces, put it around Bhushan's neck and said to him, "Kaviraj, every single word of yours deserves to be rewarded with a fistful of pearls. I am mesmerized. Your compositions are striking!"

"Please treat him with due honour." Sambhajiraje instructed Mahadeopant. Kulesh and Mahadeopant left with Bhushan.

"Let's go." Raje said to Sambhajiraje. Yuvaraj put his hands on Ramraje's shoulder, who stood next to him. Prabhakarbhat and Anantbhat had carried cooked rice in a platter and spread it along the fortification of Raigad to ward off the evil eye.

The first round of rituals of the coronation ceremony was going to begin today. Crowds thronged Raigad. Raje's kith and kin from Faltan, Talbeed, Shringarpur, Chouk, Sindakhed, Bhuinja, Pali and other places had arrived on the fort.

All sardars including Bandal, Jedhe, Shirke, Malusare, Pasalkar, Shilimbkar, Kank, Jadhav, Dahatonde and Bhosale had ascended the fort with their entourage. The British vakeel of the Mumbai durbar, Henry Oxenden was present at the fort too.

Big and small tents, shamianas had been erected wherever place was available. The Nagar Khana, Maha Darwaja and the Balekilla were festooned with garlands of flowers and mango leaves. Special tents had been erected under many sprawling trees, in which food was being prepared. Smoky flames soared high from under the cauldrons placed on the stoves. The sound of beating drums pierced through the curtains of smoke and dispersed all over the fort. The tunes of trumpets mingled with the beating of the drums and spread everywhere. The saffron Jaripataka pennant, looking larger than usual, stood tall on the flagpole near the Nagar Khana. The small triangular orange flags hoisted on top of all the temples on the fort kept fluttering in tune with the Jaripataka pennant.

Silver anklets were fastened around the front-right legs of the horses in the royal stable and rich brocaded cloths were placed on their backs. Attendants carrying leather water bags sprinkled water on the streets to settle the rising clouds of dust. A square wooden stool was placed in the Aabdar Khana, and holy water, collected from seven rivers such as Ganga, Sindhu, Yamuna, and seven oceans such as the Eastern, Western and Southern Ocean was filled in the golden and earthen containers. Raje, clad in puja clothes, left his palace with Ramraje, Yuvaraj Sambhajiraje and Gaga Bhatt. Behind them walked the eight ministers, and chief sardars such as Yesaji Kank, Anandrao, Firangoji, Pilaji Shirke, Rupaji, Sarjerao; Kavi Bhushan, Kulesh, Parmananda and Nischalpuri also walked along and were followed by loyal Mavalas such as Gomaji, Khandoji, Rayaji, Antoji!

After getting blessed by Jijau, all of them came to Ramji Dutto's workshop. Soyarabai arrived with a few suvasinis and a bevy of maids.

The royal throne was covered with a saffron cover and placed in the central chowk of the workshop. A golden Ganesh murti was placed on its right. They were going to be worshipped and installed today. The bow given by Samartha was also going to be worshipped.

Ramaji stepped forward and gently removed the saffron cover.

"Jagadamb! Jagadamb!" With the first glance at the throne, Raje's hand unwittingly touched his chest. Sambhajiraje saw the tiger faces carved on the arms of the throne and remembered Raje's words, "We are Bhosales first, and hunters later! The tiger is Goddess Jagadamba's mount."

Raje, Soyarabai and Sambhajiraje sat on sandalwood seats. Gaga Bhatt chanted a shloka from the Ganesh Atharvashirsha.

The puja of Lord Ganesha and the royal throne was performed. The puja of the bow was performed, and flowers of gold were showered.

"Please come forward and give the customary touch of your hand to the royal throne." Gaga Bhatt urged the royal family. Raje and Soyarabai stepped forward. Ramraje watched everything, standing aside.

"Come, let's touch the throne together." Sambhajiraje affectionately held Ramraje's hand and ushered him close to the royal throne.

"Har…har…Mahadeo!" The assembled Mavalas shouted at the top of their lungs. The royal family gave the customary touch of their hands to the royal throne.

Hambirarao, Anandrao, Moropant, Annaji, Ramchandrapant, Yesaji, everyone stepped forward. "Jai Bhavani" they all roared in unison, and carried the golden royal throne to a chariot embellished with flower garlands. Five embellished white horses were harnessed to the chariot. Raje leaned forward, picked up the Ganesh murti and held it close to his chest. Sambhajiraje carried the bow.

The vibrating beats of tabors resounded. The lezims started jingling rhythmically. The guns and the cannons boomed. The royal cavalry marched in a disciplined manner. The swords in the hands of the cavalry troopers sparkled in the rays of the sun.

Raje, carrying the Ganesh murti, Soyarabai holding the puja platter, Sambhajiraje holding the bow of Samartha and Ramraje holding his hand, the royal family bound to the royal throne by blood, walked behind the chariot carrying the throne.

The chariot procession proceeded through the Nagar Khana Darwaja and came to the courtyard of the durbar. The frame of the royal throne's platform was built in gold. The centre of the platform was left vacant for the unique royal throne. Raje handed the Ganesh murti to Sambhajiraje.

The chariot came close to the platform. Gaga Bhatt climbed up the platform with the royal circle. Prabhakarbhat climbed up with a platter containing the auspicious sand collected from the sole of an elephant.

Ramaji Dutto climbed onto the platform with a platter containing a golden nail. A ladder was carried onto the platform. Gaga Bhatt picked up the golden nail from the platter Ramaji Dutto was holding. He chanted some mantras, looked at the nail and handed it to Raje.

Raje held the nail and came close to the ladder. Hambirarao, Yesaji and Anandrao supported the ladder. Raje climbed up the ladder, holding the nail and the hammer and reached the roof of the Meghadambari. Everyone raised their heads high and looked at the roof.

Raje hammered the golden nail in the hole of the roof. He climbed down the ladder and the ladder was removed. The ritual of spreading the auspicious sand collected from the sole of an elephant began. Mantras were chanted.

Gaga Bhatt took the platter of the auspicious sand from Prabhakarbhat. He picked a fistful of sand and poured it in Raje's palms.

He signalled Raje to sprinkle it on the vacant base where the throne was going to be installed. Raje sprinkled the sand on the vacant base. Soyarabai stepped forward. Gaga Bhatt poured a fistful of sand in her palms. Soyarabai spread the sand on the vacant base. Sambhajiraje handed the Ganesh murti and the bow to Prabhakarbhat. He stepped forward and spread the sand that Acharya Gaga Bhatt had given him.

Gaga Bhatt was about to place the platter down when Soyarabai pulled Ramraje forward and held his palms in front of acharya. Acharya hesitated for a moment. Then he poured some sand in Ramraje's palms. Soyarabai ushered him to the vacant base and said, "Here, pour the sand here now!"

Raje came to Jijau's chamber with Soyarabai and Sambhajiraje, before starting the pre-coronation rituals. Their faces looked radiant as they had been consuming fruits and milk only. Jijau sat on a seat in the centre of her chamber, leaning against a bolster. For the last fifteen days, she had been receiving the guests arriving at the fort, though she was feeling weary.

Raje and Yuvaraj leaned forward together to touch her feet. Jijau stroked their faces affectionately. Her words were exhausted. They got stuck in her throat.

"Swari should have been here to witness this ceremony!"

Shahajiraje's memory brought tears to Jijau's eyes. Her sorrowful tears trickled through her wrinkles. So many glorious rituals are taking place on the fort, but I cannot even watch one, only because I am a widow! It is like being surrounded by sea water; you can't drink a single drop to quench your thirst! I am here but I cannot participate in any ceremonies. 'Jagadamb, Jagadamb!' Jijau composed herself and blessed Raje and Sambhajiraje wholeheartedly, "May god bless you with a long life!"

"May you have a blissful married life!" Jijau blessed Soyarabai with trembling hands.

"Masaheb, you should stop attending to the guests now and rest." Raje said earnestly.

"How can I stay away from the guests? I am going to be a Rajmata now. More people will come to visit me now. Raje, I will never stop the guests coming to the fort!" Jijau said determinedly.

"Let us take your leave now." Raje left Jijau's chamber with Sambhajiraje and Soyarabai.

The three of them offered milk to Lord Jagadishwar and came to the grand altar in the courtyard of the durbar. The main rituals of the pre-coronation ceremony began. Gaga Bhatt, Balambhat, Anantbhat and many other holy men guided them to perform various rituals. Many rituals were performed.

By the royal hands of Raje, Yuvaraj and Soyarabai, sacrificial sticks of various trees such as Bael, Audumbar, Pimpal, Aamra were offered in various pits of sacred fire. Milk, ghee, curds and honey were offered to the fire.

Though he was married, had daughters, two sons and a daughter-in-law, Raje's thread ceremony was performed! Mighty Raje became a 'Batu'. He wore the sacred thread. Raje who had rejuvenated the Marathi region, was himself reborn.

All the marriages of Raje were annulled by the thread ceremony. Therefore, he had to get remarried to his queens Soyarabai, Sakawarbai, Putalabai and others as per religious rituals. Raje expressed a desire of his heart to Gaga Bhatt – "As I am from the Suryavansha dynasty, I would like you to consecrate me with the Savitru mantra."

Gaga Bhatt agreed. A yajna pit was raised for the Savitruhoma. As this ceremony was not propitious for women, Soyarabai was excluded from the homa ceremony.

After the Savitruhoma the Shantihoma and many other homas such as Vinayak, Nakshatra, Indra, Graha, and Purandar were performed. The grand altar abounded in the aromatic fragrance of milk and ghee poured in the yajna pits.

At the centre of the grand altar, a large scale of silver pans, embellished with flower garlands was fastened to a sturdy pillar. Its puja was performed.

The ceremony for performing Raje's Tula began. Raje put

his right leg in the right pan and sat in the pan. Gaga Bhatt, Balambhat, Anantbhat started pouring fistful of sparkling gold coins in the left pan. The gold coins kept striving to raise the golden Sun of the Bhosale family.

The pan Raje sat in got raised. Raje's Suvarnatula was done. Various mantras resonated in the air. Gaga Bhatt collected the seventeen thousand gold coins in various platters and offered flowers atop them.

Fifteen more tulas of Raje were performed with various materials such as silver and copper coins, camphor, lead, fruits, honey, spices, sugar and other things.

"Yuvaraj, please offer the flowers to the scale pans." Gaga Bhatt put some flowers in Sambhajiraje's palms.

Sambhajiraje offered flowers and haldi-kumkum on the pans and paid respects to it. Then, he put his right foot on the right pan and sat in the pan. Mantras resonated in the air again.

Gaga Bhatt, Balambhat, Prabhakarbhat poured gold coins in the left pan. Sambhajiraje watched the jingling coins falling in the pan, and out of the blue, a thought occurred in his mind, 'My Masaheb will come here, place a single Bael leaf that is usually offered to the Shivlinga, in the other pan, and throw a loving glance at me. Then, my pan will rise and reach the sky!"

The pan Sambhajiraje sat in got raised. Sambhajiraje stepped out of the pan.

"Maharani, please come." Acharya handed some flowers to Soyarabai. Soyarabai performed the puja of the pan. As she placed her right foot in the right pan, she wanted to tell Acharya Gaga Bhatt, 'If you really want to do my tula, let Ramraje sit in the pan with me. Without him, this tula means nothing to me.' But she remembered acharya's hesitance when he handed Ramraje the sand from the elephant's sole. And without saying anything, she sat in the pan alone.

The thirteenth day of the bright fortnight of Jyeshtha was about to break.

Raje and Sambhajiraje, both got ready early in the morning and came together to Jijau's chamber to seek her blessings. Jijau blessed both and as she embraced them, her heart was filled with turmoil, 'By the primordial mother's grace I can witness this day. Swari should have been here to witness the ceremony today. Raje's elder brother and my eldest Soonbai should have been alive.'

She gasped for breath. Jijau resolutely tried hard to control the bout of coushing, as Raje and Sambhajiraje were in front of her. She panted and felt an irritation in her throat. She had been able to control herself so far, but today she could not. She started coughing hard.

Raje and Sambhajiraje held both her arms and tried to comfort her,

"Masaheb."

"Thoralya Aausaheb."

The father and son forgot about the coronation ceremony for a moment. Dharau and Putalabai stood behind Jijau. All of them supported her and seated her on the bed. Everyone felt distressed. Just then, Balambhat entered the chamber with acharya's message. As she saw him, Jijau said, "Raje and Yuvaraj, you should leave now. Acharya has summoned you. You no longer belong to me, but to the royal throne! The pandit is waiting for you."

Sambhajiraje made an obeisance to Putalabai and Dharau. They were about to leave and go to the grand altar. As Sambhajiraje was about to turn, he saw Jijau wiping her eyes with the edge of her sari. He was unable to move.

"Let's go." Raje's hoarse voice fell on his ears. He turned around and started walking towards the Jagadishwar and Bhavani temple.

"This cough is bringing tears to my eyes." Jijau said to Dharau who stood quietly behind her. She did not realize that Dharau's eyes had already filled with tears, without any cough at all.

The pandal of the grand altar was crowded with sages who had attained divine knowledge, pandits and the scholars of Shastras. At the centre of the pandal, round pitchers made of gold, silver, copper and clay were placed in the eight directions. Mango leaves and coconuts were placed on top of the pitchers. They were filled with five ambrosial ingredients – milk, curds, ghee, honey, sugar and also water. All pitchers were arranged together in a square for the Abhishek ceremony. To the right of the square, a large seat made from the wood of an Audumbar tree, was erected, on which Raje, Yuvaraj and Soyarabai were going to sit for the Abhishek ceremony. Elaborate arrangements were made for the Abhishek ceremony.

The ceremony commenced with the puja of Lord Ganesh. The royal family offered haldi-kumkum, put their right foot forward and entered the chowk. Gaga Bhatt, Balambhat and others entered after them. Moropant, Hambirarao, Annaji, Ramchandrapant, Tryambakpant, Duttaji Trimal, Nirajipant, Raghunath Pandit and other ministers followed. The pandal was thronged with crowds.

Raje approached the seat; the ministers followed him. Raje performed a ceremonial puja of the seat and sat on it, making sure his feet didn't touch it. Soyarabai and Sambhajiraje followed suit.

From all the materials arranged neatly for the ceremony, Annaji picked up the parasol, Tryambakpant took the peacock-feathered fan and Duttaji held the golden chowri. The three of them stood behind the seat. Moropant holding the golden pitcher, Hambirarao with the silver pitcher, Ramachandrapant holding the copper pitcher, Raghunath Pandit carrying the clay pitcher and judge Nirajipant holding the diamond-studded, golden royal sceptre, stood on either side of the seat.

Acharya Gaga Bhatt commenced the Abhishek ceremony.

Moropant handed the golden pitcher of ghee to Balambhat.

Raje, Samhajiraje and Soyarabai were drenched under the trickling streams of ghee, milk, curds, honey, and the waters of the holy rivers such as Ganga, Sindhu, Yamuna, and the invincible waters of the roaring oceans of the east, west and south.

After the Abhishek ceremony, the royal family donned rich attire and viewed their faces in the mirror of melted ghee spread in a round salver. Raje and Yuvaraj performed the puja of their weapons and wielded them.

Accompanied by Sambhajiraje, Raje started walking behind Gaga Bhatt, in the direction of the royal throne. The ministers, pandits, sardars and others followed him. Faraway, in the distant mountain ranges, a new day had dawned.

Raje, Soyarabai and Yuvaraj approached the platform of the royal throne. On the first step of the platform a silver vessel was placed on a wooden stool. A copper pot was placed in it to indicate the time of the Mahurat.

Raje cracked open the coconut that acharya had given him, on the first step of the platform and tossed the two pieces on both sides. Then he performed the ceremonial puja of the royal throne.

"Jagadamb, Jagadamb" Raje whispered and put his right foot on the first step of the platform and started climbing the stairs. Soyarabai and Sambhajiraje followed him.

Raje made an obeisance to the oversized golden royal throne studded with gems and diamonds. Then, he sat on the throne without touching his foot to it.

Sambhajiraje sat on the golden step near the base of the throne. Soyarabai sat on the left of the throne, in the curtained section for the royal ladies. The eight ministers took their respective places near the golden poles. The spear-holders, chowri-holders, and fan-holders took their respective places.

Acharya Gaga Bhatt removed the Jiretops of Raje and Yuvaraj and placed them in an empty platter. He picked up Raje's white

Jiretop, charmed with mantras, from another platter. Mantras resonated. As the time measuring pot sank in the water vessel, acharya placed the royal Jiretop on Raje's head, and an orange Jiretop on Sambhajiraje's head. The Ukhali cannons on Raigad boomed, gun shots were fired. The drums and other instruments resounded.

The spear-holder raised the spear in his hand and called the appellations in a clear voice, "The sovereign king of the Hindus, from the lineage of the Kshatriyas, the crowned king and the saviour of the cows and the Brahmins, Shriman Chhatrapati Shivaji Maharaj!"

"Victory to him! Victory! Victory! The entire durbar responded in unison.

The rays of the rising sun arrived to make obeisance to the royal throne. The golden throne, basking in the sunlight, glowed radiantly. Sambhajiraje was captivated by the sight of the rising sun and kept gazing at it.

His reverie was broken as he heard the tinkling of golden coins falling to the floor around him. Raje sat on the royal throne and Peshwe Moropant was showering golden coins over him. The coins kept bouncing over Raje's head and dropped around Sambhajiraje who sat on the step at the base of the royal throne.

All the guests started presenting valuable gifts to Raje. The British officer, Henry Oxenden, made his way through the crowd and stood in front of the royal throne.

He removed his hat and bowed low to make obeisance to Raje and Yuvaraj. Then, he spoke in his mother tongue, "Your excellency, Raja Shivaji may shower his mercy and accept the gifts of the Company!"

His attendants presented the salvers of gifts which included a diamond-studded aigrette, two precious pearls and two bracelets studded with gems for Raje. Sambhajiraje was gifted with two bracelets studded with gems and a diamond-studded necklace.

The presentation of gifts concluded, and the offering of alms began. Raje and Yuvaraj began offering alms to the assembled Brahmins, ascetics, sages, bhutyas, torchbearers and fakirs. After receiving the alms, all of them blessed Raje and Yuvaraj wholeheartedly, "May your wishes be fulfilled! May Lord Bholanath bless you with happiness", "May Allah always protect you!"

After the charity session, various artists presented their select compositions such as ballads, bhajans and dances. At the end of the programme, Kavi Bhushan fastened a scarf around his waist and stood in front of the royal throne. He started beating his hand-drum vigorously.

The audience in the durbar began applauding Bhushan's glorious tribute to Shivajiraje. Bhushan had closed his eyes and, raising his hand, he started singing Raje's glory in dazzling words.

Sambhajiraje forgot his royal status and lauded Bhushan's brilliant, dazzling compositions, by raising his hand. In the chowk behind them water fountains kept surging, and fountains of words kept gushing in front of them. Bhushan got excited while describing the Raje's achievements and got lost in the moment.

"Wah, Brilliant!" the poet in Sambhajiraje responded spontaneously. Bhushan concluded his presentation. A platter of gold coins was presented to Bhushan, who was drenched in sweat.

Raje rose from the royal throne. Sambhajiraje stood on the step he was sitting. Soyarabai left her seat in the royal ladies' section. The royal circle was now going to visit the Jagadishwar temple.

"Hail Shriman Chhatrapati Shivaji Maharaj..."

"Victory to him! Victory! Victory!" The peals of triumph created ripples on the sheer curtains around the hall. With every step the royal family took forward, hundreds of loyal heads on both sides bowed down in obeisance.

The entourage for the journey of the royal family was in

position near the Nagar Khana. The royal elephant 'Trishul' stood there in a trance, flapping his ears and swaying his body. A tinking golden bell was tied around its neck and a silver anklet was placed on the right leg. Colourful tracery designs were inked on its trunk and temples. A rich brocaded cloth covered its back, and a golden howdah was placed on it; it was shining in the rays of the sun. In front of Trishul stood a snow-white royal horse. A rich brocaded cloth embellished its back, a golden garland was put around its neck, and a golden anklet on the right leg. The honourable guests of the durbar had donned exclusive attires, held bare swords, and had lined up on either side of the path. The royal elephant was surrounded by the parasol-holders, flag-bearers, chowry-holders, and spear-holders. The mahout goaded the royal elephant to sit down. A ladder was placed against it. First, Sarlashkar Hambirarao, holding the golden goad, climbed the ladder and took charge of the royal elephant as the mahout. After him, Raje and the royal family mounted and took their seats in the golden howdah. Moropant, holding a bunch of peacock feathers, sat behind them.

Hambirarao goaded the elephant to stand up. Golden flowers, gulal powder and fresh flowers were showered on the elephant. In a grand style, the procession of the royal family set out. The bands of lezims started playing in various formations; tabors and drums started beating; shotguns and Ukhali cannons boomed. Men wielding various weapons, showcased their talents aggressively in front of the royal family sitting in the howdah. The spear-holders announced the royal appellations. The ocean of assembled mavalas in red turbans began moving. 'Shiva' and 'Shambho' were going to take the darshan of Lord Shankara. The procession came in front of the Jagadishwar temple.

With Maharani Soyarabai on one side and Yuvaraj Sambhajiraje on the other, Maharaj entered the courtyard of the Jagadishwar temple.

After taking the darshan of Lord Jagadishwar the royal

procession returned to the Balekilla. The royal family went to Jijau's chamber, to take darshan of the Rajmata.

"Chhatrapati Maharaj is on the way." As Jijau heard the message, goosebumps arose on her aged body. Putalabai, Dharau and Yesubai stood around her seat.

Chhatrapati Shivaji Maharaj knelt in front of Jijau to place his head on her feet. Sambhajiraje knelt next to him. Both bowed down in front of the idol of benevolence as tall as Raigad. Tears slid from Jijau's closed eyes, over the wrinkles on her face and landed on Maharaj's royal Jiretop. The royal Jiretop got purified by the holy water.

Jijau wanted to give her blessings, but she couldn't utter a word. Her entire body trembled. Her heart was crowded with thousands of memories. Her mind was reeling in the turbulence of countless thoughts. Maharaj placed his head on her feet and waited for a few moments. Then, he raised his head with determination. His eyes were full of tears, and he could barely see Jijau. He raised both his hands and placed them on his royal Jiretop. Then, to the astonishment of everyone around, he removed that eminent Jiretop and placed it at Jijau's feet. His entire body was trembling.

"Shivaba...!" Jijau quickly wiped her tears and promptly picked up the royal Jiretop. She placed it back on his head and embraced him, and instead of any blessings the only word she could utter was, "Shivaba...!"

Jijau's trembling hand kept stroking Maharaj's back. The embrace seemed very calm but was charged with overwhelming emotions. Only Sambhajiraje who had been nurtured by the love of Maharaj, and Jijau, could understand the emotions behind that embrace.

The concluding rituals of the coronation ceremony were performed. Maharaj offered one lakh twenty-five thousand hons to Acharya Gaga Bhatt in Dakshina and dispatched a security troop of armed soldiers with him.

In Rajmata Jijau's chamber, the influx of visitors increased. The Jedhes, Bandals, Kankas, Shilimbkars… all started visiting Jijau and making an obeisance to her. Jijau, the mother of the people of Swaraj was getting drenched in the showers of the pure, simple love of the Mavalas.

The assembled guests went back. The advent of monsoon brought dark, clouds. A chilly, cold wind started blowing unhindered in Raigad. Jijau had determinedly sustained so far, but now she became ill and took to her bed. Her asthma worsened. Despite being covered in warm blankets she kept shivering. It was essential to move her from the fort to Pachad.

Covered palanquins were kept ready. Jijau was wrapped in a shawl. Maharaj and Sambhajiraje ushered her out of the chamber. Putalabai, Dharau, Yesubai, Soyarabai, Ramraje…everyone gathered around her.

"Raje, could you please take me to the hall of the durbar?" Jijau said.

"Ji." Jijau took the support of Maharaj and Yuvaraj on both sides and started walking. They came to the decorated hall of the durbar that still flaunted the signs of the coronation ceremony.

Jijau stood in front of the east-facing, diamond-studded, golden royal throne that weighed thirty-two mounds. Her body trembled and her eyes got misty. Her heart was in emotional turmoil. She looked at the embellished parasol above the royal throne and said in a hoarse voice, "Raje, finally you were crowned a king…"

Jijau's palanquin left from the Palakhi Darwaja. Maharaj and Sambhajiraje walked on both sides of the palanquin followed by more palanquins of the royal ladies. Jijau was leaving Raigad. Walking along the palanquin Sambhajiraje was lost in thought, 'The coronation ceremony is over now. I will spend this monsoon in Pachad with Thoralya Aausaheb. I will read my poems to her.

I will massage her sore muscles. Whenever she has a bout of coughing, I will hold a spittoon for her. She will smile even while gasping for breath and say to me, "Sure, read me your poems. Shivaba never composed a lyric, but Shambhooraje, you have certainly made up for that." Then, in the end I will read her the lyric which I composed on her. She will listen to it with closed eyes and utter "Jagadamb, Jagadamb!" She will tap her hand on her bed and tell me to sit near her. She will not say anything openly, but her hand stroking my back will speak a great deal to me.'

The lamps in the palace of Pachad were burning faintly. Jijau lay on her bed. Dharau sat on the floor, grinding a medicinal herb on a small round stone slab. Jijau's mind mused on a peculiar thought, to the rhythm of Dharau's jingling bangles, 'So many medicinal herbs withered in the treatment of Thoralya Soonbai. She was fed up of taking the herbal potions. At that time, I used to chide her lovingly and force her to consume the potions. I didn't realize then that in the end one feels an aversion to the medications. Today, all my family members are not listening to me and forcing me to take the potions.'

"Come in." Jijau murmured as she saw Soyarabai crossing the threshold of her chamber. She herself had summoned Soyarabai.

Outside the chamber, Maharaj and Yuvaraj sat on the veranda, anxiously listening to the vaidya from Mahad. Soyarabai made an obeisance to Jijau. Her golden bangles jingled with her movement; a few moments passed in silence.

"Soonbai, I wanted to share my thoughts with you, that is why I have summoned you." Jijau gasped for air. Her eyes were fixed on the ceiling; her hands resting on her abdomen. Soyarabai frowned; the kumkum stripes on her forehead furrowed. She pricked her ears.

"Soonbai, these might be my last words to you!" As Dharau heard those words, her hands grinding the herb stopped at once.

"This is the last time I am going to tell you anything. I am not free to die until I pour my heart out to you. Soonbai, you must understand that now you have not one but three sons, Raje, Shambhooraje and Ramraje!" Dharau's hands stopped and ears pricked.

"It is difficult to handle the men of the Bhosala family, and now you have to deal with three of them. Try and understand them. This kingdom is growing, you should help in expanding it further. Take especially good care of Shambhooraje. After his mother's demise, I became his mother. Now that responsibility lies on your shoulders. Dharau…!" Jijau's throat was parched, so she called Dharau. Dharau realized what she wanted and promptly came forward with a pitcher and a glass. Jijau felt better after sipping some water.

"I am contented that you have become the Maharani. Be the mother of the masses! Be gracious and generously accept everything that comes your way. A mother should never be vain. Pray to Goddess Jagadamba to give you that strength. You may or may not remember me, but never forget Goddess Jagadamba. I am sure that she will guide you through rough times. That is all I want to say. You may leave now." Jijau closed her eyes.

Soyarabai's nose ring twitched; her golden bangles jingled again as she made obeisance and left the chamber.

"Masaheb, here, take this." Dharau put the ground herbal paste on Jijau's tongue; Jijau swallowed it. Dharau was standing near the head of Jijau's bed, so Jijau could not see her. She could not resist herself and said, "Masaheb, you will get better. Then why do you speak like this? I am here for you!" And she stuffed the edge of her sari into her mouth, so that Jijau could not hear her muffled cries.

Pachad got drenched in monsoon showers. The Savitri, Kaal and Gandhari rivers were flooded with red water. Drops of rain kept trickling from the branches of the trees.

Yesubai was pressing Jijau's legs. She was waiting for Jijau to finish her siesta.

"Yesu." Masaheb's soft voice broke her reverie.

"Ji." Said Yesubai and got up. She picked up a pitcher from a wooden stool and went near Jijau. "Masaheb, have the tirtha of the goddess." Yesubai took the spoon close to Jijau's lips.

Jijau sipped the tirtha. "Yesu, whenever I went to the courtyard here, I always wondered if you were also standing on the western machi on the fort!"

"Yes Masaheb, once when Swari was on the fifth floor of the tower I had dared to come to the machi to take your darshan. Aabasaheb was not on the fort at that time."

Jijau smiled slightly as she heard Yesubai's reply. She wanted to say to Yesuabai, "That was the first and last time you took my darshan in that manner!" But she knew very well how hurtful those words would be to Yesubai, so she said, "My dear granddaughter-in-law, I never got a chance to talk to you. Years ago, my Swari had done a tula. In Nangargao, near the confluence of River Indrayani and Bhima, by placing an elephant cub in a boat." A bout of cough stopped Jijau from speaking.

Yesubai tidied her sari and stood up, because Maharaj was entering the chamber with Yuvaraj. The royal family vaidya and Moropant followed them. The story of the elephant cub's tula that Jijau wanted to share with Yesubail remained untold.

Jijau affectionately looked with weary eyes at Sambhajiraje and Ramraje who had held his hand and whispered, 'always stay like this – like Rama and Bharat!'

"Raje, why do you trouble him so much?" Jijau looked at the vaidya and asked.

"Looking after a mother is no trouble for a son." The vaidya tried to reassure Jijau. Maharaj sat on the bed and held Jijau's hand.

Sambhajiraje and Ramraje stood on the other side of the bed. Jijau patted her hand on the bed and signalled to them to sit on the bed. Sambhajiraje picked up Ramraje and placed him on the bed. Jijau's trembling hand stroked Ramraje's back. She said in a calm voice, "Balraje, don't let go of your Dadamaharaj's hand."

"Masaheb, how are you feeling?" Raje asked, realizing that Jijau was trying to avoid him.

"Raje I am beyond feeling anything now. It felt good to see you all. One thing, Raje..." Everyone felt as if there was detachment in Jijau's voice.

"What is it Masaheb?" Maharaj stroked her hand with affection.

"I – I want to see Mother Jagadamba's Gondhal!"

Maharaj was surprised by her wish. Then he glanced at Moropant. Moropant understood what he meant and left to summon the Gondhalis. The vaidya opened his pouch and pulled out some medicinal herbs.

At night a Gondhal dance was organized in the palace of Pachad. Jijau distributed the betel leaves and garments to the Gondhalis. The Gondhalis accepted them and began the opening prayer. Their leader started singing the tribute of the goddess in a melancholy voice.

Sambhajiraje was pressing Jijau's legs. His eyes filled with tears as he heard the prayer. Raje's heart got heavy, but Jijau lay peacefully with her eyes closed. The beating of the Sambal drums and the vibrations of the Tuntune dissipated in the clatter of the rain pouring outside.

The melancholy night of the ninth day of the dark fortnight of Jyeshtha enveloped the palace of Pachad. The downpour continued outside. Inside, everyone had gathered around Jijau's bed with heavy hearts. The potions had lost, poultices had given up and the herbs had surrendered in the battle against Aausaheb's stubborn asthma.

Constant coughing had left Jijau exhausted, and she had dozed off. Sambhajiraje sat next to her, holding her hand. He did not want to disturb her sleep. Maharaj and Ramraje sat near him.

Moropant, Annaji, Changoji, Hambirarao, Antoji, Rayaji, all near and dear ones surrounded the bed. Putalabai, Yesubai, Dharau, Soyarabai and other ladies stood anxiously near the head of the bed.

Around midnight a feeble voice called from the bed, "Raje..."

"Ji." Maharaj leaned forward.

"Give me the holy water of Ganga." The feeble voice became resolute. "And the holy basil too."

Maharaj rose, went near the sanctum and brought the vial of the holy water of Ganga and the holy basil leaf to the bed. He fed Masaheb the holy water of Ganga. The golden bracelet on his wrist trembled.

The water of Ganga and the basil leaf attained holiness indeed, by serving Jijau in her final moments. "Shivaba, come close." A resolute voice called.

Maharaj stepped forward.

"Give me your hand." A dignified lady demanded something from Raje. She had never done this before. Maharaj placed his hand in Jijau's hand.

"Shivaba, I have never asked for anything before, but today I am asking for something. Promise me that you will do it."

"Masaheb, your wish is my command...." Raje's heart got heavy.

"Shivaba...now you must become Shambhooraje's mother! I have promised so to Thoralya Soonbai. Now you must fulfil that promise."

As Sambhajiraje heard these words, he could not control himself. He shook Jijau's hand that he had held and said while weeping, "Aausaheb, Maharajsaheb and I, we both want you..."

"Shambhooraje, calm down. Listen to one thing carefully. You...you look just like my Swari. But you should never abandon Yesubai alone, like he abandoned me!"

"Raje, I saw everything in my life, except for one thing –

Ramraje's wedding! Get him married soon… and don't go risking your life anymore. No one is going to pray to Goddess Jagadamba for your safety now!"

"Raje, summon Keshav Pandit and let me listen to the *Dasbodh* of Samartha!"

The obstinate darkness of midnight had spread across the town of Pachad. The patrolling guards who had finished their shift were handing over their spears to the incoming guards. Torrential rain continued to pelt down on the roof of the palace.

Keshav Pandit placed the *Dasbodh* on the bookrest and sat on a wooden stool. Dharau placed a burning lamp near the bookrest so he could read easily.

The ascetic words of Samartha started flowing from Keshav Pandit's trembling lips, "There's a thin line between life and death. As soon as the Karma accrued in one's life is over, one must go without a moment's delay.

The men who were powerful in their time and renowned in their prime, the kings of many great dynasties, all have walked on the path of death.

After going through many cycles of birth and death we acquire this human body by good fortune. Hence this life should be spent with the virtue of morality and justice."

Keshav Pandit's voice became tremulous. With every word, the hearts of the assembled people were becoming numb. The flames of the burning lamps were shivering, "One should practice empathy and love others wholeheartedly. Our soul should be united with the soul of others, and we should strive to understand their heart's desires."

Keshav Pandit's hands trembled, his eyes got misty. His voice was cracking, and he struggled to utter each word, "I rest my quill here. This book which candidly advises are to surrender yourself to the Sadguru, comes to end here."

"Pandit, please stop…" Sambhajiraje uttered in anguish. The tears gathered in Keshav Pandit's eyes fell on the page he was reading. He could not read any more. Everyone was speechless.

Neither Chhatrapati Shivaji Maharaj, nor Yuvaraj Sambhajiraje, nor anybody else around knew that with her eyes closed, Jijau's soul had already departed. The flame of her glowing soul was surrounded by a bright light – the final light!

She saw the eight-armed, weapons-wielding Goddess Jagadamba astride a tiger coming towards her. She was accompanied by a grand procession of torch-bearing Bhutyas, hollering "Ude...Ude..." They were clad in churidar and jama, had cowrie necklaces on their chests, with foreheads daubed in haldi paste.

The procession of Goddess Bhavani came straight in front of Jijau. The din of the musical instruments subsided. Jagadamba, astride the tiger spread all her arms towards Jijau. The Bhutyas hollered in fervour, "Ude...Ude..."

Resolute Jijau left the throne of her body. She tidied the orange border of her sari. Then, she gazed at Goddess Jagadamba and voiced a notion she had held for a long time, "I never thought that you would come in such a grand manner. I thought you would come with a saddled horse and drag me along with it to your durbar. The same way you dragged my husband in the woods of Hodigeri...! I am ready for you. Let's go!"

Raje, Sambhajiraje and all others felt that Jijau was uttering, 'Jagadamb! Jagadamb!'

Raje, who had been crowned in a grand ceremony, who had got drenched in the holy water of the seven holy rivers, was orphaned in the true sense. An embellished parasol was held over his head, but he was bereft of the parasol of his mother's love! Raje had lost his mother...and...what about Sambhajiraje? He violently shook Jijau's cold, lifeless hand and looking at Maharaj with tearful eyes, Sambhajiraje wailed in a voice that left even the stone-hearted dark night heartbroken, "Aaba, our Aausaheb is gone!"

Dharau struck her tattooed forehead a few times on the

wall behind her, and exclaiming, “Masaheb…. Masaheb” she slumped on the floor. Even the flames of the burning lamps shivered with the loud wailing. Maharaj and Sambhajiraje fell on Jijau’s lifeless body and began sobbing.

Chapter 7

Aashadh was over and Shravan arrived with the sun and the rain playing hide and seek with each other.

Maharaj had masterfully ransacked Kokaltash Jafarjung's fortress at Bahadurgad and was on his way back with a booty of one crore.

Lost in thought, Sambhajiraje was pacing back and forth in his chamber. Yadav Namaji, who was a former personal attendant of Sambhajiraje, entered his chamber. He made an obeisance and announced – "Dhakale dhani, Shankaraji Bhavar, the deputy minister of Karyat Maval has arrived. He wants to meet you." The announcement broke Sambhajiraje's reverie, and he frowned momentarily. He remembered his duty as a Yuvaraj and commanded, "Present him in front of me."

Shankaraji entered the chamber and made an obeisance courteously. He broached the intent of his meeting, "Yuvaraj, the post of the officer in charge of Karyat Maval's office of Deshkulkarni has been vacant for the lack of an official royal decree. At present, Maharaj is not available at the fort…"

"Is there any problem in obtaining the royal decree? Sambhajiraje asked Shankaraji.

Yadav Namaji intervened, "Rangabhat Thakar, the descendant of Karyat Maval's Deshkulkarni is no more. Shankaraji has been employed in Rangabhat's office as a deputy minister. Rangabhat has no heir to succeed him. As his deputy minister Shankaraji knows the specifics of his office. That is why he is here to plead…." He stopped talking.

"Plead what?" Sambhajiraje asked calmly.

"If the hereditary rights of Karyat Maval's office of Deshkulkarni are transferred in my name, this humble servant will be better able to serve Maharaj."

Yadav Namaji came forward and took the bag of documents that Shankaraji was holding. He took out all the documents and showed them to Yuvaraj. He convinced Yuvaraj that Shankaraji was the deputy minister of Rangabhat and it was essential to transfer the rights of the office in Shankaraji's name.

"Yadav Namaji, convey my message to the Chitnis. Tell him to prepare the royal decree and send it to me for the official royal seal. Shankaraji, make sure that the office of the Deshkulkarni runs efficiently."

"Ji." Shankaraji and Yadav made an obeisance to Sambhajiraje and left.

By evening, the royal decree was ready. Sambhajiraje read it and affixed it with the royal seal. Shankaraji Bhavar, the deputy minister of Rangabhat Thakar, descended Raigad as the Deshkulkarni of Karyat Maval.

Maharani Soyarabai, Sambhajiraje, Yesubai, Putalabai, Ramraje and the entire royal family had gathered to pay the evening tribute to Jijau's seat. They were waiting for Maharaj.

Raje got late as he was occupied in the assessment of damage caused by the Mughal army in the Kalyan-Bhiwandi region. He entered the chamber in a rush.

Moropant Peshwe also accompanied him with an attendant holding a platter covered with a cloth. This was unusual.

Everyone bowed and made an obeisance to Jijau's seat. Raje glanced at Yesubai who stood politely among the royal ladies and said, "Soonbai, come forward."

Yesubai puckered her forehead in wonder. She tidied her already neat sari to show respect to Maharaj and approached the seat.

"Soonbai, every time I see you, I remember Masaheb!" Maharaj glanced at the empty seat and said, "That is why, in front of her seat, I want to allocate one duty to you. Will you accept the responsibility?"

"Ji." Yesubai nodded in affirmation, looking at the floor.

"Today, I want to bestow on you the responsibility of my 'Shikke-katyar'. Always remember that hundreds of lives depend on this 'Shikke-katyar'. Make sure that you seek Masaheb's blessings to shoulder this responsibility. I am sure that you will fulfil your duties successfully."

All eyes in the chamber were riveted on Yesubai, who stood still like Goddess Bhaveshwari. Yesubai was overwhelmed to hear that Aabasaheb found her worthy of such responsibility. She barely said, "Aaba…"

"Don't say anything. Just come forward and accept it." Maharaj said pointing to the platter of 'Shikke-katyar' that an attendant was holding. Moropant had removed the cover of the platter.

Naïve Yesubai was baffled. She wondered how to receive this unexpected honour.

Everyone expected Yesubai to give the customary touch of her hand to the platter and accept it. Instead, she looked at the dagger sheathed the scarlet scabbard, the silver box of the royal seal, and she spread the pallu of her sari in front of her. As mother earth would spread her sari, to accept a majestic gift from the firmament.

The attendant was bewildered.

"Yesu…" Raje was overwhelmed. He stepped forward in a trance and picked up the 'Shikke-katyar'. As he placed it in the lap of Yesubai's sari he spontaneously blessed her just like Jijau, "May you always be victorious!"

Yesubai bowed three times and made an obeisance to Jijau's seat. Then she paid respects to all the queens of Maharaj, and her husband. Maharaj left the chamber contentedly. All the members of the royal family left too.

Soyarabai came to her own chamber, fretting and fuming, and untied her golden cummerbund. As she handed it to Chandra, she groaned and muttered, "Shikke-katyar!"

Maharaj sat in the court hall of his palace. Moropant, Annaji and Balaji sat in front of him.

"We have received news that Nirajipant's health is on the decline. He is bedridden in his hometown." Moropant shared the news. Raje got worried.

"Balaji, dispatch a messenger to Nirajipant's home and check how he is doing now. Tell him not to spare any treatment." Maharaj instructed the Chitnis.

"Dhani, a lady from Karyat Maval wants to meet you." Khandoji Dabhade, Maharaj's personal attendant announced.

"Bring her here." Maharaj said and glanced at everyone in front of him. Everyone understood his signal and left the court hall.

Khandoji presented an elderly widow in a red sari.

Maharaj asked with concern, "Bai, who are you? Why have you come here? If you would have sent me intimation from Pachad, I would have sent a palanquin for you."

I am the wife of Karyat Maval's Deshkulkarni! Since my husband's demise, I have been cheated. I have come here to seek justice from you."

"Yes, Bai, please don't hesitate." Raje's voice was firm. Maharaj, who was leaning against a bolster, leaned forward as he heard her plea. His words reassured Janakibai. She took a moment to think about how to present her case.

"My husband was in your service, as the Deshkulkarni. His deputy minister, Shankaraji Bhavar, has obtained the hereditary rights over his office without my knowledge and has assumed the office of the Deshkulkarni! He has been harassing and coercing me to leave Maval. I was speechless when I came to know that he got the royal decree from your durbar. Swami, where should a widow like me go? Please grant me a decree too and let me know where to go!" Her eyes were filled with tears due to utter humiliation.

"Rest assured, Bai! You are like my own mother! You will get justice. It is my duty to serve justice. Can you please tell me one thing? Who has signed the royal decree?"

Janakibai hesitated as if she was in a tight spot. She remained silent, looking down.

"Bai, you must tell me who has signed the decree, without fear." All his ministers' faces lingered in front of Raje's eyes.

"Ji, I have heard that the decree has been signed by…by Yuvaraj!" Janakibai spoke courageously.

"Bai…!" Maharaj's voice cracked as if his tongue was caught between his teeth. His nostrils flared.

"Khandoji, summon Yuvaraj immediately." Raje commanded in an intimidating voice.

Alarmed, Khandoji promptly bowed down and responded, "Ji." He gingerly left the chamber.

Sambhajiraje was conversing in his chamber about the Anupurana, Matsyapurana, Ramayana and Mahabharata with Umaji Pandit and Keshav Pandit. Khandoji's announcement obliged them to stop their discussion. Unaware that a different Mahabharata was awaiting him, rugged Sambhajiraje went to the court hall with a smile on his face.

"Do you recognize her?" Maharaj didn't even let him bow down and make his obeisance. Sambhajiraje's smile vanished instantly as he noticed the change in Maharaj's tone and the look on his face. He glanced at Janakibai.

"Ji. No." He replied in a low voice.

"She is Janakibai. The widow of Karyat Maval's Deshkulkarni!" Each word of Maharaj felt like a whiplash to Sambhajiraje. Shankaraji Bhavar and Yadav Namaji's faces flashed in front of his eyes. Unknowingly, his breath intensified, and his chest heaved.

"Bai, you may go now. Rest assured that your rights will be protected. Khandoji, take her to Aausaheb's chamber and treat her with honour." Raje said kindly. Khandoji left with the lady.

Raje immediately admonished Sambhajiraje, "Did you sign the royal decree in the name of the deputy minister, setting aside the rights of this lady?"

"Ji." Sambhajiraje couldn't raise his head.

"Why?"

"Yadav Namaji misled me that Ranganathbhat had no successor."

"And you believed him! I have already told you, that a king cannot commit a mistake and if he does, he cannot justify it. Have you already forgotten that? What if someone misleads you that something bad has happened to me while I am on a military campaign? Will you believe it? Every single word stressed the importance of public welfare. There was no disputing it.

Sambhajiraje was shocked to hear Maharaj's words, he immediately raised his head. He could not see his Aabasaheb as he was in tears; his lips were trembling.

"Sorry…I made a huge mistake." He barely uttered each word in a hoarse voice.

Thann… Thann…Thann…! The timekeeper in the palace of Pachad was tolling the bell indicating the hour. The sound of the bell penetrated the royal hall, as if Jijausaheb had entered the royal hall.

She had put her hand on Sambhajiraje's back and pleaded to Raje, "Raje…I have never asked for anything, but today I want one promise from you. You must become Sambhajiraje's mother now. I have given my word to Thoralya Soonbai!"

The Chhatrapati rose from his seat and approached Sambhajiraje. He gently patted his shoulders and said, "Come, let's go the machi!" And both of them started walking towards the machi. In the evening, Balaji presented the written firman to be approved by Raje. It read, "… The hereditary rights of

Karyat Maval's office of Deshkulkarni have been hereby bestowed upon Janakibai, the wife of late Rangabhat Thakar. Take note that the royal decree in the name of Shankaraji Bhavar has been revoked henceforth. Shankaraji will remain the deputy minister in the office of the Deshkulkarni. Ensure that he does not harass Janakibai in any way."

Janakibai took a copy of the firman with her and descended Raigad with a contented heart, looking at the Jaripataka pennant fluttering atop the Nagar Khana.

Nyayadhish Nirajipant breathed his last. In recognition of his service, Maharaj had convened the durbar and appointed his son, Prahlad Niraji as the next Nyayadhish. Prahladpant was young, noble and sharp-witted. He was the youngest office bearer in the ministry.

One day, after the durbar was over, Maharaj put forth a proposal to his ministers, "Just as my thread ceremony was performed, it is important to perform the thread ceremony for Yuvaraj. The religious rituals should be performed at the right time, otherwise it can cause problems in the future." Maharaj was speaking from his own experience.

All the ministers endorsed the proposal. Maharaj assigned the responsibility of finding a good mahurat to Anantbhat and Prabhakarbhat. The atmosphere in the fort was buzzing with the preparations for Yuvaraj's thread ceremony. The wise ones in the durbar realized that Yuvaraj, who had been sitting at Maharaj's feet in the durbar, was going to succeed to the throne in the future. Maharaj himself had clearly expressed that this was his wish. He had taken the decision to perform the thread ceremony of Yuvaraj, so that no objections could be raised during his coronation ceremony. When she heard this decision, Soyarabai, who was sitting in the curtained section for the royal ladies, immediately left for her chamber. No one came to know about it in the main durbar outside.

After dispatching the invitations for the thread ceremony,

Maharaj had come to visit Soyarabai.

He pulled Ramraje close and said with a smile, "I have been sending invitations of your Dada Maharaj's thread ceremony, and what are you doing here in the chamber?"

Since Maharaj had already broached the subject, Soyarabai grabbed the opportunity and said to him smilingly, "I am a bit puzzled. Why do we have to do the same thing twice?"

Maharaj did not understand her intent. He puckered his forehead.

"The Abhishek ceremony was performed twice. Now, it looks like you want to perform the thread ceremony twice too."

"What do you mean?"

"I feel that if Yuvaraj and Balraje's thread ceremony is performed at the same time it will save time and effort." Soyarabai looked at Ramraje and said with a smile.

"Balraje's thread ceremony? He is too young for that right now. Let him grow up and prove his mettle first, then I will perform his thread ceremony with a grand celebration. Right Balraje?" Raje said, patting Ramraje's back lovingly. Maharaj did not realize that the tip of Ranisaheb's nose had flushed on hearing his words.

But Soyarabai's livid words gave away her anger, "Indeed, our Yuvaraj has proved his mettle by assigning the office of Deshkulkarni to the wrong person!"

"Quiet!!" Maharaj's intimidating voice startled Ramraje. Raje pulled him close and admonished Soyarabai, "You don't have to interfere in the official matters. I am capable of assessing his mettle." The next moment, Raje put his hand on Ramraje shoulder and calmly said to him, "Let's go."

Soyarabai was petrified and trembling in fear. She kept staring at Ramraje leaving her chamber. "Balraje stop." She wanted to say, but she was too stunned to say anything.

On the fifth day of the bright fortnight of Magh,

Sambhajiraje's thread ceremony took place on Raigad in a grand celebration. As the Yuvaraj, Sambhajiraje started participating actively in the official matters. Winter over, Gopalshet Vani, a merchant from the Purandar region came to Raigad with a grievance. Maharaj delegated Sambhajiraje to run the trial and give the verdict. He wanted to test Sambhajiraje's acumen.

The trial took place in the court hall of Raje's palace. Raje was present in person, and sat next to him to see how Sambhajiraje conducted the trial.

The hearing began. Sambhajiraje heard both the plaintiff and the defendant's arguments. He listened to the witnesses and checked all documents carefully. In accordance with the law of inheritance, Gopalshet was the rightful successor to the post of the chief of the trading office in the Purandar region.

Sambhajiraje started dictating the verdict to the deputy minister Mahadeo Yamaji. Maharaj listened to it carefully without interfering.

Every word that Sambhajiraje dictated, echoed the diction of Maharaj. After the verdict was ready, Sambhajiraje asked Mahadeopant to read it one more time. Then, he signed and stamped it with the royal seal. The document was then kept in a pouch and placed on a platter. Jotyaji Kesarkar held the platter in front of Gopalshet.

Gopalshet made an obeisance to Sambhajiraje, picked up the pouch and touched it to his forehead. He stood courteously in front of Sambhajiraje.

Maharaj was satisfied with the result. He reminded Gopalshet, "You got what you wanted, now don't forget to pay the trial fees. You can leave the fort after making the payment of five hons to Yuvaraj and one hundred and twenty-five hons in the state treasury.

"Ji Dhani." Gopalshet nodded in affirmation, made an obeisance to Maharaj and left the court hall.

Maharaj had recently delegated the Fonda campaign to

Annaji Dutto and Duttaji Trimal. Maharaj immediately planned two more crucial campaigns. One mission was for Sambhajiraje; to strike through the Adil Shahi region as far as Bhaganagar of the Qutub Shahi sultanate. The other one was for himself, to fall upon Fonda via Rajapur-Kudal.

Sambhajiraje's army was set in Pachad. In this campaign, Yuvaraj was going to be accompanied by twenty thousand cavalry.

Sambhajiraje bade farewell to all members of the royal family, took the darshan of Jagadishwar with Maharaj and descended Raigad. In the memory of Jijau, a stone Samadhi had been raised in Pachad, near her palace. Sambhajiraje offered flowers and haldi on it and touched his forehead to it.

"May you be victorious." Maharaj pulled him up.

Along with Anand Makaji, Rupaji Bhosale, Jotyaji, Antoji and Kondaji Farzand, twenty thousand -riders sprinted forward.

This campaign was organized with the intention of launching a surprise attack on Bhaganagar, the capital of the Qutub Shahi sultanate. To that effect, Sambhajiraje was first going to travel to Miraj via Panhalgad, plundering the Adil Shahi region on his way to Bhaganagar. Sambhajiraje ascended Panhalgad with his army through Teen Darwaja. Tryambakpant, the custodian of the fort, came to receive him.

There was a small temple to Lord Shiva in front of the Balekilla. As they came near the temple, Tryambakpant said, "Yuvaraj should visit the temple before going to the royal palace." Sambhajiraje followed Tryambakpant and bent down to enter the small sanctum.

"Yuvaraj, this is a colour-changing Shivlinga." Tryambakpant provided information about the uniqueness of the Shivlinga. Sambhajiraje didn't understand what he meant and said, "I didn't get you."

"Cover this Shivlinga with your palms for a few moments, and then pull your palms away. You will see that this black Shivlinga appears white at first, and then the colour changes to purple, silver, and dark blue, before becoming black again!"

"Jagadamb! Jagadamb! Is it true, Pant?" Sambhajiraje's eyes widened in astonishment.

"Yuvaraj should try it himself." Tryambakpant gingerly removed the Bael leaves and flowers from the Shivlinga and placed them on the Shalunka.

Sambhajiraje leaned forward and placed his hands on top of the Shivlinga. Tryambakpant picked up a burning torch from a corner and held it close to the Shivlinga.

After some time, Sambhajiraje gently moved his hands away. Pant brought the burning torch very close to the Shivlinga. The area of the Shivlinga that Sambhajiraje had touched with his hands turned white first and started reflecting various colours. Sambhajiraje's heart was filled with devotion. The Shivlinga turned black again. Yuvaraj joined his hands in prayer and closed his eyes. He thought, 'Aabasaheb's face is just like this Shivlinga. Expressive! Changing colours according to the emotions!

Sambhajiraje was pleased to see the Lake Someshwar, Sajja Kothi, the granaries and the cannons on the bastion walls of Panhalgad. After spending two days on the fort, he bade farewell to Tryambakpant and descended the fort with his army through Chou Darwaja. Yuvaraj's cavalry marched in the direction of Miraj via Battis Shirala. Miraj was a well-equipped military base of the Adil Shahi sultanate. Sambhajiraje's army circumvented Miraj and infiltrated the Adil Shahi region, ravaging the territory around Miraj. His raiding troops collected booty on their way and kept moving towards Bhaganagar, camping at places such as Athani and Etaggi. Sambhajiraje's twenty thousand armed forces travelling at the speed of wind surrounded Bhaganagar's borders, near the Golconda fort. Tana Shah, the ruler of the Qutub Shahi sultanate had never imagined such a crisis.

"The Marathas have come…run for your lives!" Chaos erupted in Bhaganagar.

"Onward! Attack! Har…Har…Mahadeo" Sambhajiraje roared, wielding his bare sword shining in the sun.

A lofty shamiana was erected for Yuvaraj, on the southern border of Bhaganagar. Sambhajiraje was drenched in sweat; he took a ride through the encampment and approached the shamiana. He dismounted and tossed the reins of his horse to the groom. Anandrao, Rupaji, Jotyaji followed him.

"Anandrao, dispatch an envoy to Qutub Shah with a warning. Our forces will not retreat until we acquire the desired tribute. Yuvaraj took his seat and commanded.

"Ji." Anandrao bowed.

Anandrao dispatched an envoy to the Golconda fort.

Tana Shah convened a council to discuss the demands. His advisors had heard tales of Maharaj's coronation and the ransacking of Bahadurgad. They advised him to accept the terms and pay the tribute. His Wazir Madannapant went to Sambhajiraje's encampment for negotiations. Sambhajiraje met him.

The tribute of two thousand hons arrived in the Maratha camp from the Golconda fort. The Marathas also received one thousand florins from the alarmed Dutch traders in Bhaganagar. Sambhajiraje amassed the booty and was about to fall upon the Adil Shahi sultanate again, but the informers brought news that Pathan Bahalol Khan was coming after them with a well-equipped army.

Sambhajiraje evaded the Pathan's army and plundered Adil Shah's prominent trade centre in Hubli. After that Sambhajiraje's army conquered the post at Raibag and marched towards Panhalgad with the booty.

Yuvaraj ascended Panhalgad with his triumphant army. The kettle drums on the fort resounded in his welcome. After ascending the fort, Sambhajiraje dispatched the booty to Raigad in the custody of armed troops. He summoned an honour assembly and offered bracelets, robes of honour and weapons to the soldiers for their military exploits.

An elaborate account of the campaign was dispatched to Maharaj who was engaged in the campaign of Fonda, "... I have reached Panhalgad after successfully concluding the campaign. I am looking forward to seeing you in person."

Sambhajiraje was dictating letters to Parashurampant in the court hall of the Balekilla on Panhalgad. Anandrao stood nearby.

Just then, Tryambakpant, the custodian of the fort, arrived and made an announcement, "Yuvaraj, the four brothers of the Inamdar family, Nilaji, Shankaraji, Viasaji and Trimbakji, are seeking permission to meet you in person. They are from the Chambali village of the Karhepathar region."

"Pant, let them in." Sambhahiraje granted permission.

The Inamdar brothers from Chambali entered the court hall, made an obeisance and stood in a line.

"Why did you want to meet me?" Sambhajiraje asked them.

"We have come all the way from Raigad to seek justice in a matter. The elder brother Nilaji broached the subject.

"Justice in what matter? Tell me everything clearly." Sambhajiraje glanced at the four brothers.

"Maharaj has been imposing the coronation levy on the Mirasdars. The Inamdar families have been exempted from the coronation levy. Though we are from the Inamdar family, Ragho Bhaskar, the Hawaldar of Pune, is compelling us to pay the coronation levy. He is charging a twenty-five per cent levy. Though we tried telling him that we are the Inamdars and we are not required to pay the coronation levy, he disregards our pleas and keeps harrasing us. Yuvaraj, please solve our problem. We seek justice."

"Do you have documentary evidence of being the Inamdars?" Sambhajiraje asked cautiously. Nilaji stepped forward and placed a pouch of documentation of their Inam at Sambhajiraje's feet. Sambhajiraje examined the documents, and said to them, "Rest assured. You will not be required to pay the coronation levy; the exemption will continue."

"Anandrao, who is the Subedar of the Pune region?" Sambhajiraje asked.

"Ji. Ragho Ballal Atre." Anandrao bowed down and provided the information.

Sambhajiraje started dictating the letter to Parashurampant. The guests from Chambali village, Tryambakpant and Anandrao kept listening.

The quill in Parashurampant's hand started squeaking – "To Ragho Ballal, Subedar of Pune region, greetings from Yuvaraj Sambhajiraje – It has come to my notice that Ragho Bhaskar, the Hawaldar of Pune region, has been wrongfully imposing a coronation levy of twenty-five hons on the Inamdar family of Chambali, despite the fact that they have been exempted from the said tax. Therefore, I inform you hereby, to write a letter to Ragho Bhaskar and warn him of the consequences of his actions. You should send him an official warning. You are wise enough to understand the situation. What more can I say?"

Parashurampant wrote a similar letter to Hawaldar Ragho Bhaskar. Sambhajiraje read both letters and signed them.

Tryambakpant handed the rolled parchments of the official letters to Nilaji.

"Present these letters to Peshwe Moropant on Raigad and get them stamped with his seal. Then deliver these to Subedar Ragho Ballal in person." Sambhajiraje instructed Nilaji.

"Ji. You have done us a big favour." The four brothers bowed down and made an obeisance.

"It is my duty. You may leave now." Sambhajiraje corrected Nilaji. The Inamdars of Chambali left the court hall. The coronation levy which had been imposed on them was revoked.

A letter arrived from Fonda, with Maharaj's message – "Leave immediately for Fonda with your army and bring Tryambakpant with you."

Sambhajiraje descended Panhalgad accompanied by

Tryambakpant, with his rejuvenated army and proceeded in the direction of the Konkan coast.

Maharaj descended the fortified fort of Fonda with Annaji, Dharmaji Naganath and others, and came to receive him. Sambhajiraje's face was tanned due to the travel in the hot summer.

As he saw Maharaj, Sambhajiraje walked forward briskly to touch his feet. Maharaj didn't let him bend. He pulled Sambhajiraje up, embraced him and said, "I have called you for a special reason. Come, let's talk at length." Both went inside the fort.

Maharaj had skilfully conquered the fort of Fonda by defeating the Adilshahi custodian, Mohammed Ikhalas. The Portuguese of Goa were alarmed by the attack and would definitely take some action. The Marathas having control over Fonda was a big threat to the Portuguese.

After taking some rest, Maharaj summoned a meeting with Sambhajiraje and explained the plan to him, "I am going to charge upon the Karvar region. You should take charge of this campaign with your rejuvenated army. The Portuguese are keeping tabs on this fort. You must intercept their forces and keep them in check."

"Ji. As you wish." Sambhajiraje's eyes beamed with pride with the realisation that Maharaj had given him the charge of another campaign. "Rest assured, I will do my best." Sambhajiraje reassured Maharaj.

Maharaj appointed Tryambak Pandit as the Subedar of Fonda, gave the charge of the mission to Sambhajiraje and left from Fonda. He was going to charge upon the Adil Shahi regions of Ankol, Shiveshwar, Kadra and Karvar.

Sambhajiraje dispatched a letter of warning to the Portuguese viceroy of Goa, Louis-da-Mendos-e-Albuquerque, "Better vacate the sixty villages in the Fonda region, including Hemadbase, Antruj, Bali, Kanakon, Ashtagar, Chandrawadi, Kope or else, the Maratha army will invade the region!"

The viceroy disregarded the warning. Hence, Sambhajiraje left the fort of Fonda with Tryambakpant, Dharmaji Naganath, Anandrao and the cavalry unit. He penetrated the Portuguese region via Antruj. Several skirmishes broke out and plundering continued.

The viceroy had anticipated as much. He had kept his region combat-ready. The Maratha army faced staunch retaliation at every post in the region. In addition to that the rainy season began. Sambhajiraje decided to retreat to the fort of Fonda with his army and await further instructions from Maharaj.

Maharaj had returned to Raigad after finishing the campaign in the Adil Shahi sultanate. Sambhajiraje received his letter, "Dharmaji Nagnath has been hereby appointed, as the custodian of the fort of Fonda. You should send Tryambakpant to Panhalgad, to secure the fort and you come to Raigad. The monsoon has began."

Sambhajiraje executed all the instructions given by Maharaj and bade farewell to Dharmaji. Accompanied by Anandrao, he started his journey towards Raigad, getting soaked in the rains. He was going back to Raigad after almost two and a half months. Even during this return journey, Sambhajiraje plundered Ankola and the region of Sarup Naik with his cavalry.

Sambhajiraje had just finished his composition. As he looked at the paper, his face emitted a unique radiance. He gently placed the quill in the stand and spread a pinch of soft sand on the paper to absorb the excess ink. Then he flicked the paper to shake off the sand.

"Dharau, could you please send for my better half?" Sambhajiraje said in a trance, gazing at the paper.

A smile cracked on Dharau's face; she tidied her sari and left the chamber.

After some time Yesubai entered the chamber. Sambhajiraje

smiled at her and said, "Can you guess why I sent for you at this time?"

The episode of the list of ornaments was lingering in Yesubai's mind. She was baffled to see the smile on her husband's face.

"Looks like you can't guess it! Fine, let me tell you. I have composed a poem." Sambhajiraje's eyes glowed as he looked at the paper. The doubt in Yesubai's mind was cleared, and her eyes started shining with pride.

"May I read it to you?"

Yesubai nodded in affirmation.

Sambhajiraje started reciting the poem. Titled 'Nakhashikha', it was a romantic description of a beautiful woman, from head to toe.

Yesubai was flustered to hear it and kept glancing at the door frequently in fear that somebody might show up any time.

Sambhajiraje finished his reading, looked at Yesubai and asked her, "How is it? Do you like it?"

Bashful Yesubai did not respond and continued gazing at the floor. She was embarrassed.

Sambhajiraje realized that she had misconstrued the poem to be about her. He smiled and stretching her patience further he said, "Well, how could you like it? This is not your portrayal."

"Can I go now?" Yesubai was feeling awkward.

"Okay, you can go." Yuvaraj smiled, stretching the thin line of his moustache.

As Yesubai was about to leave, Sambhajiraje gazed at the golden design on her sari and shared the subject of the poem with her.

"But listen before you leave, this is the description of Radha in Gokul, who was madly in love with Krishna! Nakhashikha! I am quite sure that you also find Radha the same, like a trail of shining stars! Like the sharp edge of the sword!" Sambhajiraje laughed heartily.

Yesubai felt like turning around and saying to him, "Why didn't you tell me that before?"

Sambhajiraje left the Balekilla with Rayaji and Antoji, to take the darshan of Lord Jagadishwar. This tradition of visiting the Jagadishwar temple in the wee hours during Shravan had been followed for years.

As he entered the courtyard of the Jagadishwar temple Sambhajiraje bent forward to touch the stone threshold at the entrance gate. Thoralya Aausaheb's memories flashed in his mind, 'Thoralya Aausaheb was alive when we moved from Rajgad and came to this fort. She was with me when I crossed the same threshold for the first time. Today, everything is the same as before, but she is not here. How can I say she is not here? She is indeed here. Just like this faint sunlight in the early morning is dispersed everywhere, even though the Sun is hiding behind the mountains, she is present here too.'

Lost in thought, he came near the stone tortoise in the courtyard. The feet of the tortoise were drawn inside its shell. It was telling him silently that it had been installed there to remind all devotees entering the temple to curb their desires just like it had drawn its feet into its shell.

As he looked at the tortoise, Sambhajiraje's mind cleared.

He devoutly tolled the bell hanging over his head. A trembling melody dispersed over the summit of Raigad.

Sambhajiraje kept gazing at the Shivlinga in the sanctum and started walking forward to offer Bael leaves and flowers to the Shivlinga.

Suddenly, the Shivlinga in front of him disappeared. A beautiful young woman, clad in a white sari, was coming out of the sanctum after finishing her early morning puja. She carried a platter of puja materials in one hand and an empty cane basket in the other. She looked like the morning of Shravan breaking out from behind the mountain range. Nakhashikha!

Her forehead bore the kumkum tilak; she wore green bangles

in both hands that married women wore traditionally; she had a Mangalsutra around her neck and a few golden necklaces; silver toe rings and a pearl-studded nose ring. As soon as she saw the sandalwood paste stripes on Sambhajiraje's forehead and his brocaded Jiretop, she immediately turned her gaze down and left promptly, swishing like the early morning zephyr! The trail of shining stars disappeared. "Nakhashikha! Nakhashikha!" Sambhajiraje's poetic heart throbbed with a strange beat of the kettle drums.

The lady who looked like the character of Radha depicted in Sambhajiraje's poem Nakhashikha, was a relative of Surnis Annaji. She had come to Raigad to spend time with her parents. Her name suited her pure beauty and gracious personality–Godavari!

It was a Friday in the month of Shravan. Maharani Soyarabai had invited Suvasinees at her palace for the haldi-kumkum ceremony. Maharani offered fruits and sweets to all women. After the ceremony, all the women left Maharani's palace one by one. Godavari was in the group of the Brahmin women.

All of them crossed the veranda in front of the seven palaces and came to front yard surrounded by water channels. Sambhajiraje was engrossed in watching the play of light and shadow on the surface of Lake Ganga Sagar, from the fifth floor of the tower. As he was strolling in the spacious passage in the tower, he saw Godavari in the group of ladies standing in the front yard. He kept gazing at her. The tranquil lake of his artistic mind quivered. 'Nakhashikha! Who is she? Where is she from? What is she doing on the fort?' The next moment, he briskly climbed down the spiral staircase of the tower. Bystanders kept making an obeisance to him as he passed them by. Sambhajiraje climbed down the five floors of the tower and came to the front yard. No one was there! But as they saw him, all the guards of the palaces stood at attention and straightened their spears.

He could hear some women chit-chatting nearby. Maharaj

had installed the 'Maruti' idol that Samartha had gifted him, in a shrine built on the Balekilla. All the women had gone to that shrine. Sambhajiraje kept watching the fish in the water channels. After some time, the women started coming out of the shrine one by one. Godavari also came out. Sambhajiraje wanted to talk to her, ask her something. But how could he do it? Would it be appropriate?

He quickly moved towards the shrine. All the women saw him and moved aside respectfully. Sambhajiraje touched the first step of the stairs leading to the shrine. He climbed the first step and stopped; then turned around and glanced at Godavari. All women stood quietly looking down.

"You – who are you? What brought you here?" Sambhajiraje asked Godavari. Her head was still bent low. Somebody nudged her. Baffled, Godavari lifted her head. As soon as her eyes met Sambhajiraje's radiant eyes; she immediately looked down at his feet.

Without losing his regal bearing, Sambhajiraje graciously asked her again, "Who are you? What brings you here?"

"Ji. I am related to the Surnis. My name is Godavari. I have come here to visit my family." With her heart beating faster, Godavari answered him with due respect. Sambhajiraje smiled, entered the shrine and disappeared in an instant.

The women left the Balekilla whispering among themselves. They were wondering why Yuvaraj had inquired about Godavari alone. They weren't saying anything wrong, but still, Godavari felt embarrassed and quietly walked alone behind them.

Neither she, nor Sambhajiraje who was taking the darshan of Maruti in the shrine, had any inkling that Maharani Soyarabai had watched everything from her balcony. She entered her chamber calmly, pulled the pallu of her sari tight and mumbled to herself, "So, our Yuvaraj engages in such activities too!"

Now Soyarabai started making strange moves. She did not know that with every move she made, she was thrusting the royal family's future into an entangling mess.

She started sending invitations to Godavari at Annaji's home under the pretext of festival celebrations or religious rituals. Godavari could not refuse the invitations as they were from the Maharani. Soyarabai's maids and personal attendants started tracking Godavari's movements whenever she came to the palace. An intricate scheme was cooking.

Sambhajiraje was a candid, open person. He talked to Godavari occasionally. There was no pretence. Indeed, an elephant should not pay attention to the dogs barking around him, but at the same time it should be alert not to trample an anthill under its feet. Otherwise, a single resentful red ant might use its trunk to move into its ear and sting at a tender spot that could even kill it. Straightforward Sambhajiraje did not understand it. A man should be benevolent, but more than that, a man should be vigilant.

In the form of Soyarabai, the royal palace itself was all set to ruin the royal reputation. As it is, revenge is a terrible emotion. A woman's revenge is much more dreadful, and a royal woman's revenge is catastrophic.

From Soyarabai's chamber, toxic rumours started trickling slowly and steadily all over the fort. This was going to consume the Jaripataka pennant, the haldi of Goddess Bhavani and the stripes of the sandalwood paste. Above all, it was going to destroy the thriving Swaraj that had been nurtured by Jijau's tears and the sweat and blood of countless Mavalas.

Annaji, who had no idea about what was transpiring at Raigad, had left the Fonda region and arrived at Raigad. Maharaj had assigned him the mission of reconstructing the ramparts of the fort of Fonda. Annaji was going to report the progress of the mission to Maharaj. Annaji arrived at the fort and within a short time he realized that the guards and personnel in the eighteen departments were looking at him strangely and whispering among themselves. Furthermore, he was unexpectedly summoned by Maharani Soyarabai. Annaji presented himself in Maharani's chamber with an unknown fear in his heart and countless doubts in his mind.

"Surnis, I feel embarrassed to accept your obeisance, but what else can I do?" One cannot bite one's own tongue with one's own teeth!" Soyarabai said very calmly, taking the blame upon herself, increasing Annaji's curiosity and confusion.

Annaji was holding the edge of his shawl as usual. Unknowingly, it slipped from his hand. "Sarkar should tell me if I have committed any mistake. I have been unable to understand what is going on here. The people in the fort are looking strangely at me." Annaji spoke courageously as a diplomatic politician.

"Surnis, you successfully completed the mission of strengthening the ramparts of the fort of Fonda, but how are Maharaj and I going to reward you for that? With humiliation and disgrace! You strenghthened the fort there, but here everything has collapsed. You are like a family member, so try to understand the situation here." Soyarabai spoke evasively while acknowledging his service to Swarajya.

"Please forgive me, but I still haven't understood what is going on here. I am your humble servant. Please tell me what I should do."

"Annajipant, the fault lies with our own family member. The disgrace that he has brought to the family has shamed me more than the pain this news is going to inflict upon you. You should forgive Yuvaraj with a large heart. He has committed a huge crime, but still, he belongs to you, too. He has fallen for Godavari, the married woman who is currently staying with your family. Everyone on the fort is talking about it..." Soyarabai stopped for a moment and glanced at Annaji to check his reaction. Annaji's forehead had puckered as if it had been touched by a burning incense stick. His eyes widened and he pressed the edge of his shawl tightly.

"Surnis, you must have understood now, how painful it is for me to share such terrible news with you. But please be patient. Please don't share this with anyone else. I have come to know that Godavari wants to leave the fort. It will be a big mistake to do so, as it will spread more rumours about her. Swari doesn't know anything about this. Nobody has the guts to tell this to him. Even I am afraid to do that!" Soyarabai stopped decidedly.

"I will investigate the matter and report it to Maharaj in person." Stunned Annaji said with resolve. He lowered his head and said, "Let me take your leave now." He stepped backwards and left the chamber.

The first thing Annaji did after going home, was to beckon Godavari in the ladies' chamber and take her to task. "Did you and Yuvaraj meet frequently?" Annaji's eyes turned red with anger.

Godavari lowered her head and nodded in affirmation. Tears trickled from her eyes.

"Don't you feel ashamed of yourself?" Annaji bellowed at her in anger.

"Please listen to me. I…" Godavari gathered her courage and tried to speak.

"Shut up, you should have at least thought about your marriage! You had better not step out of this house now." Annaji couldn't even look at her, and left the chamber hastily. Godavari was weeping; she felt suffocated and utterly helpless.

Now, the people on the fort couldn't see Godavari anywhere. 'Yuvaraj has transferred her somewhere else to cover up his illicit affair.' Scandalous rumours spread around the fort. Soyarabai's lackeys were actively working to that end. Annaji's visits to the Maharani's chamber increased. He was quite confounded by the situation and couldn't think of a solution. Soyarabai kept persuading him in various ways to convince Godavari to testify in their favour.

Yuvaraj got an inkling that a slanderous plan against him

was cooking in Maharani's chamber. He planted his informers around Annaji's residence and the Maharani's chamber.

One thought kept vexing Sambhajiraje–. 'Godavari should not stay at Annaji's residence anymore. It can prove disastrous for her and myself too. She would be subjected to deceit. She should be kept away from Annaji and the Maharani's chamber. But how can I do it? How can a married woman be taken away from a house full of people?'

Restless and agitated, Sambhajiraje was nervously pacing in his chamber. He would suddenly stop walking, look at the stone ceiling and whisper 'Jagadamb, Jagadamb' to gather courage. This peculiar dilemma had confined Sambhajiraje to his chamber and Godavari to Annaji's residence in Brahmanwadi. Any moment this news was going to reach the Chhatrapati Maharaj. What exactly was Maharani Soyarabai planning with Annaji could not be known. The tension was rising, and the problem remained unresolved.

Soyarabai had summoned Godavari for a meeting in her chamber. What was going to transpire now? Only Goddess Jagadamba would know.

"Dhakale Sarkar, Maharani's maid Chandra has gone to the residence of the Surnis. A palanquin has left from there. The woman in the palanquin is travelling to the Balekilla, to Maharani's palace." As an informer reported this to Sambhajiraje, countless apprehensions filled his mind.

Sambhajiraje folded his hands behind his back and paced back and forth like a wounded tiger. He couldn't think straight. Things were getting out of hand. He wanted to rush to the Maharani's chamber and demand an explanation from her.

He didn't even realize that the informer was still waiting for his next command. He decided something in his mind, and as he was getting out of the chamber, he commanded the informer, "You may leave now and keep me informed of every small news that you collect from the Maharani's palace. No mistake will be spared." The informer made an obeisance and left. Sambhajiraje started walking determinedly towards the sanctum.

The torch bearer of the sanctum saw Yuvaraj coming and made an obeisance. Without looking at him Yuvaraj said in an intimidating voice, "I want to be left alone in the sanctum. I want to pray to the goddess in solitude. You should leave now." Yuvaraj looked benumbed. The torch bearer was startled to see his cold face and left immediately.

Sambhajiraje dragged his feet like a stone statue being dragged. The murti of eight-armed Goddess Bhavani stood still, enveloped by the light of the burning lamps; her eyes were wide open, and she looked as if she was ready to attack. Sambhajiraje's numb yet determined eyes met the eyes of the goddess. He was not afraid of the destructive, fiery eyes of the mother of the universe. He felt he had an inexplicable bond with her, and hence wanted to demand answers from her. He wanted to shake her eight arms vigorously and ask her, "These burning torches are dancing around you through days and nights, and how come you don't see what is transpiring?"

'Thoralya Aausaheb…!' A wave erupted from the deepest recesses of his heart. The omniscient eyes of Goddess Jagadamba looked like Thoralya Aausaheb's eyes to him. His numbness faded, and the doors of his mind opened instantly.

"Even if she deviates from deference, you should not lose your patience!" Jijau's royal words came swirling towards him like a feather through the air.

Yuvaraj's royal heart was in turmoil. "Thoralya Aausaheb… you should have been alive today! Then I would have asked you, how to deal with this situation. I would have tolerated anything else, but this is beyond my power. Thoralya Aau, I have been cornered. I am going to do whatever Goddess Jagadamba prompts me to do. Trust me, I vouch in your name, whatever I do, I will do courageously, and will remember my promise to you." Sambhajiraje closed his eyes. His mind was now calm and stable. He offered the Bael leaves and flowers at the feet of Goddess Jagadamba and showered a fistful of haldi on her divine murti. He bowed in front of the murti, took a few steps backwards and came out of the sanctum. No one on the fort could now stop him from doing what he had decided.

Yuvaraj summoned his personal secretary Mahadeo Yamaji, and instructed him, "Present ten swordsmen from my personal troop urgently. Select a few proficient infantry and cavalry men too. You climb down the fort in person and keep one cavalry troop ready in Pachad. I am going to climb down the fort right after you."

"Ji." Mahadeo Yamaji responded. He made an obeisance to the Yuvaraj and left.

An attendant picked up an iron armour from the platter and standing behind Sambhajiraje he placed it on his rugged, muscular body. Another attendant placed a brocaded orange jama over it and fastened his wrist guards. Then, he placed the shield on Sambhajiraje's back, pulled its straps on his chest and handed them to him. Yuvaraj pulled the straps tight on his chest, tied a knot and wrapped the scarf around his waist. He fastened the scabbard at his waist and inserted his straight, heavy sword in it. The Rudra incarnate, born on the high-rising fort, got ready to face the storm that was coming. Those who live at great heights, must always be ready to face the storms coming their way!

All alone, Sambhajiraje started pacing in a trance. The troop of swordsmen sent by Mahadeo Yamaji presented themselves and made an obeisance. In a calm and steady voice, Sambhajiraje began sharing his plan with them. The soldiers listened to him attentively.

The informer keeping a close watch on the Maharani's palace came and said, "Dhani, the Maharani has tightened the security of her palace. There is no scope to break through. What should I do next?"

Sambhajiraje stood still for a moment. Then, coming to a decision, he said, "There is no need to get news anymore. When the lady leaves the palace, inform me immediately."

Raigad seemed apparently calm. The Jaripataka pennant atop the Nagar Khana kept fluttering in the winds. Every moment led to an unknown future that no one could have anticipated. The fearless and loyal swordsmen of Yuvaraj, with whom he had just shared his plan, left the chamber. They went separate ways and gathered near the huge gate of the Nagar Khana, keeping out of sight.

A benumbed Godavari followed Annaji out of the Maharani's palace. Her face looked as if she had been tortured by someone. She could not prove her innocence either to Annaji or to Rani Saheb. Soyarabai had cunningly declared her guilty and made a pretence of kindly granting her immunity. Now, Annaji was going to seek Maharaj's permission and present her in front of him. She was going to keep silent there, and only Annaji was going to talk on her behalf. She was only supposed to nod in agreement him.

Annaji made sure that Godavari had sat in the palanquin and left for his office. The palanquin started travelling towards the Nagar Khana. Two swordsmen of Annaji accompanied the palanquin. The palanquin-bearers started walking briskly.

As soon as Sambhajiraje received intimation about the palanquin, he left his chamber. His face looked rigid and stern, as if it had transformed into a burning torch. He was oblivious to the people making an obeisance to him. He walked rapidly and approached the huge gate of the Nagar Khana. His swordsmen bowed to him and made an obeisance.

As soon as the palanquin-bearers brought Godavari's palanquin out through the gate of the Nagar Khana, Sambhajiraje's swordsmen surrounded it from all sides. As the palanquin-bearers saw Sambhajiraje in person gesturing them to stop, they stopped and made an obeisance to him.

Sambhajiraje approached the curtained window of the palanquin and said in an imposing voice, "Bai, this is Yuvaraj speaking. I have taken you in my custody. Don't be scared at all. No harm will come to you. I vouch in the name of Thoralya Aausaheb."

Annaji's swordsmen had already been moved aside.

"Pick it up!" His intimidating words left the palanquin-bearers sweating. They picked up the palanquin on their shoulders, and silently started walking in a hurry, in the direction of the tower, where Sambhajiraje was pointing.

Ferocious Sambhajiraje took the lead. The palanquin, surrounded by bare swords went past the trading market of Raigad and travelled towards the tower. Occasionally, a few people passed the palanquin. They believed that some member of the royal family was travelling and hence made an obeisance to it. The Maha Darwaja passed. Sambhajiraje's swordsmen were not letting the palanquin bearers slacken the pace even a bit. The palanquin crossed the Lahana Darwaja and landed near the Pachad border. Mahadeopant had kept a cavalry troop ready for the Yuvaraj. They were waiting for him. They brought a few horses to Yuvaraj. Sambhajiraje chose a white horse, caught hold of its reins and brought it near the palanquin.

"Bai, please step out of the palanquin." Yuvaraj commanded looking at the curtain. Godavari stepped out of the palanquin. She could not raise her head. She was completely numb.

"Mount the horse, please." Sambhajiraje pointed to the horse. Godavari trembled as if struck by lightning. She just couldn't do it. Neither could she voice her dilemma openly. Sambhajiraje realized her predicament, and hesitated for a moment. He felt distressed, thinking that all his determined efforts so far were going to come to nought. He immediately came to a decision. In a flash, he leapt onto the white horse. As he pulled its reins, the magnificent animal reared up and whinnied. Sambhajiraje wrapped his arm around Godavari and pulled her up onto his horse. The horse was prodded so hard, it felt a pang of pain and darted forward. The cavalry troop followed the horse. Torrents of dust arose. The Rudra of Raigad sprinted forward, racing with the stormy wind, towards Fort Lingana.

The foothills of Fort Lingana came in sight. Fort Lingana was connected with Raigad. Godavari was transported to Lingana. As Sambhajiraje left her confined in a room heavily guarded by his loyal soldiers, he was moved from the bottom of his heart. He couldn't even look directly at her.

He said to her, "Please forgive me for bringing you here in such a manner. There was no other option left. You are in my captivity. You and I, both will have to face Maharaj Saheb. When that time comes, do as Mother Jagadamba and Lord Jagdishwar guide you. I believe that you will not give in to pressure from anybody's. I am the Yuvaraj, and I regret that I have to keep you in captivity. If possible, please forgive me for my actions. Farewell."

Yuvaraj Sambhajiraje had decided that he would not regret the things that he had done consciously. He descended Fort Lingana with that determination in his heart.

On Raigad, there was complete pandemonium. A strong man like Annaji was completely shaken and felt utterly helpless. Ashamed, he had covered his mouth with the edge of his shawl and had left his residence to visit Maharaj. He had decided something to himself. In a flash he felt like a stranger on the fort on which he had lived with pride so far.

"Swami, please release me from your service and let me go." With a lowered head Annaji opened his heart's wound in front of Maharaj. Tears trickled from his eyes and got absorbed in the carpet below. The Chhatrapati Maharaj was not aware of the fire burning in Annaji's heart.

"What do you mean?" Maharaj gazed at Annaji's turban.

"Swami…Swami…" Annaji couldn't speak further. He

started sobbing like a child and covered his face with his shawl.

The Chhatrapati was startled to see him like this. He rose from his seat and called Annaji in a strange voice – "Surnis..." His voice brought Annaji back to his senses making him realize his duty as a minister. He controlled his sobs with great effort.

Maharaj walked calmly and slowly and approached Annaji. Meanwhile, he had planned what to say to Annaji. Maharaj placed his hand on Annaji's shoulder and asked him, "Annaji, people grow tired of me and abandon me. Netaji abandoned me, Prataprao left me, Sambhaji Kavaji deserted me. I never got an opportunity to understand their anguish. At least, you are giving me that opportunity. Tell me Annajipant, what fault is there in me, that people who have been close to me like my own shadow, have abandoned me? Let me at least understand it for once in my life!"

"No Swami, you are not at fault. Nobody is at fault. It is just my misfortune. Please let me go." Annaji leaned forward and touched the mojaris of the Chhatrapati.

"Annaji, Masaheb should have been here to hear you talk of misfortune." Raje remembered Jijau and all calamities she had faced and fought determinedly.

"Annaji, even Mother Bhavani cannot stop a person who has made up his mind decided to leave. Just tell me the reason before you go. What is making you leave your duty midway? Answer me." Chhatrapati shook Annaji's shoulders vigorously.

"Swami, I am lost for words. I cannot forget that I have survived so far only by your grace. I have no complaint. No one is at fault at all." Annaji couldn't speak further.

"You say, you have no complaint means that the complaint is serious. You say, no one is at fault means someone is at fault. Surnis, I command as the Chhatrapati, that you disclose the reason for your request for release you from the duty, in front of our family deity." Raje's words gradually became formal.

Annaji was in two minds. He hesitated for a moment. The

word 'Surnis' gave him some unknown confidence. Annaji wiped his eyes with the edge of his shawl, and said in a resolute voice, "My reputation has been ruined Maharaj. That is why I request the release from my duty.

"Tell me clearly. What happened? Who ruined your reputation?" Maharaj became alert.

"Maharaj, forgive me, Maharaj – It's Yuvaraj!"

"A…nna…ji!" Raje was shocked as if scorched by a burning torch.

"What – what has Yuvaraj done, Annaji?" Raje's heart shook with an unknown fear.

"Please forgive me, Swami. He has done the deed, but I am ashamed to even talk about his actions with you. Please forgive me."

"I forgive you, Annajipant. Tell me, what Yuvaraj has done!" Chhatrapati's face was turning rigid. The vein on his forehead throbbed noticeably.

"Maharaj, Yuvaraj has abducted a married woman of my family who had come to stay with us. We cannot show our faces to the world. Our honour has been completely ruined. It is difficult for me to leave you, yet I request you to let me go." Annaji knelt at Raje's feet. His words failed to make an impact on the Chhatrapati

The moment he heard the words, 'abducted a married woman' Raje's entire body trembled with rage. His breathing intensified. He felt trapped between intense guilt and uncontrollable wrath.

His face became red with rage and fiery words erupted from his lips, "Annaji, if this is the reason, then someone will have to leave, not just this fort, but perhaps this world. But it won't be you – it would be Sambhajiraje Bhosale! In this Swaraj, that has been run in the name of God, you will get justice. Trust me." The Chhatrapati went to the inner chamber to be alone.

Sambhajiraje climbed up Raigad, gasping for breath. As far

as he remembered, he had never experienced such a thing in his life. The personnel of the eighteen departments did not make an obeisance to him as usual. Many of them, in fact, looked at him quite contemptuously, and quite a few had pity in their eyes. But he could not see respect in anyone's eyes. The firmament that usually seemed small to him in front of Raigad, seemed frightening today. Only one thing on that populated fort helped him build his courage again – the Jaripataka pennant fluttering on the wind atop the Nagar Khana.

He had travelled to Lingana so spiritedly, but now every step had become heavy for him as if he was shackled in heavy chains. Only one thought occupied his mind, 'For the first time, today, I will have to justify my actions to Maharajsaheb'.

Yes, he was going to present himself in front of Maharaj. He was going to confess everything in front of him and do whatever Maharaj wished.

He threw a contemptuous glance at Soyarabai's palace and turned to Maharaj's palace. There was nobody with him. He felt lonely as he had never felt before.

As he was crossing the door of Maharaj's palace, Khandoji Dabhade made an obeisance to him and told him, "Maharaj wants to be alone. He has told me not to send anybody in!" He placed his spear across to stop Sambhajiraje. Sambhajiraje pushed it aside with his wrist, without looking at him.

He was going to appeal to his Aabasaheb in the same way he had appealed to Goddess Jagadamba in the sanctum. Today, he was courageously going to protest in front of his father who was the Chhatrapati, against Soyara Masaheb's conniving ways of conduct. He was going to pour out his heart today.

Yuvaraj Sambhajiraje – who had lived in Mirza Raja's Rajput encampment as hostage, who had not been afraid to stay behind and live alone in Mathura, who had conducted the Bhaganagar campaign, was going to prostrate in front of his Aabasaheb and say to him, "You are my father as well as my mother. I don't want to live on Raigad anymore. Please take me with you on your campaigns. I surrender the title of Yuvaraj at your feet. It should be assigned to Ramraje and he should be given the honour of sitting on the golden step at the base of the royal throne in the durbar. Just give me your mojaris. They are closest to my heart. I would like to request only one thing. No one understands me in this fort. Therefore, please take me in your embrace just as you had done in Mathura. Thoralya Aausaheb, who understood me had told me many tales of wisdom. The only thing I need now is your support."

"Maharajsaheb" Sambhajiraje knocked on the closed door of Maharaj's personal chamber.

The door did not open. It was not going to open.

"Thann…Thann…Thann…!" the sound of the bells tolling in the courtyard of the Jgadishwar temple penetrated the palace. Sambhajiraje, standing out and anxious, Maharaj sitting on his bed inside, both could not resist the memory of late Jijau Saheb. They could not see each other or could not know it, but both had placed their hands on their chest. Inside, a thought flashed in Maharaj's mind, 'Masaheb, it is better that you are not alive to witness this dilemma I am facing now. You would not have been able to watch your son prosecuting your grandson.'

Outside, Sambhajiraje's heart was in turmoil, 'Thoralya Aau, you should have been here today. Even if all doors would have been closed to me, I would have come to you. Just hearing you call me 'Shambhoobal' would have given me the strength to face any crisis, no matter how big.' Yuvaraj Sambhajiraje went back. At that moment, the fortunes of the Maratha Empire turned for the worse. The family bond of the Bhosales was shattered. Truth turned its back on itself due to the game of fate.

As soon as he came back to his chamber, Sambhajiraje was put under house arrest by Maharaj's armed soldiers, as he was an accused. Even Putalabai and Yesubai who had come to meet him, were prohibited from seeing him.

Another dark day in Raigad's life broke. The day of Jijau's demise had been first dark day and today was the second. Today, Sambhajiraje was going to be prosecuted in the durbar in front of the Chhatrapati. The father-son duo who were like a figure and its shadow, were going to face the truth courageously.

Putalabai, Sarlashkar Hambhirarao and Yesubai tried very hard to visit Maharaj, but they failed.

"Yuvaraj is going to get the death sentence. The news left everyone terrified. Sambhajiraje who had spent the night in anguish had prepared his mind for the 'death penalty'.

Anxious people were gathering in the durbar. No one was speaking. In no time, the courtyard in front of the durbar thronged with crowds.

Maharaj was dressed in the royal attire and stood calmly in front of Goddess Bhavani's idol in the sanctum. The yogi king of the Marathas offered some bael leaves and flowers at her divine feet and left the sanctum. He started walking slowly towards the royal throne in the durbar. With every step he took, the seemingly unbreakable bonds of relationships, were breaking easily. Suddenly, two hands clasped the yogi's feet, and he heard an earnest feminine voice calling him, "Aaba..."

The royal daughter-in-law, Yesubai, stood against the stone wall of the sanctum, waiting for Maharaj to come outside. Those few moments had tormented her heart gravely. She could not bear the stress and clasped the feet of Maharaj who had treated her with a father's love. She wanted to plead for her husband's life.

The great king had prepared himself to deal with this situation, but in that moment, he too hesitated. The Chhatrapati closed his eyes to control his emotions that were about to erupt.

Maharaj himself had placed the Shikke-katyar in the lap of her sari. Now, his soonbai had spread the same pallu of her sari before of him. As if Masaheb was trying to communicate with him through her. That thought moved Raje from the bottom of his heart. He wanted to take a step forward, but he hesitated.

"Soonbai..." The Chhatrapati put his trembling hand on Yesubai's back. His trembling touch left Yesubai sobbing.

"Stand up and calm down." Raje pulled her up. Yesubai was tongue-tied, she could not speak a word. Her sobbing expressed everything she wanted to say.

"Listen to me and get a grip." The warmth in his wise words had enough strength to give courage to a feeble man in the face of death.

"Indeed, I remember Masaheb when I see you. You are just like her. At this moment, you are the only one who can understand what I'm going through." The tension between them dissolved in that instant.

"Yesu, never forget Masaheb. She faced severe crises throughout her life but never lost courage. Among the people on this fort, only you have that kind of great courage that befits our family. Trust me. If at all Goddess Jagadamba compels me to take your husband's life, I will never sit on the royal throne again! I will treat you as Masaheb and spend my entire life serving you!

"Now go and beseech Goddess Jagadamba to prevent me from having to do anything like this. I have already appealed to her.

"My dear, wipe your eyes. We should not weep like this. Farewell." Maharaj calmly patted Yesubai's shoulders and left. Just as calmly, Yesubai started walking towards the sanctum. If someone would have seen her from behind, they wouldn't have believed that Jijau was no more!

Maharani Soyarabai had arrived in the section for the royal ladies in the durbar. She had purposely brought Ramraje with her today. Except for her, no other ladies of the royal family were present.

On the platform of the royal throne, seven ministers including Moropant, Duttaji, Prahladpant, Hambirarao,

Raghunath Pandit and others had taken their places. Only Surnis Annaji Dutto's place was empty. As he was the plaintiff in today's case, he could not take his usual place. He was standing in the durbar with lowered head.

As per the custom, an attendant blew the horn and its sound dispersed all around the durbar. Following that, the drums in the Nagar Khana resounded.

An attendant holding the golden spear, came to the platform of the royal throne. He pounded the shaft of the spear on the floor and called out the customary appellations three times. The entire durbar became alert. As the attendant pounded the shaft of the spear on the floor, the scales of Justice shook slightly. A few moments passed in complete silence, as people waited with bated breath. Then, like an eagle, the king of birds, perching on the summit of Mount Mainak, the Chhatrapati Maharaj appeared on the platform of the royal throne. The entire durbar bowed down promptly and made an obeisance. Maharaj raised his hand and blessed his ryots present in the durbar. He didn't realize that Ramraje had come onto the platform and making an obeisance. Soyarabai had sent him. When he realized it, he hesitated for a moment. Without turning his head, he said, "Pant, take Balraje with you and have him stand next to you!"

"Ji." Moropant stepped forward, held Ramraje's hand and had him stand by his side. Soyarabai saw it from the royal ladies' section and her neck twitched. She had wrongfully thought that Maharaj would smilingly make Balraje sit in the vacant seat of Yuvaraj.

Maharaj bowed down to the royal throne, and without touching his feet to the throne, he sat on the royal throne. His right foot rested on the footrest. Maharaj raised his hand and signalled his minsters to commence the durbar.

Sarlashkar Hambirarao did not want the trial of the Yuvaraj to take place at the very beginning of the durbar. Therefore, he put forth some military requirements of his troops at first.

Chhatrapati raised his hand and approved his proposal. Chitnis Balaji Aavaji, who sat on a seat in front of the royal throne, noted down the approval.

Two platters of royal gifts had arrived at the fort. Peshwe Moropant requested the Chhatrapati to accept the royal gifts. As per protocol, one of the platters had arrived in the name of Yuvaraj Sambhajiraje. Maharaj accepted his platter with the customary touch of his hand. The gift platter for Yuvaraj was placed on his vacant seat. As Maharaj realized that time was passing by, he reminded Prahladpant, "Chief Justice, let the legal proceedings of the durbar start now.

Prahladpant bowed down and said, "As you wish". The entire durbar was as tense as a taut bowstring. "Present the accused Yuvaraj in the durbar." Prahladpant ordered an officer from the justice department.

All eyes in the durbar turned towards the path from the Balekilla leading to the durbar, passing by the side of the royal ladies' section. Countless hearts throbbed in fear with every moment that passed.

Ten swordsmen who had surrounded Yuvaraj Sambhajiraje brought him in front of the impartial royal throne of Swaraj. Sambhajiraje, clad in an orange jama and a dotted scarlet churidar, shining orange Jiretop on his head, forehead smeared with stripes of sandalwood paste, the cowrie necklace resting on his chest, and both his wrists tied with a blue scarf, entered the durbar.

He held his head high, and his eyes were glowing with determination. He walked steadily and took firm steps with his bare feet. It was the fearless mien of a young lion cub stepping out of the cave.

When they saw him like this, many courtiers felt deeply grieved. Even in that condition, a few soldiers from his troops made an obeisance to him. The swordsmen presented the accused in front of the royal throne and took a few steps back.

The handsome son of the Maratha king stood before him as an accused! Jijau's grandson 'Shambhoobal' was presented in front of her son 'Shivba' as a criminal! The proud Yuvaraj was presented before Chhatrapati Maharaj as a culprit.

Utter silence that could have been broken even by the sound of breath prevailed in the durbar. The next moment, a distressed cry of affection broke the silence. "Dada Maharaj…!" Five-year-old Ramraje, who stood next to Moropant on the platform of the royal throne was terrified!

Sambhajiraje felt dispirited. His eyes welled up and his heart felt heavy. He wanted to go forward, pull Balraje into his embrace and have him sit in his empty seat.

"Pant, please take Balraje back to his chamber." Maharaj instructed Moropant. Moropant quickly took Balraje outside from the back, handed him to the personal secretary of Maharaj, and returned to his place.

Sambhajiraje stared at the gift platter kept in his seat. Only one thought left him dumbstruck, 'When I had sat on that seat for the first time, it never occurred to me that I might have to stand up here, like this!'

Prahladpant was utterly confounded and didn't know how to break the silence in the durbar.

"Pant, give a warning to the accused. He hasn't made a formal obeisance yet!" Chhatrapati's neck straightened, and his voice became stern.

As Sambhajiraje heard his words, he felt embarrassed and looked around awkwardly. As his hands were tied, he bowed down to make an obeisance before Pant could give him a warning. Maharaj saw it and calmed down. He broached the subject that had got sidelined.

"Pant, read the charges against the accused."

"Ji, as you wish." Nyayadhish Prahladpant started reading the charge sheet – "The accused, his Royal Highness Sambhajiraje, the son of… of…" Prahladpant hesitated…how could he announce Maharaj's name in his presence?!

"Please go ahead and read." The royal throne reassured him.

"The defendant, his Royal Highness Sambhajiraje, the son of Sivajiraje Bhosale, aged eighteen, currently residing at Raigad." Pralhandpant continued reading.

"The plaintiff, his highness Annajipant, the son of Duttoji Prabhunikar Surnis, Raigad, aged approximately fifty years, currently residing at Raigad, has filed a complaint against you that…" Prahladpant took a deep breath before doing the most difficult thing and wiped his sweat with the shawl.

"You have forcibly abducted a respectable married woman named Godavari from Raigad, who is a relative of his. The aforementioned woman is currently in your custody on Fort Lingana." Prahladpant stopped.

"Do you accept your crime?" Maharaj asked Annaji.

"Ji." Annaji made an obeisance and responded keeping his head low.

"Defendant Sambhajiraje, do you accept the charge?" Maharaj stared at Sambhajiraje. No one had dared to look at Maharaj directly in the durbar so far, but today Sambhajiraje looked directly in his eyes.

"No! I do not accept this charge!" Yuvaraj's words were loud and clear.

"Do you mean that the woman is not in your custody?" Maharaj was confused for a moment.

"Ji. She is!" Sambhajiraje was just not ready to step back today.

"Then why do you deny the charge?" The two royals clashed. Fiery words started flying.

"She is not in my 'custody', she is my 'prisoner'. I have not abducted her but detained her." He answered slowly.

"For what reason and in what capacity?" Maharaj's mind was entangled in conflicting thoughts. In frustration, he thumped his fist on the hand rest of the royal throne.

"Some crafty people were scheming against me and wanted to use her as a pawn in the game – they were going to spread scandalous rumours about us. That is why using my rights as the Yuvaraj, as the son of the Chhatrapati Maharaj, I arrested her. If need be, the Bhosales have to sacrifice their lives to defend their honour. Keeping that in mind, I have imprisoned her."

The entire durbar was abuzz, hearing his fearless, fiery words. There was commotion in the durbar.

"Who are those crafty people? What had they planned?" Maharaj asked the key questions that would lead to the root of the case. His questions left the durbar in utter silence. Everybody pricked their ears.

Sambhajiraje threw a fierce glance at the sheer curtain of the royal ladies' section. As he remembered Ramraje and Thoralya Aausaheb he got tongue-tied. Unbearable silence prevailed in the durbar.

"I am asking you, who are the people who were going to use the woman as a pawn against you? What was their plan?" Raje asked intimidatingly.

Now, for the first time Sambhajiraje dropped his head. He shook his head and said, "No, Maharaj, I cannot take their names here in this durbar!"

"Then your defence does not stand." A determined response came from the royal throne. About to be resolved, the case got complicated again.

"Maharaj, please forgive me. Please let the woman be present in the durbar as a witness in this hearing. In my opinion, she should be granted impunity and investigated thoroughly." At the last moment, Sarlashkar Hambirarao voiced what Yuvaraj had wished in his mind.

Hambirarao did not know that through the sheer curtain of the royal ladies' section, two eyes were glaring at him.

"No…I don't find it appropriate to present a respectable lady in the durbar." For the first time Annaji Dutto spoke hastily.

"Annaji, you are forgetting that even Yuvaraj was brought to the durbar as an accused!" The Chhatrapati reminded him.

"Pant, grant impunity to the woman and tell her to present herself in the durbar. You personally make sure that it happens." Maharaj ordered Peshwe Moropant.

"Defendant Sambhajiraje, what right do you have to wield a sword and wear the cowrie necklace that is the pride of the Bhaosale clan until, you are proved innocent?" That sharp question posed by Maharaj left the durbar stunned.

Sambhajiraje's shackled hands touched the cowrie necklace in shock. His eyes betrayed a fear, and he pleaded from the bottom of his heart, "No…! Please cut my head if you wish!"

"Silence!" Chhatrapati stood up at once. Everyone in the durbar was startled. No one could tell what was going to happen next.

After seeing the pain in Yuvaraj's eyes, only one fearless person felt the need to open his mouth at the cost of risking the outcome of his action. It was Sarlashkar Hambirarao Mohite.

"Maharaj, pardon me. Even Goddess Jagadamba cannot remove the cowrie necklace from Yuvaraj's neck unless he is proven guilty. I am sure, if such a thing happens, Yuvaraj himself will not hesitate to cut off his head like he said!"

Maharaj looked at loyal Hambirarao who had bowed down in front of him. He raised his hand and concluded the durbar. All the courtiers bowed down. Sambhajiraje also bowed down. When he raised his head, Maharaj had left the durbar. The ministers were leaving the durbar one by one. Hambiraro was among them; Sambhajiraje looked gratefully at his back. There, in the sanctum, Yesubai still sat with her head placed at Jagadamba's feet, and Putalabai's tremulous hand still stroked her back to console her.

Moropant had gone to Fort Lingana to bring Godavari, but he returned empty-handed and with a heavy heart. Godavari had reached that durbar from where no one could ever return!

Godavari's mind had been clouded by countless frantic thoughts. She was feeling tormented. Her beautiful, delicate feminine heart had become harsh. In a desperate moment, she had decided not to show her face to anyone. Under the pretext of relieving herself she got out of the room she was confined in and went away from the armed soldiers of Sambhajiraje. She went to a high cliff on Fort Lingana, tucked the edge of her white sari, joined her hands and prayed to her family deity. As she opened her eyes and looked at the bluish black deep valley before her, it appeared like the tranquil Shivlinga in the Jagadishwar temple. With an intense desire to offer the bael leaf of her body on that Shivlinga, she threw her body that was pure from top to toe but wounded by countless mental afflictions, into the valley before her.

Moropant sent some Bhillas in the valley and had her scattered remains collected. They were covered by a cloth and kept at the foothills of Lingana. Moropant had returned, wondering how to convey this heart-wrenching news to Maharaj.

The news he had brought drowned the entire Raigad in a strange stifling sorrow. Godavari had left everyone speechless by her actions. The sentinels guarding Sambhajiraje's chamber were removed. The Chhatrapati left his palace with Moropant, Hambirarao, and Prahladpant. The palanquin-bearers brought a palanquin in front of him, but he signalled them to take it back. He started climbing down the fort on foot.

After arriving in Pachad Maharaj ordered Sais to saddle the horses and keep them ready. First, he went to take darshan of Jijau's Samadhi.

The Chhatrapati Maharaj mounted the horse that Sais had kept ready and started galloping towards Fort Lingana. The ministers who had accompanied him and a few select swordsmen followed him. Along with everyone, Maharaj came near the place where Godavari's remains were kept, covered by a cloth. As per the advance intimation sent by Moropant, a funeral pyre had been erected at the foothills of Lingana.

The swordsmen put Godavari's remains on the funeral pyre. The pyre was lit. Maharaj kept staring at the funeral pyre.

"Pant, Tell Aabaji Mahadeo to raise a memorial in the name of this virtuous lady." Chhatrapati instructed Moropant.

A benumbed Sambhajiraje stood at the Bhavani point on Raigad and stared at the funeral pyre burning at the bottom of Lingana. That pyre, burning at a faraway distance, was burning his heart. A radiant woman, holding a puja platter, walked towards him. That fearless glowing woman came in front of Sambhajiraje. She looked at Yuvaraj's feet and did not raise her eyes. She was clad in a married woman's attire. She said to him, "Yuvaraj had to bear a lot because of me. If possible, he should forgive me for that!"

Godavari took her own life, leaving Yuvaraj in perpetual pain. Her death left a deep impact on him, and he realized that Soyarabai could go to any length to accomplish her goal. Since that incident, he harboured a deep grudge against Soyarabai. Maharaj was in a predicament as to how to console Yuvaraj who was deeply hurt by the chain of events. During this whole incident, Annaji had surrendered his allegiance at Maharani Saheb's feet. Now there was no way out for him.

Sambhajiraje felt exhausted thinking about the events that had transpired. He came into his sleeping chamber and lay on the bed. He had dozed off. Yesubai was pressing his feet. Suddenly, in his sleep, a wrinkle appeared on Sambhajiraje's forehead. His breathing intensified. Drops of sweat gathered on his face and as if he was desparately trying to stop someone, he screamed out loudly, "Wait…! Stop…!". His screaming startled Yesubai. He woke up at once shaking violently.

Yesubai wiped his face with a cloth and asked him affectionately, "What happened? You screamed out so loud…"

Without responding to her, Yuvaraj shook his head to dispel his thoughts. He had a terrifying dream in broad daylight!

Yesubai gave him water; he drank it. After he composed himself, Yesubai said in a soft voice, "Kaviraj is waiting for you in the guest room."

Sambhajiraje did not wait to tidy his dishevelled hair and came to the guest room. As he entered the room, Kavi Kulesh and another Hindustani person made an obeisance to him.

"Yuvaraj, he is Udho Yogadeo- Goddess Durga Kali's devotee." Kaviraj introduced the new guest. Kavi Kulesh was speaking in his Hindustani tongue.

Udho Yogadeo bowed down. He had applied horizontal stripes of sandalwood paste on his forehead. He had donned northern style attire. The round face of fair complexioned Udho Yogadeo looked resolute, owing to his bright eyes.

"Yuvaraj, please accept Mother Kali's prasad." Udho Yogadeo said. He pulled out a pouch of holy ashes and prasad wrapped in a leaf from his handbag and placed it in Yuvaraj's palms.

"I was saved from this situation only by the grace of Goddess Durga Bhavani. She will save me from such problems in future too." Sambhajiraje thought and touched the prasad to his forehead.

"Yuvaraj, if it is okay with you, I would like to say something to you." Kulesh's tone had changed.

"Sure, please feel free Kaviraj." Sambhajiraje had not forgotten his assistance during the stay in Mathura.

"Yuvaraj, whatever has happened, happened dur to Goddess Bhavani's wish. You should forget it. Your Maharaj is indeed great. You are fortunate to be born as his son. You are a poet. Remember that creativity is the holy prasad of Brahmadev. Forgiveness and forbearance are its foundation." He wanted to speak more, but he resisted, thinking that as he was from the north, he may make some mistake while speaking and end up being disrespectful.

"Kaviraj, I am not angry with Aabasaheb, and I'm not worthy enough to forgive him. But I cannot forgive Masaheb for what she did. You look at me as a poet, but I consider myself the Yuvaraj first and then a poet. Sambhajiraje stopped speaking.

Kavi Kulesh could understand the Marathi language a little bit, but he could not speak it. The handsome, brilliant prince standing before him had won his heart back in Mathura itself. He had come to the Marathi region in the hope of serving the father and son from Deccan as much as he could.

"Please take some rest. I will take your leave now." Kavi Kulesh said. He did not want to continue the unpleasant topic. He bowed down, took a few steps back and left the room with Yogadeo.

'This Kavi Kulesh reminds me of the time in Mathura. How many years have passed!' Sambhajiraje sighed and went to his chamber.

"Here, eat this." The moment he entered his chamber, a loving hand came in front of him. His reverie broke. Sambhajiraje extended the hand in which he had held Goddess Durga's prasad. A peasant hand placed a piece of coconut and jaggery in his palm. It was Dharau. She had also pleaded to Shambhoo Mahadeo of Kapurhol and promised to do something for him. Today she had fulfilled her promise.

Turbulent winds started blowing on the fort. They displaced the triangular flags on top of the Jagadishwar and Shirkari temples.

The inclement weather made Maharaj shiver. He fell sick. Whooping cough and high fever left him bedridden. The royal physicians got busy preparing medicines for him.

As the Maharani, Soyarabai took control of the palace of the Chhatrapati, under the pretext of taking care of him.

Putalabai, Sakawarbai, Yesubai, Dharau – were allowed to wait in Maharaj's chamber only for a short while.

Maharaj had drifted off in the afternoon. Sambhajiraje was desperate to meet him, so he decisively came to Maharaj's chamber.

As soon as the swordsmen guarding the chamber saw him, they made way for him.

Soyarabai sat near Maharaj's head. The moment she saw Yuvaraj, her forehead creased. She got up at once and walked out of the chamber. As she passed Yuvaraj, she did not even bother to look at him.

But the moment she passed by him; pure-hearted Yuvaraj bowed down to pay respect. He was surprised at his own action. As he saw Maharaj sleeping, he was about to go back. When he threw a sweeping glance around, his eyes fell upon the shawl spread over Aabasaheb. Maharaj's feet had got exposed while turning on his side in his sleep. His feet caught Sambhajiraje' attention. He gently entered the chamber. He touched Maharaj's feet with his fingers and touched them to his forehead. He sat on the bed, at Maharaj's feet.

Maharani's maid, Chandra, came twice to check and went back.

After a while Maharaj woke up. As he opened his eyes, he saw Sambhajiraje's shining Jiretop, and sat erect. He said to him, "How come you are here?"

Yuvaraj promptly stood up and made an obeisance.

"It's okay. Have a seat. I knew that you would come to visit me. I should thank my illness for that." Maharaj started coughing while talking. Though he knew that he couldn't do anything to stop it, Sambhajiraje stepped forward in worry.

The coughing stopped, but the strain had flushed Maharaj's face.

"Shambhoo, I really like your fearlessness. If I had the same fearlessness at your, I would have done so much more with the grace of Goddess Jagadamba, than I have done so far." Maharaj was reminiscing.

After some time, he said, "But you should clearly remember now, that if such audacity is used at a wrong time, in a wrong place, everything goes wrong. You are bound to a married woman's sacrifice now, and nothing you do can bring her back. Her life was more precious than anybody's reputation." The Chhatrapati started coughing hard. That cough was stifling Sambhajiraje from all sides, it was smothering him.

"The only thing I regret is that you don't speak about your problems openly to me. You feel scared of me. You too consider me as the Chhatrapati just like everyone else, but you forget that I am your father." Raje was feeling pain, he paused.

"Just think about it, how could we have faced Masaheb if she were alive, after a married woman had sacrificed her life for the wrong reasons? It is okay if you forget me, but never…never forget her." The Chhatrapati closed his eyes.

"Aaba…" Sambhajiraje had put his forehead on the edge of the bed and was sobbing in the memory of Godavari. Chhatrapati's words had clearly touched his heart.

"Calm down, Shambhoo, get a grip." Maharaj's hand kept consoling Yuvaraj by stroking his shoulder gently.

"Get up, the physician is here." Raje commanded. The physician had come to administer the medication. Maharaj looked at him with a smile and said, "I think, I don't need any more medication now. My cough has almost stopped now." Maharaj controlled the bout of cough in his throat while saying it. Sambhajiraje could clearly see on his face the stress it was causing. Somewhere in his mind the words of Kavi Kulesh echoed, "Your Maharaj is indeed great!"

Maharaj's cough was brought under control. The physician advised him a change of place and plenty of rest. The Chhatrapati decided to go to the fort of Satara for vacation.

The travel preparations began on the fort. The cold season was almost over. Sambhajiraje was discussing the religious scriptures, the Puranas and politics with Kavi Kulesh, Keshav Pandit and Udho Yogadeo. He received intimation from Maharaj's palace.

Sambhajiraje wondering why he had been summoned and

entered the seating chamber of the palace.

As he bowed to make an obeisance to Maharaj, his eyes fell upon a person standing in the chamber. He was wearing a turban.

"Yuvaraj, this is pandit Umajipant. I have invited him here on purpose." Maharaj pointed to the person who was wearing a turban.

The pandit bowed down to Sambhjiraje.

"I am leaving for Satara. You should spend your time with him and Keshav Pandit. He is proficient in the Shastras and well-versed in the scriptures. I think your literary talent will develop in his company."

Maharaj had gathered detailed information about the Godavari episode. He had realized that Rani Saheb resented Shambhooraje's appointment as the Yuvaraj and was trying to cause trouble for him.

"As you wish." Sambhajiraje had observed Umaji Pandit thoroughly in the meantime.

"Pandit, please come with me." Yuvaraj was about to leave with him.

"Listen!" Maharaj called him affectionately.

"Ji."

"I have heard that you have composed a poem 'Nakhashikha' on the character of Radha, but you haven't recited it to me! Now, in the company of these two pandits, you should compose something that you can share with me!"

Sambhajiraje's face flushed; he hastily said "ji" and left quickly.

Maharaj went to Satara. Soyarabai took charge of Raigad. Sambhajiraje was engrossed in the company of the pandits, in the study of the Shastras and the Puranas.

After a fortnight a messenger climbed up Raigad. He was panting. The entire fort became anxious because of the worrisome news he had brought. Maharaj had taken very ill. He was throwing up all the food he ate. He had headache and high fever.

The administrative officer had sent an urgent message that said, 'Leave immediately after getting this letter. It is very urgent.' An anxious Sambhajiraje was in Putalabai's chamber. The maids were packing their luggage for the journey. Yesubai was pacing back and forth and instructing them.

Putalabai's face was full of concern. She handed a small container covered with a cloth to Yesuabai and said, "Take this with you in the palanquin, it won't last if kept with other luggage."

Yesubai raised her eyebrows wondering "What is this?"

"It is a special herbal extract. I have heard that it's very useful in controlling nausea." Putalabai showed her that her heart was already on the fort of Satara.

Yesubai carefully put the container in one corner.

As everyone was anxiously waiting, Soyarabai's maid came and delivered Maharani's message to Putalabai, "Everyone should have their meal and climb down the fort and go ahead. Maharani is going to start her journey in the late afternoon." As she heard the message, Putalabai just glanced at Sambhajiraje and Yesubai and did not say a word. No one could disregard her wish.

Sambhajiraje did not wait to have a meal and instructed the palanquin-bearers to get the palanquins ready.

They went to the sanctum and took darshan of Goddess Jagadamba. Putalabai and Yesubai sat in the palanquins. Sambhajiraje walked beside Putalabai's palanquin. The menials carried the luggage on their heads. The armed soldiers stood guard. The palanquins started descending the fort.

They arrived at Pachad. Everyone took the darshan of Jijau's samadhi to clear their heads. The menials placed the luggage on the beasts of burden. More security troops were added to the entourage. Sambhajiraje mounted a scarlet horse. The palanquin-bearers started walking.

On the fort of Satara, Maharaj lay restlessly on his bed. He was in intense pain. The windows of his chamber were closed, and the curtains were drawn. Two dimly burning lamps stood in a corner so the Chhatrapati could see the person visiting him.

Putalabai pressed his legs to ease his pain. She was lost in thought. Yesubai held the container and stood near the foot of the bed. Maharani Soyarabai stood behind her. Sambhajiraje sat near the head of the bed and held the Chhatrapati's hand which was scorching. It seemed as hot as a cannon heated in strong sunlight.

"Shambhoo…" Chhatrapati moaned in pain. He tightened his grip on Sambhajiraje's hand. His tight grip told Sambhajiraje that he wanted to say something.

"Ji." Sambhajiraje leaned forward.

"Aabasaheb, how are you feeling?"

Maharaj just shook his head left and right in unbearable pain. Shivaramshastri Vaidya entered the chamber. He had brought some ground herbal paste in a shell.

"Swami…" The vaidya approached Maharaj's bed and called him gently with sheer affection. Maharaj opened his eyes.

"Here's some medicine." The vaidya extended the shell in front of Maharaj while looking at Sambhajiraje, so he could help Maharaj to get up.

Sambhajiraje put his hand under Aabasaheb's neck and helped him to sit on the bed. The vaidya took the shell near his lips and put some medicine on his tongue.

Putalabai promptly wiped Maharaj's mouth with a cloth. A few moments passed and Raje's guts got churned like clouds churned by gusty winds. He spread both his arms wide. His throat shook.

The nervous vaidya supported Maharaj and exclaimed, "The spittoon please."

Putalabai quickly picked up the spittoon from under the bed and held it in front of Maharaj. Maharaj instantly vomited the whole medication with the phlegm. The vaidya gently stroked

Maharaj's back.

"Please help him lie down." The vaidya put his hand under Raje's arm. Sambhajiraje supported his neck and helped him lie down.

"Oh Lord Shiva..." The vaidya whispered to himself and left the chamber with a heavy heart.

Instantly, Sambhajiraje's mind swarmed with countless thoughts like a hive swarming with bees. He got up from the bed and followed the vaidya. He was checking the grinding slab on which the herb had been ground.

"Vaidyabuva, I am very worried. I cannot even look at Maharajsaheb. What kind of illness is this?" Sambhajiraje asked.

"I am trying my best to treat him, but Yuvaraj, now I am feeling like this is beyond my limits." The vaidya dodged his question and said in a solemn voice.

"But what exactly has happened to him? Should we summon any other vaidya for your assistance?"

"Sure, I don't mind it, but this is getting serious now." The vaidya's forehead puckered.

"What?" Sambhajiraje screamed in a muffled voice as if stung by a scorpion.

"Yuvaraj...Yuvaraj...I don't know how to tell you this."

"Buva, just tell me what to do. I will sacrifice my own life to save Aabasaheb." Sambhajiraje held the vaidya's hands and shook them vigorously.

"If that would have saved Maharaj, then I would have sacrificed my own life for him, Yuvaraj!" The vaidya said calmly.

"Then what should we do? Tell me Vaidyabuva."

The vaidya lowered his head, "We can do only one thing."

"What is it?"

"To pray to the family Goddess Bhavani." The Vaidya's eyes welled up.

"Buva..."

"Yuvaraj, you will need to brace yourself to hear the diagnosis of Maharaj's illness. Are you ready for it?"

Sambhajiraje was deeply concerned.

"Janardan..." The vaidya called his disciple who was putting the levigating slab in a handbag.

"Ji." He exclaimed and came forward.

"Bring the spittoon from Swami's chamber." The vaidya instructed him.

Janardan left promptly and within a short time returned with the spittoon. Vaidyabuva held it and came near a window. "Yuvaraj, check this spew!"

Sambhajiraje went near the window. He saw the yellowish-purplish mixture of spew and the medicinal paste. As he saw it his eyes changed colour.

"Buva!" A muffled scream escaped from Sambhajiraje's mouth.

"Yes Yuvaraj, Swami has been poisoned. His disease is very peculiar. The food he has eaten hasn't been digested and has curdled in his stomach. I tried hard to make him vomit the lumps of food in his stomach, but that did not work. If I administer medication to dilute the lumps in his stomach, he is throwing it up. The benumbed Vaidya spoke as if he was talking to himself.

Chhatrapati Shivaji – the radiant Sun of Kavi Bhushan was eclipsed by the shadow of death! All people gathered on the fort of Satara were bound in the shackles of worries.

The hourly toll of the time-indicating bell echoed in the middle of the night and dispersed in the darkness. The guard at the entrance of the fort hastily entered the ramparts of the Balekilla. He whispered something in the ears of the armed soldiers guarding the Chhatrapati's chamber. Then, carrying a spear, he went inside.

Sambhajiraje, Putalabai, Yesubai, Hambirarao, Shivaram Vaidya… everyone was deeply concerned and had surrounded Chhatrapati's bed. Their faces were distressed. Maharaj had dozed off. Soyarabai stood near him keeping a keen eye. "Dhakale Dhani, a sanyasi disciple of Ramdasbuva has arrived at the main gate of the fort. He insists on meeting Thorale Dhani right now. He is not ready to listen to me." The guard informed Sambhajiraje in a low voice. Sambhajiraje glanced at Hambiramama. Hambirarao understood his gesture and left the chamber with the guard.

Hambirarao came to the main gate of the fort, peeped out of the wicket and examined the person standing outside in the dim light of the torch. A clear voice pierced the darkness and echoed in the air, "Jai Jai Raghuveer Samartha…!"

Hambirarao stepped outside, Kalyanswami, the disciple of Samartha stood outside.

"Senapati, Samartha has sent me. Please don't waste any more time and take me directly to the Chhatrapati."

"Please come!" Hambirarao opened the wicket for him.

Kalyanswami took off his wooden sandals near the threshold of the Chhatrapati's chamber and entered inside. As soon as they saw him, the royal family members gathered to receive him. Sambhajiraje touched his feet. The royal ladies tidied their saris, leaned forward and touched his feet three times. Everyone was silent, but their faces were urging him earnestly – "Swami…please save our Maharaj."

Kalyanswami gazed at the radiant Kshatriya lying on the bed. It seemed as if God Himself had sent him. He sat on the edge of the bed, placed his soft palm on the Chhatrapati's head and called him as lovingly as Jijau would have called him – "Shivbabaraje!"

A wave of vibrant energy engulfed Raje and he opened his eyes. As soon as he opened his eyes, he saw Kalyanswami. Though he was feeling fatigued, he tried to get up and pay respect to Kalyanswami.

"Raje, I accept your greetings. No need to get up." Kalyanswami did not let him get up.

"Bring the shell and some milk please." Kalyanswami said.

He pulled out two pouches made of Palash leaves from his shoulder bag.

"Swami cannot consume any medication. He feels nauseated and throws up instantly. He…he…" As Shivaram Vaidya saw the pouches, he could not resist speaking.

"I know that. Gurudeo has sent me here with the ashes and the powder to treat the very same condition.

Kalyanswami mixed the powder in the milk and made the Chhatrapati drink it while chanting 'Jai Jai Raghuveer Samartha'.

The Chhatrapati whispered in a feeble voice that seemed like coming from the depth of a cave, "Jai Jai Raghuveer Samartha!"

Without taking support from anybody, Maharaj balanced his own body and lay himself down. The Vaidya let out a deep sigh. Sambhajiraje kept gazing at the bearded, radiant ascetic face of Kalyanswami as if he was gazing at the murti of Goddess Bhavani in the sanctum. The Maharani gently left the chamber.

"Shambhoo!" A calm voice floated over the cool morning breeze. Sambhajiraje was awake all night, sitting on the edge of the bed. In the early morning the cool breeze had lulled him into slumber. The Chhatrapati's voice brought him out of his slumber.

"Maharaj Saheb, how are you feeling?" So many questions were hidden in that one question.

"I am feeling much better." The Chhatrapati's oblong, pale face showed a fleeting vay of hope.

"Where is the swami?"

"Ji. He is still here. He has been meditating in front of a burning fire pit in a chamber. Should I summon him?" Sambhajiraje's face was glowing with joy. Outside, the chirping of birds had enlivened the trees.

"No, not right now. Give him my message immediately after he finishes his meditation. Tell him that I am yearning to see him."

"Ji!" Sambhajiraje left the chamber and started walking towards the Hammam Khana. After getting refreshed, he kept pacing in front of Kalyanswami's chamber, waiting for him to finish his meditation.

In the late morning, he heard swami's voice from the chamber. Sambhajiraje himself was now yearning to meet Kalyanswami. He came into the chamber.

"Swami..." As Sambhajiraje placed his head at Kalyanswami's feet, he was speechless.

"Yuvaraj, how is the Chhatrapati?" Swami gently picked him up and asked.

"Maharaj Saheb is feeling much better. He spoke to me. He is eager to meet you.

"Let's go Yuvaraj. Some time ago the Chhatrapati had the same feeling that you are having now. He wanted to renounce everything. Gurudeo had guided him at that time. I would tell you the same. You must fulfil the duties of a king. Your path will be full of obstacles. You too are a devotee of Goddess Jagadamba! Those who are trying to kill you and your Maharaj, have only two hands, but don't forget that the primordial mother has eight arms. Come with me." Swami had read his mind. He went out of the chamber.

Kalyanswami visited Maharaj and gave him blessings. He handed the medication to the Vaidya, and after bidding farewell to all he descended the fort.

Sambhajiraje accompanied him to the Maha Darwaja.

Yuvaraj stood still at the gate till he disappeared. Swami's pious words kept echoing in his heart, 'You too are a devotee of Goddess Jagadamba!'

Two weeks passed. Maharaj was gradually regaining his energy. He could digest light food now. Meanwhile, from the western coast the British were dispatching letters containing the joyous news, to their warehouses all over, "Rebel Shivaji has died of toxic poisoning at the fort of Satara! But all our problems are not over yet! His son Sambhaji has taken charge of the kingdom now! He is as troublesome as his father! Word is that he had his father killed by poisoning!!"

The Mughal messengers were cheerfully galloping in the direction of Surat, Burhanpur carrying letters that contained the following message, "Infidel Shiva has been poisoned and banished from this world. His wicked son got him poisoned. Merciful Khuda planted this idea in the mind of wretched Sambha!"

These were obviously rumours, but not fleeting rumours. These rumours were purposely spread from the fort of Satara itself.

Sambhajiraje came to make the evening obeisance to Maharaj. Maharaj could now walk slowly in his chamber.

Yuvaraj made an obeisance to Maharaj. An attendant carrying an incense burner came into the chamber. He waved the incense around the chamber and left.

"Maharaj Saheb…" As Chhatrapati heard Sambhajiraje speak he stopped pacing.

"Yes, what is it?"

Yuvaraj threw a quick glance at the guards standing still like statues. Maharaj understood his gesture and clapped gently. The chief guard heard the clap and presented himself. He made an obeisance and waited for the instruction.

"We want privacy, Hawaldar." As Raje spoke to him, he realized that his jama had become a bit too loose for him. He became restless for a moment.

The guards standing still like statues started moving. One by one all the guards left the chamber.

"Don't let anyone in, till you receive further instructions and close the door after you." Maharaj commanded the last guard.

The chamber was empty. A few moments passed in awkward silence.

"Go ahead and speak." Raje's voice cracked the silence. But

Yuvaraj was still quiet. He didn't know where to start. Inadvertently, words slipped from his mouth, "Aabasaheb…"

"Hmmm!"

"Aabasaheb, I could not resist coming here. I have come here to caution you…"

"What are you talking about?" The Chhatrapati was as tranquil as a Shivlinga.

"Aabasheb, I want you to live long. I fear for your…your life. The illness…"

"Shambhoo, I know that my illness was not a normal one. I'm aware that there's a conspiracy behind it. I am only enduring this because my hands are tied. I should be alert, but more than that you should be vigilant!"

"Do you know what the wagging tongues are talking about you?" Raje was sounding unwell yet daunting.

"Ji. What…what are they saying about me?" Sambhajiraje was terrified of thinking about what the Chhatrapati was going to say. The thought itself sent chills down his spine. His eyes welled up and voice cracked.

"That you…you got me poisoned!" Raje's tone was cold. He let out a deep sigh.

"Aaba…!" Sambhajiraje was shocked as if struck by a sharp whiplash. His head started spinning. His ears, throat…face flushed as if molten lead had been poured on him. That devotee of Goddess Bhavani trembled like a flaming torch. The next moment his hands clasped Maharaj's feet. His entire body shivered.

"Shambhoo, get up and calm down!" Maharaj patted Yuvaraj and pulled him up.

"Look at me now." The walls of the chamber trembled to hear Maharaj's resolute voice.

The moment Sambhajiraje looked into Raje's eyes, he remembered the Aabasaheb who had eagerly come down to the foothills of Rajgad to receive him when he had returned from

Mathura. In a cracking voice Sambhajiraje exclaimed, "Maharaj, now…now you should give me a glass…full of poison! I cannot refute these claims to prove my innocence! I would prefer death; that would be much less tormenting.

Maharaj intensely pulled Yuvaraj into a deep embrace and quickly said in a hoarse voice, "Jagadamb, Jagadamb. Shambhoo, calm down! Neither you nor I am free to die. Get a grip." Maharaj's touch spoke to Sambhajiraje and his hands kept consoling him. Many memories of Sambhajiraje flashed in Chhatrapati's mind – young and fearless Sambhajiraje who had gone as a hostage to the Rajput encampment in Karhepathar with Netaji; Sambhajiraje, who emotionally placed his mojaris in front of him outside the durbar in Agra; Sambhajiraje, who had stayed in Mathura as a sanyasi clad in saffron clothes, his forehead smeared with stripes of ashes; Sambhajiraje lost in dancing the torch of Mother Jagadamba on Pratapgad; Sambhajiraje who looked directly into his eyes and exclaimed fearlessly with his head held high in the durbar full of courtiers, "I refuse to accept the allegations against me"….

"You have no idea; I have such high hopes from you."

Sambhajiraje had calmed down by now. Maharaj gazed at his orange Jiretop and started pacing in the chamber. He wanted to say something, but his words choked in his throat. He remembered Saibai and unwittingly stopped walking.

"I have given my word to your…your Masaheb. I have taken care of you as a father, but I am falling short while fulfilling the duties of a mother. When my Masaheb passed away you lost a major support in your life. That is why you should be very vigilant." A dreaded silence prevailed in the chamber.

"I will never harbour any suspicions against you, not even in my dreams. I know you very well, and that is exactly why I am more worried about you today. Yuvaraj, if the ceiling above your head betrays you and collapses without warning, who will you complain against? Be aware of your circumstances and be alert. You should go now and have your supper without any worries. Don't be afraid, I am recovering now. I am going to live long by the grace of Mother Jagadamba and Samartha. Farewell." The Chhatrapati gently patted his son's shoulder. Sambhajiraje left the chamber with a calm and contented heart.

Lost in thought, Maharaj lay on his bed. His face was drawn. He did not feel at ease. So, he got up and came near the crystal Shivlinga placed on a wooden square stool. The sight of the Shivlinga gave him courage and he resolutely decided something in his mind.

An attendant carried a covered platter of food for the Chhatrapati on his shoulder and a jar of water in the other hand. He placed the platter on a wooden square stool and removed the cover; the food was steaming.

The attendant tasted a bite of everything in the platter and took a sip of water. He quietly stepped back, made an obeisance and left the chamber.

Another attendant came in with a platter and a jug of water. Maharaj washed his hands in the platter and wiped them with a cloth. Then, Maharaj sat down to have his meal.

The attendant left the chamber and closed the door behind him.

Maharaj placed a few bites of food around the platter for the forefathers and offered Chitrahuti by circling water around it. He closed his eyes, whispered the Bhojan mantra, and took two sips of water. As he was doing all this, he had a fleeting regret, 'I didn't realize in all this chaos, I should have told Yuvraj to stay back and have dinner with me.'

Just then, the door of the chamber creaked. Maharaj looked at the door. It was Maharani Soyarabai Saheb. At her sight Maharaj quickly glanced at the platter of food in front of him and decided something to himself.

Soyarabai hesitated for a moment and turned around to go back.

"Come in…" Maharaj did not let her go.

The calmness in his voice reassured Soyarabai and bearing a slight smile she walked in with her usual graceful gait.

"Good to see that you decided to have dinner alone," she said standing near him.

"Yes, now I can trust only myself! Haven't you heard the rumours yet?" Maharaj spoke in a normal tone and started placing the bowls in his platter on the wooden stool.

"Ranisaheb, it's been a while since you and I had dinner together!" Maharaj said calmly. He looked at the door and called out to an attendant, "Anybody there?"

An attendant standing outside came in promptly and said, "Ji."

"Go and get another platter of food for Rani Saheb and place another square wooden stool here." Maharaj instructed him.

Soyarabai sensed her plan backfiring on her. She was stunned.

"Rani Saheb, you didn't bring Ramraje with you to meet me?" Maharaj distracted her and asked her without betraying his agitation.

"Travelling does not suit him." Soyarabai had to say something.

As per the command, the attendant came in with another platter of food. He placed a wooden stool, put the platter and water jug on it and left the chamber.

Maharaj pointed to the wooden square stool and without looking at Soyarabai said, "Come, have a seat."

Her feet, decorated with henna, hesitated for a moment. Drops of sweat gathered on her face. The royal lady barely managed to say, "I forgot to tell you that I am fasting today. I have taken a vow."

Maharaj's eyes were breathing fire, but he looked at the platter and calmly said, "Is that so? Then should I start?"

"Ji."

"What vow have you taken?"

"I had prayed for your good health to Goddess Waghajai. I feel afraid for your life. I have come here to caution you."

"What caution?"

"Yuvaraj…Yuvaraj is not as naïve as he looks!"

"Quiet!" Maharaj pushed his dinner platter aside and stood up at once. His whole body was trembling. "Don't you feel ashamed of saying such things about Yuvaraj?"

The Chhatrapati was shaking with rage. He could not even speak clearly. Soyarabai felt as if someone had poured boiling oil on her. She also began shaking in fear. She had never experienced such fear before!

" What are you saying, about whom, and in whose presence? Better watch your tongue. Yuvaraj is not an orphan as you think. He is not a traitor, or a cunning person. You are a mastermind and trying to play a very clever game, but one day it will backfire on you. Though you have forgotten the fact that a married woman from Annaji's family unnecessarily lost her life, I haven't forgotten it. I know very well why you presented Ramraje in front of me on the day of Yuvaraj's trial. How far you will go, only you know it better than I do." Maharaj could not speak further.

Soyarabai stood still; her head hung low. Warm tears flowed from her eyes. The furious Chhatrapati who had controlled his rage so far, started castigating her, "You consider Shambhooraje as your stepson, and are jealous of him. You forget that it was a step-mother who brought about the Ramayana. This kingdom does not belong to me, or to Yuvaraj or to Ramraje. Many people have sacrificed their lives to raise this kingdom, in the name of Goddess Bhavani. Balraje, Yuvaraj, and I… all Bhosalas are her devotees. That is our legacy. Your power-hungry attitude has taken over your senses. You are spreading rumours to damage Yuvaraj's reputation. You are conveniently assuming that I will not understand your moves!" Maharaj laughed to himself. It was a strange laugh. A strange stifling silence filled the chamber. Raje could not bear it. He walked towards the wooden stool on which the crystal Shivlinga was placed. As he got a glimpse of the crystal Shivlinga through the bael leaves covering it, Masaheb Jijau's memories soared from the deepest recesses of his mind. His eyes were riveled to the Shivlinga and his heart felt heavy.

Maharaj had turned his back to Soyarabai. Heart-rending, raspy words slipped from his lips, "When Masaheb passed away, I thought you would try to fill the gap caused by her demise. You would treat everyone affectionately and console them. You obtained all the privileges that she had, but you could never make your heart as large as hers. At least, try not to forget that you are the Rani Saheb. I am the Chhatrapati, the guardian of one and all. You are the Maharani. My partner in my duty. If you cannot fulfil your duties, then at least keep quiet. Don't create needless confusions and cause discord in the family. If your obstinate and spiteful behaviour continues regardless, I will not spare you even as the Maharani. You may leave now…" Maharaj started stroking his cowrie necklace restlessly. Soyarabai stood still behind him, stunned, like a statue. She had got the final warning.

"Tomorrow morning your palanquins will leave for Raigad. There is no need for you to stay here anymore. I have instructed Hambirarao accordingly. Before you leave let me tell you how you speak falsely even in front of me. You have already fulfilled the vow you had taken before Goddess Waghajai, back when my health had started improving by the grace of Samartha. You must be fasting for some other reason now. You think and decide what that reason is!"

Now it was extremely difficult for Soyarabai to stand there. She felt like her legs were giving way. She stuffed the edge of her sari in her mouth and was about to leave, when the Chhatrapati heard the tinkling of her bangles and turned around. "Stop…" He commanded her in an intimidating voice that made her stop right at the threshold of the chamber.

His fiery, resolute words fell on the ears of the Maharani of Swaraj, "Open your ears and listen to me carefully, if at all Yuvaraj Sambhajiraje hands me poison I will consume it happily, in front of the durbar full of courtiers and ministers ... because...because for the sake of this royal throne, at the age of nine, he had lived in the Rajput military camp as a hostage. He had travelled alone, in arduous conditions, from Mathura to this kingdom disguised as an ascetic!"

After bidding farewell to Maharaj, Sambhajiraje descended the fort of Satara and started his journey to Raigad. Yesubai and Putalabai's palanquins were surrounded by armed soldiers. Sambhajiraje was lost in thought. No matter how hard he tried, he could not stop thinking about Masaheb Soyarabai. Whenever it got too painful, he pulled hard on his horse's reins. With each pull, the metal nose band bit into the horse's muzzle and it whinnied in pain. Countless thoughts kept racing in Sambhajiraje's mind, and deeply pierced his heart harshly. His mind dragged him aimlessly.

'Why is this happening to me? Who is at fault? Why does Masaheb treat me like this? Don't I mean anything to her? Forget about me, how is she behaving with Aabasaheb? Where is her greed going to lead us? Ramraje never seemed a stranger to me and she never seemed like family. Why so? Maharaj Saheb gets poisoned, and I get blamed for that? I don't understand what is going on. I am not afraid of anybody but myself now! I might end up doing something wrong! I want to meet Masaheb and pour my heart out to her. If she is so disturbed about my being the Yuvaraj, I am ready to surrender my title to Ramraje.

'I miss Thoralya Aausaheb terribly. Each word of hers was so comforting! What if she would have been alive now? No! Had she been alive, no one could have dared to play such cruel games with Maharaj Saheb's life. People would have been compelled to think twice before accusing me!

'...No way! They say that I... I poisoned Maharaj Saheb! Instead of all this, it would have been better if I had been given the death sentence at the time of my trial! At least I wouldn't have to hear such unimaginable accusations. Masaheb... Masaheb, you have broken my heart for a reason that was so uncalled for. This is beyond the limit of my tolerance. I wonder how Aabasaheb could remain silent through all this. How could he endure so much suffering? Or have the circumstances rendered him speechless? I was presented as an accused in front of the durbar full of courtiers. Will the same happen to Masaheb? No! Not possible. Even I could not declare her name in the durbar! Aabasaheb simply cannot do it. Oh, what kind of a dilemma is this?

'... What if something bad would have happened to Aabasaheb when he was unwell?! No... no!'

To dispel the disturbing thoughts from his mind, Sambhajiraje earnestly muttered, "Jagadamb, Jagadamb." He prodded his horse. It sprinted forward and galloped for quite a distance.

When Sambhajiraje realized that the entourage was left way behind, he pulled the reins of his horse and reduced its speed. He kept his horse trotting slowly until the entourage came close, and he mingled with the entourage. As his horse passed by Putalabai's palanquin he found courage again. He wanted to stop the entourage for some time and pour his heart out to Masaheb Putalabai, but he didn't do it. When he left the fort of Satara, he had realized one thing. Though Maharaj had come to see him off in person to the Balekilla, many people on the fort were giving him strange looks! Many contemptuous glances were piercing his heart like arrows and damaging his reputation. Those disdainful glances were accusing him of poisoning his own father, the Chhatrapati of Swaraj.

Slowly, the feeling of guilt and being trapped, dissipated from his mind and was replaced with feelings of anger and revenge. He started seeing Soyarabai everywhere on the path. But he also visualized young Ramraje standing behind her and calling out to him, 'Dada Maharaj'. As he saw Ramraje, the feeling of revenge dissipated from his mind. He felt cornered.

The turmoil in his heart left him restless and he could not think straight. He simply kept muttering… "Jagadamb! Jagadamb!"

Sambhajiraje's heart was heavy when he visited Jijau's Samadhi in Pachad. He did not want to go to Raigad immediately. So, he stayed in Pachad for a couple of days with Putalabai and Yesubai.

The news of his arrival had already reached Raigad, but none of the ministers bothered to come and see him. Only Kavi Kulesh came to visit him. After four days, Sambhajiraje climbed Raigad with his entourage. The rumour from the fort of Satara had already spread to Raigad too. People in the fort were giving him strange, disdainful looks and were reluctantly making an obeisance.

A fortnight passed. Sambhajiraje left his chamber only twice a day to make an obeisance to Jijau's seat and to visit the Jagadishwar temple. He spent most of his time in his palace discussing the holy Puranas with Keshav Pandit, Umaji Pandit, Udho Jogadeo and Kavi Kulesh. He found comfort in those discussions.

Dharau kept checking his chamber frequently. When she found him alone, she approached him and said, "Dhakale…"

"Yes, what is it?" Sambajiraje gazed at the tattoo on her forehead and responded.

As Dharau looked at his radiant eyes and the thick, curly hair spread around his neck, she completely forgot what she wanted to ask him. Nowadays, whenever she looked at her youthful 'Dhakale dhani' who looked like his father, she remembered Shambhooraje as a child.

As he saw that Dharau was quiet, Sambhajiraje became

restless. He turned his back to Dharau and said in a heavy voice – "Dharau, I know what you want to ask me! You feel that I… I poisoned Maharaj Saheb…"

Dharau promptly stepped forward and putting her forefinger on his lips she stopped him from talking further. Her eyes welled up. "Dhakale dhani – I have fed you my milk. I know you cannot be disloyal or deceitful. I am not here to talk about that. It's been fifteen days since you came on the fort, but you haven't visited Soonbai yet. She must be feeling sad. You don't even meet Dhakalya Rani Saheb. What should she do?"

Dharau was trying to mend strained relationships with her credulous affection.

"Dharau, I don't feel like meeting anyone."

"How can you say such a thing? Dhakalya Rani Saheb got tired of waiting for you and is herself coming here to meet you. Balraje is also with her."

As Sambhajiraje realized that Putalabai was coming to see him, he was lost in thought. She was the only person among the royal ladies whom he could trust; the only one he could open his heart to.

Dharau left the chamber. In a little while, Putalabai entered the chamber with Ramraje. Sambhajiraje saw her with Ramraje and felt that Balraje should have been born to her!'

The moment he saw her, he remembered how she had carried the herbal extract for Maharaj to Satara. He promptly approached her, touched her feet and gently held Ramraje's hand in his hand.

"Yuvaraj…" Putalabai stopped, wondering how to broach the subject.

"Ji!"

"I can understand if you are upset with me, but… but… what is Soonbai's fault? She is here, in the fort, but you haven't gone to visit her. Why?"

"Masaheb…everything I have done so far is wrong. I

abducted a married woman forcefully… I poisoned my own father. How can I face her? I can't even think about what she must be feeling, while applying the kumkum in my name!" Sambhajiraje stared in another direction and stiffened.

"Yuvaraj…" Putalabai's voice touched his heart. "At least men have the freedom to blame and rebuke themselves, but women don't even have that freedom! You are the Yuvaraj. If you start blaming and isolating yourself, what should Soonbai do? Being a woman, she is already confined. She is blaming herself."

"Dada Maharaj…" Ramaraje had been listening quietly so far. He swung Sambhajiraje's arm to say something. Sambhajiraje thought he was going to say something about Yesubai. So, he responded softly, "What is it, Balmaharaj?"

"You…you gave poison to Maharaj Saheb only… but you didn't give it to me since you came here! I am waiting for Aabasaheb. Even if you didn't give me the poison, he will surely give it to me!!"

Sambhajiraje's ears went numb on hearing his words. His hand holding Ramraje's hand trembled strangely. He promptly picked up Ramraje and kissed him on his cheek. His eyes welled up; he couldn't even see Ramraje's face.

Putalabai could not bear to see them like that. She trudged towards the window and kept gazing at the dome of the Hanuman temple visible at a distance. She realized that her efforts to improve the situation had been inadequate, and she felt dejected. She remembered Maharaj and thought, 'Only Swari can improve this situation.' She grabbed the thread of that one hope and tried to console herself. Her eyes were stuck to the dome and her mind kept wandering in the memories of Raje.

Yesubai stood in Putalabai's chamber, her head bowed low. Sambhajiraje paced back and forth in front of her. Both could feel the awkward silence in the chamber. Both were hesitant about broaching the subject.

"You must be ashamed of me after hearing the rumours." Sambajiraje came straight to the point.

Yesubai was startled, she looked up. She noticed how drastically his face had changed. Her heart ached for him. "I have heard everything, and I feel proud that I am fortunate enough to have a husband like you!" Yesubai voice was firm and clear.

"What?" Asked a baffled Sambhajiraje.

"At the trial, you kept your lips sealed and did not disclose Masaheb's name in the durbar. During Aabasaheb's illness on the Satara fort, despite hearing the rumours against yourself, you did not bluntly break your bond with Balmaharaj. I am realizing it now that…" Yesubai stopped talking.

"What?"

"Why that married woman in Annaji's family must have thrown herself from the cliff of Fort Lingana!"

"Why? Why did she do it?" Sambhajiraje's voice broke with her memory.

"You are so good-natured; not just she, even I would have jumped off the cliff. That courageous woman embraced death rather than hearing something offensive about you or saying something false against you in the durbar full of people. I feel sad that our own family members couldn't understand what she had understood!"

Each word of hers touched Sambhajiraje's heart. His assessment of Yesubai had been completely wrong. He felt deeply happy that he had been proved wrong. He approached her, put his finger under her chin and gently pulled her face up. He said to her, "Even I am coming to know now, why Aabasaheb handed you the responsibility of the 'Shikke-katyar'!"

Yesubai's face flushed, she stepped back and freed her chin.

"You are good at the game of chess. Remember, I was complaining about the game?" Sambhajiraje asked.

"What complaint?" Yesubai did not understand.

"That the game of chess doesn't include the Queen and the Yuvaraj. Today I feel that it's better that the game doesn't include those pieces!" Sambhajiraje let out a deep sigh and went closer to the window. He looked out and said to Yesubai, who stood behind him, "You and Aabasaheb play the game of chess prudently, but I did not realize until now that there was another player whose skills surpassed yours by a mile."

"Who?" Confused Yesubai looked at him and asked.

"Soyara Masaheb!" Cold words floated from Sambhajiraje's mouth.

"You play the game of chess on the chessboard. She plays a game of relationships. She makes such crafty moves that the person who is put in check gets smothered! In her game there is no shortage of pawns and there is no restriction on putting anyone in check."

Yesubai didn't know how to respond. Just then, a maid came in to announce the arrival of a visitor.

As Yuvaraj was facing the opposite direction, she shared the news of the guest's arrival with Yesubai, "Duttajipant has come from Satara. He wants to meet Dhakale Sarkar."

"Let me take your leave." Said Sambhajiraje and left the chamber.

In the visitor's chamber of Maharaj's palace, minister Duttajipant was waiting for Sambhajiraje. He saw Sambhajiraje coming and made an obeisance to him.

"Duttajipant, how is Maharaj Saheb's health?" Sambhajiraje asked him.

"Ji. Maharaj is doing fine by the grace of Lord Vyankatesha. He recently visited Pali and solved a case there. I was with him. Now he is at the Satara fort. Swami is devising some big plan with Raghunathpant Hanamante who had come from the Karnataka region."

Sambhajiraje's face lit up to hear the news.

"Yuvaraj, Swami has given me a confidential letter for you.

I have been strictly instructed to hand it only to you." Duttajipant pulled out the pouch tied in the scarf around his waist, bowed down to Yuvaraj and handed it to him.

Sambhajiraje touched the pouch to his forehead and untied it. He pulled out the roll and opened it. As he read the letter, Sambhajiraje's face glowed like gold.

"By the grace of God, I am in perfect health. I am sending Duttajipant with this letter, for a reason. Take him with you on this mission. You are to infiltrate and fall upon the territory of the Bijapur sultanate via Miraj and Athani. You need not take any unnecessary risks. Focus on quickly capturing their territory."

Maharaj had devised a plan to take advantage of the discord between Wazir Khawas Khan and Sardar Bahlol Khan of Bijapur sultanate. He had instructed Sambhajiraje to undertake this campaign.

"Duttajipant, take rest today. We will leave tomorrow for Miraj." Yuvaraj forgot about everything else.

"Ji! Swami has instructed me likewise. I will stay in Pachad and gather our troops. I have brought some troops from Satara."

"Okay. Join me for dinner today. I will descend the fort with you." Duttaji made an obeisance and left. The letter was in Sambhajiraje's hand, and he was lost in thoughts of the campaign!

Ten thousand armed soldiers assembled at the border of Pachad. Sambhajiraje, astride his horse, was leading the army with Duttajipant, Rupaji Bhosale and Kondaji Farjand.

Sambhajiraje's army passed by Miraj, raided the villages nearby and with all speed stood at the borders of Athani, the prominent commercial centre of Adil Shahi. The Adil Shahi ryots started running helter-skelter in panic.

Sambhajiraje's face glowed in the rush of the war. He pointed his bare sword in the direction of Athani and shouted, "Har…Har…Mahadeo! Attack!"

The Mavalas attacked the ryots and in a short time, poured booty worth one lakh hons in front of Sambhajiraje. As per

Yuvaraj's instructions, Duttajipant dispatched a letter of the mission's success to Maharaj. The booty was secured and dispatched to Raigad. Informant Karmaji made an obeisance to Sambhajiraje and went in the direction of Panhala. From Satara, Maharaj had arrived at Panhalgad.

After completing the mission successfully, a triumphant Sambhajiraje returned to Raigad. Duttajipant fell upon the region of Belgaum with his troops. Maharaj was still at Panhalgad.

Sambhajiraje's success in the Adil Shahi mission restored his tainted image as the Yuvaraj.

The days of summer arrived. Sambhajiraje started relishing the joy of reading literary works such as *Siddhant-Koumudi*, *Muktawali*, *Raghuvansha* and *Amarkosh*. He started spending and enjoying his time in the company of Keshav Pandit, Umaji Pandit, Kavi Kulesh, and Udho Yogadeo. In one of their discussions, the topic of heroines in lyrical compositions came up.

Pandit, how many types of heroines are mentioned in the Poetics?" Sambhajiraje asked Keshav Pandit.

Keshav Pandit disclosed three major kinds of heroines according to the Poetics – Sweeya, is one's wife; Parakiya, is any woman other than one's wife, and Samanya, is a courtesan. Poetics gives prominence to the 'Sweeya' heroine; it mentions three types of 'Sweeya' heroine."

"What are those?"

"Those are – Mugdha, Madhyama and Pragalbha."

"Yuvaraj, with your permission, I would like to share the eight types of the 'Sweeya' heroine according to aesthetics." Kavi Kulesh spoke, taking everyone by surprise.

When Keshav Pandit heard him, a slight wrinkle appeared on his forehead and disappeared quickly.

"Sure Kaviraj, go ahead." Sambhajiraje twirled the flower in his hand.

Kavi Kulesh tidied the shawl that had slipped from his shoulder and leaned forward.

"Yuvaraj, aesthetics describes eight types of the 'Sweeya' heroine according to her mood – Khandita, Abhisarika, Swadhinpatika, Vipralabdha, Vasaksajja, Kalahantarita, Preshitbhartruka and Virahotkantha. Kulesh described each type in detail, revealing the whole gamut of feminine emotions.

As Sambhajiraje heard Kavi Kulesh's description of the feminine emotions, his face lit up and he kept gazing at Kavi Kulesh. He unwittingly expressed his desire, "Kaviraj, I would like to compose a lyric about the eight types of heroines."

"Ji. May Goddess Chandi grant you success in your new endeavour." Kulesh bowed.

Sambhajiraje offered everyone the betel leaves brought by Rayaji and bade farewell to all. The session concluded. Sambhajiraje occupied himself in composing the lyrics of 'Nayikabhed'.

One evening the kettle drums at Maha Darwaja started beating suddenly. Sambhajiraje's clerk, Parashurampant came into his chamber and announced, "Jadhavrao has come from Sindakhed. Akkasaheb has also arrived with him."

Sambhajiraje's sister, Ranoobai, married into the Jadhav family, and her husband, Rustumrao Jadhav, were waiting at the Palakhi Darwaja with their entourage.

Sambhajiraje came to Palakhi Darwaja with Parashurampant to receive them. Rustumrao approached him and embraced him. Ranoobai came out of her palanquin. Sambhajiraje approached her with a smile. He touched her feet and said, "Akkasaheb, we didn't receive any letter about your arrival. I could not come to Pachad to receive both of you."

"Balmaharaj, you wouldn't understand the joy of giving a surprise visit to your parents' home." Ranoobai said smilingly.

Ranoobai had brought good luck to Raigad. Just a couple of days after her arrival, a messenger from Panhala arrived at

Raigad. He had brought good news – "Chhatrapati Maharaj is coming to Raigad!"

Sambhajiraje went to Pachad with select men to receive Maharaj. The warm weather indicated the advent of monsoon. The air was still.

Late in the afternoon, suddenly, the wind began to pick up. Clouds of dust arose in the air. Making his way through the clouds of dust, Maharaj entered the borders of Pachad with Moropant, Raghunathpant, Janardanpant, Hambirarao, Yesaji and Anandrao. The horns resounded, announcing his arrival.

Maharaj saw Sambhajiraje and dismounted.

By now, the wind had picked up from all sides. Unmindful of his jama fluttering in the wind, Sambhajiraje walked through the clouds of dust and leaned forward to touch Maharaj's feet. This meeting was long due.

Maharaj did not let Sambhajiraje bend down and embraced him with affection. He looked at Raghunathpant and Janardanpant Hanamante standing to his right and asked Sambhajiraje, "Do you recognize them?"

"Ji…" Sambhajiraje hesitated.

He could not recognize them. Maharaj told him, "This is Raghunathpant Hanamante, the subedar of the Karnataka region, serving under your uncle, Ekojiraje. He has left your uncle and joined us; he has come here to discuss something important." Maharaj narrowed his eyes to prevent dust from entering his eyes and said, "And this is his brother, Janardanpant."

Robust Raghunathpant and Janardanpant had donned a Karnataka-style turban on their heads. They smiled and made an obeisance to Yuvaraj saying, "Jai Vyankatesh, please accept our obeisance, Yuvaraj."

"Aabasaheb, the wind has picked up. Looks like it will rain soon. We should leave now." Maharaj had just recovered from his illness. Samhajiraje did not want him to get wet, so he insisted.

"Let's go." Maharaj started walking towards the palace of

Pachad, with Raghunathpant and Janardanpant on one side and Sambhajiraje on the other. The rain drops pattered on the leaves of the trees. Maharaj listened to the patter of the rain and the whooshing wind as he walked. He said to Sambhajiraje, "Shambhooraje, it gives me hope when I see people like Raghunathpant coming from a distant region to join the service of Swaraj. I am satisfied that my extensive travel has paid off."

Sambhajiraje gazed at Raghunathpant with reverence.

"Maharajsaheb, Akkasaheb from Sindakhed has arrived at Raigad. Rustumaji is also with her." Sambhajiraje shared the news with Maharaj.

Maharaj stopped walking momentarily. Ranoobai's face flashed in front of his eyes and he asked, "How is Ranoobai doing?"

"She is doing fine." Sambhajiraje responded; his words were drenched in affection.

Everyone arrived at the palace of Pachad, and within a short time heavy monsoon showers enveloped the Pachad region. The skies were overcast, and thunder started rumbling. The next day, they climbed Raigad which was drenched in the monsoon showers.

Maharaj performed the puja of the crystal Shivlinga and summoned Rustumaji to his chamber. Rustumaji had planned something in his mind. He came to visit the Chhatrapati.

Maharaj made general enquiries about his family. Rustumaji answered his questions courteously. Maharaj realized that he wanted to say something and was waiting for an opportunity to broach the topic. To open him up, Maharaj affectionately said, "Here I am talking all alone, Rustumaji. Don't you feel that you should enquire about my health too?"

Rustumaji felt confused. He hesitated and said, "Ji..."

Maharaj looked at him with a smile and encouraged him to speak his mind... "Go ahead and say what you want to say."

"Ji – I would like to put forth a proposal."

"I already know that. Tell me what it is."

A few moments passed in silence.

"I... I have come with a marriage proposal for Yuvaraj!" Rustumaji revealed what was in his mind.

"Rustumrao, the plan sounds good. Even I would like it if our families united in a familial bond one more time, but I will tell you my decision tomorrow. Okay?" Maharaj wanted to check with Yesubai and Sambhajiraje first and then tell his decision to Jadhavrao.

"Ji. There is no hurry." Rustumrao said happily, as he felt hopeful from the way Maharaj spoke.

Yesubai was in Putalabai's chamber. Dharau rushed to Putalabai's chamber to inform Yesuabai – "Thorale Dhani is coming to visit you."

Yesubai couldn't believe her ears. She smiled and exclaimed, "Aau, don't make such fun of me!"

"I swear in the name of Shambhoo Mahadeo. Dhani called me in person and told me." Yesubai became anxious and rushed to get ready.

Maharaj entered the chamber. Yesubai touched his feet and made an obeisance to him. She was quite puzzled and wondered 'Why would Aabasaheb come to meet me?'

"May you live a happy married life." Maharaj blessed her. He realized that she was confused. Without further delay, Maharaj broached the delicate subject astutely, "Soonbai, do you remember the time when I handed you the Shikke-katyar?"

Yesubai had no idea where the discussion was headed. She just nodded in affirmation.

"Now Rustumaji from Sindakhed has come to the fort. He wants to hand you only a katyar! Will you accept it?" Maharaj said smilingly.

Yesubai did not understand. But the way Maharaj spoke touched her heart and she unwittingly responded "Ji" to Maharaj out of respect.

“Rustumaji has put forth a marriage proposal for Yuvaraj. I am going to agree to it only if you are ready to accept it. So, tell me, are you ready to accept this challenge? You know how complicated family relations can become, in such cases.” Maharaj paused, remembering Soyarabai bitterly.

Yesubai was trying to dig the stone floor with her toe, obviously without success. Her ears flushed. An image flashed in her mind, ‘A big orange Jiretop was drifting away on the waters of River Kal coursing along the foothills of the fort. She was stretching her arms and struggling to capture it, but her arms just couldn’t reach it!’ The image baffled Yesubai for a moment. She felt as if Thoralya Masaheb was standing next to her. She had gently put her hand on Yesubai’s shoulder and spoken to her in a soft voice, “Dealing with the men of the Bhosale clan is like carrying the flaming torch of Goddess Jagadamba! Pray to her to give you a heart as big as the skies to take the mantle!”

Maharaj took Yesubai’s silence for disapproval and turned to leave. He said, “Farewell.”

“Aabasaheb did not hear my reply. I accept the proposal presented by the Jadhav family of Sindakhed from the bottom of my heart.” Yesubai said calmly.

Yesubai wanted to tell Maharaj who was leaving the chamber and had always loved her like a father, “Aabasaheb, I am not at all worried about the golden katyar that the Jadhav family is handing over to me, but… but… if you offer me burning embers, I will accept them too with a smile!”

Maharaj returned to his palace and immediately summoned Sambhajiraje, but he did not ask Sambhajiraje anything in the way he had asked Yesubai.

As he glanced at Sambhajiraje standing courteously in front of him, the image of a young boy clad in the saffron cloak of a Sanyasi, flashed in his mind.

Maharaj decided how to broach the topic and said, “Raje, you compose lyrics of your own, but I would like to offer you a living lyric!" Maharaj stopped.

"…" Sambhajiraje was baffled.

"A poet needs an additional quill at hand while composing lyrics, likewise a man needs another companion for his life. Rustumaji has brought a marriage proposal for you. I am thinking of forming another bond with the Jadhav family."

"But…" The stone statue of the woman with anklets in the caves and the fair, round face, flashed in front of Sambhajiraje's eyes. Yesubai's memory left Sambhajiraje hesitant.

"I understand! I have already met with Soonbai and she is ready to accept the proposal, but what about you?" Sambhajiraje was cornered. He didn't know what to say.

"Does this mean you are not ready for this marriage? Should I consider this as a 'No'?" Maharaj put Sambjajiraje into a tight spot.

"No… I didn't mean to say that."

"You haven't said anything at all. What does that mean?"

"Maharajsaheb's wish is my 'command'!"

"Command! You mean you accept this as my command! But this is not a command!" Raje wanted a genuine affirmation coming from Sambhajiraje and he gave it.

"Ji. I accept the proposal from the bottom of my heart!"

Sambhajiraje left, but on his way out he felt, "At least today Thoralya Aausaheb should have been alive. I could have taken her advice in this matter!"

Rustumaji bade farewell to Maharaj and went back home. Ranoobai stayed at Raigad. After fifteen days, Rustumaji returned to Raigad with a palanquin surrounded by armed soldiers.

The betrothal ceremony for Sambhajiraje's second marriage was organized in the palace. Clad in a fine sari, the girl who came with Jadhavrao, presented herself in front of the family. She made an obeisance three times to the elders of the family and stood politely.

The ladies of the Bhosale family were stunned by her beauty.

All royal ladies including Putalabai, Sagunabai, Sakawarbai were present for the ceremony. Except for Soyarabai. She had suddenly taken ill.

Everyone gathered for the ceremony affirmed their approval of the bride-to-be in unison. Maharaj put his finger under her chin, lifted her face up and said, "In the memory of Masaheb and in front of all present here, I accept this daughter of the Jadhav family of Sindakhed as the bride for my son, Yuvaraj Sambhajiraje."

Putalabai applied kumkum on the girl's forehead. The engagement was fixed. The royal priest consulted the almanac and found an auspicious mahurat for the wedding.

On the auspicious day of Akshay Tritiya, the wedding ceremony took place with royal pomp. The new Soonbai was named Durgabai. Sambhajiraje who was in the process of composing a lyric of about eight kinds of heroines, was blessed with another heroine in his own life!

Sambhajiraje's lyrical composition 'Nayikabhed' was finally ready. He was engrossed in discussing poetics with Kavi Kulesh in his chamber. It was raining outside. Khandoji Ballal, Rayaji and Antoji stood around.

Just then he heard indistinct commotion outside, breaking through the pouring rain. Something was going on. The personnel of all eighteen departments were rushing towards the Palakhi Darwaja. Vague, indistinct words fell upon Sambhajiraje's ears.

"When? Soaked to the bone…can't even recognize him…so pathetic!"

No one understood what was happening. Some commotion was going on all over the Balekilla. 'What's happening?' Sambhajiraje frowned. Just then, his personal secretary Mahadeo Yamaji, dashed into his chamber.

"Sarkar, the Sarlashkar has ascended the fort." He made an obeisance and announced. He was unable to express himself properly; his words did not make any sense.

"What do you mean?" Sambhajiraje reminded him that Yesaji and Hambirarao were still on the fort.

"Not our Sarlashkar, Swami…the Mughal Sarlashkar… Ne…Netajirao!"

"What? Netajikaka? On the fort?" Sambjiraje's eyes widened in astonishment, and he stood up in shock.

Sambhajiraje left his palace and started walking directly towards the Palakhi Darwaja. The people who were with him followed him unwittingly.

Meanwhile, Mohammed Kuli Khan, alias Netaji Palkar had arrived at the central square of the Balekilla with two more people. All three of them were dressed in the Mughal attire. They were soaked in the rain and their clothes were stuck to their skin.

Mohammed Kuli Khan had furtively tried to climb the fort, but the former brave Sarlashkar of Swaraj, Netaji Palkar could not hide his distinctive gait. The sagacious people on the fort had recognized him at the Maha Darawaja. Like monsoon winds, the news had spread all over the fort.

All buildings around the central square were thronged with crowds within no time. Mohammed Kuli Khan stood in the central square between the two people who accompanied him. His head hung low and the Mughal kimosh on his head was getting drenched in the rain. The rain showers had flared up the fire burning in his heart instead of subsiding it. Warm tears streamed down his cheeks and blended with the drops of water caught in his beard. Such a big crowd had gathered there, but no one dared to come forward and speak with Netaji who had become 'Kuli Khan'.

Netaji, who was earlier considered the crown of Fort Raigad, was now soaking in the rains like a doormat, in the central square of the Balekilla. Every single person gathered in the square was deeply grieved to see his plight.

One of the two people who had accompanied him whispered something in Mohammed's ears and leaving him alone, they both started walking towards Maharaj's palace. They were the Kulkarnis of Wai, top informers from Maharaj's surveillance squad. They had cleverly followed Netaji from the Maratha kingdom to the Kabul-Kandahar region. They had kept a keen eye on Netaji and kept Maharaj informed his whereabouts every now and then.

Aurangzeb had sent Kuli Khan on the Kabul-Kandahar campaign. During that campaign Kuli Khan felt guilty and humiliated. He tried to escape from the Mughal camp but was captured.

Converted to Islam, the Sarlashkar of the Maratha kingdom, used to whisper 'Shiv…Shiv…' habitually at bedtime every day to muster courage. He had spent countless nights tossing and turning in bed. The Kulkarnis of Wai had shared all this information with Maharaj. As per Maharaj's instructions, the two Kulkarnis revealed themselves to Kuli Khan near Agra. "Maharaj has a big heart. He will forgive you, provided you surrender yourself to him. The plant of Swaraj should be nurtured. It is not wise to wield your weapon against Swaraj." The Kulkarnis had persuaded and convinced Kuli Khan in several ways and had brought him to Raigad with them. This had happened at the right time, because Aurangzeb had ordered Kuli Khan to fall upon the Deccan region. Mohammed Kuli Khan had contemplated his options and had taken a wise decision to come to Raigad, after ten long years!

Followed by the courtiers, Sambhajiraje walked briskly and came to the stone railing by the side of the central square. Everyone bowed down and made an obeisance to him, but he did not notice it. When he saw Netaji standing in the square, his feet grew heavy as if he himself was shackled.

'He is related to Dhakalya Masaheb but what has he done to himself? He has destroyed his own life! Is this really Netajikaka?

No, even death would have been much better than this!' Sambhajiraje's heart was in turmoil. He commanded Mahadeo Yamaji, "Get an attire ready."

Mahadeo Yamaji realized who the attire must be for. "Ji" he said and went back to fetch the attire.

Sambhajiraje walked slowly and approached Mohammed Kuli Khan. Kuli Khan's head was hanging low. He saw the curved orange mojaris on Sambhajiraje's feet and thought that Maharaj himself was standing in front of him. His entire body shuddered in shame.

Mohammad Kuli Khan tried to control his sobbing and stepped forward to clasp Maharaj's feet. Sambhajiraje promptly leaned forward and stopped him. Words slipped from his lips unknowingly, "Netajikaka…!"

A startled Kuli Khan raised his head. He wondered, "Who is this?" The round, full face and the same radiant, fire-breathing eyes! Mohammed recognized him – 'Dhakale Raje!

'I… I don't deserve to touch his feet. Why did I come here, to make such a mess? I should better go back.' Agitated Mohammed turned around to leave.

Sambhajiraje quickly held his hand and gazed at him. He ushered Kuli Khan to the stone railing. Seeing that everyone's tension released.

Sambhajiraje pointed to the platter that Mahadeo Yamaji had brought and said to Kuli Khan, "Change your attire first, and rest assured."

Sambhajiraje asked his attendants to look after Kuli Khan and started walking towards the queens' palaces. Rayaji followed him. Sambhajiraje came to Sagunabaisaheb's palace. Rayaji went ahead and gave intimation of his arrival.

Sambhajiraje entered Masaheb's palace to deliver the news of Netajikaka's arrival. Sagunabai stood in front of him, she only knew that there was some commotion in the fort.

Yuvaraj made an obeisance to her as usual. As he stood in

front of her, he realized that he was at a loss for words.

"Masaheb, he has arrived." Sambhajiraje couldn't say what he wanted to say. Sagunabai or he had prudently avoided talking about Netaji in their conversations so far.

"Who?" Sagunabai's forehead puckered.

"Mohamm...Netajikaka...!" Sambhajiraje corrected himself.

"Really, is that true?!" Sagunabai's round face glowed like a fully blossomed Prajakta tree but only for a moment. Then, at once, her royal face looked pained, and she turned around to hide her face from Sambhajiraje. Netajirao was Sagunabai's kaka.

"Let me take your leave." Sambhajiraje also couldn't speak further.

The Kulkarnis of Wai presented Mohammed Kuli Khan in front of the Chhatrapati Maharaj. Large-hearted Maharaj took the decision of reconverting the Sarlashkar of the Marathas who had lost his way, back to the Hindu fold. He got his decision approved by his council of ministers.

A messenger was dispatched to Nashik to invite Anantbhat on the fort. He and the royal priest Prabhakarbhat found a mahurat for the reconversion ceremony. It was going to take place on the fourth day of the dark fortnight of Aashadh. This was the first ever ceremony throughout Bharatvarsha that was going to drastically transform the religious beliefs of the society. Until now, the Hindus who had been forcefully converted to Islam were forbidden from reconversion to the Hindu fold. With the royal throne of Raigad as witness, the Chhatrapati Maharaj was going to perform the purification ceremony and open the door for reconversion to all! The fort was abuzz with the news of the ceremony.

The ironsmiths were sweating in the forge, hammering and shaping the blades of the weapons. Maharaj had appointed Sambhajiraje to examine the weapons. Accompanied by Kondaji

Farzand, Rupaji Bhosala, Khandoji Ballal, Rayaji and Antoji, Sambhajiraje came to the forge.

The sweating ironsmiths stopped their work to make an obeisance to Sambhajiraje. He raised his hand, and signalled them to continue their work. He came to the pile of the weapons that were ready.

"Dhakale Dhani, have a look at this piece." The chief of the forge, Dagadoji, held a weapon in front of Sambhajiraje. Sambhajiraje took it and examined it keenly.

"Dhani, you should have seen it when it was put on the bellows. It was completely rusted.

The weapon reminded Sambhajiraje of Netajirao. His mind was filled with innumerable thoughts, 'Maharaj Saheb is such a great, accomplished ironsmith! Not just me, but nobody else can comprehend his vision. No pincers, no bellows, no hammer holders at his disposal, but he wipes out the corrosion of people's minds simply with his words! I thought that he would only reinstate Netajikaka, but he took the decision of his reconversion. He did not just remove the rusti in people's hearts but also cleaned the rust that had gathered on dharma. Only he can dare to play with fire so daringly!' Sambhajiraje's eyes glowed with pride.

Though it was the dark fortnight of the month, the revolutionary day of Netaji's reconversion broke out.

The reconversion ceremony began amidst the chanting of mantras. Netaji had spent the previous day fasting. Prabhakarbhat conducted him to the courtyard and seated him on a flat wooden seat. The royal barber removed his Mughal style beard and shaved his hair, leaving only a tuft. Netaji took a bath and sat for the purification ceremony. Anantbhat and Prabhakarbhat started sprinkling holy water over Netaji's head while chanting the mantras. Netaji had a strange feeling that the layers of sins accumulated over his skin were getting washed away with this sprinkling. Overcrowded with courtiers, the entire durbar was moved while observing the ritual. Maharaj rose from his seat and approached Netaji. He put the holy thread in his hand around Netaji's neck and across his chest. Maharaj's fingers touched Netaji's skin slightly while doing that. Goosebumps rose on Netaji's skin, at the touch of Maharaj's fingers, more than at the touch of the holy thread. The disgraced Sarlashkar of the Marathas was purified by that touch.

Maharaj placed the pieces of attire on Netaji's shoulder one by one. Emotionally overwhelmed, Netaji controlled his tears and embraced Maharaj's feet in front of all. His action stunned the Chhatrapati for a moment. He leaned forward and gently pulled Netaji up.

"Dhani…" He barely managed to utter in a heavy voice. His voice stirred Maharaj's heart.

"Yes?" Maharaj glanced at Netaji's shaved head.

"Dhani, I would like to make a request." Netaji struggled to pour his heart out.

"Feel free to speak your heart."

"Please…please…"

"What do you want?"

"Dhani, just once…only once call me 'Netaji'! I am eager to hear it coming from your lips!"

Maharaj held his head high. He held Netaji's shoulders tightly and said, "Now… now you have realized the value of your name! Hold your head high, Netajirao, you belong to us!"

Netaji believed that he would be purified in the true sense not by the enchanted water, but by Maharaj calling out his name. Netaji's ears, eagerly waiting to hear his name from Maharaj's lips, flushed. He felt overwhelmed, and tried to hide his face in his palms. Maharaj did not allow him to do it and held him in a deep embrace. Lost in thought, Sambhajiraje observed the scene from his seat. It was etched on his heart.

In observance of the ceremony, a luncheon was organized. Netajirao received the honour of sitting between Maharaj and

Sambhajiraje for the luncheon.

Putalabai and Sagunabai were serving the guests. Maharaj glanced at all the guests and signalled them to start eating.

Maharaj started placing each bowl from his plate on the wooden stool. Everyone did the same. Only Netaji, who was lost in thought had directly put his hand in the plate and started eating in the Mughal style.

Maharaj commenced a secret conference. All assembled people listened to him earnestly. The precious words of Shiva Chhatrapati fell upon Sambhajiraje's ears, he started grasping them ardently, "All of you have been convened to this secret conference; to discuss a plan of action I have in mind. We should strive to expand this kingdom. Heretofore, Adil Shah had sent his acclaimed sardars after me, but by the grace of Goddess Bhavani I could overcome every perilous situation.

"At present, the Adil Shahi is on the decline. It's been crippled by internal conflicts. Hence, I have devised a plan to seize as much territory of the Adil Shahi as we can. Our kingdom will never survive unless we wield our weapons against our enemies and attack them. Therefore, I have planned to capture the Adil Shahi region between River Tungabhadra and River Kaveri.

"On the auspicious day of Vijayadashami, I am personally going to initiate the Karnataka campaign with the army. Just as all of you have showed your support for me so far, continue your support for this campaign too. It is Goddess Jagadamba's wish that this kingdom should achieve greatness. All of us are Her devotees. If we act with courage, she will surely grant us success."

Maharaj spoke with shining eyes. He shared the particulars of the campaign with all present, and assigned Hambirarao, Yesaji and Anandrao to test and assemble troops of expert swordsmen, spear-holders and horse riders.

Maharaj instructed Moropant about the responsibilities of Raigad and the rest of the kingdom in his absence, "Peshwe, during the entire time I will be engaged in the campaign, Raigad and the rest of the kingdom will be under the leadership of Sambhajiraje. Should any kind of dilemma arise, all of you should resolve it collectively."

"Ji, as you wish." Moropant affirmed. But… Annaji did not approve of this arrangement in his heart. Maharaj had planned everything so meticulously that Annaji didn't dare voice his objection. Sambhajiraje was pondering over how to successfully implement the responsibility that Maharaj had placed on his shoulders.

Everyone was offered the betel leaf to conclude the conference.

"Shambhoo, I wanted to tell you something. Hope you will understand it." Maharaj had summoned Sambhajiraje on purpose and was talking to him.

"Ji. Your wish is my command." Sambhjiraje couldn't gauge what Maharaj was about to say.

"Rani Saheb doesn't approve of the idea of Raigad being under your command. You know her nature very well. She has expressed her wish to go to Talbeed, her parental home, in my absence. If she does that, it won't look good. I am tired of convincing her. I have already spent two days in vain. I am hoping that at least you will understand the situation and make a compromise. Will you?" Each word was drenched in heart-wrenching pain.

"Rani Saheb! The mere mention of her smothered Sambhajiraje. His chest heaved in rage… 'Not just for me, but she also frequently creates obstacles in Maharaj Saheb's path! She does it so astutely every time! Have I wronged her in any way? What is my fault? I become the cause of Maharaj Saheb's agony. Everybody thinks that I am at fault. I am heartless. Neither I, nor Aabasaheb can challenge her openly. What kind of a Yuvaraj am I? I cannot even complain about the insults I suffer. How long can I tolerate such humiliation, and why? I never wished to be the Yuvaraj. Just because I was born as the elder son, I became the Yuvaraj as per the tradition, and she detests it. She colludes with Annaji and complicates the situation to such an extent that it becomes impossible to sort it out.

"Why are you so quiet?" Maharaj noticed his reticence and said in a cold voice.

"Ji. Your word is like the prasad to me." He thought that Maharaj should not be bothered at this time.

"I knew you would agree with me. I am going to leave the fort on the day of Dussehra. You accompany me to the border of the kingdom. Then you should go to Shringarpur and stay with Pilajirao. I am going to give you the charge of the Prabhanvalli subah and the region around Fort Panhala. Keep a keen eye on the region. Keshav Pandit and Umaji Pandit will accompany you. For the implementation of administrative matters, take Vishwanath, Khandoji Ballal, Parashurampant, and Mahadeo Yamaji with you. Develop your poetic skills in the company of Keshav Pandit and Umaji Pandit."

Maharaj remembered Yesubai and Bhaveshwari, the family deity of the Shirke family. He stopped talking.

"I have one request to make. May I present it to you?" Sambhajiraje said determinedly.

"Go ahead. What is it?" Maharaj gazed at the necklace on his chest.

"I would like to personally join Maharaj Saheb in this campaign. Masaheb can singlehandedly take the charge of Raigad and the kingdom. All problems will be solved if I join you in this campaign."

Maharaj smiled to hear his words. "Shambhoo, I knew very well that you would make such a request, but this is politics. Being sentimental in such situations doesn't help. Remember how you and I were captured in Agra? It is not wise to repeat the same mistake. I have made a cautious decision to give you the charge of the Prabhavalli subah. You just follow my instructions and fulfil your responsibility well."

"Ji, as you wish. May I request one thing? The ministers should not interfere in my matters."

"If you wish so, that can be done. But remember, holding grudges against them is not going to be beneficial for you. In the future, these are the people whom you are going to work with. A leader has to astutely bring about a change of heart in the people and bring them over to his side."

"Maharaj Saheb, I am not holding any grudges against anyone. I would have made amends and convinced the people who opposed me to join me, but how can I deal with people who purposely put hurdles in my way? Aabasaheb, you are soon going to leave on a major campaign. Please don't get stressed thinking about anything else. Rest assured, that I will follow your command to the best of my ability."

"Yuvaraj, one should not be proud of inherited property. My father also gave me the charge of the desolate jagir of Pune. I kept building relationships with people. Moropant, Annaji, are men of great calibre. You don't approve of them, and they can't deal with your audacity. But I get caught between the two sides. The Siddis are on the prowl, hiding in the ocean. If they come to know that I am out on a campaign, they might grab the chance to attack the Konkan shores. Ambitious and greedy Aurangzeb might charge upon our kingdom any time. How are we going to deal with him? I have to take so many crucial decisions. To accomplish this mission, I must bring people together. Samartha's advice always echoes in my ears, 'Unite the Marathi people and spread the Maharashtra Dharma in the world.' You should not forget it too.

"This kingdom does not belong to me, to you or to Rani Saheb. It belongs to Goddess Jagadamba. Many faithful people have sacrificed their lives for it. The Bhosales are only the staunch devotees of the kingdom. When this fact is disregarded, conflicts arise. Rani Saheb doesn't have such foresight, but you should act patiently.

"For the sake of the kingdom, I the responsibility had given you to stay as a hostage in the Rajput encampment of Mirza Raja. After that, I gave you responsibility to face death all alone in Mathura in the disguise of a Sanyasi. And even today I am placing the responsibility on you. I am not doing this willingly. The men in the Bhosale family are born to carry responsibilities on their shoulders. More than anybody else, you and Ramraje belong to me. He is a young child; you are a grown-up now. Try to understand the situation."

Maharaj's agonizing words touched Sambhajiraje's heart. He quickly came forward and touched Maharaj's feet. His voice choked as he spoke, "Aabasaheb, I state from the bottom of my heart that I am not at all interested in ruling over the kingdom. Your word means everything to me. Everything will happen as you wish."

"Shambhoo…" Maharaj barely managed to call his name as he embraced the young, rowdy Bhosale standing in front of him.

The auspicious day of Dussehra broke out. At daybreak, Maharaj descended Raigad in a palanquin surrounded by Sambhajiraje, all ministers and select sardars, and arrived in Pachad. Putalabai had decided to live in Pachad after Maharaj left for the campaign. She put a blob of curds on the palms of the father and the son.

Maharaj left the palace of Pachad with Sambhajiraje and select men such as Raghunathpant, Janardanpant Hanamante, Hambirarao, Yesaji, Dhanaji Jadhav, Suryaji Malusare, Santaji Ghorpade, Netaji Palkar, Balaji Aavaji, Babaji Dhamdhere, Annaji and Moropant. The bell hanging in the courtyard was at rest. It was blessing them silently.

"Har…Har…Mahadeo!" the assembled soldiers shouted in excitement. The sound of booming cannons mingled with their peals. Bahirji Naik's surveillance troop at the front line galloped ahead.

The army of thirty thousand soldiers followed the Bhosale father and son. The war horns resonated.

In time, the entourage arrived at Chiplun. Maharaj and Sambhajiraje visited the temple, performed Abhishek and offered alms.

The troops left Chiplun and travelled towards Shringarpur. On the outskirts of Shringarpur, which was surrounded by mango orchards, Pilaji Shirke came with Ganoji to receive Raje. Maharaj and Sambhajiraje entered Shringarpur with their kith and kin.

At night, Maharaj talked with Pilaji at leisure. He informed Pilaji that Yuvaraj was going to stay at Shringarpur to take charge of the Prabhanvalli subah. He requested Pilaji to support Yuvaraj in every possible way. Pilaji readily concurred. Maharaj inquired about his son-in-law Ganoji and daughter Rajkunwarbai. The Shirke and Bhosale family dined together at night.

The next day, Maharaj left the palace at daybreak. Sambhajiraje accompanied him to take the darshan of Goddess Bhaveshwari. Maharaj sought the blessings of the Shirke family deity, bade farewell to Pilajirao and left Shringarpur. The father and son went in the direction of the Amba ghat. Moropant and Annaji returned to Raigad.

As they approached the incline of the Amba ghat, Maharaj pulled the reins of his horse 'Vijay' and dismounted. Sambhajiraje also dismounted. The entire army following them, halted.

"Yuvaraj, you should go back now. Farewell." Maharaj put his hand on Sambhajiraje's shoulder. A few moments passed in silence. It was time to say goodbye.

"Maharaj Saheb, take care of your health. Send me messages from time to time. Rest assured that everything will be fine in your absence. Don't worry."

"Shambhoo...why should I worry about anything? Everything happens according to Goddess Bhavani's will. You carry out my orders. Bring your family with you and stay at

Shringarpur. When I return, I would like to hear Pilajirao complimenting you. Farewell. Jai Bhavani!"

Sambhajiraje stepped aside with Khandoji, Rayaji, Antoji and his swordsmen. The mammoth army started climbing the ghat.

Sambhajiraje kept staring at Maharaj's horse 'Vijay' climbing the ghat.

Sambhajiraje spent a couple of days at Shringarpur and bade farewell to Pilajimama and Ganojiraje. He returned to Raigad. Raigad was now under the leadership of Rahuji Somnath. Putalabai was already living in the palace of Pachad. She had given her palace in Raigad to Yesubai and Durgabai. Ranooakka from Sindakhed was still on the fort. She did not approve of Soyarabai's tactics. She had stayed back to give full support to her brother, Sambhajiraje.

Maharaj had advised him to keep the company of Keshav Pandit, Umaji Pandit and Vishwanath. Without Parashurampant, Khandoji Ballal and Mahadeo Yamaji, it would be difficult to handle the administration of the subah. Sambhajiraje instructed all of them to go to Shringarpur. Kavi Kulesh bade farewell to Sambhajiraje and left Raigad with Udho Yogadeo. Keshav Pandit started his travel to Shringarpur with Umaji Pandit. His menials carried the Vishnupuran, Matsyapuran, Ramayana, Mahabharata and other great books on their shoulders. Sambhajiraje's day of departure from Raigad was approaching. Till Maharaj's return he was going to spend his days in Shringarpur. Therefore, Sambhajiraje tried to spend most of his time with Ramraje, but Soyarabai did not approve of it.

Sambhajiraje selected armed troops for his convoy. He sent advance intimation to Pilajimama at Shringarpur that he was coming soon with his family. He visited the temple of Lord Jagadishwar and prayed to him.

Sambhajiraje came to Putalabai's palace to tell Ranooakka

that he was going to leave Raigad soon. Yesubai, Durgabai and Ranooakka were living together in Putalabai's palace now.

Sambhajiraje made an obeisance to Ranooakka and said, "Akkasaheb, as per Aabasaheb's wish I am going to Shringarpur with my family."

Ranooakka listened to him patiently and told him determinedly, "I know that. I have decided to come with you!"

"What do you mean?" Sambhajiraje was baffled.

"Balmaharaj, I have been silently watching everything since I came here. I did not think that the situation here would be far worse than the rumours I had heard so far. Masaheb envies you. I have realized that far worse than what has already happened is going to happen in the future. Everyone here thinks there is no one to support you. But now I am going to be with you like your shadow. I am going to confront everyone who opposes you. Balmaharaj, whether you want it or not, I am coming to Shringarpur with you!"

"Why are you so quiet? Say something." Akkasaheb insisted.

"As you wish, Akkasaheb." Sambhajiraje complied.

On the day of departure, three draped palanquins were kept ready in the square in front of the queens' palaces. Yesuabai, Durgabai and Ranooakka's palanquins left from the Palakhi Darwaja.

Yuvaraj bade farewell to Rahuji Somnath. No matter how hard Soyarabai tried to forbid him, Ramraje came with Annaji and Moropant to bid farewell to Sambhajiraje. Sambhajiraje kissed his forehead, patted his back and said, just as Maharaj had said to him a few days before, "Balraje, you should go back now. Farewell."

"Dada Maharaj…" Ramraje wanted to say something.

"Yes. What is it?" Sambhajiraje patted his shoulder gently.

"Can I…I come with you?" Ramraje looked at him expectantly.

Sambhajiraje unwittingly removed his hand from Ramraje's

shoulder and glanced at Annaji, Moropant and Rahuji. Everyone looked at the ground. Sambhajiraje remembered the time on Rajgad when he was going to the Rajput encampment as a hostage. Maharaj had come to bid farewell to him at that time, and unexpectedly he had removed his cowrie necklace and put it around Sambhajiraje's neck!

Sambhajiraje's eyes lit up with an unknown resolve. He removed his cowrie necklace, put it around Ramraje's neck and said, "Keep this with you as my rememberance. Farewell!"

Sambhajiraje set up the administrative offices of the Prabhanvalli subah in Shringarpur, at the Shirke residence. Many sardars in the region of the subah came to visit Yuvaraj at Shringarpur with their retinue. In the misty, wintry weather, Shringarpur bustled with visiting guests.

On an auspicious day, Sambhajiraje sought the blessings of Goddess Bhavani and commenced the composition of a lyrical work, 'Budhabhushanam'.

Sambhajiraje sat in the drawing room, with Keshav Pandit, Umaji Pandit and Kavi Kulesh. The holy scriptures were arranged in front of them on wooden book rests. Sambhajiraje commenced the work with a tribute to Lord Shiva's son, Ganesh, 'Oh, Lord Ganesh, you destroy the evil spirits and remove the obstacles in the path of your devotees. The gods and the demons extol you and you feel content to hear their praise. Oh, son of Shiva, I bow down to you!'

After paying tribute to Lord Ganesh, Sambhajiraje described the glory of his grandfather, 'Many years ago there was Raja Shahaji who was as mighty as the ocean, illustrious, benevolent and valiant!'

Now, his Aabasaheb's visage appeared in front of Sambhajiraje's closed eyes and spontaneous words poured from his mouth, 'Shahajiraje had a great son named Shivaji who was the master of vast lands, a prodigious leader to his people, as strong as a majestic mountain. Raje Shivaji was a great man like

Lord Shiva in the Puranas!

'Hail, oh Raja Shiv Chhatrapati, a visionary who had transcended the boundaries of time, who was perturbed to see the degeneration of Dharma in the world and reincarnated as the saviour of the world! Victory to you!'

Sambhajiraje remembered the legacy of the Bhosale clan and described his own disposition, 'I am Raja Shivaji's son, Shambhooraje, hailed as an icon by the surrounding kingdoms, who is well versed in poetics, literature, Puranas, music and archery. I have selected relevant shlokas from the Puranas, and I am expounding those in this lyrical work named 'Budhabhushanam'.'

As Sambhajiraje drew the attention of the audience to his book and pointed out how the reader should grasp the content, his round, manly face lit up. 'The swan separates pure milk from water and consumes only that. Likewise, fine and wise people accept only the truth and discard the untruth.'

Sambhajiraje dictated the shloka intended for the audience; Parashurampant noted it on paper, drew two horizontal lines below it and spread a pinch of soft sand on it. The first canto of the lyrical work was completed.

Sambhajiraje opened his eyes. Kavi Kulesh had been gazing at him for a long time. He was in awe of Sambhajiraje. He rose from his seat and made an obeisance to Sambhajiraje.

"Yuvaraj, I travelled from the north and came to this kingdom, but I have never heard or seen a single Yuvaraj who composes such lyrical works." Impressed Kavi Kulesh said.

"Thank you for the compliment Kaviaraj. You may sit down. Sambhajiraje signalled Kavi Kulesh to sit down. Now, I would like to see if I can write a tribute to my family deity, Goddess Bhavani."

Pilajirao had entered the room and was standing by a wall. Nobody realized it. Pilajirao saw that Sambhajiraje had closed his eyes and was dictating something in Sanskrit. He felt very proud, and kept watching the meeting quietly without disturbing it.

"Jagadamb, Jagadamb!" Sambhajiraje closed his eyes. Sanskrit words glorifying Goddess Bhavani gushed forth, "The dark-skinned Goddess Bhavani is sitting on a white crystal seat. A blood-red kumkum tilak adorns her forehead. Her visage is round like the full moon. Her breasts are shaped like a kalash. She is lotus-eyed and has a resplendent complexion. Her navel is deep-seated, and her waist is slender. She has donned a blood-red sari. I, Shambhooraje earnestly sing the glory of the Goddess Bhavani!"

"Wah! Wah!" Kavi Kulesh responded spontaneously. Pilajirao's shining eyes were already riveted on Sambhajiraje's face.

Sambhajiraje opened his eyes. He saw Dharau waiting at the threshold. He realized that she was about to go back. He called her and said, "Yes Aau, what is it?"

Dharau hesitated for a moment and said, "I don't want to disturb you, but just wanted to let you know that supper is ready!"

Sambhajiraje smiled and rose from his seat. A thought occurred in his mind, 'Which one is better – the Sanskrit language in which I compose the lyrics or Dharau's simple, pure, peasant tongue?'

Yesubai, Durgabai and Ranooakka dressed in the finest of saris and got ready. It was the day of Makar Sankrant. They were going to visit the temple of Goddess Bhaveshwari with their retinue and worship her.

Yuvaraj arrived in the courtyard and gave darshan to the ryots of his subah. As it was a festive day, he came to Ranooakka's chamber to meet her and seek her blessings. Yesubai saw her husband coming and tidied her sari. Demure Durgabai turned around to go to the inner apartment.

"Bai, wait." Yesubai stopped her.

Sambhajiraje came in with a smile and made an obeisance to Ranooakka. He glanced around and saw a piece of sweet made of sesame and jaggery, shaped like a crocodile placed on a silver platter. It was going to be offered in the puja of the goddess today. Later, it was going to be broken into pieces and distributed among people. Sambhajiraje went near the platter and kept gazing at the crocodile.

"Balmaharaj, you were so occupied in hunting, archery and the discussion of the Puranas that I was wondering whether you were going to remember the sweets made by your family." Ranooakka looked smilingly at Yesubai and Durgabai who were looking at the floor.

Sambhajiraje kept staring at the crocodile and said, "Akkasaheb, when I decide something in my heart, I can't let it go, just like this crocodile. I am going to compose a lyric and present it to Maharaj Saheb."

"Well, I don't understand anything about poetry. I would like to watch you shooting the gun today. Would you show it to me?" Akkasaheb said looking at Yesubai and Durgabai. Sambhajiraje spontaneously said, "Ji, as you wish. This evening some coconuts are going to be hung on the Peepal tree. I am going to shoot them down with my gun. I will show you my shooting in the evening. Please be there." Sambhajiraje looked at Ranooakka first and then at Yesubai and Durgabai. He meant to tell her to bring them with her. Ranooakka understood his gesture and smiled. What she was implying earlier, Balmaharaj had finally understood it.

"Farewell!" Sambhajiraje left the chamber.

In the evening, the courtyard of Goddess Bhaveshwari's temple on the outskirts of Shringarpur, echoed with gun shots. Sambhajiraje sat in the Veerasana pose placing the stock of the gun on his right shoulder. He closed his left eye and aiming at the coconuts hanging on the Peepal tree, he shot them down.

He shot down five coconuts in successive shots. The broken

pieces of coconut shells fell on the ground. The leaves of the Peepal tree were drenched in coconut water. Yesubai and Durgabai were watching the spectacle. Their hearts were drenched in pride.

Sambhajiraje's second meeting for 'Budhbhushanam' was in session at the Shirke residence. Today he was going to compose the canto of 'Rajniti', the principles of diplomacy. This was the core of the composition.

"Pandit, what are the characteristics of a true 'king'?" Sambhajiraje questioned Umaji Pandit.

Umaji Pandit browsed through the scriptures in front of him and said after a while, "Ji, a king must subjugate the feelings of anger, avarice, fear and malice. He should have the wise counsel of the elders and also virtues acquired of on his own."

Sambajiraje browsed through the scriptures placed in front of him. After some time, he gazed at Parashurampant and started expounding the characteristics of a king in an eloquent style, "A king should possess the qualities of brilliance, vigilance, mercy, and a warm heart. He should be the follower of Dharma, and free from malice; grateful, emulate his elders, valiant yet free of vice. He should be a visionary, who has conquered his anger and who has complete control over his senses. A king should support his people and destroy the evil."

Kulesh, Keshav Pandit, Umaji Pandit... everyone spontaneously praised the lyrics. Sambhajiraje's eyes were shining with the pride of his ancestors. He was about to continue dictating the lyrics when Pilajimama entered the chamber.

"Yuvaraj, some peasants are waiting outside to take your darshan. They have some complaint." Pilaji had assumed that the session was not going to end soon. So, he took a chance and delivered the message. The session was concluded.

"I will be there soon. Please convey my message to them, mama saheb." Sambhajiraje smiled to himself and whispered, 'A king should support his people'.

"Pandit, I will be back." Sambhajiraje left the chamber and started walking to the court hall. Rayaji, Antoji and Khandoji Ballal followed him. Yuvaraj came to the court hall. A group of fifteen to twenty peasants made an obeisance to Yuvaraj. Sambhajiraje took his seat. Khandoji, Rayaji and Antoji stood around him deferentially.

Sambhajiraje glanced at the peasants in expectation that they would present their grievance. But their heads were hanging low. It looked like they were under pressure. Sambhajiraje gestured Khandoji Ballal. He stepped forward and told the peasants, "One of you come forward and put forth your complaint."

An old man gathered his courage and opened his mouth, "But will we get justice?"

"Tell us your complaint first." Khandoji reassured him.

"Sarkar, we are the sons of the soil, you are like a father to us. This year there was drought and we could not grow any crops. We cannot pay the levy this year. We tried to tell this to the officer-in-charge in our village, but he simply dismissed us. We went to the fort to report this. We met Pant and Surnis there. They said, 'This is the administrative levy. You can ask for reduction, but you must pay the levy. Sarkar, we don't have anything. We will have to sell our cattle to pay the levy. Our cattle are like our children. What should we do Dhani? We have come from a faraway place. Please help us in the absence of Maharaj. Please pardon the levy this year." The old man's eyes were misty. He bowed down.

Sambhajiraje's poetic expression transformed into a resolute regal expression and he said determinedly, "Khandoji, I have pardoned the levy for these people and it will be pardoned for all people who are in a similar situation. Prepare the orders to this effect and send to me for my seal. Send skilled messengers to spread the message everywhere."

"Ji, as you wish." Khandoji bowed.

"Baba, you may go now. I have pardoned your levy. Feel free to come and meet me anytime you have any problem. My door is always open for you."

Sambhajiraje got up. The assembled peasants bowed. They were very happy. They had no worries now.

As Sambhajiraje walked back to the drawing room Surnis Annaji's face danced in front of his eyes – 'This man is going to be a nuisance for me!'

Sambhajiraje came back and joined the meeting with the pandits. Despite the unrest in his mind, he dictated another shloka to Parashurampant, 'Men who perform small but difficult actions lead the kingdom on the path of success.'

Sambhajiraje's face was full of mixed emotions. Neither he, nor the people gathered in the drawing room, knew that meanwhile the Chhaptrapati Maharaj astride his white horse, Vijay, had entered the western borders of Bhaganagar with a glorious parade. The musical instruments resonated, the cannons boomed, and an embellished elephant walked in front of him. Thousands of Mavala soldiers followed him. The ryots of Tana Shah had gathered in the balconies of their havelis and were eagerly taking the darshan of the Maratha king.

The second canto of 'Budhbhushanam' was concluding in Shringarpur, and the final canto of Maharaj's life saga 'Shivabhushanam' was commencing in Bhaganagar.

'Mishrakniti' – the third canto of 'Budhabhushanam' was finished. The meeting was over. Everyone made an obeisance to Sambhajiraje and left the room. But Keshav Pandit wanted to tell him something, so he stayed back.

"Keshav Pandit, what is it? Feel free to speak." Sambhajiraje surmised that he wanted to say something.

"I…I would like to request one thing, if it is okay with Yuvaraj." Keshav Pandit said hesitatingly.

"Yes, what is it?"

"A Shiv yogi, who is also a devotee of Goddess Kali, lives in

Shringarpur. He would like to meet Yuvaraj. If it is okay with you…"

"Certainly. Pandit, do bring him to visit me." Sambhajiraje consented.

One day the pandit brought the Shiv yogi, the devotee of Goddess Kali and his disciple, Ganeshbhat Jambhekar, to the palace. The Shiv yogi was clad in a saffron cloak, and his matted hair was tied with a Rudraksha necklace. He had smeared his upper arms and forehead with horizontal stripes of holy ashes.

Keshav Pandit ushered the Shiv yogi to Sambhajiraje's chamber. Yuvaraj promptly came forward and touched his feet.

"Jai Bhadrakali!" the Shiv yogi uttered and placed his hand on Sambhajiraje's Jiretop to bless him. Sambhajiraje courteously ushered him to a seat covered with tiger skin.

"Yuvaraj, I have held a wish in my heart." The Shiv yogi closed his eyes and said to Sambhajiraje.

"Ji, your wish is my command." Sambhajiraje responded with humility.

"It is my wish that a murti of Goddess Bhadrakali should be installed in this palace and she should receive prasad from your valorous hands."

"Ji, as you wish." Sambhajiraje bowed down in front of the yogi.

The contented yogi and Ganeshbhat bade farewell and left the palace.

At the Shirke residence, preparations for the installation of the Goddess' murti were in full swing. Under the keen eyes of Pilajimama, Ganojiraje and Sambhajiraje preparations were done in great detail.

An accomplished sculptor in Shringarpur carved a tall murti of Goddess Bhadrakali in black stone. The Shiv yogi found an auspicious mahurat for the installation. On that day the murti of Goddess Bhadrakali was taken to the palace in a grand procession. She was clad in a blood-red sari. Ranooakka, Yesubai,

Durgabai and Rajkuwarbai offered fruits and flowers to the goddess.

The Shiv yogi picked up a bare sword placed in a platter, and handed it to Sambhajiraje. Sambhajiraje gazed into the eyes of the goddess. Mesmerized, he stepped forward. He knelt in front of the goddess and touched his forehead to the floor. Then, he raised his head and touched the sword to his forehead. He held the sword in his left hand and shouted, 'Jai Bhadrakali'. Then, he quickly pulled his right thumb on the sharp edge of the sword. The warm blood of the Bhosale spurted out. Yuvaraj held his dripping thumb near the feet of the goddess and offered his royal blood to her. The murti of Goddess Durgabhadra was officially installed.

But something else was cooking in Raigad. Annaji Dutto had left the chamber of Maharani Soyarabai and handed a sealed letter to a loyal messenger. The letter stated, "Yuvaraj interferes unnecessarily in the matters of levy collection. How can the administrative treasury sustain the burden if all people were pardoned from paying the levies?"

The Chhatrapti had no idea of what was going on in his absence. He had successfully made a treaty with Tana Shah in Bhaganagar and had left Bhaganagar. He was going to attack the Adil Shahi sultanate now. The omniscient Goddess Kali was unmoved, watching everything with eyes wide open.

The murti of Goddess 'Kali', devoutly installed by Sambhajiraje, reigned in Shringarpur. But on Raigad utter malice reigned in the hearts of Surnis Annaji Dutto and Maharani Soyarabai Saheb.

Chapter 8

The entire Shringarpur had assembled in the courtyard of Goddess Bhaveshwari's temple. A platform bedecked with rich mattresses and pillows, was raised facing the murti of the goddess. Sambhjiraje sat on the platform leaning against a bolster. The men of the Shirke family including Pilajimama, Ganojiraje, and Kanhojiraje, sat behind him. Keshav Pandit, Umaji Pandit, Kavi Kulesh, Udho Yogadeo, Mahadeo Yamaji, Parashurampant, Khandoji, Antoji and Rayaji had lined up on the left. The ladies of the Shirke and Bhosale family including Yesubai's mother, Yesubai, Rajkunwarbai, Ranooakka, and Durgabai sat together on another platform raised on the right.

A pole laden with coconuts was basking in the moonlight in the courtyard. Near it, a Holi of wooden logs had been arranged in the centre of the courtyard.

"Dhakale Dhani, please honour us by lighting the Holi." The town-chief of Shringarpur approached Sambhajiraje and urged him politely.

Yuvaraj Sambhajiraje rose from his seat and removed his footwear gently. He took the torch from the town-chief.

He shouted "Jai Bhavani" and touched the torch to the Holi. The fiery flames of the Holi soared in the starlit skies. The town-chief encircled the Holi and tossed a few coconuts in the scorching fire. The excited players circled around the Holi and started piercing their hands through the blazing fire to extract the coconuts.

The spectators ardently watched the players battle with the fire. Three rounds of Holi players had surrendered to the blazing fire. No one had been able to extract the coconut from the fire.

Sambhajiraje who had been leaning against a bolster so far, was sitting upright now. His stern eyes challenged the blazing flames.

Rayaji, Antoji, even Ganojiraje Shirke, made an effort to defend the honour of his town but could not succeed.

Sambhajiraje threw a glance at all the players of Holi. Their heads were bent. The fire kept flaring. He had a sudden rush of blood to his head.

He rose from his seat at once. Many people raised their heads. The scorching fire of the Holi was burning brightly in Sambhajiraje's eyes now, reflecting his resolve.

'I will extract the coconut from the fire. Give me your blessings.' He said to himself. He rapidly approached the Holi and encircled the fire passionately.

"Jai Bhavani!" He roared and thrust his hand into the flaming fire. His roaring peal raised goose bumps on everyone's body. Sambhajiraje kept assessing the intensity of the heat and to pull out the coconut. His singeing hands moved vigorously. Within a short time, he pulled out a scorching dark object from the fire. In a flash he hurled it to the ground shouting "Jai Bhavani". The coconut broke into pieces.

The jubilant peals of "Jai Bhavani" filled the atmosphere. Kavi Kulesh, Khandoji, Rayaji, Antoji all rushed to check the Yuvaraj's hand. Sambhajiraje did not let anyone touch his hand and held it behind his back. He looked at the section of the royal ladies with a sparkle in his eyes. All the ladies, including Yesubai had stood up.

As soon as he saw Yesubai, Sambhajiraje smiled slightly but Yesubai couldn't see it as her eyes were filled with tears.

Sambhajiraje planned a hunting expedition in the woods

today. He had dispatched a team of shouters ahead. Rayaji, Antoji and Khandoji were going to accompany him.

Yesubai had wrapped Sambhajiraje's wounded palm in a bandage. Khandoji handed a lubricated rifle in the same hand and said, "Yuvaraj, this one has a perfect aim."

Sambhajiraje put the stock of the rifle on his shoulder, closed his left eye and checked the aim.

"Okay, Khandoji, you begin the preparations. I will leave in the late afternoon." Sambhajiraje entered the palace, holding the rifle in his hand, to inform Yesubai before leaving for the hunting expedition. Yesubai and Durgabai stood in the balcony. They saw him coming and stood up straight.

"I am leaving for a hunting expedition." Sambhajiraje said as if he was saying it to either one of them.

A few moments passed in silence. Yesubai wiped the drops of sweat on her throat with the edge of her sari and said, "Looks like it's going to rain today!" She meant to say, "Wouldn't it be better if Swari doesn't go today?"

"It is really thrilling to hunt in the rains." Just then, Pilajirao's personal secretary came onto the balcony and announced, "A messenger has come. He wants to see Yuvaraj."

Many questions arose in Sambhajiraje's mind, but he followed the personal secretary quietly.

Sambhajiraje instructed the personal secretary to bring the rider in the court hall. The rider presented himself in the court hall and made an obeisance.

"What brings you here?" Sambhajiraje asked in an intimidating voice.

"Please forgive me, but I have been instructed to meet you in private." The rider said calmly.

Sambhajiraje glanced around. The personal secretary, Parashurampant, Khandoji…everyone picked up the cue and left.

"You can speak now." Sambhajiraje said resolutely while

observing the rider.

The brocade design on the rider's attire sparkled. He pulled out a sealed letter hidden in his outfit. He gingerly approached Sambhajiraje, bowed down to him and handed him the letter. It was from Aurangzeb's Lashkar-e-Salar, Diler Khan, who had come to attack the Deccan. It was sent from his encampment in the Aklooj region; an appeal to Sambhajiraje to come and join hands with the Mughals.

Sambhajiraje went numb while reading that letter. His hands trembled. 'Join the Mughals – to conquer Deccan? How is it even possible?' His nostrils flared and breathing intensified.

Sambhajiraje stared at the closed door and clapped loudly. Parashurampant came in. "Pant, bring a quill and paper to write a letter."

"Ji." Parashurampant picked up the quill placed near his seat. He handed a plain paper to Yuvaraj and placed the ink bottle in front of him.

"You may leave now!" Parashurampant obeyed the order and left.

Sambhajiraje thought for a moment, decided what to write and then started writing in his royal hand.

"To Lashkar-e-Salar Diler Khan, Subah Deccan, from His Highness Yuvaraj Shambhoo –

I am in receipt of your letter. At present, father is away on a military campaign. He has appointed me as the guardian of the kingdom in his absence. You have astutely sent me the message at a very opportune time. But I swear by my ancestors that I will never join hands with you. How could you even expect that of me? Regards."

Sambhajiraje reviewed the letter contentedly and sealed it. He placed it in the same pouch in which it had arrived, and, from his seat he tossed it to the Mughal rider. The rider caught it in his hands, made an obeisance and left.

Sambhajiraje rose from his seat and picked up the rifle

leaning against a wall. He had completely lost the urge to go hunting now.

As he opened the door, Khandoji made an obeisance to him. Yuvaraj handed the rifle to him and said, "Khandoji, I have cancelled the plan of hunting. Inform the team so."

Khandoji stared at his Dhakale Dhani in astonishment.

Heavy monsoon showers began. The Mughal messenger left the Shirke palace, in the pouring rain. He released his horse chained outside the gate, and went eastwards.

A Mavala rider followed him from the Shirke residence. He was Vishwanath! A faithful informer that Maharaj had appointed, to keep a keen eye on the movements in Shringarpur. Braving the gale, the deluge, the thunder, Vishwanath was going to find out where the Mughal rider had come from. He was then going to travel to Raigad and report everything to Surnis Annaji.

"Yuvaraj, there is some alarming news. Vishwanath has disappeared from Shringarpur. No one knows his whereabouts." Kavi Kulesh bowed down and said.

After hearing the news Sambhajiraje jolted from his seat.

"Who's there?" An intimidating royal voice called. A guard at the door presented himself.

Sambhajiraji commanded, "Summon Khandoji here right away." Lost in thought, Sambhajiraje started pacing back and forth again. Kavi Kulesh got confused.

In a short time, Khandoji Ballal entered the chamber.

"At your service Swami," he said and made an obeisance.

"Khandoji, present Rayaji and Antoji in front of me immediately. Get two faithful riders ready. They are going to undertake a risky task."

"Ji." Khandoji left promptly. Kavi Kulesh also left the chamber.

Vishwanath, Annaji Dutto and Soyarabai's faces flashed in front of Sambhajiraje's eyes. Yuvaraj made up his mind.

"Please accept our obeisance, Dhakale Dhani." Rayaji and Antoji, his reliable men stood at the door of the chamber. As soon as Sambhajiraje saw them he rushed towards them. He placed his hands on their shoulders and observed them for a moment. The two brawny sons of Dharau seemed to him like his own brother Ramraje.

"Keep the door closed." Sambhajiraje instructed the guards at the door.

"Rayaji, Antoji, something is cooking against me in Raigad. Both of you should immediately travel to Raigad. Khandoji will provide skilled horse riders to you. Keep a keen eye on Surnis Annaji and Masaheb Soyarabai. If you hear anything that concerns me, send me a message immediately. When you leave from here tell people that you are going to Kapurhol to prepare your farms. Explain everything to Dharau. You can go now."

Sambhajiraje patted their shoulders and embraced them. Both brothers left without uttering a word, but they had fully realized their responsibility.

That afternoon, four riders left from the Shirke residence. They trotted slowly till they passed Goddess Bhaveshwari's temple and reached the borders of Shringarpur. As soon as they crossed the borders, their horses sprinted in the direction of Raigad.

Raigad was now caught in a family feud. It was inevitable. The eight-armed Goddess Bhavani of Pratapgad and Tuljapur kept watching everything calmly.

Shringarpur started receiving a barrage of news of the Chhatrapati's successful conquests from the Deccan.

"The Chhatrapati persuaded the custodian, Nasir Mohammed, and conquered Jinji. In Somottar Perumallam many temples had been converted into mosques. Maharaj Saheb restored the temples and installed Shivlingas there. Maharaj attacked Vellore and Tiruwadi. He conquered the forts at Valdur and Tevenapattam."

With every piece of news that Shringarpur received, the kettle drums at the Shirke residence resounded amidst the pouring rain. As the farmers working their fields heard the drums, they stopped their work momentarily, looked at each other and shouted in unison, 'Hail Goddess Bhavani! Hail Goddess Bhaveshwari!" And with new vigour, they resumed their work.

The Monnsoon was in full swing. One day, Khandoji Ballal presented two completely drenched Mavalas in front of Sambhiraje and left the chamber. They were Rayaji and Antoji. They had returned from Raigad. Rayaji and Antoji made an obeisance to Yuvaraj. Drops of water kept dripping from their turbans and soaked into the carpet below. Sambhajiraje saw them and approached them eagerly in anticipation of the news from Raigad. "What's the news? Tell me." He commanded.

"Dhani, the queens' palaces on Raigad are heavily guarded. No one can enter. Surnis' office is also surrounded by armed guards. His visits to the Maharani's palace have increased." Antoji shared the information that he could gather.

"Messengers carrying letters for Thorale Dhani are leaving the fort in the wee hours in the direction of the Karnataka region." Rayaji added.

"We could not gather any information from the queens' palaces but…but…" Antoji stopped talking.

"But what? Say it, Anta." Sambhjiraje comforted him.

"A rumour has spread on the fort among the personnel that…"

"What rumour?" Sambhajiraje pressed his shoulder tightly.

"That you…you are going to join the enemy, Diler Khan's camp!" Antoji dropped his head.

"Antoji!" A raging roar erupted from Sambhajiraje's mouth, leaving the Gaade brothers frozen. He started pacing in his chamber like a wounded tiger.

The monsoon was over. Shringarpur was shrouded in the thick blanket of wintry fog. Around the time of Dussehra, the farmers smeared the threshing grounds with cow dung and started the threshing process.

At Pilaji's residence, the evening round of drums resounded and dispersed in the darkness around. Yesubai carried a bowl of hot porridge in a silver plate, and entered Sambhajiraje's sleeping chamber. She placed the plate on a stool, the bangles on her wrists tinkled. Sambhajiraje had wrapped a shawl around himself. He approached Yesubai. She quietly handed him the bowl of porridge.

Sambhajiraje kept gazing at Yesubai. She looked enticing, like a couplet of a lyric. Yesubai looked at the light falling on the floor and played with it with her toe. Yesubai broke the warm silence and said, "The porridge is still waiting!"

"Well, not only the porridge, but I am also waiting!" Sambhajiraje smiled gently and touching the bowl to his lips he took a sip. Yesubai felt happy and stole a glance at him. She saw a speck of the porridge stuck in Sambhajiraje's moustache, and quickly looking down she pressed the edge of her sari over her lips to suppress her laugh.

Sambhajiraje kept pacing in the chamber while sipping the porridge. He came in front of Yesubai and extending the bowl to her he said, "Here, taste it. See how delicious it is!"

Bashful, Yesubai did not move from her place.

"Have it, it hasn't become salty just because I tasted it!" Sambhajiraje laughed out loud. Yesubai grabbed the bowl from his hand in haste; in a single sip she emptied the entire bowl like one consumes the sip of tirtha and placed it in the silver plate. Then she picked up the plate and briskly walked out of the chamber.

Sambhajiraje smiled to himself. He removed the shawl he had wrapped around himself, shook it and wrapped it around himself again. He came to the drawing room. Kavi Kulesh was present there, writing something. He saw Yuvaraj and got up to make an obeisance.

"What are you writing, Kaviraj?"

"Just trying to solve a Sanskrit puzzle, Swami."

Sambhajiraje started walking towards a seat. Some baskets full of vegetables were lined up against the stone wall of the chamber. The farmers had sent them to the palace. They were going to be stored in the kitchen soon. Sambhajiraje casually picked up a piece of ivy gourd and sat on his seat. He was observing the piece when an idea occurred to him. Sambhajiraje smiled and got up from his seat. With the piece of ivy gourd still in his fist, he left the chamber to have dinner.

The cool starlit night descended on the Shirke residence. The midnight tolls rang. Sambhajiraje was tossing and turning in his bed. He came to a decision and left his sleeping chamber. He started walking in the direction of Yesubai's sleeping chamber.

He stopped in front of Yesubai's sleeping chamber. The maid, standing guard at the door, was half asleep. seeing him, she promptly got up.

"Announce my arrival to Rani Saheb."

"Ji." The maid rushed inside. She came back in a minute and said, "Rani Saheb is still awake."

Sambhajiraje entered the chamber and closed the door. Brawny Sambhajiraje walked slowly to Yesubai. She was standing near the bed. He sat on the bed, removed his cowrie necklace and placed it in a platter on the stool. Then he glanced at Yesubai. Demure Yesubai was looking at the floor. She had covered her head with the pallu of her sari. She looked like the crescent moon. She could not believe that her Swari had come to her chamber after the midnight hour. Such a thing had not happened before. She was completely baffled.

A few moments passed silently. Then Sambhjiraje said in a husky voice, "Will you do me a favour?"

"Ji." The edge of Yesubai's sari shook subtly.

"It is not a very easy thing to do." Sambhajiraje said suggestively.

"I will do my best." Yesubai responded.

"I want you to cut this piece of ivy gourd in half."

Sambhajiraje held the piece of ivy gourd in front of Yesubai.

"Hmm..." Yesubai wondered if Swari was making fun of her. She smiled and said, "A very difficult task indeed, but I will do it for sure."

"Promise? You should not back out later!" Sambhjiraje's eyes sparkled.

"A daughter of Goddess Bhaveshwari would never break her promise." Yesubai said solemnly.

"Okay then, go ahead and cut the ivy gourd, but there is one condition. You should not use your hand or any tool to cut it. It's a very delicate vegetable." Sambhajiraje smiled.

"Of course, no need of hands or tools to cut this piece." Yesubai said innocently.

"I knew that you would never back out. Hmm?" Sambhajiraje said with a smile. "Let's test the determination of Goddess Bhaveshwari's daughter!" Sambhajiraje said and quickly held the piece of vegetable between his teeth exclaiming "Hmm!" Still, Yesubai did not get his impish mischief. She stepped forward innocently. Her hands fidgeted for a moment and stopped. She got baffled. She couldn't figure out how to cut the simple piece of vegetable. Her face displayed a medley of emotions.

Sambhajiraje removed the piece from his mouth and laughed loudly. He said, "Didn't I tell you that it's not an easy task!"

His words provoked Yesubai. She felt ashamed. She gazed at the flames of the burning lamps and wondered how to cut the vegetable. Her heart was pounding, and she had goose bumps all over her body. She feigned anger, and threw a glance at Sambhajiraje that meant, "Oh, so naughty!" Her body trembled.

Sambhajiraje held the ivy gourd in his teeth and his eyes smiled. Yesubai's round face started moving towards the piece of ivy gourd. She was entering the world of romance; her eyes closed involuntarily. Her white teeth grabbed the piece of ivy gourd and she feverishly cut a piece of the vegetable that had bothered her so much. The deep red juice spread on four royal lips. A romantic night descended on Shringarpur.

Winter was over. The month of Pausha arrived. Sambhajiraje concluded his discussion with the pandits about poetics, politics and revenue collection. He came to the court hall to handle administrative matters. Parashurampant stood up and made an obeisance to him. Khandoji Ballal, Rayaji and Antoji took both sides of the hall.

"What is the news, Chitnis?" Sambhajiraje sat on his seat and asked.

"Most of the revenues from the region of Rangana, Vishalgad via Kolhapur in the Panhala subah have been collected, Yuvaraj. But due to heavy rains, crops in some of the western regions have been destroyed. Those peasants have appealed that they should be exempted from paying their levies. Parashurampant presented the case.

"Please inspect the region, confirm the facts and then give them the exemption." Sambhajiraje instructed.

"These messengers have arrived from the Karnataka region. They have brought news of Maharaj's victory." Parashurampant pointed at the messengers.

Sambhajiraje, who was leaning against a bolster, straightened up.

"Sarkar, Thorale Dhani visited the samadhi of the late Shahaji Maharaj and offered charities." A messenger stepped forward and made an obeisance.

"Thorale Dhani captured the region of Kolar, Arani, Torgal, Gadag and attacked Belwadi. Queen Mallamma spared no effort in protecting her fortress. The widow of Ishwar Prabhudesai fought ferociously against our army for more than a week. In the end, our sardar Sakhujirao conquered the fortress, but..." The second messenger hesitated for a moment.

"But what?" Sambhajiraje got curious.

"But Sakhuji made a mistake. He tried to molest the queen. Thorale Dhani ordered in front of the entire army, that hot iron rods should be thrust into his eyes."

The entire court hall fell silent on hearing that news.

"Mallamma was brought in front of Maharaj. She was holding her only son in her arms. She courageously approached Maharaj, placed her son in Maharaj's lap and said, "You have won our fortress, now accept the responsibility of this heir of the fortress too, and throw me in the prison." Maharaj's eyes filled with tears when he heard it. Dhani patted the child in his lap and said, "Bai, you are indeed brave. You are like a sister to me. I am giving this fortress back to you as a gift from a brother!" Maharaj released Mallamma with honour." The messenger's voice choked while recounting the tale.

"Jagadamb! Jagadamb! Chitnis, that child is indeed fortunate, he got the privilege of sitting in Aabasaheb's lap. Gift this messenger with an attire of honour." Sambhajiraje honoured the messengers and they left. Sambhajiraje was about to get up from his seat when the Chitnis said in a low voice, "A messenger has arrived from the Mughal kingdom. He wants to meet you."

Sambhajiraje frowned. He got upset, but outwardly he spoke in a calm voice, "Please bring him here."

A messenger clad in Mughal attire came in the court hall. He made an obeisance and said, "Huzur, I have been instructed to meet you in private!"

"Silence! I don't meet any commoner in private. Just tell me what you are here for." Sambhajiraje's eyes breathed fire.

"Ji." The messenger muttered, shaking in fear, and put a green pouch at Sambhajiraje's feet. Sambhajiraje untied the pouch and pulled out a letter. He scrolled through the letter. It was from Diler Khan and had the same content as the previous one – "To His Highness Shahjada Shambhoo… Come and join us. We will honour you." Sambhajiraje stood up instantly from his seat and furiously hurled the letter towards the messenger. His thunderous words echoed in the hall, "What does Diler Khan take me to be? Tell him my response is the same as before. You had better leave, before I throw you out."

Sambhajiraje left the court hall hastily and went to his chamber. He kept pacing restlessly in his chamber. For quite a while, he didn't even realize that Yesubai was standing near the window in his chamber. When he realized that he approached her and gently asked her, "How long have you been standing here?"

"Quite a while, but you look very upset today."

Yesubai were worn a green sari, green blouse and green bangles. Her face reflected a unique glow.

"Why are you dressed so enticingly today?" Sambhajiraje asked with a smile.

"Oh no! It's not what you think. This is a 'Chorcholi' offered by my Aau."

"Meaning?" Sambhajiraje did not understand the meaning of 'Chorcholi'.

"When a mother secretly gifts a sari and blouse to her daughter, without letting any other woman know about it, it is called 'Chorcholi'. Yesubai smiled and turned around. As she moved, Sambhajiraje observed her sluggish movements and realized why her mother had offered her the 'Chorcholi'.

In an ashram on the outskirts of Shringarpur, the Shiv yogi sat on a high seat covered with tiger skin. Sambhajiraje sat on a step near his feet. Keshavbhat and Ganeshbhat Jambhekar stood on both his sides. Vapours arising from a burning incense stick had filled the atmosphere with a strong fragrance.

"Yuvaraj, you installed the murti of Goddess Kali in Shringarpur. Her daily worship continues religiously. But as the Goddess of War, she would like an Abhishek of blood." The Shiv yogi spoke in a solemn voice.

"Your wish is my command. I will perform the Abhishek

under your guidance."

"Yuvaraj, no matter how valiant a man is, he should seek the support of the divine powers. You should perform 'Kalash Abhishek' in front of the goddess. You will obtain the powers of 'Tantra siddhi' by performing the ritual, and your child to be born will be protected from the evil forces." The Shiv yogi continued pulling the beads in his rosary.

"Ji." Sambhajiraje thought for some time and said, "Swami should give detailed instructions to Keshavbhat and Ganeshbhat about the rituals and decide upon the mahurat for Kalash Abhishek."

"Yuvaraj is going to perform the Kalash Abhishek." The news spread all over the subah. It reached Raigad as well. After hearing the news, Surnis Annaji Dutto presented himself in front of Soyarabai. He shared his views about the Kalash Abhishek with the Maharani –

"I feel this Kalash Abhishek is ill intentioned! Sending our informers to Shringarpur and finding out their intention, would be a wise thing to do at this time." Soyarabai followed his advice and took action accordingly. The informers from Raigad infiltrated Sambhajiraje's subah in the disguise of Gondhalis and fakirs.

Sambhajiraje kept a fast on the eleventh day of the bright fortnight of Pausha. The day of Kalash Abhishek broke out. The kettle drums in the Shirke residence began resounding.

The ceremony commenced under the guidance of the Shiv yogi. The Kalash was carried from Goddess Bhaveshwari's temple to the Shirke residence in a lavish procession. At the threshold of the Shirke residence, a goat was sacrificed in front of the Kalash. The Kalash was placed in front of Goddess Kali, on a square drawn with rice grains. Sambhajiraje, dressed in a red dhoti and a red shawl, sat on a flat wooden seat next to the Kalash, facing Goddess Kali. The Shiv yogi sat on a wooden high seat and began giving him instructions about the rituals to be performed. Keshavbhat and Ganeshbhat started chanting mantras to protect the heirs of the royal family from evil forces. With a contented heart Sambhajiraje started sprinkling the water of holy rivers, honey and milk on the Kalash with mango leaves.

"Yuvaraj, now you have to give the final offering." The Shiv yogi instructed Sambhajiraje.

"What should I offer?" Sambhajiraje looked at the Shiv yogi expectantly.

"Your virtuous royal blood!" The Shiv yogi glanced at Ganeshbhat. Ganeshbhat picked up a platter with a naked sword in it and held it in front of Sambhajiraje.

"Chant the name of Goddess Bhadrakali and offer the blood from your thumb on the Kalash."

The Shiv yogi closed his eyes and started chanting mantras himself.

"Jai Bhadrakali" Sambhajiraje ran his thumb on the sword and sprinkled the warm blood dripping from his thumb. He joined his palms in prayer and closed his eyes. The image of Goddess Bhadrakali stood in front of his eyes. He observed her intently.

The Kalash Abhishek ceremony concluded. The Brahmins were offered alms.

This ceremony was going to avert the effects of evil forces on Sambhajiraje's heir…but it was also going to result in unexpected challenges for Yuvaraj Sambhajiraje. A messenger astride a horse was on his way from Raigad to Karnataka. He was carrying a secret letter with him. It was a message from Maharani Soyarabai. It stated–

"I must convey the malicious activities of Yuvaraj to you. He has performed the 'Kalash Abhishek' ceremony in Shringarpur in aspiration of the quick demise of his noble father and seizing control of the entire kingdom!!"

With the advent of the monsoon Shringarpur got drenched in exhilaration. Joyous news had arrived in the subah, "The

Chhatrapati Maharaj has conquered the region from Jinji to Gadag-Torgal. He has begun his journey back home. He has assigned Raghunathpant Hanamante as the custodian of the Karnataka subah. The victorious Chhatrapati is returning after almost two years, after conquering territories from Jinji to Gadag-Torgal."

As Sambhajiraje heard the news, he came to the court hall with much excitement and summoned Parashurampant and Khandoji. He gave quick instructions, "Pant, erect an archway of mango leaves to the south of Shringarpur and keep the kettle drums ready for the welcome. Dispatch a messenger to Aabasaheb to convey that I am looking forward to receiving and welcoming him to Shringarpur. Khandoji, keep some select horse riders ready to accompany me and you stay with me. Be alert. Aabasaheb is on his way."

The day that Sambhajiraje had estimated for Maharaj's arrival in Shringarpur dawned. The ryots raised Gudhis in front of their houses. The triangular saffron flag was fluttered on the dome of Goddess Bhaveshwari's temple. Sambhajiraje took the blessings of Ranooakka and Yesubai's Aausaheb and left the palace. Khandoji had kept a troop of select horse riders ready for him.

"Jai Bhavani," Sambhajiraje whispered and mounted his horse. Pilajirao, Ganojiraje and Khandoji were behind him astride their horses. Behind them were Umaji Pandit, Keshav Pandit and Kavi Kulesh. A troop of hundred horse riders stood behind them.

A palanquin bedecked with flower garlands was placed in front of the entourage. As Sambhajiraje signalled them the palanquin-bearers picked up the palanquin. It was for the Chhatrapati. The entourage left. Sambhajiraje was going to wait two miles beyond the borders of Shringarpur to receive his victorious father.

The entourage crossed the border. After the entourage had

covered a distance of two miles, the palanquin stopped. Everyone dismounted. Khandoji had carried a pouch of gold coins in the scarf wrapped around his waist. Everyone's eyes were focused on the path coming from Amba ghat to Shringarpur.

Quite some time passed. The sun ascended in the sky. The covering of the palanquin heated up. The flower garlands wilted; all eyes got weary. Everyone saw that one of the messengers who had been stationed in the ghat was riding towards them. All felt hopeful. The rider approached them. Sambhajiraje immediately questioned him, "Where has he reached?"

"Dhani, our informer will be coming here soon."

Everyone waited for the informer. The afternoon was almost over. People got worried. After a while the informer came into sight. As soon as Sambhajiraje saw him, he mounted his horse and dashed forward to catch up with him. He asked the informer hastily, "How far away is Maharaj Saheb?"

The informer somehow managed to dismount. He made an obeisance, nodded his head and handed a pouch to Sambhajiraje. Sambhajiraje opened the pouch hastily. There was a letter in it.

"What is this?" Sambhajiraje frowned.

"I could not meet Dhani in person. He is on the way to Pune via Samangad, Kolhapur, and Satara.

"To Pune!" Sambhajiraje's expression changed instantly.

'Has Aabasaheb forgotten me? Or is he angry with me? Did something happen in Raigad?" Sambhajiraje's mind was full of doubts, his heart pounded.

"Let's go back now." An aged hand wearing a silver bracelet patted Sambhajiraje's shoulder. It was Pilajirao who had understood the pain of his son-in-law and tried to console him, putting aside the royal protocol.

Sambhajiraje did not speak to anyone. He entered his chamber quietly. He did not realize that Ganojiraje was walking right behind him. The chamber was lit with lamps. Sambhajiraje removed his Jiretop and placed it in a platter.

"Yuvaraj..." Sambhajiraje was startled to hear Ganoji's voice, but he composed himself and said, "Yes, what is it?"

"Oh Yuvaraj, indeed you are so naïve just like Lord Shankar."

"What do you mean?" Sambhajiraje stared at Ganoji.

"I will tell you what has happened, why the Chhatrapati avoided meeting you. A rumour has been circulating on Raigad that you performed the Kalash Abhishek in anticipation of Maharaj's early demise. People on the fort are gossiping that Yuvaraj performed the Kalash Abhishek to seize control of the kingdom!"

"Ganoji...stop it!" Sambhajiraje put his palms on his ears and screamed in a tremulous voice.

"Just be careful! That's all I want to say." Ganoji left.

Sambhajiraje's heart shattered into countless pieces. Annaji Dutto and Masaheb Soyarabai's faces lingered in front of his eyes. He could not stop thinking about them.

"What happened?" Yesubai had been standing in the chamber for quite some time.

Sambhajiraje did not respond to her. He went to the window and kept stared at the darkness outside.

Sambhajiraje turned around and faced Yesubai standing behind him. He removed the cowrie necklace, placed it in her palms and said in a subdued manner, "I am afraid that I may not be able to defend the honour of this precious ornament. You are more capable of handling that responsibility!"

The dark night was embracing Shringarpur. A dejected Sambhjiraje started walking towards Durgabai's sleeping chamber.

At Raigad, a conference had been convened in the court hall of the Chhatrapati's palace. Outside, the deluge continued. The Chhatrapati who had returned from the successful Karnataka campaign was collecting information from the administrative offices of the eighteen departments.

"Maharaj, Pant captured the Nashik and Tryambak region." Annaji reported Moropant's valiant feat. Balaji Aavaji presented some crucial letters from the Portuguese, Qutub Shahi and British durbars that needed immediate attention.

After discussing the matters of the royal stable, treasury and armoury, finally the discussion turned to revenue collection. Annaji was the head of the revenue department. While presenting the report of his department, Annaji complained about Yuvaraj Sambhajiraje, "Maharaj, Yuvaraj interferes in the process of revenue collection. I have already informed you about it."

"And exactly how does the Yuvaraj interfere?" Maharaj calmly asked Annaji.

"He waives the taxes as he wishes." Annaji responded.

"Does he approach the people or do people approach him to get their taxes waived?" Chhatrapati asked a pointed question.

"People approach him all the time."

Maharaj smiled and to point out Annaji's mistake to him without hurting his feelings, he said in a soft voice, "Annaji, you are the head of the revenue department. If our ryots have any problems, they should approach you directly. I don't understand why they keep going to Yuvaraj instead!"

Annaji was stunned. He kept quiet. Then Maharaj consoled him and said, "Annaji, the people of this kingdom are like God to us. They are the ones who fight for us, who fill our granaries with food. They are the ones who suffer during the enemy attacks. You and I should try to understand and solve their problems. We should support them in their hour of need. If Yuvaraj has done the same, I don't find anything wrong with it. I will check the matter personally."

"Ji. He may be right in this case, but I doubt his intentions when he corresponds with Diler Khan, our staunch enemy; and performs the ceremony of 'Kalash Abhishek' under the influence of the followers of Shaaktism, to ruin Swami's health. I consider it my duty to draw attention to such things at the right time."

Under a façade of concern, Annaji spewed the venom in his heart, Maharaj became solemn. He didn't know how to respond. Everyone was unsettled.

"Have you validated your claim Annaji?" The Chhatrapati said with caution.

"Ji. How could I not fulfil the duty that Swami had delegated to me?"

Pin-drop silence prevailed in the hall. Everyone was quiet. Just then, Hambirarao courageously put forth his proposal, "Annaji could not be wrong, but I think Dhani should speak to Yuvaraj in person and directly ask him the truth."

Many people in the conference agreed with Hambirarao and nodded in affirmation. But the Chhatrapati said, "Hambirarao, I agree with you, but do you think, if all this is true, Yuvaraj will readily accept it in front of me? And if the accusation is false, what will he think of my treating him like a culprit? The Chhatrapati became restless. As nobody spoke up, he said, "I am not at all afraid of the 'Kalash Abhishek' ceremony. The Rajput, Mirza Raja too had come to annihilate me after performing the 'Lakshabhishek' ceremony of Goddess Chandi. If at all something bad is going to happen to me, it is not because somebody wishes so, but at the wish of Goddess Jagadamba. But I am more concerned about the kingdom. If Yuvaraj has become power-hungry and it is confirmed that he is corresponding with our staunch rival Diler Khan Pathan, I will be forced to forget our blood relation and punish him severely. I want to give him a second chance before I take further action. Goddess Jagadamba has guided me so far, and will continue to guide me." The Chhatrapati stopped talking. Annaji's eyes brightened with hope to see his resolve. The conference concluded; all the courtiers left the hall. Annaji Dutto left the hall with his personal secretary. On the way to his residence, people were making an obeisance to him, but he did not notice it. He was wondering about only one thing, 'What kind of a second chance is Maharaj going to give Yuvaraj? What exactly is the Chhatrapati's plan?'

The month of Shravan arrived. Golden sunlight pervaded the ambience. Yesubai's baby shower ceremony took place. Yesubai received two royal gifts from Raigad for the baby shower, one from the Chhatrapati and the other from Putalabai Saheb. Putalabai Saheb had sent a message, "I really wish to be there with you, but it is not possible this time. Please don't get us wrong. Take good care of yourself."

Dharau accompanied Yesubai all the time. She was taking utmost care of her. The festival of Shrikrishna Janmashtami passed. The eleventh day of the dark fortnight of Shravan broke out. A baby's first cry echoed in the maternity room of the Shirke residence.

"It's a girl, by the grace of Goddess Bhaveshwari." The midwife announced.

Yesubai became 'Masaheb'! Sambhajiraje became 'Aaba'! The kettle drums resounded; the cannons boomed. Pilajirao, who had become a grandfather, stood in the courtyard and distributed sugar to the people of Shringarpur. He exclaimed smilingly, "Now that my grandchild is born, I have officially become an old man."

Sambhajiraje heard the news and got lost in thought, 'Had Thoralya Aau been alive today, she would have rushed to me and badgered me with many queries! And my Masaheb…I don't even remember her face. I have become 'Aaba' today! Oh, what an exhilarating feeling! Is it a reality or a dream? Aabasaheb has become a grandfather! He must be exhausted by the arduous Karnataka campaign. He will feel jubilant to hear this news and will leave for Shringarpur immediately. I will see him again, after so many days. I am dying to see him in person.'

"Yuvaraj, what would you like me to do?" Parashurampant presented himself and said courteously.

"Pant, dispatch messengers to Faltan, Sindakhed, and Raigad with the news that a daughter has been born to us. Please convey to Aabasaheb – 'You have become a grandfather. Your granddaughter is waiting to see you in person.'"

The day of the naming ceremony dawned. The Shirke residence was abuzz with joy and excitement today.

As the mahurat to put the baby in the cradle drew close, Sambhajiraje got anxious. Just then, Khandoji rushed into the courtyard and announced – "The royal gift from Raigad has arrived!"

Sambhajiraje's eyes sparkled, 'Aabasaheb has arrived! I must go to receive him.' He commanded, "Khandoji, we have to go ahead to receive them. Get everything ready."

Khandoji realized that Yuvaraj had misconstrued his words. He looked down and said, "Thorale Swami has not come…"

Suspicion started gnawing at Sambhajiraje's heart. He was stunned and muttered unconsciously, "He didn't come?"

The royal gift from Raigad arrived at the Shirke residence with grandeur. The riders accompanying the royal gift made an obeisance to Sambhajiraje. They presented the covered platters of gifts for the baby and the new mother in the courtyard and delivered the message of Raigad to the Yuvaraj with lowered heads, "Dhani is not keeping well. He has sent these gifts and has said that the baby should be named 'Bhavanibai'.

Sambhajiraje was stunned. He left the courtyard and walked towards his chamber.

The time-indicating vessel sunk in the big container. At the auspicious mahurat, Rajkunwarbai placed her niece in the cradle and whispered her name in her ears, "Bhavani! Bhavani! Bhavani!"

Durgabai was not present during the ceremony. As she was sick with nausea and vomiting, she was resting in her chamber.

Dussehra was over. This time, Sambhajiraje did not participate in the Dussehra celebrations. He stopped speaking to people and started spending more time in solitude. He was having a private conversation with himself, and he became frantic. Countless doubts arose in his mind, 'Why does it always happen to me? Why does the gold in my hand always turn into ashes? If Aabasaheb himself has doubts about me, then nothing else matters! Who has poisoned his mind against me, and why? Did I ever bear Masaheb any ill will? What troubles have I caused for Annaji?

'While leaving for the Karnataka campaign, Maharaj Saheb stationed me in Shringarpur. Though it was very difficult for me, I accepted his decision as I did not want to cause any trouble while he was leaving for the campaign. On his way back from the campaign, Maharaj Saheb didn't come here to visit me. He didn't even come to see my newborn daughter, his granddaughter. Why is this happening to me? What is the mistake for which I am getting punished so severely? Is it my fault that I was born as the elder son? Or that I am the designated Yuvaraj of the kingdom?

'I am quite sure that Aabasaheb has misjudged me. Who can defend my side in Raigad? Why doesn't he summon me to Raigad? Does Aabasaheb want me to spend the rest of my life at my in-laws' residence in Shringarpur? I have spent almost two years here. I don't want to stay here anymore, but where else can I go, and how?' He couldn't think straight.

"Yuvaraj, a messenger has arrived from Raigad. He is waiting for you in the court hall with a letter from Maharaj." Parashurampant entered the chamber and announced the news.

'A messenger from Raigad! For sure Aabasaheb has invited me to Raigad.' The anxiety he was feeling a moment ago vanished instantly. He walked briskly to the court hall. The courtiers made an obeisance to him. The rider from Raigad stepped ahead politely and handed a pouch to Yuvaraj. Sambhajiraje touched the pouch to his forehead for a moment and quickly opened it. He held the letter in his hand and started reading it.

"To Yuvaraj Shambhooraje, many heartfelt blessings. We

received the news that dear Soonbai has delivered a daughter. It has brought us great joy.

Now, the most important thing, as soon as you receive this letter you should travel to Sajjangad. Visit Samartha and present yourself in his service. Listen to his advice attentively and follow it cautiously in your life. Surrender all your thoughts at Samartha's feet. What more should I write?"

With each word in the letter, Sambhajiraje's left eyebrow kept arching. An emotional turmoil erupted in his heart, 'This clearly means that Aabasaheb has misjudged me. I should go to Sajjangad and listen to Samartha's advice. Why? To clear all doubts in my mind. What have I done? Was it wrong to handle the subah administration successfully? Or to waive the taxes for the people who were facing financial problems? Or was it wrong to perform the 'Kalash Abhishek' ceremony so that no harm befalls my child? Aabasaheb…Aabasaheb…why are you telling me to do this? I don't need anybody's advice right now. What I need is to see you in person. Why should I go to Sajjangad and for what?'

Sambhajiraje left the court hall with the letter in his hand. He directly went to Yesubai's chamber. He showed her the letter and said, "Here, Aabasaheb's letter from Raigad. He has ordered me to go to Sajjangad and surrender at Samartha's feet. Why should I go there?"

Yesubai was nursing Bhavani. She gently separated her daughter from her bosom and said with a smile, "Why are you so upset about it? Sajjangad is a holy place. Please listen to me and go to Sajjangad as per Aabasaheb's order. I am busy with the baby, otherwise I would have also come with you, to visit Samartha."

Sambhajiraje was surprised at her calm attitude. It made him think twice and he started pacing in the chamber. After some time, before leaving the chamber, he said in a calm voice, "Fine then, I will go to Sajjangad."

The day to go to Sajjangad dawned. Khandoji had selected three hundred armed riders to accompany Sambhajiraje. They stood in front of the Shirke residence. A palanquin with sheer curtains was prepared. Ranooakka and Durgabai were going to accompany Sambhajiraje to Sajjangad to meet Samartha in person. Durgabai was glowing. She was with child now.

Sambhajiraje took Pilajimama and Mami Saheb's blessings and bade farewell to them. He came to Yesubai's chamber to bid farewell to her. Yesubai lay on her bed. As she saw him, she promptly got up and sat on the bed. Baby 'Bhavani' was fast asleep in the cradle. Dharau stood near the cradle.

Sambhajiraje avoided Yesubai's gaze and said in a heavy voice, "I have come to bid farewell. Please take care of yourself".

"Looks like you are still angry, but that anger will subside after meeting Samartha on Sajjangad. You might even compose a poem there!" Yesubai tried to cheer up Sambhajiraje.

Sambhajiraje did not respond to her with his usual smile. He sounded heartbroken when he said, "I don't think I will ever be able to compose a poem again!"

An unbearable silence prevailed in the chamber for a few moments. Yesubai broke it and said, "You are going to see Samartha. Please convey my obeisance to him. If he says something harsh to you, please don't take it to your heart. I believe that by the grace of Goddess Bhaveshwari everything will be alright."

As Sambhajiraje heard her words, he smiled in a very strange way. He said to Dharau, "Farewell Aau, take good care of them."

"Please don't forget to get an amulet blessed by Samartha, for Bhavanibai." Yesubai said, looking lovingly at the cradle. She pressed her palm against the edge of the bed and stood up. She went to a corner of the chamber and picked up a wooden casket from a recess in the wall. She opened the casket, took out the cowrie necklace and calmly approached Sambhajiraje. She spread her palms in front of him and said, "This is a very precious ornament. Your chest looks bare without it. I am not capable of taking care of it. You should take it back. Please take good care of Dhakalya bai."

Sambhajiraje kept observing his wife. He picked up the cowrie necklace and wore it.

Sambhajiraje left the chamber without looking back. Ranooakka and Duragabai bade farewell to all, and sat in the palanquin placed in front of the palace. Sambhajiraje mounted a white horse. Pilajirao, Ganoji, all pundits, Khandoji, Rayaji and Antoji accompanied him to the northern border of Shringarpur to bid farewell. On the way, Sambhajiraje visited the temple of Goddess Bhaveshwari's. The entourage came to the northern border. Sambhajiraje said to Pilajirao, "Since you are there to take care of everything in my absence, I have no worries."

"Don't worry. Come back soon after visiting Samartha. We will be waiting for you." Pilajirao said affectionately. Sambhajiraje bade farewell to all and left Shringarpur. The armed riders surrounded the palanquin and started travelling towards the Koyana ghat.

The evening descended. Sajjangad was now within reach. At the foothills of the fort, the custodian of the fort, Jijoji Katkar was present with his retinue to receive Sambhajiraje. He came forward and welcomed them. Sambhajiraje started climbing Sajjangad with Ranooakka and Durgabai. Jijoji walked behind them.

Sambhajiraje arrived at the fort. The news of his arrival spread in the fort. Sambhajiraje came to the entrance of the ashram. He removed his mojaris and washed his feet. He walked with Ranooakka and Durgabai through a pandal full of Samartha's disciples and took the darshan of Lord Hanuman. He touched the feet of Kalyanswami, Samartha's disciple, and said, "Please give me your blessings."

"Jai Jai Raghuveer Samartha" Kalyanswami chanted and

pulled him up. Ranooakka and Durgabai touched Kalyanswami's feet and paid respects.

"Yuvaraj, I will bring tirtha and prasad for you all. Till then, take some rest in the veranda." Kalyanswami said affectionately.

"Ji." Said Sambhajiraje and started walking towards the veranda. Samartha's disciples observed Yuvaraj with curiosity.

Yuvaraj sat on the seat arranged in the veranda. Ranooakka and Durgabai went to the ladies' apartments with the female disciples of Samartha.

After some time Kalyanswami came to the veranda with a bowl of prasad and a container of tirtha. He smiled and said to Yuvaraj, "Here, have the prasad." Sambhajiraje hesitated for a moment and said to him, "First…I would like to visit Samartha and then…"

Kalyanswami gave him a peaceful smile and said, "Gurudev is not in the fort at present. He has undertaken a journey. Here, have the prasad." He placed a morsel of the prasad in Sambhajiraje's palms. Yuvaraj was not expecting this, and it made him forget about the prasad in his hand.

"Have the Prasad, please." Kalyanswami reminded him. Yuvaraj consumed the prasad and sipped the tirtha.

That night, Yuvaraj did not have dinner in the ashram. Maybe because it was a new place, Yuvaraj couldn't sleep that night. He kept tossing and turning in his bed.

Sambhajiraje was gazing in the direction of Raigad, his palms placed on the stone ramparts of Sajjangad. He looked utterly anxious. It was a week since he had arrived at the fort. Sambhajiraje moved away from the ramparts impatiently. Jijoji, the custodian of the fort was standing politely behind him with a few swordsmen. Sambhajiraje said to him in a solemn voice, "Dispatch a letter to Raigad and convey to Aabasaheb that Samartha is not present at the fort, and I am waiting for further instructions."

"Ji." Jijoji responded. Sambhajiraje started walking towards the meeting room of the ashram. Jijoji followed him.

The armed guards made an obeisance to Yuvaraj. Jijoji instructed an attendant to summon the Chitnis. The Chitnis presented himself and started writing the letter to be sent to Raigad.

"Dhakale Dhani, Sadanad Gosavi wants to see you. May I present him?" Jijoji made an obeisance and asked for Yuvaraj's permission.

Sambhajiraje's forehead puckered. He stroked the pillow he was leaning on and said calmly, "Let him come in."

Sadanand Gosavi came in and made an obeisance to Yuvaraj. He gathered the handbag hanging on his shoulder and raising the staff in his hand he said, "Yuvaraj, I have a complaint!"

Sambhajiraje straightened up and glanced at Sadanand Gosavi who was clad in a saffron cloak. He wanted to tell him, "Buva, I have a complaint too. Who should I present it to? How can someone who has a complaint of his own resolve the complaint of another?" But he composed himself and to comfort Sadanand Gosavi he said, "Please tell me what it is."

"The administrative office has annulled our Inam. Please assist me in getting that decision repealed." Sadanand Gosavi said firmly.

Sambhajiraje instantly remembered Samartha, who had detachedly refused the invitation to the coronation ceremony. On the other hand, here was his disciple, Sadanand Gosavi! Even the Gosavis yearn for the Inam! The trees that grow tall, strive to reach the sky; the grass growing in the meadows cannot reach sky-high! There will always be only one Samartha.

"Who has annulled your Inam?" Sambhajiraje asked him.

"The Surnis!" Sadanand Gosavi replied.

Sambhajiraje was agitated to hear that name, but composed himself, and said, "Yes, this matter comes under his authority. I will convey your complaint to him. You may leave now."

Sadanand Gosavi left. Sambhajiraje instructed the Chitnis,

"Write one more letter to the Surnis and dispatch it to Raigad. Let him know that – 'The Inam of Sadanand Gosavi has been annulled at present. In my opinion it should be reinstated, but this matter does not fall under my authority. Please resolve the matter as you feel appropriate.'"

Both the letters were ready. Sambhajiraje signed and sealed them. The messenger left with the letters.

The bright fortnight of Pausha arrived. The crescent moon started waxing. Though Sajjangad was bustling with activities, Sambhajiraje was feeling left out and utterly lonely. Only one thought took over his mind, 'I must leave this fort, but where should I go? Should I go back to Shringarpur? No! Anywhere else but there!'

Sambhajiraje kept pacing back and forth anxiously. The guard at the door came in and said courteously, "Somebody form the ashram is here."

Sambhajiraje stopped pacing and said, "Let him in."

A disciple entered the room with the message of Kalyanswami. He said, "I have brought a message from the Swami for Yuvaraj."

"Yes, what is it?"

"There is an auspicious mahurat after two days. Yuvaraj should take a bath in the confluence of Krishna and Venna rivers near the holy place Mahuli. He should also offer alms with his own hands; it will earn him religious merit."

Sambhajiraje hid the turmoil in his heart and said in an outwardly calm voice, "Please tell Swami that I will take advantage of this 'auspicious mahurat'! You may leave now."

The disciple left contentedly. Unbeknownst to him he had agitated Sambhajiraje's heart. He folded his hands behind his back and started pacing like a wounded animal. His own countless images shadowed his heart.

'The day Thoralya Aau passed away, the Yuvaraj in me was orphaned. Masaheb became the Maharani, and was envious that

I had been declared the Yuvaraj. Because of her actions, I had to stand in the durbar as an accused; I became the cause of a married Brahmin lady's suicide. Masaheb craftily planned to charge me with the heart-wrenching accusation of poisoning my own father. She did not let go of a single opportunity to separate Ramraje from me. I waived the taxes for the people caught in financial trouble. She misrepresented this to Aabasaheb with Annaji's help. I performed the 'Kalash Abhishek' ceremony with a very different intent. But again, my actions were misconstrued and conveyed to Aabasaheb in Karnataka. How did all this come to be, and why?

'On his way back from the Karnataka campaign, Aabasaheb did not come to Shringarpur. He did not feel like giving his blessings to his dear Soonbai who had delivered his first grandchild. Is it because of me? Maharaj Saheb must have wanted to hold Bhavani in his arms and give her his blessings, but he didn't do it, because of me. The wise Maharani of Raigad and the Surnis convinced him that I am power-hungry, and that is why he told me to go to Sajjangad.

'Doesn't Aabasaheb want to see me? Does he think the same of me? Then why should I bear the burden of being the Yuvaraj. How long am I supposed to tolerate this torture and why?' He sat on his bed; his heart throbbed with pain. He felt as if his head was going to burst, he grabbed it with both hands and closed his eyes tightly.

"All bonds are broken! And I am going to break the last bond myself!" He consoled himself. "Yes, I have decided to join the camp of Diler Khan Pathan! I won't be looked upon as a son, a husband, a brother or a Yuvaraj there! I will only be Sambhajiraje Bhosale, who has faith in his own mettle!"

Sambhajiraje sat on his bed and began writing a letter to Diler Khan, "To the Mughal Lashkar-e-Salar Diler Khan, Deccan Subah, greetings from His Highness Sambhajiraje Bhosale.

I am visiting the holy place Mahuli in two days. From there,

I will come to meet you in person. Be ready to receive and welcome me appropriately. We will talk in detail when we meet in person."

Outside, the night guards of Sajjangad were wide awake. They were keeping a vigilant watch around.

The tenth day of the bright fortnight of Pausha dawned. It was the darkest day in the history of the Maratha kingdom. Sambhajiraje had selected two hundred armed soldiers. They descended the fort with the containers of hons to be distributed in charities.

Sambhajiraje removed his royal attire and wore simple clothes. He was unsure about whether to wear the cowrie necklace or not. He rubbed the cowrie necklace in his hand momentarily. Then he whispered, 'Wherever I go, I will always be a Bhosala. Who else is going to protect me now, but Goddess Jagadamba?' and wore the necklace.

"I heard that you are going to bathe in the holy place of Mahuli." Ranooakka's words broke Sambhjiraje's reverie. He responded to her, "Ji."

"I would also like to take a bath in the holy confluence." Ranooakka expressed her desire with a smile. Sambhajiraje's forehead creased and he kept gazing at Ranooakka. He couldn't figure out what to tell her. After some time, he said, "As you wish. I will get the palanquin ready for you. Please get ready."

"I am not coming alone. Durgabai is also coming with me." Ranooakka gave a pleasant smile and exclaimed.

"As you wish." Sambhajiraje had nothing else to say.

A palanquin was kept ready. Sambhajiraje went to the ashram and took darshan of Lord Hanuman. He touched Kalyanswami's feet and sought his blessings.

"Jai Jai Raghuveer Samartha" Kalyanswami chanted and pulled Yuvaraj up. He gave Yuvaraj a pleasant smile and poured some tirtha on his palms.

Sambhajiraje threw a woeful glance in the direction of

Raigad. He signalled the palanquin-bearers to pick up the palanquin of Ranooakka and Durgabai. Keeping the palanquin in the front, and Jijoji Katkar and a troop of armed soldiers at the back, Yuvaraj Sambhajiraje began climbing down Sajjangad of Samartha. With each step of the fort that he climbed down, Sambhajiraje went further on a descending path of life. Every step he took, his mind kept questioning him, 'Should I go ahead or come back? For what? What is left for me to come back?'

'What will Aabasaheb feel when he will come to know that I have joined hands with the Pathan? No! I should go back. And then…? Should I spend my time in Shringarpur enjoying the hospitality of Pilajimama? Or should I spend time in the company of the pandits discussing poetics?... No! That's not possible! That's not going to happen ever! The decision I have taken is the right one for me.

'The entire Maratha kingdom will be shocked by the news of my defection, but only two people will be overjoyed – the supposedly wise Maharani of the kingdom and the so-called clever, faithful Surnis Annaji!

'Is it just my imagination that the Maratha kingdom will be shocked after I am gone!' The kingdom needs a king, only a king. After Aabasaheb, Ramraje can become the king. I…I will build a new kingdom of my own…on the power of my strength. No one will doubt my intentions there. Even Aabasaheb did not have his own kingdom! I still remember his words, "Yuvaraj, the wealth inherited from your forefathers doesn't prove your merit!" After all, I am his son. I have got an opportunity to prove my mettle now. Twice before I denied it, but destiny thinks otherwise. That is why I don't have any other option but to join hands with Diler Khan. The path I have taken is an arduous one, but isn't it better than no path at all?

'…Aabasaheb, I have never asked myself before, but today I wonder, what would you have done, had you been in a similar situation? Imagine that you are the same age that I am, and a cunning lady like the Maharani is your Masaheb! How would you have faced her? Would you have confronted her and warned her, "You may be the Maharani, but I am also the Yuvaraj of the kingdom! The future king! Mind your manners when speaking to me!"

'The flowing river neither laments the ghats that have been left behind nor fears the obstacles that lie ahead. The only thing that I carry with me now, is my sword and the blood in my veins. I am the scion of a royal family too. I am not meant to lead an oppressed life. Aabasaheb was sent away from my grandfather and grew up without his counsel. I am going away from Aabasaheb too…is it even possible to abandon him like this? No! No matter wherever I go, I won't be able to forget him, even for a moment…but still…I can't stay in this kingdom anymore. I must go now, wherever the path takes me…I must go. Aabasaheb left me behind in Mathura; today I am leaving him behind. Aabasaheb played a cunning move when I was in Mathura. He purposely spread the rumour of my death in the kingdom, and to convince the enemy about it, he performed my obsequies on Raigad, though I was very much alive! Today, I am telling him myself, "Aabasaheb, my actions have proven that I am dead to you, so don't hesitate to perform my obsequies again! Forget that I am your son!" There is no politics involved in this, it is only my heartfelt appeal…

With every step he was climbed down, Sambhajiraje's heart was dragged like a prisoner tied to a horse's leg. As the foothills of the fort came close, he signalled the entourage to take a short break. He raised his head high, gazed at Sajjangad reaching sky-high and wiped his sweaty forehead.

He ordered the palanquin-bearers to get ready. The entourage began the journey ahead. The sizzling sun of Pausha kept shining in the sky.

They reached the holy place of Mahuli near the confluence of the Krishna and Venna rivers. The stone ghat of the confluence was buzzing with people. Tents had been raised for the entourage under a sprawling tree. The news that Yuvaraj had come to bathe in the confluence spread across the ghat. The masses vacated the north side of the ghat for the royal guests. In a corner, Jijoji had erected an enclosure for the bathing of the royal ladies.

Sambhajiraje removed his jama and Jiretop and tucked his breeches. He wrapped a shawl around himself to cover his body. He came out of the tent and started climbing down the ghat. The troop of soldiers that had already reached the confluence were making an obeisance to him. He reached the last step that was under water, quickly removed the shawl and handed it to an attendant standing behind him. His body shone briefly like a gold bullion in the bright sunlight of Pausha. Instantly, the gold bullion dived in the whitish blue waters of Krishna and Venna. Yuvaraj began swimming. The moment the water touched his body, the storm in his heart dissipated.

Ranooakka and Durgabai took a bath in the enclosure. Sambhajiraje came out of the water. He threw a quick glance at the shining sun, and wrapped the shawl around himself again, climbed the steps of the ghat briskly and came to his tent. He dried himself and got dressed again.

Ranooakka and Durgabai performed the puja of Krishna and Venna rivers and came to the tent.

Jijoji had erected a special seat for Yuvaraj in front of the tent for the distribution of alms. Covered platters of gold coins, food grains and attires were placed near the seat.

Yuvaraj came out of the tent. Akkasaheb and Durgabai were behind him. Yuvaraj sat in his seat. The ladies took their seats and the charity offering began.

Yuvaraj started distributing alms with a calm, contented and smiling face. The Brahmins, priests, ascetics, fakirs…everyone who received charities started blessing Yuvaraj from the bottom of their hearts. The royal ladies distributed coconuts and blouse pieces to the women who had gathered.

"Jijoji, take a look around and check if anyone has not received alms." Sambhajiraje instructed the custodian.

"Ji." Jijoji nodded and went to take a look around. Immediately, Sambhajiraje summoned the troop of soldiers that he had chosen, and gave them a command that no one understood, "Put all our animals in the boats and carry them to the other side. Carry all luggage to the other side of the confluence. Hurry, move fast!"

"Ji." The soldiers nodded and started working.

"A few Gosavis remain, but they don't want any alms. They want food grains." Jijoji reported.

"Okay then, give them food grains." Sambhajiraje left his seat. He came to the banks and checked the boats crossing the confluence. He made sure that everything – the animals, the soldiers, and the boxes had reached the other side. Only four-five boats were floating near the bank on this side waiting for him.

Sambhajiraje entered the tent and said to Ranooakka, "Akkasaheb, can you please come to the bank with me?"

"Let's go." Ranooakka said casually. She had no clue about what was happening.

Sambhajiraje started climbing down the steps of the ghat with Ranooakka and Durgabai. Jijoji followed them politely, wondering, "Why have the soldiers crossed the confluence and why are they waiting on the other side of the river?" They reached the bank. The boatmen sitting in the boats made an obeisance to Yuvaraj.

Unexpectedly for Ranooakka, Sambhjiraje touched her feet and said, "I am leaving now. You should take her with you and return to Sajjangad!"

"What? What do you mean?" Startled, Ranooakka asked.

"I...I have decided to team up with Pathan Diler Khan and I am going to his encampment right now!" Sambhajiraje answered in a clear voice.

"Balmaharaj…!" Ranooakka screamed as if hit by lightning. Jijoji was stunned. Durgabai had never done it before, but today she raised her head and looked at her husband questioningly.

Ranooakka stared at her younger brother and asked, "What are you talking about? Have you even thought about Aaba?"

"Ji. I have. I don't belong to anyone at this moment. I am not going to be confined to any place, be it Raigad, Shringarpur or Parali. I am not going to implore anyone for anything at all. My decision is firm. You should go back now, and feel free to tell me, 'Instead of having a brother like you, I would have preferred not having a brother at all!' I have prepared my mind for such words."

Ranooakka was stunned. She said, "Balmaharaj, how can you do such a thing? Did I support you so far, to hear this? Instead of confronting your foes you are running away from them. With your actions, you are playing into their hands. Have you thought about it? How will your wife who is with a child, survive without you?" Ranooakka asked pointing to Durgabai.

"I have thought about everything. I don't care about who will get an advantage and what will happen to anyone anymore! I am leaving now. You should go back."

Sambhajiraje turned his back to Ranooakka and hopped into the boat. "Let's go." He ordered the boatmen. The boats left, swayed on the waves and went a bit ahead.

"Balmaharaj, wait…" Akka's trembling voice raised goose bumps on the waters of the confluence. The boat stopped for a moment. Sambhajiraje signalled the boatman to take the boat back. As soon as the boat touched the shore Sambhajiraje questioned Akka, "What is it? Tell me quickly. I don't have time to waste."

"I…I am also coming with you!" Words drenched in pure love, echoed on the ghat. Durgabai's eyes conveyed the same concern to her husband.

"You want to come with me? Akkasaheb, I am not going to

visit a temple…Why do you want to be an obstacle in my path?"

"Balmaharaj, I might abandon myself, but I cannot leave you alone now. I have decided to support you all the way, and to go with you wherever you go. Please take me with you. I have never asked for anything, but today I swear in the name of Goddess Bhavani and ask for this one thing. Take me with you."

Stunned Sambhajiraje kept staring at Akkasaheb.

"Fine, as you wish. Let's go." Sambhajiraje got off the boat and assisted Akka and Durgabai to climb in. The three of them, bound to each other by birth sat in the boat and sailed on the waters of the confluence.

"No, Dhakale Dhani, please don't do this!" Jijoji Katkar, the custodian, loyal to the Chhatrapati, called out to Sambhajiraje from the bottom of his heart.

"Jijoji, take the remaining property back to Sajjangad."

"Dhani…"

Sambhajiraje's mind had gone astray and at that moment fiery words escaped from lips, "Follow my orders and tell your Maharaj that I will return only to conquer the Sahyadri!" These acidic words fell on the holy waters of Krishna and Venna.

As soon as they reached the opposite shore, Sambhajiraje, Ranooakka and Durgabai mounted three horses. The entourage of Yuvaraj Sambhajiraje Bhosale marched towards the Mughal encampment. The scion of Shiva was going to join hands with the evil forces; not alone, but taking the daughter and the pregnant daughter-in-law of the Chhatrapati with him.

Yuvaraj Sambhajiraje Bhosale had abandoned the Chhatrapati!

He was orphaned today, in the true sense!

Chapter 9

The entourage travelled past the Mughal camp at Supe. Three hundred Mavala soldiers were drenched in sweat in the blazing sun. Sambhajiraje had sent advance intimation of his arrival to Diler Khan who had camped at Bahadurgad in Pedgaon.

At the border of Pedgaon, Diler Khan waited with his entourage to welcome Sambhajiraje. Earlier, Rajput Mirza Raja had coerced 'Shiva' to sign a treaty and had brought 'Sambha' to the Rajput encampment as a hostage. The Rajput had gifted a royal elephant to Sambha, and Pathan Diler Khan had ridiculed him by asking, "Sambhooraje, how will you carry this mammoth elephant with you?" Shivaji's son had haughtily replied, "Your elephant walks slowly. It is easy to carry it, but the forts that our Maharaj Saheb has surrendered to you, don't walk! It is impossible to carry them!"

The Pathan smiled at the memory today and thought, 'Oh pugnacious prince, forts don't walk, and it is indeed impossible to carry them, but a man can walk, and it's quite easy to make him move.'

As Sambhajiraje arrived at the border of Pedgaon the kettle drums in the Mughal camp resounded. Diler Khan tidied his green brocaded khilat, spread his arms wide and approached Sambhajiraje saying, "Welcome…Sambhooraje, welcome." The Pathan embraced the Bhosale. The soldiers thronged the area to witness the bizarre scene. The Pathan took Sambhajiraje's hand

and ushered him to his lavish shamiana.

The royal ladies were sent to Bahadurgad in bedecked palanquins with armed guards.

The next day, a grand platform was raised in the camp for the ceremony of offering the royal gift to Sambhajiraje. It was adorned with lavish carpets.

Diler Khan ensured that his eminent sardars such as Ikhalas Khan and Iraj Khan were present in the ceremony. In front of them, Diler Khan gifted Sambhajiraje with an embellished elephant that the Alamgir had sent from Delhi, three Arabian stallions, a sword sheathed in a green scabbard, kettle drums and a royal attire. A proclamation was issued in front of all assembled sardars that the Mughal Durbar had bestowed the Mansab of seven thousand cavalry and the Varad-Khandesh region upon Sambhajiraje. Diler Khan introduced Sambhajiraje to the Faujdars and Hawaldars who would work for him in his Mansab.

Sambhajiraje, who, as the Yuvaraj of the Maratha kingdom, used to accept the obeisance of the Mavalas, now began accepting the obeisance of the Mughal soldiers as the 'Royal mansabdar, Shambhoo Khan'. The darkest period in the life of the noble, young Bhosala had begun.

His great grandfather, Malojiraje, grandfather, Shahajiraje, Aabasaheb, Shivajiraje – none of them had escaped the dark fate of serving under the Mughal rule. Only one person was anxious on seeing the gifts and the mansab offered to Sambhajiraje. It was Mahadaji Nimbalkar, the son of Bajajiraje Nimbalkar, the son-in-law of the Chhatrapati, who was also a maternal cousin and a brother-in-law to Sambhajiraje.

Sambhajiraje returned to his tent after the ceremony. Immediately, the guards at the door announced, "The Nimbalkar from Faltan wants to see you."

Mahadaji came in. He were a triangular turban on his head and the Khilat. Though he was senior in age, he made an obeisance to Sambhajiraje with courtesy.

"I have come to meet you personally, to have a talk with you."

Mahadaji broached the subject.

"Sure. Go ahead."

"Raje, what have you done?" Mahadaji didn't know how to express himself.

"What do you mean?"

"Why did you come to this dreadful place?"

Sambhajiraje looked piercingly at Mahadaji and asked him, "You are wearing the Khilat, and you are asking me this question? Why are you serving here?"

"No one will ever understand my predicament. But you had the staunch support of your elders. You shouldn't have come here, Raje."

"That's enough, Daji Saheb, when the road in front of you is blocked, you are forced to take an untrodden path. No one will understand my predicament, and even if they do, they won't be able to solve my problems."

"Raje, please think about this again. You still have time. In my opinion, you should go back. This is not a place for a designated Yuvaraj."

"I have taken my decision, and don't call me Yuvaraj." A grim silence prevailed in the tent.

"You will repent your decision eventually. That's all I want to say. Farewell." Mahadaji was about to leave when he heard Yuvaraj say, "Please convey my respects to Akkasaheb. Not as the Yuvaraj, but as an unfortunate young brother!" Sambhajiraje's voice choked as he remembered Sakhoobai.

Mahadaji left. Diler Khan had received the news about this visit from his informers. As soon as Mahadaji entered his own tent, it was surrounded by armed guards. Mahadaji was detained.

Diler Khan's stars were on the rise. Siddi Masood, the Wazir of the Bijapur durbar and the commander, Sarja Khan were at odds. Sarja Khan, who had previously battled four powerful commanders such as Mirza Raja, Diler Khan, Shivaji Raje and Netaji Palkar to protect Bijapur, had now deserted Bijapur and joined hands with Diler Khan. As one prince and one commander had united with him, Diler Khan was in an advantageous position.

Aurangzeb's son, Muazzam, alias Shah Alam was the subedar of Deccan. He was in Aurangabad. He felt that Diler Khan's success was going to be disadvantageous to him. Diler was now dreaming of overthrowing the Bijapur sultanate. Shah Alam didn't want him to earn the credit of such a huge success. Therefore, he kept giving Diler Khan the unsolicited advice of attacking the Maratha kingdom. They both were at daggers drawn.

Diler Khan left Bahadurgad with Sambhajiraje and camped at Aklooj. It was a perfect place from where Adil Shahi and the Maratha kingdom could be invaded. In anticipation of Diler Khan's attack on Bijapur, the fearful Wazir, Masood Khan started diplomatic negotiations with the Chhatrapati Shivajiraje. Raje sent a letter of support to Masood Khan. He had two objectives behind this move. Firstly, if the Mughals conquered the Bijapur sultanate it would be disadvantageous for the Marathas. Secondly, he wanted to try in every possible way, to break Sambhajiraje away from Diler Khan and bring him back.

Two regiments of the Maratha army under the leadership of Sarlashkar Hambirarao and Anandrao entered the Adil Shahi territory. Informers from these regiments had risked their lives to meet Sambhajiraje in the encampment of Diler Khan, but Yuvaraj was adamant. He did not budge. The informers had returned empty-handed.

Sambhajiraje was anxiously pacing in his tent at the Aklooj camp. He was thinking about Bahadurgad; he was lost in memory.

'Some people are very unlucky! I lived in Shringarpur with Yesubai. She was loved and pampered at her parents' home, but what about her...' Sambhajiraje felt heartbroken as he remembered Durgabai.

'Yesu, you always said – I am wedded to the wild wind! It is true indeed, not in your case, but in case of Dhakalya bai! When we left Shringarpur, you told me to take care of Dhakalya bai. But I am myself trapped in a storm, then who is going to look after her?' Sambhajiraje's mind ran amok.

'Akkasaheb, such a big dilemma you have put me in! Had she stayed back, Yesubai would have taken good care of her.'

Sambhajiraje came out of his tent to avoid his own thoughts. Two horse riders had entered the camp; they had come from Bahadurgad. They came directly to Sambhajiraje's tent and delivered the news that Durgabai had delivered a baby boy on Bahadurgad. He was named 'Madan Singh'.

Sambhajiraje appealed to Diler Khan and got Mahadaji's confinement revoked. The Mughal forces were now consolidating. The herds of bulls carrying the food grains of the Mughal forces started travelling back and forth in the Malashiras, Indapur, and Baramati region. One such flock collided with the Mavala troops near Bhupalgad. There was an altercation between the two troops. The Mughal soldiers reported the incident to Diler Khan, "The Kafir Mahrattas of Bhupalgad are resisting our efforts of gathering food grains for our army; they are threatening us frequently."

That was more than enough for Diler Khan. He was already waiting for an excuse to attack. This was the only chance for Diler Khan to test Sambhajiraje's loyalty. "Has Seva's son turned a Mughal mansabdar in reality, or is this a ruse planned by the father and son together? Besides, the agitation caused by the Maratha army in the Bijapur territory was not going to be curtailed easily unless they were taught a lesson. After all, Diler hadn't come to Deccan to entertain himself.

On the first day of the bright fortnight of Vaishakh, at the Aklooj camp, Diler ordered his army to attack the Maratha kingdom. Troops of soldiers started departing from the encampment one by one. The cannons started moving in the direction of Bhupalgad.

Diler Khan himself came to visit Sambhajiraje and said smilingly, "Sambhooraje, come, let's see how lucky you are for us. We have to capture Bhupalgad. The Shahjada Muazzam questions your loyalty sitting at Aurangabad. It's time to prove your loyalty to him."

As Sambhajiraje heard Bhupalgad's name, he said hesitatingly, "But Khan Saheb…" Diler laughed out loud and said, "Raje, you are right. Your hesitation is quite appropriate, but I am not giving you an order to do it yourself. In fact, I am coming with you on the mission. Everything is fair in war. You must come with us. Tell your forces to get ready." Diler left the tent like a roaring storm.

Sambhajiraje gave orders to his forces. Marching to the beat of the war drums, the Mughal army of Varad-Khandesh got ready to proceed.

Pathan Diler Khan and Sambhajiraje sat together in a howdah on an elephant. The elephant was leading the army. Diler pulled his sword out and raised it high. The army behind him caught his cue and responded in unison – "Attack…"

Like a boat caught in a storm, a disoriented Sambhajiraje got ready to attack Bhupalgad with the Mughal army behind him and the Pathan commander with him. Shivajiraje's own son, Sambhajiraje was going to attack his Swaraj! The panic-stricken ryots in the vicinity of Bhupalgad took shelter in the fort. The gates of the fort were locked. The custodian of the fort, Firangoji Narasala, got ready to defend the fort dauntlessly. He was a very old, reliable soldier of Raje. He had looked after Sambhajiraje in his childhood. The same Sambhajire was coming to attack him today.

"Balraje, what have you done?" The pain in his heart did not reach Sambhajiraje at the foothills of the fort, and even if it had reached him, it would have been futile.

The second day of the bright fortnight of Vaishakh had barely broken when Diler's cannons started breathing fire on Bhupalgad. The battle commenced. Firangoji's soldiers started shooting arrows and stones from the fort. The sun kept ascending, and the Mughal cannons continued firing at the fort. The Mughal soldiers were attempting to reach the ramparts of the fort. A fired-up Firangoji was moving around the fort swiftly and wasn't giving the Mughal army any chance to move forward even an inch.

Diler, who had conquered a strong fort like Purandar, was feeling inadequate here. As the scorching heat of Vaishakh increased in the afternoon, Diler ordered the cannoneers to stop firing. Silence prevailed in the battlefield.

Diler came to his tent, wiping the sweat on his forehead. An attendant placed a platter of food in front of him. He dipped a piece of the roti in one of the bowls and gave a command, "Summon Sambhooraje right now. The fort will fall for sure, and it will fall today!"

Sambhajiraje came to Diler's tent. As if nothing had happened since the early morning, Diler said to him, "Rajasaab, will you take the lead of the battle?"

"Yes. Certainly." Sambhajiraje agreed.

"The fort is quite impregnable. Don't lose heart." Sambhajiraje only smiled in response.

In the late afternoon, Diler played his ultimate move. He gave his elephant to Sambhajiraje. The regular enclosed howdah on the back of the elephant was replaced with an open howdah for Sambhajiraje.

Sambhajiraje came to the forefront with his army. On the fort, the loyal archers took aim to attack the enemy. The gunmen wielded their guns and got ready to fire. Firangoji, who was observing from the bastion walls saw Sambhajiraje sitting on the elephant. He immediately shouted and ordered his men to stop – "Soldiers, we are in big trouble. The Pathan has played his move. He has sent our Bal Dhani to the forefront. Put down your arms!"

Emotional attachment became the hurdle in the way of duty. The scene on the battlefield changed instantly. Sambhajiraje's forces collided against the ramparts of the fort. Firangoji raised the white flag on the ramparts and let down a rope from the ramparts. One soldier climbed down the rampart wall and delivered Firangoji's message to Sambhajiraje, "We cannot wield our weapons against you. Please go back the way you came."

Sambhajiraje roared in response, "Tell the custodian of the fort that I am not going to retreat until I conquer the fort! Either I will fall while fighting or the fort will fall!"

The soldier delivered the message to the custodian of the fort. Firangoji got caught in a dilemma. If we continue to fight, we will have to use our weapons against Sambhajiraje, and if we don't, we will lose the fort!

Firangoji took the decided to vacate the fort after getting a promise from Sambhajiraje that he would spare the lives of all people on the fort. The white flag on the ramparts started fluttering in the wind. As the Mughal army saw the symbol of surrender, the kettle drums started beating in the encampment and cannons were fired to proclaim victory. Firangoji came to the entrance of the fort with Vitthal Bhalerao and opened the door. He hung his head low as he didn't feel like looking at Sambhajiraje directly.

Firangoji vacated Bhupalgad with Vitthalrao and his troop of Mavala soldiers. The green flag with the symbol of the crescent moon and the star was now fluttering atop the fort. Sambhajiraje stayed in the Balekilla and Diler Khan remained at the foothills with the army.

The night descended. The torches and campfires in the

Mughal camp were lit. Seven hundred Marathi people shackled like cattle were brought in front of Diler's shamiana. They stood with their heads bent low and were surrounded by armed guards. The fearful ryots who had taken shelter on the fort were left without any refuge after the fort was surrendered. Their future was in the hands of the Pathan now.

Diler, who had just consumed a delicious meal with liquor, came out of the shamiana. The prison chief made an obeisance to him and asked, "Huzur, what should be done with these people?"

Diler threw a glance at the bunch and ordered, "Cut one hand of all these Kafirs!"

A group of executioners arrived on the plains of Manjara. The hands of the kafirs were forcefuly pressed against a wooden stump. While slicing their hands with the wide-bladed sharp knife, the executioners were asking them maliciously, "With which hand did you hurl the stones, you scoundrel?!" When one executioner got tired, he passed the knife to the next one and said, "So many of these scoundrels are here, damn it! They should have been just pushed down from the rampart walls; it would have saved us much trouble!"

Scream after scream echoed on the plains. No saviour came to their rescue.

Maharaj had dispatched an army of sixteen thousand for Bhupalgad's aid, but they did not reach there in time. As they saw the Mughal flag fluttering on the fort they went back. Diler Khan destroyed all the important posts on the fort from where an attack could be launched.

The Monsoon was about to begin. After setting up the administration of the fort, Diler and Sambhajiraje began their journey towards Bahadurgad. Sambhajiraje was perturbed that Khan had ordered the cutting of hands of the common Marathi people. He could not sit quietly. Sitting in the howdah on the back of the elephant he said to Khan, "It was a bad decision to order the cutting of the hands of the common people."

Khan dismissed his concern and said, "Be thankful Raje, that I did not order their killing. Do you know how many soldiers we have lost just to capture this single fort?"

Sambhajiraje couldn't argue after that, but something kept pinching at his heart. They reached Bahadurgad. After making sure that his soldiers were taken care of, Sambhajiraje came to visit Ranooakka and Durgabai. They both were talking about something. As soon as they saw Sambhajiraje, they stopped talking instantly.

Sambhajiraje touched Ranooakka's feet. Ranooakka didn't speak anything at all. She turned her back and said in a tremulous voice, "You have conquered the fort. I don't know how to welcome you now!"

Durgabai stood looking at the floor, crumpling the edge of her sari, expressing her disapproval of his actions.

Sambhajiraje was stunned. His face went dark with guilt, and he dropped his head, "Akkasaheb, listen to me please..."

"What more should I listen to? What will Aaba feel after he comes to know that you captured the fort of Swaraj? Is that why you chose this path?

You put me on the spot on the Mahuli fort and you did the same to Firangoji on Bhupalgad! It must be quite difficult for Yesubai in Shringarpur to deal with such news. What about Aabasaheb on Raigad? I loved you with all my heart. It doesn't mean you are free to behave in any way you want! Bal Maharaj, I cannot put up with such actions!"

"I have made a big mistake." Sambhajiraje couldn't stand in the room; he left immediately.

The skies were overcast; it started pouring. In the pouring rain, Diler Khan was planning a big mission. Meanwhile, he received a firman from Shah Alam from Aurangabad. Diler summoned a conference of his allies. In the court hall of Bahadurgad, Diler's conference took place in the presence of

Sarja Khan, Sambhajiraje, Ikhalas Khan, Khairat Khan and Iraj Khan.

"I have received a message from the Shahajada from Aurangabad." Diler broached the subject.

"He has ordered us to capture Fort Panhala, in this pouring rain!" Khan stopped to gauge the reactions of others. Sarja Khan and Sambhajiraje glanced at each other.

"This is insane, Salar. The Mahrattas have blocked our food supply." Sarja Khan voiced his candid opinion. He wanted a campaign to attack Bijapur, to get even with Siddi Masood, the Wazir of Bijapur.

Sambhajiraje seconded him as it served his own purpose, "I cannot go against the Maratha kingdom anymore. I am even ready to renounce my mansab to that effect."

"But this is the royal order! How can we just disregard it?" Diler could not arque with two strong forces at the same time. He did not want to lose the once in a lifetime opportunity. "Salar, send a letter to Aurangabad with a message that Bijapur is on the decline at this moment. It would be better to attack it right now. We will leave for the mission before we receive any response from the Shahjada." Sarja Khan openly declared his agenda.

Diler Khan became alert; he realized that if he didn't accept the proposal, it might offend his allies. Therefore, he took the decision to attack Bijapur. The conference concluded.

Regardless of the pouring rains, Sambhajiraje, Diler and Sarja Khan's armies got ready to march.

Sambhajiraje came to bid farewell to Ranooakka, but she had decided not to stay back. She firmly told Sambhajiraje, "I have decided to accompany you wherever you go. You get carried away by your emotions and do things that cannot be undone later. Therefore, I am coming with you.

"As you wish." Sambhajiraje couldn't go against her wish.

Durgabai carried five-month-old Madan Singh in her arms and sat in the palanquin with Ranooakka. The armies of Diler,

Sambhajiraje and Sarja Khan marched together in the direction of Bijapur.

"Pandit, if veterans of your calibre have lost hope and given up, what should I do? I can't even believe the news that I am hearing. That is why I have summoned all of you. I have lost my sleep over this." Yesubai poured out the pain in her heart. Kavi Kulesh, Keshav Pandit, Umaji Pandit, Parashurampant, Rayaji, Antoji... all stood in front of Yesubai, their heads bent, in the ladies' chamber of the Shirke residence in Shringarpur.

"Swari abandoned me and joined hands with the enemy. He took Ranooakka Saheb and Dhakalya bai with him too. He came to strike our kingdom and captured Bhupalgad. What more are we waiting for now? Dhakalya bai has delivered a boy. How long are we going to allow her life to be dragged in all this mess? More than Swari, my heart aches for them."

Yesubai's raging words fell upon everyone's ears like flaming embers. All the elders were at loss for words.

"We will put our lives on the line but will not come back without Dhani." Antoji tried consoling Yesubai.

"How are you going to do it Antoji?"

"No matter what, we will sneak into Khan's camp." Rayaji said firmly.

"Then I will lose both of you too!" Yesubai sighed deeply.

"Yuvaradnyi, Maharaj has tried everything possible to convince Yuvaraj and bring him back, but hasn't succeeded yet. I will write a letter on your behalf. Please seal it with your signature. Maybe, by Bhaveshwari's grace he will change his mind!" Parashurampant voiced his opinion.

"If he won't change his mind, I will have to change mine. I will mount a horse and go in search of Swari. Please write this clearly in the letter." Yesubai expressed her concern openly and raised her hand to conclude the meeting.

At Raigad, the Chhatrapati had also called for a secret meeting. Utter silence prevailed in the room. Maharaj sat reclining against a bolster. He looked concerned. Hambirarao, Moropant, Annaji, Anandrao and Pralhadpant stood around him.

"Diler is marching towards Bijapur, Hambirarao. It's his long-harboured wish to vanquish Bijapur. We must stop him from doing that." Maharaj stopped. He wanted to say, 'Diler wanted to destroy me earlier, but that did not materialize. Now he has avenged it by separating Yuvraj from me.' But he determinedly refrained from saying so.

"Ji. We need to teach him a good lesson. He has taken our Yuvraj under his wing." Hambirarao indirectly expressed his concern for Sambhajiraje.

"He is not at fault, Sarlashkar. Had I been in his place, I would have done the same. A true statesman finds an opening in the smallest opportunity and takes advantage of it."

"But we have to somehow close this opening." Hambirarao did not give up his point.

"It won't work, Hambirarao. I have tried everything possible in case of Yuvraj, but to no avail. My consolation will not open Yuvraj's eyes. His eyes will open only after Khan betrays him. I am not worried about Yuvraj, but I am more concerned about something else."

"What do you mean Maharaj? I don't understand."

"Hambirarao, Yuvraj will be safe as long as he is under the wings of Diler. But if Aurangzeb summons him for any reason, it will be risky for him. What happened to Netaji? In fact, remember what was going to happen to me?" The Chhatrapati was feeling quite anxious.

The Chhatrapati pushed aside the dilemma in his mind, and firmly said, "Moropant, you march towards Bijapur with twelve thousand cavalry. Remain in the Mughal territory near the Varanda ghat and keep them in check. Pralhadpant, dispatch a message to Siddi Masood that it is my duty to protect the Adil

Shahi sultanate. The Chhatrapati offered betel leaves to all and concluded the meeting. Hambirarao stepped forward and knocked on the boulder with the hilt of his sword. The boulder was pushed aside, and all attendees came out. But Hambirarao lingered behind. He was worried about Maharaj and said to him, "Maharaj, can I say something?"

"Yes, go ahead."

"You seem to be in low spirits. You should take rest in the fort. We will take care of Diler."

"Rest! Hambirarao, now I will get rest only on my deathbed!" Hambirarao felt as if someone was pouring molten lead into his ears.

Annaji left from the meeting and went towards the queens' palaces. He presented himself in Soyarabai's palace and reported to her, "For the sake of Yuvraj, Swami is going in person on the mission to save the Adil Shahi sultanate!"

Hearing that, Soyarabai bitterly exclaimed, "Looks like a father's love for his son is taking precedence over everything else. Even if he converts to Islam, he will be brought here at the fort and reconverted just like Palkar!"

Annaji was startled to hear such a thing. He shared another piece of news with the Maharani to divert the subject, "Yuvraj…Yuvraj has been blessed with the birth of a son in the Mughal camp. The baby has been named 'Madan Singh".

The so-called big-hearted Maharani tugged the edge of her sari and exclaimed haughtily, "Annaji, you must have heard it wrong. It must be 'Madan Khan'!"

Sambhajiraje's army moved from Dhoolkhed with Diler's army. It conquered the Mangalvedhe city and marched towards Bijapur. It camped at the town of Halsangi. At the same time, under Moroapant's leadership twelve thousand Mavala soldiers arrived in the Adil Shahi territory. The Maratha army geared up to assist Bijapur. Soon, with an army of sixteen thousand soldiers, Shivajiraje arrived in the Adil Shahi region with Hambirarao and Anandrao.

The negotiations that Siddi Masood had held out of fear with Diler failed. Diler and Sarja Khan who were hell bent on overthrowing Bijapur, left from Halsangi and camped at Bahamanhalli. Sambhajiraje who was left behind, was given the task of transporting food grains to the army.

The Chhatrapati Maharaj had travelled rapidly and encamped at the town of Shivapur near Bijapur. The Chhatrapati dispatched his vakil to Masood with the message, 'Let me enter the Bijapur fort with my army.' Masood's advisers warned him, "The Mahrattas will seize the fort before the Pathan arrives here!" Masood sent his reply to Shivajiraje, 'You can come to Bijapur with four-five hundred soldiers!"

Maharaj did away with the pretence of aiding Masood and commanded Moropant, "Attack the Adil Shahi region and seize as much territory as you can."

Maharaj divided his army in two troops. He infiltrated the Mughal territory with Hambirarao and Anandrao via Dharangao, Jalna. Moropant's troops plundered the Adil Shahi territory.

Sambhajiraje, his family and the army, left Halsangi to deliver the food grains and fodder to Diler Khan. On the way, unexpectedly, his army clashed with the Adil Shahi sardar, Sabaji Ghatage. Sabaji attacked Sambhajiraje's army to seize the food and fodder that was being delivered to Diler. An altercation took place. Sabaji Ghatage and Sambhajiraje, both were Maratha sardars, but were fighting against each other on behalf of the Adil Shahi and Mughal sultanates. Sabaji got wounded in the battle and retreated immediately. Sambhajiraje reached Bahamanhalli with the convoy of food and fodder.

Diler was waiting for the rains to stop. His forces were congregating from all sides. He was dreaming of vanquishing Bijapur with the aid of Sarja Khan and Sambhajiraje. Many skirmishes kept taking place between the Adli Shahi and Maratha sardars. Meanwhile Diler received the first news from the Mughal territory that destroyed away his plans – "Dharangao has been ransacked!"

Monsoon was over and winter had arrived. In the camp at Bahamanhalli, Sambhajiraje, wrapped in a shawl, sat on a bed in the ladies shamiana. He kept staring at a burning lamp. The entire camp was engulfed by the darkness of the night. The calls of the night sentries patrolling at a distance could be heard occasionally. Ranooakka's tent was right next to Sambhajiraje's tent. She was fast asleep there with Madan Singh. Sambhajiraje got lost in memories of Yesubai's. He kept seeing many of her miens in the burning flame of the lamp.

Diler's Pathan army was marching towards Bijapur breaking through the clouds of mist. At the front line, Diler, Sambhajiraje and Sarja Khan were sitting in a howdah on an elephant.

The Mughal army had set up camp a few miles away from Bijapur. The Maratha army was already plundering the Bijapur territory. Complete mayhem had broken out in Bijapur.

Cold-blooded Diler Khan was deliberating the mode of attack on Bijapur. He had been receiving frequent letters from Shah Alam from Aurangabad, "Seva has infiltrated the Mughal region. You should immediately strike back with your army and save us from disgrace."

Diler was very close to achieving his objective of overthrowing Bijapur. He did not want to lose this opportunity and hence disregarded all the messages.

He sent an ultimatum to Masood, the Wazir of Bijapur. The Mughal army awaited at the outskirts of Bijapur in anticipation of Masood's response. They were all set to attack Bijapur any time.

Diler was feeling exultant. By conquering Bijapur, he was going to prove to Aurangzeb that only he deserved to be the subedar of Deccan. The Shahjada should be appointed in the north.

But Shivajiraje destroyed all his sweet dreams! Raje ransacked Jalna, a prominent Mughal marketplace close to Aurangabad, in broad daylight. Jalna was vanquished! Shah Alam dispatched a message to the Delhi durbar and blamed it all on Diler.

Diler received a castigating letter from Delhi! It read – "Stop the infidel! Withdraw your troops!"

Diler crumpled the letter in frustration and exclaimed, "Oh, the devil Seva and the Shahjada have spoiled all my plans!"

Diler ordered his army – "Dismantle all the tents and shamianas and march to Miraj. Let's destroy the Adil Shahi region!

Town after town was getting ravaged by the army of Diler, Sambhajiraje and Sarja Khan. In each town, Diler and Sarja Khan tied the defenceless Hindus with ropes and humiliated them by parading them on the streets. Sambhajiraje felt suffocated by the cruelty. He felt trapped and was angry with himself. Akkasaheb, who was travelling with the entourage of the Pathan ladies, was burning in anger to see the destruction. There was no one with whom she could share her anger and frustration. Therefore, she had to restrain her anger.

The army arrived in the Tikota village. Diler's savage soldiers plundered every house. The entire village was burning in broad daylight. It had not happened before but this time Sarja Khan's soldiers crossed all limits. They molested defenceless Hindu women who had lost their homes. The Pathan and the Mughal soldiers were chasing the women on the streets like lascivious predators, calling them 'sluts' and 'whores'. About three hundred women defenceless women ran everywhere in fear, screamed for help, and jumped into wells to save their honour.

Diler and Sarja were intoxicated by the looting and plundering. They immediately left Tikota and went to Athani. Sambhajiraje was travelling to Athani with his army. His heart was burning with rage. He was prodding his horse harder than usual, and the horse kept dashing forward groaning in pain.

Sambhajiraje arrived at Athani. It was burning! Sambhajiraje raised his hand and signalled to his army to stop. The fire burning in Athani reflected in his eyes and they started breathing fire. It set aflame his entire body, and his blood boiled. Withou turning around he called out all his troop leaders and made them stand in front of him. He threw a fiery glance at each one of them and lashed at them, "You had better make sure that no one dares to enter the village, or else you will lose your life. Everyone stops right here!"

Sambhajiraje selected a few skilled swordsmen and commanded them, "Follow me!" He dashed forward and entered Athani. The fierce Bhosale dashed through the burning streets of Athani. He seemed driven by passion.

Diler, Sarja and Ikhalas had ravaged the entire village and were waiting under a sprawling tree, astride their horses. Some Pathan soldiers were sorting out the booty in front of them. Enraged, Sambhajiraje directly approached Diler. He pulled the reins of his baffled, panting horse and dismounted.

"Welcome Raje…" The Pathan dismounted with a smile on his face.

"Khan, what is going on?" Everyone felt the change of tone in Sambhajiraje's indignant voice. Sarja and Ikhalas also dismounted.

"What are you talking about?" Diler raised his eyebrows and growled.

"Why are your soldiers killing my innocent people and molesting women in front of me?"

"Whose people? Yours?" The Pathan threw his head back and laughed haughtily.

"Pathan…! I demand an explanation." Sambhajiraje's wrathful words froze Diler's arrogant laughter.

"You want an explanation? I don't give explanations to anyone; I demand explanations from others! You better stay within your limits!" The Pathan raised his head like a serpent's hood.

"Limits? What limits? If the Pathan women are molested like this…"

"Raje…you better watch your tongue! These are not the women of the infidels. We Pathans put our lives on the line for our women! You are merely a mansabdar, I am the commander of the army! Remember that your family is with our women! So be careful."

"You…!" Sambhajiraje was shaking in anger. He pulled out his sword and ran towards Diler. Diler had struck a tender nerve.

"Be careful. Get hold of yourself!" Sarja Khan exclaimed and moving forward quickly he deftly clasped Sambhajiraje's arm. Meanwhile, Ikhalas, Khairat and Iraj had pulled out their swords too. Diler signalled to them to lower their swords.

In utterly cold words, Diler said to Sambhajiraje, "I have heard that your father showed temerity in the royal durbar of Agra in front of the emperor! Indeed, you are his true son!"

As Sambhajiraje heard Aabasaheb's name from Diler's mouth, he felt as if he had been struck by lightning! His heart broke; his eyes reflected a jumble of emotions like humiliation, anger, guilt, despair and regret, about his own actions. He could not face the Pathans. He turned around and leapt on his horse like a cheetah. The horse reared and dashed forward.

Ikhalas, Khairat, and Iraj mounted their horses quickly to follow him. Diler stopped them and said indifferently, "He is a young man, and he loses his temper quite easily, but he will calm down."

In the evening, Diler and Sarja's forces marched towards Ainapur. Sambhajiraje camped at the foothills of the mountain near Athani. The menials had erected a tent for Sambhajiraje. He was pacing anxiously in the tent. Desolate Athani was enwrapped in darkness.

Many thoughts crowded Sambhajiraje's mind and lashed mercilessly at his heart,

'You are a mere mansabdar! Whose people? Yours? These

are not the women of the infidels…! Diler… Diler…who on earth is he and where has he come from? The hundreds of hands that were severed in the camp of Manjara! The swollen dead bodies of hundreds of women floating in the wells of Tikota! The huts and houses burning in the fire!… Defenceless cries for help coming from all directions!…

A benumbed Sambhajiraje slumped on the bed squeezing his head tightly. His royal heart was trapped and writhing in pain.

"Yuvraj…" a tremulous voice called his name from the entrance of the tent.

Sambhajiraje raised his head. His brother-in-law Mahadaji Nimbalkar stood at the entrance.

"Please go away and leave me alone. Don't rub salt into my wounds." Sambhajiraje pleaded earnestly.

Mahadaji whispered, "I cannot leave you alone in this situation. I haven't come here to rub salt into your wounds, but to remind you of the value of salt."

"What do you mean?"

Mahadaji came close to Sambhajiraje and whispered in an even lower voice, "Yuvraj, you have been betrayed! The Pathan has received orders from the Delhi durbar. You will be shackled and dispatched to Delhi! The Pathan can arrest you at any moment on the grounds of the dispute you had. So, get hold of yourself and take quick and cautious action immediately. Leave this camp tonight and go anywhere else. Be careful. Let me take your leave now." Mahadaji was about to leave, when Sambhajiraje called out to him in a whisper, "Dajisaheb! I insulted you. I am sorry for that."

"Don't worry about that and take care of yourself." Mahadaji vanished in the darkness outside.

Now, Sambhajiraje's mind was occupied in thinking about the escape. He remembered Aabasaheb's vigilant insight in the prison of Agra. He kept pacing to the entrance of the tent and checking if Akkasaheb and Durgabai's palanquin had reached the camp or not. His dinner plate was just sitting on the wooden stool; he had not touched the food at all. Suddenly, he thought of something and beckoned the Pathan guard standing at the entrance. He instructed the guard, "Let your men take some rest. I will appoint another group of guards to replace them."

"Ji." The guard removed his men keeping watch in the cold weather and told them to take a break.

Sambhajiraje selected a few men who had come with him from Sajjangad and instructed them to guard his tent. Weary of the cold weather, the Pathan soldiers ignited small fires and sat around them in groups, warming themselves.

A couple of hours passed. The panting palanquin-bearers brought the palanquins of Akkasaheb and Durgabai in front of Sambhajiraje's tent. Akkasaheb and Durgabai, holding six-month-old Madan Singh in her arms stepped out of their palanquins.

The Mavala guards made an obeisance to Akkasaheb, but she didn't pay much attention to that and rushed inside.

Wrapped in a shawl, Sambhajiraje sat on the bed wide awake.

An intimidating voice echoed in the tent like the echo of the thunder, "Bal Maharaj, I am utterly ashamed of your actions!"

"Akkasaheb?"

"Yes. I have come here to give you a final warning. I have seen with my own eyes, the so-called valour that your army exhibited in the Tikota village. I cannot support such actions of yours anymore!" Despite the cold weather, Akkasaheb was trembling with rage.

Sambhajiraje approached her and hanging his head, low he said, "All that was Sarja Khan's doing Akka...I am completely trapped. I have been betrayed. I have only one night at my disposal."

Instantly, Akkasaheb's rage turned into concern.

"I don't understand what you are saying."

"Any moment now, Diler can arrest me and send me to Delhi. He has received official orders from the emperor."

"Bal Maharaj…" Akksaheb couldn't even scream due to fear.

"Calm down! I am not worried if I get punished for my actions, but I am worried about the three of you. You must leave this camp safely, before daybreak." Akkasaheb was stunned. She looked at Durgabai holding the baby in her arms and exclaimed anxiously, "Bal Maharaj, what crisis have you pushed us into?"

"You have just arrived after a long journey. Take some rest. I am here." Sambhajiraje composed himself and consoled her. Grave silence enveloped the three of them.

Akkasaheb and Durgabai sat on the bed. Durgabai put sleeping Madan on the bed. The three of them were lost in thought. They didn't know what to do. Every passing moment was taking them closer to doom. They kept gazing at each other helplessly. At midnight, a guard came into the tent and said, "Dhani, an informer has come from our kingdom. Should I send him in?"

"Yes, go ahead."

One of Arjoji Yadav's informers of presented himself in front of Sambhajiraje. He made an obeisance and handed two letters to Sambhajiraje. One was from the Chhatrapati Shivaji Maharaj and the other from his daughter-in-law Yesubai Saheb!

The Chhatrapati had said in his letter – "Whether it is the Mughal empire, Adil Shahi or Qutub Shahi sultanate, you won't be able to fulfil your wishes in their service. Leave as soon as you receive this letter and come back home. You will be suitably honoured! Have no doubt about it."

Yesubai's letter said, "Whatever I have heard so far, is very difficult to take in. You should come back now. If you don't, I will have to come to you! If not about yourself, please think about the ladies who are with you."

"Who has sent the letters?" Akkasaheb whispered.

Sambhajiraje wiped his eyes with the edge of his shawl and handed the letters to her, "From Aabasaheb and Yuvardnyi Yesubai, requesting me to come back."

As he saw the tears in Sambhajiraje's eyes, the informer felt hopeful and he spoke courageously, "Dhani, we are mere servants, but I earnestly request you to listen to Maharaj. Our troops are waiting at the village borders. If you are ready to leave then..."

"That's what I am going to do. You go back to the troops and give my message. Wait for me and my family till daybreak. Go back carefully."

"Ji, as you wish." The informer was pleased to hear his words. He left quickly.

As the night progressed Sambhajiraje instructed the guard at the entrance of his tent, "Keep the Mavala troops ready. We are going to leave soon."

Sambhajiraje took of his shawl and the Mughal khilat and tossed it in a corner. He wore a simple attire.

He pointed to the inner section of his tent and said, "Akkasaheb, grab some men's attire from the box and get dressed in it. It would be difficult to escape in women's attire."

Akkasaheb and Durgabai got dressed in men's attire.

Sambhajiraje glanced out of the tent to gauge the situation. About three hundred Mavala soldiers had gathered outside. A few skilled swordsmen were chosen from the troops. He instructed them, "Follow me when I leave from here. All others should stay behind and leave the camp when they are ordered to do so.

It was almost morning now. A chill breeze was blowing. The Pathan soldiers were fast asleep in their tents.

Sambhajiraje touched the cowrie necklace on his chest and muttered, "Jagadamb!"

"Let's go! Three people dressed in men's attire left the tent. One of them carried a bundle close to his chest. The troop of select soldiers picked up the palanquin. Sambhajiraje walked briskly; two men followed him and left the camp. They reached the temple at the village borders.

The leader of Arjoji Yadav's troops came forward promptly. He made an obeisance and asked, "Should we leave?"

"Wait." Sambhajiraje signalled the palanquin-bearers to come forward.

"Akkasaheb, please sit in the palanquin." The curtain of the palanquin was pulled aside.

Akkasaheb and Durgabai, dressed in men's attire, came forward. Sambhajiraje leaned forward and touched Akkasaheb's feet. "Bal Maharaj!" Ranooakka pulled him up and embraced him warmly. "Be careful and come safely." Akkas's voice was heavy. Sambhajiraje kissed the cheeks of sleeping Madan and said to Durgabai, "Take care."

Both the royal ladies dressed in men's attire sat in the palanquin. The palanquin-bearers picked up the palanquin and armed guards surrounded the palanquin quickly. The retinue started travelling in the direction of Panhala.

Sambhajiraje kept watching the palanquin in the early morning haze till it disappeared. Then he sent a message to the soldiers waiting at the camp. The Mavalas quickly dispersed and vanished from the camp.

With the troop of three hundred Mavalas, galloping in the cold weather of the wee hours, Sambhajiraje started his journey in the direction of Bijapur!

He had no courage to face Chhatrapati Shivaji Maharaj directly! Therefore, he was going to appeal to Siddi Masood to be the mediator to return to Swaraj.

As Bijapur came in sight, Sambhajiraje signalled his troops to stop at the borders. They had been travelling continuously for two days and two nights.

Sambhajiraje selected a loyal informer from the troops. Yuvraj took off his royal ring and putting it in the informer's hands, he said, "Show this to the guards at the entrance. Meet Wazir Masood Khan and give him my message, "I have come in person to meet him. I request a private visit with him."

"Ji." The informer clasped the ring in his palm and entered Bijapur on his horse.

The informer returned from Bijapur. The Wazir, Masood Khan had sent a few armed soldiers and a message with him, "Come immediately!"

Sambhajiraje started moving towards the Bijapur fort with his retinue. The fort was well protected by ramparts built in stone. On every bastion wall, armed soldiers stood guard wielding bare swords in their hands.

News of Sambhajiraje's arrival was sent to Siddi Masood. He came with his advisors to receive Yuvraj. As Masood saw Sambhajiraje's round, radiant visage with a dark beard, he tried to guess what Shivajiraje looked like.

"Welcome Shahjada," Masood said and embraced Sambhajiraje. He held Sambhajiraje's hand and ushered him to the seat in the seating chamber courteously.

"Wazir, there is a discord between the Pathan and me. I have left the Mughal sultanate." Sambhajiraje broached the subject directly.

"I have heard about it. That is why, I brought you to the fort as quickly as possible. I would like to give you some advice. Could you please lend an ear?"

"Absolutely." Sambhajiraje looked at Masood wondering what he was going to say.

"You should go back to your father as soon as possible. I have received news that Diler Khan's envoy Abdul Razzak is coming to Bijapur with an army, to capture you."

Shivajiraje had recently plundered Siddi Masood's kingdom. Sambhajiraje himself had also ransacked his territory with Diler and Sarja Khan. But the same Siddi Masood was giving him prudent advice now.

By giving political asylum to Sambhajiraje, he did not want to provoke two powerful enemies such as Diler and Shivajiraje and give them an opportunity to charge upon Bijapur. He also did not want to incite their anger by capturing Sambhajiraje treacherously. He probably thought that Sambhajiraje was like a 'golden dagger', handsome to look at but so sharp that one could not dare to touch it.

After hearing Masood's advice, Sambhajiraje was lost in thought. If he wasted time he would have to fight with Abdul Razzak. All his ways were blocked. He did not have enough time to mediate with Maharaj through Siddi Masood. He didn't know what to do. Finally, he took a firm decision, got up from his seat and said, "Wazir, I agree with you. I will take your leave now."

A flicker of satisfaction flashed on Masood's face. He held Sambhajiraje's hand and said, "Shahjade, this is the royal palace. You will be suitably honoured." Masood clapped and summoned his personal secretary.

The personal secretary arrived. Masood whispered something in his ear. He exclaimed, "Ji" and left the chamber.

Within a short time, some menials entered the chamber with gift platters. Masood looked at them and said, "This is a gift for the son of Raja Sivaji. My soldiers will also be at your disposal."

Sambhajiraje gave the customary touch of his hand to accept the gift platters, but he was speechless as he realized that he had nothing to give as a return gift to the Wazir. He was no more a Mughal mansabdar. Sambhajiraje bade farewell to Siddi Masood and left the fort. He began his travel towards Panhalgad with an entourage of one thousand soldiers.

Yuvraj Sambhajiraje's heart was dragged with the rattling hooves of the horses. It had not been easy to desert Swaraj, but it was harder to return.

'How will Aabasaheb punish me now? Will I be tied to a

horse's leg and get dragged with it? Will I be shackled and confined to a prison for my lifetime? Or will he order to slice off my hands and feet? Will he order my execution by pushing me from the Takamak point? Will I be tied to the muzzle of a cannon and fired to bits and pieces? Or will I be trampled under the feet of the royal elephant?

'Whatever punishment he gives, I will accept it as the prasad. Only that punishment will purify my body which has been defiled by the Mughal khilat. I wish only one thing. Maharaj Saheb should come in front of me, even if it is for punishing me severely. For three years, I have not seen him in person; now I am dying to see him in person.

'This is the only reason I am going to Panhala. Nothing else matters to me now. I have ruined my reputation by my own dreadful actions. My arrogance has led my life astray. I have tormented Maharaj Saheb so much despite being his son. Even Netajirao, Prataprao did not hurt him so much. I don't have any right to seek immunity. In fact, I don't even consider that as an option.

'But… but would Maharaj Saheb even consider meeting me in person? Would he care to see my face? Or…or as usual will my fate seal my chances?

'No! I am nobody's mansabdar, no Yuvraj. I am just a human being, a member of the Bhosale family. Even with my head hanging and my lips sealed, I have the right to meet my father. If Maharaj Saheb doesn't meet me, I will die of a broken heart.'

They arrived at the foothills of Panhalgad surrounded by dense woods. Sambhajiraje signalled his entourage to stop and dispatched a soldier to the fort with the intimation of his arrival.

The entire fort was excited. Vitthal Trimbak Mahadkar, the custodian of the fort went to the Chou Darwaja with Hawaladar Bahirji Ingale, Hiroji Farzand, Krishnaji and Somaji Banki.

Vitthalpant sent a message to Sambhajiraje, "Please feel free to climb the fort with your entourage."

Sambhajiraje started climbing the fort with his entourage. They arrived at the stone-built Chou Darwaja.

Vitthalpant came forward. He hesitated for a moment, wondering whether to pay obeisance or not. Then he made up his mind, bowed down and made an obeisance to Sambhajiraje saying, "Welcome Yuvraj". Then all the people came to their senses and made an obeisance to him. But Hiroji Farzand stood still. Sambhajiraje followed Vitthalpant to the Balekilla.

They came to the seating chamber in the Balekilla. Sambhajiraje took of his mojaris outside and entered the chamber. He told Vitthalpant in a calm voice, "Pant, please send a letter to Raigad with the message that I have arrived at Panhala with my family."

As Vitthalpant heard his words, he bent his head and was quiet. Sambhajiraje noticed the silence and said, "Have you heard what I said? Send the letter immediately."

"Ji, but…" Vitthalpant said in a dejected voice.

"But what?"

"How can I say it Yuvraj, I can't dare say it out loud. I am a mere servant of the Chhatrapati. It breaks my heart to deliver any bad news about the royal family."

"What are you talking about? Pant, tell me clearly what it is."

"Yuvraj, your…your family…has been captured by the Pathan soldiers of Diler Khan! Akkasaheb and Durgabai Rani Saheb have been caught! The worst thing that was not supposed to happen, has happened."

"Pant…!" Stars flashed in front of Sambhajiraje's eyes in broad daylight. The entire Panhalgad whirled around him like lamps whirling in river water, and from the waves words emerged and echoed in his ears, "Bal Maharaj, what have you done?"

"Leave me alone." Sambhajiraje exclaimed and turned his back to Vitthalpant. As soon as Pant left the chamber, Sambhajiraje's legs gave way, and he collapsed on the bed. Pathan

Diler Khan stood before his closed eyes. He was laughing loudly with his head thrown back and he was lashing out at the Mughal mansabdar, Sambhajiraje, "Beware, your family is living in the camp with our ladies!"

In frustration, Sambhajiraje bit his lip and muttered helplessly, "Alas! Aabasaheb, the Pathan has punished me for my deeds before you could!"

In the family shrine at Raigad, the Chhatrapati Shivaji Maharaj devoutly offered bael leaves to the crystal Shivlinga. He offered a pinch of haldi at the feet of Goddess Bhavani, joined his hands in prayer and closed his eyes saying, 'Jagadamb!' It was a fortnight since Sambhajiraje had returned to Panhalgad. The Chhatrapati was going to leave Raigad today, to meet him.

Many miens of Yuvraj flashed in front of his closed eyes. The time when he lived in the Rajput encampment as a hostage. When he was left alone in Mathura, he had said to Maharaj, "I will behave like your son." He had fearlessly declared in the durbar, "I have taken the lady as a prisoner within my rights as Yuvraj, Sambhajiraje Bhosale." He wailed his heart out near the lifeless body of Aausaheb. He has changed completely now. Why, and for what?

The anxious Chhatrapti came out of the shrine and came to the seating chamber of his palace. A palace maid entered the chamber and announced, "Ranisarkar is coming." The Chhatrapati frowned to hear the announcement. It was almost time for him to descend the fort.

"I came to know that you are going to Panhala. I couldn't help myself and came here to meet you." Soyarabai entered the chamber and said with a fake but beautiful smile.

"Hmmm."

"I came here to tell you to be patient on Panhala!" Soyarabai stopped deliberately.

Maharaj threw a startled glance at her.

Soyarabai didn't keep him in suspense and exclaimed, "You

are such a conscientious man. I am afraid something untoward might happen. When the Patil of Ranze behaved inappropriately, you punished him by cutting his hands and feet! When Khandoji Khopade betrayed you, you got his hands and feet cut too! You were going to tie Firangoji to a cannon and fire him to his death when he abandoned Bhupalgad. Then, this is the biggest offence, of forsaking Swaraj and joining hands with the enemy. That too, despite being a Yuvraj! I am afraid that you won't forgive such an offence and will punish him severely! That is why, I came here to tell you to be patient!"

Every single word of Soyarabai was drenched in utter sarcasm. She was implying, 'You have given severe punishment to people who had committed lesser offences, now I would like to see what punishment you are going to give for this grave offence'. Maharaj immediately realized what she was implying. He stared at her keenly and said in a calm voice, "Had it been Ramraje in place of Yuvraj, you wouldn't have let me descend the fort today! Rani Saheb, I never seek the advice of the ladies in the family in case of judicial decisions. I will punish Yuvraj as I deem appropriate. You can leave now." Maharaj dismissed Soyarabai.

The Chhatrapti descended Raigad with select men such as Hambirarao, Suryaji Malusare and Jotyaji Kesarkar.

Putalabai Saheb had been living in the palace of Pachad since Jijau's demise. Maharaj came to meet her.

"I am leaving for Panhala." Maharaj said to Putalabai calmly.

"Ji. I have been eagerly waiting to meet you for the same reason."

Maharaj felt the concern in Putalabai's eyes. Suddenly, Putalabai moved forward, touched his feet and said in a heavy voice, "I have never asked you for anything, but today I ask for only one thing. Though he has made a mistake, he is our child. You should forgive Yuvraj and reassure him."

"Arise." He urged Putalabai.

“I have been giving something or other to everyone around me… and I will keep doing it. But…but I can’t give you anything.” Putalabai’s motherly love, despite being childless, had touched the Chhatrapati’s heart. He bade farewell to her and left the palace.

The kettle drums resounded, and the horns resonated at the Chou Darwaja on Panhala announcing the arrival of the Chhatrapati. The custodian of the fort, Vitthalpant came forward to receive the Chhatrapati. Maharaj threw a quick glance at the people around him to see if Yuvraj was present. He was not there.

“Pant, Yuvraj?”

“He is in the Sajjakothi.” Vitthalpant replied.

“Okay, let’s go.” Maharaj sighed in contentment and started walking towards the Balekilla with Hambirarao, Hiroji Farzand, Somaji Banki and Jotyaji Kesarkar.

After visiting the Someshwar temple near the lake, they arrived at the Balekilla. Maharaj took the darshan of the colour-changing Shivlinga with Vitthapant and came to his palace.

The custodian of the fort presented the report of the fort to the Chhatrapati sitting in the court hall.

After sorting out the official matters, Maharaj broached the main subject of his visit, “Pant, send intimation to Yuvraj. I am going to Sajjakothi to visit him.” Maharaj had realized that Sambhajiraje was not going to face him out of guilt.

“Ji.” Vitthalpant said and made arrangements to send the intimation to Sambhajiraje.

“Hambirarao is nowhere to be seen. Where is he?” The Chhatrapati glanced at the people assembled in the court hall and asked.

“Sarlashkar has gone to Sajjakothi.” Pant replied.

Even in that condition, Maharaj thought, ‘Hambirarao is Maharani’s brother. She envies Yuvraj excessively, but Hambirarao tries to comfort Yuvraj.’

"Let's go." Said the Chhatrapati and left the court hall. He started walking to Sajjakothi. He came to the Sajjakothi adjacent to the ramparts of the fort. Hambirarao saw Maharaj coming and promptly left Sajjakothi. He approached Maharaj and made an obeisance to him.

"Hambirarao, your wish is coming true today. I am going to meet Yuvraj."

"Ji. It does not befit me to speak in front of you, but I feel we should use his comeback to our advantage. He repents his actions. His life is in your hands now."

Maharaj gave him a faint smile. He wanted to tell Hambirarao, "Even my own life is not in my hands, then who am I to take control of his life?" but he didn't say anything. The Chhatrapati signalled Vitthalpant to stop at the bottom of Sajjakothi and went in alone.

Maharaj reached the open seating chamber. Sambhajiraje stood near a window, lost in gazing at the plains below. The moment Maharaj saw him he stopped in his tracks. His heart was in turmoil. The father and son were meeting after three long years.

For the first time ever, the Chhatrapati intensely felt that he was not a crowned king but just a defeated father!

Sambhajiraje was lost in thought. He sighed deeply and turned around. He saw Maharaj Saheb standing at the door of the chamber. His heartbeat intensified. 'Is this Aabasaheb? He...he looks so worn out!' His heart was overwhelmed, and his eyes welled up. He quickly approached Maharaj and placed his head on Maharaj's feet.

Maharaj closed his eyes with that touch. He controlled himself and without pulling him up as usual he said in a dry tone, "Arise."

Maharaj entered the chamber. For quite some time he kept pacing in the room, his hands hold at his back. The Chhatrapati who used to speak directly could not figure out today what to say and how to say it. There was a turmoil of countless thoughts and memories in his heart. For some time, he even forgot that Sambhajiraje was in the chamber.

Sambhajiraje stood near the stone wall with his head bent. He could not bear Aabasaheb's agitation.

The Chhatrapati stopped walking. His words echoed in the chamber like the peals of a bell, "Did you succeed in conquering the Sahyadri and raising your own kingdom? Did everything happen as per your wish after you joined the Mughals?

"Despite being the Yuvraj of Swaraj, the future Chhatrapati, you joined the Pathan! You brazenly watched the Mughal soldiers cut the hands of our patriotic Mavalas on the plateau of Manjara! Three hundred helpless women jumped in the wells fearing the Pathans and you. The Pathan captured your own family. I am utterly ashamed of you! Despite being a Yuvraj and a warrior, you risked your reputation and lost it in the worst possible way; that too at such a young age! I had such grand dreams for you! You made a huge mistake in considering this kingdom as my sole property. This is the kingdom of God, raised for the welfare of the people. The Bhosales don't own it. You are, first the Yuvraj of the Swaraj, and only then my son.

"You felt no regret when you befriended the Mughals, notwithstanding your status as the Yuvraj of Swaraj. You did not feel ashamed to launch an armed attack on Bhupalgad, and when you spoke arrogantly to elderly Firangoji! Keep in mind that relationships are the first to break and physical death comes much later!" As the enraged Chhatrapati was giving an earful to the Yuvraj he had a bout of coughing. As Sambhajiraje watched him press his palm on his chest trying to comfort himself, he was heartbroken. He was so tongue-tied that he couldn't even utter a single word, and he couldn't tolerate Aabasaheb's agony.

"You deserted Swaraj to raise your own kingdom and when you came back you had lost your own family! You lost your sister Ranoobai, married in the Jadhav family, to the enemy!

What if someone questions me tomorrow that how is a king who can't even protect his own family, going to protect his people, then how am I going to answer them? The Rajput set our territory on fire and coerced me to surrender, but I eventually got out of that crisis. But the plight you have brought upon me by setting all my dreams on fire is impossible to come out of. Thankfully, you escaped from Diler's clutches and did not get sent to Delhi. Otherwise, seeing you in the same condition as Netaji would have left me with no option but to consume poison! Why aren't you speaking up now? Answer me. I am talking to you." Maharaj approached Sambhajiraje and stood in front of him. Sambhajiraje's head still hung low in intense heartache; tears rolled down his eyes and trickled over his beard onto the carpet below.

"You should worry that the Siddis who have a strong grip on Janjira are trying to conquer the Konkan coast, and we are unable to keep them under our thumb. The British are constantly confronting us and not letting us build the water fort on the Khanderi island. Understand that sometime in the near future, Aurangzeb is going to attack the Deccan with his mammoth army. He is going to leave no stone unturned to overthrow Adil Shahi, Qutub Shahi and Swaraj too. It is easy to desert me at once, but it is not that simple to face the challenges that time throws your way.

"You think too much about your own dignity and tend to forget that even the gods had to face humiliation sometimes and spend their time in forests. All you see is the royal throne and not the prickling thorns spread on it. You are good at finding fault in others' behaviour, but you never realise your own faults. You tend to forget that a king should not be too emotional." The Chhatrapati's voice was cracking. His fiery words were incinerating the misguided thoughts in Sambhajiraje's mind.

"You don't get along with the ministers like Annaji; you are at odds with the Maharani. Annaji is a veteran statesman of the kingdom, but you can't make amends with him. I transformed people like Murarbaji and Baji Prabhu who were in the enemy camp and convinced them to join my side. How are you going to do that?

"What if you have to face situations similar to my meeting with Afzal Khan or getting stranded in the prison of Agra, how are you going to deal with them?

"It is okay if you don't think about me, but at least think about the departed soul of Aausaheb, who nurtured you since your childhood. Of good think is that she is not alive today! Otherwise, after hearing the news that you, who used to sleep peacefully in her lap, deserted me and joined hands with the Pathan, she…"

"No Aabasaheb, please stop!" Heartbroken Sambhajiraje embraced Aabasaheb's legs instantly and started sobbing. Words of repentance spurted out of his mouth like pearls.

"I…I made a huge mistake. I don't want to hold the post of Yuvraj. All I want is to be with you. I surrender myself at your feet. I am utterly ashamed of myself. Please punish me whichever way you want, but I cannot bear your lashing words anymore. Aaba…Aaba!"

"Though he had gone astray, he is still our child. Please forgive and spare him." Putalabai's words echoed in Maharaj's mind.

"We should use the comeback of Yuvraj to our advantage. He repents his actions." Sarlashkar Hambirarao's words made an obeisance to him.

"Aabasaheb, could you extract the coconut from the Holi fire?" A young boy was raising his hands and asking him.

That young boy was scorching in the fire of repentance and the mistakes he had made. The Chhatrapati's royal pride dissolved. Absolute affection replaced the royal wrath. His tapering eyes welled up. He quickly leaned forward and pulled Sambhajiraje up. He gazed at his son's tear filled eyes and spoke a lot to him through his eyes. The next moment, hoarse words soaked in affection, slipped out of his lips – "Oh my dear son, where were you? How could you make such a mistake?"

Chhatrapati Shivaji Maharaj embraced Sambhajiraje tightly as if the eastern horizon was eagerly embracing the sun at daybreak.

Panhalgad was content to witness the divine union.

Chapter 10

Maharaj sat in the court hall of the Balekilla on Panhalgad. Sambhajiraje sat on a seat near his feet. VItthalpant, the custodian of the fort, Hambirarao, Hiroji Farzand, Sonaji and Krishnaji Banki, Bahirji Ingale, Babaji Dhamadhere and Suryaji Vichare stood courteously in the hall. Janardanpant Sumant from Kolhapur and Ravaji Pandit, the subedar of the Konkan suba stood nearby, wondering why the Chhatrapati had summoned them. Umaji Pandit stood near them.

"Janardanpant, please come in front of me." Maharaj instructed Janardanpant.

"Ji." Janardanpant joined his palms and came before Maharaj.

"Yuvaraj, he is the officer in charge of the Kolhapur region. You are going to stay here henceforth and oversee the Panhala region. Ravaji Pandit from Konkan subah will assist you." The Chhatrapati pointed to Ravaji.

"As you wish, Swami." Ravaji said and bowed down to him.

"Swami, I would like to share a problem that I am facing in my subah. May I have your permission?" Ravaji broached the topic of his subah.

"Yes, go ahead."

"A few ships of the Europeans have been docked in the Rajapur harbour. The sailors are neither getting off the ships nor sailing them. What should be done? Should we confiscate them?"

"Yuvraj, you should recommend the solution for this problem as it comes under your purview!" Maharaj encouraged Sambhajiraje with a smile.

Sambhajiraje thought for some time and asked Ravaji, "Whose ships are those? The Firangis, British, Dutch or French? Any idea?"

"Ji. Those belong to the French." Ravaji replied.

"Then we should send our sailors on those ships to check if they have come here for trading purposes, and if that is the case, then we should befriend them. They supply us with arms."

"Good solution." Maharaj smiled with satisfaction.

"Yuvraj, you should monitor the naval forces in the coastal region with the aid of Ravaji." The Chhatrapati looked satisfied.

"Sonaji Banki, Babaji, your guru, Umaji Pandit... all of them will stay with you at Panhalgad. You should safeguard the Panhala region until further notice from me. Keep in mind that Diler and Sarja Khan may strike this region any time."

Everyone listened to Maharaj attentively. They all felt that the Chhatrapati's voice was not as spirited as usual. His face looked dull and gaunt.

"Vitthalpant, please give everyone the betel leaf to conclude the meeting. Yuvraj, let's go and take the darshan of the Shivlinga." Maharaj arose from his seat.

Maharaj left the Balekilla with Sambhajiraje. As Vitthalpant, Hambirarao and Ravaji started walking behind them, Maharaj signalled them to stop.

Sambhajiraje had already figured out that Aabasaheb was going to say something personal to him, as he did not allow anyone to join them. But he couldn't guess what exactly he was going to talk about.

They came to the temple. The temple priest made an obeisance to them. Until they reached the temple, the Chhatrapati had not realized that the temple priest would be present there. He instantly planned how to dismiss him from there.

"Pujaribuva, please deliver my message to the custodian of the fort that I am coming to visit the temple near the Someshwar tank soon, and you wait for us at that temple."

"Ji." The priest exclaimed and quickly left for the Balekilla. The father and son took off their mojaris.

"Come in." The Chhatrapati instructed Sambhajiraje and entered the sanctum making sure that his Jiretop didn't touch the entrance of the sanctum. Sambhajiraje followed him. The colour-changing Shivlinga was covered in bael leaves and flowers. The stone lamps in the sanctum were burning gently and the water from the Abhishek vessel kept trickling onto the Shivlinga. The father and the son knelt in front of the Shivlinga, joined their palms and prayed.

"Shambhoo, this Shivlinga changes its colour; it tells us that human life is full of colours…colours of joys and sorrows." Maharaj gazed at the Shivlinga and paused for a moment. Listen carefully to what I say now, with the Shivlinga as my witness.

"I don't know how long I am going to live now. That is why, I am going to do something that I never imagined I would have to do. You and Rani Saheb will never get along. Earlier, you were angered by her behaviour and that affected your actions. If you do the same after my demise, no one will ever understand or support you. Therefore…therefore, I am going to divide the kingdom of Swaraj between the two of you!"

"Aabasaheb, I promise that I don't want anything. All I want is to be with you. Why are you talking like you are going to depart soon? I will never go against your word anymore. I will be with Ramraje like his shadow no matter what. Since seeing you in poor health my heart is grief-stricken. I can't think of anything else."

"Let's not talk about that. I don't have enough time to look after my own health. Even if you say you don't want any rights or privileges, I cannot avoid the responsibility of the administrative matters of the kingdom. You have been crowned the Yuvraj of Swaraj. In fact, you are the real successor of the entire kingdom, but Maharani won't let you have it so easily. And the ministers have lost faith in you due to your own actions. That is why I am going to delegate to you the kingdom of Jinji from River Tungabhardra to River Kaveri and Ramraje will rule the kingdom in the north from River Godavari to River Tungabhadra. The ministry will administer the kingdom till he comes of age. This will avoid any disputes between you and the Maharani. You don't have to worry about what happens behind your back. So, what do you think about this?"

"Aabasaheb, my words have lost meaning. I am earnestly and sincerely beseeching you to believe that I am not at all interested in power. I consider Ramraje my own. I have made you suffer so much, and all my life I am going to carry the burden of that guilt. You should take care of yourself. You are a father not only to me, but to countless people. I ask for only one thing…"

"Yes, what is it?"

"You should go to some other place to take rest; you won't get it in Raigad."

"Raje, where else am I going to get repose but Raigad? Aausaheb's samadhi is located at the foothills of Raigad. You don't have to worry about me any longer now. I am worried about you, as I am leaving Panhala – will you follow my advice?"

"Your wish is my command." Sambhajiraje gazed at Maharaj. Whenever Maharaj spoke, he usually felt that Maharaj should never stop talking, but for no reason today he felt that Aabasaheb should not speak any more as his words were filled with deep pain and agony.

"Shambhoobal, never forget what I am going to tell you now. On two earlier occasions, you have escaped successfully from the clutches of our arch enemy – Aurangzeb. You should never commit the mistake of getting caught in his clutches again. Now don't leave Panhala till you get further instructions from me. Goddess Jagadamba will always bless you. Let's go."

Before leaving, Maharaj leaned forward, picked up a bael leaf from the Shivlinga and placing it on Sambhajiraje's palm he said,

"When you were born the astrologer had told us that you are Rudra incarnate. You will live at sky-rising forts, and perform valiant feats…but…but- "

"But what Maharaj Saheb?"

"But you will be deceived by your own people just like Rudra was deceived by his own people! When you were two years old you were deceived by your Masaheb! After becoming the Yuvraj you were tricked by your Thoralya Aausaheb! Who knows, even I might deceive you one day and punish you severely! I am confident that you are the incarnation of Rudra, you will endure that punishment with fortitude.

Sambhajiraje did not understand much of Aabasaheb's deep and mysterious talk. When the father and the son came out of the temple, the entire Panhalgad was enveloped in mist.

The palanquin-bearers had kept the palanquin ready at the Chou Darwaja for the descent from the fort, From Panhalgad, Maharaj was going to Sajjangad via Koyana ghat–Satara, to visit Samartha Ramdas Swami. The Chhatrapati left the Balekilla with Sambhajiraje, Vitthalpant, Hambirarao, Ravaji, Hiroji, and Umaji Pandit. Sambhajiraje came forward and touched Aabasaheb's feet.

Maharaj pulled him up, embraced him tightly and patted his back silently. "Farewell, Shambhooraje. Take care. Jai Bhavani!" He said in a calm voice.

"Aabasaheb, please take care of your health. Jai Bhavani!" Sambhajiraje couldn't resist saying.

Maharaj glanced at all the people who had come to bid farewell and like never before, he brought his palms together and said, "Farewell, everybody! Jai Bhavani!"

The Chhatrapati turned around and walked towards the

palanquin. Everyone bowed down and made an obeisance to him; their loyal hands waved to say goodbye.

Suddenly, a gusty breeze of the wild wind on Panhala rushed on the fort. It plucked one of the eagle feathers adorning his Jiretop. The auspicious feather drifted on the wind towards the deep cliff on the fort. Sambhajiraje was startled to see it. He touched the cowrie necklace on his chest and muttered in a tremulous voice, "Jagadamb! Jagadamb!"

The palanquin-bearers picked up the palanquin. Sambhajiraje's great, wise Aabasaheb, who Samartha had described as 'the possessor of determination as great as Mount Meru and the guardian of the masses', started climbing down the fort. Hambirarao, Hiroji Farzand and others surrounded the palanquin astride their horses. All the people gathered at Chou Darawaja went back, but Sambhajiraje stood in his place till the palanquin disappeared from his sight.

Umaji Pandit, who cared about him, stood behind him. Sambhajiraje looked at him and said, "Pandit, come with me. I want to discuss something with you."

Sambhajiraje came to Sajjakothi with Umaji Pandit. He gestured Umaji Pandit to take a seat and said to him, "Pandit, you haven't shared any news of Shringarpur yet."

Pandit kept quiet.

"How is Bhavanibai doing?"

"She is safe…"

"And what about Yesubai?"

Pandit fell silent again. He didn't know what to say.

"Say something."

"She has been grief-stricken since she heard the news that her co-wife has been captured by the Pathans. She is not meeting anyone. She has locked herself in her chamber." Umaji Pandit could not raise his head. Sambhajiraje's eyes kept wandering aimlessly over the plateau that was visible through the window.

The meeting conducted in the court hall on Raigad had

concluded. Maharaj had dismissed Moropant, Annaji, Hambirarao, Balaji and Yesaji. He had instructed Balaji to meet him in his chamber.

All courtiers had left the hall, but Hambirarao lingered behind. He approached Maharaj.

"What is it Sarlashkar?"

"You will probably not listen to me, but I can't stop myself from saying this. Dhani need not worry about Emperor Aurangzeb at all. Even if many emperors like him attack our kingdom, our people are resilient. What I am more worried about is your health. You should take care of your health, Dhani."

Maharaj kept gazing at Hambirarao. He was deeply touched by Hambirarao's pure affection; his eyes welled up, but he controlled himself and with a smile he said in a calm voice, "Hambirarao, I am fine by the grace the Goddess Jagadamba. If you really want to worry, you should worry about somebody else." Maharaj astutely diverted Hambirarao's attention from his own health.

"Who?" The rowdy Sarlashkar kept wondering.

"Yuvraj! You care about him. You will guide him better than me in a problematic situation. You should always keep an eye on him."

"Ji. Rest assured Dhani." For some reason Hambirarao felt like touching Maharaj's feet and paying respect to him. He moved forward and touched the Chhatrapati's feet. Maharaj closed his eyes and felt his touch silently. Hambirarao left.

The Chhatrapati came to his personal chamber. In the solitude of his chamber, he felt feverish. The guard at the door came in and announced, "The Chitnis is here."

"Let him in." Maharaj started pacing in his chamber. Balaji Aavaji entered the chamber.

"Balaji, dispatch a letter to Yuvraj on Panhalgad — Do not to take it to heart that you weren't invited to Ramraje's wedding. I will talk to you in detail about it when we meet. Recently, I have received confirmed news that the Alamgir is going to descend upon the Deccan. You should keep your troops ready to block Alamgir's path. I will summon you at the right time to join me."

"Ji." Balaji listened to the matter attentively and nodded.

"Get the letter ready at the earliest and send it to me for my seal. Make sure that it gets dispatched today itself." The Chhatrapati raised his hand and turned his back to Balaji. He was lost in deep thought and kept pacing in the chamber.

Sambhajiraje sat in the sitting room of Sajjakothi. Two messengers from Pachad stood in front of him with lowered heads. As soon as Sambhajiraje heard the message he stood up at once. He was racked by anxiety. One of the messengers had delivered to him a message from Putalabai from Pachad – "All entrance gates of Raigad have been suddenly barricaded, without any intimation to anyone! No one is allowed to come in or go out. I have heard that Swari has taken ill. Something suspicious is going on. I don't know what to do."

Sambhajiraje was worried when he heard the message. He could not resist the temptation to mount his horse, descend the fort and sprint in the direction of Raigad. But he remembered that Maharaj himself had told him, "Don't leave Panhala until further instructions from me."

'I cannot hurt Aabasaheb with any of my words or actions anymore.' Sambhajiraje was in two minds. He started pacing restlessly in the chamber. Maharaj's weary face when he had left from Panhala, flashed in front of his eyes.

"Rayaji, Antoji, both of you go to Raigad at the earliest possible. Whatever information you collect from there, send it to me immediately." Sambhajiraje raised his hand and dismissed them.

Maharaj, who had travelled from Surat to Jinji Peddapolum, was now alienated from his ryots and the Mavalas. The Maharani had taken complete control of his palace. Now, even for the people on the fort, it had become extremely difficult to meet their Dhani.

In the evening, Soyarabai came to the Chhatrapati's chamber with Ramraje to pay evening obeisance to him. The chamber was now under the surveillance of Soyarabai's chosen few, such as Khandoji Naik, Kanhoji Bhandwalkar and Ganoji Kavala. Even the guards standing at the doors were not aware of Maharani's evil intentions.

Soyarabai closed the window and gently approached the bed.

"Rani Saheb, would you do me a favour?" Raje asked.

"Of course, I will. You don't have to ask." Soyarabai pricked her ears to hear what he was going to say.

"Dispatch messengers to Panhala tomorrow morning and summon Yuvraj to the fort. Summon Putalabai Saheb from Pachad to the fort too. Tell Balaji to send letters to Hambirarao, Moropant and Annaji and let them know about my ill health. I want to meet all of them and discuss some things." Even this little talk left the Chhatrapati fatigued.

"Is that all? I will do everything for sure. Swari should take rest. I will send Balaji here to meet you."

Soyarabai left the chamber with Ramraje. The Chhatrapati kept gazing at the flames of the lamps in the chamber; he was lost in thought.

"Vitthalpant, any letter from Raigad...?" Anxious Sambhajiraje asked the custodian of the fort as they went around on a surveillance of the fort.

"Nothing so far, Yuvraj. Even I am waiting for it." Vitthalpant replied.

They had reached the Konkan Darwaja. Before climbing the stone steps of the Darwaja, Sambhajiraje stopped. "What do you think Pandit? Why hasn't Aabasaheb summoned me to Raigad yet? Or is nobody allowed to descend the fort?" Sambhajiraje asked Umaji Pandit who was behind him.

Umaji Pandit was talking with Bahirji Ingale and Krishnaji

Banki. As he heard Sambhajiraje's question he promptly came forward and politely said, "Ji. I don't think so Yuvaraj. Balaji Chitnis is there on the fort. He wouldn't delay the dispatch of the letters. It's possible that Swami may have recovered from his illness by now. Maybe the Chhatrapati did not want to worry you unnecessarily and that is why he did not send the letters."

"Well, if that is the case, I will offer sweets to you. But no one can play games like the human mind. I can't think of anything, but Raigad. I cannot relax until I hear that he is doing fine." Sambhajiraje trudged with a heavy heart and came to the loft.

"Vitthalpant, please send a letter to my Chitnis Parashurampant at Shringarpur and tell him to come here." Sambhajiraje decided something in his mind and ordered the custodian of the fort.

"The Chitnis here can take dictation if needed, so..." Vitthalpant was caught off guard.

"Just do as I have told you. Within two days, I want Parashurampant present at this fort." Sambhajiraje's eyes pierced Vitthalpant's eyes. Vitthalpant did not dare look at him. He simply nodded, "Ji" and freed himself from the discomfort.

"Pandit, until Rayaji and Antoji come back, my anxiety is not going to reduce." Sambhajiraje placed his hand on the fence and looked in the direction of Raigad.

"Have courage Yuvraj. Everything will be okay, by the grace of Goddess Bhaveshwari." As Umaji Pandit mentioned Goddess Bhavaeshwari, the image of the palace in Shringarpur stood in front of Sambhajiraje's eyes. A strange thought pierced his aching heart – my wife has confined herself to her chamber in Shringarpur, ailing Aabasaheb is confined within the locked gates of Raigad, my sister Akkasaheb and my wife, Durgabai imprisoned in the fortress of Nagar, and here I am, bound by the promise that I gave Aabasaheb; I can't do anything for anyone except keep worrying about them...Alas! What a miserable situation this is! Right now, I feel like I should break my promise to Aabasaheb and go directly to Raigad. He might reprimand me, but at least I will get to see him. No, I shouldn't do that. After seeing me, Aabasaheb would feel more pain than relief.'

There on Raigad, the Chhatrapti had taken Balaji Aavaji to task. Balaji couldn't bear to see his condition. Maharaj had high fever, his eyes had turned red, and he was asking Balaji – "Is this how you have been doing your duty all your life? I had told you to dispatch letters to Yuvraj, Moropant and the Sarlashkar. Though I was sick, I dictated the letters to you. Then how come not a single person has responded yet? Have they become insolent, or have you failed in your duty?"

Baffled and terrified Balaji vouched in the name of his family deity and replied, "Please trust me, Swami. I had sealed the letters with my own hands and handed them to the delivery men. I had given them all instructions."

"Then why is no one responding? Why hasn't anyone come to meet me yet?" The Chitnis was so baffled that he could not answer that question. In fact, he was never going to be able to answer that question.

Soyarabai had appointed her chosen people at all the entrance gates of the fort – the Chit Darwaja, the Palakhi Darwaja, the Nane Darwaja and other gates. They had intercepted the letters from the delivery men; had descended the fort and gone back to their homes. All of them were from the Talbeed area, from the Maharani's parental home.

The letters that Balaji Aavaji had prepared and sealed were now locked in wooden chests and were in the possession of the Maharani now.

To divert his attention from Balaji, Soyarabai came forward and said hypocritically, "Why are you blaming the Chitnis for this? How could you even expect that Yuvraj will send any response from Panhalgad or come here in person? If at all, he cared for anyone, he wouldn't have joined hands with the enemy.

You yourself had sent the Peshwe and the Sarlashkar on a campaign. We cannot anticipate where they are located right now. They will come. Be patient. Even Balraje is asking me about Dada Saheb. What should I tell him?" Soyarabai pulled Ramraje close and made him stand in front of the Chhatrapati.

Maharaj sarcastically questioned the Maharani, "What about Dhakalya Rani Saheb in Pachad? Has she gone on a campaign too? Or has she also joined hands with the enemy? I had told you to summon her here."

"I had sent some people to Pachad. But Dhakalya bai was so stressed about your illness that she herself has fallen sick!" Soyarabai told an outright lie.

A diabolical plan was cooking in Raigad. Soyarabai who had taken control of the fort as the Maharani, became the master manipulator of the plan! Maharaj and Sambhajiraje became the target. The incentive was the golden throne of Raigad. Moropant, Annaji, Balaji...all the people devoted to the throne were going to become puppets in her hands.

Sambhajiraje sat in the Sajjakothi; his lunch platter was placed on a stool in front of him. He was lost in the memory of Maharaj; he pushed aside the lunch platter and got up. He had not eaten anything for the last two days.

Rayaji and Antoji stood near him. They looked at him anxiously. The Gaade brothers had camped in Pachad for three-four days and had spared no efforts to gather information about what was happening on Raigad. No one could enter the fort except for the wind, the light and the wild birds! Sabaji Bhosale, who had come from Nagpur to see Maharaj, was also stranded in Pachad.

"Chitnis, I don't understand it. Why would Aabasaheb barricade all the entrance gates of the fort? Maybe...he was afraid that I... I might show up at Raigad." A concerned Sambhajiraje said to Chitnis Parashurampant who had arrived from Shringarpur.

“I don’t think that Swami would have given such an order.”

“Who else would dare to barricade the entrance gates of the fort?”

“I should not say so, but…but the Maharani can do it?” Parashurampant replied thoughtfully.

“Really? Do you think she would dare to do such a thing even though Maharaj is present on the fort?”

“Maharaj has taken ill.”

“But still, he is the Maharaj. I know Aabasaheb very well.”

“But Yuvraj you are forgetting that the Maharani is capable of doing this even in the presence of Maharaj!”

“Oh Pant, for some reason I am feeling anxious today. It is Hanuman Jayanti today. Let’s go and take darshan of the devotee of Rama.”

An agitated Sambhajiraje left Sajjakothi. Parashuarmpant followed him. They came to the small temple of Hanuman located to the north of the Balekilla. The murti had been installed by Maharaj. As he gazed at the murti in the sanctum, he felt like asking the son of the Wind god who was posing in a stance ready to soar in the sky, “Today is your day. Would you fly to Raigad for me today? Would you bring me the good news that Aabasaheb has recovered from his illness and is doing fine?”

Sambhajiraje was earnestly speaking in his mind with the son of Vayu. He was unaware that even though it was a full moon night, the entire Raigad was shrouded in darkness! For the last two days the kitchen of the fort was closed.

Chapter 11

In the wee hours of the day, Panhalgad received the grievous news. Though Raigad had done everything to keep it a secret, the news had reached Panhalgad through Putalabai from Pachad and Hambirarao from the Talbeed camp in the Karhad region.

Putalabai had sent a personal message, "Darkness encompassed the fort in broad daylight today. Swari left this world, leaving us forlorn. Chaos has ensued on the fort. Even the appropriate obsequies were not performed for Swari. His funeral was performed in haste without proper rituals. This is a very difficult time for us. You should not lose courage. Whatever you do now, do it cautiously and thoughtfully. Make sure that people around you are trustworthy. I am awaiting your arrival at the fort. This is the will of Goddess Jagadamba; we have to accept it. We will talk more when we meet in person."

Hambirarao had sent a message, "Dhani has left this world; Swaraj is orphaned. I am leaving for Raigad immediately. Don't lose courage. I am with you."

Though the people who cared for him were telling him 'Don't lose courage' it was indeed a crisis that would wilt one's courage. Sambhajiraje's heart was not ready to accept the fact that Aabasaheb was not alive. His smiling face kept flashing in front of Sambhajiraje's eyes.

Sometimes, a person realizes the worthlessness of life in every way. Sambhajiraje felt the same. Destiny had struck the worst possible blow; his wounded mind was running helter-skelter.

Grief, guilt, anxiety of separation, helplessness, anger, humiliation, dejection… a strange turmoil of emotions filled his heart.

'Gone… Aabasaheb is gone! Without meeting me, without talking to me. He had lost hope only because of me. A man of mountainous strength, but he crumbled due to my wrong doings. He has given me the most severe punishment… Aabasaheb, you were my own, and still you deceived me! Why? How could you?

'You should have met me at least once, just to reprimand me, to tell me that you are ashamed of me.

'Now, who will call me 'Shambhooraje – my dear son' in a voice drenched with affection? How will I hear him whisper 'Jagadamb' and visualize the idol of eight-armed Goddess Bhavani? How can I touch his feet and seek his blessings? Who will I stand with on the walls of the machi and observe the courtyard of the Pachad palace? Why should I even go to Raigad? For the sake of the royal throne? No…it's not going to happen!

'My differences with Aabasaheb were as clear as the sunlight. Though I went astray in the heat of the moment, that great man forgave and embraced me with a big heart. I had barely recovered from the regret of the pain that I had caused him, when Time snatched him away. He was the only person who understood me. You people have thrown me in the dark abyss of grief. How are you going to pay for your sins?

'Aabasaheb suffered heart-wrenching pain because me, but now I am going to repay that debt wholeheartedly; even if I have to sacrifice my life for it! I am going to tackle the enemies of Swaraj – the Siddis, the British and Aurangzeb too!'

Sambhajiraje squeezed the cowrie necklace on his chest. With a determined heart, he opened the door of his chamber calmly. A gust of fresh wind rushed inside. All the people standing outside his chamber, waiting anxiously, kept staring at his swollen eyes. No one could imagine what was going on in his mind.

"Chitnis, the lunar eclipse is not only detrimental to a great man's life, it is also an indication that his visionary dream is about to be eclipsed!" Sambhajiraje's words set Parashurampant thinking.

"Rayaji – Antoji, did you hear the evening kettle drums today?"

"No." Rayaji, Antoji were confused.

"It means the custodian of the fort, Vitthalpant, has received the news of Maharaj's demise, and yet he hasn't come to meet me and deliver the news to me! Keep a watch on him."

Everyone kept staring at Sambhajiraje. At that time, Vitthalpant was in a secret meeting with Hiroji Farzand and Somaji Banki who had come from Raigad. Soyarabai had given the charge of Raigad to Kanhoji Bhandwalkar and Sarnoubat Shahaji Bhosale. She had sealed the treasury and other offices in her own authority. She had sent Hiroji Farzand and Somaji Banki from Raigad to Panhala, with further instructions for Vitthalpant.

The game of chess was on. Sambhajiraje was making his moves from Panhala. At Raigad, Maharani Soyarabai had taken all the control in her hand, and she and her spies were making their moves from there.

The day after Maharaj's ashes were collected, Annaji Dutto who had arrived from the Konkan coast, ascended Raigad. He presented himself in front of the Maharani to offer condolences. As soon as he offered condolences, Soyarabai broached the main topic – "Maharaj is no more. Now, I am worried what is going to happen next."

"I have presented myself in front of Ranisarkar for the same purpose. I will follow your orders. Rest assured." Annaji Dutto bowed down and spoke.

"I trust you, but what about the others? Now Sambhajiraje will take action from Panhala any time. Then what about Moropant, Prahlad Niraji, Rahuji and most importantly, the Sarlashkar?"

"Sarlashkar is Ranisarkar's brother. I believe he would support Ramraje as his mama saheb. I will convince the other ministers. It would be risky if Yuvraj comes to Raigad as the successor. We should take prompt action and whatever we do, we should keep it secret. Balraje should be declared the next king and the Maharani should take all control in her hand, otherwise the kingdom will be in a precarious situation. At this time, you should hold your courage and act with determination."

"I am already firm about my decision. It would be better if you and the other ministers support Balraje. That's all."

"I swear in the name of my family deity that I will do everything in my power. Rest assured."

Soyarabai's royal hook had captured the most cunning and slithery fish among the ministers – Annaji. This fish was not one to be trapped in the net, rather he was capable of slyly weaving his net to capture his own prey. Why did Annaji want to disregard Sambhajiraje's birth right as the eldest son of Chhatrapati Shivaji Maharaj and the crowned Yuvraj and install Ramraje on the throne of Swaraj? There were many motives behind his moves. First of all, he could not forget the incident of Godavari, the married lady of his kin whose life had needlessly been cut short only because of Sambhajiraje's actions. The responsibility of revenue had been entrusted to Annaji. But he was offended because Yuvraj frequently intervened in those matters. And most importantly, he was not sure if he would be able to retain the office of the Surnis under Yuvraj. He was doubtful that even if he did retain the post of the Surnis, he wouldn't be able to exercise his rights as the Surnis completely and he wouldn't be able to hold his post permanently. But if Ramraje inherited the throne, there was a great probability of his being the Maharani's most prominent advisor.

In the evening, Peshwe Moropant who had arrived from the Nashik–Tryambak region, ascended the fort. He also presented himself in front of the Maharani to offer condolences.

He was greatly agitated to see the Balekilla bereft of Maharaj's presence. He could not even manage to utter a few words of consolation to the Maharani. He placed the edge of his shawl on his lips and sobbed like a child. As soon as he calmed down Soyarabai said to him, "Pant, if people like you lose their courage, who should I look up to? Who is going to support Balraje? I am completely shattered. I don't even know how to handle the situation!" Each word of Soyabai put Moropant more ill at ease. He wiped his eyes, bowed and said diligently, "Please don't lose courage. We are with you."

"Your support is what I need right now. I believe in you. Please meet Annaji and together you decide the next moves. What more can I say?" Soyarabai conveyed what she wanted to say without betraying her involvement.

Soyarabai and Annaji had already planned everything. Their plan was not going to work without Moropant's participation. After all, Moropant was the Peshwa of the Maratha kingdom.

At the daybreak of the fifth day of the dark fortnight, Hambirarao started ascending Raigad; he had spent the night in Pachad. He had not forgotten to visit Putalabai. During that visit he had come to know what had happened and what had transpired since the day Maharaj fell ill.

After arriving on the fort, Hambirarao promptly came to visit the Maharani in her palace. As soon as she saw him, Soyarabai, clad in a plain white sari, wept her heart out. Hambirarao's eyes also welled up in Maharaj's memory. Such a strong-hearted, brawny man but in the memory of his Dhani, he sobbed like a child. Soyarabai pulled Ramraje close to her and said in a heavy voice, "Forget about me, but what about your nephew? Who is going to console him? It is good that you came to the fort. Now my worries will reduce a bit, otherwise with whose support is he going to carry the onus of the kingdom on his shoulders?" Soyarabai astutely tried to assess Hambirarao's response.

Hambirarao never thought that the Maharani would broach the topic of the inheritance of the throne even before the last rites of Maharaj had been performed. Even he wanted to ask a lot of questions to the people on the fort – 'Why were the gates of the fort barricaded? Why didn't I receive the news of Dhani's illness? How come the funeral of Maharaj was not performed with proper rituals?' But Hambirarao was a wise man and knew that this was not the right time to ask such questions.

Hambirarao pulled Ramraje close and patting on his shoulder he tried to make Soyarabai aware of the situation, "Balraje and Yuvraj are like Dhani's two eyes. We should summon Yuvaraj from Panhala immediately. Then Yuvraj, Peshwe, Surnis, Yesajikaka, other ministers, you and I…we all should take further decisions together. Now that Dhani is no more, all our enemies will try to take advantage of the situation. Let's first perform all the prescribed final rituals for Dhani and then decide what to do."

Soyarabai realized where this was leading and became alert. She understood that Hambirarao would not support her plan. Annaji and Moropant were on her side, but she was suspicious that Hambirarao might turn them against her. She instantly started making plans of sending Hambirarao away from the fort, but outwardly said, "I agree with you. We will need your guidance for sure. Balraje, touch your mama saheb's feet and seek his blessings!" Soyarabai made a final attempt of making an emotional appeal to Hambirarao.

Hambirarao stopped Ramraje who was about to touch his feet, "Oh no, please don't do such a thing. The moment you were born as Dhani's son; I became your servant. Our family relation doesn't matter anymore. You should accept my obeisance now." Hambirarao bowed down, made an obeisance to the Maharani and Ramraje and left the chamber. Soyarabai threw a fiery glance at his broad back.

She summoned Annaji immediately and informed him in a

seemingly sweet voice, "Sarlashkar is not going to participate in our plan for sure. I am going to send him to the Karhad region as soon as the final rites are performed. Beware of him."

Annaji was worried when he heard this. He was aware of the power that Hambirarao wielded as the Sarlashkar, as he had the support of the entire army. Still, he believed that once Ramraje was enthroned, Hambirarao would not obstruct his path.

Annaji informed other ministers that Hambirarao was not inclined to join in their scheme. After that Moropant, Prahlad Niraji, Rahuji and others started speaking with Hambirarao cautiously and only when necessary.

On the twelfth day of the dark fortnight of Chaitra, the final rites of Maharaj were performed. The day after the final rites, early in the morning, Hambirarao was summoned to the Maharani's chamber. He presented himself in front of the Maharani. Yesaji Kank, Anandrao, Moropant, Annaji and Prahladpant were already present there. Soyarabai accepted Hambirarao's obeisance and spoke very formally, "Sarlashkar, we are all waiting for you."

"Ji."

"I have summoned you to discuss a plan. I am worried at what you said. Now all our enemies will try to attack us from all sides. All you veterans should take charge of your regions immediately. Anandarao, Rupaji you handle the Satara area. Yesaji, you keep a regiment of ten thousand ready in Pachad. Sarlashkar, you should immediately go to the Karhad region and take charge there. Pant, Annaji you should go back to your regions." Everyone bowed down to Maharani and exclaimed "Ji" in unison.

Hambirarao raised his head and said, "...but what about the arrangements over here? It's a huge responsibility. Everything should be done carefully."

"We will do that eventually with the assistance of all of you, but at this moment, we need to protect the kingdom. All of you should leave today."

"Ji." Everyone exclaimed along with Hambirarao. Soyarabai rose from her seat. Everyone was offered betel leaves to conclude the meeting. This meeting was especially arranged to send Hambirarao and Anandrao away from Raigad. Annaji and Moropant were going to stay back in Raigad.

Sambhajiraje had performed the final rites of Aabasaheb on Panhalgad. He stood on the banks of Lake Someshwar, joined his hands in prayer in front of the Pinda, and said, "Aaba, I accept full responsibility for my mistakes. I will strive to fulfil all your wishes."

After the final rites were performed, Sambhajiraje, who had clearly realized what was going to happen in the coming days, took some quick actions. In the Sajjakothi, he dictated a letter to Parashurampant to be sent to Ravaji Pandit, the subedar of the Konkan coast. "His Highness Ravaji Pandit, subedar of the Konkan region, Rajapur, my respects to you. Please make sure that the revenue and food grains collected from the Rajapur territory are dispatched to Panhala at the earliest possible. As soon as you receive this letter, come to Panhala with your army and meet me."

Parashurampant sealed the envelope and kept it aside. He opened the next roll of parchment and placed it on the stool.

Some Mavalas had assembled at the base of the Kothi. Their chit-chatting was faintly audible inside. Sambhajiraje started pacing back and forth and dictated the next letter,

"His highness, valiant warrior, virtuous Sarlashkar Mama Saheb Mohite, humble obeisance to you from Yuvraj Shambhooraje.

"It's been fifteen days since Aabasaheb passed away at Raigad. I have performed his obsequies here on Panhalgad. I have received information that some people in Raigad are conspiring against me. The entire ministry has united, and all ministers are plotting something under the Maharani's leadership. They all want to enthrone Ramraje, and alienate me. I suspect that my life is in danger. Except for you, nobody else is going to support me. Since Aabasaheb's time you have been loyal to the throne. Is it fair to alienate me, despite my seniority when our kingdom faces the threat of external attacks? Lend me your support and do as Aabasaheb would have thought fit. You are a father figure to me. What more can I say?"

Another letter was prepared for Pilajimama of Shringarpur – "These are trying times. Keep your forces ready in the Prabhanvalli subah and be ready."

The news of Maharaj's demise had spread in the kingdom. After hearing the news, throngs of Mavalas from Rajapur, Malkapur, Rangana, Varanakhore, Samangad, Vishalgad and nearby territories kept arriving at Panhalgad to offer condolences to Yuvraj.

Seeing the massive influx of the masses, Hiroji Farzand astutely escaped from Panhala and went to the Konkan coast.

Sambhajiraje selected a few Mavalas from the assembled crowds and seized control of Panhalgad by incarcerating Vitthalpant, the custodian of the fort, Bahirji Ingale, Somaji and Krishnaji Banki.

The conspirators, unaware of the developments on Panhalgad, had scheduled a secret meeting on Raigad. The armed sentinels of Kanhoji Bhandwalkar were guarding the door of the chamber. Maharani Soyarabai sat in the chamber. Ministers, Annaji Dutto, Moropant, Prahlad Niraji, Rahuji Somnath, Hawaldar Kanhoji Bhandawalkar, the leader of the informers - Khandoji, Ganoji Kavala, and Shahaji Bhosale stood around her.

"Tomorrow is Akshay trutiya, a very auspicious mahurat. It's perfect for the ceremony of Balraje's enthronement." Annaji commenced the meeting.

Ramraje, for who this meeting was taking place, was fast

asleep in his chamber.

"But Annaji, it would have been better if Sarlashkar were present here." Moropant expressed his concern.

"Though he is not here today, we will make sure he gets invited to the enthronement ceremony." Soyarabai who was dreaming big, was not ready to let go of her dream.

"Yuvraj is the elder son. What are we going to do if somebody objects to our plan and defends his seniority? Looks like Hambirarao himself might do the same." Moropant started voicing his suspicions about what problems might hamper their plans in the future.

"Yuvraj may be the elder son; but even when Swami was alive, he teamed up with Diler; then think of what he will do, if he comes to power after Swami's demise" Annaji started weaving his web.

"But Balraje is still young, and managing the kingdom is quite challenging." Prahlad Niraji displayed the impartiality of a Nyayadhish.

"Besides, we are surrounded by our enemies from all sides." Rahuji upheld his opinion.

"Balraje is obviously young, but Maharani Saheb who will act as his regent is sagacious. The late Swami raised this kingdom at a very young age, that too with the support of sagacious Aausaheb!" Annaji compared Soyarabai with Jijau!

"But we are doing this without knowing the final wish of our late Swami. Why would the masses accept our decision?" Moropant went to the heart of the issue.

"Swari did not send Balraje's wedding invitation to Panhalgad. Doesn't that make his wish clear?" Soyarabai astutely turned the tide.

"And despite sending him many letters, Yuvraj did not come to visit Swami on his deathbed. Doesn't that make his intentions clear?" Annaji seconded Soyarabai.

"But what if we invite Yuvraj to the fort and present our

side to him… who knows, maybe he will accept it!" Moropant said hesitatingly.

"How could you say this, Peshwe? Bringing him here with honour would be like pouring molten lead on our own bodies with our own hands! If at all that is going to happen… then I will resign from the post of Surnis!" Annaji unsheathed his ultimate weapon.

"And I will also step down as the Maharani and go to Talbeed for good." Soyarabai echoed Annaji's sentiment.

"I aver that Yuvraj is not fit to inherit the throne. If he becomes the king, our kingdom will be doomed. Swami took care of us all his life; I would never commit the sin of abandoning the kingdom in its hour of need. Ramraje's kingship will prove beneficial for the kingdom." Annaji enwrapped Moropant in his web completely.

Still, Moropant raised a very valid question, "I agree with you. But Annaji how can you assume that Yuvraj will watch all this quietly and accept it without any resistance?"

"In fact, I am quite puzzled that Swari forgave a traitor who defected to our enemy!" Soyarabai indirectly suggested that not only did Yuvraj not deserve to inherit the throne but also that he was a culprit who deserved punishment.

"Pant, what Swami couldn't do because of his love for his son, we will have to do firmly." Annaji prepared the background before striking the blow.

"What do you mean, Surnis? I don't get what you are saying." Moropant said in confusion.

"Once we enthrone Ramraje, we will have to besiege Panhala with our army and present a shackled Sambhajiraje in front of the Maharani. She will give the final judgement in his case." Annaji spit the venomous thoughts, which he had harboured deep in his heart.

"Surnis…" Moropant screamed; his body was trembling.

"Yes. I will repeat what I said. We will have to shackle Yuvraj and bring him here. Pant, two swords cannot fit in one scabbard. If we enthrone Ramraje and set Yuvraj free, he will never let us and Ramraje be at peace. In fact, he will prove most dangerous to Ramraje and the Maharani. I know Yuvraj very well." Annaji's words left everyone, including Moropant, stunned. They all had been thinking about only the first part of the conspiracy. As Annaji revealed the other part of the conspiracy everyone was taken aback and became solemn.

"Just as it is important to enthrone Ramraje for the welfare of the kingdom, this is equally important. We cannot avoid it. If we don't have the guts to do this, then we should just leave the kingdom to its fate and go back to our vatans." Annaji skilfully reminded everyone of their duty.

Now Moropant realized that he had entered way deep in a quagmire. From here, backing off was not possible, because the people who were ready to imprison the Yuvaraj wouldn't have hesitated to imprison the Peshwa. Moropant was utterly confused. He thought for a while and said, "Okay Annaji, I am ready to implement your plan." Soyarabai's face gleamed as she heard his words.

Moropant's consent encouraged Prahlad Niraji, Rahuji, Kanhoji and the others to second the audacious plot and they concurred. On behalf of the Maharani, a platter of Goddess Bhavani's sacred haldi was circulated in the chamber to assess the loyalty of the assembled men. The meeting concluded. As Kanhoji Bhandwalkar was leaving, the Maharani instructed him, "Kanhoji, tell Balaji that I have summoned him immediately."

"Ji."

Within a short time, Chitnis Balaji stood in front of the Maharani to offer his services.

"Chitnis, I will tell you the content of a few letters. Compose them as per my instructions and dispatch them at daybreak tomorrow, towards Panhalgad and Kolhapur at the hands of my loyal informers, Khandoji Naik and Ganoji Kavala."

"Ji." Balaji was oblivious of what content the Maharani was going to tell him.

"The letter to the custodian of Panhalgad, Vitthalpant, Hawaldar Bahirji Ingale, Hiroji Farzand and Somaji Banki should state that –

"We have devised a plan. Take Yuvaraj in your custody and be on the alert. Don't let the news of Swari's demise leak out!"

"Specify the following in the letters to Janardanpant Sumant and Parajipant Pedgaonkar in Kolhapur – Take your forces to Panhalgad and assist Vitthalpant in the plan that he is going to execute."

"Dispatch one letter to the Yuvraj of the kingdom too, with the following message – Swari is recovering now. He will feel better soon. Do not believe any rumours you hear! Stay calm!" This new stance of Soyarabai left Balaji stunned. Shocked, he kept staring at her! He was speechless.

"Chitnis, I am talking to you, compose the letters, put your seal on them and bring them to me." Soyarabai's voice was stern.

Balaji lowered his head and said in a firm voice, "I am a servant of the kingdom. How can I write such letters when I know that Yuvraj is the rightful heir to the throne? Please forgive me; I cannot do it."

"What did you say? The letters will not be considered valid without your seal on them. That is why you are getting so much importance. Have you forgotten that I am the Maharani?"

"Please don't misunderstand me. My son, Aavaji is at home, I will send him with my seal. Please accept his services for whatever purposes you want. Just don't involve me in this matter, that's all I ask."

Soyarabai was agitated, but she needed the letters with the seal of the Chitnis. She wanted somebody else to do her unscrupulous work.

"Send him here immediately. You can leave now!" She dismissed Balaji. Balaji left the chamber and sent his son there.

Aavaji composed the letters as per Maharani's instructions, put the seal on them, secured them in pouches and handed them to her. Khandoji and Ganoji left with the fraudulent letters.

Sambhajiraje took a round of the fort, surveyed the preparations and came to the summit of the fort with Rayaji and Antoji. He glanced at the peak of the Jotiba hill visible at a faraway distance, joined his hands in the direction of the hill and whispered, "Hail Lord Malhari!" In the light of the setting sun the silhouettes of the mountains on the horizon were dancing on the plateaus.

Suddenly, Sambhajiraje moved towards the fence and narrowing his eyes he stared at the sinuous road leading to the Chou Darwaja. Two riders were galloping in the direction of the Chou Darwaja. As soon as Sambhajiraje saw the saddles, he recognized that the horses were from Pachad's stable.

He swiftly turned around, briskly walked towards the staircase and exclaimed, "Rayaji–Antoji, follow me." He leapt over two steps at a time and quickly came down the stairs. He signalled to the groom to bring the horse out of the stable. As soon as he brought the horse out, Yuvraj quickly took the reins in his hands, leapt on to his horse and prodded it. The horse rared, neighed loudly and darted like an arrow, in the direction of the Chou Darwaja. Baffled, Rayaji and Antoji followed him.

As soon as they approached the Chou Darwaja, Sambhajiraje released the reins and dismounted. The doorkeeper made an obeisance to him, but he did not notice it. His eyes were focused on the road in front.

The riders took a turn and came in front of the Chou Darwaja. Their hearts sank to see Sambhajiraje himself standing at the door.

They were Soyarabai's loyal messengers Khandoji Naik and Ganoji Kavala coming from Raigad. They trembled with fear.

"Where did you come from?" An intimidating voice echoed from the Chou Darwaja.

Khandoji barely managed to get off his horse, made an obeisance and said, "Ji, from Kolhapur."

"What?" Sambhajiraje roared while observing the saddles on the horses keenly.

"Ji, not from Kolhapur. We went from Raigad to Kolhapur and from Kolhapur we came here." Ganoji realized the gravity of the situation and corrected Khandoji.

Though Sambhajiraje was wearing his Jiretop, they could make out that his head was shaved. They were startled to see it.

"What news have you brought from Raigad?" Khandoji and Ganoji did not reply to his question and kept staring at each other. They shook in fear.

"Why are you looking at each other? Open your mouth now."

The terrified men were dumbfounded. They couldn't speak; they didn't know what to do.

"Rayaji…give them a good lashing; that will open their mouths quickly."

His words sent a chill down their spines.

"No Dhani…please spare our lives." Khandoji exclaimed and prostrated at Sambhajiraje's feet. Ganoji also followed suit.

"Get up. Nobody will hurt you as long as you share every minute detail of what has happened."

Khandoji pulled out the letters he had hidden in his dress, near his chest, that they were supposed to deliver to the custodian of the fort and the hawaldar. With trembling hands, he put the pouches at Sambhajiraje's feet. Next to them, Ganoji put the other letter meant for Yuvraj. They both hid their faces in the palms and started sobbing. Sambhajiraje picked up the pouch that Khandoji had placed at his feet; he pulled out the letter from it and began reading it. With every word he read, his nostrils flared, his chest heaved, and his eyes breathed fire.

When he read the words, "Take Yuvraj in your custody and be on the alert." He squeezed the letter in his fist in rage, and roared in a loud voice that left Rayaji and Antoji also trembling, "Who has the nerve to shackle me? How dare…"

When he read the words, "Swari will feel better soon." in the other letter his lips trembled in Maharaj's memory and his eyes welled up. 'A fortnight had passed since the demise of that virtuous man, and for their selfish purposes these avaricious people are telling me that he will be fine!'

Rage, revulsion, shame, pain… a tumult of varied emotions arose in Sambhajiraje's heart. He realized that he was standing in the Chou Darwaja as the Yuvraj of Swaraj; he took a deep breath and commanded, "Antoji, bring the custodian of the fort and hawaldar Somaji here. Rayaji, summon Parashurampant here too. I want to see how they react when I expose them."

"Why did you go to Kolhapur?" Yuvaraj questioned Khandoji and Ganoji, to make sure he had checked every aspect.

"We delivered similar letters to Janardanpant and Pedgaonkar." Khandoji told the truth. As Sambhajiraje heard him, Sumant Janardanpant and Parajipant Pedgaonkar's faces flashed in front of his eyes.

Antoji conducted Vitthalpant Mahadkar, Bahirji Ingale, Somaji Banki, his son Bapuji, and Suryaji Kale in the custody of swordsmen, from the Balekilla.

Rayaji conducted Parashurampant and Umaji Pandit from the side of the Sajjakothi. Everyone looked quite surprised.

"Welcome, the custodian of the fort and the hawaldar. I have been waiting here to reward you for your loyalty." Sambhajiraje said sarcastically. He handed the pouches to the Chitnis and said, "Pant, here are some letters from the Maharani from Raigad, stamped with the seal of the Chitnis. Please read these for my loyal servants here!"

Parashurampant cleared his throat and loudly read the letters written to the custodian of the fort and the hawaldar.

The conspirators were already hanging their heads low; they were stunned to hear the contents of the letters.

Sambhajiraje approached Vitthalpant, held his own wrists in front of Vitthalpant and said bitterly, "Go ahead and take me into custody now! Shackle me! Will you?"

Vitthalpant shook his head in utter shame; tears trickled from his eyes.

Sambhajiraje roared like thunder in wrath, "Take these ungrateful traitors away from me! Shackle them all and throw them in the dungeons!"

Within a short time, a cavalry troop left from the Chou Darwaja of Panhala, in the direction of Kolhapur; to arrest Sumant and Pedgaonkar as punishment for their deeds.

There at Raigad, Ramraje's enthronement had taken place with religious rituals on the auspicious Mahurat of Akshay Trutiya. Annaji, Moropant, Pahlad Niraji and the Maharani had declared him the next Chhatrapati and were eagerly awaiting the arrival of the news of Sambhajiraje's imprisonment.

Raigad was shocked to hear of the events that had taken place on Panhalgad. Their plan was foiled. Annaji was not ready to waste even a moment now. He came to meet the Maharani with Moropant and Pahlad Niraji. The most gruesome phase of the conspiracy commenced.

"We have lost Panhala. Yuvaraj has taken it over. His allies are increasing in numbers day by day. We won't be able to survive unless we break them. I myself will go to Panhala now to tackle the situation." A determined Annaji hadn't lost hope yet.

"I agree with you. Moropant, Prahlad Niraji and you should take the forces assembled at Pachad with you and besiege Panhalgad. Any further delay will prove disastrous for all of us." Soyarabai showed her royal faith in him.

"I would like to go via Karhad. Conquering Panhala won't be possible unless we persuade the Sarlashkar to team up with us." After all, Annaji was more experienced in politics.

"It would be helpful if the Maharani could send a letter for the Sarlashkar with us." Moropant suggested.

"Annaji and you have high hopes of him. I will write a letter to him, but I don't think it will make any difference!" Soyarabai knew Hambirarao's mindset very well. After all, she and Hambirarao had inherited the same genes.

The conspirators descended Raigad with the letter to be delivered to Hambirarao and arrived in Pachad. With ten thousand armed cavalry, they left from Pachad.

The Chhatrapati had striven to build the Maratha kingdom. But within a month of his demise, the staunch stalwarts of the kingdom, Surnis, Peshwe, and Nyayadhish had launched an armed attack to imprison Sambhajiraje though they had witnessed him being inducted as the Yuvraj of the kingdom. Annaji and Moropant's army travelled to Karhad and arrived at the border.

Sarlashkar Hambirarao's town, Talbeed was located a few miles away from the encampment. Hambirarao was camped there with an army of fifteen thousand Mavalas. He had already received the news that Annaji and Moropant were going towards Panhala from Raigad. As soon as he had received the news, he had invited Anandrao Nimbalkar, Rupaji Bhosale and Mahadaji Mapolkar with their forces to Talbeed to strengthen his base. Annaji was unaware of Hambirarao's movements; he selected a faithful messenger and dispatched him to Talbeed to deliver the Maharani's letter to Hambirarao. He kept awaiting his messenger's return in the hope that Hambirarao would come to meet him.

As soon as Hambirarao received the letter, he called a meeting of his advisors at his residence. Anandrao, Rupaji, Mahadaji Gujar, Hambirarao's brother Shankaraji and Harifrao sat around Hambirarao. Hambirarao's Chitnis read the letter aloud – "Support Peshwe and Surnis in every way possible. Assist them with your army and provide protection to Balraje and me. You are family. You will be rewarded appropriately in time."

No one spoke after hearing the letter. Finally, Hambirarao

said, "Well – at least now the Maharani has remembered me! She sent me away from the fort because I was an obstacle in the enthronement of Balraje. At that time, she had told me, 'We will consult you when needed.' Now she is ordering us to team up with Pant and Surnis. What do you think about this?" Hambirarao tried to gauge the opinions of all those present.

"Well, now that Ramraje has been enthroned, we should treat the Maharani's order as Ramraje's too." Shankaraji Mohite indirectly took his sister's side. "But they all have snubbed the elder son completely. That is not good." Mahadaji Mapolkar said.

Hambirarao realized that these gullible men would go astray like a lost bull. He cleared his throat and said in a hoarse voice, "Well, do you think this army is going to the fair of Lord Jotiba? No! Annaji and Moropant are going to Panhalgad – to imprison Yuvraj! Have you realized that?

They all heard Hambirarao, with their mouths agape, and their heads erect. None of them had ever heard something as preposterous as this. Everyone was terribly shocked. Somebody exclaimed, "What?!! This is too much."

Hambirarao interrupted him and said, "It hasn't happened yet, but it is about to happen! Should we take part in this? We are ever ready to sacrifice our lives for our Dhani. Should we betray him like this? No matter what, Yuvraj is the elder son. He is the rightful heir to the throne. Though Ramraje is my own nephew, he is the younger son. He doesn't have the right to inherit the throne. How can I team up with them?"

"No, we shouldn't." A few voices exclaimed.

"Just saying 'No' to them is not enough. Not only will I not put Yuvraj in prison, but I will not let anybody else do that either. We need to stop them."

"How can we stop them?" Rupaji voiced his concern.

"We will invite Annaji and Moropant to Talbeed to discuss the matter and convince them to not do such a thing." Wise

Hambirarao had found a solution. Everyone seconded his advice.

Hambirarao's Chitnis sent a return message through Annaji's messenger, "Both of you come to meet us. We will discuss things in detail."

When Moropant heard the message, he said to Annaji, "This is exactly what I was telling you to do. We should go and meet the Sarlashkar."

Annaji disagreed with him and said, "You are mistaken, Pant. If the Sarlashkar really wanted to team up with us he would have come to visit us with his army. At this stage, it wouldn't be wise to take the risk of going to Talbeed. I believed that he would respect the family bond with the Maharani and comply with the royal order. We should not rely on him now. We should take further steps on our own."

Moropant became solemn. He realized what kind of a vicious circle he was stuck in and felt depressed.

"I think we should start negotiations with Yuvraj now." Prahladpant who had unwillingly teamed up with Annaji, voiced his opinion.

"Negotiations? At this stage? Do you think Yuvraj will accept any kind of negotiations?" Annaji dismissed his suggestion.

After hearing Annaji's words, Prahladpant excused himself saying, "I will be back soon" and left from Annaji's tent. He came to his tent, prepared a letter of negotiation and dispatched it to Panhala through his trusted men.

The evening was almost over. In Talbeed, Hambirarao got tired of waiting for Annaji and Moropant. He felt quite offended that the Surnis and Peshwe had not shown any respect to his request. He came to a decision; he gathered Anandrao, Rupaji, Mahadaji and his brother Shankaraji and Harifji and ordered them, "Mount your horses and penetrate the army encampment at Karhad. Incite as many soldiers as you can to turn traitor, and send them to Talbeed! Leave immediately."

In the night, Hambirarao's men penetrated Annaji and

Moropant's army. They started using all tactics in their power, to turn the soldiers against Annaji and Moropant.

When Annaji came to know about it, he lost his temper. Annaji and Moropant discussed the matter through the night and decided to attack Hambirarao! Their plan was now going haywire. At daybreak Annaji and Moropant fell upon Talbeed with the remaining forces they had at their disposal.

Hambirarao was all ready to face them. He also had a large number of forces at his disposal. Within no time, fifteen thousand Mavala soldiers surrounded Annaji-Moropant and their army. Pant realized that they had lost the battle and put down his weapons. Annaji followed suit.

Hambirarao approached Annaji and Moropant with a troop of select men. He sarcastically bowed down to them without getting off his horse and exclaimed bitterly, "Pant – Surnis, I bow down to your loyalty and judgement! You were going to put chains on the same hands from which you should be receiving rewards! You are raising arms against the person whom you should be serving! Barely a month has passed since Dhani's demise, and you are already besieging his son! Had he been alive, would you have dared to do such a thing?" Hambirarao's eyes were breathing fire.

"Anandrao, Rupaji, let them feel the shame a man feels when he is shackled! Bind them with ropes! Alas! What an awful day I had to witness because of them!" Hambirarao was upset with himself. He prodded his horse hard; it dashed towards Talbeed. Forty–fifty riders followed him. Finally, Prahlad Niraji and Rahuji Somnath were also captured with Annaji and Moropant.

Yuvraj was at Panhalgad, Ramraje was on Raigad, and the issue of succession of the Maratha kingdom was being resolved by Hambirarao in Karhad!

The late Maharaj always used to say, "May God's will prevail!" It was indeed true.

Sambhajiraje stood in the Chou Darwaja to receive

Hambirarao. Behind him stood Mhaloji Ghorpade and his son Santaji, Bahirji, Subedar of Konkan – Ravaji Pandit, Umaji Pandit, Parashurampant, Rayaji and Antoji.

As Sambhajiraje saw round-faced, brawny Hambirarao astride his horse, coming forward with Anandrao, Shankaraji and Rupaji, a commotion arose in his heart. Till today, he had experienced such commotion only when he had seen Aabasaheb. As if drawn to him, Sambhajiraje briskly walked forward. Hambirarao also saw him and raised his speed. As he came close to Sambhajiraje, he dismounted.

As Sambhajiraje realized that he was about to bow down to make an obeisance, he got emotional. He quickly held Hambirarao's hands and stopped him; he pulled Hambirarao up, gazed in his eyes and said in a hoarse voice, "Mama Saheb!" The next moment they both embraced each other. He was touched by Hambirarao's loyalty; his eyes welled up. Hambirarao gently patted his shoulder. As Sambhajiraje realized that Aabasaheb had patted his shoulder in the same manner a few months back, for the first time in a long while he felt like he wasn't alone.

As they entered the fort through Chou Darwaja, after a long time, the kettle drums resounded on Panhalgad.

Sambhairaje came to the Balekilla with Hambirarao. He graciously conducted Hambirarao to his seat and said, "Mama Saheb, what should we do next? I am not going to do anything without your advice."

Hambirarao realised that he was avoiding the prisoners and said, "That we are going to do eventually, but first you should take the prisoners in your custody!"

Sambhajiraje got restless. He had to face the subject that he had been avoiding.

"I don't feel like seeing their faces, especially after seeing you!" Sambhjiraje spoke bitterly.

"That won't do! The people who committed the mistake

are not ashamed of their actions. Then why should you feel guilty? Rupaji, present the prisoners here." Hambirarao ordered Rupaji.

Shackled and surrounded by armed soldiers, Annaji, Moropant, Prahladpant and Rahuji were brought in front of Sambhjiraje. Their heads were bent low.

The moment Sambhajiraje saw Annaji who was standing at the front, he rose from his seat at once. His eyes got red. The vein on his forehead throbbed and puffed up. His nostrils flared and his lips trembled. He wanted to say so many things, but uncontrllable rage did not let him speak properly. He couldn't even bear to see Annaji standing in front of him. He briskly turned his back to Annaji and roared, "Take them away from me and never bring them in front me again. He is the one who has shattered all my hopes. Take them away from here and throw them in the dungeon!" Sambhajiraje's whole body shook with rage. Hambirarao was shocked to see him so angry and kept gazing at him.

The armed soldiers were taking the prisoners back. Sambhajiraje saw Moropant amongst them and said, "Wait!"

Everyone, including the prisoners, froze with fear.

Sambhajiraje walked slowly, came in front of Moropant and said in a dejected voice, "You…you also came to imprison me, Pant! You too failed to understand me. Had you sent a message; I would have surrendered myself in front of you! You stood by Aabasaheb like his shadow. Is this how you perform your duty after his death?" Sambhajiraje's disappointment outweighed his anger.

The moment Moropant was shackled, his heart was broken; he did not utter a single word. His conscience was still active enough to regret his wrongdoing! His guilt started flowing through tears in his eyes.

"Pant, how did you get caught in the trap of the shrewd Annaji? The cleverest minds have not been able to decipher the conspiracies plotted by him."

Sambhajiraje came in front of Annaji; threw a fiery glance at his bulky body and roared, "Surnis Annaji Dutto why can't you raise your head now? Or are you busy plotting against the very ground on which you are standing? You are still holding old grudges against me! What were you going to do to me after capturing me and taking me to Raigad? Were you going to push me down the Takamaktok, or were you going to fasten me to a cannon's muzzle and blow me off? What…exactly what were you going to do? Answer me now." He lashed Annaji with his royal words.

Annaji was certain that his death was inevitable and there was no way out for him. He courageously exclaimed, "I don't have that right. We have enthroned Ramraje who is Swami's scion too. Even at this moment, I believe that what we did was in the best interests of the kingdom. Though I have been captured, I don't repent my actions! Had Swami been alive, he would have done the same."

"Silence! One needs a sensitive mind to repent one's wrongdoings, which you are incapable of. I am not at all interested in listening to your perception of what Aabasaheb would have done. He wouldn't have given the gift of the shackled elder brother to his young brother, like you did! You are so outrageously unrepentant of your wrongdoings! Why?"

His sharp words pierced Annaji's heart. He raised his head and said bitterly, "Why should I feel ashamed?" I haven't stolen anything from anybody, or defected to the arch enemy of the kingdom!"

"Annaji…!" Hambirao jumped out of his seat like an exploding bombshell. Trembling with rage he roared, "You had better watch your tongue or else…!" Annaji looked at Hambirarao's menacing face and lowered his head.

Sambhajiraje's eyes welled up. He couldn't bear to stand up there, so he promptly left the hall and went towards his chamber.

"Just take them away, and throw them in the dungeon." Hambirarao shook with rage and roared. He also left the court hall. The armed soldiers took the prisoners to the dungeons.

From the record office of Panhala, flocks of Mavalas were returning happily to their camps. They were paid two months' wages in advance, as per Sambhajiraje's instructions.

Sambhajiraje dictated the contents of the letter to be sent to Pilajimama in Shringarpur. Parashurampant noted it down, "Take your forces and leave for Raigad immediately. On your way, replace the previous surveillance teams with your own teams." Hambirarao, Ravaji, Mhalojibaba—everyone listened to it attentively.

Now Panhala had become a secured military post for Sambhajiraje. The subedars and hawaldars from nearby towns kept coming to Panhala to make an obeisance to him as their 'king'.

"Swami, the Biritish are expecting compensation from us. What should we do?" Ravaji Pandit who had come from Rajapur informed Sambhajiraje about the complaint of the British. Earlier, Maharaj had ransacked the British warehouses in Rajapur. The British in Rajapur were receiving remuneration for the damages caused at that time.

"Ravaji, inform them that I don't have time right now. I will first go through the previous deal and, then take a decision.

"Ji"

"Ravaji, sending the previous records from Rajapur to Kaarvaar to Panhala was outstanding. It proved quite useful for me."

"The viceroy of Goa has sent a letter of condolence on Swami's demise." Parashurampant read the letter.

"Pant, send them a reply – It is unfortunate that I have lost my father. I am the Kulekhtyar now, I will continue the previous policies with respect to you. Dispatch the letter to the Portuguese durbar at the hands of Ramaji Naik."

"Ji." The Chitnis started preparing the letter for the Viceroy of Goa, Antonio Pious de Sondes.

"Mama Saheb, we have received news from Raigad." Sambhajiraje said to Hambirarao sitting next to him.

"What news?"

"Yesaji Kank has captured some people in Raigad including Kanhoji Bhandwalkar, Shahaji Bhosale and Moropant's son Nilopant."

"Well done Yesaji Kank." Hambirarao exclaimed with content.

"Now before leaving for Raigad, I would like to fulfil one wish of mine." Sambhajiraje said with a smile.

"I am ready to shoulder any responsibility, and take any risk for you." Hambirarao said and wondered what Sambhajiraje had in mind.

"Well, take a look at it first." Sambhajiraje said and signalled to his personal secretary.

A few attendants came into the chamber holding covered platters in their hands. They placed the platters near Sambhajiraje's seat and left. Sambhajiraje uncovered the first big platter placed in front of him. He touched the platter with his hand and said, "Give this to him." That platter contained a turban, a shawl and a sword.

"What are you doing?" Hambirarao said and got up hastily.

"Please accept it, Mama Saheb. Had it been possible, I would have spread red carpets for you from the Chou Darwaja to the foothills of the fort!" Sambhajiraje didn't let Hambirarao raise any objections. Hambirarao touched the platter that the attendant held in front of him and said, "So, this is what you wanted to do, hmm…!"

Sambhajiraje touched another platter with his hands and the attendant presented it to Mhaloji Ghorpade. "Mhalojibaba, I appoint you as the Sarnoubat of Panhala from today. I believe you will perform your duty well with the assistance of Santaji and Bahirji."

"Ji." Mhaloji and his sons Santaji–Bahirji made an obeisance to him.

Sambhajiraje honoured Ravaji Pandit, Anandrao, Rupaji, Jotyaji and Antoji with gifts such as swords, apparel, and bracelets. He designated the custodian and hawaldar of Fort Panhala. While watching this, all the spectators felt as if they were present at Raigad.

"Mhalojibaba, keep a keen eye on the fort. After you receive my message, dispatch the prisoners to Raigad with armed surveillance. Farewell." Sambhajiraje embraced Mhaloji.

The kettle drums at the Chou Darwaja reverberated; the horns resonated. Sambhajiraje mounted a white horse named 'Chandravat' that looked as bright as the moon. Raje left from the Chou Darwaja with Hambirarao and twenty thousand pugnacious, brawny soldiers and began descending the fort. He was going to Raigad after a long three and a half years! So much had come to pass in those years!

Sambhajiraje's army crossed River Varana and via Battis Shirala it arrived at Karhad. They took the first sojourn. The tents and shamianas were erected. The cooks built stone stoves for cooking and ignited small fires. Cauldrons were placed on the stoves and curries simmered in the pots.

Sambhajiraje took a round of the encampment and came back. Hambirarao affectionately said to him, "Yuvraj, I have a favour to ask. If you may…"

"Mama Saheb, why are you talking so formally? Tell me, what is it?"

"I am your humble servant. I should not forget my status. My town is close by. If you would like to take the darshan of our family deity, Vagheshwari, and visit my residence…"

Sambhajiraje felt overwhelmed to see Hambirarao's affection. He approached Hambirarao and said, "Mama Saheb, forgive me. I should have expressed the desire to visit the family deity of the Sarlashkar. I actually wanted to say it, but...I hesitated as Talbeed is the Maharani's parental home. But...I will surely come and visit your home."

In the evening, with a retinue of fifty people, Sambhajiraje visited the Mohite residence at Talbeed. At night, he had dinner with Hambirrao, Anandrao, Rupaji and Shankaraji.

The next day, they all left early in the morning and returned to the encampment.

Sambhajiraje took a few Mavalas with him, and went to take a bath at the confluence of Krishna and Koyana rivers.

After taking a bath, he came back to the encampment. He came in front of his shamiana, dismounted, and threw the reins to the groom. As he was about to enter his shamiana, an ascetic clad in a saffron cloak approached him and made an obeisance. He said, "I have come to meet the Yuvraj from Korati, from Malharbaba Gosavi's ashram."

"Yes, I have heard about Malharbaba. How is he doing?"

"He is fine. He has sent a special message for Yuvraj."

"What message?"

"Baba's ashram had received the Nadoli village in reward, but it has been taken over by the civil office. That is why, the ashram is suffering financial hardships. Therefore..."

"Why was the rewarded village taken over?" Sambhajiraje wanted to know the details of the case.

"Malharbaba had received a letter from the late Chhatrapati that stated, 'the practice of granting villages in rewards had been discontinued and therefore the town is being taken over."

"How could it be? Aabasaheb was the patron of religious institutions. Gosavi, something doesn't seem right. I will come to meet Malharbaba in person and will take care of the matter. Rest assured." Sambhajiraje raised his hand and dismissed the ashram disciple.

After lunch, the army continued the journey. Sambhajiraje went to Kotari with Hambirarao and his retinue. Malharbuva's ashram was located near a stream. As Sambhajiraje approached the ashram, he dismounted and started out on foot.

The ashram was enclosed by a sturdy fence. Malharbuva stood at the gate with his disciples. He had a beard and matted hair; his face looked tranquil and contented. Sambhajiraje placed his head on his feet and said, "Please give me your blessings."

"Arise, Yuvaraj..." The ascetic remembered the late Chhatrapati and was overcome with emotions. He put his trembling hand on top of Yuvaraj's Jiretop. Sambhajiraje followed baba in the ashram and sat near his feet.

"Yuvraj, the Chhatrapati is no more. I am an ascetic. I know very well that death is an inevitable part of life, and still, I feel sad about the Chhatrapati's demise. You are his son. I can understand your pain. You should follow his legacy. Look after your kingdom, and take care of your people. Strengthen your heart so you can go one step ahead of him." Malharbaba's words were flowing as freely as the stream next to the ashram.

Sambhajiraje had heard such words after a long time. He felt peaceful and contented.

Sambhajiraje had a heart-to-heart chat with Malharbuva and left from the ashram. He felt contented. Trotting on the horse, he said to Hambirarao, "Mama Saheb, tell the Chitnis to send a letter to the officer in charge of Karhad, Bhanaji

Gopal –

"I have met Malharbaba Gosavi in person and have talked to him. He is a righteous, honest devotee of God. Please grant the Nadoli village to his ashram without any hesitation."

"Ji." Hambirarao also felt satisfied to hear the decision. Chandravat kept galloping towards Wai to join the army.

Sambhajiraje joined the army at the Wai camp. After resting for a day the entourage travelled via Mahabaleshwar, Radatondi ghat and arrived at the foothills of Pratapgad.

As Sambhajiraje saw the summit of Pratapgad where the murti of the family deity Goddess Bhavani had been installed, he made an obeisance to the fort. With five hundred soldiers and select men such as Hambirarao, Rupaji, Mahadaji, Rayaji and Antoji, Sambhajiraje started climbing Pratapgad to take darshan of Goddess Bhavani. The remaining army camped near the foothills.

The custodian of Pratapgad came to receive Sambhajiraje. With him, Sambhajiraje came to the fort summit. He visited the temple of Kedareshwar and on while his way to the Balekilla, he instructed the custodian of the fort, "Make preparations for the puja of Goddess Bhavani. I am going to spend some time here. I will visit the fort later."

"Ji." Said the custodian of the fort, and went to meet the priest of the temple of Goddess Bhavani.

It was late afternoon. Sambhajiraje washed his hands and feet and came out of the Balekilla. He stood alone near the rampart wall, and kept gazing to the north, in the direction of Raigad.

"Should we leave for the temple now? Everything is ready for the puja." Hambirarao said.

"Let's go."

Yuvraj entered Goddess Bhavani's temple with the Sarlashkar. He performed the puja and consumed the tirtha and prasad. He took a round of the fort and descended the fort with his retinue. Now he was looking forward to visiting Raigad.

Sambhajiraje joined his army and travelled to Mahad. Just then, heavy rains started, and the army got drenched in the deluge.

"Yuvraj has arrived!" Thunderous lightning delivered the news to Raigad.

Pilajimama who was on his way, had kept all the forts battle-ready. He united with Sambhajiraje's army. The torrent of armed Mavala soldiers gushed towards Raigad. As the army came to the borders of Pachad a cacophony of war horns and kettle drums ensued.

Sambhajiraje pulled out his sword out and raised his hand high. The Mavala soldiers following him shouted in unison "Har Har Mahadeo!"; the war cries shook the overcast skies.

Sardar Malsawant confronted Sambhajiraje with his forces at the borders of Pachad. It was as if a pack of wolves was trying to strike at a shrieking elephant who was charging upon them while trampling trees in its path. Sambhajiraje's eyes were breathing fire. He came forward and charged upon Malsawant himself.

Within a short time, Sambhajiraje threw him off his horse, on the muddy ground. The barrier was broken. Yuvraj and the Sarlashkar's army rushed into Pachad.

"Mama Saheb, you climb up the fort and meet with Yesajikaka. Take charge of the entire fort." Astride his horse, Sambhajiraje pointed his sword towards Raigad and instructed Pilajimama. Pilaji started ascending the fort with his forces.

Sambhajiraje came to Thoralya Aausaheb's samadhi with Hambirarao and Anandrao. He touched his head to the base of the samadhi; he didn't want to lift it. But with great effort, he got up and started walking towards the palace, to meet Putalabai Masaheb!

He came into the courtyard where the bell was hanging on a hook and stood under the bell; his heart was numb. He walked like a statue towards Putalabai's chamber. Putalabai stood near a window in the chamber. She looked like Jijau in a white sari.

"Masaheb, I'm here..." The chamber shivered.

Putalabai placed her palms on her face and started sobbing.

Unaware of his own tears trickling down his cheeks, Sambhajiraje stepped forward. He came to Putalabai and said in an agonized voice, "I – I am here Masaheb."

Sambhajiraje leaned forward to touch Putalabai's feet. She stopped him, took him in a deep embrace and said, sobbing, "How did all this happen, Yuvraj? Swari left this world without meeting you or me! Life seems meaningless, and I feel so weary now!" In her affectionate embrace Sambhajiraje felt, 'what if…I had been born to you…'

Putalabai came to a decision; she composed herself and held Sambhajiraje's shoulders. He was still looking down. She said to him determinedly, "Raise your head."

Sambhajiraje gazed into Masaheb's eyes. A moment ago, her eyes had been overcast like the skies, but now they looked clear skies. Her eyes were shining like the sun.

"You call me 'Masaheb', then will you fulfil a wish of mine?" She spoke in a voice just like Maharaj.

"Ji. Your wish is my command." Sambhajiraje said courteously.

"Then consider this as my first as well as last command. Place your hand on the cowrie necklace and promise that you will fulfil my wish."

"Ji. I promise."

"Shambhoobal, Swari has left us, now–now I want to end my life too!! I want to hold Swari's mojaris close to my heart and go Sati! Make preparations for that." Putalabai's eyes were fixed mid-air; she looked like a statue! Motionless and determined.

Heartbroken, Sambhajiraje fell at her feet and clasped them. He sobbed helplessly, "What did you say Masaheb! Why did you make me promise such a thing?!" But the statue standing tall could not hear a single word he said.

"We have taken charge of the fort. Please come at the earliest possible." As soon as Sambhajiraje received the message of Yesaji Kank and Pilajimama, he left Pachad and began climbing up Raigad. Five thousand Mavalas followed him.

It was raining. Whenever the rain showers halted, Hambirarao signalled the palanquin-bearers to take the empty palanquin in front of Sambhajiraje. Sambhajiraje signalled them with his hand and kept refusing to take the palanquin. Instead, he took shelter under a nearby tree. As soon as the rain lessened, he started climbing up the fort again. Lahana Darwaja passed;

the manors at the forefront of Raigad were visible.

Sambhajiraje glanced at the inundated Lake Gangasagar and came to the tower. All the personnel and employees of the eighteen departments had swarmed there. Aged Yesaji Kank approached Sambhajiraje. He was about to bow down to Sambhajiraje, when Sambhajiraje stepped forward quickly, touched his feet and said, "Yesajikaka, you should give me your blessings!" Yesaji pulled him up and embraced him. In an overwhelmed voice he said, "Oh, what took you so long! The fort has lost its dignity. It's good that you are back now. We have captured everyone who was plotting against you. You should now take charge of the fort and its administration."

"Well, we are going to do it together Yesajikaka. I can't do it all alone."

'Yuvraj has arrived at the fort!' People in the fort had come to know about it and thronged both sides of the path. Taking the light rain showers on his body and accepting the obeisance from the people around him, Sambhajiraje entered the temple of Jagadishwar. He took the darshan of the Shivlinga and came to the Maha Darwaja. The kettle drums in the Nagar Khana of Raigad resounded for the first time in three months.

The royal throne of Swaraj stood vacant. It looked like an orphan without its master.

Sambhajiraje took one step at a time and came to the royal throne. He had to stand as an accused in the same durbar. He stopped momentarily at the same spot. Sambhajiraje felt restless and glanced all around.

He started climbing the steps leading to the royal throne. Hambirarao, Anandrao, Yesaji, Madari...everyone looked at him with bated breath. No one had ever climbed those steps from the durbar hall.

Sambhajiraje stopped at the step where he used to sit as the Yuvraj. His own image sitting on the step flashed in his mind.

He stepped forward and stood in front of the royal throne.

The people standing around got restless, and stared at each other in bewilderment. They thought Yuvraj was going to sit on the royal throne without a formal coronation. They waited with bated breath.

The vacant royal throne looked utterly gloomy. The images of the lions with open jaws on the hand rests looked lifeless. The parasol looked unsteady.

At that moment, Sambhajiraje deeply felt Aabasaheb's absence.

Sambhajiraje untied the sword fastened around his waist. He touched the scabbard to his forehead and placed his sword at the base of the royal throne. He knelt down and touched his forehead to the base as if he was touching Maharaj's feet. He was overcome with emotions.

The people had gathered in the durbar hall and watched the scene. It moved their hearts. Many among them immediately enthroned Sambhajiraje in their hearts.

Those people buried deep the bitter truth that Sambhajiraje had once defected to an enemy like Diler Khan. They wanted to have a mighty king who could carry the onus of the royal throne on his shoulders – just like Sambhajiraje, young, brawny, pugnacious, and above all ready to put his own life on the line for the sake of the late Chhatrapati's love, pride and honour. A king who could defend the grace of the royal throne. A king, in whom they could see the Shivachhatrapati in their memory; a king who belonged to the same lineage. Sambhajiraje's heart was overburdened with the events happening in his life. He had placed his head at the base of the royal throne in an emotional moment to get some peace of mind. But his action won over the hearts of all people assembled in the durbar hall. For the last three months the durbar hall had been spiritless, but today it was taking a new breath; it was coming back to life.

The ryots could not visit Maharaj during his illness; they could not witness the enthronement of Ramraje, but today their wish had come true. They were looking at the future king that they had dreamed of.

Sambhajiraje left the platform of the royal throne and began walking towards Maharaj's chamber.

The court hall where Maharaj used to sit came in sight. Some platters were placed on Maharaj's seat containing his jama, Jiretop, breeches and weapons. Sambhajiraje kept gazing at everything. He imagined Maharaj dressed in the royal attire standing in front of him. He had spread his arms wide and was asking him, "Oh my dear son, where were you?"

Sambhajiraje kept a respectful distance from the seat and took another seat in the court hall. People from the durbar hall entered the court hall one by one through the Palakhi Darwaja. Yuvraj instructed Changoji Katkar from among them, "Changoji, prepare a platter with royal gifts."

"Ji." Changoji left to make the preparations.

"whom have you captured so far?" Yuvraj glanced at Yesajikaka and Mama Saheb and asked.

"Bapuji Mali, Suryaji Nimkar, Bhandwalakar and Ghatage." Pilajimama provided the details.

"We have also put Balaji Chitnis, his son Aavaji and Hiroji Farzand under house arrest." Yesaji said

"Okay, Yesajikaka, you took prompt actions, otherwise..."

"I was really tired of their deceitful actions. They locked down the entrance gates of the fort, they put Dhani under surveillance! I have many men at my disposal, but these people didn't even bother to seek my opinion."

"Kaka, you were a hindrance to them. Your loyalty was an obstruction for them."

Sambhajiraje was waiting for Changoji. As he saw Changoji coming from the side of the treasury, with an attendant carrying the gift platter Sambhajiraje said to Hambirarao, "Mama Saheb, come with me."

He left the court hall and started walking to the queens'

palaces. Hambirarao, Changoji and the attendant carrying the platter followed him.

The maids serving the queens' palaces saw Yuvraj approaching. This caused a commotion among them.

The door of Maharani Soyarabai's palace creaked shut. Sambhajiraje approached that closed door and glanced at Hambirarao. Hambirarao understood his gesture and came forward.

"Open the door!" Hambirarao thumped his hand on the door. The silver bracelet on his wrist collided on the door making a clanking sound. Hambirarao continued thumping the door.

Somebody was whispering inside; fleeting words could be heard outside, "…Listen to me. Don't go!"

"Leave me…let me go!"

After a while the door opened and Ramraje stood in the door. His face was flushed; he was about to cry. He called out to Sambhajiraje as he always used to call him, "Dada Maharaj…!"

Sambhajiraje approached him quickly. Ramraje was about to touch his feet, when Sambhajiraje embraced him and exclaimed, "Balraje!". He stopped Balraje and said, "Don't be scared. Look at me."

Ramraje looked at the towering figure of his Dada Maharaj; he choked but the words slipped out of his mouth, "You…are you going to kill my Masaheb?"

Sambhajiraje trembled to hear those words; in deep anguish. he embraced Ramraje tightly. When he heard those unthinkable words, he froze. His hand stroked Ramraje's back and conveyed to him, "No matter what she does, she is still my Masaheb."

Ramraje was still sobbing. Sambhajiraje consoled him and said, "Calm down! Be quiet! Accept the gift your Dada Maharaj has brought for you."

Ramraje touched the gift platter and touched teary-eyed Hambir mama's feet.

Sambhajiraje took Ramraje with him and started walking

towards Sakawarbai's palace. Soyarabai was sitting in front of the family deity, Goddess Vagheshwari, in the sanctum of her palace. She had placed her head at the feet of the Goddess; she was sobbing, and her entire body was shaking. She had neither understood Goddess Vagheshwari and Sambhajiraje nor her own son Ramraje!

"Thann…thann…thann…." Sambhajiraje closely listened to the sounds floating on the early morning wind. The cacophony of birds mingled with the sounds of the bell. In the temple of Lord Jagadishwar, the early morning arti had commenced. Yuvraj touched his chest with his hand and prayed to Lord Jagadishwar. He gazed at his own palms, removed his shawl and got up from his bed.

He called a guard, "Anybody there?"

A soldier came in. Sambhajiraje ordered him, "Summon Changoji here at the earliest." He went to the Hammam Khana to freshen up.

Within a short time, as Sambhajiraje came out of the Hammam Khana wiping his hands and his face, Changoji presented himself in front of Yuvaraj.

He was wondering, 'Why did Yuvaraj remember me so early today?'

"Changoji, does the bell in the courtyard of Pachad still continue to ring in memory of Thoralya Aausaheb or not?"

Half asleep Changoji came to his senses in an instant.

"Ji." He faltered.

"Why the hesitation?"

"Since the time Thorale Dhani fell ill, no one even realized that the practice had discontinued." Changoji told the truth.

"Oh, so the situation had deteriorated to that low level… hmmm! Katkar, such family practices should not be discontinued so easily. Whenever that bell rings, it gives me a sense that Thoralya Aausaheb is still present in the vicinity of the fort. You go to Pachad today itself, and make sure that the practice resumes."

"Ji." Changoji bowed down and was about to leave.

"And take a palanquin guarded by armed soldiers with you."

"Ji" said Changoji and left. Sambhajiraje kept gazing from the window, in the direction of Pachad. It was pouring outside; nothing was visible at a distance.

A maid came in with a steaming bowl on a platter. She placed the platter on a wooden stool and said, "Shirke mama is waiting outside."

"Send him in." Sambhajiraje picked up the steaming bowl from the platter; it was porridge. Pilaji mama stood at the door. Sambhajiraje placed the bowl back on the platter and went forward to receive him. When he touched Pilajirao's feet, his heart was filled with memories of Yesubai.

"Yuvraj, what about your wife? My daughter has been in poor health. It's been more than a year since she's saw you." Pilaji's voice was heavy.

"Mama Saheb, my fate dragged me to strange places. You know that I am coming back to Raigad after three and a half years. Please send your men to Shringarpur and bring Yuvaradnyi here. Also summon Keshav Pandit, Udho Yogadeo and Kavi Kulesh.

"Ji." Pilaji smiled after a long time.

"Why did you put it back? Have it." Pilaji mama pointed to the bowl sitting on the platter and said affectionately.

"Ji…that…" Sambhajiraje didn't know what to say.

"Let me take your leave now. I will send my men to Shringarpur today itself." Pilaji left.

Sambhajiraje kept gazing at the vapours rising from the bowl. He saw Bhavanibai's tender face in it. 'She must have grown up a bit by now; and Yuvaradnyi? Mama spoke about her poor health. Yes Yesu, what you say is true, that you have been married to the wild wind. Not just you, but your co-wife too! At least, you are living at your parents' home, but she…?' Sambhajiraje's heart became heavy with the memory of Durgabai and Madan Singh who were confined in the fort of Nagar.

After having his bath and taking Goddess Bhavani's darshan, Sambhajiraje came to the court hall. All courtiers made an obeisance to him. Yuvraj took his seat.

"With your permission I would like to present some news received from Aurangabad…" Ragho Swanand, the record-keeper said.

Sambhajiraje raised his hand and granted permission. All the courtiers listened to the news carefully.

"The Delhi Durbar has called back Shah Alam, the subedar of Deccan, and has appointed Khan Jahan Bahadur Kokalatash in his place. Khan has arrived in Aurangabad and is in the process of assembling his army."

Sambhajiraje's forehead puckered; he was lost in thought. This was a significant change after Maharaj's demise. As the subedar, Shah Alam had never left Aurangabad.

"Convey this information to all forts located near the Mughal borders and tell them to be battle-ready and stay alert."

"Ji." Ragho Swanand bowed.

"Mama Saheb, send a message to Panhala to send the prisoners here." Sambhajiraje instructed Hambirarao.

"Ji. The treasury, record office, jewellery warehouse… everything is sealed. The personnel of all departments cannot perform their duties until the offices are reopened." Hambirarao stated the problem the personnel at the fort were facing.

Sambhajiraje felt sad to hear it, but he composed himself and said with determination, "Sarlashkar, you take the initiative and break the seals of all departments in front of their chiefs and tell them to make a detailed list of goods in each department. Aabaji, you take charge as Surnis."

"Swami, a complaint has been lodged." Ragho Swanand presented another case in front of Sambhajiraje.

"Who has lodged the complaint?"

"Manaku Rudrappa, the Desai of the Murgoad town near Bailhongal."

"What does he have to say? I had sent a letter to him from Panhala that I will continue the agreement of the levy formulated by Maharaj Saheb."

"He has no complaints about that. Manakoji collects the levy to remunerate expenses and pay the salaries of the people who maintain the estates on Katorgad in the Belgaum region. But recently, our officer, Vitthal Hari, has been interfering in that area and collecting levy as an intermediary. Due to this, there is a dearth of funds in the Katorgad treasury." Raghopant provided the details.

"Raghopant, send a letter of warning to Vitthal Hari and tell him, "You have no right to collect any levies! If you interfere in the levy collection process in the Murgoad area, you will not be spared.' Also, tell Manakoji to continue the collection of levies as before and not to have any deficit of funds."

"Ji."

The courtiers assembled in the court hall were satisfied with Sambhajiraje's prompt, cautious and flawless decisions.

"The palanquin of Pachad's Rani Saheb has reached near the tower." An attendant sent by Changoji delivered the news. Sambhjiraje rose from his seat and left.

As she saw him, Putalabai stepped out of her palanquin. Sambhajiraje touched her feet. Hambirarao, Raghopant, Yesaji, Anandrao and others made an obeisance to her.

"Let's go, Masaheb." Sambhajiraje pointed to the Palakhi Darwaraja leading to the queens' palaces. Putalabai walked as if she had yielded her all in Lake Gangasagar. She came to Sakawarbai's palace and said, "Yuvraj, summon the royal priest at the earliest. Swari's obsequies were not duly performed. I am going to consult him and get all necessary rituals performed duly." She sounded as if she was not in this world.

Sambhajiraje summoned the royal priest, Balambhat. Balambhat presented himself in Sakawarbai's palace. Putalabai asked him, "Shastribuva, which rituals of Swari's obsequies were not performed duly?"

"Swami's funeral pyre was set alight without performing proper rituals. His thread ceremony had been performed according to the Shastras; his funeral pyre too should have been lit as per the Shastras."

"You were present here at that time, then why didn't you make sure it happened properly?" Putalabai's eyes flashed with righteous anger.

The royal priest was startled; he hastily said, "Masaheb, it was not my presence that mattered at that time. As the elder son of Swami, Yuvaraj had to be present to light the funeral pyre."

Sambhajiraje felt restless and asked, "Then what can we do now? What do the scriptures say?"

"We can still perform the due obsequies for Swami."

"How?" Sambhajiraje asked. Deep down, He felt satisfied.

"Yuvraj can perform Swami's funeral rites on his wooden statue." Sambhajiraje and Putalabai kept staring at each other.

"Okay Shastribuva, then you should start the preparations as per the Shastras." Putalabai said with resolve.

"Ji." The royal priest was about to leave.

"And one more thing, find a Mahurat for me. I am going to commit Sati…"

"Masaheb…" Sambhajiraje was going to say something, but Putalabai raised her hand and said, "Yuvraj, you have promised me, now don't say anything to prevent me from implementing my decision." Putalabai left calmly.

A benumbed Sambhajiraje was pacing back and forth in his chamber.

"Dhani…" Rayaji entered the chamber.

"What is it?"

"Rani Saheb has arrived from Shringarpur. Her palanquin

is climbing up the fort!"

Sambhajiraje was lost in thoughts. Many memories of Yesubai instantly flashed in front of his eyes.

"Let's go." Sambhajiraje started walking towards the tower. From the second floor of the tower, his eyes were riveted on the path leading to the entrance of the tower.

A draped palanquin, surrounded by Keshav Pandit, Udho Yogadeo, Changoji, Kavi Kulesh and Pilaji stopped at the base of the tower. First, Dharau stepped out of the palanquin, holding eighteen-month-old Bhavanibai in her arms.

Yesubai touched the stone threshold of the entrance to the tower and entered the Balekilla. Sambhajiraje left the tower.

Yesubai went to the queens' palaces, to seek the blessings of Putalabai, Sakawarbai and…and Soyarabai too!

Dharau, carrying Bhavanibai in her arms came to Sambhajiraje's chamber. Sambhajiraje took Bhavanibai from her and, holding her in his arms, he touched Dharau's feet. Dharau pulled Raje close affectionately; stroked his face with her shaking hands and said, "Oh my dear child, you have lost so much weight!"

As she saw Sambhajiraje kissing Bhavanibai's cheeks, tears started trickling from her eyes.

"Dada Maharaj!" A loving voice called from the door. Yesubai was coming with Ramraje. She looked peaceful, tranquil and solemn. As she approached her Swari, she leaned forward and touched his feet.

"Yesu…" Only one word, full of so many emotions, barely came out of Sambhajiraje's mouth.

As she heard his voice, Yesubai pressed the edge of her sari to her lips and started sobbing. Her entire body trembled. They wanted to say so much to each other, and yet neither of them could utter a single word. Sambhajiraje kept stroking Bhavanibai's back; his mind wandered somewhere else.

The eleventh day of Aashadh struggled to break through

the overcast skies. People from the nearby villages started climbing up Raigad in flocks. Despite the thronging crowds, silence prevailed on the fort.

Putalabai took a bath early in the morning, took darshan of Lord Jagadishwar and Goddess Bhavani and sat on the seat raised for her in the court hall. She had donned a fresh green sari, a necklace of black beads and had applied horizontal kumkum stripes on her forehead. Yesubai, Sakawarbai, Dharau and other ladies stood behind her. Sambhajiraje, Ramraje, Pilajimama, Hambirarao, Yesaji, Anandrao, and Keshav Pandit stood in front of her with their heads bowed low. The royal priest, Balambhat kept glancing at the time-measuring copper pot placed near him while chanting mantras. His voiced mingled with the mantras chanted by the priests from Nashik and Tryambak. Some gift platters were lined up nearby. Yesubai handed them to Putalabai one by one. Putalabai distributed the gifts to suvasinees as a part of the ritual of becoming Sati. As the suvasinees touched Putalabai's feet with their foreheads daubed with kumkum, her feet were covered in kumkum. Her face glowed.

The royal priest placed a golden platter in front of her. It contained a pair of orange mojaris of the late Chhatrapati which had served their master lifelong. Putalabai imagined as if Maharaj was standing in front of her and offered haldi-kumkum and flowers to the mojaris.

Putalabai joined her palms and closed her eyes. Amidst the chanting of mantras, the water of holy rivers was poured on her head. Balambhat saw that the time-indicating pot had sunk halfway in the big vessel and said, "It's time to leave…" Four Mavalas picked up the big vessel with the time-indicating pot.

Putalabai rose. Yesubai clasped her feet and sobbed, "Masaheb…"

Putalabai placed her hand on Yesubai's head and blessed her dispassionately, "May you have a happy married life. Look after Yuvraj and Balraje."

The retinue approached the stone pillar erected near the queens' palaces – 'The Pillar of Sati!' It was erected along with the queens' palaces as per the Rajput custom. It was going to be worshipped for the first time today. Putalabai offered flowers to the pillar. There was a tradition regarding this pillar. Once a royal lady who desired to commit Sati, determinedly offered kumkum to the pillar and worshiped it, there was no turning back for her. She had to become Sati.

Putalabai glanced at the pillar. She was about to offer kumkum to the pillar; her hand stopped for a moment. Her heart, deeply involved in Sambhajiraje, was trying to pull her back. Putalabai painstakingly controlled her heart, composed herself, and calmly offered kumkum to the pillar that was waiting to be honoured.

Putalabai who was all drenched held her palms in front of her. The royal priest placed the orange Mojaris of Maharaj in her palms.

Putalabai was departing for the last time, leaving behind all bonds. Holding the Mojaris of Maharaj in her hands, a determined Putalabai was about to follow her husband's footsteps to the heavens! Sambhajiraje was moved from the bottom of his heart. He didn't realize when Ramraje's hand slipped from his hand. His numb feet turned around, and he started walking back… towards his chamber!

Countless people called out to Putalabai, "Aausaheb… Masaheb…" and prostrated at her feet. The whole area thronged with crowds. Numerous people holding their turbans under their arms, had gathered there to honour the Sati.

A tall funeral pyre of sandalwood logs had been erected in the centre of the yard. Putalabai came to the pyre. From all four sides, ladders were placed against the pyre to climb on it. The time-indicating vessel had almost sunk to its brim. The royal priest signalled the Brahmins to stop chanting the mantras. He approached Putalabai and said, "Masaheb, the mahurat is approaching soon. Who do you wish should light the pyre?"

"Yuvraj." Putalabai said firmly without moving her eyes from the pyre.

The royal priest shook his head in negation and said in a heavy voice, "Forgive me, but Yuvraj is not present here!"

"What? Summon him here immediately. Send him a message that – though he is the Yuvraj, I am the Rani Saheb! I order him to come here and light my funeral pyre! Her eyes looked as bright as the ignited torches of Goddess Jagadamba.

"Ji." The royal priest promptly sent a messenger to Yuvraj. The messenger delivered the message verbatim to Sambhajiraje.

Sambhajiraje wiped his eyes, and obediently presented himself at the Kala Haud. He touched Putalabai's feet and said, "Masaheb, I am here!"

"May you have a long life! May you be victorious!" Putalabai gave her blessings for the last time.

"Light my funeral pyre."

"Ji."

"Farewell! Take care of Balraje and Soonbai! Remember me in the difficult times! You are my son. Jagadamb!" With her forehead daubed in kumkum, wet Putalabai calmly climbed up the ladder and set foot on the pyre. She took her seat on the pyre facing the east. She touched the Mojaris of Maharaj to her forehead and placed them in front of her. She remembered the family deity and closed her eyes!

A few men stacked sandalwood logs around the Sati up to her neck. Sambhajiraje was smothered by unbearable sorrow; he dragged himself up the ladder onto the funeral pyre. Putalabai's palms were visible through the stack of logs.

The royal priest followed Sambhajiraje. Sambhajiraje bit his lip to suppress his sobs and picked up a fistful of camphor pieces from the platter the royal priest held in front of him. With teary eyes he placed the camphor in the palms of the Sati and lit it. He kept putting fist after fist full of camphor in the palms of the Sati. The Sati had been duly honoured by her family member. The birds of fiery flames arose from the sandalwood pyre and soared in the sky.

Benumbed, Sambhajiraje climbed down the ladder, still holding the last fistful of camphor. He did not look at the people around him but started walking to the Balekilla with lowered head. Ear-splitting cannon blasts honouring the Sati echoed over Raigad.

Shambhooraje came to the Pillar of the Sati and helplessly touched his numbed forehead to it. His body shivered with the feel of the wet kumkum from the pillar on his forehead. The pieces of camphor slipped from his fist and scattered on the ground. He had managed to suppress his pain so far, but now the agony was bursting out. His burning heart cried in silence, 'Masaheb…Masaheb!' Benumbed, he stood still in the same position for a long time.

"If you lose heart like this, what will the others do?" He had not even realized when Yesubai had come there and was standing behind him.

Sambhajiraje lifted his head, looked at the pieces of camphor scattered on the ground and said, "No Yesu, though you are my better half, you wouldn't understand my grief. The hands that used to put a blob of curds on my palms every time I left Raigad, today I put pieces of camphor in the same hands! My hands are indeed so unfortunate! Please leave me alone." He kept gazing at his own hand as if it was the culprit and started walking towards his chamber.

On the way to his chamber, his eyes fell upon Soyarabai's palace. A shooting pain filled his heart as he saw the closed doors and windows of her palace. 'Putala Masaheb, who could not spend much time with Aabasaheb, committed Sati with the Mojarais of Aabasaheb, and this Masaheb who sat next to Aabasaheb to get herself coronated as the Maharani stays in her palace; she didn't even come to the Kala Haud to pay last respects to the Sati! Oh, Goddess Jagadamba, why do you play such a game?' Even She did not have an answer to that question.

The day of Aashadhi Ekadashi had broken its customary fast by devouring Putalabai.

Sambhajiraje had put Soyarabai's palace under surveillance so that people would not be able to take disadvantage of Ramraje's innocence and do something treacherous. But Soyarabai was deeply hurt by his actions. Whenever somebody came to visit her, she started claiming that she was not the Maharani but a prisoner.

Sambhajiraje came to know about her grievance. So, he summoned Yesaji Dabhade in his chamber. Yesaji was the personal secretary of Ramraje and was a trusted sardar of the Maharani. Yuvaraj explained the situation to him and said, "Yesaji, placing the Maharani's palace under surveillance was the toughest thing to do, and only I know how I felt while taking that decision. Balraje is still young. I would like you to continue serving him as before. Keep a keen eye on him."

"Ji. I will make sure that he doesn't fall into wrong company." Yesaji reassured him and left.

After some time, Hambirarao, Kavi Kulesh, Keshav Pandit, Udho Yogadeo and Khandoji Ballal entered the chamber. Sambhajiraje frowned to see Khandoji bowing down to him. Khandoji quickly realized that Sambhajiraje had misunderstood him. He promptly said, "Please don't misunderstand me, Swami. I haven't come here to seek pardon for my brother or my father. These are difficult times, and I am here to tell you that I am at your service." Balaji was Khandoji's father.

Sambhajiraje's eyes glowed to hear his resolute words. He approached Khandoji, placed his hand on Khandoji's shoulder and said, "You behaved just as I had expected you to. You and I, in fact, everyone has a lot to learn from my mama saheb. Family relations should not hamper your duty to the kingdom." Sambhajiraje honoured Hambirarao duly.

Hambirarao took the opportunity and broached the subject that was on his mind and that of many others, "Not just family relations, in fact, nothing should hamper our duty towards the kingdom. You should take the decision now and solve this problem."

"What decision are you talking about Sarlashkar?" Sambhajiraje didn't get what Hambirarao was implying.

"How long should the kingdom remain without a king? You should now ascend the throne." Hambirarao voiced the wish of many people and the practical problem in implementing decisions.

"What Sarlashkar says is right. How can the administration run unless the Yuvraj is enthroned?" Kavi Kulesh seconded him.

It was indeed a significant concern. It wouldn't be wise to hand over the administrative power to young Ramraje. There was no guarantee what Soyarabai would do in his name. It was easy to bow to the throne of Maharaj, but Sambhajiraje was aware that it was not easy to inherit the royal throne. He became solemn and said, "Let me think about it. Udho Yogadeo, the administrative office needs a head. For now, you take charge of the administrative office and keep it running.

"Ji." Udho Yogadeo joined his palms and bowed.

"Mama Saheb, the prisoners will soon arrive here from Panhala. What is your advice in that case?" Sambhajiraje broached the topic that was on his mind.

"Yuvaraj should investigate them and deliver justice as he wishes."

"I have investigated them and have concluded that Prahlad Niraji and Rahuji mistakenly got involved in the situation. I am thinking of setting both free."

"As you wish." Hambirarao felt a bit relieved.

"Kaviji, let's go and take darshan of Lord Jagadishwar."

Raje left the Balekilla with Kavi Kulesh and Keshav Pandit. They arrived at the Jagadishwar temple.

Sambhajiraje went into the sanctum, offered flowers and bael leaves on the Shivlinga, consumed the tirtha and stepped out of the temple.

As Yuvraj reached the court hall in the palace, the Yadav brothers, Girjoji and Arjoji made an obeisance to him.

"When did you come, Girjoji?"

"We have just arrived of the fort. We picked up the news from Nagar and left immediately."

"What's the news?"

Girjoji hesitated for a moment and delivered the news slowly, "In the haveli of Nagar…Dhakalya Rani Saheb…"

Sambhajiraje stood up in fear and exclaimed, "What happened to her?"

"Ji. Nothing to worry about. She has given birth to a boy!"

Sambhajiraje kept staring at Kaviji and Pandit. His eyes betrayed the turmoil in his heart, "Don't I resemble that stone tortoise? How many steps do I have to bear on my back? Here, I am discussing my enthronement here and there my son, Aabasaheb's grandson has been born in the Mughal prison of Nagar."

The auspicious day of Lalitapanchami, fixed for the enthronement ceremony, dawned. Shambhooraje had cautiously taken the decision of his enthronement.

No one from the ministers stood near the golden pillar of honour today, because this was no coronation ceremony. It was only a formal ritual of enthronement to declare that Sambhajiraje had taken charge of his duties. On the mahurat, Sambhajiraje made an obeisance to the royal throne and sat on it amidst the chanting of mantras.

As an appointed king Sambhajiraje gave the customary touch to the platter containing the royal seal and the dagger. He held the spear with the image of the golden fish, till the royal sceptre had been blessed with the proper mantras.

He began distributing the platters containing gifts to honour the courtiers.

The cannons on Raigad boomed loudly in honour of the newly enthroned king. As if they were proclaiming to the British, the Siddis, the Portuguese and the Mughal sultanate, Adil Shahi and Qutub Shahi, "Shivaji is no more but now 'Sambhaji has taken the onus of the kingdom!"

"Sarlashkar, Kokal Khan of the Deccan subah has started showing his true colours. He launched a surprise attack on Ahiwantgad. Shyamaji Keshav, the record-keeper of the fort, has sent his messenger from Khandesh." Raje said to Hambirarao. He had just returned after surveying the armoury, granary and ammunition warehouses.

"Did the fort…?" The Senapati was worried.

"No, the fort did not fall. It is standing tall. The custodian of the fort fought hard and forced Khan to retreat. Mama Saheb, we should send a message to Shyamaji and the custodian of the fort should be rewarded with the robe of honour."

"Ji. Dhani, we have received some very bad news from the island of Khanderi."

"Must be the insolence of the Siddis."

"Ji. We lost our most valuable sailor, Maynak Bhandari's son. About two weeks back, with three hundred soldiers, he had raided the sea fort of the Siddi on the Underi island in the night. Due to the utter darkness and the unfamiliarity of the new place his raid failed. The insolent Siddi, beheaded Maynak's son and eighty soldiers and carried their heads to Mumbai." Hambirrao visualized the heads without the torsos and his voice choked.

Shambhooraje was benumbed when he heard the news.

"Sarlashkar, send a letter of consolation to Maynak Bhandari. Tell him, "You have lost your son, the kingdom has lost an invaluable warrior. We will take care of you." Raje got lost in the thoughts of Siddi.

"The Siddi is a rat gnawing at our kingdom. He grabs

anything he lays his hands on and hides in the Janjira fort. We should settle the score with him." Hambirarao spoke furiously.

"I agree with you, Mama Saheb, I am aware of how he had been harassing Aabasaheb. I am going to have a meeting with Maynak, Daulat Khan, Kanhoji and Govindaji Ghate. We cannot rule the seas until we overthrow the Siddis in the region." As Raje arrived at the Maha Darwaja, Changoji made an obeisance to him and shared some news, "The prisoners from Panhala have arrived at the fort."

Raje glanced at Hambirarao and thought for some time. He came to decision, and commanded Changoji, "Changoji, release Prahlad Niraji and Rahuji and send them to meet me."

"Ji..." Changoji lingered for a moment hoping to hear something more.

"That's it. You may leave." Raje abruptly closed the topic.

As Raje came to the court hall of the royal palace, Ragho Swanand approached him, holding some rolls of paper in his hands.

"Swami, the lists of materials from all departments except for the treasury have been prepared. Everyone thinks that it is crucial to break the seal of the treasury in your presence." Raghopant said while fidgeting with the rolls in his hands.

"Okay. I will review the lists of all departments myself. Inform everyone about it."

Raghopant lingered for a moment, but shared another piece of news before leaving, "The British envoy of Rajapur has arrived to ask for baksheesh."

Sambhajiraje's face turned stern, and voice became harsh. He commanded Raghopant, "Give him a warning to kick out the Siddi from Mumbai first, and then come to me for baksheesh! Don't even bring him in front of me."

"Ji." Raghopant was about to leave when another instruction fell upon his ears, "Give him a proper farewell and send him back at the earliest. Don't let him stay on the fort for long."

Raje was about to say something to Hambirarao when an attendant came and announced, "Prahladpant is here."

"Send him in." Raje raised his hand in consent; his mind was crowded with various memories. Prahladpant and Rahuji came inside, made an obeisance and stood with lowered heads. A strange silence prevailed.

Shambhooraje arose from his seat, approached Prahladpant and said, "Don't be afraid, Nyayadhish. I am not going to recount the allegations against you. I have thoroughly investigated your movements from the time of Aabasaheb's demise to the time you left for Panhala. I also received the letter of negotiation you sent, though rather late. You are the Nyayadhish. I have summoned you here to share my views about the duties of the Nyayadhish, and not to criticize you." Raje's eyes shone with the same lustre that they had when he had sat on the royal throne during the enthronement ceremony. The words that flowed from his mouth stirred Prahladpant's heart –

"Aabasaheb, who shouldered the responsibility of the kingdom passed away. After his demise, the Surnis and Peshwe conspired against me and came to capture me. You should have been the one to support me at that time. You were the Nyayadhish– the one who serves justice and stands against injustice. Sarlashkar Mohite mama fulfilled your duty at that time! I got justice at his hands…on the battlefield!

"A Nyayadhish may not be able to serve justice at times, but even unwittingly he should not uphold injustice in any way." Prahladpant, Rahuji, Hambirarao everyone felt as if Maharaj himself was standing in front of them and talking to them.

While pacing back and forth, lost in thought, Sambhajiraje spoke his heart out – "Pant, keep in mind that every person has three mothers. First, the biological mother who gives birth; second, the Mother Earth who nourishes the body throughout life and provides the final resting place and the third one is Mother Justice who keeps a close watch on a person throughout his life, even though her eyes are blindfolded.

"The first one has eyes that are full of love and can't see any flaws or defects. The second one doesn't have any eyes. The third one must blindfold her eyes. Why? So that, no sentimental mistake will be committed by her while serving justice. Pant, you were the Nyayadhish, and yet you opened the blindfold. Your conscience was compromised. You let go of the scales of justice from your own hands, and you yourself sat on one of the pans. Forgetting all the pain your actions have caused me, I am honourably reinstating you as the Nyayadhish. Please use your powers wisely. I will not spare another mistake. I cannot express the pain I felt to see the Nyayadhish standing in the place of the accused. Don't make me face such a situation again."

Prahladpant's eyes welled up. He joined his hands and shaking his head he said in a choked voice, "Swami, forgive me. I repent my misdeeds…." He could not speak further.

"Prahladpant, it reflects your sense of duty. Take charge of your office from tomorrow."

"Rahuji, you used to look after the fort's administrative affairs. Instead of worrying about who is in power, ensure that the capital keeps running smoothly! You should also resume your administrative duty."

"Ji." Rahuji and Prahladpant made an obeisance and started walking out. Prahladpant had never experienced something like this during the reign of the late Maharaj! What if he had been caught in such a situation then? … He was overwhelmed by the thought. He turned around, walked back hastily, and tried to touch Sambhajiraje's feet.

Raje quickly stepped back, pulled him up, embraced him and said, "Pant, you and I, both have a big responsibility on our shoulders. Just stand by me."

Lost in thought, Raje came to Yesubai's chamber. Yesubai held Bhavanibai in her arms and Dharau was dressing her.

Bhavanibai kept calling "Aaba…aaba…". Yesubai handed

her to Raje and said, "Swari must have known by now that Dhakalya bai has delivered a son."

Both got lost in memories Durgabai.

Raje left the palace to assess the property of all departments. He was accompanied by Prahlad Niraji, Hambirarao, Yesaji, Raghunath Narayan, Kavi Kulesh, Rahuji, Aabaji Sonadeo and Changoji.

The treasury, armoury, granary…Raje visited all departments and made an assessment of the property in each department. As Raje left the elephant camp he was lost in thought. Raghunath Narayan politely said to him, "Swami, we have received a letter from Ganoram, the officer in charge of Kudal."

"About what?"

"Yogi Namadeobhat Bakare who resided there, passed way. He has a son. Ganoram suggests that we should support the family."

Raje stopped walking and said, "Pant, send the royal gift and some horses to Bakarebuva's son. Allocate a fixed yearly amount for the family's livelihood and prepare a gift deed accordingly. After getting my seal on it, dispatch it to Kudal. Aabaji, you review the deed and give your approval for it.

"Ji." Raghunathpant felt contented to hear Sambhajiraje's words.

Raje remembered something and gave another instruction to Raghunathpant – "Pant, a representative of Subedar Damaji Raghunath had recently come from Pune to visit the fort. He had met with Mahadoba, the son of Tukarambuva of Dehu. Allocate twenty maunds of jowar and an annual allowance for Mahadoba too.

"As you wish Swami." Everyone was satisfied to see that Raje was keeping track of the religious establishments, the saints and the yogis.

In the evening, when Sambhajiraje came to the court hall, Raghunathpant handed the gift deed for the Bakare family to him and said, "Swami, please approve the gift deed and put your seal on it." Sambhajiraje reviewed the gift deed, signed it and put his seal on it.

"To Khan Jahanbahadur Jafarjang Kokaltash, Deccan subah, from His Highness Sambhajiraje" Prahladpant noted down to whom the letter was being addressed. After being defeated at Ahiwantgad, Jafar Khan had besieged the fort of Salher in Baglan. Raje started dictating the letter of warning to be sent to Jafar Khan, "I have received reports of your military hostilities in the Baglan region. I am only awaiting the end of monsoon. I am going to descend in Baglan myself to test your military prowess in person. Rest assured!"

Prahladpant sealed the letter and placed it in a pouch.

"Swami, the Portuguese viceroy has sent a letter. He has complained that Moro Dadaji, the subedar of Dicholi has broken the agreement." Prahladpant provided information to Raje.

"What has Moro Dadaji done?"

"The Subedar raided the Siolim region in Bardesh and imprisoned some people. He has also detained a European trader who was transporting jewellery from Dicholi."

Raje was lost in thought. The late Maharaj had made an agreement with the Europeans in which both parties had agreed to not attack the other party's territory. It also included unhindered commercial trading between the regions of both parties.

"Pant, dispatch a letter warning Moro Dadaji not to commit any action that will violate the agreement on our part, and order him to release the prisoners immediately."

"Ji." Prahladpant nodded seeing Raje admonishing Kokaltash Khan and warning his own officer who had committed a mistake, at the same time.

"The officer in charge of Kudal has arrived." An attendant delivered the news. Raje raised his hand and signalled the attendant to send him subedar in.

Ganoram, the officer in charge of Kudal came in.

"When did you come, Ganoram?" Raje inquired.

"Just now, Swami. I have come to deliver some special news."

"Yes, go ahead." Raje gazed at him.

"Mounibuva resides in Patgaon in our suba. A great holy man. Thorale Swami had taken his darshan during the Karnataka campaign. Could Swami do some…"

"Yes, I have heard a lot about Mounibuva. I will certainly make arrangements for his livelihood." Raje assured Ganoram. He left contented.

"Pant, prepare an order to allocate an annual sum of one hundred twenty-five Hons for expenditure to Mounibuva's ashram. Also mention that the ashram is exempt from the administrative tax. Make sure this order is delivered to buva's disciple Turutgiri." Raje instructed Prahladpant.

"The Shirkes and Mahadiks are climbing up the fort." Antoji came in and announced.

Raje brushed aside the thoughts of the administrative duties and said to Prahlad Niraji, "Let's go and receive them." Shambhooraje left the Balekilla with Prahlad Niraji, Antoji and a few swordsmen, and came to the tower.

Ganojiraje, Harajiraje and Amlojiraje Mahadik were coming with their entourage. Shambhooraje saw them coming and came forward to receive them. He embraced everyone and enquired about their well-being. Harajiraje was Sambhajiraje's brother-in-law. Raje's elder sister, Ambikabai was married to him. With Ganojiraje and Harajiraje, his brothers-in-law walking on both his sides, Sambhajiraje started walking towards the queens' palaces.

All of them came to Yesubai's palace. After meeting Yesubai and paying their respects to Sakwarbai, they came to the seating chamber in Raje's palace.

Hambirarao came to know about the arrival of the guests and came to meet them with Yesaji Kank, Anandrao, Rupaji,

Jotyaji Kesarkar, Tukoji Palkar and Tryambak Baji.

After some general conversation, Harajiraje broached the important topic, "Sarlashkar, do you think the enthronement ceremony of Raje will suffice for further governance of the kingdom?"

"I agree with you. It's been five months; the royal throne has been vacant." Hambirarao seconded him.

"Raje, when is your coronation going to take place?" Harajiraje asked directly.

"As long as that is not done, some important issues cannot be resolved." No one understood what Ganojiraje was implying.

"I understand your point. I am going to organize the coronation ceremony too. But the preparations for that can start only after the monsoon is over. This ceremony is not about me, but about shouldering the responsibility of the royal throne of Maharaj Saheb. It should be carried out with appropriate grandeur. The kingdoms around us are also anticipating such a ceremony. It should not be rushed." Sambhajiraje calmly replied to all and that was enough for everyone.

As they received the intimation that supper was ready, Raje rose from his seat and came out of the chamber. Hiroji Indulkar, the chief engineer, was waiting for Raje outside. He made an obeisance and said, "Why did Dhani summon me?"

As Raje saw him, his facial expressions changed, and he felt woeful. He gazed at his own palm and said in a low voice, "Hiroji, choose a proper place near the Maha Darwaja and erect a shrine of Putala Masaheb who committed Sati. She is no more, at least I will get to see her shrine whenever I pass by." Putalabai's memory saddened everyone.

In the evening Sambhajiraje took a stroll on the fort with Harajiraje, Ganojiraje and Amalojiraje and came to the temple of Jagadishwar. As they were entering the temple, Sambhajiraje said to Harajiraje, "I am going to entrust you with an important mission. I know that you will achieve success."

"Ji. I am your family. Whatever task you assign me I will accept it." Harajiraje reassured him.

Raje picked up a bael leaf from the Shivlinga and gave it to Harajiraje. Mahadik accepted it without even knowing what the mission was. But Ganojiraje was disappointed to hear their conversation.

Night descended on the fort. Raje lay on the bed in his sleeping chamber. Yesubai was pressing his legs. She stopped for a moment and tidied the edge of her sari. While doing so, her bangles jingled. She said in a resolute voice, "May I say something?"

"Yes, what is it?"

"I never asked for anything, but today I want to ask for something." Yesubai's voice choked while speaking.

Sambhajiraje lifted the arm resting on his forehead, sat up, and said, "Yesu, why are you speaking like this? Tell me openly what you want. You had requested me to get a charmed amulet for Bhavanibai. Instead, I brought calamity with me." Raje's voice was full of pain.

"Please don't say such things. We have been saved from the calamity by the grace of Goddess Bhaveshwari. With the immediate future in mind, I would like to propose something."

"Yesu, feel free to speak. No matter how hard it is, I will fulfil your wish." Yesubai's face lit up on hearing Raje's words. She started pressing Raje's legs unwittingly. She hesitated for a moment and then said resolutely, "Swari should do away with the surveillance of the prisoners now! These people have spent a lifetime in Aabasaheb's company. Though they have committed a mistake, they are our own people. Swari should grant them pardon and reinstate them."

"Yesu!" Raje was bewildered to hear the undesirable topic coming from a close family member.

"Had Aabasaheb been alive, I would have proposed the same thing to him too. Great men make great mistakes; therefore, only a person with a large heart can forgive such mistakes. Swari should show that large-heartedness at this time. Aabasaheb himself had shown it in case of Swari." Yesubai's voice choked as she remembered Maharaj.

Raje felt as if Thoralya Aausaheb was sitting in front of him. Raje held his dear wife's hand affectionately, patted it gently and said, "Yesu, I was struggling to reach a decision, but you have given me the strength. Your wish will be fulfilled."

"Please do it immediately. Peshwe…Peshwe has taken ill and is bedridden at his residence." Yesubai's voice trembled.

"Jagadamb! Jagadamb!" Raje uttered restlessly and lay down. Yesubai kept pressing his legs.

Harajiraje and Ganojiraje also insisted, "You are going to be coronated soon and if the ministers of Swaraj remain under surveillance at such an auspicious time, it would not seem right."

Raje summoned Changoji and ordered him, "Withdraw the surveillance of the captives and… and send the royal physician to the Peshwa's residence immediately."

As per the instruction, the surveillance of Annaji, Pant, Hiroji and Balaji's residence was withdrawn. Even the prisoners in Kolhapur and Panhalgad were released.

The royal physician came to the Peshwa's residence with a pouch of medicines. Moropant had high fever, but as soon as he saw the physician, he raised his hand and silently refused to take any treatment. After two days, the veteran servant of Swaraj, the Peshwa, started hallucinating.

His son, Nilopant, Annaji, Prahladpant, Rahuji, Ragho Swanand and Hambirarao gathered around his bed anxiously. Pant was on the brink of death. Everyone felt that Raje should meet the Peshwa in his last moments, but no one dared to propose this to Raje.

Suddenly, there was a commotion among the people gathered around Pant. Nilopant and Pant's personal secretary stayed by his bed to give him support. Everyone else stepped back. There were whispers in the chamber, "Rani Saheb is here!"

With her personal secretary and a bevy of maids, the Chhatrapati's daughter-in-law, Yesubai Saheb was entering the Mantribadi for the first time.

Moropant, who was hallucinating, mistook Yesubai for Jijau. "Masaheb!" his lips moved slightly. Even in that condition, he tried to get up and make an obeisance to her.

Yesubai quickly stepped forward and said, "Pant…kaka…!"

Pant did not hear her, but the people around him felt the pain in her voice.

"Swari is coming to meet you Pantkaka." Yesubai could not speak further. As she saw the Peshwa's condition she couldn't imagine what Aabasaheb might have gone through during his last days. Her eyes welled up; she couldn't see Pant clearly.

The people around bowed down to make an obeisance to her. Yesubai saw that; she wiped her eyes and looked behind her. Sambhajiraje was entering the chamber with Harajiraje.

"Pant…!" Sambhajiraje called in a hoarse voice. Only Yesubai realized that Raje's voice rarely sounded like this; and that was only when he called either Aabasaheb or Thoralya Aau. Pant gave Sambhajiraje a vacant look. What he was saying had nothing to do with his surroundings. It was something related to the late Chhatrapati, and nobody could understand it.

A deeply distressed Sambhajiraje left Moropant's residence. That evening loud lamentations erupted in Pant's residence. Moropant had left the world. Swaraj had lost its veteran and wise soldier.

Sambhajiraje summoned Prahlad Niraji and instructed him, "After the obsequies of the Peshwe are performed, dispatch the attire of the Peshwa and the royal seal to his son Nilopant." And without saying anything else, he trudged towards Yesubai's palace to inform her of this decision.

"Prahladpant, dispatch letters to all subahs, sarsubahs and Sarnoubats of Swaraj and instruct them to come to Raigad with their forces at the earliest. Keep a minimum force necessary for the protection of all forts, and summon all the remaining soldiers on Raigad. Ask them to follow these instructions rigorously, no mistake will be spared." Shambhooraje was lost in some deep thought; his stern face glowed radiantly.

All the people assembled in the court hall were listening to him attentively and making their own plans about how to successfully implement the responsibilities assigned to them.

"Sarlashkar, assemble the experts of the surveillance team such as Bahirji Naik, Vishwas Musekhorekar, Karmaji and Mahadeo."

Hambirarao was jubilant to hear the words. He understood what it implied and said, "The surveillance team will be here in a week."

"Keshav Pandit, take the help of the Chitnis and dispatch a messenger to Kashi with a letter to Gaga Bhatt, 'I would like to have my coronation ceremony performed by you. Just as you performed Aabasaheb's coronation ceremony, please bless me too with your presence.' Also, send a similar invitation to Anantbhat Kavale of Nashik.

The courtiers were now catching onto Raje's plan.

"Prahladpant, send messages to the sailor Daulat Khan, Mayanak and Kanhoji Aangre to come and visit me in the month of Kartik."

As Raje saw Aabaji Sonadeo, he remembered Divakar Gosavi, the disciple of Samartha. Everyone around felt the softness in his voice, "Aabaji, Samartha's disciple, Divakar Gosavi had come to meet me. In all this hustle, I couldn't issue the grants for Samartha's ashrams. That still needs to be done."

"Ji."

"Send messengers to Kashi Ranganath of Javali, Koner Ranganath of Satara and Yesaji Malhar of Wai, and convey to them that the grants for the ashrams at Chaphal, Shinganwadi, Sajjangad and Mahabaleshwar should be continued."

"Ji."

Raje approached Raghunathpant Hanamante. Usually, Raje would feel delighted to see him, but today his forehead puckered. He didn't show his feelings outwardly and said to him, "Raghunathpant, you should go to the Karnataka region immediately."

"Ji?" Hanamante was startled. But Raje smiled, and speaking in a normal tone, he diverted his attention, "Pant, who else can shoulder the responsibility of such a big distant subah, but an experienced and wise man like you?"

"As you wish." Raghunathpant let out a slight sigh that no one noticed.

But he didn't know that Raje had noticed it. Raghunathpant Hanamante had been also involved in the recent conspiracy against Raje. Raje had received the evidence a little late. As soon as Raghnathpant reached the Karnataka region, he was going to be detained.

Raje distributed the betel leaves to conclude the meeting. As Kavi Kulesh was leaving with everyone, Raje stopped him, "Kaviraj, you stay here."

Sambhajiraje had spoken ingenuously, but he didn't realize that many people who heard his words had become envious of Kulesh as they attributed his quick rise to favouritism on Sambhajiraje's part.

Raje came to Yesubai's chamber with Kulesh. He had not instructed anyone during the meeting to look after the affairs of the fort. He assigned that responsibility to Yesubai.

He shared his plan with her and said, "I am going to Kelashi with Kaviraj to get darshan of Yakutbaba. Aabasaheb had brought baba to Kelashi and got him settled there. I would feel better in his company. I think I will spend a few days there."

"Ji. Rest assured." In fact, Yesubai wanted to tell Raje about the discussion she had with her Dada Saheb – Ganojiraje who had recently gone back to Shringarpur, but as she saw Kaviji with him she did not broach the subject.

In the evening, Sambhajiraje descended the fort with Kulesh and fifty swordsmen. He left in the direction of Kelashi, observing the ripened paddies on the way.

Sambhajiraje took darshan of Yakutbaba and felt contented by his discourse. After spending five days at Kelashi, Sambhajiraje returned to Raigad.

The monsoon was now over. The paddies were replete with pendulous rice crops. The lush green fields were basking in the golden sunlight of the month of Ashwin.

The festival of Navaratri arrived. After celebrating Dussehra, the Mavala forces arrived from all sides and assembled in Pachad. About seventy-five thousand soldiers had gathered at the foothills of the fort.

Manaji More, Tukoji Palkar, Santaji-Bahirji Ghorpade, Yesaji Kank and his young son Krushnaji, Dhanaji Jadhav, Keso Trimal, Nagoji Ballal, Sarjerao Jedhe, Vithoji Chavan, Santaji Jagatap, Dadaji and Bhimaji Kakade, Naro Tryambak, Yesaji Malhar, Naroji Bhosale, Nemaji Gaikawad, Dadaji Narasprabhu…all valiant warriors ascended Raigad.

Raje had sent his skilled informers Bahirji, Vishwas and Karmaji in the Mughal, Baglan, coastal region of Javhar and Varhad. As the Sarlashkar had sent them a message, they had now returned to Raigad.

A meeting was convened in the royal court hall. To begin with, Raje affectionately enquired about all assembled subedars, jumledars and sarnoubats. As he threw a quick glance at the courtiers assembled in the court hall, his heart was filled with confidence. He stroked the cowrie necklace on his chest while deliberating the details of his plan. Then he broached the topic of his audacious campaign in a firm voice, “I am delighted to see that all you valiant warriors have reached the fort with your forces. Aabasaheb raised this kingdom by the grace of God. We should now strive for its expansion. Don't think that Aabasaheb is no longer with us. He still lives in our hearts. I am merely the dust of his feet! If all of us face our arch enemies unitedly, they will be vanquished for sure. On the strength of your support, I am devising a plan to commence a big campaign to launch an attack on three fronts. Mother Jagadamba will bless us with success for sure." Raje took a breath before sharing the particulars of the campaign. The courtiers remembered their late Swami.

"Rupaji, you penetrate the Nashik region with Manaji, Santaji and seven thousand soldiers. Hansaji of Salher and the forces at Trimbakgad and Songad will be at your disposal. Your own army may have to gallop either to the east to join the division in the Varhad-Khandesh region or to the west in the coastal region of Javhar. So, keep your forces ready accordingly. But make sure to spread the rumour that you are going to attack Surat."

"Ji." Rupaji Bhosale accepted the responsibility.

"Nilopant, you cover the territory of Javhar, Manor and Ganeshphata. Dadaji Prabhu, Tukoji, you safeguard the region from Sudhagad to Kalyan; the Siddis in the coastal area might try to take advantage of the current situation and attack us, you keep them under control. Mhaloji, you assist Venkoji Rudra of Karhad and Ambaji Moradeo of Satara and keep a watch on the Adil Shah's camp at Miraj.

"Sarlashkar, with Anandrao, Keso Trimal, Nagoji Ballal, Dhanaji and thirty thousand soldiers, you ambush the Varhad-Khandesh region. Keep the rumour circulating continuously that you are going to attack Aurangabad. The Mughal forces in Burhanpur will come to assist the Varhad region. That is when we are going to fall upon Burhanpur. I will penetrate the Baglan region, and with your forces, both of us will conquer Burhanpur!"

All the courtiers were presented robes of honour. Betel leaves were offered to everyone, and the meeting concluded.

Burhanpur was the prominent city that the Mughal sultanate

considered as the gateway to the Deccan. The Chhatrapati had already disfigured the beautiful city of 'Surat', now his son was ready to turn the bustling city of Burhanpur into a desolate one.

The horses were groomed, and the Marathi forces got ready with all the provisions. Raje descended Raigad and came to Pachad. He bade farewell to all the sardars going on the campaign. He embraced Hambirarao and said to him, "As soon as you take control of Varhad, send me a message. I will be waiting for the news."

"Ji." The Marathi forces left Pachad to spread in different directions like red ants dispersing from an anthill. The mighty Sarlashkar of the Maratha kingdom, Hambirarao, was going to fall upon Varhad-Khandesh.

Now, preparations for the coronation ceremony began on the fort. The painters started painting the courtyard and the temples on the fort. Sacks of food grain were taken out of the granary for drying, winnowing and sifting. The royal priest, Balambhat descended the fort with the Brahmins of Nashik, to collect the waters of the holy rivers for the Abhishek ceremony. He travelled north with his group of disciples.

After eight days, the news arrived,"Raghunathpant Hanamante has reached Jinji."

Raje was in a meeting. When he heard the news, he said to Harajiraje, "This Hanamante conspired with his brother Janardanpant and tried to detain me at Panhala. I want to entrust the responsibility of the Karnataka subah to you. I would like to appoint a family member like you in the Karanataka subah. Hanamante is going to be detained."

Haraji exclaimed, "Ji", but was lost in some thought. He advised Sambhajiraje frankly and said, "Whatever duty you assign me, I will accept it. But Raghunathpant was the Majumdar; he handled the crucial office of record-keeping. How can we keep such an important post vacant?"

Raje smiled, glanced at Nilopant and gestured him. Nilopant

picked up his cue and went out. Raje said to Haraji, "I have made arrangements for the office of the record-keeper. You will also approve of them."

Haraji could not gauge Raje's intention.

Within a short time, Nilopant presented Annaji Dutto and Balaji Aavaji in front of Raje.

Annaji could not lift his head. Balaji was anxious about what was in store for them now.

"Annaji," Raje approached Annaji and stood in front of him. "Raise your head, Annaji. I would like the Majumdar of Swaraj to always hold his head high!"

For a moment, Annaji felt that he was dreaming or hallucinating. Though he wanted to speak, he could not utter a word.

"You are an expert in keeping and maintaining records, Annaji. You are perfect for the position of the Majumdar. There would be no question of pardoning taxes to the farmers; no interference from me. I know your potential, and that is why I am honourably offering you the post of the Majumdar. I hold no grudge against you. You spoke in the interest of Swaraj, befitting Aabasaheb's loyal minister." Raje's eyes flashed a pained look; he stopped for a moment.

"You rightfully reminded me of my misdeed; of my defection to the camp of the Pathan. I am obliged to correct that mistake, and I promise to do so. You established a great revenue system under Aabasaheb's leadership. Now, take charge of his record office too. I am confident that you will perform your duty faithfully."

"Ji." Annaji who had been prepared to face death, didn't know how to respond to Raje who was honouring him.

"But remember one thing Annaji, your duty is to manage the accounts and records of Swaraj, and not my relationship with Balraje! Just keep that in mind."

Raje came in front of Balaji. For no reason, he compared

Khandoji and the Chitnis. "Chitnis, Aabasaheb appreciated your neat handwriting skill and employed you for the same. You served Swaraj faithfully as the Chitnis. You are a veteran, a senior member of the ministry. You refused to write the secret letter ordering my imprisonment, but you sent your son, Aavaji with the seal and stamp of the Chitnis to Masaheb, to do the same job. You committed three mistakes when you did that, Chitnis. First, you handed the seal and stamp of the Chitnis to another person. Second, you expected your son to approve of the same actions that you did not approve of, and third, you thought that you had found a perfect solution to the problem, by neither accepting nor denying your participation in the plot.

"Chitnis, two things are of crucial importance for a kingdom: the quill and the dagger. The quill you hold is a lethal weapon. Handle it cautiously so that it does not bite the hand that holds it. I am honourably reinstating you as the Chitnis of Swaraj. Discharge the responsibility with utmost caution!"

"Ji. Your wish is my command."

Haraji's face lit up in contentment. The Chitnis and the Majumadar left.

Nilopant broke the silence and said, "Swami, we have received a complaint from Moreshwar Gosavi of Karhepathar."

"What is it?"

"The Gosavibuva says that the soldiers of the Maratha army have been harassing his people and farmlands."

Raje's face became stern. He inquired, "Who is the Hawaldar of Karhepathar, pant?"

"Jivaji Narayan."

"Give a strict warning to Jivaji, not to harass Gosavibuva's people, farmland or the cattle, henceforth. One more complaint against him, and he will not be spared."

Raje received news that the Mavalas in the Solapur region had confiscated twenty-five cannons that were being transported from the fort of Solapur. The news reminded him of something, and he said, "Nilopant, Sarlashkar's informer will reach here. Let me know when he comes. I am going to travel to the Solapur–Sangola region."

Nilopant came to meet Raje with Anantbhat from Nashik, Keshav Pandit, Umaji Pandit, and Kaviji. Anantbhat threw a final glance at the almanac spread in front of him and said, "Swami, the upcoming seventh day of the bright fortnight of Magh is very auspicious for the coronation ceremony. The rituals can be started from the fifth day."

"Nilopant, get the invitations ready for this mahurat."

"Ji. Hawaldar Nagoji Ingale of Bhimgad in the Fonda region has sent a recommendation, Swami." Nilopant presented the case.

"What is the recommendation, pant?"

"One Nagoji Naik Sardesai resides in the vicinity of Bhimgad. He tenaciously defended the villages around the fort against the Portuguese assault. Therefore, the Hawaldar of Bhimgad recommends that he should be appointed as the Sardeshmukh of the Hemadbarase and Chandrawadi villages in the Antaruj region."

"Pant, collect all information regarding the attack. Consult Dharmaji Naganath, the officer in charge of Fonda, and only then prepare the documents to be handed over to Sardesai."

"As you wish, Swami." Nilopant made an obeisance and left with everyone. Raje started pacing the empty hall.

Just then, an attendant came in and announced, "Divakar Gosavi has arrived." Raje stopped walking and raised his hand to indicate his permission.

Moreshwar Panditrao, the head of the office of charity, entered with Divakar Gosavi who was clad in a saffron cloak. Raje enquired about the Gosavi's health and asked him about Samartha, "Gosavi, where is Samartha located nowadays? How is he?"

"He is at Sajjangad. Since the demise of Thorale Chhatrapati he has been grief-stricken." Divakar Gosavi replied.

"Gosavi, since you are going back, Ragho Anant will accompany you to take darshan of Samartha. Please convey my respects to Samartha. I am getting crowned on the seventh day of the bright fortnight of Magh. I would feel grateful to receive his blessings. There is no one in my life now, whose blessings I can seek." Raje looked dejected. Divakar Gosavi also felt his grief. He insisted, "Raje, if you come to Sajjangad in person…"

"I had planned the same, but I might have to travel to Varhad sometime soon now. Please convey this to Samratha, and take Ragho Anant with you when you leave. Panditrao, send the invitation of the coronation ceremony to Samartha at the hands of Raghopant. Also send the robe of honour for Samartha and garments and ornaments for Lord Rama.

After two days, Hambirarao's informer came from Varhad with good news, "The Sarlashkar has initiated the campaign of Varhad. Raje should leave the fort now."

Sambhajiraje bade farewell to Yesubai, descended the fort with Khandoji Ballal, Krishanji Kank, Jaanrao and Himmatrao and arrived at Pachad. Ten thousand soldiers, astride their horses left the royal stable of Pachad. The roaring army sprinted forward.

Raje travelled via Bhor, Pune, Chakan, Khed, Narayangaon, Sangamner, Ahiwantgad; crossed the rivers Bhima, Ghod, Pravara and Godavari and penetrated the Baglan region. Here, he received news from the informers of Rupaji Bhosale, "Only about five hundred soldiers are in Burhanpur. The rest of the army is fighting in the Varhad region."

Raje ordered his army to rest and recover and sent a message to Hambirarao, "Leave from Varhad immediately and come via Dharangaon-Chopada to Khandesh."

Hambirarao deceived the Mughal army and left the Varhad region, as per the instruction. Bahadur Khan couldn't figure out the sudden disappearance of the Maratha army that was fighting ferociously in the region. He tightened the security of Aurangabad and let out a sigh of relief.

Hambirarao entered the Dharangaon–Chopada region while terrorizing the villages such as Jalna, Deulgaon, Fardapur and Erandol. Sambhajiraje left from the Baglan region and united with Hambirarao's army. The consolidated Maratha army now consisted of thirty thousand soldiers, besides the ten thousand soldiers engaged in the Varhad region. The army started marching towards Burhanpur, which was an imperial platter full of delicacies, waiting for a connoisseur to savour them!

Khan Jaman was the Mughal subedar of this gateway to the Deccan. The Khan was not present at Burhanpur, as per protocol. His representative, Kakad Khan was present. He used to collect the Jizya tax. Now, it was time for Kakad Khan to repay the tax that he had collected so far, with interest. The Maratha forces besieged Burhanpur. Kakad Khan, already shivering in the cold weather, was completely frozen by the terrifying uproar. He found a solution for himself. He gave refuge to the people who entered the Balekilla, and then locked the entrance gates. The wealthy traders outside the Balekilla were left to die. Hambirarao, Nagoji, Keso Trimal took them into custody.

Nawabpura, Khurrampura, Shahaganj, Shahjahanpura, Hasanpura… the jewellers and traders in all market towns were plundered. Gold, silver, pearls, cash and coins were poured in separate piles in front of Raje in the central chowk. Everything was measured, poured into sacks and sealed immediately.

The first day was spent collecting the booty which was easily accessible. The next two days were spent in digging and retrieving the wealth buried underground. For three days, the market towns around Burhanpur kept burning. The Mavalas had retrieved countless sacks full of riches and carried the wealth out of the city.

For three days, Sambhajiraje and Hambirarao kept moving around the city, keeping a keen watch on the progress of the campaign. On the fourth day, an informer came with the message, "Bahadur Khan has left Aurangabad with a mammoth army. He is coming to Burhanpur's rescue."

The Mavala forces left the burning Burhanpur for Bahadur Khan and vanished from the city with the immense wealth, just as swiftly as they had arrived in the city. Many goods, such as fine garments and fragile glass items were left behind as there were no appropriate means to transport these.

The army was divided into two regiments. Sambhajiraje led the regiment that carried the booty and fell upon the Baglan region again, via Chopada–Dharangaon. Hambirarao, Nagoji and Keso Trimal went back and attacked the Varhad region again.

Sambhajiraje took a sojourn at Salheri in Baglan and captured Gajiyapur located at the borders of Baglan. Then, with the immense wealth, Raje began his return journey to Raigad via Ahiwantgad, Ramsej and Pattagad.

Occupied in the Burhanpur campaign, Raje was unaware of a small incident that took place on Raigad. Soyarabai had summoned Annaji whom Raje had entrusted with the office of the Mujumdar to her palace for inquiry.

As soon as Raje returned to Raigad, he received two pieces of unfortunate news. Keshav Pandit informed him, "Gaga Bhatt of Kashi cannot come to the coronation ceremony. He has sent a message for you; to perform the coronation ceremony as per the list of rituals he has prepared and to accept the holy book that he has sent for you."

Gaga Bhatt had sent a book for Raje titled 'Samanayan' based on the Dharmashastras. The second message was delivered by Ragho Anant who had gone to Sajjangad to meet Samartha. Samartha had sent the message, "I won't be able to come. You should wield the bow that I had gifted the late Chhatrapati and ascend the throne."

The preparations for the second coronation ceremony were in full swing at the fort. Sambhajiraje descended Raigad with the palanquin carrying the golden parasol created by Ramji Dutto. Kavi Kulesh, Khandoji and Umaji Pandit accompanied him. He came to Pratapgad to offer the parasol to the family deity Bhavani and perform a grand puja.

Raje performed the grand puja of Goddess Bhavani and offered her the parasol. With closed eyes and palms joined in prayer he sought her blessings.

At night, Goddess Bhavani's Gondhal was performed at Pratapgad. Raje performed the holy Abhishek on the crystal Shivlinga that the late Maharaj used to worship daily. After spending a day at Pratapgad, Raje returned to Raigad. Flocks of people thronged the fort. The street fortune-tellers, ascetics, fakirs and gosavis assembled on the fort in anticipation of huge alms. Brahmins from holy places such as Tryambak, Nashik, Karhad, Karavir, and Aalandi arrived at Raigad.

Hambirarao handed over the Varhad-Khandesh campaign to Nagoji and Keso Trimal and came to Raigad with Anandrao Nimbalkar. Rupaji Bhosale, Santaji Gaikwad, and Manaji More came from Baglan. Dabir Janardanpant Hanamate from the Kolhapur subah, Mhaloji Ghorpade, Santaji–Bahirji Ghorpade, and Sardar Vichare also came. From the Konkan coast came Dadaji Raghunath, Moro Dadaji, sailor Daulat Khan, Kanhoji Govindaji Kat and Maynak Bhandari. Gopal Rayaji, Maloji Itbararao, Kank, Bandal, Silimkar and Sarjerao Jedhe came from the Maval region. Yesubai's mother came with Pilajirao, Harajiraje, Achalojiraje Mahadik, Ganojiraje and Kanhojiraje Shirke.

Samartha's disciple Divakar, and disciples of other saints from the ashrams at Chinchwad, Patgaon, Marul and Kurate arrived on Raigad. The female singers came from the temples of Goddess Bhavani's at Tuljapur, Pratapgad and Mahur. More than fifty thousand people gathered on Raigad. Raigad resembled a place of pilgrimage. The Lahana Darwaja, Maha Darwaja, Jagadishwar, Shirkai, Hanumant...all the gates of the temples were embellished with festoons made of gold-plated coconuts. Triangular saffron flags fluttered atop the temple domes. The huge, saffron, golden-bordered Jaripataka pennant was fluttering at full mast in the winds of Maval atop the Nagar Khana near the Maha Darwaja.

The fifth day of the bright fortnight of Magh broke. The rituals for the coronation ceremony commenced. Sambhajiraje took a bath, wore his royal attire, and with Yesubai left the Balekilla with Yesubai along with the ministers, Peshwe Nilopant Pingale, Surnis Aabaji Sonadeo, Mujumdar Annaji Dutto, Nyayadhish Prahlad Niraji, Senapati Hambirarao and Yesaji Kank, Dabir Janardanpant Hanamante, Danadhyksha Moreshwar Panditrao and Vaknis Ramchandra Dutto Trimal. In front of him walked the erudite Brahmins such as the royal priest Balambhat, Anantbhat Kavale along with Kavi Kulesh, Keshav Pandit and Umaji Pandit.

Yesuabai sat in a palanquin with aged Dharau. Sambhajiraje walked barefoot behind palanquin and left the central tower. Thousands of eyes were fixed on him. The royal family descended Raigad and arrived in Pachad.

The entourage went towards Thoralya Aausaheb's samadhi. The royal priest and Anantbhat performed a detailed puja of the samadhi. Sambhajiraje and Yesubai offered bael leaves and flowers at Jijau's feet. Together, they both touched their foreheads in front of the samadhi. Their hearts brimmed with overwhelming emotions.

The royal family sought Jijau's blessings and returned to the fort summit. Hiroji Indulkar had erected a memorial to the late Maharaj near the Jagadishwar temple. A puja of that memorial was performed. The royal couple offered bael leaves and haldi at Aabasaheb's feet and prostrated in front of it.

Sambhajiraje took the darshan of the Sati Vrindavan, Lord Jagdishwar, Goddess Shirkai and returned to the Balekilla. Now the ritual of shanti yajnas began. The first yajna was for Lord

Vinayaka, the remover of obstacles. The royal couple performed the puja of Ganesh. Twenty-one valuable ornaments and dresses were offered to the murti of Ganesh. A rich, gourmet meal consisting of twenty-one dishes, was offered to Lord Ganesh.

Thereafter, other peace-offering yajnas took place. The divine fragrance of milk, ghee, honey and other offerings poured into the fiery yajna pit dispersed all over the fort and purified it.

By subduing the evil powers and inviting the divine powers, the fifth day of yajnas came to an end. The sixth day, the day of offering alms broke. It was Wednesday. In the central chowk of the Balekilla, a spacious weighing scale was erected on a platform. It was embellished with flower garlands and coconuts and a puja was performed.

The time-indicating vessel in the big water container was about to sink. It was the time to perform the tula. Sambhajiraje removed his mojaris, offered haldi and kumkum to the pans of the weighing scale and climbed on the platform.

First of all the Suvarntula of Raje was performed. Thereafter, many tulas of Raje were performed with various materials such as silver, copper, bronze, iron, sugar, eighteen types of food grains, cotton, coconut, salt, jaggery, spices and oils. As the soon to be Maharani, Yesuabai's tulas were performed too. One tula was performed for Dharau too.

The royal couple gave the customary touch of their hands to all materials used for the tula. Under the guidance of Moreshwar Panditrao, all the materials used in the tulas were distributed among the bhats, ascetics, fakirs, gosavis and others. Clothing, food grains, cows and coins were also distributed. The sixth day ended with the blessings of the people who had received alms.

The seventh day of the bright fortnight of Magh dawned on Raigad. It was Thursday, the day of the grand ceremony! Married women cleaned their yards and decorated them with attractive rangoli designs. Flaming lamps lit up the marketplace, the Balekilla, the Jagadishwar temple, the Shirkai temple and the ambience of the fort. The rituals of the coronation ceremony commenced at dawn. The rumble of the kettledrums originating from the Nagar Khana spread all arount in the cool early morning breeze. Sambhajiraje and Yesubai were fasting today. They left from the Balekilla with their entourage. They arrived at the platform raised for the rituals of the coronation ceremony.

In the east corner of the platform, Peshwe Nilopant Pingale stood holding a gold pitcher full of ghee; in the west corner stood Majumdar Annaji Dutto with a copper pitcher of curds; in the north corner Moreshwar Panditrao stood with a gold pitcher of honey; in the south corner stood Senapati Hambirarao holding a silver pitcher of milk; in the northeast corner was Nyayadhish Prahlad Niraji holding a golden miniature of the scales of justice; in the southeast corner, stood Sachiv Aabaji Sonadeo holding the parasol; in the southwest corner, Sumant Janardanpant Hanamante was holding a golden-handled fan in his hand; in the northwest corner was Ramchandra Duttaji Trimal with a chowrie in his hand. Thus, the eight ministers stood as a guard of every direction. Along with them, Balaji Aavaji, Kavi Kulesh, Keshav Pandit, Umaji Pandit and Yesaji Kank also stood on the platform.

Two golden seats were placed in the chowk. Sambhajiraje sat on his seat and Yesubai sat on his left, facing the east. The Brahmins started intoning the mantras. The royal couple was first bathed in the five nectarous substances such as milk, ghee, curds and honey. After that, Sambhajiraje and Yesubai were bathed in the pure holy waters of seven holy rivers amidst the chanting of mantras.

After the Abhishek ceremony, Raje viewed his face in the melted ghee spread in a round salver.

The crowds had gathered around the platform of the royal throne. The ryots eager to take darshan of their king, thronged the durbar hall.

Sambhajiraje came to his palace; Yesubai went to her chamber. Raje donned the special attire and got ready to induct himself on the royal throne. He paid respects to the bow bedecked with flower garlands and put it on his shoulder. He bore a quiver full of arrows on his back, and the Bhavani sword around his waist.

Yesubai came back to his chamber. She had donned a dark violet, golden embroidered sari. She was wearing a gold girdle around her waist and a pearl-studded nose ring. She had applied horizontal stripes of kumkum on her forehead.

With the parasol-holders, spear-holders, chowrie carriers and the proclaimers walking in front, Sambhajiraje and Yesuabai left from the palace along with the eight ministers and the Brahmins and started walking towards the platform of the royal throne.

The eight ministers took their respective places on the platform. Yesubai went to the draped section of the royal ladies. As the auspicious moment of the actual coronation arrived, the royal priest and Anantbhat signalled Raje to take his seat on the royal throne.

Sambhajiraje put his right foot forward and making sure that his other foot did not touch the royal seat, he ascended the golden royal throne facing the east. The platform of the royal throne got drenched in the chanting of mantras. Peshwe Nilopant picked up gold coins and showered them on Sambhajiraje, who was holding the royal sceptre. Anantbhat touched the parasol. As Sambhajiraje raised his hand to indicate that he had assumed the throne of the Chhatrapati the courtiers bowed down to make an obeisance to him.

The spear-holders raised the spears they were holding and pounding them three times on the floor they announced the appellations in loud and clear voice, "Here comes the sovereign king of the Hindus, the crowned king and the saviour of the cows and the Brahmins, Shrimanmaharaj Sambhajiraje!"

The cannons boomed, the guns fired and made an obeisance

to the second Chhatrapati of the Maratha kingdom.

Nyayadhish Prahladpant held the golden platter with the royal seal in front of Maharaj. Maharaj gave the customary touch of his hand to the platter and accepted it. The seal had a Sanskrit inscription on it which meant,

'This kingdom of Sambhaji, the scion of Chhatrapati Shivaji is as vast as the sky, and his reign will assure the protection of one and all. Who wouldn't want to have such a munificent king?'

Maharaj offered the eight ministers the robes of honour. Kavi Kulesh was summoned in front of the royal throne. Maharaj placed the robe of honour on his shoulder and bestowed upon him the title of "Chhandogamatya".

Maharaj gave the customary touch of his hand to another salver which was sent to Maharani Yesubai in the royal ladies' section. It contained her royal seal that honoured her as the Maharani and as his wife, his life partner. The royal seal had the inscription of "Shri Sakhi Radnyi Jayati" which meant 'Victory to the Maharani'.

Maharaj honoured the artists with attires, hons and jewellery. Three hons per person were distributed among the people.

The royal emissaries of Qutub Shahi, Adil Shahi, Portuguese, British and other durbars, presented royal gifts to the Maharaj and received gifts in return.

The second coronation ceremony was taking place on Raigad with grandeur; but Soyarabai who had boycotted the ceremony was sitting in her palace with Ramraje. She had forbidden Ramraje from participating in any rituals of the coronation ceremony.

Sambhajiraje, sitting on the royal throne faced a big dilemma, "I have been inducted as the king, but there are no elders left to seek blessings from!"

A week passed. Maharaj was pondering about two pieces of news that he had received from the north. Aurangzeb's fourth son, Akbar, who was the subedar of Rajasthan had revolted and had declared himself an 'independent Emperor'. Aurangzeb had accused his own daughter, Zebunnissa, of assisting him in the rebellion and had imprisoned her in dungeons of Salimgad.

Maharaj was oblivious to what Kaviji was speaking. Prahlad Niraji and Keshav Pandit also stood in front of Maharaj along with Kaviji. Jotyaji Kesarkar entered the seating chamber and announced, "Divakar Gosavi, the disciple of Swami Samartha wants to meet Maharaj. He has brought a message from Samartha."

"Bring him in." Maharaj stopped twirling the rose in his hand.

Jotyaji ushered Divakar Gosavi in the chamber. Gosavi chanted a mantra, pulled out a pouch from his shoulder bag and handed it to Maharaj. Maharaj touched the pouch to his forehead with respect and, pointing it to Prahlad Niraji he said, "Please read. Let me hear Samartha's advice."

Prahladpant stepped forward and took the pouch. He pulled out the letter, touched it to his forehead and started reading in a clear voice,

"Be vigilant at all times, but never malicious. Contemplate in private and plan future strategies accordingly. Keep your temper in check and don't act in haste; inculcate patience and tolerance in yourself. Always show concern for your people. Be merciful and pardon the previous wrongdoings of your ministers; reinstate and redirect them to the right path, and revive their trust in their duty towards the kingdom."

Prahladpant paused briefly pause while reading. He licked his lips, took a deep breath and cautiously resumed reading. Maharaj had closed his eyes and was listening carefully to every word.

"Remember your father. Compare your life with his and be humble. Don't be vainglorious. Perform your duties to the best of your ability and people will remember you forever.

Remember what your father looked like, how resolute he was. Remember his valiant feats and the legacy he has left behind. Remember the way he walked, the way he talked and how he inspired people. He renounced all the pleasures of life, and lived his life like a Yogi. Follow in his footsteps and rule the kingdom. If you can achieve more than what he achieved in his life, only then will you be considered his true scion. What more can I say?"

Maharaj's eyes were misty. Nobody around him could see his tears. Maharaj raised his hand and gestured to Pant to read the letter again.

Every single word in the letter pierced Maharaj's heart deeply. His heart was in turmoil wondering about a lost opportunity in his life. His aching heart silently exclaimed, 'Samartha, had you met me on Sajjangad, it would have saved me from committing the biggest mistake of my life!'

"Keep your temper in check and don't act in haste; inculcate patience and tolerance in yourself." Am I really that hot-headed? Or is that what people think of me? Does Samartha also think the same? Of course, he is not at fault. He has advised me based on what he has heard about me. It is true that I captured all the people who conspired against me. Not only Samartha, but Ramraje also felt that I was going to raise my weapon against Maharani Masaheb. How would Samatha know about the content of the letters that were sent to Panhala from Raigad? What if I would have been captured? Then…In that case, Samartha wouldn't have had this opportunity to write such a letter to me!'

"Pardon the previous wrongdoings of your ministers and reinstate them." 'Samartha, I have already done that. Whether the reinstated ministers support me and give me strength, or conspire against me and leave me vulnerable, is yet to be proved. I will wait to see that too.

'I have given my life to extend the Maratha kingdom in all

directions. I don't consider myself as the Chhatrapati, but a servant of the kingdom.

'Samartha, you established eleven idols of Lord Hanuman. Would they get an opportunity to see another Samartha rising from among your disciples? Who can predict it and how? The world doesn't get to see extraordinary people like you and Aabasaheb every day. I am fortunate enough to walk until my last breath on the path that your generation has paved for us. I bow down to you and accept your blessings.'

Maharaj felt overwhelmed as countless thoughts arose in his mind and he got up from his seat. "Prahladpant, make proper arrangements for Gosavibuva." He instructed Nyayadhish Prahladpant and took Samartha's letter from him. Then he went to his personal chamber. Pilajimama, Ganojiraje, Kanhojiraje and Yesubai were in the chamber.

As Pilajimama saw Maharaj he said, "We would like to go back to Shringarpur now."

"Why? Are you getting bored here?" Maharaj said smilingly.

"No, nothing like that. The coronation ceremony is over. The whole family is with me…so…"

"Once Maharaj takes a decision in our case, we can leave with the official documents." Ganojiraje broached the subject that he had been discussing with Yesubai.

"What case are you talking about?" Raje's forehead puckered.

"Thorale Swami had promised us that he would sign the vatan of Shirkan in my name, back at the time of our wedding ceremonies." Ganoji expressed his desire.

"What are you saying Raje? Aabasaheb was very much against giving new vatans to anyone." Maharaj looked serious.

"Thorale Dhani had said, when your daughter-in-law delivers a son, I would sign the vatan of Shringarpur in your name. Swami wanted to gift it to his daughter. Now Ganoji has fathered a son so…" Pilaji shared information about the old agreement.

"Mama Saheb, just like Ganoji, Mahadaji and Harajiraje are also the sons-in-law of Aabasaheb. What if everyone starts demanding a vatan? You are a part of our family. Please try to understand. I will offer suitable posts to Ganoji and Kanhoji, but don't ask for a new vatan. It will create more problems for us."

"What does Maharani think about this?" Ganojiraje asked Yesubai, thinking that she would take his side as he was her brother.

"In my opinion, Swari is right. Our family members should not demand new vatans, especially at this time. If Aabasaheb were alive, he would have taken the same decision." Yesuabai's reply offended Ganojiraje. He bitterly exclaimed, "Does this mean the Bhosalas have broken their promise?"

"Shirke!" Sambhajiraje's expression changed. He remembered the words in Samartha's letter that was in his hand, "Even when you are angry, don't express it in public." With an effort, he controlled himself.

"I understand what this means! Farewell. Aaba, let's go now, I don't want to drink even a drop of water here."

Ganojiraje left in haste. Pilaji mama and Kanhoji followed him silently.

Yesubai and Maharaj stared gloomily at the door.

"I would like to make a request, with your permission…" Yesubai said.

"Yes, go ahead. What is your command?" Maharaj teased Yesubai with a smile.

"Everything went smoothly. I feel that we should erect a royal temple at Pachad. There is no temple there."

The words on Yesubai's royal seal flashed in Raje's mind, - "Shri Sakhi Radnyi Jayati".

He summoned Hiroji Indulkar and instructed him, "Select a good plot in Pachad and lay the foundation for a royal temple. Use chiselled stones for the walls of the temple."

"Ji." Hiroji left the chamber, planning the design of the temple in his mind.

Maharaj came to the court hall with Jotyaji, Antoji and Rayaji.

"Moro Dadaji's employee has arrived from Dicholi. He has sent a message that the Portuguese have severed all ties with us." Nilopant presented the important news in front of Raje.

"Pant, did Moro Dadaji set their men and that trader free?"

"Ji. He hasn't. That is why the viceroy is upset."

"What? I had ordered the subedar to set the Portuguese people free. Does Moro Dadaji think that he owns the subah? Send him a message that I am coming to Dicholi in person!"

"Ji, there has been a significant change in the Portuguese durbar, Swami. The previous viceroy Antonio has been replaced by Codi-de-Alvar. The new viceroy has not yet arrived in Goa."

"Rayaji Pandit is in Goa. Instruct him to send us a message once the new viceroy arrives in Goa." *Sooner or later, we will have to deal with the Portuguese and the Siddis. If we erect ammunition factories in the Kudal, Dicholi region, it would be beneficial in the war against them* — Maharaj was lost in thought; just then Nilopant shared another piece of news with him.

"The emperor has started imposing tax on the Muslim population too. He has appointed Iraj Khan as the subedar of Burhanpur."

The news made Maharaj solemn. Aurangzeb, who was in Rajasthan, had received the news of the raid on Burhanpur. The people of Burhanpur were concerned that the Friday Namaz would be discontinued, and they had informed the emperor about it. Aurangzeb had issued an order to build ramparts around the city. Though Aurangzeb was engaged in quelling the rebellion of his defiant son, Akbar, he was not going to sit quiet.

"Pant, inform the custodians of all forts on the border of the Mughal sultanate to be vigilant and keep their forts battle-ready. Inform all subedars of Swaraj to recruit new soldiers in their army. Send a message to the Sarlashkar to plunder the Varhad–Khandesh region as much as possible. Inform him that after performing the religious rituals of Aabasheb's death anniversary, I will be travelling to Panhala, Rajapur." Maharaj kept pondering about his nemeses on all sides.

"Swami, Timaji Vyankatesh, the subedar of Cheul has sent a message." Nilopant broached the topic of the Siddis' offence.

"What does Timaji say?" Maharaj's forehead puckered.

"The Siddis had captured two of our ships and the crew, sailing to Mumbai. Timaji sent a warning to the British in Mumbai, 'I will inform the authorities at Raigad of this. Our king will not spare you.' After receiving the warning, the British seized our ships and seamen from the Siddis; mediated with us through Aabaji and handed them over to us."

"Peshwe, send a letter of appreciation to Timaji. Inform Aavaji to keep a watch on the Siddis' activities in Mumbai." The coastal region from Vengurla, Malvan to Mumbai stood in front of Maharaj's eyes and thoughts of the three sea beasts — the British, the Siddis and the Portuguese — kept nagging at his heart. It was detrimental to the Maratha kingdom to let the three naval powers form an alliance. In such a situation, building sea forts, forming an alliance with the Arabs and building ammunition factories in the coastal region were the only options that would have proved advantageous. Maharaj shared his plan to deal with the situation, "Pant, inform the sailors to keep the sea posts from Rajapur to Khanderi ready for action. Tell them to build amicable relationships with the Arabian sailors as much as possible."

Maharaj rose from his seat and left the court hall with Harajiraje. A few peasants were waiting outside. Changoji signalled them to come forward and informed Maharaj, "These fishermen are from Prachandgad; they are sentinels. They want to meet Dhani."

The men, dressed in loin cloths, vest and with coarse blankets on their shoulders, bowed down beseechingly. Maharaj gazed at them with his keen eyes.

"Tell me baba, why did you come to the fort?"

The fishermen only glanced at each other out of fear.

"Speak freely. Why are you here?" The Chhatrapati reassured them affectionately.

One of them gathered courage and said, "Some of us serve on the fort. We have been charged fees for grazing our cows in the pastures along with house tax. We don't have anything except for our cattle, Dhani. Please pardon us the fees for grazing our cows, Dhani." He stepped forward and touched the Chhatrapati's feet.

"Get up." Maharaj held his shoulders and made him stand up. His face looked firm, like he had taken a decision.

"Changoji, summon the record-keeper, Chimangaonkar." A royal command was given.

Changoji went to the record office and brought Chimangaonkar with him. Maharaj immediately shared his decision with Chimangaonkar, "Send a message to Raghoji Hirarao, the custodian of Prachandgad immediately. Tell him that I have exempted these people from the charges for grazing their cows in the pastures. All Hawaldars, Naikawadis and Rajputs on Prachandgad are hereby pardoned the charges of grazing two buffalos in the pastures. You can collect charges for grazing additional buffalos. Warn him that the house tax has also been pardoned for these people."

"Ji." The record keeper listened to the royal command attentively.

The poor peasants felt happy by Maharaj's decision. They bowed down gratefully to Maharaj.

The Chaitra Purnima arrived. Maharaj descended Raigad to perform the rituals of Aabasaheb's death anniversary. Clad in only a dhoti, he stood in the waist-deep water of River Kaal and offered water to Aabasaheb's soul.

Balambhat, Kaviji, Udho Yogadeo, Keshav Pandit and Umaji Pandit stood on the bank of the river.

Memoriy after memory was swirling in Maharaj's mind – 'One year has passed. I still can't believe that Aabasaheb is gone, but it is the truth. On his deathbed he told the others, "This world is ephemeral! Every person who is born must go some day." It is the cycle of life. But the arrival of people like Aabasaheb sanctifies the ephemeral world, and their departure leaves it orphaned. This is how life should be lived. In fact, he does not even need any kind of offerings for moksha.

'Aabasaheb, I went astray in a moment of weakness and defected to the Pathan. My actions tormented you severely, and even if I kept offering water to you, standing like this for the rest of my life, I would never be able to make it right. I can never remove this guilt from my heart. In fact, I am not worthy enough to offer this water to you. What Putala Masaheb did, and Peshwe Moropant did was the true sacrifice! I do not covet this kingdom that you have raised. I have taken charge of the royal seal to completely clear my name.'

Maharaj ascended Raigad after performing the rituals of Aabasaheb's death anniversary. He summoned Nilopant and called for a meeting in the court hall. Harajiraje, Shamaji Naik Punde, Dadaji and Bhimaji Kakade and Jaitaji Katkar were invited to this meeting with honour.

In front of the courtiers, Maharaj presented Harajiraje with a sword in the scabbard, some ornaments, robes of honour, and headgear. Maharaj placed his hand on Harajiraje's shoulder and gazing into his eyes confidently he said, "Raje, I entrust you with the responsibility of the Karnataka region consisting of Bengaluru, Jinji, Hoskot, Kolar, Velur, Doddabalapur and Chikkabalapur. It is surrounded by the Madura, Mysore, Hukkeri, and Ramnad kingdoms. Ekojikaka is in Tanjavar. With his assistance, try to extend the boundaries of Karnataka. The Karnataka region is very crucial for the kingdom. Keep the surrounding kingdoms under control. Shamaji, Jaitaji and the Kakade brothers will be at your disposal. I believe that your presence in the Karanatak region will be as good as my own presence. If needed, send me a message and I will support you. Leave the fort today. May Mother Jagadamba bless you with success." Maharaj embraced Harajiraje affectionately. Haraji reassured the Chhatrapati, "I will never deter from my duty. The Chhatrapati should rest assured."

Shamaji, Jaitaji, Dadaji and Bhimaji were also bestowed with robes of honour. Maharaj descended Raigad with Harajiraje and came to Pachad. Harajiraje left Pachad with fifteen thousand soldiers and select men. Harajiraje Mahadik marched towards Karnataka as the representative of the Maratha kingdom.

As Maharaj was gazing at Harajiraje's army marching out of Pachad, Ganojiraje's face lingered in front of him. One brother-in-law was going on a faraway campaign for the kingdom; the other had turned his back in aspiration of the vatan and had gone back to Shringarpur.

When Maharaj arrived on the fort, Vaknis Ramchandra Duttaji and Shivaji Suro came to meet him. Ramchandrapant informed Maharaj about an adoption case in Wai and the arrears related to the case. "Maharaj, there is one Keshavji Naik in Wai. As they are without children, his wife, Pilai, has adopted his brother Gangaji's son. This adoption was approved by Thorale Swami. At that time, Thorale Swami had ordered Keshavji to pay five thousand hons as the levy for the adoption. Keshavji has so far deposited two thousand honons in the record office. He wants to pay the remaining three thousand Hons in instalments."

"What kind of a person is Keshavji?" Maharaj tried to assess the person.

"He is an honest person who never breaks his promise. If permitted to pay in instalments, he will pay the duty to the last Hon." Shivaji Suro vouched.

"Then grant him the permission to pay in instalments." Maharaj announced his decision immediately. Satisfied by the decision, Ramchandrapant and Shivaji Suro made an obeisance and left.

"The Majumdar is here to see you. He is waiting outside." Jotyaji announced.

"Send him in." Maharaj couldn't guess why Annaji had come to see him. Annaji came in, made an obeisance and stood silently, thinking.

"Yes Annaji, what is it?"

Annaji who never hesitated to speadk his mind, hesitated for a moment. Maharaj realized that he was afraid of speaking out, so he reassured Annaji,

"Annaji, feel free to tell me, even if it is something personal."

"Ji, the post of the Deshkulkarni of Sangameshwar has been vacant with no heir to succeed. If Swami would be kind enough to..." Annaji was apprehensive of Maharaj's reaction while proposing the idea.

Samartha's words echoed in Maharaj's mind – fulfil the pertinent desires of your ministers to restore their faith in you and encourage them to fulfil their duties appropriately.

"Annaji, have you verified that the Deshkulkarni has no successor?"

"Ji."

"In that case, I hereby appoint you as the Deshkulkarni of Sangameshwar, Majumdar! Sangameshwar is fortunate to have an officer of your calibre as the Deshkulkarni, Annaji!" Maharaj spoke genuinely.

Satisfied, Annaji promptly made an obeisance and left.

"The leader of the surveillance team, Bahirji Naik is here to meet you." An attendant announced. The announcement broke Raje's reverie, he gestured to send him in.

Soon, Bahirji came in. He was unrecognizable in the Mughal attire and the fake beard. Nonetheless, he made an obeisance.

Maharaj took him to a secret chamber. Bahirji had probed the Agra, Burhanpur, and Baglan region with keen eyes and sharp ears and picked up crucial news from there. He whispered, "Dhani, I have brought vital information from the Rajput camp. The emperor duped his son in a blink, in the Rajput encampment of Ajmer. Prince Akbar fell upon his father with a mammoth army of the Rajputs, but he could not sustain. The emperor sent a fake letter to his son that said, "Well done! It's great that you have convinced the Rajputs to come together and have brought them in my clutches. Now, you and I will destroy the entire Rajput army together!" The emperor made sure that the letter fell into the hands of the Rajput sardars. It worked perfectly, just as he had predicted. After reading the seized letter, the Rajput sardars panicked. They abandoned Akbar's camp in the middle of the night and vanished. Out of the sixty thousand soldiers, barely twenty thousand remained behind. Despondent Akbar has been on the run. Word is that he might be coming to our kingdom."

Maharaj listened to Bahirji carefully; he was lost in thought. He asked Bahirji a probing question, "Naik, what is the emperor's next move?"

"The rumour is circulating in the Mughal region that he is going to charge upon the Deccan. Big preparations are going on in Burhanpur and Aurangabad in anticipation of his arrival.

Maharaj gazed at Bahirji with concern.

"Okay Naik, you leave after taking rest for a couple of days. Post skilled informers in Burhanpur and Aurangabad. Make sure that any information you get, reaches me at the earliest."

He summoned Changoji and gave him an order. His intention behind that order was to keep the atmosphere on the fort amiable. "Changoji, withdraw the surveillance on Thoralya Masaheb's palace." Maharaj had no idea that this order was later going to have severe repurcussions.

Aurangzeb's son, Akbar had reached the city of Maheshwar

located to the north of River Narmada. He had sent a letter to Maharaj in Persian. With the assistance of Kavi Kulesh, Prahlad Niraji created the Marathi draft of the letter, and both had come to meet Maharaj.

"Maharaj, the Marathi draft of the Mughal prince's letter is ready." Prahladpant extended his hand holding the roll of the translated letter.

"Prahladpant, go ahead and read what Prince Akbar says." Maharaj instructed him. Prahlad Niraji started reading the translation.

"To His Highness Shambhooraje, I pledge my loyalty to you, please believe me that since the onset of his reign, my father, the Alamgir, had intended to destroy the Hindus and still intends the same. After the death of Maharaja Jaswant Singh, his motive had been exposed to all.

"As every human being is the child of Allah and He is the Saviour of all; it is sinful on the part of Hindusthan's emperor to eliminate the jamindars and the ryots of Hind. Alamgir has thus crossed all limits in atrocious cruelties.

"If he continues eliminating the natives of Hindustan, my family will be eventually deprived of the throne of Hindustan. I have abandoned the Alamgir and escaped with my personal retinue from the Mughal Empire. I have travelled via Shahajahanabad, Lahor, Elgad, Baglan and have crossed the River Narmada near Bhaiswaad. The Rajpur sardar, Durgadas Rathod is with me. By God's grace, when I capture the throne of Delhi, I will become only the titular emperor. The entire kingdom will belong to you. You and I should consider the Alamgir's enmity with both of us and join hands to achieve our common goal.

"Nothing is constant in the ever-changing world, except for the reputation one earns and one's good deeds. Considering your valour and temerity, I have decided to enter your kingdom. Need I write more? A hint is more than enough to a wise person."

The picture of the father, the emperor, that his son had

sketched was indeed vivid. Maharaj was lost in thought after listening to the content of the letter.

"Kaviji, what do you think of this Mughal prince?"

"Akbar is the emperor's son! We should take as much advantage of him as we can, Swami." Kulesh expressed his opinion.

"You are wrong, Kaviji. I am not going to give him much importance. He can be just as burdensome as he can be beneficial. Until we figure out what his intention is, don't send a response to this letter, Prahladpant. Send your best spies to monitor his movements." Maharaj announced his decision.

Nilopant came to visit Maharaj with Aavaji, who had come from the British durbar of Mumbai. Aavaji presented the gift of the British durbar, worth one hundred fifty rupees, sent for the Maharaj. Maharaj gave the customary touch of his hand to the gift and asked Aavaji, "Are the British supportive of the Siddis or do they admonish them?"

"After I went there, within a month, the British sent their advocates, Gary and Tharwin to Janjira, to mediate with the Siddis. The British have warned the Siddis to stop plundering the Nagothane, Aapate and Pen region, otherwise they will be prohibited from entering the Mumbai harbour. The British are dealing with the Siddis strictly. I delivered Maharaj's message to the British officers. That is why they are admonishing the Siddis."

"Where are the Siddis now?" Maharaj asked with satisfaction.

"The Siddis have taken their fleet of ships towards the Surat harbour." Aavaji had thoroughly monitored the Siddis' movements while he was in Mumbai.

"Okay." Maharaj said and rose from his seat. Kulesh broached a topic that he had been pondering for many days. "Maharaj's coronation ceremony has taken place, but the induction of the prince could not be performed as no prince was present. Therefore…"

"What are you implying Chhandogamatya?" Maharaj didn't

understand what he was saying.

"If the Putrakameshti yajna is organized…!" Kaviji broached the sensitive topic.

Maharaj responded with a smile, "Kaviraj, you are a perfect fit for the post of the Chhandogamatya. Life is also a melody consisting of many chhandas (poetic meters). If a yajna is a part of it, then why should I refrain from performing it? You make preparations for the yajna with the assistance of the secretary." The Chhatrapati rose from his seat.

"Come Kaviraj, let's take a stroll to the western machi and take darshan of Thoralya Aausaheb's courtyard in Pachad." He ordered Kavi Kulesh while leaving.

Maharaj went to the western machi with Kaviji and Jotyaji. Kavi Kulesh was walking behind Maharaj. Maharaj brought one thing to his attention. "Chhandogamatya, I call you 'Kaviji', but the people of Maval cannot pronounce that word properly; they call you 'Kabaji'. They find it hard to pronounce Kulesh, and hence they call you 'Kalusha'. Does that bother you?" As the Chhatrapati said this, he remembered that in the Mughal, Adil Shahi, Qutub Shahi and British durbars he himself was referred to as 'Sambha'.

"It doesn't bother me, Swami!" Kavi Kulesh responded with a smile.

As Maharaj was gazing down at Pachad from the machi, only two words echoed in his mind like the tolls of the bell – 'Putrakameshti yajna'. 'Should I perform this yajna while both my sons are in prison?

The Putrakameshti yajna took place on Raigad. Raje put the responsibility of transporting Akbar from Tryambak to Sudhagad of Pali, on the shoulders of Chitnis Balaji Aavaji and Bahirji Bhosale. Raje himself descended the fort to go to Dicholi. Khandoji Ballal, Yesaji Gambhir, Kaviji and others accompanied him. Maharaj travelled via Poladpur, Mahad and after climbing the Koyana ghat, he came to Panhalgad with Kashi Ranganath, the officer in charge of Javali and Bapuji Trimbak, the officer in charge of Malkapur. He was coming to Panhala after almost a year.

As the Chhatrapati came to the court hall, Khandoji made an obeisance and informed him, "Maharaj, our soldiers have set a few Portuguese houses on fire in the Daman region and also executed a few people there. Two weeks back, the Portuguese had set one of our villages ablaze in the Bardesh region and had set alight our people in the central chowk of the village. We have settled the score in Daman."

The Chhatrapati was about to say something, when Mhalojibaba, the Sarnoubat of Panhala came in. He bowed down and said, "The Dutch officer is here. He wants to meet with Dhani."

Maharaj gestured to Mhaloji, indicating his approval. The lanky, fair Dutch advocate, Lefebvre came in with an interpreter. He had donned a flared scarlet robe, and fringed loose trousers. He knelt down in front of Maharaj, removed his wide hat in which a white feather was tucked and leaned forward to make an obeisance. He had come from Pondicherry. His interpreter presented the petition of the Dutch durbar in front of the Chhatrapati.

"Maharaj, the Dutch durbar seeks your permission to engage in trading in the Pondicherry region and to mint copper coins."

The Dutch people had an amicable relationship with the Maratha kingdom since the time of Aabasaheb. Maharaj granted permission to the interpreter with one condition, "I will grant permission on one condition. The Dutch people should provide guns and cannons to us."

The interpreter conveyed the Chhatrapati's condition to Lefebvre which he accepted politely. Maharaj instructed Kaviraj to close the deal and bade farewell to the Dutch advocate.

After having lunch, the Chhatrapati summoned the Chitnis of the fort and dictated the content of letters to be dispatched later to Rajapur, Kudal and Dicholi regions. He also instructed the Chitnis to convey to Yesubai on Raigad that he had reached Panhala safely. The Chitnis left. Maharaj was pacing in the chamber alone. He did not notice that Mhalojibaba had come in and was standing on a side. Mhalojibaba wondered whether he should stay in or go out. He turned around to go out, but his movement caught Maharaj's attention. Maharaj stopped him and asked, "What is it, Mhalojibaba? Why were you leaving?"

"Umm…nothing special, but…" Mhaloji mumbled.

"What is it? You can tell me. Don't hesitate."

"A shepherd has come to the fort. His name is Dhakalu. I tried to convince him but he is not budging. He wants to meet you."

"What for?"

"He says he wants to gift something to Dhani!"

"He wants to gift something to me. Really? Inspect him thoroughly. He probably wants some gift from me, Mhalojibaba."

"I asked him many times, but he insists that he wants to give you something."

"Then bring him in." Maharaj got curious. Mhaloji brought the shepherd, Dhakalu in. He carried a coarse blanket on his shoulder, wore a tight vest, with a red turban on his head. He wore a loin cloth and a sharp sickle tied around his waist. Mhaloji signalled to him many times to bow down to Maharaj, but the rough and tough Dhakalu did not understand it.

Maharaj asked the rugged shepherd, "Who are you, baba? Where are you from? And what brings you here?"

He tidied the coarse blanket on his shoulder and replied in his rustic tongue, "Ji, I'm Dhakalu, a shepherd…from the gorge of Mhasai. Who's the king here?" Fearless Dhakalu asked Maharaj himself, "Who is the king?"

The Chhatrapati found the shepherd standing in front of him like an elegant Arabian stallion. To put him at his ease, he said, "I am the king!"

"Oh, hail Lord Birhuba!" The shepherd exclaimed and directly prostrated in front of Maharaj.

"Oh king, here's this shepherd's gift for you." Dhakalu got up quickly, pulled out a white piece of something from the folds of his loin cloth and placed it at Maharaj's feet.

Maharaj bent down, picked up the piece and observing it he asked, "What is this Dhakaloba?"

"It is a scale of a scaly cat. I have pulled it out from the skin of a live scaly cat!"

"Why did you give it to me?"

"Very useful…not easy to find. I caught a scaly cat alive, smeared its back with limestone paste and kept it covered for the whole night. In the morning, only one scale on its back turned pure white like lamb's wool. Then, I pulled it out from its skin. It's the treasure of the forest, oh king. It cannot be bought even with a pot of gold."

"But what is the use of this?" Maharaj's curiosity was piqued.

"It's very useful in case of poisoning! Put it in a ring and wear it on your finger. The white colour changes to greenish blue when it comes near poison. That scale…is the sentry for your food." The shepherd was talking to the Chhatrapati as if talking to an equal.

As Maharaj observed the scale in his hand carefully, his face glowed. He stepped forward, patted Dhakalu's shoulder and said, "Dhakaloba, you have given me a very precious gift. Now tell me, how should I reward you? You name it and you will get it… land, animals, food grains, weapons, clothes, gold… anything."

Dhakalu's eyes sparkled with pure innocence. He nodded his head and said, "Oh king, you're our God! You put your hand on my shoulder; my life is blessed now. I don't need anything more. God Bless." The shepherd prostrated in front of the Chhatrapati again and placed his head on the Chhatrapati's feet.

Maharaj pulled him up and held him in a deep embrace; he was overcome with emotion.

Like the wild wind, Dhakalu left the chamber and started walking towards the gorge of Mhasai.

Chhatrapati Sambhaji Maharaj, who was curiously observing the scale in his hand, had no clue that Annaji had met with Soyarabai and with her consent had scheduled a secret meeting at his residence. Ragho Vasudeo, Bapu Mali, Surya Nikam, Hiroji Farzand, Annaji's brother Somaji Dutto and Chitnis Balaji Aavaji who had returned from Tryambak were discussing something with Annaji in low whispers. A dark conspiracy was taking shape in secret.

Jivaji Hari, the subedar of Sudhagad sent a message with an informer, "The Mughal prince Akbar has reached near Pali. He seeks an audience with Maharaj. He is accompanied by a unit of about four hundred horses, two hundred camels and a few menials. He is demanding provisions for his retinue. Let me know what to do."

Maharaj sent a letter to Nilopant and had summoned Hiroji Farzand from Raigad to Panhala. Hiroji has seen the Agra durbar in person. As a veteran of Swaraj, Maharaj had selected him as the emissary to meet with Akbar.

Hiroji concealed his true feelings and presented himself in front of Maharaj. Maharaj commanded him, "Farzand, as a capable veteran of Swaraj, I am sending you to visit the Mughal prince at Pali. Take one thousand rupees, a jewel-studded necklace and a diamond-studded headgear with you as a gift to the prince. Inform Jivaji to supply provisions for the prince's retinue. I have written a letter for the prince; collect it from Kaviji. Maintain the protocol when you meet the prince."

"Ji." Evil thoughts flooded Hiroji's mind; still, he bowed down and made an obeisance.

The Chhatrapati gave the customary touch of his hand to the gift platter for the Mughal prince. He was wearing a ring made with the special scale in his right index finger. There was no reason for Hiroji to notice that. Hiroji made an obeisance and left. Krishnaji Bhaskar of Battis Shirala came to meet Maharaj. He made a request, "Army recruitment is underway in the Shirala region. Maharaj should come sometime and inspect it."

In the evening, Maharaj descended Panhala with Krishnaji Bhaskar, Bapuji Trimbak, Khandoji and Kaviji and marched towards Shirala. He crossed over Varana and arrived at Shirala. He met the new Mavala soldiers being recruited in the army in front of the fort on the plains. The Chhatrapati spent a day at Shirala and came to Malakapur with all.

Maharaj sat in the court room of Bapuji's Trimbak's residence. Bapuji informed him, "Tulaji Desai Nikam has come to meet Maharaj".

Tulaji looked anxious and worried. He made an obeisance to Maharaj and blurted out in anger, "Dhani, am I in your service or that of the Mughals?"

"What happened, Desai? Tell me in detail." Maharaj calmed him down.

"I have inherited the post of the Deshmukh of twelve villages near Bilashi. This area was consolidated in the subdivision of the Shirala district, but now it has been forcibly annexed to the Varankhore region to create problems for me, Swami."

"Who has done it?" Chhatrapati's face became stern.

"The Deshmukh of Varankhore, Somaji Bandal."

"Desai, are you saying that Bandal has separated the twelve villages of one district and annexed them to another?" Maharaj asked turning to Bapuji and Krishnaji.

"Ji, it is true that the villages of Nikam belong to the Shirala district." Krishnaji Bhaskar confirmed.

"I have told Bandal many times that it is wrong and he should not do it. He disobeys me, Maharaj." Said Bapuji.

Maharaj's face turned red. He announced his verdict sternly.

It was going to add insult to injury for the Bandal. The Chhatrapati said to Bapuji Trimbak and Krishnaji Bhaskar, "I will give you the edicts. Make sure that the twelve villages of the Desai stay consolidated in the Shirala district. Somaji Bandal is encroaching upon the property of another. Let him experience the same thing first-hand and understand what it means to suffer like this. Kaviji, inform Bandal that he has been dismissed as the Deshmukh of Varanakhore and the revenue office will take over the region!"

Tulaji Desai felt joyful. Bapuji, Krishnaji, Kaviji all understood that Maharaj was prompt not only in administering justice, but also in terminating injustice.

From Malakapur, Maharaj came to Panhala and spent two days there. Maharaj bade farewell to Mhaloji, sent the subedars of Javali and Malakapur back to their Subahs and left Panhala via Konkan Darwaja. He marched in the direction of Rajapur, Kudal, with Khandoji, Yesaji Gambhir and Kaviji. But Hiroji spent a few more days on Panhala, meeting a few people.

In Rajapur, Maharaj mediated with the British through subedar Devaji Vitthal and enlisted their ammunition experts. Then he travelled to Dicholi via Kudal.

The Portuguese vakil, Narayan Shenavi came to visit Maharaj. He presented gifts to Maharaj and put forth a complaint about Moro Dadaji of Dicholi, "Subedar Moro Dadaji does not have amicable relations with the Portuguese durbar."

Maharaj admonished Moro Dadaji, "We are planning to raise an ammunition factory in the subah. How can we do that without building friendly relations with the Portuguese? The saltpetre and sulphur needed for the factory are going to be delivered from Karvar by sea. We must buy it from the Portuguese region. You better keep good relations with them, or else I will have to dismiss you from the post of subedar."

Narayan Shenavi presented one more important piece of news to Maharaj, "As per the Chhatrapati's instruction, the advocate Ramaji Thakur who had come from Panhala has been taken into custody. A new advocate needs to be appointed." As Ramaji had been involved in the first conspiracy, Maharaj had instructed the Portuguese durbar to imprison him.

Maharaj got lost in thought for a moment. Then he took a decision and shared it with Shenavi, "Yesaji Gambhir will join you, as our official vakil."

Maharaj prepared a letter requesting the Portuguese durbar to permit the release of the shipment of the saltpetre and sulphur coming from Karvar. He sent Yesaji Gambhir to Goa with his letter and royal gifts for the viceroy. He examined the region to find good locations for setting up the factory. Maharaj bade farewell to Dharmaji Nagnath of Kudal and Moro Dadaji and left Dicholi. As the Chhatrapati was marching back to Panhala he realized that Khemsawant of Kudal and Dalavi of Fonda had not come to see him.

The Chhatrapati stood on the Pusati Buruj of Panhala, gazing at the Konkan coast at a faraway distance in the west. As the Mriga constellation had gone by without rains, the sky was still clear. Maharaj had recently sent a message to Nagothane and had commanded the expert mariners of the naval forces to gather in Nagothane.

The next day a message arrived from Nagothane, "The expert sailors and mariners have assembled."

Maharaj left Panhala, travelled via Anuskura ghat, entered the Konkan coast and came to Nagothane.

At the subedar's residence, by the seashore, a meeting was organized. Seasoned mariners such as Dadaji Prabhu, Maynak, Daulat Khan, Govindji Aangre, Kondaji and Jagoji Farzand, Santaji Pavala, Mohammed Kavaji, Nagoji Waghmare and Sundaraji Baji, were present for this meeting. Maharaj glanced at all of them and presented his plan, "The Siddis' control over Janjira and Underi has shackled the naval forces of Swaraj. Why have we been unable to break the shackles of the Siddis, despite having such diehard sons of the sea like all of you? Aabasaheb's soul will not rest in peace until Janjira falls. I put forth a proposal to all of you. Whoever captures Janjira and Underi, will be rewarded with two kilograms of gold, a headgear and the honour of owning a palanquin."

The Chhatrapati threw a challenging look at all of them. Everyone was given the betel leaf of honour. Three thousand employees in the naval forces were paid six months' salary in advance. Maharaj visited the Nagothane, Pen and Aapte region and returned to Panhala. After a couple of days, as per his routine, the Chhatrapati took the darshan of the colour-changing Shivlinga at the Someshwar temple and came to the Balekilla. He dictated to the Chitnis, the contents of the letters to be sent to Baglan, Goa, Mumbai and Khandesh.

At noon, Maharaj received the intimation that lunch was ready. So, he left the court room. Outside, the skies were overcast.

An attendant placed a bowl in front of the Chhatrapati. The Chhatrapati held his hands over the bowl and the attendant poured water on them. Maharaj wiped his hands with a cloth and sat on a seat placed in the dining room. The armed guards kept patrolling outside. Khandoji and Mhalojibaba were discussing the plan about Janjira. Kavi Kulesh was leaning against the stone railing and observing the overcast skies.

An attendant came into the dining room with a covered platter. He placed the platter in front of the Chhatrapati. As he removed its cover his hands trembled a bit. Steam rose from the warm bowls surrounding the mound of rice. Maharaj pointed to each bowl and asked the name of the dish. The attendant politely told him the name of each dish. Maharaj removed the bowls he didn't want and placed them aside. But the attendant was still looking at the four bowls in his platter.

Maharaj made sure he had everything he wanted in the platter and signalled the attendant to leave. He closed his eyes, joined his palms and paid respects to the food; pulled his sleeve up and got ready to eat.

The Chhatrapati poured daal on the rice and started mixing it. He was lost in thought.

Before taking the first bite, he casually glanced at the platter. All his thoughts vanished instantly, like a gusty wind blowing away clouds. His eyes narrowed, as he noticed that the white ring on his index finger had changed colour and turned greenish blue! His eyes widened and nostrils flared. He took his hand away from the platter to verify. The ring turned white when his hand was away from the platter and was turned greenish-blue when he took his hand close to the platter.

Every time the ring changed colour, the Chhatrapati's eyes changed colour too. His whole body shook with royal wrath. Drops of sweat gathered on his forehead. He shook his hand and pushed the lunch platter away. As he rose from his seat, the Chhatrapati roared loudly. His loud voice startled the people standing outside, "Mhaloji, feed this to that ungrateful traitor! Bring him in front of me!"

Terrified, Mhaloji, Khandoji, Kaviji and the guards rushed inside. They were baffled; they did not understand what was happening.

In confusion, Mhaloji, Khandoji and Kaviji kept staring at Maharaj and the platter alternately.

"Who served me the food? Bring that backstabber in front of me. That traitor…" Raje roared like a booming cannon.

The guards rushed to the kitchen, arrested the attendant and presented him in front of the Chhatrapati. He had packed his stuff and was ready to leave the fort.

"Feed a few bites to the dog outside." Maharaj pointed to the platter and commanded a guard. The guard said, "Ji". He put some food from the platter in a bowl, took it outside and placed it in front of a dog.

The captured attendant was shaking in fear. The Chhatrapati approached him, "I cannot stomach this food. Looks like you can! Be quick. Eat that food in front us!" Maharaj pointed to the platter. His eyes were breathing fire."

"No Dhani…no." The attendant screamed, leaving everyone stunned, and fell at Maharaj's feet sobbing loudly.

"Silence!" The Chhatrapati continued to point his finger pointing at the platter. The attendant clasped Maharaj's feet while sobbing. Maharaj pushed him aside and commanded the guards, "Shove that nectar down his throat."

The guards poked the attendant with their spears from all sides; the attendant got up quietly. He mixed the food in the tears trickling from his eyes and quietly consumed the food that he had served the Chhatrapati. Everyone's eyes were fixed on him. No one could do anything except watch what was happening in front of them.

Within a short time, the attendant's eyes turned white; he began slobbering; his body turned bluish black. From a sitting position, he collapsed on the floor and his body started shaking.

Mhaloji stepped forward promptly, grabbed his barabandi tightly, shook him vigorously and asked, "Who bribed you to commit such a horrible act? Say his name. Tell me…" Just a bit of saliva trickled out of the corner of his mouth.

"Mhalojibaba, he wouldn't have told us the name of the conspirator even if we would have thrashed him. He had participated in this act after careful consideration."

All the faces of the conspirators from the previous conspiracy flashed in front of Maharaj's eyes.

Maharaj let out a painful sigh. As Maharaj left the chamber, he commanded the hawaladar, "Don't throw away the carcass of the dog outside. Bury it in a deep hole. It has been poisoned. Cremate this loyal servant near the well."

As he was walking towards the yard, the shepherd Dhakalu's face lingered in front of Maharaj's eyes. Samartha's words echoed in his ears, "Be vigilant all the time!"

The Chhatrapati left no stone unturned to get to the root

of the plot to poison him on Panhala, but to no avail. Without evidence, no one could be accused. Maharaj had barely missed being poisoned and it left him deeply hurt.

Maharaj was on the Balekilla, standing at a window in a chamber on the second floor. He was gazing at the pouring rain outside. 'Suspicion' torments man like nothing else can. It enters one's mind timidly like a rabbit and wreaks havoc like an elephant. As suspicion enters one's mind, one starts doubting even one's own shadow.

The suspicion had left Maharaj utterly restless. He could not find a way out.

"Dhani, two Muslim messengers of the Mughal prince have come to meet you. They want to meet in private." Mhaloji broke the Chhatrapati's reverie.

Maharaj felt irritated. Akbar's men must have come here to ask for some favour. He wanted to say no to Mhaloji, but since they had travelled a long distance in the pouring rain, Maharaj said, "Bring them in."

Mhaloji came with Sardar Mirza Yahuddin Shujai who was a confidant of the Mughal prince and vakil Abdul Hamid. Mhaloji sent them inside and stood himself outside.

"Assalam–e–salam" Mirza Shujai and Abdul Hamid bowed down to make an obeisance to Maharaj. Maharaj raised his hand in acceptance and responded, "What do you want? Tell me."

Both glanced around and ensured that nobody else was present.

"Ala Hazarat has sent a letter for Rajaji." Shujai glanced at Abdul. Abdul pulled out the green pouch from under his robe and handed it to Maharaj. Maharaj unfastened it and pulled out three rolls. The roll of Akbar's letter was easily recognizable as it was of a different make. Maharaj opened it; it was written in the Modi script.

"To Sambhajiraje, the scion of Shivaji Maharaj, I am eager to meet you. Enclosed herewith are two letters received from your capital. Please read them carefully and decide what to do. Have faith in me."

Baffled Chhatrapati opened the second letter. It was a letter to the Mughal prince Akbar with the royal seal of the administrative office of Raigad. It was written in the neat handwriting of Chitnis Balaji Aavaji, on behalf of Soyarabai!

Maharaj was stunned to read the letter. He read both letters quickly and kept staring at them as if he was holding embers in his hands. Those were not normal letters. In fact, they betrayed a manifesto of treason, designed by those conspiring Marathi people who had turned against the Maratha kingdom.

Soyarabai, Annaji, Balaji, Hiroji, Somaji and others had taken advantage of Maharaj's absence on Raigad and devised a pathetic, evil plan. They had planned to assassinate Sambhajiraje and join hands with Akbar! In return, they were going to offer a part of the Maratha kingdom to Akbar!" The names of all conspirators were clearly mentioned in that letter. By writing that letter, Balaji had destroyed his own reputation as the loyal servant of Swaraj. Hiroji Farzand, who had been disguised himself as Thorale Maharaj in Agra, had fulfilled the loyal service of delivering those letters to Akbar. The senior, veteran employees of Swaraj who were pardoned by the Chhatrapati once, had proved that treason flowed through their blood. Maharaj shook with royal wrath; the letters in his hands shook too. His eyes turned blood red. He barely managed to control his anger and bade farewell to Akbar's people saying, "I will look into this matter."

Maharaj felt as if the Balekilla was whirling around him. He was enraged by the intention of the plot. Poisoning him was the first half of the plot and teaming up with Akbar was the second half. The first part was extremely dark, and the second part reflected the same darkness.

"Who is there?" The Chhatrapati called the guard in an intimidating voice and commanded, "Summon Trimbakaji with his writing materials."

Trimbakji, the personal secretary presented himself in front of Maharaj. With an aggrieved heart, the enraged Chhatrapati commanded him, "Chitnis, send a message to Kudal-Dicholi immediately and tell Dharmaji and Moro Dadaji to detain Majumdar Annaji at once and present him in front of me. Send a letter to Jivaji at Sudhagad. Dispatch a letter to Raigad and instruct Nilopant to capture Balaji Aavaji and Somaji Dutto and place armed guards around Soyarabai's palace."

The letters were dispatched. The Chhatrapati dispatched a letter of appreciation to Akbar with the message, 'I will come to meet you soon.' After two days, the Chhatrapati left Panhala. Maharaj marched towards Raigad, braving the pouring rain. He was determined to cross the flooding rivers in boats.

As Maharaj arrived at Raigad, he realized why Annaji had gone to the Dicholi region even when he had not been instructed to. It was an astute move, to prove that he had nothing to do with the plot. Maharaj had sent Balaji to transfer Akbar from Tryambak to Pali, but he had returned to Raigad after devising the plan with Akbar. Soyarabai who had influenced about ten, twenty people on Raigad, Annaji, Balaji who had formulated the plan with Akbar, Somaji Dutto, Balaji's son Aavaji and roving Hiroji...such was the chain of the conspiracy. These people had lured Shamaji Naik, the subedar of Karnataka, also into this scheme and extended the link to the Karnataka region.

This time, the Chhatrapati really missed Hambirarao. He was not in the fort and Maharaj had to resolve the matter immediately. He was not going to rest until it was done. Peshwe Nilopant came to meet Maharaj with Prahlad Niraji, Aavaji and Khandoji Ballal. He shared the news of Underi, "Maharaj, a few days ago, our mariners attacked the Underi fort early in the morning. They fought for eight hours in the sea but failed. The Siddis fought hard and forced them to retreat. We have lost many sailors."

Maharaj's face turned grave on hearing that news. He hadn't

received any good news in a long time. Maharaj approached Aavaji. To assess Aavaji, he placed his hand on Aavaji's shoulder and said, "Aavaji, can you advise me about something?"

"Ji." Aavaji didn't understand the Chhatrapati's intention.

"We have unveiled a plot of treason. The plan was to assassinate me and then team up with Akbar. If enough evidence is found and the crime is proved, how should I punish the culprits involved?" Aavaji trembled in fear.

"Death sentence!" Khandoji furiously blurted out. He didn't know that his father was one of them!

Maharaj didn't say anything, just patted Khandoji's shoulder and asked a vital question, "What if Rani Saheb and Sarlashkar Hambirarao are involved in it?"

"How...how is that possible Maharaj?" baffled Khandoji said.

"Anything is possible, Khandoji! Even the Sun can get eclipsed! Think carefully and then give me your advice."

Khandoji thought that Swami was suspecting his involvement in the plot. He firmly said, "Doesn't matter who the person is – even if it's me, the punishment for such a crime is only the death sentence!"

Khandoji had passed the test of loyalty.

"What is your opinion, Nilopant and Nyayadhish Prahladpant?" Maharaj had purposely called Prahladpant Nyayadhish.

"Khandoji is right." Peshwe, Nyayadhish, Khandoji – everyone understood that whoever was involved in this conspiracy was going to pay the price.

"Okay. Khandoji, summon Ramraje's personal secretary, Yesaji Dabhade to my chamber.

Nilopant and Prahlad Niraji thought that Ramraje was going to be the first to be investigated in this case!

Maharaj dismissed everyone and started pacing back and forth holding his hands at the back. With every step a web of thoughts weaved in his mind, 'Am I afraid of death? No. Then what is this pain? This is not the pain of the fear of death. The death of loyalty is so much more dreadful than actual death! What is left after the death of loyalty? This is that pain.

Yesaji Dabhade came. He looked scared. Maharaj saw him and said, "Yesaji, please come with me."

Baffled Yesaji didn't know where they were going, but he said, 'Ji' and started walking behind Maharaj.

Chhatrapati Sambhaji Maharaj started walking towards the palace of Soyarabai Masaheb without giving advance notice. He wanted to confront her and get things clear once and for all.

The guards patrolling Soyarabai's palace made an obeisance, but Maharaj didn't notice it. As he entered the palace, the maids dispersed. Maharaj went to the inner chamber. Ramraje saw him and felt confused. He stepped forward and exclaimed, "Maharaj Saheb!"

Maharaj pulled him close, patted his shoulder and gently corrected him, "Call me Dada Maharaj!" A strange silence prevailed in the chamber.

Soyarabai saw the Chhatrapati and started going to the sleeping chamber. An intimidating voice commanded her, "Stop!" She stopped in her place. His voice was authoritative and commanding.

"I have endured a lot. It would be a big favour to me if you just stop plotting against me. That is all I wanted to tell you." The Chhatrapati said sarcastically and joined his arms at his elbows and bowed down to Masaheb.

"It has been proven by now that I cannot be defamed, captured or poisoned!" Maharaj felt overwhelmed and stopped for a moment.

"If...if only my death is going to satisfy you and going to prove beneficial for the kingdom...then please go ahead and give me a glass of poison in front of Balraje. I will consume it readily!"

Soyarabai had never heard such a thing in her life. She was

agitated. She spoke out instantly and firmly, "Yesaji, the Maratha Chhatrapati never accuses anyone without evidence, especially not a royal lady. Please explain this to him."

"Silence! Don't underestimate me just because I spoke to you politely as you are my Masaheb. The Mughal prince himself has sent me the letters that carried your royal seal. If you wish to see them, I will show them to you.

"As you are Ramraje's mother, and Aabasaheb's wife, I have come to warn you for the last time. Your greed is getting out of hand. Control it." Furious Maharaj couldn't speak any further.

The royal lady in front of him burst out like a serpent that has been provoked. She hissed, "Yesaji, tell you Chhatrapati that he has no right to admonish me like this. If he really believes that I am the culprit, he is free to punish me as he wants!"

Maharaj was stunned to hear it. Ramraje was terrified and had clung to him. The Chhatrapati gently extracted himself from Ramraje's embrace and while leaving the chamber, he said bitterly, "Yesaji, tell the former Maharani that no Maratha king who ascends the throne will ever punish his mother. The queens of the Bhosale family don't ask to be punished by others, they decide their own punishment. If at all the Maharani thinks that she has committed an unpardonable offence, then she is free to choose her punishment!"

The night of Shravan descended on the fort. Maharaj had finished his dinner and was in his sleeping chamber. Yesubai, clad in a brocaded yellow sari, came in. Maharaj was thinking about the culprits involved in the plot. As he saw her, he thought, 'Should I appeal to her that she should not put her word on the line in this case of treason…it would be really difficult if she makes any recommendation in this matter… After all she is an inducted queen now, with her own royal seal.'

"Can I say something?" Yesubai broke the silence.

"I would like to say something before that." Maharaj became cautious.

"Please listen to me. I have come to know everything about the conspiracy on Panhala. I only want to say..."

"Rani Saheb...."

"That once everything is proved beyond doubt, Swari should sentence the culprits the way he deems right. He should not spare anyone now."

Maharaj was mesmerized by her words. But he did not show it and went along with her thought, "And what if Ganojiraje is involved in this?"

Yesubai realized that Maharaj was trying to gauge her loyalty. To show him her grit she said, "Swari should definitely give me that responsibility and see how I handle it!"

Maharaj was delighted; he removed his Jiretop and handed it to Yesubai. Maharani started walking towards the wooden stool to place the Jiretop on the platter.

Maharaj observed her from an angle and remembered the 'Swakiya' heroine in Sanskrit poetry. Yesubai leaned forward to place the Jiretop on the platter. The brocade design on her sari sparkled in the light of the lamps. Maharaj felt as if a creeper of glittering stars was leaning in front of him.

As Yesubai placed the Jiretop and stood up, the Chhatrapati's muscular arms embraced her! She trembled for a moment and rested her head on his chest.

Yesaji Gambhir had sent a messenger from Goa to inform, "The Portuguese durbar is quite offended by the actions of Moro Dadaji of Dicholi. He has captured two Portuguese ships and kept them in custody indefinitely."

Maharaj summoned Nilopant and announced his decision, "Pant, inform Moro Dadaji that he has been dismissed from service. Appoint Vinayak Umaji in his place."

"Ji. How should we deal with the message that Jivaji Hari of Sudhagad has sent, Maharaj? The Mughal prince Akbar is recruiting new soldiers in his own authority." Nilopant drew the Chhatrapati's attention to Akbar's actions.

"Pant, I have summoned Netajikaka to deal with that problem." Maharaj had taken a decision in his mind.

Considering that Netaji had spent a long time in the north, the Chhatrapati said to him, "Kaka, take twenty thousand hons with you and go to Pali with a retinue of select swordsmen. Meet the Mughal prince in person and give him a clear warning. If he wants to stay in our kingdom, he cannot recruit soldiers to build his own army. Just as he considers himself the emperor of his kingdom, I am the king of this kingdom. As long as he obeys the customs, we will extend our hospitality. If necessary, give him monetary support, but don't provide personnel to him."

"Ji. I will keep a keen eye on the Mughal prince." Netaji accepted the responsibility. Maharaj dismissed him.

Maharaj realized that Nilopant wanted to say something but was hesitant to broach the topic. Maharaj reassured him and encouraged him to speak, "Yes Nilopant. Say what you want to say. Don't hesitate."

Pant licked his lips and presented the news hesitantly, "Jivaji Hari has sent another message Swami."

"What is it?"

"Majumdar Annajipant, Chitnis Balajipant, his son Aavaji, and Somaji Dutto have been captured and detained at Parali near Pali!"

Maharaj got up at once and exclaimed, "I – I was waiting for this news. Peshwe, why did you address them as Majumdar and Chitnis? Why did you affix the honourable title 'Pant' to their names? They have destroyed the reputation of these prominent posts by their own actions. Inform Jivaji Hari that I am coming to Parali in person."

"Ji!" Nilopant bowed quickly.

Maharaj left the Balekilla with Yesaji Kank and Changoji. He started walking towards the dungeon. About twenty culprits, including Bapu Mali, Surya Nikam, and Ragho Vasudeo were shackled in the dungeon. None of them could lift their heads in front of the Chhatrapati.

Maharaj threw a glance at all of them and said in a sharp voice, "Take a look at me with your own eyes. This is not my ghost. I am still alive. Goddess Jagadamba has saved me to reward you for your loyalty. Yesajikaka, rigorously execute the sentence I declare for them." Maharaj turned his back.

Maharaj handed the control of Raigad to Yesubai and Nilopant and left Raigad after two days. He was accompanied by Jotyaji, Rayaji–Antoji and only five hundred soldiers. It was the month of Shravan. Maharaj was marching towards Parali; conflicting thoughts filled his mind. 'What would have Aabasaheb done, had he been in my place today?

They reached Parali. Jivaji came to receive Maharaj. Maharaj came to the Sarkarwada of Parali with Jivaji.

Maharaj had lunch and took a siesta. In the late afternoon the Chhatrapati ordered Jivaji, "Present the prisoners in front of me."

Shackled Annaji, Balaji, Aavaji, Hiroji and Somaji were brought to the court hall of the Sarkarwada and presented in front of Maharaj. Their faces had darkened with shame. As Maharaj saw them, he rose from his seat with extreme disappointment and rage. He didn't even want to look at Annaji.

'Such a faithless and backstabbing man! He bowed down in front of me as the Majumdar, while planning a conspiracy against me. This Balaji! He used the same quill with which he wrote the invitations of my coronation ceremony, to write a letter to Akbar! And this Hiroji! He slept on Aabasaheb's bed to help him escape from the haveli in Agra, but he was preparing my funeral pyre! Are these the same people or their hideous ghosts?'

Bitter words flew from the agitated Chhatrapati's lips, "Oh loyal servants of Swaraj, look carefully. I am still alive! I pardoned you before and reinstated you in the ministry with faith, and this is how you repay me!" The Chhatrapati's lips trembled.

"Now open your mouth and tell me what kind of

punishment you are ready to go through for your actions?" Like the sound of a whiplash, Maharaj roared.

The Chhatrapati approached Annaji, and roared while shaking him vigorously, "Why are you tongue-tied now? Open your mouth. Should I reward you with another region for this valiant feat?"

Annaji felt agitated but remained quiet with lowered head.

"When it is time to speak up, you know very well how to stay tight-lipped! Tell me, what kind of penalty should I give you?" Maharaj threw a fiery glance at Annaji.

Annaji made up his mind, looked up and said in a cold voice, "Whatever penalty is given to the Maharani! My only crime was that I obeyed her command."

"Silence!" Annaji's irrefutable reply had hit a tender spot in his heart. He felt stifled for a moment; his entire body was shaking in rage. Annaji had rendered his authority worthless. Maharaj felt that it was now necessary to make Annaji understand that though she was a 'Maharani' for the world, she is 'Masaheb' for him. The Chhatrapati not only carries the royal seal, but also bears the responsibility of maintaining the honour of the cowrie necklace of Goddess Bhavani.

'Jivaji, bring me the cane-stick." Fiery royal words flew in the court room.

Jivaji gauged his mood and saying "Ji" he went inside. He handed a long, thick cane-stick to Maharaj and with a stunned heart and fearful mind he stood aside.

Shaking in royal wrath, Maharaj roared, "Hold this cane vertical and it is called a sceptre, hold it horizontal and it becomes a stick. It depends on how you view it. Just like that, the one on Raigad is the 'Maharani' for you and 'Masaheb' for me. I cannot penalize her, and I cannot let you free. You ungrateful wretch!" With a whipping sound the cane struck Annaji! Thereafter, "Filthy rogue, scoundrel, fiend"– with every strike Annaji was cursed furiously. Maharaj struck him seven-eight times; with every strike Annaji writhed in pain.

Maharaj's forehead was sweating; with trembling hands he threw the cane aside and gave a very harsh command, "Jivaji, load all of them on the horses and dispatch them to Raigad. Tell Nilopant to shackle and parade all of them with their accomplices in the fort. Make a public announcement and execute the high-level culprits under the elephant's feet in front of the public. Hurl their accomplices down Takmak tok. Do away with them." The Chhatrapati left the court room like a flash and disappeared.

Maharaj travelled to the coastal region, went back to Panhala; with Mhaloji's assistance, distributed the army in the Solapur, Pedgaon and Aurangabad region and returned to Raigad. As per his instructions, Nilopant came to meet him with Khanderao Pansambal and Khandoji.

A fortnight had passed since the conspirators had been executed. A strange atmosphere of hopelessness prevailed on the fort.

The Chhatrapati approached broken-hearted Khandoji who stood in front of him with a lowered head. Quiet, solemn words fell on Khandoji's ears, "Sometimes I feel like removing this royal attire from my body. My heart and soul suffocate under its pressure. But the question leaves me dazed, whom should I hand it over to? I have inherited this attire from Aabasaheb, and I cannot do away with it. You have also inherited the skills of the Chitnis; it is in your blood; you should not keep the quill aside. You and I, have no family relations. Serving the throne is the only relation we possess. I want to appoint you as the Chitnis. Would you accept the responsibility?"

Khandoji was not prepared to hear anything like this. His eyes welled up. This was a crucial moment in his life. Destiny was testing his loyalty. Khandoji did not waste a moment. He immediately leaned forward, touched Maharaj's feet, and said in a hoarse voice, "I am the humble servant of Swami and the royal throne. I will do my duty faithfully."

Maharaj pulled him up; his eyes also welled up with satisfaction. He said to Khanderao, "Pansambal, you are the heir of Gomajibaba. He served Thoralya Aau; in a sense, he served the entire kingdom. I appoint you as the Majumdar of Swaraj." Maharaj took the decision to present Khanderao and Khandoji with robes of honour and hand them their seals and stamps in the durbar. Nilopant felt delighted with this decision, but he immediately had to obey another command, "Pant, send an urgent message to Haraji in Jinji, to detain the crook, Shamaji Naik Punde. immediately."

Nilopant nodded in affirmation and left with everyone.

The days of Navaratri arrived. Maharaj performed the religious rituals in Pachad and on the day after Dussehra he left Raigad. He went to Panhala with a few close people. He was planning a big campaign. As soon as the monsoon was over, he was going to commence the campaign. As he was climbing up Panhalgad he felt, 'I have an unknown connection with this fort. This is where I met Aabasaheb for the last time. While I was on this fort, both conspiracies against me were exposed. This fort is so close to my heart.'

For a week, Panhala was covered in fog. After that, Maharaj received news that clouded his heart, like the fog surrounding the fort. Vishwas had picked up the news from the Mughal sultanate. It was the most dreadful news – A mammoth green cloud was moving towards the Maratha kingdom. "Aurangzeb has left Ajmer to invade the Deccan! His entourage includes three lakh infantry, three lakh cavalrly, large numbers of cannons and a treasure of thirteen crores. He is accompanied by Prince Muazzam, Kambaksh, his grandsons Bedar Bakht and Muhajuddin, and prominent sardars such as Bakshi Ruhulla Khan, Asad Khan, Ranamasta Khan, Etikad Khan, Shahabuddin Khan, Mohammed Amin, Hasanali Khan, Lutfulla Khan, Matbar Khan, Bahadur Murad Khan, Tabiyat Khan and Rao Dalpat Bundela. The cities of Burhanpur and Aurangabad are preparing for his welcome."

To face this onslaught, letters of appeal to bring together the forces in Deccan, were dispatched to the Qutub Shahi and Adil Shahi sultanates through loyal informers. Maharaj was planning to leave Panhala after getting it battle-ready, when he received another shocking news on the twelfth day of the dark fortnight of Ashwin.

Yesubai had sent Jotyaji to Panhalgad. He stood in front of Maharaj with bent head and shared the news with him, "Thoralya Masaheb is no more! She drank poison and killed herself!"

On the twelfth day of the dark fortnight of Ashwin, the door of Soyarabai's chamber did not open until mid-day. The frightened maids knocked on the door for a while and finally called the Maharani's personal secretary. He came with Ramraje, knocked on the door and called out to her, but no one responded. In the end, Yesubai came and tried calling her, but that also did not work. Ultimately, she had to give the order to break the door open.

The scene inside left the viewers stunned. A beautiful, middle-aged, royal lady was sleeping peacefully on the bed. A vial of poison lay faithfully by her side. The life of a spirited royal lady of the Bhosale family had come to an end. With tears in her eyes and Ramraje by her side, Yesubai touched the feet of Masaheb and left the chamber. As stubborn Soyarabai had realized her failure, she resolutely punished herself in a way that nobody could have imagined. She did not surrender! Putalabai's body had been engulfed by flames while Soyarabai's mind had been set afire!

Tears rolled down Maharaj's eyes, trickling onto his beard. As if they were saying, "You played a game with yourself too, that no one could ever comprehend! Even Aabasaheb did not understand you, then, how could I? You have wounded my heart deeply by punishing yourself in this way. I can never forget this pain. You did not say to me, "remember me always". But I will never be able to forget you. Just as it would have been better if I had been born to Putala Masaheb who committed Sati, it would have been much better if I were born to you. It would have solved so many problems…for you, for me, for Aabasaheb, and for all…"

Chapter 12

The Chhatrapati was grimly pacing in his chamber. Raigad was in mourning for Soyarabai. Maharaj had not met Yesubai since his arrival. As a matter of fact, he didn't feel like meeting anyone. As soon as he arrived at Raigad, he had met only Ramraje. The memory of their meeting kept chasing him constantly. Innocent Ramraje had said something that had left a deep scar on his Dada Maharaj's heart.

The moment he saw the Chhatrapati, fearful Ramraje clasped him in fear and said, "Maharaj, don't put me under the elephant's feet! I will take my own punishment, just like my masaheb!"

His words had torn the Chhatrapati's heart to pieces and brought tears to his eyes. He consoled his brother and took an impromptu decision – 'He shouldn't hear anything inappropriate for his age. He should be protected. For that, Yesaji Dabhade should be provided with more trustworthy people.

To accomplish that, Maharaj had employed more reliable people in Ramraje's service. He had taken precaution not to keep any unreliable, fickle person around Ramraje.

But his decision had sparked off a peculiar reaction on the fort – "Ramraje is placed under house arrest!" Maharaj did not know it. He was pacing back and forth, pondering Aurangzeb's next move.

"Rani Saheb is coming." An attendant's announcement broke his reverie.

Yesubai entered the chamber. Maharaj approached her. They gazed at each other. Their eyes reflected a similar sentiment – the pain of Soyarabai's death.

"I have heard something; is it true?" Yesubai posed a direct question.

"What did you hear?" The Chhatrapati was confused by her stance.

"That Swari has put Ramraje under house arrest? That too, before the mourning period of Masaheb had concluded?" As if Bhaveshwari herself was scrutinizing the Chhatrapati.

"What…did you say?" Indistinct words slipped from his lips. A painful expression covered Maharaj's face. He turned his back to Yesubai and posed a question just as sharp as hers, "And…and you believed it?"

Until now Yesubai had been holding her head high, but now she lowered her head and exclaimed, "Sorry, I made a mistake." An unnerving silence prevailed between the two royal hearts.

"It is true that I have appointed some reliable people in Ramraje's service. Ramraje is not under house arrest – just under the protection of trustworthy people. I am waiting for Hambirarao to come from Varhad, so I can fix Ramraje's marriage with his daughter! I know very well that he cannot endure the suffering that I endured in my childhood." Maharaj left the chamber. As Yesubai looked at his disappearing figure, she realized, "No matter how hard you try, you cannot fathom a person who is like the wild wind! You can only go along with him!"

The mourning period was over. The Chhatrapati left Raigad with Yesaji Kank to overcome a guilt that had been gnawing at him for a long time. He came to Pachad. Fifteen thousand cavalry soldness had assembled in Pachad. Yesaji Kank's regiment of ten thousand infantry had already marched forward with the artillery.

Maharaj surveyed his forces with select people such as Girjoji Yadav, Vinayak Umaji, Khanderao Pansambal, Bajirao Jedhe, and Yesaji Kank. He took the darshan of Jijau's samadhi and mounted his horse 'Chandrawat' standing at the front of the army. The kettle drums boomed; the pennants were raised.

As soon as the Chhatrapati raised his hand and signalled the army, the cavalry marched forward. Maharaj was going to attack Nagar; with the audacious plan to rescue Duragabai and Ranooakka who were confined in the fort of Nagar!

The cavalry regiment passed through Pune, Koregaon, crossed over river Kukadi and united with the infantry regiment. With an army of twenty-five thousand, the enraged Chhatrapati forced his way through the borders of Ahmednagar.

For three days, the Maratha army exerted efforts to break open the entrance gate. The number of soldiers getting killed kept increasing every day, but the fort did not budge at all. In the evening of the third day, the dispirited Chhatrapati commanded his army to retreat. As a despondent Maharaj left the border of Nagar, his head was bent low, and his face had turned pale. The faces of Durgabai and Ranooakka who were in imprisonment kept flashing in front of his eyes.

Maharaj appointed Girjoji Yadav to gather information about Durgabai and Ranooakka, ordered Yesaji Kank to remain in the Nagar area, and returned to Raigad extremely dejected. The Nagar mission had failed completely.

The forests were getting bedewed in the cool weather of Kartik. Six months had passed since the Mughal Prince, Akbar, had entered the Maratha kingdom. The Chhatrapati decided to meet him. He summoned Kavi Kulesh and instructed him, "Kaviji, inform Jivaji Hari of Sudhagad that I am coming to meet the Mughal prince. Make arrangements for a private audience."

"Ji." Kulesh was delighted that the long-delayed meeting

was finally going to take place. It was mandatory to meet Akbar now. Maharaj had to collaborate with any big or small kingdom that considered Aurangzeb their enemy. He had to confirm for himself whether Akbar had truly rebelled against his father or not.

During the bright fortnight of Kartik, the Chhatrapati descended Raigad with Kaviji, Prahlad Niraji and a select troop of warriors. He travelled via Nizampur, Roha and arrived at the border of Pali where Jivaji Hari had come to receive him with his men. Maharaj also saw a hefty, middle-aged Rajput wearing an orange turban, waiting to receive him.

Maharaj dismounted, accepted Jivaji's obeisance and came forward. He was gazing at the handsome Rajput man. As Maharaj came in front of him, he humbly knelt and made an obeisance. Jivaji quickly introduced him, "This is Durgadas Rathod! He has come to Deccan as an ally of the Mughal prince."

"Jai Eklingji, oh King of the Marathas, please accept my obeisance!" Durgadas bowed low again. The Chhatrapati leaned forward, pulled Rathod up with respect and embraced him. Maharaj came to the residential mansion of Sudhagad with the retinue.

After lunch and a siesta, in the late afternoon, Maharaj came to the seating chamber with Kaviji, Netaji Palkar and Prahladpant. Jivaji had embellished the chamber with luxurious mattresses, bolsters and carpets. The Chhatrapati took his seat.

The Mughal Prince, Akbar was stationed in a simple tile-roofed house, in an old town, Dhondasha in the Pali region. His men had camped on an open plateau. Jivaji had gone to Akbar's camp to bring him to the meeting place.

"Kaviji, what day is it today?" Maharaj asked Kavi Kulesh who was standing behind him.

"JI. The third day of the dark fortnight of Kartik." Kaviji replied. Maharaj picked up a rose from the platter placed on a wooden stool in front of him. He twirled it in his fingers and, lost in thought, he leaned against the pillow.

He remembered the cold days of winter, three years ago. 'The ghat on the confluence of Mahuli…the boats sailing on the water…the camp of the Pathan…hefty, arrogant Diler! The whole year that was wasted in his own folly; that had stained his reputation forever!'

'What is the difference between Akbar who is coming to meet me now and me back then? Akbar has come here after revolting against his own father. Was I rebelling against Aabasaheb? No…no. Then who was I rebelling against? It was my rebellion against my own self, a reckless and thoughtless decision.

'Aabasaheb had the capacity to understand my folly; that is why I could come back. Or else? Would Akbar ever go back to his father? Would Aurangzeb ever embrace him with the love of a father? And what would he do to his father, if by chance his wish is fulfilled, and he captures the royal throne of Delhi? Did I ever think of betraying Aabasaheb, even in my dreams? This…this is the difference between us. The power-hungry Mughal royals will not hesitate to remove any obstacles in their path to the throne, including their own family. But the Maratha royals value their family as much as their throne!'

Jivaji rushed to the chamber. He bowed down, pointed towards the door and announced, "The Mughal Prince, Akbar is coming."

The Chhatrapati rose from his seat. The young Mughal Prince, Akbar entered the chamber. He had donned a brocaded, fine-textured white jama, an emerald-studded Mughal kimosh, and pleated, fine-textured, loose trousers. He wore the necklace that the Chhatrapati had gifted him. He had a ruddy face and a trimmed beard.

With a royal smile on his face, Prince Akbar spread his hands and walking briskly he approached the Chhatrapati. The Chhatrapati embraced him and ushered him to his seat with honour. The prince's loyal men, Mirza Yahuddin Shujai, envoy Abdul Hamid and Durgadas Rathod, stood courteously by his side.

The exchange of royal gifts took place. The Chhatrapati handed the rose to Akbar and said, "This rose is from your kingdom. It is our first guest. I like it!"

Prince Akbar knew that Raje was a poet; he laughed heartily and responded, "I am sure, you would like me too." He sniffed the rose quickly.

Maharaj raised his hand and signalled his men to give them privacy. As agreed, everyone except Kavi Kulesh left. Akbar also dismissed his men, except Durgadas Rathod. The Chhatrapati broached the topic of their meeting with caution, "Prince, do you think you will be able to sustain the weather of the Deccan?"

"Raja Saab, the circumstances here are less harmful than the imperial weather!" Akbar understood the intent of the question and astutely expressed his disapproval of his father. They gauged each other's responses and opened up their hearts gradually.

"Prince, you have done me a great favour by handing me the letters of the conspirators plotting against me." Maharaj could not forget that favour of Akbar.

"That was his doing!" Akbar pointed towards Durgadas. Durgadas bowed courteously.

"I don't get it." Maharaj looked at Durgadas and exclaimed.

"That was his suggestion, Raja Saab – Durgadasji is a very reliable person. He had advised me to send the letters to you." In the first visit itself, Durgadas had impressed Maharaj; and now his respect for Durgadas had increased. Maharaj also formed a favourable opinion about Akbar who had spoken so highly of his aide.

"What do you plan to do next?" The Chhatrapati asked the crucial question.

Countless bitter memories surrounded Akbar; his ruddy face became stern. Harsh, resentful words about his father slipped from his lips, "Alamgir will annihilate Hindustan, Raja Saab! Does ruling the kingdom mean torturing the ryots? The Jizya tax, breaking of idols, torture and murder! Why would the people of Hindustan trust the imperial family? Alamgir is putting himself and the imperial family in danger. He should be stopped at any cost." He had spoken the truth, but it was quite difficult to implement. The Mughal prince had clearly understood his father's flaws, but he was incapable of assessing his father's immense power.

"Oh prince, you are right, but we should also think about Alamgir's military power. We are up against an emperor, who assassinated your grandfather, Emperor Shahjahan, and uncles Darah and Murad. How do you suggest we confront him?" Maharaj calmly and astutely reminded Akbar how Alamgir had assassinated his own family members.

Akbar stroked the pearl necklace on his chest momentarily. He put forth his plan to vanquish Aurangzeb, "You are right, Raja Saab. Alamgir is going to charge upon Deccan. I am thinking of going back to Rajasthan in the north. In the entire Hindustan, only two kingdoms have the mettle to confront Alamgir – the Rajputs and the Marathas.

Kunwar Ram Singh, the son of Mirza Raja Jai Singh, the king of Jaipur, loathes Alamgir. Alamgir got Mirza Raja Jai Singh poisoned and assassinated him; Ram Singh wants to avenge his father's death. I am confident that with Durgadasji and Ram Singh's assistance, I will unite the Rajputs. I have also written a letter to the Shah of Persia to join hands with me...

"Raja Saab, if you lend me your support, I will annihilate Alamgir." Akbar's eyes glowed as he expressed his deepest desire.

"What kind of support do you expect from me?" Maharaj asked calmly.

"Provide me twenty-five thousand Maratha soldiers. This is the time; I have to wage war against Alamgir." Akbar was eager to hear an affirmation from Maharaj. He gazed hopefully in

Maharaj's eyes.

The Chhatrapati glanced at Durgadas Rathod. Based on the information Maharaj had received, he trusted Durgadas more than Akbar. Akbar was alive because Durgadas Rathod was with him.

"Durgaji, what do you think?" The Chhatrapati had faith in Rathod's loyalty and so asked him.

"Ji. Alamgir will fall upon the Marathas first, Raja Saab. Alamgir will make his move first and you will counter it, that is how it should go. First, we will need to keep Alamgir engaged in the Deccan with his army. The Rajputs will revolt in the north, at the same time. Raja Saab, think carefully and take your decision." Seasoned Durgadas spoke Maharaj's mind.

"Very well, Durgaji. Oh prince, I agree with Durgaji's advice, but with a powerful enemy approaching the borders of our kingdom, I cannot send my forces anywhere else." The Chhatrapati announced his decision to Akbar.

Disappointed Akbar did not realize that he had crushed the rose in his hand and its petals had scattered on his seat. But Maharaj had noticed it.

Maharaj patted his hand and consoled him in a calm voice, "Oh prince, I understand your grief, but politics doesn't run on sentiments. You are our guest, and you are safe here. Trust me, your plans will materialize at the right time; have some patience. I will write a letter to Raja Ram Singh of Jaipur; you should also write to him. Only time will decide the outcome of this meeting."

"It is okay, Raja Saab. I will wait but remember that as long as I stay in your kingdom, Alamgir will not let you rest.

As Maharaj heard Akbar's words, he wanted to say, "I have never had a peaceful sleep in my life so far." But he smiled outwardly and said, "Oh prince, Alamgir has destroyed his own son's sleep, and I must accept that he can destroy mine too."

The betel leaves were presented to conclude the meeting. Maharaj accepted the betel leaf and, as Akbar was getting up from his seat, he picked up another fresh rose and handed it to Akbar with a smile.

Akbar got sentimental and embraced the Chhatrapati unwittingly. He left for his camp with his men. As per custom, Maharaj accompanied him a few steps and stopped. As he looked at the disappearing figure of Akbar, he thought, 'He has suffered a lot'. He dismissed these thoughts and said to Kulesh, "Kaviji, you stay here with the prince, and keep an eye on him. He might end up doing something, not necessarily with a political motive, but in an emotional outburst. He needs to be supported."

"Ji." Kulesh accepted the responsibility.

On the same day, sitting in an embellished howdah on the back of a bedecked elephant, amidst resounding kettle drums, Aurangzeb was entering Burhanpur with a mammoth army.

Sitting in the howdah, he was checking with his keen eyes, whether the fortification wall around Burhanpur had been properly raised or not. The fakirs, mullahs and maulvis who had received alms from him were blessing him from the bottom of their hearts.

From Pali, Maharaj arrived on Raigad. He was surveying the cannons lined up in front of the ammunition warehouse on the south of the fort. He said to Nilopant, "Peshwe, did the Dutch envoy keep his word?"

"Ji, they have also delivered the ammunition." The Dutch envoy, Lefebvre had made a recommendation to his durbar to send cannons and ammunition to Raigad.

"Pant, perform a puja of the cannons on a good mahurat." Maharaj was lost in thought; he patted the back of a cannon like he was patting his horse's back. He surveyed the security of the ammunition warehouse and started walking towards the Balekilla with Nilopant, Jotyaji Kesarkar and Yesaji Kank. Nilopant delivered an important message to him, "Harajiraje's messenger has arrived on the fort from Karnataka. Haraji has to seek frequent administrative advice from Raghunathpant

Hanamante, but Hanamante has been imprisoned, so…." Nilopant stopped halfway.

The Chhatrapati stopped and asked, "What solution does Haraji propose, Pant?"

Peshwe quickly put forth Haraji's suggestion, "He suggests that an official order should be given to him, and all paperwork in Hanamante's possession should be seized."

Maharaj pondered the problem. Raghunathpant had handled the administrative duties of the region efficiently. Only during the time of the conspiracy, had his loyalty wavered. He had received enough punishment to understand the consequences of his actions. Maharaj announced his decision, "Pant, inform Harajiraje to release Raghunathpant and reinstate him as the Majumdar of the Karnataka region. People make mistakes, but they should be given a chance to correct their mistakes."

The unexpected decision surprised Nilopant; he tidied the shawl on his shoulder and responded, "Ji."

"Kank kaka, when is Hambirarao coming back from Varhad? I am looking forward to meeting him." The Chhatrapati thought about Ramraje's marriage and asked Yesaji.

"Ji. The Sarlashkar is on his way back. He should be at the fort in about a week."

Maharaj came to the court hall, while accepting obeisance from people, on his

way. Khandoji, Prahladpant, Khandero Pansambal and Shankaraji, the grandson of a woman called Deepai Bandal from Bandal Maval, were waiting for him in the court hall.

Shankaraji had come to meet the Chhatrapati for a personal reason. He bowed down and said to Maharaj, "Sarkar, Thorale Dhani had given the village of Parher as a gift to my grandmother; apparently, she cannot enjoy the gift that she had received. It has been a personal gift. Should we just give it up?" With a fretful expression, he stepped forward and placed the pouch of documents at Maharaj's feet. He stood up and bowed his head.

Shankaraji was the grandson of Deepai Bandal. His father, Rayaji, had shown great valour during two campaigns of Thorale Swami against Chandrarao More of Javali. At that time, Aabasaheb was pleased with his performance and had gifted the village of Parher to Deepai.

Maharaj looked once at the pouch that Shankaraji had placed at his feet, and glanced at Khandoji. He promptly stepped forward and picked up the pouch. He pulled out the documents and started checking them.

Bandal, rest assured. I will fulfil Aabasaheb's promise." Maharaj comforted Shankaraji and gazed at Chitnis Khandoji.

Maharaj, these are authentic official documents with the royal seal and signature of Thorale Swami." Khandoji confirmed. Maharaj calmly asked Shankaraji,

"Bandal, who is causing a problem for you?"

"Ji. The officer in charge of Bandal Maval, Gopal Rayaji is not accepting the validity of these documents. He is telling me to bring new official documents." Shankaraji shared his problem.

"What?" Maharaj's eyebrow arched. He instantly commanded Khandoji, "Chitnis, send a letter of warning to Gopal Rayaji. Tell him that Bandal has met me in person and has shown me the authentic documents. The late Maharaj has gifted the village of Parher to Deepai. It should be treated as hereditary property. You will not be spared if there is any further complaint in this case!"

Khandoji nodded in affirmation. Shankaraji's face lit up as justice was served to him. He thanked Maharaj profusely, made an obeisance and left.

"Maharaj, our nemesis, stationed at Burhanpur has started making moves." Prahladpant broached the important topic and waited.

Maharaj was ready to hear whatever difficult news it was. He gazed at Prahladpant.

"Hasan Ali Khan has left from Burhanpur with fourteen thousand soldiers; he is travelling towards Talkonkan." Prahladpant stopped to hear Maharaj's response to the news. Maharaj was lost in thought. Prahladpant wondered whether he should share the second news or not.

"Yes Prahladpant, speak up. I am aware of everything. In the Nashik region, Shabadi Khan has reached Mulher. He has teamed up with Devi Singh, the custodian of Mulher and has attacked Salheri. Every day, Rupaji is ambushing him as much as possible, and keeps eluding him." Maharaj rose from his seat while speaking. His eyes were riveted in mid-air as if he was visualizing the battle of Salher-Mulher in front of him.

Maharaj nodded and spoke as if speaking to himself, "Pant, Chitnis, I assume that Aurangzeb will attack us from all sides. He has already anticipated that I will assault Nagar again, and hence has tightened its security with additional troops of Prince Azam, Munwar and Kilich Khan. Aurangzeb is coming with pomp to openly attack us. He has declared war upon us but…" Enraged, Chhatrapati stopped for a moment.

He was trying to solve some problem in his mind. He started pacing back and forth, oblivious to the people around him.

Khanderao couldn't help himself and asked politely, "Is there any problem? Dhani should just command us."

Maharaj who was lost in deep thought, snapped back to the matter in hand and said, "Khanderao, where is Kondaji Farzand stationed nowadays?"

"He is in the Kalyan-Bhiwandi region, assisting Tukaji Palkar, Swami." Prahladpant provided information.

"Prahladpant, summon him to Raigad immediately to meet me."

The Chhatrapti raised his hand to seek some privacy. Everyone left, wondering, 'why has he summoned Kondaji this time?"

In a secret underground room, a worried Maharaj said to

Hambirarao, "Sarlashkar, the Siddi is getting out of control." Hambirarao who had come from Varhad and Kondaji Farzand, who had come from Kalyan region, sat in front of him. They earnestly listened to their Dhani's concern.

"The Siddis set ablaze the village of Aapta. They have become insolent enough to slash the noses of our ryots that they have imprisoned in Nagothane." Maharaj's eyes were burning.

As Hambirarao heard his words, his moustache stiffened and he said in rage, "Dhani, just give me the order and I will attack Janjira immediately…I won't show you my face until I bring Janjira down, just as I brought down Varhad."

"No Mama Saheb, in this time of crisis, I cannot remove you from the Mughal front for this coastal campaign. I have summoned Kondaji for that purpose." The Chhatrapati gazed at Kondaji.

The image of the Janjira fort floated in front of Kondaji's eyes; he exclaimed, "Ji" and straightened up in his seat.

"Kondaji, you have a special talent. During Aabasaheb's reign, you used a unique strategy and conquered Panhala with only sixty men at your disposal. This campaign is harder than that. Panhala was a hill fort; this one is a sea fort. The ocean waves make it difficult for the boats to enter the Siddis' region." Maharaj stopped and glanced at Kondaji's twisted turban.

Kondaji arose from his seat at once. He bowed down three times and said in a hoarse but firm voice, "Dhani, I take a vow in the name of Lord Khandoba and accept this challenge of conquering the sea fort. Rest assured that Kondaji will set foot on this fort of the Siddi. I will blow up their ammunition warehouse and bring Janjira down with it. Only then, I will come to pay obeisance to you." With eyes shining bright, Kondaji quickly leaned forward and touched Maharaj's feet.

"Bravo Farzand! I had expected the same from you."

The attire of honour was bestowed upon Kondaji.

As Maharaj stepped outside, a cool breeze caressed him and

he stopped at the entrance of the secret room. In that moment, his thoughts about the Siddis faded and the thoughts about his family took over. He tenderly said to Hambirarao, who had come out of the meeting room, "Mama Saheb, I want to talk to you about something else."

"Ji, what is it?" As Hambirarao responded to him a puff of steam released from his mouth. Kondaji gave them privacy and left.

"Mama Saheb, Masaheb is gone. In an unexpected and unpleasant way. Ramraje has become an orphan. I am thinking of getting him married, and I have been waiting for you to talk about the same."

Hambirarao remembered Soyarabai and was overcome with emotions. He did not say anything. The Chhatrapati stopped for a moment and continued speaking, "You are not saying anything…"

"What can I say, Dhani? I don't understand why she took that step. When I met Balraje he clung to me and said…" Hambirarao remembered his visit to Ramraje and could not speak further.

"What…what did he say?" Maharaj's voice was tender.

"The same thing…tell Dada Maharaj not to put me under house arrest!" Fearless Hambirarao who had overpowered Burhanpur and Varhad, was overcome by emotions.

The Chhatrapati rushed to an attendant holding a torch nearby, grabbed the torch from him and approached Hambirarao. He hold the torch up in front of his face and said in an agonized voice, "Mama Saheb, do I come across as someone who intimidates his brother or loves him?"

The Chhatrapati's hoarse voice mingled with the fluttering of the torch and fell on Hambirarao's ears, "What Aabasaheb would have done, had he been alive, I am going to do the same for Ramraje, my brother. That is why, I have to ask a favour from you Mama Saheb."

Hambirarao was surprised to hear the word 'favour'. He wondered what favour Maharaj was going to ask from him.

"Whenever I faced a dilemma due to Masaheb's behaviour, you gave me unconditional support. Not as the Chhatrapati, but as Dada Maharaj of Ramraje I put forth this proposal. Mama...I wish to bring your daughter into the Bhosale family... as Balraje's bride!"

Seeing that he was still silent, Maharaj changed his stance and made an emotional appeal, "Give me your word, Sarlashkar!"

"Ji. I am ready to give my daughter's hand to Balraje in marriage. I vow in the name of Goddess Waghjai." Hambirarao promised in the name of his family deity, and leaned forward to touch Maharaj's feet. Maharaj quickly stopped him, embraced him and said, "Though you are going to be Ramraje's father-in-law, to me you are still my mama, and will always remain so."

Ramraje's wedding ceremony took place in grandeur, on the magnificently decorated Raigad. With pomp and splendour, Hambirarao's daughter, Tarau, entered the Bhosale household.

As soon as the wedding ceremony was over, the news that Maharaj was anticipating, reached Raigad. Vishwas Musekhorekar, who was keeping a watch on the Janjira region presented himself in front of the Chhatrapati, and shared the news, "Maharaj, Kondaji Farzand has penetrated the sea fort of the Siddis! -About fifty men are with him. Kondaji's men have very cleverly entered the fort and have started working there! Some are pretending to be carpenters; some are working in the lime-stone factory in the fort of Janjira.

As the Chhatrapati heard the news, he felt contented and muttered, "Our Tarau indeed has the golden touch."

Vishwas made an obeisance and left. The Chhatrapati felt confident about Janjira; he took a decision and summoned Peshwe Nilopant.

"Pant, Rani Saheb has decided to go to Gangoli. You

personally take care of the preparations for her journey. Maharaj instructed Peshwe.

Yesubai had decided to go to Gangoli for her delivery. It was not possible for her to go to Shringapur, so she was happy that Gangoli was located near the temple of Goddess Bhaveshwari of Shringarpur.

"Ji." Nilopant nodded in affirmation. Maharaj noticed that Nilopant wanted to say something else, so he prompted Nilopant to speak, "Go ahead, Pant. What do you want to say?"

"Maharaj, the Mughal Prince, Azam has sent Hasan Khan from Nagar with military forces. Hasan Khan has realized that we have blocked the ghat. Therefore, he has changed his plan to fall upon Konkan and has moved towards the Saswad valley. He is trying to pay off our mansabdar of the Purandar region, Sheikh Ibrahim, and lure him to his side!"

Maharaj became restless, but still said calmly, "Pant, send our informers to keep a watch on Ibrahim."

"Ji. Bahadur Khan has plundered the old town of Shivapur near Pune too, Swami." Nilopant reported another bad news to Maharaj.

"Okay, Peshwe, send a messenger to Damaji Raghunath, the public-officer of Pune. Inform him that the enemy is coming to attack the Pune region. Tell him to be vigilant in the region and make sure that two Mughal troops don't join forces."

"Ji." Nilopant was confused to hear his Swami's cool and calm decisions.

"Swami, the Portuguese viceroy, Tavera has completed the construction of a fort in Kolwal. Thorale Swami had kept a keen eye on this Kolwal."

Maharaj was lost in thought, "Pant, instruct our subedar in the Karwar region, to attack the Anjediva island and conquer it. Inform him that the Portuguese want to capture that island too."

The Chhatrapati's strategy against the Portuguese was completely unexpected for Nilopant.

Nilopant felt contented about it and put forth another topic, about the British, "Swami, the British of Mumbai are upset about one thing."

"What is it?"

"Our sardar, Sundarji Baji, has accused the British of assisting the Siddis in Nagothane and has detained two of their ships in the Nagothane harbour. That is why the British are feeling offended."

"Nilopant, it is not wise to provoke all our enemies at the same time. Instruct Sundarji to release the British ships after giving them a warning."

"Ji. The Qutub Shahi durbar has sent a royal gift of four lakh pagodas, Swami."

Maharaj smiled and said to Nilopant, "It is not a royal gift, Pant. It is financial aid sent to us, to encourage us to stand up against Alamgir. Even at the time of my coronation ceremony we did not receive such a huge amount from the Qutub Shahi. They want to destroy their enemy by any means. It's simple politics. Send our reply to Qutub Shah and let him know that we are in receipt of his aid. We might need military support from them. The Deccan cannot be protected by financial aid alone, we need to maintain our unity too."

Four days passed. On the day of the mahurat, early in the morning, Yesubai went with a bevy of maids and offered Oti to Goddess Shirkai.

Draped palanquins, travelling to Gangoli, were ready in the chowk in front of the queens' palaces. They were surrounded by armed guards.

Yesubai took the blessings of Sakwarbai and with Ramraje and Tarau she came to see her Swari in the seating chamber. As Maharaj saw Yesubai, he moved forward. The Maharani leaned forward and touched her Swari's feet three times. Ramraje tried to make an obeisance to Maharaj; Maharaj held him close and kept thinking of what to say to Yesubai who was standing in front of him, gazing at the floor. All he wanted to say was, "Take care of yourself."

In the end, Yesubai spoke, "May I take your leave now? You take care of yourself!"

"Ji." Maharaj unwittingly exclaimed in a courteous manner and said, "I am coming with you, up to the tower."

The palanquins surrounded with armed guards came to the central tower via Palakhi Darwaja; took a short break and continued their descent.

"Dhani...." Bahirji Naik stood in front of the Chhatrapati in the court hall of the royal palace. He was sweating profusely and was breathless. He could not utter a word. As they saw the peculiar expression on Bahirji's face, which was a rare sight, Nilopant, Prahladpant, Aavaji, Moreshwar and Keshav Pandit made an obeisance and left the hall gingerly.

The turban on Bahirji's head shook; for a moment, Bahirji gazed at his Dhani with misty eyes, then with lowered eyed he kept staring at his Dhani's feet.

"Naik...!" Maharaj exclaimed in an alarmed voice.

Bahirji shook his head again, as if he was witnessing something heart-wrenching. A few tears rolled down his cheeks. The coarse blanket slipped from his shoulder, but he didn't even think of picking it up.

"Naik, what happened?" The Chhatrapati rose from his seat at once.

Bahirji's lips trembled; choking words slipped from his mouth breaking the silence in the court hall, "Dhani, we are undone – our Kondaji is no more, Dhani!!" Overwhelmed with sadness, his throat choked.

The Chhatrapati's entire body trembled, and he exclaimed in agony, "Naik – how could it be? Exactly what happened, Naik?"

The staunch servant of the kingdom controlled his emotions and reported, "Maharaj, Kondaji was living vigilantly in Siddi's fort, observing everything keenly, but one of our own men betrayed all of them. We were double-crossed."

"Who did it?" The concern in the Chhatrapati's voice turned into rage.

"Evil Kumaji Desai!" Bahirji's voice was now clear. The Chhatrapati felt agitated and perturbed to hear his words.

"Ungrateful Desai exposed Kondaji's plan to the Siddi, told him that Kondaji was waiting for an opportunity to blow up the ammunition factory. That very night the Siddi captured Kondaji with all his men. Throughout the night, he whipped them and tried to make them talk.

Naik took a deep breath and shared the story of Kondaji's heroic death with his Dhani.

"As Kondaji did not budge, in the early morning, an enraged Siddi Khairat came to see him in person. He stood in front of Kondaji, spit on his face and said, "You dog, we will cut your head and hang it on the pillar. Tell your master from there – whoever casts an evil eye on Janjira suffers like hell!"

"Siddi ordered his executioners to kill all of them."

The Chhatrapati's heart was filled with grief, anger and shame.

"Dhani, Kondaji faced his death like a brave warrior. At dawn, four men of Siddi pressed Kondaji's head down on the wooden stock.

Before his neck was pressed down on the stock, Kondaji bowed down to the fort and to Dhani and shouted, 'Maharaj we have offered our blood to this sea fort! Please forgive our mistakes, and remember this loyal servant of yours…Jai Bhavani…'

"Sarkar, at sunrise, the Siddis hung the heads of fifty men, including Kondaji, on the pillar erected in front of the fort."

The Chhatrapati had closed his eyes. Tears dripped on the cowrie necklace on his chest. Benumbed Bahirji picked up his coarse blanket from the floor and went out.

Sailors from the coastal region, and other prominent warriors, had assembled in the royal court hall. Dadaji Raghunath Deshpande, the public officer of Mahad, his brother, Visaji Raghunath, Maynak Bhandari, Daulat Khan, Govindaji Jadhav, Udaji Padwal, Govind Kanho, Subhana Kharade, Bhivaji Gujar, and Manakoji were present among them. Siddi Sambul and Siddi Misri had abandoned the Siddi and had joined Swaraj by taking an oath on the Quran. They were in the front row in the meeting.

The Chhatrapati sat on the royal throne. Select men such as Nilopant, Duttaji Trimal, Khanderao, Kavi Kulesh who had come from Pali, Prahladpant, and Yesaji Kank stood on either sides of the Chhatrapati.

Nilopant commenced the meeting, "Everyone is aware why the Chhatrapati has summoned all of you here. The emperor of Delhi has charged upon Swaraj from the Aurangabad, Nagar region. His aide, Yakut Khan, has travelled via sea and has charged upon Dandarajpuri. The Siddi of Janjira and Yakut from one side and Aurangzeb himself attacking us from the other side; the enemy has thus planned to trap us in between and destroy us. With his backing, the Siddi of Janjira has become audacious enough to attack us. Siddi Khairat is committing atrocities against our people. This meeting is for planning the strategy to teach him a lesson." Nilopant took a break.

Maynak Bhandari was rewarded with a ship named 'Palakhi' by the Thorale Chhatrapati. His young son had been slain by Siddi Khairat, and that pain was festering in his heart. He proposed a hostile attack against the Siddi, "This is too much. How long are we going to wait? I suggest that Davlat Khan, Sambal Khan, Angre, and me… all of us can launch a united naval attack on Janjira."

As the courtiers discussing the matter realized that Maharaj was not speaking at all, everyone fell silent. The discussion halted. Aged Maynak couldn't bear the Chhatrapati's silence and audaciously urged him, "Dhani, why are you so worried? We are all here. Just give us the betel leaves and we will attack the seas right away."

The Chhatrapati, who had made a decision, was touched by the affection. He glanced at Bhandari, rose from his seat and exclaimed, "Bhandari kaka, I…I am going to fall upon the Siddi of Janjira myself!"

Many people raised their heads in shock. Siddi Sambul and Misri exclaimed – "Inshallah…!" Bahirji Naik, who was standing aside, nodded his head with pride.

The Chhatrapati's eyes looked as fierce as Lord Rudra himself. He started giving commands rapidly, "Prahladpant, dispatch reliable envoys at the earliest, to the coastal region to seek an alliance with the Arabian naval forces. Tell them to carry royal gifts for the Arabs with them. Nilopant, with your regiment, you will camp in the Kalyan region. Yesaji kaka, you make sure that our cannons in Pachad and Mahad are dispatched towards the sea, with the cannon shooters.

"Dadaji Prabhu, with Visaji and Antyaji, you will assemble the forces near the Mahad region and wait for me there. Nilopant, offer betel leaves to everyone." All courtiers left the court hall.

Only Maynak Bhandari, Kavi Kulesh and Bahirji remained behind, as the Chhatrapati had instructed them to. "Naik, disperse your informants in the Raigad, Janjira and Kalyan region." Bahirji got his instruction and left. On the way he planned his strategy.

"Kaviji, you send a letter to the Mughal Prince Akbar in Dhondasha and inform him to join us in this campaign. His participation will give us a clear idea about his intentions, and we will also be able to test his combative skills." The Chhatrapati dismissed Kavi Kulesh too.

Only Maynak was left behind now. Maharaj smiled and said to him, "Come, Bhandari kaka, let's have dinner together!"

The old man was hesitant to sit in front of the Chhatrapati.

Maharaj comforted him and said, "Kaka, don't be so shy. You are family, have a seat." Maynak sat courteously in front of his Sarkar. Dinner was served. The Chhatrapati offered Chitrahuti and took the first bite. But Maynak was quite confused. He was wondering why Dhani had asked only him to stay back.

Maynak ate the first morsel and Maharaj's words fell on his ears, "Bhandari kaka, you are the master of the seas. You know it very well. Tell me the weakness of the Siddi."

The white moustache of the old man trembled; he immediately understood Maharaj's intention. He straightened up in his seat and said, "Ji. The fort is well protected. It is surrounded by a thick wall. The creek side is the only weak spot for the Siddi. The creek is about 120 feet long and about 2400 feet wide. The Siddi knows that the creek side is the weakest spot and that's why he has placed his cannons facing the creek side."

With every morsel Maharaj was asking Maynak a question and Maynak was giving him every small bit of information he knew.

The Chhatrapati left Raigad; united with Dadaji and Visaji Narasprabhu's army at Mahad and the Mughal Prince, Akbar and Durgadas at Sudhagad. With an army of twenty thousand he had reached the coast of Janjira.

The Chhatrapati surveyed the encampment, which was still being set up, and the place where Yesaji had placed the unit of cannons; he came to the mouth of the creek. He was accompanied by the Mughal Prince, Akbar, Durgadas, Dadoji and Visaji, Kavi Kulesh and Yesaji. The Chhatrapati's fierce eyes were fixed on the Janjira fort, visible at a distance, in the ocean.

'This – is the same insolent power that beheaded Maynak's son, our Kondaji and so many more people; the one that abducts our poor people living on the coast and sells them as slaves in their own country far away. This is the power that deprived Aabasaheb of sleep.' Countless thoughts crowded in his mind.

At the same time, Siddi Khairat and Siddi Qasam stood on the rampart walls of Janjira and watched with wide eyes, the mammoth Maratha army spread across the coast. Their thick lips were sealed tight! They were utterly frightened in their hearts, but outwardly they kept giving orders to their men with a pretence of courage.

At the break of dawn, a cacophony of kettle drums and war horns arose in the Maratha camp. With Dadaji and Visaji Narasprabhu, Yesaji Kank, Kulesh, Mughal Prince, Akbar and Durgadas, Maharaj approached the mouth of the creek, accepting obeisance from the soldiers standing around. The cannons were lined up facing the sea fort; the cannon shooters made an obeisance to the Chhatrapati.

As the edge of the golden orb became visible on the eastern horizon, a determined royal finger pointed towards Janjira like a trident. The trembling, enraged lips under the burning eyes roared, "Sarlashkar, let the cannons boom! Let the boats sail on the ocean!"

"Har Har Mahadeo! Jai Bhavani!" the war cries echoed, and the five cannons boomed, reverberating on the shore. Heavy cannon balls collided against the ramparts of Janjira. In fleets of twenty, boats started swaying on the sea waters. They were filled with rope-climbers, ladder-climbers and gun-bearers who were expert swimmers. As per the orders, Maynak, Daulat Khan and Angre were ready in the ocean with their warships. They started approaching Janjira with the intent to attack. They were aided by the Arabian naval forces.

Finally, a war long due, broke out on the seas. The Siddi was vigilant. He instructed Yakut Khan's Mughal ships to stay put on the sea. Boats full of Siddi soldiers were dispatched from the creek. The cannon balls shot from the ramparts of Janjira kept falling on the creek shore. As the day progressed, the Marathi cannons started breathing fire. The Chhatrapati himself kept motivating the cannon shooters. The cannon balls shot from Janjira kept crashing in the creek, splashing water on Maharaj and the Mughal Prince. At noon, the cannon shooting stopped. The soldiers were ordered to take a lunch break.

The Chhatrapati was eagerly gazing at the creek. He saw some black dots swaying on the sea. They were toppled boats. Empty! Some of them belonged to the Marathas and some to the Siddi. Behind them, were some injured sailors who barely made it to the shore.

Their wounds were burning due to the briny sea water. The soldiers in the camp carried them over their shoulders and took them to the tents to tend to their wounds. The Chhatrapati had forgotten to eat his own lunch; he went to the tents of the wounded soldiers in person and inquired after them. He realized that the Siddi was going to give a tough fight.

For twelve days in a row, the roaring Maratha cannons kept firing at the fort of Janjira. Terrified sea birds flew away from the creek. The ramparts of Janjira were now considerably damaged. The British and Portuguese warehouses had dispatched letters to their durbars in Mumbai, Surat, Goa – "Siddi Khairat is in deep trouble. The Maratha king, Sambhoo, is not going to rest until he immerses Janjira in the sea!"

In the Maratha camp, the number of wounded soldiers was increasing. The dead bodies of brave soldiers smashing into the creek shore, were being cremated regularly. Only one fierce attack was going to be enough to bring Janjira down now. The Maratha and Siddi ships kept attacking each other on the sea.

The fifteenth day broke. Like every day, the Chhatrapati, wearing his armour left his shamiana with the Mughal Prince. He came to the mouth of the creek with select men. The Mavala soldiers standing there, made an obeisance to him. The Chhatrapati glanced at them once.

"Dadaji, when does the low tide start?" The Chhatrapati asked. It was a confusing question.

"Maharaj, the low tide started yesterday." Dadaji replied.

"Jagadamb!"

"Maharaj, please give order to release the boats." Yesaji Kank said politely.

"No! Kank kaka, remove those boats from the water and bring them to the shore." The Chhatrapati suddenly issued an unexpected command.

"Ji." Yesaji was shocked.

"Hurry up. Remove all boats!" Maharaj repeated his command.

Countless hands came forward and pulled the boats to the shore. The creek was now open.

All of a sudden, Maharaj's, audacious words reverberated through the air, astonishing everyone; petrifying even the sea – "As soon as this creek makes way for us, Janjira will fall soon! Sarlashkar, Dadaji – Visaji, engage every single soldier in the camp to dump rocks, pebbles, logs, sacks… anything they can get hold of and fill up the creek before the high tide begins! Janjira must fall. Aabasaheb's soul will not be at peace until it happens, and I will not relax until then."

The Chhatrapati turned around and commanded thousands of soldiers standing behind him, "Fill up this entire creek!!"

In a short time, the Mavala soldiers formed lines. Thousands of Mavala soldiers united to dump boulders, rocks, bricks, logs…whatever they could get hold of, in the open jaws of the creek.

Only two people who had never heard or seen anything like this before, kept watching the whole action in wonder, raising their eyebrows – the Mughal Prince Akbar and his loyal adviser Durgadas! The fifteenth day ended.

Siddi Khairat and Siddi Qasam wondered why the Marathas had stopped the cannon shooting. They both stood on the rampart walls to watch what the Marathas were up to. They didn't understand what was going on.

As the twenty-fifth day was coming to end, it dawned upon

Siddi Khairat! "Ya Khuda, toba...!" He screamed as if bitten by a scorpion and whispered something in Qasim's ears.

That night, terrified Siddi Khairat and Siddi Qasam sat in a boat and left Janjira leaving it in the custody of their Siddi soldiers. They sailed farther and settled on a rocky hill located in the sea.

The twenty-sixth day dawned; but the Mavala camp had no clue about what had transpired in Janjira. Thousands of hands toiled to fill up the creek. The creek water was now surrendering to their efforts; it was dispersing in all directions! Success was now within their grasp.

The twenty-seventh day broke out. Thousands of soldiers kept dumping boulders, rocks, logs, bricks, sacks in the creek. The creek water kept dispersing. Maharaj stood firmly in the sand on the shore. Akbar, Durgadas and Yesaji stood on both sides.

At noon, the Chhatrapati raised his hand and gestured to everyone to take a lunch break. Tired and exhausted, all men made an obeisance and waited for lunch to be served.

The Chhatrapati also thought, "I should have lunch with the Mughal Prince today, Janjira is going to fall soon."

He came to his shamiana. Lunch platters had been placed on wooden stools. Satisfied, the Chhatrapati removed his Jiretop and placed it on a platter. He washed his hands in the washing bowl and with Akbar he took his seat to have lunch. He said to Akbar, "Oh Prince, you are my special guest. As we are engaged in a war, we can't serve you delectable dishes at this time. Hope you are not disappointed!"

Aurangzeb's son Akbar was awestruck by the battle of the Mavalas against the sea; he gave a queer smile at first. Then, deliberately gazing at Durgadas Rathod, sitting next to him, he said, "Raja Saab, what you eat hardly matters, but your actions indeed reflect the Maratha spirit.

The Chhatrapati laughed heartily. He proudly glanced at

the creek in front of the shamiana and was about to eat his food. Just then, Yesaji Kank rushed into the shamiana. His face looked quite pale and gloomy. He gulped and politely spoke in a hoarse voice, "Dhani, Ramchandrapant has come from Raigad…"

The Chhatrapati's hand lingered in the platter.

"Who? Pant?"

"Ji."

"Send him in." Maharaj pushed the lunch platter aside. Ramchandrapant came in. He joined his hands to make an obeisance, but they trembled. Pant removed his turban and held it in his hand! Agitated, the Chhatrapati rose from his seat at once. His trembling words full of concern, raised goose bumps on the walls of the shamiana, "Pant! What happened?"

Pant stood with his head hanging tears trickled from his eyes and rolled onto the turban in his hand. His choked, broken words echoed in the shamiana, piercing the Chhatrapati's heart, "Swami, on the ninth day of Magh, Samartha…Samartha breathed his last!"

Maharaj instantly closed his eyes when he heard the news. Many holy and radiant miens of Samartha whirled around him.

Like a seashore beaten by the waves, the Chhatrapati's heart was benumbed by grief. Moreover, Ramchandrapant's concerned voice fell on his ears, "Swami, Hasan Ali Khan and his mammoth army has surrounded the region of Kalyan–Bhivandi. Lodhi Khan is also with him. What action should we take against them?"

The Chhatrapati had to set aside the grief of Samartha's demise and had to take a firm decision immediately. The same day, Maharaj handed over the Janjira campaign to Dadaji and Visaji Narasprabhu. As he left the camp, Maharaj said to both of them, "Don't let my absence weaken your resolve. Leave no stone unturned to conquer Janjira and come in person to share the news with me." The Chhatrapati embraced both of them. After dispatching Ramchandrapant to Sajjangad, to raise

Samartha's samadhi there, the Chhatrapati travelled towards Gangoli, with Yesaji Kank. The Mughal Prince, Akbar went to Shahanpura with Durgadas. The fort of Janjira and the creek, both breathed a sigh of relief to see the Chhatrapati's departure from the shore!

Gangoli came into sight. Maharaj entered Gangoli with Yesaji Kank and select swordsmen.

Accepting the obeisance of the people around, the Chhatrapati entered the palace. As soon as he stepped in, young Bhavanibai came, calling him 'Aaba…' and clung to him. Maharaj held her in his arms and kept talking to others, but people noticed that he was thinking about something else.

Maharaj washed his hands and feet and came to the Yesubai's chamber. Yesubai and Dharau were present in the chamber. Maharaj glanced at Yesubai standing in front of him and asked, "Did you get the news?"

"Ji. Hasan Khan has camped into Talkonkan. The Mughal Prince Azam has attacked the Purandar region. But how come Swari came here unannounced…"

"Yesu…Yesu… Samratha breathed his last on Sajjangad…. on the ninth day of the dark fortnight of Magh…"

"What!" Yesubai raised her head in shock. As she saw Maharaj's grief-stricken face, she lowered her head in pain. As old Dharau heard the news, she exclaimed 'Oh Lord Khandoba…' and left the chamber with a heavy heart.

The Chhatrapati kept pacing back and forth, Yesubai stood still in shock. A few moments passed in silence. Then, the Chhatrapati said with determination, "Can you do me a favour? Nobody but you will be able to fulfil my wish."

"Ji, what do you want me to do? Tell me whatever it is. I will do it."

"Since Thoralya Aausaheb's demise, Samartha's Dasbodh is just sitting in the sanctum. Flowers and haldi-kumkum are being offered to it; it's being worshipped and then wrapped in a cloth and placed in the sanctum. Yesu, now you should take it out on an auspicious day. Perform its puja and just like Thoralya Aausaheb used to get it done before, you should get it recited in Raigad regularly. Will you do it for me?"

"Ji. When I came from Shringarpur to Pachad, I took darshan of Thoralya Aau's seat. At that time the same thought had crossed my mind. I wanted to bring the Dasbodh onto the fort, but I controlled myself at that time.... until today."

"Why?" The Chhatrapati asked in surprise.

"If at that time I would have taken the Dasbodh from Thoralya Aau's sanctum then... then without understanding my intention, a rumour would have spread on the fort in no time, 'The granddaughter-in-law is trying to establish her authority indirectly.'"

The Chhatrapati was impressed by the depth of her thinking and approached Yesubai. He put his forefinger under her chin, pulled her face up and said, "Aabasaheb handed you the royal seal and the dagger. I gave you the name 'Shrisakhi' in the durbar full of people at the time of my coronation. Thoralya Aau has given you this awareness. May Goddess Jagadamba give you the strength to handle all this responsibly."

Maharaj spent two days at Gangoli, surveyed Yesubai's security personally and bade farewell to his family. At the same time, in the Panhala region, Hambirarao attacked the Mughal Prince, Azam's camp with fifteen thousand cavalry and five thousand infantry.

In the court hall of the royal palace on Raigad, the Chhatrapati was gathering information about the administrative affairs. "Swami, we have taken control of the Anjediva island. Please issue the order to take up the construction of a fort on the island." Peshwe Nilopant presented the urgent matter.

"Peshwe, send a message to Arjoji Yadav to send me the estimate for the construction of a fort on the island. Write a letter to the subedar of Karwar and instruct him to collect and provide materials such as limestone, bricks, lead etc. to build the fort. Aabasaheb has already proved how important it is to build formidable sea forts to keep surveillance on the sea. The Sindhudurg is a testament to that, and…"

"Your wish is my command, Maharaj." The Peshwe bowed.

"And just recently I have experienced it at Janjira, how the sea fort takes advantage of the sea waters. To that effect, we should form as amiable a relationship with the Arabs as possible, to continue the construction of the fort on the Elephanta island. Keep that in mind."

"Swami, the Portuguese durbar has created a problematic situation in the Ramnagar region. We have conquered the region, but the Portuguese are not ready to pay the tax as they used to pay to the Rana of Ramnagar." Khandoji put forth an administrative problem.

"What do you mean?"

"Swami, the Portuguese durbar has sent us a letter that, that they will pay us the tax only after we take possession of the entire Ramnagar region!"

As Maharaj heard the words, he rose from his seat at once. Fiery words slipped from his mouth, "Chitnis, it looks like we have to teach these Portuguese a lesson and make it clear to them that the region belongs to us. We don't need the Chauth paid by them; in fact, we don't even need their presence in our region! The Portuguese are supporting the Siddis in the Choul region and gave them permission to build a fort. They stay behind the scenes, and assist our old enemy in attacking us. Dispatch messengers to the subedar of Choul, Bahiro Trimal, and alert him to keep a keen eye on the fort the Siddi is raising there."

"Maharaj, the British of Mumbai have delivered the weapons and ammunition as per our demand!" Prahlad Niraji, the Maratha envoy in the British durbar, reported.

"Okay! Prahladpant, the British, Siddis and Portuguese will not fulfil our demands unless we twist their arm. They assist each other internally, but when we strike them, they pretend to surrender in front of us!" All the ministers in the durbar realized what was going on in Maharaj's mind.

"Swami, Hasan Khan accompanied by Lodhi Khan, has moved from Talkonkan to Nashik. They were not vigilant and Tukoji Palkar and Rupaji Bhosale's troops stormed upon their army in the Chandwad pass. Hasan Khan himself got wounded. Khan's allies, Bundela Rajput, Maha Singh, and Jadhavrao also got injured. Lodhi Khan's son, Mohammed got killed." Nilopant conveyed some heartening news.

"Pant, dispatch robes of honour to Tukoji and Rupaji, wherever they are. Give them my message – I expect more valiant feats from both of you." Maharaj sat in his seat. (contentedly)

"Hambirarao travelled from Karhad to Varhad and has taken over Akola and Karanja, Sarkar. He is collecting hefty tributes in the Malkapur region. Ruhulla Khan is getting offended by his actions; every week, skirmishes are taking place between them. In the Nanded region, the Sarlashkar clashed with Iraj Khan and Abdul Beg. The Sarlashkar is eluding the enemy and causing a commotion throughout Varhad." Nilopant reported Hambirarao's valiant feats to Maharaj. The Chhatrapati was glad to hear the promising news. Maharaj was concerned about Aurangzeb who had encamped in Burhanpur near Varhad, but he pushed aside his worries and said to Peshwe, "Pant, in a couple of days, I am going to descend the fort, and travel to Gangoli. Send a message to the Deshadhikari of Gangoli, to keep the cannons ready. Prepare for my travel. You may leave!" Maharaj raised his hand and concluded the meeting.

Maharaj instructed Yesaji Kank to go and aid the forces engaged in the Janjira campaign, and descended Raigad after two days. No one knew why Maharaj was going to Gangoli again.

At the same time, Aurangzeb had summoned Sardar Iraj Khan, who oversaw the Varhad region, to his royal palace in Burhanpur. The rosary in his hand jumped in discontent; he chastised him starkly, "The Mahrattas plunder the Mughal territory in broad daylight, and people like you strut around in your khilats and get beaten up by them! Is that how you defend the kingdom? Shame on you!"

"Dhadad…dhumm…!" on the outskirts of Gangoli, four cannons were shooting heavy-weight cannon balls on the open plateau. The recoil of launching the heavy cannon balls pushed the cannons back; heavy metal chains kept them in place.

The Chhatrapati had come to Gangoli and had ordered samples of explosives from the factories in Kudal and Dicholi. Maharaj was watching the performance in person. Maharaj felt delighted to see the explosives perform to his expectations and said to the public officer of Gangoli, "Mother Jagadamba has blessed us. I am glad that I could fulfil Aabasaheb's dream of manufacturing our own explosives. Now, keep these cannons in Gangoli– my family is here."

"Ji." Maharaj came to the palace in Gangoli with the public officer. He dispatched letters through the Chitnis to Kudal and Dicholi, "I am coming to survey the factories in person." After finishing the administrative work, the next day he bade farewell to Yesubai and Dharau and left for Kudal.

The Chhatrapati inspected the factories manufacturing explosives and talked to the skilled workers – the Dalavis, Sawants and Subedars serving in the factories. Then the Chhatrapati travelled from Kudal-Dicholi to Satara via the Koyana ghat. Maharaj started ascending Sajjangad with Jotyaji Kesarkar, Rayaji-Antoji and Kavi Kulesh who had joined him from Kudal.

Ramchandrapant who had raised Samartha's samadhi, came to receive Maharaj. Maharaj took the darshan of Samartha's samadhi on the fort with Kalyanswami, Divakar Gosavi and

Ramchandra-pant. He later listened to the challenges the ashram faced. Maharaj consumed the tirtha-prasad offered by Kalyanswami and descended Sajjangad. He dispatched Kavi Kulesh to the Konkan region and travelled towards Raigad.

After arriving at Raigad, he summoned Moreshwar Panditrao and commanded him, "Panditrao, make arrangements to ensure that Samartha's ashram on Sajjangad is well taken care of. Arrange an annual allocation of garments, food and cash for the Ramnavami yatra of the Chaphal ashram."

"Swami…" Nilopant came in, disrupting his trance.

"Yes, what is it, Peshwe."

"A man named Gangaram has come from Allahabad in the north. He is seeking an audience with you."

Before Maharaj could respond, a guard came in and announced, "The surveillance chief is here." Maharaj nodded and granted permission. Clad in the dress of a Mughal soldier, Bahirji came in and made an obeisance.

"The Mughal emperor has encamped at Aurangbad, Dhani! A few days back, prominent sardars of Qutub Shahi and Adil Shahi visited him. He has sent funds worth nine lakhs to the young emperor of Bijapur – to gather their armies. The commander of Bijapur, Sarja Khan, too, visited Aurangabad."

Maharaj, rose from his seat and started pacing back and forth. Bahirji delivered the news and left.

After hearing the news, Nilopant was worried; he made an obeisance and said, 'let me take your leave, Swami.' As he was leaving Maharaj said, "Nilopant, who did you say, someone has come to meet me? Present him in front of me."

Covered platters full of gold hons that Gangaram had brought with him as a royal gift were presented first. Thereafter, Pant ushered in the Hindustani sardar, Gangaram.

Gangaram was impressed to see the handsome, royal king in front of him; he kept gazing at Maharaj for a moment. He quickly gathered himself, brought his palms together and said,

"Jai Siyaram, oh great king." Maharaj joined his palms in response.

"Tell me, why are you here?" Maharaj directly broached the topic.

"Maharaj, I have a plan. I was employed in Bahadur Khan's army in the north before. I got fed up there. Such brutality, destruction of temples and towns, ill treatment of women!"

"What is your plan?" Maharaj became wary.

"The Mughal emperor has descended in the Deccan. I am set to start a rebellion against him in the northern region of Bengal–Bihar; come what may."

Maharaj wondered, maybe, if the Rajputs, Jats and other disgruntled people like Gangaram revolt in the north, then Aurangzeb might leave Deccan to defend the north.

"Who is your family deity?" Gangaram couldn't comprehend the sentiments in Maharaj's radiant eyes gazing at him. He was mesmerized by the gaze.

"Ji! Kashi Vishweshwar Lord Shiva of Varanasi."

"Pant, bring the crystal murti." Nilopant heard an unexpected command. He went to the sanctum, and quickly came back holding a gold platter. Maharaj stepped forward and took the platter from his hand. He approached Gangaram, held the platter in front of him, and gazing deeply in his eyes Maharaj said in a clear voice, "Place your hand on this and vouch for your loyalty."

Gangaram glanced at the platter. He quickly picked up a bael leaf from the platter, touched it to his forehead and vouched, "My life will end, but my loyalty will never end."

Maharaj glanced at rugged Gangaram dressed in the northern attire and assessed him. "This murti belonged to our Thorale Maharaj." He raised the platter and said in a calm voice.

"I am honoured!" Gangaram kept gazing at the sparkling Shivlinga in the platter. It was the Shivlinga that Thorale Maharaj used to worship daily!

Maharaj handed the platter to Nilopant and said to Gangaram, "I will give my decision later." He raised his hand to bid farewell.

Gangaram and Nilopant made an obeisance and were about to leave, when Maharaj said, "Peshwe, let him spend couple of days at the fort. Make sure you look after him 'personally'." Nilopant noticed the emphasis that Maharaj had put on the word 'personally'.

After having a discussion with Prahladpant, a determined Nilopant came to visit Maharaj. The Chhatrapati stood with his back to the door; his curly hair swayed on his neck. The Peshwa made an obeisance to him.

"Swami, a messenger has come from Karnataka, with a letter from Harajiraje." Nilopant said.

"Harajiraje achieved a great political feat in Karnataka. The Sarlashkar of Mysore, Kumaraiyya, invaded Trichenapalli, the capital of Madura's King Chokkanayak and besieged the fort. The terrified Chokkanayak sought assistance from Harajiraje and your kaka saheb in Jinji. Haraji took prompt action and with Jaitaji Katkar and Dadaji Kakade, he rushed to the aid of Trichenapalli. Not only did he defeat Kumaraiyaa of Mysore but also took over as much of the territory of Madura as he could."

"Any news about Hambir mama?" Maharaj asked.

"Ji. He clashed with Iraj Khan near Fort Qasam. As Mukarrab Khan came to the assistance of Iraj Khan, Sarlashkar evaded them, and has reached up to Akola in the Varhad region."

As agreed, in the evening, Nilopant presented Gangaram Hindustani in front of Maharaj, in the court hall of the royal throne. Mujumdar Khandero Pansambal and Surnis Ramchandra Neelkanth stood on either side. Khandoji Balaji sat on the seat of the Chitnis.

Gangaram came in, gazing at the royal throne with wide

eyes. He made an obeisance. Maharaj rose from his seat, "Majumdar, present our guest with the robe of honour." He glanced at Khanderao. An attendant holding a platter, standing next to Khanderao stepped forward. Maharaj touched the platter. Gangaram touched the platter and accepted it. As there was no durbar, the royal throne was empty. Maharaj raised his head, glanced at the royal throne and said to Gangaram, "Hindustani, I will provide ten thousand soldiers for your campaign. Our soldiers will be unfamiliar with the region. Take good care of them. May Goddess Jagadamba bring you success." Maharaj raised his hand and took his seat.

"Jai Siyaram, my heartfelt thanks to you Maharaj." Gangaram's eyes lit up; he placed his hand on the sword tied around his waist, bowed to make an obeisance and took a few steps backwards.

Maharaj had taken a decision to give him military assistance to rise in rebellion in the north.

"Dadaji is here." Nilopant, who had come back after bidding farewell to Gangaram broached the sensitive topic of Dadaji.

"Let him in." Maharaj commanded.

Hefty, broad-chested Dadaji Raghunath came in and made an obeisance.

"Dadaji, tell me why it is taking so long to conquer Janjira?"

"Ji, I have never shirked my duty and never will." Dadaji spoke firmly.

"Then why isn't the fort falling? The siege has been going on for four months now." An upset Maharaj stood up at once.

"Why did you attack Rajapurwadi when it was not on our agenda? Why did you waste our treasure on unplanned battles?" The Chhatrapati's voice was stern.

"Maharaj..." Dadaji hesitated.

"Are you aware of the consequences of your actions? The head clerk is regularly sending letters of your excess expenditure. Do you have any explanation for your actions?"

"Maharaj…what can I say…. I will share my reason, not as a explanation, but as a grievance; and only in front of you – in private."

Dadaji glanced at the prominent people standing around Maharaj. His face darkened.

The Chhatrapati raised his hand and gestured to Khandoji, Khanderao, Ramchandrapant and Nilopant. The court hall was now empty. Maharaj told Dadaji to present his side.

"What can I say, Swami?" The Siddi held a grudge against me and plundered my town Aapta in broad daylight. I feel ashamed to share this…but the fiend took advantage of my being engaged in the campaign and shattered my heart into pieces." Dadaji suddenly hid his face in his palms; Maharaj was stunned.

"Dadaji, get a grip on yourself and tell me clearly – what happened?"

"Swami, that scoundrel seized my wife! In that rage, I attacked Rajapurwadi – not once but many times. I was hoping that I would get hold of him sometime and take my revenge on him. Indeed, I have committed a mistake, Swami. Please chop my head off, right in front of this royal throne, with your own hands!" Dadaji's body was trembling with rage, grief and a feeling of inadequacy.

Maharaj kept staring at Dadaji with a strange look in his eyes. Dadaji vanished from his eyes. In place of Dadaji, he saw himself! The entire royal hall around him was screaming at him – "Durga…Durga…!"

Meanwhile, Raigad received some unpleasant news. The Portuguese captain, Pereira, launched a sudden attack on the Maratha soldiers who had encamped on the Anjediva island to raise a sea fort. He had launched fierce cannon fire on the island and forced the Marathas out of the island. He had also demolished a temple and erected a high-rising church on the site.

Moreover, Chimanaji, the jamindar of Khed, had defected

to the Mughals for selfish reasons, and Saeed Nijavat, the Mughal custodian of Hanamantgad who was in captivity, had escaped from the Maratha prison.

At Raigad, Chitnis Khandoji was taking dictation from Maharaj. Maharaj was pacing back and forth, rubbing his palms, lost in thought, and dictating a letter to him.

"To His Highness, scion of the Rajput dynasty, Suryavanshi, king of Amber, Ram Singh, from Hindupadpadshah, scion of Kshatriya dynasty, king Shambhoo.

"At present, the Mughal emperor, Alamgir, has launched an offensive attack on the Maratha kingdom, with his mammoth army and enormous treasure. In disapproval of his actions, I have given political asylum to the Mughal Prince Akbar who had approached us for aid. I have met him in person and discussed the matter with him. At present, if you initiate an armed rebellion in the north, I plan to induct the Mughal Prince on the royal throne of Delhi. The prince has already sent a letter of appeal to the Shah of Iran requesting his support. If the prince succeeds the royal throne of Delhi, it will prove beneficial to us. Awaiting your response in this matter...." Khandoji got the letter ready, and Raje signed it.

As the Chhatrapati came out of the office of the Chitnis, Jotyaji Kesarkar made an obeisance and reported, "Rupaji and Manaji clashed with Shabadi Khan near Nashik in the pass close to Ganeshgaon. A fierce fight took place. The Khan has marched towards Fort Ramsej."

"I am going to the Jagadishwar temple. Send Peshwe there immediately." Maharaj instructed him while walking. He came to the Jagadishwar temple. The temple priest approached the Chhatrapati and placed some bael leaves and white flowers in his palms. Maharaj entered the sanctum and offered the leaves and flowers to the Shivlinga. He knelt in front of the Shivlinga and placed his forehead on the Shalunka. Somebody tolled the bell in the courtyard outside. As Maharaj heard the tolling of the bell, Aabasaheb's words echoed in his mind, "Keep in mind that sooner or later, Aurangzeb will fall upon Deccan – therefore, first of all, you should become a Mavala soldier!"

He raised his head and gently picked up a bael leaf on the Shivlinga, touched it to his forehead and placed it in his waistband. As he came out of the sanctum, Nilopant approached him. Maharaj said to him, "Take the darshan of the Lord first. I need to talk to you."

Nilopant took the darshan and came back. Maharaj was lost in thought; in the courtyard of the temple, he asked Nilopant, "Pant, who is the Mughal custodian of Fort Mullher, in the Nashik region?"

"Ji. The Rajput, Raja Devi Singh."

"Okay. Send a message to the custodian of Fort Salheri to be vigilant. He might think of going to the defence of Fort Ramsej, and put Fort Salheri in jeopardy."

"Ji. I will send a messenger today." Nilopant was about to say something; just then the kettle drums on the fort began booming. Maharaj's forehead puckered.

"Pant, looks like Haraji has arrived." exclaimed Marahaj, glancing in the direction of the sound.

In a few moments, somebody came rushing to the temple. Rayaji came in; his eyes were glowing, and his chest was heaving up and down. He hastily removed his footwear, tossed it aside, stood in front of Maharaj and exclaimed, "Hail Lord Khandoba! Dhani, Rani Sahebb delivered a baby boy in Gangoli. The prince is born!"

Maharaj turned around; with a delighted heart, he faced the Shivlinga, closed his eyes, joined his palms and touching them to his forehead, he uttered, "Jagadamb!"

The palace in Gangoli was decorated with festoons. Near the court hall of the palace, the throbbing kettle drums echoed with the resonating trumpets. Tall plantain trunks were fastened to both sides of the entrance door. Sindakhed, Faltan, Kagal,

Karnataka…guests had arrived in the palace from everywhere.

The day of the naming ceremony dawned. It was Monday – the holy day of Lord Shankar. Gangoli thronged with crowds like never before. Clad in an exclusive attire, Maharaj sat in the court hall on an embellished seat. Ramraje stood on his right. The ministers and courtiers stood politely on both sides. The name of every guest, relative and sardar was announced to Maharaj. Whenever a prominent person arrived, Maharaj rose from his seat and received him in person. The cannons located on the border of the town, boomed at regular intervals. Bedecked Tarau placed the baby in the cradle; gave a gentle push of her back to the cradle three times and whispered the name in the baby's ears… 'Shivajiraje!'

The trumpets and kettle drums boomed. The cannons roared. Sugar was distributed to everyone. The town of Gangoli was ecstatic. In the court hall, the royal family got busy distributing clothes, gold coins and food grains. Even after sunset, people kept coming. Finally, Dharau came out, placed her hands on her waist, glanced at Raje and exclaimed, "Could you please come in now and see my grandson?"

"Oh yes, I still haven't done that!" Raje said with a smile and rose from his seat. Dharau had spoken his mind. Maharaj left the court hall and started walking to the maternity room; he glanced at Rayaji and gestured to him. Rayaji picked up the royal gift platters brought from Raigad, for the baby and the mother and started walking behind Maharaj.

Maharaj entered Yesubai's chamber. Yesubai got up from the bed. Balraje was in deep sleep; Yesubai gently picked him up and handed him to Maharaj. Maharaj got lost in observing the baby's face. As Yesubai saw them, she felt happy and remembered Aabasaheb and Thoralya Aau. Her eyelashes fluttered and eyes got misty. She controlled herself firmly and said, "He has been named after Aabasaheb."

"Yes, I was informed. Aabasaheb successfully implemented

hundreds of missions during his lifetime; may he be as successful as Aaba!" Maharaj said while handing the baby to Yesubai; he glanced at Rayaji. Rayaji presented the gift platter in front of Yesubai. Yesubai put the baby on the bed. She touched the gift platter as per custom. Just as Rayaji was about to leave with the platter Maharaj exclaimed, "Wait Rayaji." Maharaj stepped forward and picked up the small decorative wooden casket from the gift platter. Rayaji left. Raje gave the casket to Yesubai and said, "Here's a special gift for you."

As Yesubai saw the casket, she chuckled in amusement.

"Why did you chuckle?" Maharaj realized that she was mistaken and asked her.

"No, no…nothing – I like it!" She said while hiding her feelings.

"Only the casing is wooden; inside there is a special Kumkum casket for you!" Maharaj said teasingly.

Yesubai curiously opened the chest. A big, fish-shaped gold ring was sparkling inside. Two rubies were studded in place of the fish's eyes. Yesubai looked at the ring and said laughing, "Oh… looks like the goldsmith has made a mistake, or maybe its magic. The Kumkum casket has turned into a ring!"

Without saying a word, Maharaj picked up the ring. The rubies sparkled in the light of the lamps. Maharaj held it and pulled the tiny peg on the side opening the back of the fish. The Kumkum inside glowed like rubies!

"Did you like the gift?" Maharaj did not wait for Yesubai's response; he held her left hand and placed the ring on her little finger. Yesubai picked up a pinch of Kumkum from the open back of the fish, applied it to her forehead and silently declared her appreciation for the gift.

The next day, Dharau came to meet Maharaj in the afternoon. and said, "My dear son, I have one favour to ask of you. Could you please listen to me?"

Maharaj touched her feet, held her hand and ushered her to

the centre of the chamber and said, "Aau, why are you talking in such a formal way? Am I not your family? Then, why do ask for a favour; why don't you just tell me what you want?"

"Of course, you are my family. That is why I am so sentimental about this. Now, listen to this old woman."

"Just tell me. Whatever you want will happen." Maharaj had no idea what she was going to say.

"I am quite old now, and I am tired. My heart yearns for my village. Let me go to Kapurhol!" With some unknown determination Dharau, whose back was bent, stood straight and gazed into Maharaj's eyes.

"Aau..." Maharaj exclaimed and turned his back to her.

"My dear, I have experienced things that I had never dreamed of in my life. I don't know whether I deserved it, but you and your family have given me plenty of love."

Raje could not bear to hear her candid words; his heart was in turmoil. Maharaj quickly turned around and came close to her. He put his palm on her wrinkled lips and said, "Aau, in the name of Lord Khandoba, don't say anything more..."

"I had only one wish, to see Soonbai nursing a baby boy. Khandoba fulfilled my wish." Dharau lovingly held Raje's hand in her hand.

"Are you so tired of me, Aau? I could bear the absence of Thoralya Aau, only by looking at you. Please don't leave me like this!"

"You are young. How will you understand what an old woman feels? I just want to spend my last days in the place where I spent my early life and gave birth to my children. My life will be fulfilled if I die in my village. Let me go to Kapurhol." She looked like a monsoon evening. Maharaj could not bear to hear her speak like this anymore; he left the chamber silently. Nobody could stop her now.

A palanquin was readied for Dharau, to take her to Kapurhol. Rayaji and Antoji stood on either sides of the palanquin with armed guards. Maharaj honoured the old lady with fine clothes and gold coins. Yesubai touched Dharau's feet, embraced her affectionately and started sobbing. Dharau lovingly stroked her back and let her get a grip on herself. Her words, drenched in affection, fell on Yesubai's ears like a trickle of milk streaming on a Shivlinga, "Oh my dear, your heart is still bleeding. So many gifts you received from all over the kingdom, but not even one came from Shringarpur!" As soon as Yesubai heard her words, she put her palms on her face and sobbed. Dharau held her close to her bosom and spoke in a voice that reminded everyone of the tolling bell at Pachad, "Don't cry, my dear daughter, a woman must keep walking forward while bearing the burning sun above and the stones and thorns spread below. Remember your mothers-in-law always." She approached the cradle, picked up Balraje and held him in her arms. She kissed him a few times and put him back in the cradle. The Chhatrapati touched the feet of Dharau Gaade of Kapurhol…who had now become a member of the Bhosale family.

From Gangoli, Maharaj came back to Raigad; he was pondering only one thing – Fort Ramsej. Maharaj performed the puja of the crystal Shivlinga and Goddess Bhavani and came to the court hall. The courtiers made an obeisance. Yesaji was present with the envoy of the Portuguese durbar. He came forward, pointed to the Portuguese envoy and said, "Maharaj, the Portuguese durbar has sent a gift and a letter for you; on the occasion of Balraje's birth." The envoy presented the gift of the Portuguese durbar. Maharaj gave it the customary touch of his hand.

"What's does the letter say?" He asked Yesaji.

"Ji. They have given us permission to purchase the materials for our ammunition factories and have promised to break their alliance with the Siddis."

Maharaj smiled knowingly. The Portuguese envoy was offered a gift in return and dismissed.

"Swami, Ruhulla Khan, the sardar of the Mughal emperor has started marching towards Nagar." Maharaj received the first big news from Nilopant.

Maharaj could see the nemeses charging upon the Maratha kingdom from all sides. As he was aware of the fact that Aurangzeb was going to move heaven and earth to overthrow the Maratha kingdom; he asked a crucial question to Nilopant.

"The battleships of the British are nowadays encroaching upon our territory in the sea. What steps are our Siddi Sambul and Siddi Mistri taking to trap them in Mumbai, Pant?"

"Sambul and Mistri have raided their ships frequently and forced them to retreat to the Mumbai region."

"Pant, Aurangzeb is going to charge upon us not only from the ground level, but also from the sea by forming an alliance with the Siddis, the British and the Portuguese. We must continue our fight on the sea on three fronts; ambush Aurangzeb at the weakest point on the ground and overthrow him."

"Three fronts on the ocean!" Prahladpant exclaimed.

"One team of Angre and Kate in the region of Dabhol, Kudal and Dicholi who will deal with the Portuguese of Choul-Goa, the second the team of Maynak, Dadaji Prabhu, Pavala-Padwal and Kate in the region of Nagothane, Aapte and Dandarajpuri, will face the Siddis of Janjira, and the third fleet of Jivaji Vinayak, Sundarji Baji, Sambul-Mistri will keep sailing on the sea keeping the British of Mumbai in check."

"Pant, inform Yesaji kaka to remove the infantry unit from Dandarajpuri now. He is much needed here, to face the imminent attack of the enemy." Aurangzeb's possible sneaky movements on the sea kept lingering in front of Maharaj's eyes. Everyone kept listening to his plans keenly.

Maharaj ordered the Sais to keep select horses ready at the stable in Pachad and came to the court hall. Panditrao Moreshwar approached him. He showed the roll of papers in his hand to the Chhatrapati and said, "Swami, there has been a conflict between the disciples of Samartha in the ashram on Sajjangad.

"In the ashram?" Maharaj was pained to hear that.

"Ji. Samarth had stated that Divakar Goasavi should supervise the maintenance of all ashrams after his demise. But he had appointed Bhanaji and Ramaji Gosavi to look after the ashram on Sajjangad. Divakar Gosavi was complying with his wish, but Uddhav Gosavi interfered and spoiled everything. The custodian of Sajjangad, Jijoji Katkar has sided with him and done what he should not have done."

"Jijoji? What has he done?" Maharaj listened to the matter carefully.

"Jijoji has given Bhanaji and Ramaji's rights to Uddhav Gosavi in his own authority!"

"How dare he?" Maharaj's eyes started breathing fire. "Panditrao, send a royal decree to Katkar – Swami's last wish is the final word! Uddhav Gosavi makes selfish demands; he is after riches. On what grounds did you confer Bhanaji–Ramaji's rights to him? Restore the rights of Bhanaji and Ramaji. I will discuss the matter with Divakar Gosavi and take a decision after that. You have no right to interfere in the dispute of Samartha's disciples!" Moreshwar left to prepare the royal decree. But Maharaj was wondering, 'Samartha has just breathed his last, and his disciples are already fighting amongst themselves! Rotten seeds will not sprout even if the hands that sow them are holy!

Maharaj descended Raigad with Yesaji Kank, who had come from Janjira, Himmatrao, and Naruji Trimbak. It was summer. Just before the advent of the monsoon, Maharaj left Pachad with the cavalry. He travelled via Khed, Chakan and descended in Pattagad near Nashik. The massive army of Mujaffar Khan, Ranamast Khan, Moharrem Singh was stationed here to aid the Ramsej campaign. The Maratha cavalry attacked the camp.

Rupaji–Bhanaji received the news that Maharaj had arrived

in the Pattagad region; they came to meet Maharaj with select horsemen.

Maharaj embraced Rupaji with pride and said, "You have lived up to your name. Rupaji, I am proud of you."

"He is named 'Rupa Mojada' meaning 'The Devil's son' in the enemy camp." Manaji glanced at Rupaji and said smilingly.

"You are right Manaji. One should not respond to the Devil's actions with virtuousness!" Maharaj smiled and responded on behalf of Rupaji. After honouring Rupaji and Manaji, Maharaj took them with him to survey Trimbakgad, Baglan region. He also checked the moving defence troops that were protecting Ramsej. Maharaj promised to provide fresh soldiers, weapons, explosives and provisions to Rupaji and returned to Raigad. Before the advent of the monsoon, Aurangzeb played the same moves that Maharaj had anticipated – he besieged the Maratha kingdom on all sides.

He sent Meer Mohammed Momin in the direction of the Surat harbour, with six thousand Turkish soldiers.

A special envoy was sent to the Portuguese viceroy with a letter that said, "Don't provide any assistance to the infidel Sambha. In fact, whatever assistance the Portuguese durbar seeks against Sambha, will be provided to them at the earliest!"

The most vicious move was the letter sent to Ruhulla Khan in Nagar. The Alamgir had ordered Ruhulla Khan, "Pay off mansabs and khilats to the Marathi Deshmukhs, hawaldars, jumledars and custodians of various forts and immediately engage them to work for the Mughal Empire!"

Aurangzeb appointed his son, Azam Shah on the special campaign of attacking Sambhajiraje with the support of Anirodh Singh and Kishor Singh. In Aurangabad, in a durbar full of courtiers, Aurangzeb rose from his royal throne, sat on the carpet and prayed for the success of his son.

As the monsoon was about to begin, Hambirarao from Varhad, Kavi Kulesh from Konkan and Anandaro from Solapur had returned to Raigad. The Maratha navy had launched an attack on the ocean and plundered the British ships. In the Pen region, about eighty ships were docked in the sea waters, under the leadership of Maynak and Siddi Sambul to keep a keen eye on Siddi Qasam. Dadaji Raghunath's forces still surrounded Janjira. In the Thal region, five thousand naval forces were vigilantly guarding the sea fort of Khanderi.

Heavy monsoon showers began. The Mughal emperor had sent Khanbahadur Kokaltash, Qasam Khan, Dalpat and Karan Singh to Shabdi Khan's aid in the Ramsej campaign. Their armies were forced to encamp in Nashik.

Maharaj was observing the pouring rain from the window in the record-keeping office and dictating to Khandoji the letters to be sent to the Adil Shahi and Qutub Shahi durbars. An attendant came in, and breaking his link, made an announcement, "Bahirji is here." Maharaj glanced at the door and stopped. Drenched from head to toe, covered in a coarse blanket, Bahirji came in. As he made an obeisance, he shivered in the cold weather on the fort. He firmly controlled his chattering teeth and said, "Dhani, our source of receiving news from Aurangabad has been cut off. Our ten skilled informers were caught by the enemy. The scoundrels cut off everyone's head in the central square of Aurangabad!"

Ten informers were like ten moving forts! Devastated Maharaj didn't know how to console the leader of the surveillance team. He approached Bahirji, placed his hand on his shoulder and said with a heavy heart, "Bahirji, first change your clothes and get warmed up...."

Through days and nights, the smithies on the fort were engaged in making new weapons. The ironsmiths were sharpening them on a rotating wheel. Two days after Bahirji came to the fort, the informer sent by Sambhaji Jagtap came to Raigad. With lowered head, he reported to Raje news even worse than Bahirji's– "Rupaji Bhosale has been wounded in the raid on Rajput Padma Singh's camp. He is bedridden in the camp of Trimbakgad!" As Maharaj heard the news, he felt as if his own right hand had been wounded.

Jaitaji Katkar sent by Harajiraje from Karnataka arrived on Raigad. Mujumdar Khanderao Pansambal presented him in front of Maharaj. Meanwhile, a lot had happened in Karnataka. Harajiraje was expanding the borders of Karnataka audaciously.

"Kabiji is coming." Kulesh's personal attendant announced. Kulesh came in and made an obeisance.

"Kaviji, how is the Mughal prince doing in Konkan?" Raje asked him immediately.

"Ji. The Mughal Prince has sent a letter to Raja Ram Singh in the north."

"I have also written to him, but Kaviji, I don't see Mirza Raja's potential in his son."

"Ji. Mirza was a warrior; Ram Singh's skills lie in administrative matters."

For a while, Maharaj discussed politics with Kaviji. As he was leaving, Kulesh shared news of the Choul region with Maharaj – "Jivaji Vinayak has seized a Portuguese ship in Choul. It carries the treasure of Ramchandradas, a trader from Khambayat. He doesn't own the ship. The Portuguese want their ship back."

"That is okay. But what right do the Portuguese have to disapprove of our alliance with the Arabs?" Kaviji realized that Maharaj was not in a good mood, and left silently.

Maharaj summoned Peshwe Nilopant to finish the matter and ordered him, "Send a letter to Jivaji and tell him to return the Portuguese ship that he has seized in Choul, and place select informers around Choul!"

Nilopant understood the first command but not the second one.

Maharaj kept pacing back and forth. The issue of Janjira was still unresolved. Janjira was located at such a place that one could see it but could not reach it. Ramsej was already surrounded. "Pant, what's the news of Ramsej?" Maharaj was lost in thought.

"Swami, despite the heavy monsoon showers, Shabadi and Qasam Khan attacked Ramsej three times, but the custodian of the fort overthrew them."

"Pant, send one thousand cavalry for the assistance of Ramsej today itself."

"Ji. Salabat Khan has come with two hundred maunds of explosives, to assist the siege of Ramsej. That is what is encouraging the enemy to keep attacking the fort."

"Inform Ganoram of Kudal, Moro Dadaji of Dicholi, to provide as many explosives as they can to Keso Trimal of Trimbakgad to defend Fort Ramsej.

Whenever the custodian of Fort Ramsej got a hint of an imminent attack, he pushed heavy boulders, rocks and wooden logs down the slope of the fort. The monsoon showers from above, and the rocks rolling down the fort had left Shabadi Khan quite frustrated. The explosives he had buried around the ramparts got blown off and his own men were buried under it. Fort Ramsej stood tall like Hanuman, the devotee of Lord Rama, ready to soar high.

Chapter 13

"Oh the devil Siddi, Siddi, Siddi!" An agitated Chhatrapati had clenched his fists and was pacing back and forth in rage. Dadaji had sent an informer from Dandarajpuri. Kavi Kulesh, Prahladpant, Nilopant, Khanderao…everyone was stunned to hear the news he had brought. Siddi Khairat had invaded the Nagothane harbour in broad daylight and sliced off the noses of the people he had captured!

"Since we removed the infantry of Yesaji Kank from the siege of Janjira, the Siddi has gone completely out of control." Prahladpant advised that the siege of Janjira be strengthened. Maharaj was lost in thought. The treasury was already in crisis owing to the siege of Janjira.

"Nilopant, send a letter to Dadaji and instruct him to withdraw his forces from Janjira and go to Mahad. Tell Daulat Khan, Maynak and Jivaji to be on the alert and keep a vigilant watch on the sea." Maharaj announced his decision.

The Siddis were becoming audacious due to the backing of the Portuguese of Choul and Goa, and the British of Mumbai. Nilopant received the final instruction to resolve this issue, "Send a strict warning to the Portuguese and the British, that I am well aware of their scheming tactics."

"Hambirarao has sent a message from Kolhapur. The Adil Shahi Commander, Sarja Khan has encamped in Miraj with twenty thousand soldiers. His intentions are unclear." Khanderao Pansambal expressed concern.

"Peshwe, inform mama, at such a difficult time, we should maintain an amiable relationship with the Adil Shahi sultanate. He should keep a keen eye on the Panhala, Kolhapur and Karhad region until the monsoon is over. Keep Azam Shah in check."

"Qasam Khan invaded Ramsej from the Balkunda ghat. The custodian of the fort dumped rocks from above and forced him to retreat. The news is that the emperor has ordered Qasim Khan and Ranoji to enter Talkonkan from the north and south sides respectively." Nilopant reported the emperor's strategic move.

"Pant, I want most of Aurangzeb's forces restricted to the Talkonkan region. Tukoji, Rupaji and Manaji will make them suffer just like Hasam Khan." Even after hearing every move of Aurangzeb, Maharaj was not at all unnerved.

"We have received news that the custodian of Kankadkilla, Shah Alil Khan, has escaped from our prison and has gone to Bahadur Khan's camp in Nashik." Khandoji reported.

Maharaj's nostrils flared. "Chitnis, prisoners don't escape because of their skills, but by offering bribes. Inform the custodians of all forts that such kind of treachery will have serious consequences."

Maharaj said this, but an apprehension lingered in his mind, 'Despite being the Chhatrapati, how am I going to handle relatives like Shirke–Nimbalkar abandoning the kingdom openly?' Maharaj pushed the dark thought aside and dismissed everyone except Kulesh.

"Kaviraj, send intimation to the Mughal Prince, Akbar that I am coming to visit him." Maharaj commanded Kulesh.

"Ji." Kulesh nodded. He wanted to say something. He had clearly felt the discontent of many people as the Chhatrapati had dismissed all of them and told only him to stay back. But as he saw that Maharaj was worried, he kept quiet. Even when he invited them to his home, not a single minister showed up. Many of them disapproved his presence around Maharaj all the time.

In two days, braving the rains of Shravan, Maharaj left Raigad with Kavi Kulesh. He travelled via the Mahad ghat, Mahabaleshwar, Chiplun, Sangameshwar and Khelana and arrived at Akbar's camp at Rajapur. A few select horsemen accompanied him. Akbar came to receive him with Durgadas Rathod and ushered him to his seat courteously. This was their second meeting.

"Raja Saab, I am utterly bored. For a lion, surviving on grass is the worst kind of punishment," said a distressed Akbar.

"I agree with you. The lion goes foraging the woods and finds his own prey. You will feel restricted here." Maharaj exclaimed.

"What do you suggest Raja Saab?" Though he lived in Konkan, Akbar still dreamt of the royal throne of Delhi. Maharaj only wanted to exploit Akbar.

"What do you think, Durgaji?" Maharaj included Rathod in the discussion.

"Ji. Aurangzeb is now stuck in the Deccan. He won't move from here. Raja Saab, I will return to Rajasthan with the prince and unite the Rajputs."

"Very well. How can I assist you in this plan?" Maharaj observed Rathod carefully. He assumed that Rathod would ask for military assistance.

"Just make provisions for our return journey." Rathod said wisely, knowing well that Maharaj wouldn't be able to provide military assistance.

"What do you mean? The enemy is spread all over the kingdom. How are you going to take the prince to the north? Are you aware that the emperor has issued firmans from Aurangabad to capture the prince at sight?"

"He won't be able to catch me. I am his son after all. I will escape via the sea. Will you help me escape?" An agitated Akbar said with determination.

Maharaj glanced at Kavi Kulesh intentionally and announced his decision, "Okay, I will provide armed guards and military assistance to you. Durgaji, may Goddess Jagadamba bless you with success."

Maharaj rose from his seat. He bade farewell to Akbar and left Rajapur.

In the private chamber in Raigad, Maharaj was discussing with Kavi Kulesh, the details of the assistance to be provided to Akbar. A male attendant named Purusha and Jotyaji Kesarkar stood guard at the door. As it was very cold, the Chhatrapati had wrapped a shawl around his shoulders. "Kaviraj, have you gauged the Mughal prince's motive? Is he ready to go to Gujarat in Hindustan? Does he have the grit to unite the Rajputs of Hindustan?"

"I have talked to the prince. He is ready to do whatever we want. He is a member of the royal family. We should take advantage of his royal status." Kulesh said.

"Sending him away with some military assistance is our best option. That is why, I am looking for a sharp person who will keep a keen watch on our soldiers."

Now, Kulesh also been thinking about Akbar. He made an obeisance to Raje and left. Maharaj kept pacing alone. He kept seeing Aurangzeb everywhere around him.

"The Peshwa is here." The attendant named Purusha announced.

"Swami, two prominent persons have arrived at the fort. From the Miraj–Akola side Sarlashkar has sent Dhanaji Jadhav, and the Mughal Prince has sent Durgadas." Peshwe informed as soon as he came in.

"Good. Present them at the same time tomorrow morning. I have to discuss something of utmost importance with both of them. You leave for Kalyan with your forces."

Ji. Maharaj…" Nilopant hesitated and stopped talking.

"Why did you hesitate, Peshwe – tell me, what is it?"

"Siddi Qasam had captured our mariners, and beheaded all those who were not ready for conversion, and…."

"And...what...go ahead and speak, Peshwe."

"Word is, our wounded sailor Siddi Mistri has gone to Mumbai!"

The Chhatrapati dictated to Khandoji the letter to be sent to Raja Ram Singh that stated – "The Mughal Prince had come to the Deccan; I am sending him to you with Durgadas and armed forces via Ahmedabad. Our experienced commander will accompany him. You are a judicious person. Unite all the Rajputs and retaliate against the Mughal emperor in Hindustan. If at all Aurangzeb returns to the north, be ready to capture him..."

Khandoji spread the soft sand on the finished letter.

"Chitnis, send this letter at the hands of a reliable messenger. It is going a long way." Raje said glancing at the letter.

After the demise of Aabaji Sonadeo, Maharaj convened the durbar and offered the attire of honour and the seal of the Surnis to Ramchandra Nilkanth Bhadanekar. He was made in-charge of the region from Kudal to Tungabhadra.

Maharaj descended the fort and came to the stable of Pachad with Khandoji, the custodian of the fort, Changoji, Kulesh, Rayaji and Antoji. He met Dhanaji and Durgadas there. Twenty thousand cavalry and infantry were lined up in front of the stable. Raje bade farewell to them, and came to the court hall of Pachad.

Informers coming from all corners of the kingdom presented themselves in front of Maharaj. The court hall was filled with people.

"Dhani, we lost Manakoji Ballal during a skirmish with the emperor's grandson, Muijuddin, at the foothills of Purandar." An informer shared the news hesitantly.

When Khandoji Ballal heard the news, he lifted his head at once. As he politely lowered his head again, his eyes brimmed with tears. Manakoji was his brother. Maharaj was also stunned. He approached Khandoji, patted his shoulder and said in a heavy voice – "I have lost a gem today and you have lost your right hand. Khandoji, I have no words to console you."

Near the foothills of the fort, on the banks of the river of Birwadi, Arjoji Yadav, Annaji Malkare and Hiroji Indulkar had erected a grand shamiana. It was built for Raghunathpant Hanamante who had come from Karnataka to meet Raje.

The day of the meeting dawned. With Maharaj's arrival the entire camp of Birwadi got energized. The public were wondering what was going to happen next. Everybody knew that Raje had ordered Harajiraje to detain Raghunathpant in Karnataka.

As Maharaj arrived in the camp, kettle drums and trumpets resounded. Raghunathpant stepped forward from among the group of people that had arrived from Jinji. As Raje saw him, many memories crowded his mind. He walked briskly and approached Raghunathpant. Raghunathpant leaned forward to make an obeisance to him. Maharaj quickly stepped forward and stopped him. He himself leaned forward and was about to touch Raghunathpant's feet. He had no one left to seek blessings from. Raghunathpant quickly stepped back and pulled Raje up. The Chhatrapati embraced Raghunathpant directly. Pant affectionately stroked his back. Maharaj held his hand and ushered him to the shamiana. Special seats had been arranged inside. An exclusive seat was placed at the centre of the shamiana for Raje and Pant. Raje and Pant took their seats. The others sat around them courteously.

Raghunathpant presented to the Chhatrapati, forty lakh hons he had brought from Karnataka. Maharaj gave it the customary touch of his hand and glanced at Nilopant. Peshwe Nilopant presented Raghunathpant the robes of honour, a shield and a sword. Pant accepted them. Raje asked Raghunathpant, "Pant, what is the situation in Karnataka?"

"Excellent. Harajiraje is managing the region very well. You have nothing to worry on that front. If possible, you should go and visit Karnataka once.

"How did Harajiraje treat you?" Maharaj couldn't help thinking about the recent unavoidable events that had taken place.

"Ji. He treats me with respect; considers me like his own father. That is why I have come here with a particular intention." With eyes that had seen and experienced a lot in life, Pant gazed deep into Maharaj's eyes.

"Pant, feel free to speak your mind, without any inhibitions. No elderly people are left anymore who I can seek advice from. Aabasaheb, Thoralya Aau, Samartha… everyone has departed." Everyone present turned solemn as they realized that Maharaj was caught in a difficult situation.

Pant took a moment to start speaking. He had already made up his mind at the camp itself, but now he was struggling to find words. Pant glanced at the Chhatrapati and started speaking, candidly, fearlessly,

"It hasn't been long since the demise of Thorale Maharaj. Why is our territory turning desolate? The number of brutes, thugs and traitors is also on the rise. Why is this happening?"

"The sardars and ministers who had turned traitor, deserved to be punished. You should have executed them behind closed doors; why did you punish them publicly?" Pant asked.

Now, the meeting turned tense. Everyone got anxious.

Hambirarao was present in the meeting. He also held the same stature and status as Raghunathpant. He could not keep quiet and exclaimed, "Pant, those who were penalized were sentenced after thorough investigations. Why, in Belwadi, Thorale Maharaj had ordered Sakhuji Gaikwad's eyes to be removed in front of the whole army. Do you think that the culprits who wanted to assassinate Raje, deserved to be honoured like we are honouring you?"

Now, everyone wondered if there was going to be a dispute between Sarlashkar and Pant. But the Chhatrapati raised his hand and stopped Hambirarao, "Let it be Sarlashkar, let Pant speak. It is his right to speak freely."

His words reassured Pant and he fearlessly said, "I am an old man; I may or may not be here tomorrow. But Sarlashkar, have you thought about the powerful enemy who is at our doorstep now?"

His straightforward question compelled Maharaj to speak, "Pant, you have posed a very crucial question. Only I know what efforts I am taking to deal with the problem. Aurangzeb's frequent attacks are turning our territory desolate. We have recruited more than thirty thousand fresh soldiers in our army. Skirmishes with the Mughal forces are taking place all over. Our treasury is depleting due to the financial burden. On the one hand, Aurangzeb's forces have infiltrated our kingdom from all sides. On the other, the Portuguese and Siddis are taking advantage of the situation and are launching attacks from the sea. The Adil Shahi and Qutub Shahi kingdoms are not taking any action. Pant, I am not holding any grudge against you. You notify Haraji to continue to manage the region… and…you… don't go to Karnataka now."

In the afternoon Maharaj started his journey to the fort. His mind was crowded with countless thoughts. He did not speak with anyone.

At night, Yesubai brought a bowl of porridge in the sleeping chamber. She saw him lost in deep thought and asked, "Is something bothering you?"

Maharaj looked at Yesubai. He remembered the seal and the dagger that Aabasaheb had bestowed upon her; the inscription on her royal seal and the responsibility he had entrusted her with. As he looked at her, he remembered the whole discussion he had had with Raghunathpant. Raje shared the details of their meeting with Yesubai and asked her, "What would you suggest in case of Pant?"

Yesubai thought for some time and said firmly, "I think…."

"What?"

"That we should appoint Pant as the Majumdar!"

"... and what about the current Majumdar, Khanderao?"

"Meet him in person and convince him.

Yesubai's advice was implemented. Raghunathpant was honourably offered the position of the Majumdar. His son, Timaji Raghunath, was offered the position of the Majumdar of Karnataka. Everything was done with Khanderao's consent.

Maharaj was pacing in the court hall of the royal throne. Nilopant, Prahladpant, Khanderao, Raghunathpant stood around him, worried and with lowered heads. Raje stopped pacing and asked Prahladpant, "Pant, you came from the British durbar. What is their future plan?"

"Ji. They have agreed not to aid the Siddis. They have promised that the Mughal ships will not be allowed to cross the sea." He pointed to the British envoy, Henry Smith, standing next to him, and introduced him to the Chhatrapati, "This is Henry, the British envoy." Henry knelt, took off his tall hat and waved it.

Prahladpant realized that he had no gifts to present and hastily said, "Swami, the British durbar had sent royal gifts with him, but..."

"I left with him from Mumbai via Karanja, but four ships of the Siddi, blocked our way. We had to hide in the ship. I am quite embarrassed to tell you that the Siddi pirates seized our belongings and transported them to Underi."

Prahlanpant hung his head in fear that Maharaj would be furious to hear the news. Maharaj recognized his fear. He approached Prahladpant and said, "Pant, don't be ashamed of losing the royal gifts. Your safe arrival back home is the biggest gift for me." Raje pointed to Henry and said, "Treat him with the royal protocol." A royal gift was offered to Henry.

Kavi Kulesh came to visit with Akbar's envoy, Abdul Hamid.

"Swami, the Mughal Prince could not reach Hindustan. Ruhulla Khan blocked all his paths. The prince barely managed to come back." Kulesh reported how Aurangzeb had ensnared his son from all sides. Maharaj's forehead puckered. He quickly asked, "Where is Dhanaji?"

"Ji. Dhanaji has reached Gujarat. He has plundered Bhadoch. Durgadas is with him."

"Kulesh, you told me about the prince's defeat. Is there anything else?" Dhanaji's success was a solace to Maharaj amidst the anguish. He kept his consolation to himself and asked Kulesh.

"I don't understand." Kulesh was baffled by the question.

"Kaviraj, remember I had sent a royal gift to the prince with Netaji. It included a precious pearl necklace for the future 'emperor' of Delhi. What happened to that necklace? Do you know?"

Startled, Kulesh glanced at Akbar's envoy, wondering how this trivial news had reached Maharaj in all this turmoil.

"Aakah Ali gave it to a concubine, Huzur!" Abdul Hamid spoke as irreverently as he would speak in front of Akbar.

"How dare you?" the Chhatrapati roared in rage. He was furious that Akbar had considered a precious necklace as an ordinary one. More than that he detested the fact that Akbar's ordinary employee was addressing a woman of the Maratha kingdom as a 'concubine'.

"Kulesh, demand an explanation from the prince!" Lost in thought, Maharaj rapidly walked away. Abdul lowered his head in shame.

Ranamast Khan and Bahadur Khan have been wreaking havoc in the Kalyan-Bhivandi region. To deal with them, Maharaj especially summoned Hambirarao, Manaji, Kesopant, Rupaji and Tukoji Palkar and invaded Kalyan himself. A small fortress was located in Kalyan. To defend it, Maharaj kept moving from troop to troop, encouraging the soldiers, throughout the day. One evening, an exhausted Maharaj returned to the encampment. Rupaji, Kesopant, Nilopant came to receive him.

Wounded Hambirarao and Tukoji were not present. Maharaj came to a decision and said, "Summon Tukoji. This battle is getting harder."

"Ji, Swami, Tukoji is no more!" Everyone felt deep sorrow.

News kept arriving from Choul, Goa and Varhad region. Continuing the campaign in Kalyan was not possible. Maharaj performed the final rites of Tukoji; handed over the campaign to Nilopant and Hambirarao, and left for Raigad.

After arriving at Raigad, the Chhatrapati received the reassuring news of the successful attack of the Mavalas on Berur in Khandesh; of the bountiful booty that revived the treasury and the collection of the taxes in Bidar. Raje's sardar, Bhikulal had clashed with Qasim Khan near Naldurg. Khan's diwan, Meer Abid, was killed.

Yesaji Gambhir came from Goa and met Maharaj in private. He reported the havoc the Portuguese were wreaking there, "Dhani, Goa is in a disastrous state. The Portuguese keep launching early morning attacks in the Antruj, Salset and Bardesh region near Panaji. They have the backing of the Kannada people and advanced guns at their disposal. If this continues…" Yesaji paused, wondering how to speak further. He squeezed the edge of his shawl in his fist, in utter agony.

"What will happen then, tell me, Yesaji." Maharaj raised his head at once.

"The Portuguese are not just plundering the villages, Swami. They are burning alive our people who are not ready to convert to Christianity. When the head of the family dies, they confiscate the family property. They drop pieces of half-eaten bread in the wells and claim that people who drink that water have been converted to Christianity. They convert young girls and employ them in the churches as nuns. They force them to wear white cloaks and use them for religious propaganda during the day and at night…" Yesaji lowered his head.

The Chhatrapati became utterly restless when he heard all

that. He started pacing back and forth like a wounded tiger.

"Maharaj, if this continues, all of Goa will become a Christian state. Many people are abandoning the region and taking refuge in Karvar, Belgaum, and Varghat. They are barely surviving there." Yesaji's tears trickled onto his shawl.

Kavi Kulesh came to report Akbar's response to Maharaj. Raje had demanded an explanation in the case of the pearl necklace. Akbar had sent an insolent response to that – "I am the Mughal emperor. I will do as I wish". After hearing his response, the Chhatrapati immediately withdrew the cavalry and infantry provided to Akbar. He also stopped the allowance granted to him. Akbar felt offended by these actions, and after burning down his camp, he journeyed to Banda to travel in the direction of Goa.

Kulesh reported the plans of Akbar, who was considerably upset as Raje had withdrawn the forces and monetary support given to him, "Word is that the Mughal Prince has gone to Goa."

Raje kept thinking. He wanted to take as much advantage of the Mughal Prince as he could.

The heart-rending news of the large-scale destruction in Goa had left the Chhatrapati restless; he started walking towards the central tower with Rayaji and Antoji. He had taken many important decisions in the lofty tower.

Khandoji looked for Maharaj in the record-keeping office, the court hall of the royal throne, the private chamber and finally climbed up the tower. As Maharaj saw Khandoji, he talked about his future plans.

"Chitnis, send a message to the subedar of Choul to surround the Portuguese fort."

"Ji." Khandoji wanted to share the news he had heard but was hesitant.

Maharaj noticed his hesitation. "What is it Khandoji? Tell me."

"Swami, twenty-two ships and more than a hundred war

vessels are docked in the sea near the Bhoom port."

Maharaj heard it and announced his decision, "Khandoji, instruct our naval chief to send more than a hundred ships equipped with provisions and crew on that front."

"Ji. From Aurangabad, Aurangzeb's envoy, Sheikh Mohammed visited the Portuguese viceroy in Panaji. He appealed to them to revolt against our kingdom. He has advised them to detain the ships that deliver the materials to our ammunition factory." Khandoji reported Aurangzeb's crafty move.

"Khandoji, the pugnacious sardars of Adil Shahi such as Miya Khan, Sayyad Khan, Hasan Khan are just sitting idle in the Mangalvedhe region. Write to them to assist us. Make it clear to them that Aurangzeb wants not just the Maratha kingdom, but all kingdoms in the Deccan, and…" Raje looked at Khandoji and said, "I am planning a big campaign. I want you to accompany me; be prepared." Khandoji and Maharaj started climbing down the tower.

At the same time, the Mughal Prince, Akbar had met with the Portuguese viceroy. The Portuguese had agreed to assist him. They were going to provide him with vessels equipped for the long journey to Mecca, but…

After meeting Aurangzeb's envoy, Sheikh Mohammed, the viceroy changed his mind, and withdrew the aid. Akbar was stranded in Banda.

The cold season was in full swing now. Raigad was enveloped in thick fog every night. One such cold day, Yesaji Gambhir, who had left Raigad, entered the Portuguese durbar.

The Portuguese viceroy, Conde-De-Alvor, wrapped in a warm Portuguese coat, sat on a tall wooden seat surrounded by his courtiers. Through the interpreter, Shenavi, Yesaji posed a direct question to the viceroy, "Why are the Portuguese forming an alliance with the Mughals?"

Raje had conquered two ground forts in the Choul, Tarapur

regions in Firangan. On the strength of that success, Yesaji asked, "What are the negotiations going on between Aurangzeb's Mughal envoy, Sheikh Mohammed and the Portuguese durbar? Why is the Portuguese durbar permitting the Mughal ships to cross the sea?"

As the interpreter conveyed the questions to the viceroy, he lost his temper. Instead of replying he asked a counter question to Yesaji, whether he had any official proof that he was from Raje's durbar.

When Yesaji said, 'No', he kicked Yesaji out of the durbar. Yesaji sent the report of the humiliating incident to Raigad.

As soon as Maharaj heard about the humiliation of Yesaji, he ordered the united navy of the Marathas and the Arabs to "capture Portuguese ships wherever they were sighted."

Maharaj's mind was occupied with thoughts of the Portuguese. He was pacing in his personal chamber, pondering over how to pressurize the Portuguese viceroy into complying. Surnis Ramchandrapant came to visit him with a letter in his hand. It was a letter of the Portuguese durbar from Panaji.

Ramchandrapant made an obeisance and started reading the letter, "Your durbar has still not released our ships that were captured in the Vengurla harbour. We have not received any compensation for the villages in 'our' Goa that your forces burned down. Your envoy doesn't carry official identification with him. It is impossible to have amiable relations with you in such conditions. Take a prompt decision about making a deal with us, and convey immediately. Or else, we will make a deal with the Mughal durbar."

It was not an official letter, but an indirect warning from the Portuguese viceroy to the Maratha durbar!

Right from the moment Maharaj heard the words, 'Or else' the vein on his forehead started throbbing. "Pant, don't even bother to send a response to this letter! We will directly show our reply to them." Maharaj announced his decision.

"… but at such a time when Aurangzeb has stood against us…?" Ramchandrapant couldn't resist saying.

"I have already thought about it, Pant. This is not a letter to form an alliance. The Portuguese are going to team up with Aurangzeb in any case. We should break them before they do that. Otherwise, the Portuguese who are wreaking havoc in Goa today, will start capturing the surrounding region and take over entire Talkonkan, and we will be left with only the hope of forming an alliance."

"Pant, inform Changoji that I am going to descend the fort today to go to Gangoli."

Changoji made preparations for Raje's journey. Raje descended the fort; accompanied by the infantry in Pachad, Raje reached the first sojourn, Padshahpur at night.

The British envoy who had come with Prahladpant, was on his way back to Mumbai. He had also stayed in Padshahpur. The British envoy, Henry Smith came to visit Maharaj at night, with the interpreter Ram Shenavi.

Shanavi said, "Maharaj, I request you to send the documents of the accord that Prahladpant made with the British in Mumbai at the hands of this envoy."

Raje was angry that Shenavi had come to meet him at a sojourn during his journey, at an unreasonable time in the night to plead with Raje that he should send the documents of the accord, with the British envoy who had come with him. He exclaimed, "Shenavi, are the documents of the accord going to vanish with me? The British are renowned for observing the royal protocols strictly. How come this envoy brought you to a wrong place at such an unreasonable time?"

Shenavi trembled in fear. He stammered and barely managed to clarify, "I brought him here. Please forgive me for my mistake. He will go ahead. I will stay back and meet Maharaj when he wishes."

"You don't need to stay back either. You will receive the

required documents of the accord at the hands of Prahladpant from the record office on Raigad. You may go now." Maharaj dismissed Shenavi.

Raje left at night from Padshahpur, travelled via Kalyan, and reached Gangoli. Two thousand cavalry and two hundred infantries accompanied him. The entourage camped in Gangoli.

Maharaj was discussing further strategy with Prahladpant who had come with him, in the court room of the palace. "Nyayadhish, send a letter to Bahirji. Instruct him to send his select informers in the Choul–Tarapur region of the Portuguese. Tell him to deliver any news he collects at the earliest."

"Ji. One good news is that our forces have conquered Fort Dharur in the Beed region." Prahladpant said.

Just like Panhala, the Gangoli town was close to Raje's heart. Whenever the nobility visited Gangoli, the subedar of Gangoli arranged boats for them to sail in the river.

Raje's mind was occupied with the thoughts of Aurangzeb, the Portuguese, the Siddis, and the British. After a couple of days, he said to Prahladpant, "Nyayadhish, let's go boating together."

The subedar of Gangoli arranged a couple of boats for them. Maharaj and the Nyayadhish boarded the boats. A few swordsmen were also with them. They were discussing various political matters. The boats were sailing gently on the waters.

"Saheb…Sarkar…Maharaj…" From the shore somebody was shouting at the top of his lungs, waving his arms frantically. Everyone, including Maharaj, was surprised to see that. Maharaj signalled the boatman and all the boats rapidly rowed towards the shore. The person standing on the shore, clad in a saffron cloak, prostrated in front of Maharaj and spoke in heart-wrenching words, in a hoarse voice,

"Saheb, you are well versed in the Shastras. You administer sound justice like any scholar. Why is it then, that my case has not been resolved?" He was Krishanjipant of Chiplun who had protested in Raigad.

"Calm down, Baba. We are alone here. Tell me freely what your complaint is. I will solve it."

Krishanjipant shared his story of how Rahuji Somnath had taken advantage of his high position and usurped his post of Chief Accountant of Chiplun. Maharaj listened to the entire account calmly and glanced at the Nyayadhish.

"Maharaj, Krishnaji is telling the truth. Even Thorale Maharaj never confiscated one person's vatan and assigned it to another. Rahuji had misinformed you, and this is the result of that fabrication." The Nyayadhish gave detailed information.

"Nyayadhish, you, Ramchandrapant and Kulesh discuss the matter together. Prepare a royal decree stating that Krishnajipant should be reappointed as the Chief Accountant. And…and inform Rahuji – you have been serving the Swaraj since the time of Aabasaheb, such dishonourable conduct is unbecoming of you. You should hand over the vatan to Krishnajipant without any argument."

Krishanji was delighted to hear the justice served by Maharaj.

In the royal palace of Aurangabad, Aurangzeb was pacing back and forth anxiously. Ramsej, Kalyan–Bhivandi, Kolhapur–Panhala… he had invaded the Maratha kingdom from all sides, but had not received any reassuring news from anywhere yet.

The only solace was that his sardar, Ruhulla Khan had discharged the responsibility assigned to him, far beyond Aurangzeb's expectations. Ruhulla Khan had bribed many Maratha sardars and brought them over to the Mughal sultanate.

The Marathas were wreaking havoc now. They were attacking Aurangzeb's prominent military posts such as Jalna, Nagar, Pedgaon, Varhad, Khandesh and Solapur.

The Portuguese in Tarapur were terrified. From Gangoli, Raje himself fell upon Tarapur with one thousand cavalry and two hundred infantry. Prahladpant accompanied him. The war cries of 'Har…Har…Mahadeo' echoed in the air, terrifying the

Portuguese. The auxiliary forces already stationed in the Daman and Vasai region united with Raje's army. Tarapur was being plundered and burned in broad daylight. The Kannada and Portuguese soldiers started running helter-skelter to save their lives. The Portuguese of Tarapur suffered the same fate that the Mughals of Burhanpur and Aurangabad suffered.

Some troops of Raje's triumphant army fell upon villages such as Aserim, Dahanu and Saivana in the Daman–Vasai region and looted and burnt them down.

Raje's army encamped on the plateau of Tarapur. In his shamiana, Raje and Prahladpant were discussing the moves of the Portuguese, Aurangzeb, and the Adil Shahi and Qutub Shahi durbars. An attendant interrupted their discussion and announced, "Hari Shivadeo of Daman has come to meet Maharaj. A prisoner dressed in a white cloak is with him."

Raje raised his hand and granted permission. Hari Shivadeo came in the shamiana with a prisoner shackled in chains. It was a Portuguese pastor.

Hari Shivadeo made an obeisance and said, "If it were an item confiscated in the loot, I would have packed it in a sack and sent it to the treasury on Raigad. But what should I do with this useless pastor? Please tell me Maharaj."

Maharaj observed the pastor from head to toe and rose from his seat. He approached the prisoner. The rosy fair, grey-bearded pastor uttered something in a strange language. He looked up and touched his right hand to his forehead, left and right shoulder. One could clearly see extreme fear in his eyes. Maharaj stood in front of him and gazed into his blue eyes sharply; Yesaji Gambhir's report of the atrocious treatment of the people of Tal Firangan kept echoing in his ears.

Raje kept staring at the pastor. He was still trembling. He had heard many things about Raje. He thought he was going to be beheaded.

Raje turned around and took his seat again. He glanced at

Prahladpant who stood nearby and said to him, "Nyayadhish, what do you suggest we do with this Christian pastor?"

"Ji. We should release him. He is not a soldier." Prahladpant stated his opinion and further added, "Besides, our Yesaji Gambhir is an envoy in the Portuguese durbar. If we punish him, they will certainly torment him."

Maharaj thought for some time. He looked at Hari Shivadeo and announced his decision, "Dispatch him to Raigad, Hariji. Keep him in a cell there. We will see how the Portuguese durbar reacts after hearing of this arrest. We will come to know if they are really interested in forming an alliance with us or not."

Maharaj had returned to Raigad. He was pondering two grave incidents. The first incident was the news of Raghunathpant Hanamante's demise in Velvan.

With high hopes, Maharaj had assigned the office of Majumdar to Raghunathpant who had come from Karnataka. Raghunathpant! The memories of their meeting at Birwadi lingered in Raje's mind. Such a fearless person!

Finally, Raje himself took the decision and appointed Rughanathpant's son, Narayan Raghunath as the next Majumdar.

The second critical news was, the Portuguese had imprisoned Yesaji Gambhir in Panaji. As soon as Raje heard the news, he understood the motive of the Portuguese. It was now confirmed that the Portuguese were going to team up with Aurangzeb.

'The Portuguese! The Portuguese!' Constantly thinking about the Portuguese, Raje kept visiting the treasury, the ammunition factory and the stable of Pachad frequently.

One day, Maharaj was surveying the horses in the stable of Pachad with Peshwe, Khandoji, Rayaji and Antaji.

"Khandoji, Ram Singh of Amber is not giving us enough support. Many times, people don't support us, but animals respond and support us immediately." Maharaj said with a heavy heart.

"Ji. The animals always focus straight ahead…human eyes wander in all directions! You never know where they will be focused!" Khandoji spoke in his rustic language.

An informer rushed through the gate to attract Raje's attention. He made an obeisance to Raje and politely said, "Good news, Dhani; the enemy's camp at Kalyan-Bhivandi is moving. All Khans including Ranamast, Bahadur, Ruhulla are on the way back to Aurangabad. Our Sarlashkar, Rupaji, and Manaji are ambushing them at every possible place in the ghats and valleys."

The faces of everyone standing around Raje lit up. "Jagadamb!" Raje exclaimed, touched the cowrie necklace on his chest, and closed his eyes for a moment.

Aurangzeb was now going to berate Ranamast and Bahadur Khan who were returning from the Kalyan–Bhivandi region without any success. He was going to bestow a precious dagger and a horse only on Bakshi Ruhulla Khan, as he had accomplished the invaluable feat of luring the traitors of Swaraj to the Mughal sultanate.

Heavy monsoon showers started. The Mughal encampments at various places were hit by the deluge. Aurangzeb's military activities in Talkonkan reduced considerably. Raje decided to take advantage of the opportunity and braving the rains he fell upon Rajapur via Mahad ghat. He had eight thousand cavalry with him.

In the pouring rain, the warriors of Tal Konkan gathered for a meeting in the royal shamiana. Raje commenced the meeting and shared his plan with the attendees, "Our enemy, Aurangzeb, has retreated from Kalyan–Bhivandi. Now we have to teach a lesson to the Portuguese who keep attacking us with his support. I am going invade Revdanda myself. All of you should remain alert, wherever you are stationed and be ready to support us as needed. Ragho Vishwanath, you are from Revdanada. What is the news in the region?" Raje asked Ragho.

"Ji. Dom Francisco is the custodian of the Portuguese fort. He has heavy cannons at his disposal, but he won't be able to use them in the pouring rain. We should surround him right away." Ragho Vishwanath seconded Raje's plan.

The plans for the 'Revdanda campaign' were discussed and the meeting was concluded. Braving the pouring rains, the informers covered themselves with coarse blankets and dispersed in the Revdanda–Daman region.

Right in the middle of the rainy season, the battle of the army of Swaraj against the Portuguese, sparked off.

To take over the Revdanda fort, in the pouring rains, the swordsmen fetched their ropes and secured ladders against the ramparts of the fort. Dom Francisco, the Portuguese custodian started hurting rocks and arrows from the rampart walls. Dom grabbed his gun and started shooting the Mavala soldiers himself. Previously, Siddi Jauhar had besieged and trapped Aabasaheb on Panhala; similarly, Raje had besieged and trapped Dom Francisco now. The viceroy of Panaji, Conde-De-Alvor was caught in a tight spot when he heard the news.

Every day, Raje kept moving around the siege, astride his horse, and comforting the wounded soldiers. He would return to his shamiana in the rainy evenings. One evening, subedar Ragho Vishwanath came to visit him in the shamiana. He said in a choked voice, "Swami, Dabir Janardanpant Hanamante who has been running the administration of the Kolhapur–Panhala region efficiently, has passed away."

As Ragho Vishwanath saw the anguish on his Swami's face, he wondered whether he should share the next piece of news or not. Finally, he made up his mind and said, "Qazi Haidar, who has been in the service of the Munshi, since the time of Thorale Swami, has defected to our enemy in Aurangabad. The Mughal emperor has offered him ten thousand in cash, and the mansab of two thousand cavalry."

Raje thought for quite some time, and said to Ragho, "Send

a messenger to Raigad today and inform them to delegate the office of Dabir to Janardanpant's son, Vasudeopant."

The siege of Revdanda continued for one and a half month. Dom Francisco was giving a tough fight. Raje was not ready to back off. Kalyan–Bhivandi, Malakapur, Panhala, Solapur, Ramsej, Varhad, Khandesh, Raigad…news kept coming from all sides. Hambirarao, Keso Trimal, Naruji, Santaji Jagtap, Kulesh…all warriors leading various campaigns were performing their duties with due diligence despite the pouring rains.

The downpour continued throughout the night. The exhausted people of Revdanda were resting in their homes. In the early morning, just when the Portuguese soldiers, irritated with the rains, were changing the guard, Sambhajiraje pointed his sword and roared, "Har Har Mahadeo" prompting the Mavala soldiers to attack. The Mavala soldiers fell upon the fort.

At dawn, battles broke out at three places, the Mary church of Revdanda, the fort of Revdanda and the fort of Morav. The chief Portuguese sentinel of the Church, Domigo Gomes forced the Kannada cannoneers to walk in the mud and got the cannons transported to the church tower!

The viceroy panicked when he came to know of the infiltration of Raje's army in the Revdanda, Daman, and Vasai regions. He ordered his ryots as well as the pastors, "Sambhajiraje is coming to attack. Be prepared to fight wherever you are with whatever weapons you have!"

Meanwhile, Aurangzeb had honoured Ranamast Khan who had come back after accepting defeat in Kalyan–Bhivandi and bestowed him with the title of 'Bahadur Khan'. Why? Because he was now going to send Ranamast Khan to attack Bijapur of Adil Shahi.

The end of the monsoon was approaching; a three-way game of chess was on; Aurangabad, Panaji and Raigad. The players were the Mughals, the Portuguese and the Marathas.

From Revdanda, Raje had to return to Raigad. He had

received confirmed news that the viceroy of Panaji was recruiting fresh soldiers and building new weaponry to invade Tal Firangan. Two war ships with military provisions for the Portuguese, had sailed from Portugal and reached Panaji.

As Raje had surmised, Aurangzeb's retreat from Kalyan–Bhivandi was a ploy.

Raje summoned Nilopant to his personal chamber and said, "Peshwe, send message to Akbar in Bicholi and instruct him to visit the Dutch durbar in Karvar with Durgadas.

"We should use the Mughal Prince to receive as much aid from the Dutch as we can. For that purpose, send a royal gift to Bicholi, but...but don't include any pearl necklaces in the gift."

"Ji. The siege of Revdanda continues in the heavy rains, without a leader. Therefore..." Nilopant broached a critical topic.

"Peshwe, unfortunately I had to leave that campaign halfway and come back. The Portuguese are going to charge upon Tal Konkan to break our hold on the Var Firangan region. I have received confirmed news that if required, Aurangzeb is going to provide them military aid from Ram ghat via Belgaum."

"Maharaj, if the Mughals and the Portuguese join hands, Aurangzeb will definitely take over the entire Var Konkan and Tal Konkan." Nilopant said exactly what was going on in his Swami's mind.

"That is why, I want you to take over the siege of Revdanda."

"As you wish. I will proceed to Revdanda with the army."

As decided, Maharaj descended Raigad with the Peshwa. In the pouring rain, Maharaj provided eight thousand soldiers to Nilopant and bade farewell to him from Pachad.

Just as Maharaj had surmised, Aurangzeb's favourite prince, Shah Alam, had left Aurangabad with a grand display of pomp. He was leading an army of forty-five thousand soldiers including the Turks, the Pathans, the Mughals and the defectors. The leader of the cannonry, Aatash Khan and Lutfulla Khan, Ikhlas Khan, Jan Nisar and Sadat Khan accompanied him. A well-informed

Maratha sardar named Nagoji Mane from the Satara region was also with Shah Alam to provide him accurate and reliable information about the rocky region. He was going to receive food provisions and weaponry via the sea from Surat to Panaji.

The rainy season was over. The Portuguese started making their moves, revealing their intentions. Day and night, they started crossing the Mandavi creek of Panaji and kept destroying nearby towns. They were forcefully converting their prisoners. Every day, Raigad started receiving the news of atrocities committed against the ryots. Nilopant was stationed in the Choul region. When he received the news of the atrocities, he pounced upon the entire stretch of Revdanda, Daman and Vasai. His attacks terrorized the Portuguese people and more than four thousand Portuguese sought shelter in Mumbai.

Maharaj had noted the hostile activities of Panaji and summoned Yesaji Kank. He and the subedar of Fonda, Dharmaji Nagnath came to meet Maharaj. When Maharaj saw Yesaji's young, brawny son Krishnaji with him, he remembered Dhanaji Jadhav. Krishnaji had a dark complexion and a muscular physique.

"Kank kaka, the Portuguese are going to attack the fort of Fonda sooner or later. You and Dharmaji should stay vigilant and protect that fort." Maharaj said to Yesaji.

"As you wish Dhani. Now that you have appointed me for the defence of Fonda, rest assured. I have brought my son for the same purpose." Aged Yesaji said in a clear voice, pointing to Krishnaji.

Raje shared the specifics of the provisions, auxiliary forces and the war techniques of the Portuguese with Dharmaji Nagnath. Dharmaji, Yesaji and Krishnaji spent a day on the fort, and marched towards Fonda.

Raje was standing on the Hirakani machi, lost in looking at the sunset. Mudhoji, Changoji, and Khandoji stood around him. Everyone was silent. Just then Jotyaji Kesarkar rushed to the machi. As he saw Raje lost in thought, he wondered whether to share the news with him or not. Maharaj turned around in his thought. Jotyaji approached him.

"Dhani, I have news about Diler Khan…" He stammered.

"Jotyaji, don't even mention his name in front of me." The year he had spent with Diler instantly flashed in front of Maharaj's eyes.

"Ji, now no one will ever have to do that. Diler has killed himself by swallowing a diamond in his camp, Dhani!"

"What? Jotyaji, what did you say?" For the first time, after quite a long time, Raje's heart was stirred.

"It's true, Dhani. The emperor reprimanded him in front of the durbar. He said, 'You are a disloyal commander. Why couldn't you bring us any success in your region?' Khan was upset at the insult. He went back to his shamiana and…"

After hearing the news, many memories of Diler Khan lingered in Maharaj's mind.

On the one hand, the auxiliary forces that Raje had summoned were joining the army in Rajapur. On the other, news kept arriving that the Portuguese had tightened the siege around the Fonda fort. Rajapur had now become a massive camp of the Maratha forces. More than thirty thousand soldiers had assembled in the camp. Dharmaji Nagnath, Hambirarao and Khandoji were supervising the entire camp. Raje summoned Dharmaji and ordered him, "Subedar, you visit the French warehouse and meet their viceroy. Warn him not to provide any kind of assistance to the Portuguese. The number of our forces here has increased considerably. Urge him to grant us an emergency loan of fifteen hundred Pagodas."

Raje was about to tell Dharmaji something else, when he heard loud bawling outside.

Raje gave Dharmaji a startled look. In a few moments, Khandoji brought a person in, holding his upper arm. He presented the person in front of Raje and said, "This is Naikawadi from Fonda fort. He has a complaint but is not giving us any details despite requesting him repeatedly. Therefore, I had to bring him in front of you." Khandoji looked quite upset.

Dharmaji recognized the Naikawadi from his region. He went to him, released his upper arm from Khandoji's hand and exclaimed, "Chitnis, the people of Talkonkan register their complaint by bawling. He is not doing anything unusual."

Maharaj approached Naikawadi. He directly prostrated in front of Raje. Raje said to him, "Get up and speak. Tell me about your complaint without any fear."

"It's not just my complaint!" Reassured, the Naikawadi put forth his complaint. "It's the complaint of my whole region. Why is Dhani still here? The Portuguese will not just capture our Fonda fort, but they will take over the surrounding region too. Whatever needs to be done, should be done today."

The Naikawadi had expressed Raje's sentiments exactly. Raje turned around and asked, "Anything else?"

"The Portuguese have tightened the siege of Fonda fort today. They will make the final fierce attack on the fort tonight."

"Khandoji, summon Hambirmama. Dharmaji, keep five thousand cavalry ready. Send as many foot soldiers as you can to Fonda immediately. I myself will go to aid Yesaji kaka!" Raje said firmly.

Hambirarao came in. "Sarlashkar, I am leaving Rajapur to go to the aid of Fonda. You join me afterwards with your forces when you get my message. Not just Fonda, we are going to attack the entire Firangan!" Raje said to him.

"If I come with you..." Hambirarao didn't want Raje to go ahead without him.

"It will take time to move the entire camp. That is why you should stay back."

Raje left the shamiana in the attire of a warrior. He left Dharmaji, Khandoji and Hambirarao in charge of the forces and mounted his horse 'Chandravat'.

'Jai Bhavani…' He bade farewell to Hambirarao and the others, and prodded his horse.

The viceroy, Alvor was all set with his army, to make the final attack on the damaged ramparts of the Fonda fort. His drum players were beating the drums to motivate the soldiers.

From the rampart walls of the fort, anxious Yesaji and Krishnaji Kank watched them, moving around comforting their soldiers. Fonda was now on the brink of collapse. Even a moment's delay was going to be fatal…

Suddenly, the roaring war cries of 'Har Har Mahadeo' echoed in the air, touching the sky. From the rampart walls, Yesaji and Krishanji saw the saffron Jaripataka pennant fluttering in the air visible through the rising clouds of dust. The entire Fonda fort erupted in excitement to see that and responded unanimously with, 'Har Har Mahadeo…'

Caught between the two, the Portuguese soldiers were baffled and started whispering among themselves – "Run, run, the king is coming!" In no time, the army that the viceroy had lined up with rigorous efforts, scattered all over.

The Mavala soldiers standing on the rampart walls hollered with joy.

Finally, keeping the infantry in the lead, with five thousand cavalry, Sambhajiraje reached the ramparts of the Fonda fort. The situation now changed dramatically.

Not a single Portuguese soldier standing around, dared to raise his weapon. It was not even a counterattack by Raje to save the fort, just a regular arrival. Kettle drums started beating in the fort now.

After eight days, Yesaji opened the gates of the fort. "Kank kaka, send the soldiers inside the fort immediately. The Portuguese army is going to retreat. We must follow them right now!"

"Ji. Yesaji and Krishnaji took prompt action.

What Raje had surmised came to happen. As the viceroy commanded his army to retreat, his soldiers who were waiting for the command, started running back the way they had come.

The Mavala riders caught up with the Portuguese soldiers running away near Durbhat. The Portuguese took up positions and started shooting with their guns. The exploding gun shots startled the Mavala horses, and they began to retreat. Yesaji's son Krishnaji lost his temper when he saw that. He raised his head high and roared loudly, 'Har Har Mahadeo'; his battle cry inspired the soldiers again. The battle was between the Mavala spear-wielders riding their horses, and the Portuguese soldiers shooting from behind their shields. The Portuguese army was completely scattered. The viceroy himself was luckily spared twice from the spears of the Mavala soldiers.

And…and Krishnaji who was sweating, completely soaked in blood, kept galloping ahead slaying the enemy. A bullet hit him in the chest; Krishnaji fainted and collapsed from his horse. The Mavala soldiers carried wounded Krishnaji and lay him down on a blanket next to wounded Yesaji.

Both armies were exhausted now. Many Portuguese and Mavala soldiers had been killed. As twilight was approaching, the battle had stopped.

Maharaj approached Yesaji lying on the coarse blanket. Aged Yesaji looked at him and said in a feeble voice, "Are you all right?" Raje didn't know how to respond to him. He came to Krishnaji, whose blanket was soaked in blood. Weary Krishnaji tried to open his eyes. Raje sat next to him, stroked Krishnaji's wounded body with motherly affection and exclaimed, "Krishna, how did you get wounded so badly?" He commanded the people around him, "Arrange palanquins for them immediately and transport both the father and son to their village in Karhad."

Hambirarao fell upon the Salset, Bardesh region. Dharmaji Nagnath penetrated via Durbhat–Agashi. Raje's army marched from three sides to infiltrate Goa. Raje and Khandoji charged upon the Juve island and captured it in one attempt.

The viceroy was shocked when the Marathas captured the Juve island. Once the Marathas crossed the creek from the island, they were going to be able to enter Old Goa. As per the viceroy's instructions, the terrified Portuguese priests tolled the bells in the St. Xavier's church throughout the night.

Akbar, who had come from Bicholi was also with Raje during this attack. He knew in his heart that Goa wouldn't last long now.

The next day, after the Marathas conquered the Juve island, the viceroy crossed the creek and with four hundred soldiers, attacked the island determinedly to recapture it.

Raje was stationed on the hill; he took no action at first and let him climb up the hill. Once he was in the range, dumping rocks from the top of the hill Raje started descending the hill.

"Run… run!" the Portuguese soldiers abandoned their horses, who couldn't go down the hill properly and started running for their lives.

Additionally, the auxiliary forces of three hundred Mavalas united with Raje's forces.

The Portuguese people of Goa were watching a strange scene from the hills near the Juve island. The Mavala soldiers running down the slopes of the hills wielding their swords and the Portuguese soldiers running for their lives with the viceroy. A few Mavalas surrounded the viceroy's horse; the Portuguese soldiers were terrified to see that. Dom Rodrigo, astride his horse, came to the rescue of the viceroy and saved his life. But still, a stroke of a sword hit him slightly on the side and he was wounded.

Rodrigo screamed out loud, "Run for your life, go towards the creek."

The terrified, blood-soaked viceroy turned his horse and galloped in the direction of the creek. Raje kept an eye on him while fighting with the Portuguese soldiers in front of him; he skilfully pulled his horse 'Chandravat' out of the commotion on the battlefield and started chasing the viceroy.

The spectators watching from the hills were forced to watch an unprecedented scene. In the front, the wounded and terrified viceroy, Conde-De-Alvor, running for his life and the devil 'Samba' wielding his sword, running after the viceroy to catch him.

As clever Khandoji saw that Raje was chasing the viceroy alone, he followed Raje on his horse.

The terrified viceroy pushed his horse in the roaring, foaming waters of the high tide. The completely terrified viceroy, desperate to save his life, started swimming with all his might, through the salty waters to catch the boat sailing in the middle. The boat also started moving towards him.

Raje riding on 'Chadravat' shouted, "Don't let him go! He has burned and converted many villages of ours…"

And in his rage, furious Raje prodded Chandravat to enter the creek waters. The saline water splashed all over. Chandravat entered a few feet in the creek and got caught in the strong current of the high tide.

The spectators on the hills saw that the viceroy had reached the boat and 'Samba' who was trying to kill him was drifting in the water with his horse; they started applauding with joy.

Raje removed his legs from the stirrups of Chandravat. Controlling Chandravat with one hand and floating above water with the other Raje was drifting with Chandravat. The applause on the hills intensified now.

And then suddenly the spectators on the hill fell silent. They saw a man leaping from his horse, with all his might, into the creek waters. He swam swiftly and quickly reached 'Samba'. He supported drifting Samba with his hands and started bringing him to the creek shore. As Raje let go of Chandravat's reins, he also swam on his own towards the shore.

That bold soldier who had leaped from his horse in the

water, was Khandoji Ballal! All drenched, Raje and Chitnis safely reached the shore. Raje gazed at Khandoji and embraced him tightly with affection.

Now Raje joined Hambirarao in Salset, Bardesh region. This was the place where the Portuguese had wreaked havoc with religious persecution.

In this area, the Portuguese were forcibly converting the young girls of the destitute fishermen and using them for religious propaganda during the day and violating them sexually at night. The Mavala army broke open three service churches of such nuns. The biggest church was in Racholi. When that church was unlocked, the fisherwomen who had been converted into nuns, started running freely everywhere. As Raje astride his horse, saw them running freely, he gazed at the Sarlashkar in satisfaction and said, "Mama, Thoralya Aau should have been here to witness this scene."

But a bitter truth poked at his heart, 'If only I had been fortunate enough to free Ranooakka and Durga too!'

A scene that Bardesh had never witnessed, manifested in front of Raje. A Mavala unit presented seven Portuguese priests tied to a single rope, in front of Raje.

"What should we do to them, Dhani? Should we just dump them in the sea like a fisherman throws his net in the water?" The leader of the unit asked.

Their heads were hanging low. Raje observed them carefully. "Forget Samartha, not one of them looks like even Divakar Gosavi. Why? I always felt that Samartha's footprints were a beacon that steered the path of Dharma! What about these people? Such people make Dharma a path to be trampled upon. What kind of Dharma tramples upon the rights of others?"

"Dhani, what should we do with them?" The leader said with irrepressible earnestness.

A furious Raje roared, "Lash their backs with whips and take them out in a public procession!"

There, in Panaji, in the old church, the terrified Portuguese people had gathered. They were touching their shoulders and forehead and raising their arms high, they were praying to their god. For the first time ever, the viceroy, Conde-De-Alvor, opened the coffin of St. Xavier and took the golden sceptre from the hands of St. Xavier's corpse into his own hands. He raised it high towards the sky frequently and muttered to himself, "Please, please save the honour of Goa. Do something to make this 'Samba' go away. Let him conquer Goa, if he wants to but…but spare our lives!"

In the sea of Panaji, the Portuguese ships were loaded with the treasure of gold and cash, and ready to sail in the direction of Portugal. The Portuguese women and children had already boarded the ships. This was the viceroy's final prayer to St. Xavier. He was going to take the coffin with him once he left the church. The big bells in the church were tolling.

The Mavala forces of Durbhat, Juve, Antruj and Bardesh were merging. Raje was going to send them off to Panaji. But…

The Ramoshi messenger sent by Kavi Kulesh came searching for Raje, gasping for breath. He shared the news, "Shah Alam is coming from Ramghat with an army of one lakh soldiers. A long line of soldiers has occupied the ghat."

"What...?!!" Raje's eyes widened and he screamed in shock.

He was facing the same situation where he would plan something, but he would be forced to back off before executing it. He had no option but to leave Firangan with the army that had penetrated Goa before they got caught between the armies of Shah Alam and the Portuguese viceroy.

The Portuguese were ready to make an accord. Raje appointed Kulesh and Akbar to handle the responsibility of the accord and returned to Raigad; only two pieces of news occupied his mind – Shah Alam who had entered Konkan and the British of Mumbai. Previously, the Portuguese had complained that

Yesaji Gambhir did not have official identification with him. Therefore, as he was leaving Goa, Raje officially appointed Kulesh as the 'Kulekhtyar' and gave him the responsibility to make the accord. The title given to Kulesh was for political convenience, but many people did not like it. Rumours were on the rise that… 'Chhandogamatya – Kulekhtyar' – Kanoja is receiving undue favours.

As per the instruction, Kulesh and Akbar met with the Portuguese envoy at Fonda, Bhimgad and started negotiations for the accord.

The news was that Aurangzeb was going to keep Shah Alam stationed in South Konkan and was himself going to invade the region of Adil Shahi.

It was essential to defend Adil Shahi, just like Aabasaheb had done. Raje summoned Peshwe Nilopant and Hambirarao to plan the strategy for the same.

"Peshwe, looks like Aurangzeb is planning to invade Adil Shahi. If we provide support to it, Adil Shahi can fight for a long time." Raje said.

"Ji. With your permission I will go to assist Adil Shahi." Hambirarao agreed with Raje's strategy.

"Mama Saheb, it is only you that I will send, but not now, at the right time. Nilopant, you make sure that a regiment of eighteen thousand freshly recruited soldiers marches towards Bijapur." Raje was pondering the motive behind Aurangzeb's move.

Just then, informer Vishwas who had travelled from South Konkan, came to meet Raje. The news that he brought reduced Raje's stress.

"Distressed by frequent defeats, Shah Alam is going back, Dhani. Only forty-five thousand soldiers from his army of one lakh have survived. He doesn't even have the guts to wield his sword now. He has sent a message to his father at Nagar – 'Send me more horses and mules, or else I will die in these mountains'."

Raje listened to the news calmly and said to Hambirarao, "Sarlashkar, now you and I will travel together to Palatatta near Mumbai."

Nilopant interrupted and shared news that broke Raje's line of thought, "Swami, Yesaji Kank, who had returned to Karhad, is recovering faster…but Krishnaji's wounds got infected and he passed away."

Krishnaji! Raje was heartbroken. For a few moments he was lost in thought. As Raje realized that Krishnaji was survived by his wife and three-year-old son, he said to Peshwe, "Peshwe, arrange an annual allowance of one thousand hons for Krishanji's family and Yesaji too. Reward Khandoji with one thousand hons and bestow on him the honour of palanquin."

From Mumbai, governor Keigwin wrote a letter to King Charles of London describing the adverse conditions. In the letter he said, "Our neighbour, the powerful king 'Shambhooji' has destroyed a forty-mile stretch of the Portuguese territory. More than thirty thousand of his forces have surrounded the region, targeting Mumbai. We have only about two hundred soldiers of our own and two hundred Abyssinian soldiers. Shambhooji has demanded sixty cannons, four hundred barrels of explosives, small boats, big ships and garments from us. He has threatened that he will attack Mumbai if his demands are not fulfilled. What should we do? I feel that keeping in mind the destruction of the Portuguese region, we should make an accord with him."

After travelling through Palatatta, Karanja and Elephanta, Raje, who was planning to attack the British and the Portuguese in the Mumbai and Vasai region at the same time, returned to Raigad.

At night, he received intimation – "Kulekhtyar Kulesh is coming to visit with the Portuguese envoys who have come from Panaji."

Kulesh had gone to Patgaon to take the darshan of Maunibaba. The team of Portuguese envoys met him there and he came to Raigad with them. He was accompanied by Fryer, Conseco, Themudo, priest Augustine and Albuquerque.

The envoys presented royal gifts to Raje. They were courteous and filled with awe. The interpreter converted the details of the discussion that took place between Albuquerque, Kulesh and Akbar, through Ram Naik.

In fact, Raje did not want to make an accord with the Portuguese. Under some pretext or the other, Raje kept delaying the talks with the Portuguese envoys for three nights.

On the third night, an agitated Albuquerque announced his firm decision, "Our durbar is not going to vacate the Anjediva island! Raje's demands will not be fulfilled!"

"What do you mean?" When Raje heard it, he stood up at once. His face flushed in anger. "Kulesh, better tell his Portuguese man, if my conditions are not approved, our Peshwa will not move out of Var Firnagan. The prisoners of Bhimgad will not be released. We will not return the cannons that we seized in Bardesh! And if needed, we will launch another attack!"

Albuquerque shook with fear seeing Raje's rage. An enraged Raje's image made an impact on Fryer's mind.

Raje came to Birwadi. Prahladpant came to meet him with the British envoy Gary.

The London durbar had sent a reply to the letter that Keigwin, the governor of Mumbai had written to them. That is why Keigwin had sent his envoy immediately.

"The British are seeking our permission to build warehouses in Karnataka. They want us to return their ship named 'President' that we had seized thinking it belonged to the Portuguese." Prahladpant said presenting Gary in front of Raje.

Raje made peaceful negotiations with Gary through Prahladpant. As Thomas Wilkins and the interpreter Ram

Shenavi were there to assist Gary, they held the talks of negotiations for three whole days in Birwadi. Raje instructed Prahladpant to create a draft of the accord and travelled to Raigad. But after submitting the draft to the British envoy, Prahladpant did not ascend Raigad as he would usually do. He had a personal meeting with Manaji More, Gangadharpant, Rahuji Somnath and Vasudevpant.

Meanwhile, Aurangzeb and Shah Alam, the father and son, were meeting each other in Ahmednagar. With the aid of the horses and mules that his father had sent, Shah Alam had barely managed to cross the ghat. Out of one lakh soldiers, he had only forty thousand soldiers left at his disposal now.

In the Ahmednagar fort, the prince presented himself with a lowered head in front of his father. Aurangzeb condescendingly said to him, “At least the rebel Akbar went alone. You went with the army and lost half of it. How dare you come back? Why didn’t you vanish with him too?”

Poor Shah Alam! What could he say? He left his father’s chamber in shame.

The women of Sambha’s family were detained in Khuldabad. The Mavalas were took advantage of that and kept raiding the region up to Jalna. Aurangzeb was frustrated with their raids; he summoned Wazir Asad Khan and instructed him, “Dispatch the women of Sambha’s family to Bahadurgad. Make sure to send them with armed guards.”

As per the emperor’s command, Durgabai and Ranooakka were transferred to Bahadurgad. The custodian of Pedgaon sent an official acknowledgement to the emperor.

The monsoon was about to begin. From the Ramsej, Kalyan, Bhivandi, Baglan and Pune regions, informers such as Bahirji, Vishwas and Mahadeo started arriving at Raigad. News kept arriving at Raigad from all sides. “Aurangzeb had kept a limited army at Ramsej and a few forts in Tal Konkan and was withdrawing the rest of his forces. His sardars stationed at various places were travelling towards Aurangabad."

"Send messages to Hambirarao, Rupaji, Kulesh, Ramchandrapant and other prominent men to come on Raigad as fast as they can. Send the letters at the hands of the informers who have reached the fort." Raje walked briskly and gave quick commands to Nilopant. He wondered, 'Why is Aurangzeb withdrawing his forces? What could be his motive behind it? Is he backing off due to the advent of monsoon, or is he going to attack more forcefully once monsoon is over?'

Raje became extremely busy now. The British in Mumbai kept insisting on getting permission to build their warehouse, "Send us the documents of the accord with your official seal." Raje had no time to investigate the matter. He handed over the entire mission to Prahladpant.

Prominent men such as Hambirarao, Rupaji, Kulesh, Santaji and Dhanaji who had returned from Gujarat, Ramchandrapant, and Daulat Khan gathered for a meeting in the court hall of Raigad, at the height of summer. Peshwe Nilopant commenced the meeting and said, "For now, our enemy is withdrawing his forces all over the region before the advent of the monsoon. News is, that he is going to invade Adil Shahi. We should not rely on such news and be negligent. You have been invited to discuss further strategy."

"Shah Alam has left from Nagar and is travelling via Solapur. This indicates that the emperor is planning to attack Adil Shahi." Ramchandrapant suggested.

"We should catch up with him before he does that." Raje exclaimed firmly.

"Even if he attacks Bijapur, as the Peshwa says, we should not be negligent." Hambirarao spoke Raje's mind.

The meeting continued for a long time. Everyone was given specific instructions. Betel leaves were offered to all and the meeting concluded.

In the hustle nobody realized that Prahladpant who would

usually voice his opinions was quiet today. After the meeting, Rahuji and Manaji More met Prahladpant at his residence and kept discussed something in low voices.

The monsoon arrived; the ryots, who had been hard hit by drought throughout the year, were relieved. More than anything else, they were relieved that the Mughal forces had withdrawn from the region. Now the peasants got down to work in their farms.

In the personal chamber on the Balekilla, Raje was lost in thought gazing at the trickling streams of rain visible from the windows.

"Maharaj, a Pathan has arrived on the fort despite the rains. He wants to meet you." The attendant named Purusha announced. In a short time, he presented a gallant, pugnacious Pathan in the chamber. As soon as Maharaj saw him, he thought he had seen the Pathan before. But where? He couldn't remember.

"My obeisance to you, oh king of the Marathas." The Pathan made an obeisance.

"Who are you? Why did you seek an audience with me?" Raje was observing him and trying to remember who he was.

"Don't you remember me, Raja Saab?" The Pathan laughed heartily.

"No. Remind me."

"I am Mirbat Khan!" Diler's brother. Raje remembered the banks of River Bhima. He stepped forward and directly embraced Mirbat saying, "Khan…is that you?"

"How are you doing?" Though Raje knew everything, he purposely asked.

"What can I say, Raja Saab! The emperor is not an emperor! He is a heartless devil! He humiliated my brother and took his life! I am done with his atrocities!" Mirbat spoke earnestly.

"Khan, I know everything. You spend a couple of days on

the fort and enjoy our hospitality."

"Couple of days? Raja Saab, did I come here in this deluge, only for the sake of enjoying your hospitality? I am here to surrender my life at your feet." Mirbat removed his waistband, knelt and placed his sword at Raje's feet.

Raje placed his sword in his hands and wondered, 'When I returned to Panhala from Diler's camp, at least Aabasaheb was there to ask me 'Where were you, my dear child' and embrace me. But this man has no one.'

Raje employed Mirbat in his service.

Peshwe came to meet Raje with Akbar's letter that had come from Konkan.

"The prince says, we should send the documents of the accord to the Portuguese at the earliest." Peshwe reported the matter of Akbar's letter.

"Anything else?"

"Ji. He says…says…" Nilopant hesitated.

"Yes, what is it? Tell me." Raje thought the prince is demanding something more."

"Ji! The prince says, Kulesh is a very loyal servant of Raje. May Allah always bless him, and no evil eye should ever fall upon him." In fact, Nilopant did not like Akbar's praise of Kulesh.

"That's all?" Raje sighed deeply. The subject of the discussion, Kulesh himself arrived. As Nilopant saw him, he made an obeisance and left.

"Maharaj, even while going back, Aurangzeb has bribed some of our men." Khandoji said with concern.

"Who are they, Chitnis?"

"In the Nagar fort, the emperor has given mansabs to people who joined hands with him such as, Nayab Shahkuli, Khanduji and Rambha Shankaraji."

Raje was concerned when he heard the news.

Outside, the game of rain and sunshine was in full flow.

The chowk in front of the court hall of the royal throne was getting drenched in the rain showers one moment and basking in sunlight the next.

In a few days, the news that Raigad was anticipating, arrived – "The emperor has begun a campaign against the Adil Shahi sultanate. Hasan Ali Tana Shah was surrounded in Golconda to keep Qutub Shahi and Adil Shahi sultanates from coming together." When Aurangzeb sent his son Azam with the Mughal army, to attack Sikandar, the young king of Bijapur, both sultanates came to their senses. It was clear that despite being Islamic powers they were considered 'Southerners'. 'Just as both the sultanates had remained indifferent and watched the Maratha kingdom battle against the Mughals, should the Maratha kingdom return the favour?' Maharaj was facing a big dilemma.

Hence, Raje had summoned the prominent guests that he had invited on the fort for the Dussehra celebrations, in the court hall of the royal throne.

The Peshwa commenced the meeting, "We have received news from the fort of Nagar. Our rival is sending his army in the direction of Adil Shahi. He has conceded defeat in our kingdom and has withdrawn almost all of his forces from our kingdom…"

All the courtiers listened to the Peshwa attentively. Raje sat on a separate seat observing everyone in the meeting. The memories of the days when he had left Panhala after Aabasaheb's demise, whirled in his mind.

"The late Swami never desired the downfall of Adil Shahi. We are facing the same situation today. All of you have been summoned to this meeting to discuss the matter." The Peshwa continued speaking. He raised the question, 'What action should we take now?' Kulesh suggested, "Why should this durbar worry about Adil Shahi? They did nothing to help us when we needed it!"

"I agree with Chhandogamatya. Though I was stationed in

Karnataka, every day I was worried about the situation here. That is why I had sent Raghunathpant here." Harajiraje sitting next to Raje seconded Kulesh.

"In my opinion, we should launch a thorough investigation of the traitors. At least that will reduce the risk for us in the future." Prahladpant who had been quiet so far, spoke up.

"Following the strategy of Thorale swami, we should give as much military assistance to Adil Shahi as we can. That sultanate has sustained for a long time; it will give a tough fight to the emperor. Besides, they have prominent sardars such as Sarja Khan at their disposal. With the aid of our Sarlashkar, sardars like him will continue fighting with Aurangzeb." Nilopant assessed the situation correctly.

Maharaj was quietly listening to everyone's suggestions. His heart was in turmoil.

'Aabasaheb launched this kingdom of Swaraj by rebelling against Adil Shahi. When he attacked Bijapur with Mirza Raja, it was because he was left with no choice. Despite all these events, he who had invaded Surat, never invaded Bijapur on his own. In our last meeting at Panhala he frequently said to me, "Sooner or later, Aurangzeb is going to fall upon our kingdom. You should be concerned about that."

Everyone's eyes were on Raje now. "I agree with Peshwe, we should not turn our back on Adil Shahi at this time. We should support it to fight with Aurangzeb. I have sent Sarlashkar for the same purpose. Sikandar Shah has welcomed him too. Aurangzeb might fall upon our kingdom again, any time. It would be better if he is occupied in another war." Maharaj gazed at the eastern horizon and said firmly.

Everyone agreed that though Aurangzeb had withdrawn his forces, the Maratha kingdom was not out of danger yet. The meeting concluded after taking the decision of recruiting fresh soldiers in the army, and that all prominent sardars should be vigilant and prepare the forts for war.

Peshwa Nilopant came to meet Raje; he looked quite distressed. He did not say anything for quite a while.

"Nilopant, whatever it is, please share it with me. I am used to bad news. Tell me who else has defected?" Maharaj kept pacing quietly in his personal chamber. Even the guards standing nearby pricked up their ears to hear the names of the traitors.

"Swami, I am also used to the news of people turning traitor, but…the news I have is not one of defection…!" Pant sounded very distressed.

"What?" Raje instantly stopped walking. He approached Peshwe and gazed in his eyes deeply.

"Maharaj, this is serious news; news of a conspiracy!" Peshwe lowered his head.

Maharaj was repulsed by those words. His eyes strained wide; benumbed, he kept staring into the vacuum. Then he roared at once,

" What?! Are you telling the truth, Peshwe? Who thought that Aurangzeb, the Portuguese and the Siddis were not enough trouble for us? Who plotted against us and why?"

"Maharaj, I feel ashamed to share the names, but many prominent people are involved in it. Our…our own Manaji More! Rahuji Somnath, Gangadharpant, Vasudeopant…"

"That's enough Peshwe… Please stop. I cannot hear any more." Maharaj who was standing so far, sat on his seat.

"These so-called loyal servants, who stayed behind took advantage of Maharaj being engaged in the campaign against the Portuguese and used their brains to plot against the kingdom." The Peshwe himself was heartbroken to share the news.

"For what reason? What was their motive?" Maharaj composed himself and listened to their plan. This was the third conspiracy against him.

"These people want to induct Ramraje on the royal throne and take control of the kingdom. I have investigated the matter thoroughly. I am quite sure that someone very powerful is behind this plot. But we haven't found that person yet."

"Nilopant, please go and bring Ramraje here." Maharaj said.

"Ji. As you wish." Nilopant made an obeisance and left.

Nilopant came with Ramraje and Yesaji Dabhade. Ramraje, who had just matured into a young man, looked fair but delicate. He had a freshly sprouted moustache. Maharaj approached him. Ramraje was about to make an obeisance to him; Maharaj held his hands and ushered him to a seat and sat next to him.

Raje enquired about Tarau and gently asked him, "Ramraje, can I ask you something?"

"Ji. Why is Dada Maharaj so tense today? I know that our kingdom is surrounded by enemies from all sides. Like Harajiraje, I would also like to go on a campaign. I am not a child anymore!" Ramraje spoke just like his Matoshri, but his expressions and words were innocent.

"Sure, I will send you on a campaign at the right time. If I don't do it, Goddess Jagadamba will!" It was confirmed that Ramraje had no clue about the conspiracy. Maharaj struggled with himself for some time.

"Yesaji, take Ramraje with you. You have a great responsibility of taking care of him. Some of my men will accompany you from now on." Yesaji Dabhade was ordered. After he left with Ramraje, Nilopant was ordered, "Peshwe, send royal orders to capture Manaji, Rahuji and other conspirators at sight, and find out with caution who is the 'powerful' man behind the plot." Raje's heart was in turmoil.

The intensely cold season began. Akbar and Kulesh scheduled meetings in the Fonda, Bhimgad, Mardangad region and finalized the accord with the Portuguese.

The main conditions of the accord were – the Portuguese should not permit the Mughal ships to travel through their ports. Both durbars should release the political prisoners they had detained. Free trade should be permitted in both regions. Raje should not raise any forts at the borders of the Portuguese region. The final negotiations of the accord took place on Mardangad. Raje sent Akbar, Ray Kiran Singh and Mahadaji Naik to Panaji to sign the accord.

The Portuguese viceroy sent a letter of peace with the Mughal Prince Akbar to Raje. He had written, "Raje should comply with the conditions in the accord. We will follow the accord strictly. Free trade should be permitted between both durbars and mainly; 'peace' should prevail in the region." The viceroy who had launched a sudden attack on Fonda, was saying this. To comply with the conditions of the accord, Raje withdrew his forces from Vasai. The people of Vasai were relieved from the clutches of the Mavala army but were stricken by disease. The epidemic of plague engulfed Vasai.

Raje summoned Prahladpant who was dealing with the British durbar.

"Nyayadhish, the accord with the British..."

"Ji. I have finalized it and handed it to their envoy." Prahladpant let out a sigh and started sharing, "Two important conditions are included in the accord – one is the approval to build warehouses in the Karnataka region and the second is maintaining amiable relations with the Maratha kingdom."

Raje listened calmly to all conditions of the accord that the Nyayadhish was sharing with him. Then he asked, "Will the British comply with this accord, Pant? What do you think?"

"Ji. The British viceroy has agreed that they will comply with the accord strictly. Word is that Viceroy Keigwin is travelling back to his country to present the documents of the accord to their king. An officer named Grantham has travelled from Surat to take his place."

Pondering the British, Raje came in front of Prahladpant. The shawl on pant's chest shook imperceptibly.

"Nyayadhish, you seem a little unwell. You have been under

a lot of stress while finalizing the accord with the British envoy." Raje said to Prahladpant affectionately.

"Ji. It's nothing big. Just that I cannot bear the cold since the Siddi pirates attacked me on the sea when I was coming back from Mumbai."

"You deal with politics every day, pant! You are the Nyayadish. You need to be in good health to deliver justice. The Mughal forces have retreated from our kingdom. You should rest."

"Ji." Prahladpant said and left. He was lost in deep thought.

Chapter 14

Raje was informed that Nilopant's personal secretary had come to visit him. This was unusual; the personal secretary had never come to visit Raje before. Wondering what was wrong, Raje granted him permission to come in. He stuttered in fear, "Dhani wants to meet you, but he cannot come here, Maharaj."

"Why? What happened to Peshwe?"

"He is tossing and turning in his bed with severe stomach pain." The personal secretary responded.

"What?" His words had pierced Maharaj's ears like an arrow.

He took Raya, Anta, Khandoji, Purusha and Jotyaji with him and went to the Mantribadi. The colony was excited to hear of Maharaj's arrival. In this colony the residences of Surnis, Dabir, Nyayadhish and Amatya were built in a line. Every residence had armed surveillance.

Nilopant's brother, Gangadhar Moreshwar approached Raje. Raje entered the residence with him. Though in pain, Nilopant tried to get up to make an obeisance to Raje. Raje stepped forward and made him lie down. He sat near Nilopant and enquired about his health. Peshwe closed his eyes in severe pain and exclaimed, "Swami, this stomachache has occurred at such a wrong time."

"Pant, take rest till you feel better. Until then, Gangadharpant will handle your official duties." Raje consoled the Peshwe.

After Raje returned from the Mantribadi, Changoji Katkar

presented a man in front of Raje. He was from Karvar; his name was Santaji Pawala.

"Dhani, with the help of your army, we suppressed the revolt of Ram Dalavi in Karvar." Santaji reported and made an obeisance. Maharaj's face lit up to hear the news.

The hot days of summer arrived. In the middle of summer, Aurangzeb besieged Bijapur from all sides. The Bijapur fort had a huge trench around it. Taking advantage of that, the Adil Shahi army staunchly defended the fort. Qutub Shahi sent thirty thousand auxiliary forces to Bijapur's defence. Now the attention of the three kingdoms and the Mughals of Delhi was focused on Bijapur. This was the place where Shahajiraje had been shackled and paraded on the streets. It was here, in Badi Begum's durbar that Afzal Khan had picked up the betel leaf and vowed to 'present Seva alive or dead'. And to protect such Adil Shahi, Hambirarao was galloping around Bijapur with his cavalry. Melgiri Pandit was working as a mediator.

In the court room of Raje's personal palace, Kulesh presented a bearded person named Gangadhar Nagnath who had come from Harsul. Introducing him to Raje, Kulesh said, "Bade Swami had got Netajirao purified. This poor man should be purified too."

Gangadhar Nagnath was a Mughal servant from Harsul. He was a Brahmin who had been forcefully converted to Islam. He had travelled a long distance and come to Raigad to get himself purified and reconverted to the Hindu fold.

"Maharaj have mercy on me. Help me become a Hindu again." He exclaimed as he sobbed and fell in front of Raje. Raje came forward and pulled him up; patted his back and asked Kulesh, "Chhandogamatya, what can we do to get him reconverted?"

"Ji. He will have to seek atonement first. After that he can enter the Hindu fold by performing the prescribed reconversion ceremony."

"Explain the ritual to him. Perform his reconversion ceremony under the guidance of Moreshwar Panditrao." Raje patted Gangadhar's drooping shoulders to comfort him. He was thinking about something.

'Why do only my people have to face forceful conversion? Netaji was the Sarnoubat yet he suffered the same fate. This simple man could be reconverted because he reached here. What about others who cannot or dare not come here? Why don't I feel like forcefully converting the Mughals, Portuguese, British, and Siddi prisoners in my custody?' Maharaj was lost in thought for quite a long time. He didn't even realize that Kulesh and Gangadhar had left.

Raje summoned Gangadhar Moreshwar, who had recently taken charge as the Peshwa and instructed him about the concessions to be given to the ryots in the Choul region.

To keep the Siddis in check, he said to Gangadhar Moreshwar, "Peshwe, dispatch letters of new appointees to Janjira fort. Appoint competent men like Mankoji at Khanderi, Udaji Padwal and Subhanji Kharade at Sagargad, and Bhivaji Gujar at Kulaba fort. Instruct them to reach the places of their appointment at the earliest."

Gangadhar Moreshwar was listening to Maharaj's instructions attentively. Maharaj realized that he wanted to say something important. He stopped talking and asked, "How is Nilopant doing now?"

"Ji. He is doing better since yesterday. He will have to take more rest. I wanted to tell you…" Gangadhar hesitated, as the news was serious.

"Go ahead. What is it?" Raje had no idea what he was going to tell.

"From Karnataka…the news of Tanjavur…"

"What news? Go ahead." Raje's forehead puckered.

"Ekoji Maharaj's son, Arjunji has left Thanjavur and defected to the Mughals!"

Raje exclaimed 'Jagadamb' and got up from his seat. His face was in pain, as if stung by a scorpion. His heart was numb.

Aurangzeb moved his entire encampment from Nagar to Solapur to keep Bijapur within reach.

Qutub Shah had sent Aurangzeb a letter in an effort to reach a compromise. Aurangzeb put forth two significant conditions in response to that letter. The first condition was, Qutub Shah who had given him a tribute of twenty lakh Pagodas previously, should now pay him one crore twenty lakh Pagodas. The second condition was to dismiss the Hindu sardars Akkanna and Madanna from the Qutub Shahi durbar immediately. Those were not just conditions but a direct warning that very soon his army was going to fall upon Golconda.

Aurangzeb's single move of withdrawing his forces from the Maratha kingdom, drastically changed the scenario. The Adil Shahi king was a young child and there were a lot of disputes among the sardars. Aurangzeb took advantage of the messed-up situation and charged upon the vulnerable Adil Shahi sultanate. Qutub Shahi and the Maratha kingdom were striving to defend it.

In Konkan, Sachiv Ramchandrapant was tied up in crushing the uprising of the vatandars. He didn't even have time to come to Raigad. Therefore, Raje summoned Shankaraji Narayan, and appointed him as the new Sachiv.

Just like the matter of reconversion, another matter was pricking at Raje's heart. The Siddis and the British were trafficking flocks of vulnerable and helpless Bhillas, fishermen and shepherds from the Varghat of Baglan to Karvar as slaves to distant places via the sea. It was as if these people had no saviour. It was crucial to stop this. Therefore, Raje summoned the newly appointed Shankaraji Narayan.

"Shankaraji, the Siddis and the British purchase the people from Varghat as slaves and sell them in distant places. Do you have any idea why these people go with them?" This was an unexpected query for Shankaraji.

"Ji. They pay the custom duty of three Pagodas per head for the slaves. The poor, food-deprived people are ready to become their slaves for even such a small amount!"

"Three Pagodas for one person! Shankaraji, instruct our subedars in this region to connect with such tribes and recruit them in our army. Even though these people prefer slavery to the military service and are ready to go faraway, charge the custom duty of twelve Pagodas per head to the buyer!" Raje spoke determinedly. Shankaraji left to implement the order immediately.

'Slavery! The biggest blemish on humanity! People are sold like animals and timber and live a life like bulls tied to an oil mill. Where did these Siddis and British come from? They purchase the local people without any qualms. Where should the slaves seek shelter?

Lost in thought, restless Maharaj was pacing back and forth in his chamber. Just then Jotyaji Kesarkar entered the chamber with Balraje. As soon as he placed Balraje on the floor, he rushed to Raje and clasped his legs. Raje affectionately picked him up, stroked his back and said, "It is good that you are nobody's slave."

Balraje did not understand the meaning of the word 'slave'. He stared at his Aaba in confusion.

"Jotyaji, why are you not speaking?" Raje realized that Jotyaji was quiet for a long time and asked him.

"Ji, it's nothing related to us, but I have heard some news this morning."

"What news?" Raje stopped stroking Balraje's back and asked.

"… word is, in Bhaganagar, the Qutub Shahi sardars provoked by Aurangzeb killed Akkanna and Madanna; stabbed them in public!"

Raje felt as if struck by lightning to hear the news.

Since Aabasaheb's time with the mediation of Akkanna and Madanna, the Marathi kingdom had maintained an amiable relationship with Golconda.

The monsoon commenced; rain showers would start anytime unannounced. Aurangzeb's army was putting pressure on Adil Shahi. Melgiri Pandit had returned from Bijapur after meeting Sarja Khan and Sikandar Shah. He had brought a message from Sarja Khan seeking immediate aid.

Now there was no option left, but to send shrewd and expert politician Kulesh to Adil Shahi. Raje summoned Kulesh and said, "Chhandogamatya, Adil Shahi is not going to survive without our military aid.

"I am thinking of going in person to defend Adil Shahi." Kulesh was ready to shoulder the onus even before Raje asked him.

"You have spoken my mind, Kulesh. Descend the fort today and march towards Panhala. Take the auxiliary forces there with you and travel to the Adil Shahi sultanate. Prince Azam's army might clash with you in the Miraj region.

"Ji. I will descend the fort today." Kulesh accepted the order and left.

Raje stationed the forces of Hambirarao and Kulesh through the region of Miraj, Solapur, Akluj and Indapur region in support of Adil Shahi.

The fort was getting drenched in rain showers. Raje's mind was flooded with thoughts. Meanwhile, a ship had reached the Surat harbour with a letter from the London durbar. The London officers had clearly mentioned in that letter, "You must join hands with king Shambhuji and build a close friendship with the pugnacious king. You will not have to fear the Mughal or Portuguese then. Do not allow the Siddis or the Mughals to come close to Mumbai. We have sent guns and gunpowder to fulfil the accord made with him. If needed, take more materials from the sea fort of Madras."

Beyond the sea, the London durbar had recognized the power of Raje's strength, but many of his own relatives and country men had not understood it! The London durbar had called Raje 'a pugnacious king'.

Nilopant and Prahladpant came to meet Raje.

As soon as he recovered from the stomach ache, Nilopant went with Prahlad Niraji to Vanapur for negotiations with the Brtisih envoy Richard Stanley. Nilopant reported the details of the negotiations with Stanley to Raje, "Maharaj, this envoy is complaining that our subedar charges taxes to the British traders."

"Peshwe, these are the octroi duties. This is their usual complaint."

"Ji. I have warned the British envoy about it. Now, they are afraid to build more warehouses and are bickering to pay the taxes. But it seems, he has received some instructions from his bosses. He is speaking in a much humbler manner."

"What was the final result of your negotiations, Peshwe?"

"The British have agreed to keep our envoy in Mumbai. They will also send their envoy to us." Pant glanced at Prahlad Niraji and replied.

"Now, we should not keep the Nyayadhish engaged in the British durbar. Peshwe, send somebody else to Mumbai. What do you say Prahladpant?" Raje sought the advice of the Nyayadhish.

"As you wish. We should train new people as envoys." Prahladpant wondered whether Raje had not liked his plight as the envoy last time.

"We have demanded two guns from the British envoy. He has accepted it, Swami." Peshwe exclaimed with a bright face.

"They will certainly provide the guns to us, Nilopant, but what about the fact that they provide support to the Siddis and the Mughals?" Raje asked a direct question.

"The British have already banished the Siddis. The British

envoy says that the Siddis are entering our territory in the sea via Underi. They have also given a strict warning to the Mughal navy recently.

Raje realized that Prahladpant had been quiet for a long time, so he asked, "Nyayadhish, why aren't you speaking? Are you okay?"

"Ji. It's nothing. I am doing fine." His throat was parched as he responded, his eyes fluttered. They both made an obeisance and left.

Khandoji Ballal came to visit Raje with a letter from Santaji Nimbalkar, the Hawaldar of Vichitragad. The matter was related to Sarjerao Jedhe of Kari. The Jedhe family of Kari had been serving the Maratha kingdom since the time of Kanhoji Jedhe.

When Aurangzeb descended in the Deccan, Jedhe had a change of heart! Family feuds divided the family. Sarjerao Jedhe's brother Shivaji Jedhe, defected to the Mughals. He abducted Sarjerao's cattle and destroyed his territory.

The case was within the jurisdiction of Swaraj, but Sarjerao Jedhe also sought justice from the Mughals. He sent Santaji Nimbalkar, the Hawaladar of Vichitragad to the Mughal officer in Shirval as his mediator and tried hard to solve the conflict with his brother. Raje was notified about this case of the Jedhe family.

Khandoji started reading the letter of Santaji Nimbalkar defending Sarjerao's position – "… My loyalties lie with his highness, Swami. If Swami could be so generous as to grant me pardon and hand over my office of Deshmukh to me, I will serve him with loyalty."

As Raje heard the hypocritical words of Jedhe, the vein on his forehead started throbbing. He walked briskly and said, "Chitnis, take your quill. Note down the matter I dictate and dispatch the letter immediately.

Khandoji got ready and Maharaj started dictating the letter as if Sarjero Jedhe was standing in front of him, "… You sent a letter at the hands of Santaji Nimbalkar, the Hawaladar of Vichitragad stating that your brother Shivaji Jedhe had defected to the Mughals in Shirval. He abducted your cattle. He was going to torment you further, and hence you went to Shirwal yourself. Nevertheless, your loyalties lie with me… therefore I am sending you this order.

"First of all, you yourself behaved deceitfully. Despite being the vatandar of Swaraj, you did not serve Swaraj with honesty. You have been in the service of Swaraj, but instead of reporting the problem to your Swami, you went to the Mughal officer whom you don't know well. Your brother defected to the enemy. Had you come to me and reported his treachery to me, it would have proved your loyalty towards me. But you did not do it. If you still want to stay with the enemy, then go ahead and do as you please. Your actions have shown your lack credibility. You better keep in mind that at my command, my soldiers will slay you too, along with the enemy.

"If you still want to serve me truthfully, send me your complaint in writing. Better not take your grievances to somebody else.

"Once your loyalty to me is determined, I will send you my instructions and you must implement them honestly."

Khandoji sprinkled a pinch of sand on the envelope and sealed it.

"Swami, in response to the Peshwa's attack on the warehouses of Dharangaon in Khandesh, the British of Mumbai have changed their approach." Khandoji reported another piece of news.

"What is their changed approach, Khandoji?" Raje was vexed.

"They are trying to conquer our coastal region, but our mariners are quite vigilant."

Raje let out a deep sigh of relief.

"There is news from Choul. The Siddis are attacking Choul

at many places. Bajaji, the son of Pilaji the barber, launched a strong attack on the Underi island of the Siddis. It has upset the Siddis and they have infiltrated Choul and slain many locals.

Khandoji was dispirited to share the news and Maharaj was heartbroken to hear it.

The face of his loyal soldier, Siddi Mistri, who had been abducted by the Siddis and killed in Mumbai, lingered before Raje's eyes.

The traders coming for the yatra in the Chaphal ashram of Samartha were lodging complaints. They were being charged with exorbitant taxes. It was necessary to stop the exploitation. Therefore, Raje summoned Moreshwar Panditrao with his Chitnis. "Pandit, what is the problem at the Chaphal ashram?" Raje asked Moreshwar.

"Ji. The problem of the ashram management remains unresolved. Uddhav Gosavi indulges in arbitrary administration. He provokes the civil officers, and they levy exorbitant taxes on the traders coming there for business." Moreshwar reported the situation in the Chaphal ashram. His own heart was also heavy while reporting the deplorable state of the ashram after Samartha's demise.

Raje was concerned. He looked at the Chitnis and said, "Write a letter of warning to the Deshadhikari of Karhad, Rango Vishwanath and Ambaji Moradeo of Satara."

Raje started dictating the letter to the Chitnis, "I am in receipt of a complaint about the yatra in honour of Lord Rama conducted at the Chaphal ashram. It has been brought to my notice that you are not taking proper measures with regard to the said yatra. All tax received should be collected at Singanvadi without fail. The civil officers are levying exorbitant taxes on the traders. Such an attitude would affect the yatra. This should be avoided as far as possible. The yatra should be conducted as before, under the guidance of Divakar Gosavi. Uddhav Gosavi has no right to meddle in administrative activities. There is a temple of Lord Hanuman at Shahapur. Krishnaji Patil of Wahgaon and the temple priest, usurp the revenue of that temple. You should give them a strict warning. If Patil continues to usurp it, seize his Inam and hand it over to Divakar Gosavi." Raje gave his decision about every minor matter of the ashram, but his mind was occupied in Samartha's memories.

Due to the military activities during the last four-five years, the farmlands at many places had turned barren. In addition to that, drought had struck the region recently. The peasants of the region were concerned about their livelihood. It was crucial to support them and bring the farmlands back under cultivation.

Hambirarao who was covering the territory around Bijapur had sent many messengers and requested for more auxiliary forces. Raje summoned Nagoji Ballal and sent the auxiliary forces in the direction of Bijapur.

Maharaj was unsettled ever since Bahirji had delivered the news of the encounter in Ramghat. Khem Sawant of Kudal had defected to the Portuguese and was plundering the region around Goa with their aid. Ram Dalavi of Sonda had provided him with fifteen thousand soldiers; he was plundering the Karvar region.

Raje was pondering how to handle the challenge of the Desais and Dalavis in Konkan. Just then, Prahlad Niraji came to visit Raje. Two men from Choul, Vithoji Bapuji and Govind Narayan accompanied him. They made an obeisance to Raje.

"Swami, a great injustice has been done to these two men. Suryaji Visaji Prabhu coerced them to sign the deed of ownership, and usurped their properties." Prahladpant reported the details of the case.

Vithoji and Govind joined their hands in prayer and started pleading their case – "Please serve justice to us. Don't abandon us."

"Nyayadhish, who is the Deshadhikari of Choul?" Raje asked pant.

"Ji. Yesaji Anant."

"Send him an official order immediately to revoke the deed of ownership signed by them under duress. Who was the Deshadhikari when this deed was signed?"

"Hari Shivadeo Maharaj." Prahladpant had not expected Maharaj to probe so deeply.

"Nyayadhish, give him a strict warning – Vithoji Bapuji and Govind Narayan have approached me. I have heard the case of usurpation. You are the subedar! How could you be only a bystander and support Suryaji at the same time. Your actions betray your attitude. Seizing someone's property by force and handing it to another is no public service!" Furious Raje instructed Prahladpant how to warn Hari Shivadeo.

On the one hand, Raje was taking great pains to serve justice to his defenceless ryots and on the other, with misty eyes, Goddess Bhavani of Tuljapur was witnessing the event in Aurangzeb's huge encampment in Solapur. But she could only watch.

Aurangzeb's luxurious shamiana suspended by silk ropes was fluttering in the cool breeze of winter. The green pennant with the moon and the star was fluttering atop it. Tents of sixty thousand soldiers were spread across the plateau. Armed soldiers were guarding an elephant. The elephant was swaying at leisure clinking his fetters.

Inside the shamiana, prominent men such as Mohammed Azam, Muijuddin, Bedar Bakht, Ranamast Khan stood in line looking at the ground. Aurangzeb sat on a high seat. A group of maulanas was sitting on his left.

Surrounded by forty to fifty horse riders, two horse riders astride two magnificent Arabian stallions approached the shamiana. The guards made an obeisance to them. Both entered the shamiana and made an obeisance to the emperor three times. Aged Aurangzeb was intently watching the lofty, young man. The other old man stepped forward. He picked up the platter placed to the right of the emperor and held it in front of him. The emperor touched the platter with the hand he was holding his rosary in. The person who had held the platter was Wazir Asad Khan. He picked up the green Khilat from the platter and placed it on the shoulder of the young sardar who had come with him. The brocade design of the moon and the star on the attire sparkled. The young sardar bowed and made an obeisance to Aurangzeb again. He was bestowed with the mansab of five thousand cavalry, and rewarded with the things placed outside the shamiana along with the elephant. The big man was shackled by the gift of the elephant. He was Achaloji Mahadik! Aabasaheb's son-in-law's brother!

Raje didn't even get enough time to feel hurt at the news of Achloji's defection; Siddi Qasam of Janjira became active again. He sent his soldiers to infiltrate Choul, Rajapur and massacred people mercilessly. He left Janjira and fell upon Kalyan via the sea. Furthermore, in the Dabhol harbour, his naval attack on the troops of Govindaji Kanho, resulted in the death of Govindaji.

Prominent places of Adil Shahi were falling one by one. The land fort of Miraj was a mighty fort, but the custodian of the fort, Asad Khan, surrendered it to Ranamast and Ruhulla Khan. As soon as they captured the Miraj fort, in the Kolhapur–Panhala region, the military activities of the Mughals increased. Hambirarao was fighting alone, travelling from Panhala to the Adil Shahi region of Hukkeri, to defend the Adil Shahi sultanate.

Perturbed by bad news from all sides, Raje came to his personal chamber. Yesubai realized that he had been quiet for a long time and said, "A messenger has come from the Patgaon ashram. The news is, Mounibaba has been taken ill."

Raje looked at Yesubai in surprise. He didn't say anything. During all this time of turmoil, he had been unable to take darshan of Mounibaba, Moraya Gosavi, or Malharbaba. He felt guilty about it. Raya and Anta came in with Balraje. Balraje called her 'Masaheb' and clung to her. Raje remembered Thoralya Aau as he witnessed the affection between the mother and son.

Raje came to the court hall; Mhalojibaba Ghorpade's young son, Santaji who had come from the Panhala region approached him. Hambirarao had sent him. Recently, Hambirarao had been engaged in a fierce battle with Ranamast and Ruhulla Khan near Panhala. Santaji reported the news of the battle to Raje and said, "The Sarlashkar has forced both Khans to retreat in the direction of Belgaum. He has sent a message to Murad Khan, the custodian of the fort of Belgaum to defend the fort resolutely."

As Maharaj looked at Santaji's spirited face, and heard the news he had brought, Maharaj felt satisfied. Raje approached Santaji, patted his shoulder and asked him, "How is our Mhalojibaba and Fort Panhala?"

"Ji. Aaba has gone to Kapashi – to our village. And the fort is under my control for now."

In the pouring rain, covered in a coarse blanket, a messenger sent by Nilkanth Naryan of Kudal, climbed up Raigad. The letter he had brought read, "The Mughal mariner, Yakut Khan, has sent a message to Khemsawant – come and join hands with the emperor. He will reward you as graciously as he rewarded Arjunji and Achaloji." Nilkanth Narayan was the Deshadhikari of Kudal. He had astutely sent the detailed news of Yakut Khan's association with Khemsawant.

Raje's mind was overwhelmed with countless thoughts. He felt as if surrounded by something ominous. He was not talking to anyone freely.

The month of Shravan was over. The royal durbar of Raigad was in session. Maharaj sat on the royal throne. His face looked solemn. The eight ministers stood near the eight pillars. Young Shivajiraje sat on the first step of the royal throne. Chhandogamatya Kulesh stood next to him. Many prominent men such as Rupaji, Krishanji Naras Prabhu, Yesaji, Mhalojibaba, Santaji – Dhanaji, Janrao, Baradmal stood in their places. Though packed with people, a grim silence prevailed in the durbar.

The reason was obvious. One of the three kingdoms had fallen. The Adil Shahi sultanate had lost Bijapur. Young Sikandar had surrendered himself to Aurangzeb. Aurangzeb sat in a howdah on an embellished royal elephant, surrounded by soldiers wielding bare swords, and paraded through Bijapur to celebrate the victory. A proclamation was issued in the city – "The people of Bijapur are now under the control of the Delhi durbar. No one will be persecuted. Everyone should pledge their allegiance to the Mughal sultanate."

As soon as Raje received the news, he convened the durbar, to discuss the gravity of the situation.

Everyone assumed that as usual Nilopant would commence the durbar, but that did not happen. Maharaj firmly pressed both his hands on the hand rests of the royal throne and himself spoke – "All of you know… Adil Shahi collapsed." Maharaj exhaled deeply and emptied his lungs.

"To keep Aurangzeb occupied, I left no stone unturned to defend the throne with which our kingdom had an intriguing relationship. Our kingdom is now going to face more challenges. Word is, that the Mughal army will now march in the direction of Golconda. But it could be a ruse. That is why I have summoned all of you. Whoever wants to speak their mind, feel free to speak up. You all know, to raise this kingdom, countless soldiers have sacrificed their lives, including Aabasaheb. This kingdom does not belong to me alone; it belongs to Mother Jagadamba, to Thoralya Aau and Aabasaheb who gave their all to it, to the people who work hard in the forests and the soldiers who fight from Khandesh – Varad to Jinji. Now the onus is on us to protect it with our lives." Maharaj wanted to speak so much more; he rose from his seat.

Everyone in the durbar was listening to him intently.

Hambirarao saw Raje and remembered his Thorale Dhani when he had surrendered to Mirza Raja and had gone to meet him in his camp. His clear voice echoed in the durbar, "Maharaj should not be so worried. Adil Shahi did not collapse on its own. The emperor slyly took advantage of the feud between the Pathan sardars and brought it down. As long as I am here, I will not let even a single Mughal soldier stay back in our kingdom. All these crooks and scoundrels who are abandoning the kingdom for the sake of the Khilat today, will come to know tomorrow what a thorny path they have chosen. Maharaj should rest assured. I am with you." Hambirarao's robust words comforted the entire durbar.

"I am keeping a vigilant watch on the brutes in the coastal region of Konkan. I will make sure, even at the cost of my life that they do not join hands with the Mughals." Ramchandrapant seconded the Sarlashkar. Dharmaji Nagnath showed his approval by nodding his head. The durbar that had fallen silent now began to open up.

"I will support the kingdom in every possible way like I have been doing so far. I am ready to do anything for the sake of the kingdom." For the first time, Khandoji Ballal stood up from the seat of the Chitnis and showed his support.

"I take the responsibility of keeping the Portuguese under control with the aid of the Mughal Prince, Akbar; I will also connect with the zamindars and make sure they stay on Raja Saab's side. Raja Saab should not be worried about the Panhala, Khelana and Malakapur region." Kulesh expressed his support. Nyayadhish Prahladpant standing near a pillar and a few ministers became restless on hearing his words.

Hambirarao spoke up candidly now, "I don't understand much of politics. Maharaj should forgive me for speaking my mind." Hambirarao hesitated.

"Go ahead Sarlashkar, you are family. Feel free to speak your mind."

"Forgive me Maharaj…but that Mughal prince is of no use to us now. In fact, the Mughal emperor might try to take advantage of his living in our kingdom and charge upon us. The Chhandogamtya should let go of him now and…"

Now the entire durbar's eyes were focused on Hambirarao. Only Hambirarao could dare to say things that others could not express in front of the durbar. He could do it because of his age, experience and thanks to the sacrifices he had made for the kingdom.

"What do you want to say Mama Saheb? Say it openly." Raje gave him the permission to speak freely.

Today, for the first time Hambirarao broke protocol and abruptly cleared his throat before speaking in the durbar. He threw a fearless glance at the seven ministers around him and the Chhandogamatya. The seven ministers, Kulesh, the courtiers, and Maharaj himself, stared at Hambirarao.

"Maharaj, this matter doesn't fall under my authority, but somebody needs to say this sometime or the other. I have spilled my blood for this royal throne of Thorale Maharaj; that is why I am saying this – I have heard that there is a discord between the ministers, the civil officers and Chhandogamatya Kaviji!"

All the ministers standing near their pillars, looked at each other in shock. Kulesh's face went pale; a painful expression manifested on his face, and he lowered his head.

"What kind of discord, Sarlashkar?" Maharaj's forehead puckered.

"I have come to know that since the Chhandogamatya is from Kanauj, none of the ministers were ready to dine with him! He also does not mingle with anyone. Many people don't like his closeness with Maharaj. At this difficult time, this problem should be solved right away." The ministers felt that they would rather face Hambirarao on the battlefield than deal with his sharp words.

Prahladpant spoke firmly, "What Sarlashkar says is right. The Chhandogamatya does not mingle with anyone. He considers himself more special than the other ministers. He thinks he is Maharaj's confidant. He invites everyone for feasts at his residence, but no one goes there."

As the Chhandogamatya heard his words, he shook in anger and exclaimed, "Sarkar, the Nyayadhish is lying! Is it my fault that I was born in Kanauj? I have dedicated my loyalties to Raja Saab and I will be loyal to him till my last breath. Why should I be concerned about any of the ministers?" Kulesh couldn't speak properly in anger.

At that moment, a melee of many conflicting thoughts arose in Maharaj's mind. He was utterly saddened when he realised that while he was planning for the future his ministers were holding grudges against each other.

"I am proud of the Sarlashkar." Raje glanced over Hambirarao and the ministers. "This is such a difficult time, yet my ministers are fighting over their own prestige. I bestowed the title of Chhandogamtya upon Kulesh and appointed him as the 'Kulekhtyar' because he had the expertise, and he could speak the Hindustani language fluently! If Kavi Bhushan were in my durbar, I would have honoured him too with the title of 'Chhandogamatya'."

Raje's heart broke to see the ministers standing with heads bowed. He threw a sharp glance at Kulesh and said, "It is a mistake to say that you need not be concerned with any of the ministers! Sarlashkar is right. This issue should be solved right away. If I ever hear of such contentions again, I will not spare anyone!" The tip of Maharaj's nose flushed in anger; he stood up unwittingly. The entire durbar looked at him. A different expression manifested on his face. Words as sharp as the edge of the sword trickled from his mouth, "I don't even have time to worry about the fall of Adil Shahi. I am making a final declaration to all who are present here that I am going to do everything possible in my power to defend this kingdom of Aabasaheb. All of you should behave conscientiously and give me your support. Keep your egos aside now and speak about dealing with the problem we are facing currently."

Hambirarao broke the silence and said, "We should now try to save Golconda with all our might. All our eastern posts should remain vigilant through days and nights. We should keep our cavalry circulating around Golconda."

"The king of Bijapur is still a child. Hasan Shah of Golconda is a young lad. Qutub Shahi will not surrender in front of Aurangzeb." Nilopant expressed his opinion.

"Peshwe, it is only speculation that the Mughals will fall upon Qutub Shahi. It will not necessarily happen. There's a possibility that he might launch an attack on our kingdom claiming that we have given refuge to the Mughal Prince." Prahladpant seconded Hambirarao's opinion that seeking Akbar's assistance is not a good policy. Now the real discussion about the problem started.

For a long time, the courtiers discussed the problem; one thing was clear. Everyone realized that the fall of Adil Shahi was a big setback to the alliance of the kingdoms in the Deccan.

It was also evident that the ministers and Kulesh had reservations about each other. It became apparent that many people, including Hambirarao thought of Akbar as an obstacle that could cause more problems for the kingdom.

Raje had relieved Ramchandrapant from the office of Surnis and had assigned to him the responsibility of the Konkan coast. He wondered if Pant was displeased by his decision, so he asked, "Pant, I appointed Shankaraji in your place in the office of Surnis. Are you upset by my decision?"

"Ji. Not at all. I know that Swami has appointed me to deal with the grave challenge of the rebellion in the coastal region of Konkan. The task of fulfilling this responsibility is quite agonizing. I cannot share the details of the incidents taking place over there."

"What do you mean? Ramchandrapant, please be clear." Maharaj gazed at Ramchandrapant.

"Ji. Please forgive me, but...but our informers have captured a rider with the letter he was going to deliver to Khemsawant of Kudal."

"Letter from whom?

"Ji... ji..." Ramchandrapant took out the roll of paper from the fold of his shawl, but he could not speak the name of the person.

Raje snatched the roll from Pant's hands. As he quickly browsed through the letter, his face flushed, and drops of sweat gathered on his face.

Referring to the fall of Adil Shahi, Aabasaheb's son-in-law, Raje's brother-in-law, Mahadaji Naik-Nimbalkar of Faltan, had written to Khemsawant of Kudal – "Adil Shahi collapsed in front of the emperor of Delhi like a clod of earth. Sambhaji too will not be spared! After the Bhaganagar campaign the emperor of Delhi will certainly deal with him. I will join you with ten thousand cavalry. All military posts up to Rayari will be thoroughly equipped."

The letter in Raje's hand started shaking; his nostrils flared in rage. He thrust the letter back in Pant's hands and muttered, "Ungrateful traitors."

Ramchandrapant lowered his head and reported as it was his duty – "A similar letter has been written by the Mughal sardar, Sheikh Mohammed Bakshi.. he has told Sawant..."

Raje wanted to close both his ears. He did not utter a word and started walking from Maha Darwaja to the Dussehra chowk. Ramchandrapant, Changoji Katkar, Khandoji, Raya and Anta followed him. He saw Moreshwar Panditrao and Nilopant walking hastily towards the Maha Darwaja, so he stopped.

Moreshwar pointed to a person clad in a saffron cloak and said to Raje, "He has come from Patgaon..." Panditrao glanced at Peshwe and paused. He licked his parched lips.

"He is the disciple from the Patgaon ashram." Nilopant also paused.

"Peshwe, why did you trouble him so much? He is already tired after climbing the fort. I would have met him in the court hall. Baba, how is Mounibaba doing? Is he unhappy that I did not come to visit him in a long time?" Raje asked the disciple.

With every word of Maharaj, tears trickled down the disciple's eyes onto his cloak. He barely managed to speak, "Mounibaba has left his body, Maharaj! He breathed his last at Patgaon near Bhudargad."

'Jagadamb' Raje exclaimed, touched his hand to his chest and closed his eyes. Many images of tranquil ascetic Mounibaba lingered in front of his closed eyes.

After the fall of Bijapur, the Mughal forces dispersed in the surrounding region of Pandharpur, Sangola and Mangalvedha. All the sardars of the Bijapur sultanate including Commander Sarja Khan teamed up with Aurangzeb.

Aurangzeb appointed his sardars to keep watch around Bijapur with armed forces and left Bijapur. He marched towards Solapur.

Harajiraje was sending frequent messengers from Karnataka. As Raje had speculated, Aurangzeb started bribing the sardars in Karnataka and posting his sardars with armed forces near the borders.

Raje summoned Keso Trimal and Santaji Ghorpade to send them to the aid of Harajiraje. Raje who was thinking about the fort of Jinji said to them, "Kesopant, take Santaji with you and go to Karnataka with your forces to assist Harajiraje. Since the demise of Raghunathpant, Harajiraje has been managing the entire region alone. Jaitaji Katkar and Kakade are working with him. You are like Raghunathpant to them. All of you defend Karnataka collectively." Raje offered the robes of honour to Keso Trimal and Santaji and bade farewell to them as they were leaving to join Harajiraje in Karnataka.

Peshwe came to visit Maharaj with Qutub Shah's envoy who had come from Bhaganagar. He was accompanied by a few attendants carrying covered platters in their hands.

"Maharaj, the royal envoy of Qutub Shah has requested an audience with you." Nilopant introduced the envoy to Raje who sat in the court hall. The envoy made an obeisance to Raje, and conveyed the message of his royal highness Tana Shah, "My lord sends the gift of one lakh hons to Raja Saab." The envoy glanced at the attendants accompanying him. They approached Raje and bowed to let him touch the platters and accept the gift. Raje glanced at the platters and the envoy once and gave him an unexpected response – "Nilopant, looks like this is the specialty of the Qutub Shahi sultanate. Madanna and Akkanna who tried hard to maintain amiable relationships with the Maratha kingdom and the Bhaganagar durbar were assassinated in the Qutub Shahi sultanate in public. Why? Only because they were 'infidels' in the eyes of Aurangzeb? And now that it is evident that the same Aurangzeb is soon going to launch an attack on Golconda, I am being offered this gift of one lakh hons. Why? To seek my support for the Qutub Shahi sultanate during these challenging times?"

The Qutub Shahi envoy was unable to answer the question; he glanced at Nilopant expecting him to say something. Nilopant expressed his opinion.

"Swami is right. The Qutub Shahi durbar will soon realize how invaluable Madanna and Akkanna were, but in my opinion, our durbar should not follow the same stubborn attitude that they had shown."

"That is why, I have been supporting the Golconda durbar for a long time. I implemented Aabasaheb's strategy in case of Qutub Shahi and I will continue to follow it." Maharaj observed the gift platters and gave them the customary touch of his hand.

The envoy let out a sigh of relief.

Maharaj offered a return gift to Tana Shah and said, "Tell your Hazrat that I will give full support to Qutub Shahi." Maharaj bade farewell to the envoy.

Maharaj was pondering whom he should send to the aid of Golconda. Just then the fort custodian, Changoji Katkar came to visit him. He announced, "Sundarji Baji from Goa is here to see you."

Maharaj raised his hand and granted permission. Changoji presented Sundarji. Raje mentally prepared himself to hear some kind of bad news such as the Portuguese have plundered the region around Goa, they have forcefully converted villages or the vatandars have defected to them. But he kept his face calm and affectionately enquired about Sundarji, who had travelled far. Sundarji gave a pleasant smile and said, "I travelled this far to deliver special news to Swami."

"Yes, go ahead." Maharaj couldn't guess what he was going to say.

"The ships carrying the prominent people must have sailed from the Panaji harbour by now."

"Who are you talking about?"

"The viceroy Conde-De-Alvor and his family!"

"What do you mean?" Maharaj was surprised.

"The durbar of Portugal received the detailed news of how Swami attacked and made the people of Goa suffer. The durbar had sent a letter to the viceroy and criticized him for the unjustified attacks on the Maratha kingdom. They have demanded the clarification of his actions.

Sundarji was reporting ardently. As Raje heard his words, the image of Krishnaji Kank, lying on a coarse blanket, drenched in blood, looking like a Palash tree lingered in front of his glowing eyes.

"The Portuguese durbar has summoned the viceroy back, Swami. A new viceroy named Dom-Rodrigo-De-Costa has been appointed in his place."

The bluish white waters of the Mandavi creek flashed in front of Raje's shining eyes. He said to Sundarji, "I haven't been receiving any positive news so far. Sundarji, let's go and take the darshan of Lord Jagadishwar. You have brought good news."

Maharaj started walking towards the Jagadishwar temple with Sundarji and Changoji.

At that time, the three of them had no idea that Neknam Khan had captured the fort of Salher in Baglan for Aurangzeb, by bribing some Maratha sardars.

This was the second time Aurangzeb had descended in the Deccan. The first time, he had come here as the subedar of Deccan and returned as a rebellious prince. Now, he had come, the second time, as the emperor of Delhi, to obliterate the entire Deccan. Adil Shahi had crumbled in front of his mighty force.

He had now started making simultaneous moves. On the one hand, he wanted to overthrow Golconda, and on the other, he wanted to capture as much of the region of Karnataka as possible. He had continued to use bribery to crush the Maratha kingdom.

Harajiraje's leading sardars, Gopal Dadaji and Vitthal Pilaji who were equally valiant, kept charging on the Mughal forces that had infiltrated the Karnataka region.

Raje was in the court hall of his palace. He was trying to comprehend the news he had received so far and was dictating letters to Khandoji to be sent to various places. As he was lost in some deep thought, his dictation did not flow freely. Just then, Girjoji came and announced, "The Peshwa is coming."

Soon, Nilopant came with his assistant.

"Maharaj, in the battle of Jaitapur, Siddi Qasam was barely saved, by the grace of his Khuda, and escaped alive." Peshwe reported excitedly.

"Give me the details, Peshwe." The Jaitapur creek lingered in front of Maharaj's eyes. Peshwe shared the details of the battle. Silence prevailed for some time.

"Jedhe wants to come back and serve Swaraj again. He has sent a message to that effect at the hands of Baji Gholap of Purandar." Peshwe broached the topic of Sarjerao Jedhe.

"What is he waiting for, Peshwe?" Raje's face was vexed.

"Maharaj, Jedhe wants a letter of assurance of immunity."

"Letter of assurance of immunity?" Maharaj smiled in despair.

"Pant, Jedhe did not seek immunity from Aurangzeb when he defected to Aurangzeb. What makes this descendant of Kanhoji Jedhe seek immunity now?"

Peshwe didn't know what to say.

"Peshwe, though he abandoned us at the wrong time, I cannot repeat the same mistake. Though he was wrong and deserted us, he was once a loyal servant of the kingdom. Send him the letter of immunity and tell him, 'You defected to the enemy. How did you commit such a mistake? Such a mistake is not to be repeated. You are now suffering in the service of our enemy. Come back to us immediately; your efforts will be rewarded. You are a veteran. You have served the kingdom before. I have faith in you. It is good that you want to come back to us. Don't hesitate to return, and don't worry about the consequences of your earlier actions. Join us without delay. You will be appropriately compensated."

Nilopant was revising the matter in his mind and was about to leave. Raje stopped him and shared a plan with him that had been on his mind for quite some time.

"Pant, send messages to Harajiraje and other prominent sardars and summon them for an important meeting."

Peshwe left, wondering about Maharaj's plan.

Maharaj was pondering the news that had arrived from Mumbai. The envoy of the Maratha kingdom in Mumbai had passed away. Raje summoned Prahladpant to seek his advice about nominating the next envoy. "Nyayadhish, you must have heard the news about our envoy in the British durbar. You were associated with that durbar. Who do you suggest should be appointed as our next envoy?

Prahladpant let out a sigh of relief that he himself had not been assigned the duty.

"In my opinion, Trimbak Gopal would be the right person. He is well acquainted with the interpreters in the British durbar. Besides, he had also visited the durbar with me a couple of times."

Raje and the Nyayadhish discussed Trimbakji's appointment thoroughly.

"Pant, give Trimbakji the official documents of identity as our envoy." Raje declared his decision.

Prahladpant left. Raje thought of taking a round of the armoury, and so he came to change his clothes. One of the attendants placed the Jiretop on his head. As Raje looked at his reflection in the mirror he strongly felt, 'My Jiretop does not look like Aabasaheb's Jiretop; it looks rather like the Mughal kimosh!'

"Bring Aabasaheb's Jiretop out of the storeroom. I would like to take its darshan." Raje exclaimed.

The salver of Thorale Maharaj's Jiretop was brought out of the storeroom and presented in front of Raje. For a moment, Raje imagined Aabasaheb standing in front of him, wearing the Jiretop. Raje touched the Jiretop with his fingers and touched them to his forehead.

Engrossed in the moment, the Chhatrapti didn't realize that someone was calling him, "Swami… Swami…"

"Hmm…" He turned around at once and saw Kavi Kulesh and Devaji Vitthal, the subedar of Rajapur making an obeisance to him.

"You?" He looked at Kulesh and exclaimed in surprise. Kulesh realized that he had broken the protocol and had directly come to the changing rooms to meet Swami. He courteously said, "Forgive me Swami. An urgent matter compelled me to come here."

"What is so urgent?" Raje glanced at Subhedar Devaji Vitthal and asked.

"Ji. What I witnessed should be urgently reported to Sarkar.

Or else, I would have been accused of negligence of duty. Therefore, I have come here directly from Rajapur."

"Go ahead, Devaji. Speak up." A crease appeared on Raje's forehead.

Devaji momentarily glanced at Kulesh, who glanced back at him reassuringly.

"Maharaj, in the creek of Rajapur, the Mughal Prince Akbar boarded a ship and… and sailed for Iran!" Devaji delivered the news.

"He is accompanied by Ziyauddin Mohammed Shujai and fifty men." Kulesh provided additional information.

Many memories of Akbar from his first meeting, swirled in Raje's mind. Countless thoughts erupted in Raje's mind. He asked Devaji calmly, "Subedar, did Durgadas also accompany him?"

"No. He didn't. Durgadas went to Ratlam with his men." As Raje heard it, he let out a sigh of relief. He held Durgadas in high regard. What if he would have also gone to Iran with Akbar under pressure?

"Kaviji, do you think that Shah Abbas of Iran will assist the Mughal Prince? Will both of them charge upon Delhi?" Raje asked Kulesh.

"Impossible Swami! The prince will be digging his own grave in Iran now. No royal family member will be present there to offer final prayers for him."

Though bitter, it was the truth. As he heard it, Raje got lost in thought.

Meanwhile, Keso Trimal and Santaji Ghorpade had reached the northern borders of Jinji with twelve thousand soldiers. Jaitaji Katkar and Gopal Dadaji, who were sent by Harajiraje were receiving them on the outskirts of Jinji. The kettle drums were resounding. Now, with the joint forces of Harjiraje and Keso Trimal, Karnataka was going to fight against Aurangzeb.

Raje met prominent men such as Kulesh, Rupaji, Khandoji

Ballal, Nilopant, Prahladpant, Gopal Pandit who had come from Karnataka, and Dhanaji Jadhav in the secret meeting room on Raigad.

Nilopant commenced the meeting, "Adil Shahi has fallen – the enemy has lured the Adil Shahi sardars to his side and has planned a two-fold attack. On the one hand he has planned to seize the Golconda territory and on the other he intends to conquer our Karnataka region…"

"That is why, I am going to Karnataka in person with the army." Raje took charge of the meeting and glanced at everyone.

"We have to teach Yachappa Nayak of Mysore a lesson. He had assisted Aurangzeb in the siege of Bijapur and is waiting for the right opportunity. I have already sent Keso Trimal and Santaji to aid Harajiraje. Now, I will go in person to support him. Dhanaji, Rupaji, and Khandoji, you will accompany me. Peshwe will judiciously run the kingdom from here under the leadership of Rani Saheb."

Everyone present was listening attentively to Raje.

"Peshwe, dispatch a messenger to Harajiraje at Jinji with the message of my arrival there. Whoever is going to remain behind, should perform their duties diligently. Aurangzeb's forces will try to infiltrate our kingdom; you should try to entrap them and crush them."

The ministers present in the meeting thought that Raje would take Kulesh with him on the Karnataka campaign, but Raje assigned him another critical mission.

"Kulesh, the Portuguese will try to take advantage of the situation after the Mughal prince has left. Keep a keen eye on them."

The meeting continued for a long time. Raje gave detailed instructions to everyone who was going to stay behind. The meeting concluded. Raje left the meeting room basking in the light and the wind. He was thinking about the Karnataka campaign. He had no idea that in Jinji, at the residence of

Harajiraje, an altercation had taken place between Keso Trimal and Harajiraje, leaving the audience terrified. What was the reason for the argument?

Harajiraje had appointed Gopal Dadaji for monitoring the British warehouse at Saint George. Kesopant had replaced him with Chimaji Pandit. As Gopal Dadaji was a strict disciplinarian, his appointment would not have proved beneficial to the British.

The British officers in the St. George warehouse had decided to reward Keso Trimal for the transfer of Gopal Dadaji. When Harajiraje came to know about this settlement he had rebuked Keso Trimal for his actions. Consequently, their relations were strained.

Raigad got ready for the Karnataka campaign. Advance intimation of Raje's arrival was sent to Harajiraje. Khandoji, Rupaji, Dhanaji, Gopal Pandit… everyone who was going to accompany Raje on the campaign gathered in the court hall.

Raje came to the sanctum to bid farewell to Yesubai. He prayed to Goddess Jagadamba and the Shivlinga that Aabasaheb used to worship daily. Yesubai stood nearby with Balraje; she offered him the Tirtha. Raje sipped it. He spread his arms, pulled Balraje close and asked him, "Would you like to come to Jinji with me?" and patted his back with a smile.

"You should take good care of your health during the arduous journey." Yesubai said, pulling Balraje close to her again. Aabasaheb, too, had gone to Karnataka for a military campaign. The water that he drank during his journey proved harmful for his health. Moreover, after returning to the fort, on the day of the solar eclipse, he stood in the neck-deep water of the Kushavarta lake and distributed alms. All this resulted in typhoid, and he got bedridden…"

"I am quite used to these campaigns. Don't worry about my health. You look after the administration over here. I have instructed Peshwe, to take all decisions in consultation with you.

May I take your leave now?" Raje turned around to leave.

"Wait a moment." Yesubai came forward and touched Raje's feet three times.

"I have one favour to ask. Please fulfil my wish without fail." Yesubai exclaimed.

"Yes, tell me what it is."

"A wish of mine has long remained unfulfilled. At least Swari should fulfil it on my behalf." Yesubai paused and glanced at the shrine.

"Tell me. Which wish could not be fulfilled till now?"

"I have only heard that Thorale Aabasaheb's samadhi is there in Hodigeri in Karnataka. It has been my wish for a long time to go to Karnataka with you, and perform the puja of that monument together. Now that you are going there, remember to perform the puja."

Raje gazed at Yesubai. He had already planned to do it. He tried to visualize Shahajiraje's face that he could not recollect. "I will keep your wish… no 'command' in mind. In fact, I would have taken you with me, but…" Raje did not say anything further, and left the chamber.

He met Ramraje in his chamber, gave important instructions to Yesaji Dabhade and came to the court hall.

Thirty thousand cavalry and infantry travelled via Mahad ghat and came to Fort Panhala for their first stop. Mhalojibaba and Hambirarao came to receive Raje at the Pach Darwaja. Raje was visiting Panhala after a long time. As soon as he reached the Pach Darwaja, he dismounted Chandravat and said to Mhaloji and Hambirarao, "Sarlashkar, let's go and take the darshan of the colour-changing Shivlinga first."

"Let's go." Hambirarao, Mhaloji, Khandoji, and Dhanaji followed Raje.

"Mama Saheb, now Aurangzeb is targeting Golconda and our territory in Karnataka. That is why I am travelling to Jinji myself." Raje expressed his concern while walking.

"I know that. Ranamast and Ruhulla Khan tried hard to conquer Panhala and Belgaum. But Mhaloji and I chased them away.

"Because of you two, I am not worried about the Panhala–Kolhapur region."

While talking they all came near the dome of the colour-changing Shivlinga located near the entrance of the Balekilla. Everyone went inside.

Raje gave instructions to Mhaloji and Hambirarao about the administration of the Panhala region. He spent a day on Panhala and left with the army to go to Belgaum.

Hambirarao came to bid farewell to him; he embraced Hambirarao. Hambirarao couldn't resist asking, "How are things at Raigad, Dhani?"

Raje realized that Hambirarao was trying to get information about Tarau and said, "Everything is good, Tarau is doing fine."

Raje bade farewell to all and descended from Panhala.

Raje's entourage arrived at Jinji via Doddabalapur, Tiruvanmalai. Harajiraje stood at the entrance to receive Raje. Keso Trimal, Santaji, Jaitaji Katkar, Dadaji Kakade, and Timaji Hanamante were with him.

As soon as Raje dismounted from Chandravat, the cannons in Karnataka boomed in welcome; kettledrums resounded. Raje moved forward and embraced Harajiraje. He sat in the palanquin and set off in the direction of the Jinji fort with the men who had accompanied him, and the men of Karnataka who had come to receive him.

The people of Jinji had gathered in their balconies and porches to see the son of Shivaji Maharaj. They were feasting their eyes on their king who had forced Aurangzeb to retreat. They all felt proud of the gallant, young king. Raje entered the Jinji fort.

On the Balekilla, in the central square of Harajiraje's residence, Raje's sister approached him with a platter of lighted lamps. She waved a bag of gold coins around Raje and performed her brother's aukshan. In the light of the glowing lamps, both brother and the sister saw the pain in each other's eyes – reminding them of Ranooakka and Durgabai in the Mughal prison of Khuldabad.

Raje shook off his pain and leaned forward. He touched Akkasaheb's feet and asked her in a hoarse voice, "How are you doing?"

"Ji. I am doing fine. How about Yesubai and Balraje?" Ambikabai handed over the platter to a maid, held Raje's shoulders and asked him while pulling him up. The brother and sister were meeting after such a long time! They both had not got a chance to see Aabasaheb during his last days. Both had many questions in their mind.

After lunch, Raje and Harajiraje called a meeting in the court room.

Harajiraje enquired about Chhatrapati's journey and provided information about the Akera, Sondipatti and Kotwara region of the Golconda sultanate that he had conquered recently.

Harajiraje pointed towards Santaji Ghorpade and, "By the way, you had sent Santaji to assist us; he is indeed a very competent soldier."

"And what about Kesopant?" Raje glanced at Trimal and asked.

Harajiraje hesitated momentarily. He pulled a bowl in front of him and under the pretext of preparing a betel leaf for himself, he dodged the question that Raje had asked and broached another critical topic.

"Such a powerful Adil Shahi, but it crumbled in front of Aurangzeb. Now he is targeting Golconda. What will happen next, Raje? What do you think?"

Raje realized that Haraji had evaded his question. But the topic he had broached was equally important, so he gravely replied, "You should capture as much of Adil Shahi and Qutub

Shahi territory as possible. The Mughal forces will soon charge upon the region with the same purpose. Golconda won't sustain for long now."

Everyone became anxious to hear it. Harajiraje tried to alleviate their anxiety, "I clashed with Yachappa Nayak on the Vandivash battlefield near Kanjivaram. Santaji was with me at that time. We forced Yachappa to retreat to Mysore. Chikkadeo Wodeyar from Mysore is requesting military assistance from me. Mughal sardar Qasam Khan is in the Bengaluru region. Chikkadeo wants to defeat him.

"What kind of a person is Chikkadeo?" Raje asked Haraji.

"Ji. He is not to be trusted. Chikkadeoray wants to come in person to meet Raje. But he aspires to conquer Bengaluru."

Raje and Harajiraje had a long discussion about the Karnataka region.

"How far is Bengaluru from here?" The Chhatrapati asked Haraji.

"Ji, about seven-eight Majals." Haraji was baffled as he did not understand the purpose of the question. "What does Raje intend to do?" He asked.

"Come, let's inspect the Jinji fort." Raje stopped speaking, and rose from his seat to leave the court room. He inspected all bastions on the fort with everyone. The fort was well protected. Cannons were lined up neatly on every bastion wall. Harajiraje had made good security arrangements on the fort; he had placed enough guards all over the fort. Raje surveyed the armoury, granary and treasury with Harajiraje. He felt satisfied with the arrangements and said, "Aabasaheb had told me in our last visit to Panhala, that this fort is a key fort. You have kept it well secured. I am satisfied with your arrangements."

After couple of days, an envoy of Queen Chennamma of Ikkeri came to visit Raje. As the queen had a mentally impaired husband, she was ruling the kingdom on her own. Chikkadeoray of Mysore was troubling her. Chikkdeoray was in fact a shrewd ruler. He felt offended by the fact that Thorale Maharaj had invaded and conquered most of the territory in Karnataka. He kept attacking the Ikkeri, Ramanad and Madura kingdoms located around his kingdom. He had coveted Bengaluru since Ekoji kaka had shifted his capital from Bengaluru to Tanjavur. Queen Chennamma's envoy had come with the request to send Harajiraje to their assistance against Chikkadeoray. He offered royal presents to Raje and delivered the queen's message.

Raje promised to support Queen Chennamma who was courageously ruling the kingdom despite being a woman and sent her presents with due respect.

He sought information from Harajiraje about the rulers of Madura, Mysore and Ramanad located near Jinji.

Those were sultry summer days. After dinner, Raje sat on a swing with Harajiraje in the mansion. Harajiraje had speculated about Raje's further actions by now. But he was not sure of it, as Raje had enquired about Bengaluru out of the blue. Harajiraje was worried that he would get enraged by Achaloji's defection and charge upon Bengaluru.

The iron chains of the swing were creaking. Armed sentries stood guard at various places. Haraji raje tried to gauge Raje's intention and asked him, "Raje, you had asked how far Bengaluru is from here. Achaloji is young. We should consider Kakasaheb's age and…"

Raje stopped the swing with his feet and interrupting Harajiraje he asked, "Now tell me, how far Srirangapattan is from here?"

Raje had voiced the same thought that Harajiraje had surmised. Harajiraje was now convinced that Srirangapattan, which was a prominent city in the kingdom of Mysore's Chikkadeoray would not be spared any more.

"Ji. It is about seven-eight Majals away too."

"I am thinking of besieging Chikkadeoray's Srirangapattan myself. Just provide me with your select warriors and army too.

Inform the rulers of Moras, Tigud, Kodag and Maley to charge upon Srirangapattan once I besiege it. Unless this is done, Chikkadeoray will not learn his lesson."

"This is a good plan. Chikkadeoray has been a thorn in the flesh for others as well as for me. I would also like to join you in this campaign." Harajiraje said zealously.

"No need to do that. You should continue the defence of Jinji. The forces of Qasam and Ranamast Khan are circulating in the region. Start the campaign preparations from tomorrow. Send your best informers with your army." For a long time, Raje kept devising the plan of the siege of Srirangapattan in his mind, and Harajiraje kept planning the arrangements he needed to make for the campaign.

The slogans of 'Har Har Mahadeo' echoed around Srirangapattan. Raje fell upon Srirangapattan with warriors such as Santaji Ghorpade, Trimbakaji Bhosale, Dadaji Kakade, Keso Trimal, Dhanaji and Khandoji. As Chikkadeoray had already gotten the intimation about the attack he escaped towards the eastern region.

Raje's army began plundering Srirangapattan of Chikkadeoray. They attacked the auxiliary forces coming to his aid from Madura and isolated him.

Raje's regiment from Karnataka surrounded the Srirangapattan fort. The army from the Maratha kingdom started plundering the territory of Mysore. Confined in the Mysore fort, Chikkadeoray didn't know what to do. He remembered his neighbour now, and sent a message to the ruler of Ramanad to come to his assistance.

At the time of leaving for the campaign, Raje had dispersed his informers from Jinji to Srirangapattan. He himself was leading the siege of Srirangapattan. As Chikkadeoray came to hear about Raje's reputation in Goa, Janjira and Burhanpur, he was petrified. He was convinced that he was going to lose

Srirangapattan. Other rulers in the region were terrified too, on hearing the news of the siege. Santaji, Dhanaji and Khandoji's forces had spread swiftly across the Mysore kingdom. The custodian of Srirangapattan fort was fighting determinedly, but he had given up hopes too.

A shamiana was raised on the plateau around the fort. The Mavala troops galloping all over Mysore kept pouring heaps of booty in front of this shamiana. Every day, Raje kept moving around the fort astride Chandravat. But, as always, bad luck caught up with him. One day a messenger entered his shamiana and delivered some news to him. It was not the news of Karnataka but news about the Maratha kingdom – "Aurangzeb is planning to besiege Fort Panhala!"

Now it was critical for Raje to leave Karnataka and go back immediately. Still, he surveyed the Vandivash, Vruddhachalam and Tiruvanmalai region around Jinji with Harajiraje. Two days before starting his return journey, in the court room of Harajiraje's residence, he was giving important instructions to Harajiraje about the regional administration. Only Keso Trimal and Santaji were present in the room.

After giving all instructions, Maharaj broached the subject that had been bothering him. "I have heard about some discord between you and Kesopant." Haraji and Keso Trimal lowered their heads when they heard Raje's words.

"What is the reason for it, Santaji?" Raje asked Santaji. Santaji shared the specifics of the discord. Raje got restless to hear that. He advised Harajiraje as the in-charge of the region, "I have experienced first-hand the problems of discontent between people. When people's hearts break, so do their bonds. It adversely affects their focus on their duty and people end up wasting their energy where it is not required. You are a veteran. I would just like to share with you the advice that Samartha gave in his letter to me.

It is up to you to take whatever you want from it." Raje

took a breather. Just the memory of Samartha had stirred his heart. He glanced at Harajiraje and said, "Pardon the previous wrongdoings of your ministers; redirect them to the right path and reinstate them in their posts."

Harajiraje was lost in thought as he heard those words. Raje rose from his seat, approached Kesopant, and warned him moderately, "Kesopant, you must be aware of the penalty that Aabasaheb had imposed on the first Peshwa Shamraj. It hurts me every time I remember the occasions when I had to testify in the royal court. May the grace of Goddess Jagadamba save you from such disgrace. I hope no such situation will ever arise between you and Haraji! You should support Harajiraje in every possible way."

"Now both of you should leave discontent behind and embrace each other in front of me." Raje glanced at Harajiraje and Kesopant with bright eyes. Both of them glanced at each other momentarily, and spreading their arms wide they embraced each other in front of their Swami. Raje's face lit up to see that, and Santaji felt happy.

Raje stayed with Harajiraje and Ambakka for two days and left from Jinji. Harajiraje went with Santaji and Kesopant to bid farewell to him. Raje commanded the army to march towards Bengaluru. Harajiraje was baffled to hear the command; Raje cleared his misunderstanding, "I know what you are thinking about right now. I am not holding any grudge against Achaloji. I am not going to attack Bengaluru. I am going to Hodigeri; to take darshan of my grandfather's samadhi, perform puja and seek his blessings.

Harajiraje let out a sigh of relief. Raje's army marched in the direction of Bengaluru and reached the forest of Hodigeri.

They arrived at the place where Shahajiraje's samadhi was raised. Ekojiraje had made arrangements to perform the daily puja of the samadhi. Raje dismounted and walked towards the samadhi. As he stood in front of it, his mind was full of thoughts.

He removed his mojaris. The priest handed him some flowers; Raje offered the flowers on the padukas engraved in the memory of his grandfather.

After Raje, everybody else took the darshan of the samadhi. As Raje embraced Harajiraje to bid goodbye to him he couldn't resist saying, "This Karnataka region is a very prominent and powerful place. Take good care of it. Farewell."

As soon as Raje arrived on Panhala, Mhaloji informed him that the news of Aurangzeb coming to attack Panhala had been a ruse. His forces were moving about in the Miraj, Karhad and Belgaum region. Hambirarao had gone there to keep his forces in check.

Raje stayed on Panhala for a few days, then bade farewell to Mhaloji and returned to Raigad. As the monsoon was approaching, many places on the fort were being covered with haystacks. The grains spread out to dry were filled in sacks and stacked in the granary.

Nilopant provided Raje with detailed information about the actions taken in the fort in Raje's absence. Kulesh was at Khelana, Ramchandrapant in Konkan and Hambirarao in Desh. Everyone had taken their positions at the assigned places and were vigilantly guarding them even in the rainy season.

Raje came to Yesubai's chamber to visit her and shared with her the events that had taken place during the Karnataka campaign. Yesubai wanted to hear about the darshan of Shahajiraje's shrine. Raje shared that with her in the end.

News of Harajiraje's Karnataka region kept coming, across the overflowing rivers such as Pennar, Tungabhadra and Krishna.

The most important news was that Qasam Khan had conquered Bengaluru of Ekojikaka and had sold it for three lakh rupees! To whom? Chikkadeoray of Mysore. Ekojikaka was distraught to hear the news that he had lost his prominent city Bengaluru and he passed away in shock.

The month of Shravan arrived. Raje summoned Moreshwar

Panditrao to his palace to take decisions about two things he had been pondering. From Chinchwad, Morayababa's disciple had recently visited Raje to file a complaint on Morayababa's behalf. During the time of military campaigns in the Pune region, some military officers had insolently harassed Baba's ashram.

Raje was pacing in his chamber. He asked, "Panditrao, who is the current subedar of the Pune region?"

"Ji, Vinayak Umaji is the current subedar." Moreshwar replied wondering why Raje was asking the question.

The moment Raje heard Vinayak's name, he remembered Vinayak's father Umaji. When Raje was a child, Umaji had taught him the Puranas in detail.

"Panditrao, issue a decree to Vinayak and tell him to warn the Jumaledars, Hawaldars, Bargirs, Hashams and other units of his army. Include the following matter in the decree… All of you unnecessarily harass the people coming to the ashram. The ashram in Chinchwad belongs to Morayababa. He has been revered since the time of late Aabasaheb. It has been brought to my notice that you have been extorting money from the people of the ashram. Henceforth, such unlawful conduct will not be tolerated. Whoever continues to indulge in such behaviour will be executed. Take this as a strong warning and stop harassing the ashram."

The festival of Ganesh Chaturthi arrived. The painters began painting the temples in the fort. As the monsoon had just ended, the rays of the sun began occasionally illuminating the fort. But the trails on the fort were still slippery. Walking on those slippery trails, two British envoys of the Mumbai durbar came to the fort with the interpreter Shenavi to visit Raje. They were George Weldon and Robert Graham. Tryambak Gopal, the envoy of the Maratha kingdom, recently appointed by Raje, accompanied them.

The British envoys who had heard about Shivajiraja's famous attack on Surat were wondering what his son, Sambhaji, would look like in person and how he would treat them. Prahladpant conducted the four of them to the court hall of the royal throne to visit Raje.

The British envoys presented the royal gifts that they had brought. Tryambak Gopal introduced them to his Swami.

"These British envoys have come from Mumbai to finalize the accord of Karlas island." Prahladpant conveyed the purpose of their visit to Raje.

"What condition are they putting in for the accord?" Raje asked while observing both of them intently.

"The British have agreed to protect the Karlas island from the Siddis. To that effect, they are also ready to station their army on the island. But they have put forth one condition to our durbar." Tryambakpant reported.

"What condition?" Raje's forehead puckered.

They are asking for two thousand Maund of rice grains and fifty thousand rupees cash in return.

"Is that all?" Raje leaned against the back of his seat and said with a smile. He remembered the faces of his own ryots who were desperately in need of rice due to the draught for last two years. He remembered the money that he had to spend to fight with Aurangzeb's army and force them to retreat. Yet he asked, "Prahladpant, what would your advice be?"

"We don't have to accept the proposal just because they have put it forth. If we negotiate, the British will reduce their demand for the rice grains and the cash." Prahladpant advised.

"Tryambakpant, what do you think about those conditions?" Raje asked his envoy to check his opinion.

Tryambakpant was hoping that Swami would take the decision; he hesitated for a moment and said, "Ji, our treasury is already exhausted by from battles with Mughal forces." If the issue of the island is getting resolved by accepting the accord, we should approve it.

"You are new, but quite capable Tryambakpant!" Raje smiled

and approving Tryambakpant's advice he said, "Nyayadhish, why negotiate if we have to ultimately of make the accord? Tell them, we will fulfil their conditions. They should urgently send their forces for the protection of the island." Tryambakpant and the Nyayadhish were quite surprised that the accord was finalized so quickly; they kept staring at Raje.

Graham and Weldon were delighted to receive gifts. They were now free to tell their new viceroy that they had succeeded in bringing about the treaty quickly.

Bhaganagar! The place where Abul Hasan Tana Shah of Golconda had welcomed Aabasaheb during his last campaign of Karnataka, had offered him gifts and embraced him as a friend. In that same place, Tana Shah was imprisoned by Aurangzeb. It was obvious now, that with the Bijapur and Golconda armies at his disposal, Aurangzeb was soon going to fall upon the Maratha kingdom.

"We don't even have time to breathe now. Both sultanates neighbouring the Deccan have collapsed. Right from the beginning, the enemy had his eyes upon our kingdom. Baglan, Khandesh, Konkan…dispatch messages to the subedars and hawaladars all over the kingdom to make them aware of their responsibility at such times. Tell them to recruit as many new soldiers as possible. I am going to Choul in person, to offer concessions and reassure the oppressed ryots of Choul. Send the intimation of my arrival to subedar Rayaji Sadak Prabhu." The Chhatrapati's mind was full of varying thoughts; he was giving commands to the Peshwe in quick succession.

Nilopant, Yesaji, Ramchandrapant… everyone vouched their unconditional support to Raje.

Lost in thought, Raje instructed Nilopant as a cautionary step, "Pant, send a message to Harajiraje in Karnataka to keep the forces ready at the border. After all, he is Aurangzeb! You can never guess which direction he will turn to."

"You all are veterans of the kingdom; you are pugnacious.

We may have to sacrifice our lives to defend this region spread from Baglan to Jinji. Aabasaheb did not own this kingdom, I don't own it; this kingdom belongs to its people. Don't lose your heart. Once, I was confined in the same Aurangzeb's haveli in Agra with Aabasaheb. All of you must understand the impending danger of our entire kingdom getting caught in his clutches. Come with me. Let's all take the darshan of Lord Jagadishwar."

Raje left the court room of the royal throne in his reverie and started walking in the direction of Maha Darwaja. Everyone followed him. But Nyayadhish Prahladpant broke away and walked towards the palace of Ramraje stealthily. Only he knew what justice he was seeking there!

After the morning bath, as Raje was applying the horizontal stripes of sandalwood paste on his forehead his left eyelid had fluttered involuntarily. Since morning he had been having a bizarre feeling. He had even shared his uneasiness with Yesubai during lunch, "I don't know why, but I am feeling quite restless today. I am worried that Aurangzeb's army might have infiltrated Harajiraje's region."

At dusk, Raje came to the central tower with Raya-Anta and Purusha.

Raje was walking towards the Jagadishwar temple for the evening darshan; he met Yesaji Kank and Khandoji on the way. They wanted to say something.

Raje kept walking towards the Jagadishwar temple with Yesaji and Khandoji.

Khandoji said, "Ramsej – our fort Ramsej that has been fighting resolutely for so long..."

Raje stopped walking. Khandoji hesitated. He wondered how to break the news.

"Was conquered? Right, Chitnis?" Raje asked him.

"Ji. It was not won in battle but was conquered by treason. Ramsej was such a powerful fort, Dhani." Khadoji lowered his head for a moment; then quickly raised it and to reassure Raje he said, "But there is good news about Harajiraje, Swami. He has annexed to Karnataka as much territory of the fallen Golconda kingdom as he could."

Khandoji's words kept falling on Raje's ears. He reached the entrance chowk of the Jagadishwar temple.

They all took the darshan and returned to the Balekilla. The sun had set now. At the Lahana Darwaja and Maha Darwaja, the evening round of kettle drums resounded. It got dark. As usual, the doorkeepers began closing the gates. A rider from Talbeed passed through all the gates and arrived at the Balekilla after crossing the Maha Darwaja with a few people accompanying him. His clothes were all drenched in sweat and his face was drawn. He gestured to the gate keepers with his hands to stop and barely managed to cross all the gates to come to the Balekilla.

Maharaj had just returned. He had placed his Jiretop on a platter. He was instructing Majumdar Hanamante on how to distribute foodgrains to the drought-affected ryots from all forts. Yesaji and Khandoji were listening to him attentively.

"Maharaj…we are ruined." Wailing words cut through the court room of the palace, leaving Raje and everyone rattled. As the soldier who had climbed the fort, saw Raje, he fell at Raje's feet and began sobbing. He was Shankaraji Mohite of Talbeed.

Raje's entire body trembled. He quickly leaned forward, patted Shankaraji's shoulder and asked him, "What happened Shankaraji?"

The touch of Raje's hand overwhelmed Shankaraji and he couldn't speak for a moment. Sporadic words came out of his mouth, "Not just me, but the entire kingdom has been orphaned. Dhani…your… your Mama Saheb… the Sarlashkar of all… my brother…" grief-stricken Shankaraji closed his eyes tightly and shook his head in sorrow. "Sarlashkar is gone Dhani!!"

The Mughal army had infiltrated the Wai region. Hambirarao had fallen upon the Mughal army to chase them away. In that skirmish, a hot and heavy iron cannon ball had struck Sarlashkar Hambirarao's brawny chest. That was a devastating blow for Thorale Swami's kingdom.

The moment Raje heard Shankaraji's words 'Sarlashkar is gone' he closed his ears tightly. Innumerable memories of Hambirarao kept flashing in front of Raje's eyes.

"Mama Saheb, Hambirarao Mohite, who was ready to give his daughter Tarau's hand to Ramraje; when I was a defendant in the durbar, in front of Aabasaheb, he supported me and said that the lady should be called in as a witness; he shackled the Surnis and the Peshwa who were going to capture me and came to meet me on Panhala; he was the Sarlashkar of the kingdom, but he loved me as much as Aabasaheb!" Raje placed his hands over his face and started sobbing; his entire body was shaking. He had faced so many calamities before, the Chhatrapati had never been so emotional. But today he could not control himself.

"Where is Mama Saheb? How could he leave without even meeting me or talking to me? Whom can I look up to now?" misty-eyed Raje spoke with a heavy voice.

Meanwhile, the news had spread all over the fort. People kept coming to the palace. As Yesubai brought young Tarau, Raje moved forward. He patted Tarau's shoulders without uttering a word and looked at Yesubai. He forced the tears in his eyes back and said to Shankaraji, "Come with me."

Raje sat in the palanquin, surrounded by torchbearers and went towards the Mahad ghat with Yesaji, Nilopant and Khandoji, to take the last darshan of Sarlashkar Hambirarao Mohite.

Hambirarao's cremation took place. His demise caused a huge void in Raje's heart. He stopped speaking freely to people. His daily bath, puja of the crystal Shivlinga, administrative work, meals… his entire schedule was disrupted. He was unable to focus on anything. He had lost interest in everything.

Countless thoughts filled his mind! "What does 'Swaraj' exactly mean? Who was Aabasaheb? Thoralya Aau, Putala masaheb who became Sati, Samartha… who were they? Kondaji, Krishnaji, Hambir mama and the countless soldiers that I never saw, who sacrificed their lives, Shirke, Nimbalkar, Achaloji, Arjunji who defected to Aurangzeb, and accepted khilats from him, the rebellious vatandars of the Konkan coast… What kind of game is this? Why am I playing it? Who will continue it after me? Ramraje? My son? Will this newly raised kingdom survive Aurangzeb's onslaught? Or will it crumble just like Adil Shahi, Qutub Shahi…? No… No.'

A strange loneliness enveloped Raje. When people came to visit him, to share their complaints as usual; Raje signalled them to stop and asked them to be brief. People were taken aback by Raje's demeanour.

One day, as Raje got up from his seat leaving his lunch unfinished, Yesubai couldn't stop asking him, "Swami is not paying attention to anything. You haven't finished your lunch! How long are you going to continue like this?"

Raje looked at Yesubai, pointed towards his lunch platter and exclaimed, "Even I don't know why I am doing this. You had told me once – I will never be able to visit Shringarpur now. I have the same feeling that you must have had at that time!" Raje whispered, glancing out the window, gazing at the summits of distant forts around Raigad.

Yesubai was frank and outspoken, but she too, fell silent. What was she going to tell him anyway? She strongly felt that Aabasaheb's kingdom had been orphaned by the demise of the Sarlashkar.

Raje came out of the dining room and summoned Ramchandrapant. His face looked distressed and annoyed.

Ramchandrapant came to see Raje with Shankaraji. He

timidly put forth a case, "Swami, Pilaji Desai of Devarukh has arrived on the fort. He... he wants to talk about the vatan…"

"Enough Shankaraji, you listen to his side and solve the matter as per your discretion. Don't even bother to bring anyone to me…" Raje spoke abruptly. A grave silence filled the room.

"Ramchandrapant, when are you going to the Konkan coast?" Raje asked.

"Ji. Today." Ramchandrapant couldn't guess the intent of the question.

"While going take a detour to Khelana. Kulesh is posted there. Meet him in person and tell him that I have summoned him here."

"Ji. I will go in person." Ramchandrapant who had left the court room couldn't guess what was going on in Raje's mind. He, Shankaraji, Raje himself did not know that Aurangzeb had received the news of the Maratha commander's death. He had received the news with delight and whispered, "By the grace of Allah!"

The Mughal emperor had convened an honour assembly in the Golconda fort he had conquered. He offered mansabs and distributed Khillats to the Mughal and the Bijapur sardars who had brought the downfall of Qutub Shahi. In the end, he offered a Khillat to his son, Prince Mohammed Azam, and addressed him in front of the durbar, "My prince, I hereby appoint you to destroy the cursed Sambha. I am looking forward to the news of your success."

Azam knelt, kissed the rich, soft jama of his Abbajan and reassured him, "Rest assured Abbajan. I will present Sambha in front of you either dead or alive."

Now Aurangzeb's army started moving in the direction of the Maratha kingdom. Their encampments spread along the borders of Belgaum, Solapur, Miraj, and Aklooj. Matabbar Khan attacked and conquered Pattagad. About twenty of the emperor's Khans including Ruhulla, Shabadi, Zulfikar, Ranamast and

Nekanam dispersed in various places of the Maratha kingdom. They started bribing the Maratha sardars with mansabs and Khilats. Every day, Raigad started receiving the news of sardars abandoning the Maratha kingdom.

As per the instructions, Kulesh came to Raigad. He was wondering why Raje had summoned him, and he felt drained. He presented himself to Raje in the afternoon.

"I heard the news about the Sarlashkar. I came as soon as I received your message, Swami." Kulesh remembered Hambirarao, and became solemn.

"That is why I have summoned you Kaviji. I feel... feel..." Lost in thought, for quite some time Raje kept pacing back and forth while rubbing both his palms together.

"Kulesh..." Raje said after a long time. "I feel a lack of strength. Not military strength, but the strength of blessings."

Even Kulesh was lost in thought when he heard it and said, "What would you like to do, Swami?"

"Kulesh, I need the support of divine power. These are trying times, just like it was in Agra."

"Swami, you provide enough support to religious institutions. But still, I think some kind of rigorous religious service should be performed."

"What kind of service? I am ready for anything."

Kulesh was lost in thought. He stopped.

"Tell me, what kind of religious service?"

"Ji. The worship of the Goddess! But as per Shaktism..." Kulesh hesitated.

"Tell me, what is the problem?" Raje asked gazing at his turban.

"Swami, your coronation has taken place on this fort, you will have to leave the fort."

Raje was lost in thought. But after some time, he said, "That is okay. I will leave Raigad. We can go to Gangoli or Sangameshwar. But what is the rigorous service that you were talking about?"

"Swami, as part of this service we will worship Goddess Ranachandi. It involves rituals like, fasting, offering sacrifice, puja and..."

"And what? Speak up, Kulesh. I am ready to do anything."

"During the puja of other gods and goddesses one drinks purified water, but in these rituals, one has to drink alcohol. If Raja Saab does that, it will raise a hue and cry. Therefore..."

"Kulesh, I will do everything as you say. You may not know it, but since the time I defected to Diler Khan – when my family was captured, I have been drinking alcohol occasionally. That should not be a problem. You start preparations for the penance of Goddess Chandi. We will descend the fort tomorrow and go to Gangoli."

"Ji. The Shivyogi of Shringarpur knows the rituals of this service."

Shringarpur! Raje's forehead puckered. But still he said, "Then summon him too. Go ahead and start the preparations for the religious service."

Kulesh left to make further preparations. The murti of Goddess Ranchandi wielding the weapons lingered in front of Raje's open eyes.

Harajiraje was relentlessly fighting against the Mughal army that had infiltrated Karnataka. As per his instructions, Santaji went to Kanjiwaram with twenty thousand soldiers. The Mughal forces that had arrived near Madras had frequent clashes with Harajiraje's sardars. A big battle took place among both armies at Vandivash for the second time.

Azam, who had left Bhaganagar, seized the land fort of Belgaum from the Bijapur sultanate. Hambirarao had spared no efforts to defend that fort.

Aurangzeb's intention was now clear. He himself was stationed in the Bijapur, Golconda region and had sent his mammoth army to the Karnataka region.

Raje descended the fort with Kulesh to travel to Gangoli. Raya–Anta thought they would join the entourage as usual. But they were ordered to stay back, and the male attendant Purusha was recruited as the personal attendant. Along with him there were about twenty menials from Kulesh's residence.

Raje bade farewell to the people in the Pachad palace and left Pachad. But he did not tell anyone where he was going. Not even Yesubai! He had sent a messenger to the subedar of Gangoli via Changoji Katkar. Kulesh had also sent a messenger to the Shivyogi in Shringarpur and had instructed him to come to Gangoli with his disciples. In the message he had mentioned the rigorous religious service. Gangoli came in sight. This was the birthplace of baby Shivajiraje; it was very close to Yesubai's heart. As the palace here had received intimation of Raje's arrival, the menials had bedecked it. The Shivyogi had already arrived here; he came with his disciples to receive Raje.

He had brought the murti of Goddess Ranachandi with him and placed it in the basement of the palace, facing the east. A yajna pit was raised in front of it and tiger-skin mats were spread on the floor.

Raje entered the palace with his personal assistant, Shivyogi, his disciples and Kulesh. He sat on the seat arranged in the court room. Shivyogi introduced him to the men who conducted tantric practices and whom he had summoned from various cities such as Chiplun, Rajapur, Sangameshwar and Devarukh. The sun was eclipsed by the clouds.

The palace in-charge had prepared everything for the worship as per Shivyogi's instructions. Soldiers wielding bare swords surrounded the entire palace. The Shivyogi was going to look for a mahurat, when they could commence the rigorous religious service.

Meanwhile, from Malakapur, the personal secretary of Kulesh came to Gangoli to visit him. He had brought a civil complaint against Tulaji Desai of Malakapur. Kulesh handed him the warning letter to be given to Desai and bade farewell to him.

Goddess Jagadamba of Tuljapur was eyeing Gangoli, wondering how Ranachandi was going to bless Raje to fill the dearth of grace.

Chapter 15

On the mahurat chosen by the Shivyogi, the religious ceremony invoking Goddess 'Shakti' commenced in front of the murti in the palace. It was a rigorous ceremony but as it was to be done in private, the entire palace was closed to the public. This ceremony was being performed to invoke Lord Shiva, the god of destruction, in the form of Goddess Shakti. As per the norms of the sect, sacrifices had to be offered to the goddess. Amidst the chanting of mantras, oblations were to be offered in the yajna pit.

Raje removed his royal attire, donned the saffron robe and commenced the rituals of the ceremony. He performed all rituals as per the Shivyogi's instructions. Indeed, he also consumed the alcohol that he was offered. Every day, amidst the chanting of mantras, new rituals were being performed in the palace. In the evening, after finishing the rituals for the day, Raje would sail in a boat with Kulesh and Shivyogi on the river on the outskirts of the town.

As a result of the rigorous ceremony, Raje was isolated from the aides who accompanied him daily. Kulesh himself did not allow Raje to meet anyone in the palace. Though he had no bad intention, many people around them felt that Raje was under the influence of Kulesh. Furthermore, the disciples of the Shivyogi who had returned to Shringarpur kept talking about Raje's rigorous worship in public. This news reached Ganoji Shirke.

Rumours spread like wildfire, "Kabji Kalusha has cast a spell on our king! Raje drinks a lot! That Brahmin doesn't allow anyone to meet him!"

The pre-monsoon gales arrived and drifted away. One day, after the pre-monsoon flurries had stopped, the scent of the wet mud dispersed in the atmosphere. It reached Raje, who was sitting on the swing near the court room in the palace of Gangoli. He asked Kulesh who was standing nearby, "Kaviraj, how many pre-monsoon flurries would this earth have experienced! Why does the earth warm up? Why do we have pre-monsoon flurries? How does an enchanting fragrance bloom from the wet mud? We are worshipping Goddess Shakti rigorously. Will our prayers be answered?

Kulesh himself was a poet, but he was mesmerized by the royal words and kept listening in awe. He didn't know how to respond, so he changed the subject and said, "Swami, I have heard some rumours People are saying that I.... have cast a spell on you."

Raje instantly stopped the swing. He stared at Kulesh and asked him curtly, "What do you think? Are you capable of doing such a thing?"

"I would never even think of it, Swami!"

"I really pity those who say these things about you and me. Aabasaheb was such a great man, but in a dark moment I deserted him too. Diler Khan conquered Fort Purandar, but even he couldn't keep me under control. And here people are claiming that you are doing what they couldn't! I really don't know whether to laugh or cry! Kulesh, the world could never see Lord Shankar's throat turning blue after consuming the poison that came out of the ocean churning. People don't easily accept that Shiva also has 'Parvati' in his life."

Maharaj remembered Yesubai, and pushed the swing again.

The monsoon arrived. Usually, with the advent of the monsoon, Raje would travel to Raigad from wherever he was.

But this year that did not happen. Naturally, on Raigad, Yesubai, Nilopant, Yesaji Kank and Khandoji got concerned about Raje.

In Gangoli, Raje had summoned Kulesh in the court room. Kulesh dutifully reminded Raje, "The monsoon has begun. It is time to return to Raigad. Swami, everyone on Raigad must be awaiting your arrival!"

"Kaviraj, not the people, but this monsoon will guard my back. Aurangzeb's army will get stuck wherever they are stationed. You should find a better place for the rigorous worship." As a matter of fact, Raje didn't want to go back to Raigad. Every moment, he wished to lead his army, and charge upon Aurangzeb's encampment.

Kulesh was surprised to hear Raje's thoughts. He wondered why he had suggested the religious ceremony to Raje. But there was no way out. Raje's wish was his command. Kulesh sent select trustworthy men to Sangameshwar. They brought news that the Desai residence of Sangameshwar was a good place.

As per Raje's command, Kulesh and Shivyogi went to Sangameshwar and established one more branch of the Shakta sect. Now, at the peak of the monsoon, Raje kept travelling between Gangoli and Sangameshwar. In the Shringarpur and Shirkan region the Shirkes spread rumours, "Kalusha is Aurangzeb's spy! He stays close to Raje, but is loyal to the emperor."

Two months passed. The people on the fort became anxious. The month of Aashadh arrived. The fort kept receiving only the news of Raje's wellbeing through the messengers. The rigorous worship continued in Gangoli and Sangameshwar. Shivyogi and Kulesh had tried their best to convince Raje to return to Raigad. Raje was neither listening to nor talking to anyone. He was engaged in a conversation with himself. What was he saying?

'Purandar! The place where I took my first breath; the fort located near the samadhi of Sopandeo on the banks of River

Karha of Saswad. I have travelled so much since taking birth on Purandar! I can't remember my mother clearly. Thoralya Aau and Dharau took care of me. How unfortunate that I couldn't meet Aabasaheb and Dharau in their last moments. Thoralya Aausaheb breathed her last in front of me in the palace of Pachad. And with my own hands I had to ignite the funeral pyre of Putalamasaheb who committed Sati. Really, what if the Mughal soldiers would have captured me during my journey from Mathura to the Maratha kingdom, with the Trimal family? What if the plot to poison me on Panhala would have succeeded? What if Diler would have arrested me in his encampment? What a turbulent life!

'Did I covet the forts, the treasury and the royal throne of Raigad? Why did Hambirarao desert his own sister and support me?

Would Aabasaheb have surrendered to Aurangzeb, had he charged upon the Deccan with his mammoth army? Never.

Is this a personal war between Aurangzeb and Aabasaheb and me? No. Why am I the only who feels that this is a war of attitudes? Why are prominent men deserting our kingdom? Do they believe that this kingdom belongs only to the Bhosalas?

Question upon question kept arising. But no solution was in sight. The heavy rains of Aashadh were lashing the land of Maval.

"You may be the Chhandogamatya, the Kulekhatyar, but I am the Maharani. The Peshwa is at the fort. The enemy's forces are intruding into our territory despite the rain. Our prominent forts are being surrounded. And you…you have taken Swari away from the fort to wallow in luxury! How dare you?" In the royal palace of Raigad, Yesubai was shaking with rage. Even the palace maids were terrified to see her anger. They had never seen Rani Saheb furious like this before.

Kavi Kulesh who stood in front of her, began shaking in fear after hearing her words. He didn't know what to say, so he had lowered his head. Yesubai had sent a trustworthy messenger urgently and had summoned him on the fort from Sangameshwar. As soon as he arrived, she had taken him to task.

"But Rani Saab…let me...tell you…" Kulesh was trying to speak. But the Maharani didn't even want to listen to him. She was lashing at Kulesh in rage.

"Did Goddess Chandi answer your prayers? Did she give her blessings? Why did Aabasaheb never perform such rituals? He had faced so many calamities! You are a poet, yet how could you be so insensitive?"

Yesubai had heard the rumours too. She was furious. She was observing Kavi Kulesh from top to bottom with suspicion.

"Kalusha is the emperor's spy!" The venomous news that she had heard was gnawing at her heart. She didn't know what to say and how to say it.

"I have heard about your doings. I know very well of your greed, acting in favour of the emperor, and leading Swari onto the wrong path. Chhandogamatya, you should be ashamed of yourself. If you are betraying your Swami in any way, then you will have to first deal with me!" Yesubai was so enraged that she could barely speak.

Kulesh shivered and his eyes filled with tears. What had he not done for this kingdom? He had faithfully assisted Thorale Maharaj, at the cost of his own life, to make young Raje's travel from Mathura safe. On behalf of Raje, he had gone to the Portuguese durbar with the Mughal Prince Akbar, and successfully made a treaty with the Portuguese. He felt agitated. He quickly moved forward and touched Rani Saheb's feet. He was unable to speak.

"Rani Saheb, if you wish, chop off my head! I vouch in the name of my family deity…I…I am not a traitor! Please…please do something…anything…to save Raja Saab and this kingdom of Bade Swami." He started sobbing like a child.

Yesubai was stunned to hear him. Kulesh was not at fault for what had happened. Had he been the culprit, he wouldn't have come to meet Rani Saheb at all. If he hadn't presented himself, Yesubai would have sent Nilopant and Khandoji with the army and would have had him arrested without hesitation.

Yesubai did not say a word. She made a decision and while leaving the chamber she said to Kulesh, "You are going to take my place now. Stay with your Swami like his shadow. Go back immediately."

Kulesh returned to Sangameshwar. As soon as he reached, Raje commanded him, "Go to Khelana at once. There is some problem in the Shirkan region. Keep a close watch on that region. This is a family matter. If needed, send me a message. I might have to solve the problem myself." Raje had come to know about the rumours the Shirkes were spreading and their suspicious activities. The Mughal Prince, Azam, had moved in the direction of Kolhapur after conquering the fort of Belgaum. Ganoji and Kanhoji were visiting him frequently and having long secret meetings with him.

Though Kulesh was told to go to Shirkan, he remained with Raje as per the Maharani's instruction. The rigorous worship that involved consumption of alcohol continued in Gangoli and Sangameshwar. Everyone wondered if it was ever going to end. The Desais of Sangameshwar, the officers of Gangoli, Raje's personal attendant, Purusha, even the Shivyogi dared not speak in front of Raje. Kulesh felt trapped between the wishes of Raje and Maharani.

Raje was not speaking to anyone. Many events in the past were flashing in front of his eyes rapidly. The scene was so terrifying that anyone would have been appalled to watch it. But, like a farmer glancing at his field from a corner, Raje was looking at his own life as an outsider. Only one face kept recurring in front of his eyes – that of Aabasaheb! He kept remembering their last visit on Panhala when Aabasaheb had embraced him and said, "My dear son, where had you gone?"

He evaluated his entire life – 'I deserted Aabasaheb and joined hands with Diler – he probably broke down due to my reckless decision. Aabasaheb, it is such a big stigma. Will I ever be able to rectify my mistake? Will I get that opportunity?

Shravan arrived; the game of rain and the sun began. One moment, the entire Konkan coast was glowing with yellow plateaus and green meadows and the next moment it was overcast. An epidemic of cholera had broken out in Bijapur.

Bahirji Naik, the chief of surveillance had galloped from Raigad, and braving the rains of Shravan, entered the Desai residence in Sangameshwar. He was out of breath. Come what may, he had to bring Raje back to Raigad. He had brought with him an important and stern letter from the Maharani with him. Disregarding everyone around, holding the coarse blanket on his shoulder tightly, a concerned Bahirji directly entered the chamber of Goddess Chandi's worship.

He was startled to see Raje clad in a saffron robe, sitting near the yajna pit, and stopped for a moment. Raje's face had changed so much! Bahirji couldn't help but say, "Dhani, I have travelled here from Raigad despite the rain showers. Rani Saab has given this letter. She has told me to bring you along." Bahirji had forgotten to make an obeisance.

Raje got up from the tiger-skin mat. From the yajna pit he walked towards Bahirji. Everyone thought Naik was going to get an earful. Everyone knew Bahirji's dedication to the kingdom since the time of Thorale Maharaj. Bahirji had travelled from Surat to Madras to serve the kingdom. Since Ganoji had forsaken Yesubai, Bahirji had become like her own brother to Yesubai.

As Raje was about to say something, Bahirji quickly knelt, and held his feet. The turban on his head shook and he said in a choked voice, "In the name of Biruba, please stop this worship of power. If Dhani starts feeling lonely, who should the people of the kingdom look up to? Enough of this Chandi puja, Jagadamba is waiting for you there. Either you come with me, or throw this old man in the yajna pit."

The bunch of sacrificial sticks slipped from Raje's fist. He leaned forward. Everyone thought he was going to pick up the bunch of sticks. But he put his hand on the back of Bahirji who had held his feet and was sobbing. His halting words fell on Bahirji's ears, "Naik, prepare for my journey. I will leave with you." He held Bahirji's shoulders and pulled him up. He opened the letter that Bahirji had given him and read it himself. The words of Yesubai sparkled in front of his eyes. She had written for the sake of the kingdom –

"... You have worshipped Goddess Chandi for a long time now. It would have been great if the ritualistic worship of one goddess would have achieved the desired result. But the entire kingdom has lost its vigour. As soon as you receive this letter, leave with Naik and come to the fort. Otherwise, I will have to come there myself. I will offer the royal seal and the dagger that Aabasaheb had given me in the yajna pit and leave the fort for good!"

The Chhaptrapati squeezed the letter in his fist. As per his instructions, everyone started preparing for the journey. Kulesh breathed a sigh of relief and left for Khelana with his troops.

Meanwhile, Aurangzeb had returned after performing his Namaz in the royal masjid of Bijapur and was telling his Wazir Asad Khan, "While doing Namaz at the masjid today, I took an oath in the name of the Quran-e-sharif, that we will overthrow the royal throne of Seva's son and just like we did here in Golconda, we will hoist our flag with the insignia of the crescent moon and the star atop Raigad."

The rigorous worship was concluded and the murtis at both Gangoli and Sangameshwar were transported as per the royal command. The Shivyogi left with his disciples.

As soon as Raje arrived at Raigad, he received news from

Nilopant that had left him agitated. With a lowered head, the Peshwe had reported to Raje that Hasan Ali Khan has captured Honagad and Matabbar Khan has conquered Tryambakgad." The intention was clear. The Mughal army had reached up to Nashik.

Thorale Maharaj, Shahajiraje, had taken shelter on the Mahuli fort when he went to the Adil Shahi sultanate. But now, after the Nizam Shahi sultanate was overthrown, the custodian of the same Mahuli fort was deceiving Swaraj. He was scheming to team up with the Mughal sardar, Abdul Qadar who was stationed near the fort. He was ready to surrender the fort to Abdul Qadar for a hefty sum.

Every news Raje heard was gnawing at his heart.

Maharaj had not met Yesubai since arriving at the fort. How could he meet her? The ritualistic worship of Goddess Chandi weighed heavily on their minds. As the monsoon was ending, the activities of the Mughal forces had increased. Raje had appointed Mhaloji Ghorpade as the new Sarlashkar after Hambirarao's demise. He was taking shelter at Panhala and was keeping the Mughal prince at bay.

The Chhatrapati was pondering the details reported by Khandoji, Peshwe and the informers. Changoji Katkar broke his trance and announced, "Suryaji and Bopaji Prabhu, of the Kalyan region have come to meet you." Raje granted permission to Changoji and summoned the Prabhu brothers. The Prabhu brothers presented the case of their real estate properties in the parganas of Sakse, Panchmahal and Pune. Raje heard their case calmly and summoned Nyayadhish Prahladpant to handle the case.

Pant came. One observant look at him, would have made anyone notice the nervousness in his eyes.

"Nyayadhish, take a look at the case of the Prabhu brothers." Raje said simply as he was lost in thought. The Nyayadhish observed the Prabhu brothers and breathed a sigh of relief.

"Come with me to the office." Prahladpant said to the Prabhu brothers, and turned around to leave.

"Nyayadhish, I had told you once that the trees and bushes may swing with the gusts of wind, but the mountains of the region should not quiver. Just keep that in mind and serve justice to them accordingly." Raje was merely giving an instruction. But as Prahladpant responded "Ji" to him, his eyelashes fluttered, and his eyeballs rolled for a moment.

Raje was pacing in his chamber thinking about Aurangzeb, the Khans he had sent, the custodians of various forts who had turned traitor, and the Desais, Sawants and Dalavis of Fonda, Kudal and Karvar. Just then chamber maid, Rupa, arrived and announced, "Rani Saheb is coming."

Raje's heart was in turmoil. He wanted to share so many things! How was he going to say it? So many explanations to give! As if someone had pushed him, Raje unwittingly moved close to the window.

Yesubai came. She threw a glance around the chamber. The attendants serving in the chamber, got the hint and left. A strange silence prevailed between them. "I wanted to say one thing." Yesubai said in a hoarse voice. Raje turned around and glanced at her.

Yesubai nodded and said, "Please listen to me. I am quite ashamed. I have heard all the rumours that were cooked up and spread from my parental home in Shringarpur.

"Yesu..." Raje's eyes brimmed. They both didn't know what to say. The faces of Ganoji and Pilaji flashed in front of their eyes.

"You went through a tough time because of me. What the people of Shringarpur say about me, bothers me in the least, when I look at you." Raje spoke in a slow, hoarse voice, gazing at the blue skies visible at a distance from the window.

"My brother and father have no right to speak ill of Swari.

Swari should forget the past. Current conditions are tougher than the time when Aabasaheb and Swari, both were imprisoned in Agra. The enemies are infiltrating our kingdom from all sides, and our own people are turning against us!" Yesubai was overcome with emotion. Her voice got heavy; she paused for a moment.

"Do you remember? You had said once that you were married to the wild wind." Raje said without turning.

"Does Balraje ever visit Ramraje's palace? Do they talk to each other like a family?" Raje said, changing the topic altogether.

"Ji." Yesubai exclaimed cheerfully as she visualized the three faces of Ramraje, Tarau and Balraje.

Raje and Yesubai kept chatting for a long time. The lamp lighters came and lit the torches in the corners of the chamber and left.

Winter intensified. Despite the difficult circumstances Raje kept summoning Khandoji, Nilopant, Chimangaonkar and sending letters to Vatandars of various villages. He kept meeting prominent sardars in person either with Shankaraji, Nilopant or Khandoji. He was urging everyone from the bottom of his heart, "Don't join hands with the enemy who will go away sooner or later. Protect your region with your life, and give them a fitting fight just like our Fort Ramsej did."

Raje kept visiting the military encampments of Yesaji Kank, Rupaji Bhosale, Bardarmal, Santaji Jagatap, Janrao, and Dhanaji. If Harajiraje sought his advice on military matters, he sent appropriate recommendations to Karnataka through the informers. He wanted neither the Maratha kingdom nor the Karnataka region to surrender to Aurangzeb's onslaught. Sarjerao Jedhe, who had returned to the service of the Maratha kingdom, was serving him faithfully.

One cold day, Yesubai entered Raje's chamber with a bowl of hot, steaming porridge that was his favourite. She placed the bowl on the wooden stool. Raje glanced at the steam rising from the bowl and asked her, "It's been quite a while since I had porridge. Isn't it? Yesubai quickly picked up the bowl, gave it to Raje and said, "Swari doesn't eat properly nowadays. Please taste it and tell me if you like it." Raje sipped the porridge and said with a smile, "It's delicious."

Just then Balraje entered the chamber holding Raya-Anta's hands while asking them something.

As soon as he came in, he started complaining, "Whenever I go Kaka Maharaj's chamber, the Nyayadhish and two other people are always there. They stop talking when they see me. Why? Don't they like my coming to the chamber?"

Maharaj became solemn on hearing the childish complaint. 'Why does the Nyayadhish visit Ramraje's palace frequently? Most probably it's nothing! The news of treason coming from everywhere, has made me suspicious of everyone. He dismissed his doubt instantly.

He pulled Balraje close to him, patted him and said, "You should go and meet your Kaki Saheb. Then, nobody else will be there to disturb you." As he mentioned Tarau's name, Hambirarao's face flashed in front of Raje's eyes. He was still not ready to accept the fact that Hambirarao had died in the battle of Wai.

Balraje kept asking him for a long time, "Maharaj Saheb… Maharaj Saheb, Thorale Aaba had taken you on a long journey to the north when you were a child. But you don't let me go down the fort. I had a dream…"

Raje handed talkative Balraje to Raya-Anta and asked them, "You told me many times that Dharau's monument has been raised in Kapurhol, but I couldn't come and visit it. I would like to visit Kapurhol one day. Who else is there in Kapurhol?"

"Ji. Everyone is there, our wives, our old man and our children too." Everyone got lost in the sweet memories of Dharau.

One year had passed since the fall of Bhaganagar of Qutub

Shahi. Aurangzeb's sardars had dispersed all over the eastern region of the Maratha kingdom with their armies…Baglan, Khandesh, Varhad, Pune, Satara and Panhala. Now, Sarja Khan of Adil Shahi, Firajajung and a few other sardars of both sultanates had joined hands with Aurangzeb. Yet, he had barely managed to win a few forts by giving bribes. He had not met with any major success.

Raje's naval forces had kept the British and the Portuguese under control. Aurangzeb knew very well that Visapur and Golconda could be conquered on the strength of his mammoth army, but not this kingdom of Shiva and Sambha. Two years back he had experienced it first-hand. That is why, he was warning Prince Azam constantly, "Follow him, spend as much money as you want, but get the subedar of the Marathas arrested. Present him in front of me alive or dead. Then his kingdom will fall quickly."

Raje had also realized that Aurangzeb's power lay in bribing the people. That is why, he was rewarding people even for the smallest effort. Every town and village in the Maratha kingdom was giving a tough fight to the Mughal forces.

As per Raje's command, Surnis Shankaraji, Ramchandrapant, the officer in-charge of the Konkan coast, Majumdar Narayan Raghunath and other prominent people arrived on the fort.

As promised to Raya-Anta, Raje descended Raigad with his entourage. He was accompanied by Khandoji, Narayan Raghunath and Raya-Anta. Raje travelled with all to Kapurhol via Varanda ghat. Raya-Anta had sent advance intimation to Kapurhol that Dhani was coming to visit Kapurhol.

Raje had mounted Chandravat. As the horse was trotting, Raje said to Khandoji, "After returning from the campaign in Firangan, I rewarded you with the honour of a palanquin, but I never saw you sitting in the palanquin. Why so?"

"Ji. Swami bestowed the honour of a palanquin but… but…"

"But what?"

"But I have been travelling constantly. What can I do?" Khandoji replied smiling.

The summit of Purandar came in sight. The entourage arrived at Kapurhol. Baji Gholap came at the border of the village, to receive Raje.

Raje started walking towards the residence of Raya and Anta. Many memories of Dharau whirled in his heart. Raya and Anta's wives came out with vessels full of water. They poured it on Chandravat's hooves bedecked with golden anklets. Raje dismounted. Dharau's daughters-in-law performed his aukshan and applied kumkum to his forehead.

Raya and Anta felt very contented today. The simple, peasant Gaade brothers had held a wish for a long time. It was fulfilled today. Both brothers wished that their mother could have been alive to witness this day.

Both the brothers were standing among the crowd. Raje touched his chin to his chest and gestured to the elder brother Raya to come close. He didn't get it at first.

"Raya…" Raje called him gently. "Ji." Raya exclaimed and came forward.

"Rayaji, remove the shield on your back." Everyone was startled to hear Raje's words except for Narayan Raghunath. They wondered, "What mistake has Raya committed that Raje is discharging him from service?"

Stunned Raya couldn't help but exclaim, "Dhani, but…" The shield he was holding trembled.

Raje turned at an angle and glanced at Narayan Raghunath. He came forward with a rider. The rider was holding a covered platter. It had been carried from Raigad. Raje pinched the cloth and removed the covering. The golden treasure in the platter glowed in the rays of the sun. The whole platter of full of golden Hons.

Raje placed the platter on the shield that Rayaji was holding in front of him. He exclaimed in a hoarse voice, "Raya, string up a bell near Aau's samadhi. Make sure that the village of Kapurhol hears its tolls twice a day. Let's go there."

Raya and Anta kept gazing at the platter on the shield. Anta moved forward and poked Raya. Raya immediately realized his intention and quickly said, "Dhani, why are you giving this to us? We don't need it." Pure-hearted Raya stepped forward with the shield to return the platter.

As Raje touched it with his hand and returned it to Raya The diamond in his ring sparkled in the sun and words even brighter than the diamond spilled from his lips, "Raya-Anta, even if I would have sacrificed my own life and offered it at Dharau's feet, I wouldn't have been able to repay the debt of affection that she showered on me. Please keep this for her sake."

Raje took the darshan of Dharau's monument. As he touched his forehead to the monument, a thought occurred in his mind out of the blue, 'It would have been better, if I would have been born in Kapurhol instead of Purandar!'

Raje spent a night at the Gaade residence and returned to Raigad.

"Swami, the emperor has moved from Bijapur with his army. They are travelling in the direction of Aklooj to assist Prince Azam." Nilopant reported the emperor's activities to Maharaj.

"Harajiraje has sent Santaji back to the kingdom. He is stationed at Panhala with his forces." Khandoji reported Harajiraje's activities.

The Chhatrapati listened to both the pieces of news and started pondering over it. He wondered if Aurangzeb would charge upon Panhala via Miraj, Kolhapur with Azam's forces. He said to Khandoji, "Chitnis, send a message to Mhalojibaba at Panhala – it looks like Aurangzeb is planning to charge upon Panhala. You and Santaji be vigilant."

"Pant, spread your expert informers in the Solapur, Aklooj region. I should promptly receive the news of every movement of Aurangzeb without fail." Peshwe, Khandoji were listening to the commands attentively. Yesaji Kank, who had come from the Kalyan-Bhiwandi region, came to meet Raje. He was quite aged now. He said to Raje, "Please give me a new responsibility!"

Raje observed Yesaji and said to him gently, "Kank kaka, you should take some rest at your age. You… you should not leave Raigad now. I have to descend the fort any time. Who else is there to look after fort, but a veteran like you?"

Old Yesaji Kank responded "Ji" to the Chhatrapati and kept observing him. He remembered Thorale Maharaj. He had already lost his own son, Krishnaji in the Goa campaign while serving Swaraj. Yesaji had buried his son's memories deep down in his heart. He promised Maharaj and said, "Maharaj, rest assured about this fort of Thorale Maharaj. If at all any help is needed, I will call Dhanaji Jadhav who is stationed in the Satara province. I know very well that you have to travel all over the kingdom frequently."

"Kaka, since Hambirarao's death, I have been feeling very lonely. He was my staunch supporter!" Both Raje and Yesaji were moved by Hambirarao's memory.

"Kaka, go to the administrative office with Peshwe. The papers for Krishnaji's reward have been readied. Take them with you, and place this on Krishnaji's samadhi on my behalf." Raje pulled out the ring from his index finger and held out to Yesaji.

Rugged Yesaji was baffled. He exclaimed, "I don't want this. Who is going to wear it? And even if there was someone, he wouldn't dare wear it."

Raje put the ring back on his finger. Yesaji, Nilopant and Khandoji left.

Lost in thought, Raje came to Yesubai's chamber. Yesubai sat on her bed, talking to someone; as soon as she received intimation of Raje's arrival, she stopped her talk and stood up to receive him. She was talking to Kulesh's wife. As Raje saw her, he turned around to go back. Yesubai realized why he was going back and said to him, "It's nothing special. We were just having a casual conversation. Swari should stay." Still, Raje hesitated for a moment. Yesubai told him, "I was asking her about Chhandogamatya. He is stationed in the Panhala–Khelana region and is keeping a keen eye on Shirkan."

Kulesh's wife said to Yesubai, "Let me take your leave now" and left the chamber quickly to give Maharani and Raje privacy.

Silence prevailed in the chamber for some time.

"What is the news from Kulesh, about Shirkan?" Raje broke the silence, while gazing at the mountain range from the window.

"His wife was telling me that there has been some discord between Chhandogamtya and Shirke." Today, Raje realized that Yesubai refered to her parental family as 'Shirke.'

"What is the reason for the discord?" Raje asked.

"That is not clear." Yesubai was trying to guess the reason of the dispute. While talking to her, Raje remembered something and said to her, "Where is your personal secretary? Tell him to give intimation to Yesaji Dabhade that I am coming to visit Ramraje."

"Why does Swari want to visit Ramraje? I don't understand." Yesubai asked. A bizarre thought came to in Raje's mind – 'What if I would have been arrested in Panhala? What if Ramraje would have been enthroned?' Raje shifted his gaze from the mountain range and looked at Yesubai. Instead of answering her question, he asked her a question, "What do you think of Ramraje?"

"I don't understand." Yesubai was baffled.

"What if Ramraje would have been enthroned in my place? What if, you and I would have been content with the post of Subedar at Panhala?"

Yesuabai was taken aback to hear the unexpected question from Raje and exclaimed, "Why are you thinking about such a thing at such a wrong time?"

Yesubai's personal secretary came. Maharani instructed him to give the intimation to Ramraje and, to change the topic, she broached a different subject,

"News is, that the Mughal Prince stationed at Miraj is sending many of his sardars to the Panhala region to find out the whereabouts of Swari. You should take precautions at every sojourn, to evade them.

As Raje heard her words, he laughed and said, "You worry so much about me. I wish, your Dada Saheb would have worried so much about this kingdom, the people of Faltan would have supported him, Arjunaji and Achaloji would have come to Raigad instead of going to Aurangabad…anyway…. I will go visit Ramraje now."

As Raje was leaving the chamber, he saw Balraje coming with Bhavanibai and Rupa, the chambermaid. Raje held him close, patted his back and asked, "Would you like to visit your Kaki Saheb?". As Balraje nodded in the affirmative, both started walking to Ramraje's palace, with their guards.

They reached Ramraje's palace. Yesaji Dabhade came to receive Raje. Raje entered the seating chamber of the palace with him. Ramraje, who was seated, got up. He came forward, knelt and touched his Dadamaharaj's feet and pulled Balraje close to him.

As Raje looked at Ramraje's ruddy, fair complexion he remembered Ramraje's Masaheb. 'What was my relationship with her? She was the cause of so many undesirable incidents, but I never had any ill will towards Ramraje! He is Hambirarao's nephew, but I too consider him my own brother.'

"Summon Tarau too." The Chhatrapati said to Ramraje, who was patting Balraje's shoulder. Young Ramraje blushed; his cheeks went red. He glanced at Yesaji. Yesaji went to the inner chamber and brought Tarau with him. Tarau also touched Raje's feet. She placed the edge of her saree on her mouth and started sobbing in Hambirarao's memory. A grave silence prevailed in the chamber.

"Be calm. I have especially come to meet both of you. If you hear any rumours, don't pay much attention to them. We may have to make more sacrifices. If you notice anything wrong, feel free to talk to the Maharani. I might have to descend the fort anytime. Our enemies are spread all over." Tarau listened to every word of Raje attentively.

As Raje left Ramraje's palace, he signalled Yesaji to come with him. Raje left the chamber with Balraje; Ramraje and Tarau kept gazing at their backs for a long time.

Kulesh descended Fort Khelana, entered the Shirkan region and came to the borders of Shringarpur with his army. He sent his personal secretary with four to five riders, into the town, to meet Ganoji. Kulesh had come to meet the Shirkes as a mediator, on behalf of Raje. After all, the Shirkes were Yesubai's family.

Kulesh waited at the outskirts, for his secretary to come back. He knew that the Shirkes had become Aurangzeb's mansabdars. Still, he was hoping that as a senior member of the family, Pilaji would persuade Ganoji and Kanhoji. That in such difficult times, he would use his discretion and support Raje.

Kuelsh' secretary came to the court room of the Shirke residence.

The secretary of the Shirke family went inside and gave the intimation. Aged Pilajirao came to the court room. The personal secretary of Kulesh informed him about the purpose of his visit.

Pilaji's heart was flooded with memories. He remembered Yesubai and was overwhelmed. He remembered Thorale Maharaj. "Why should I long for the vatan? I barely know the Mughals; then why should I surrender my loyalty to them? Should I desert my daughter's husband in such difficult times? What was my standing earlier? Whatever I am today, is because of Maharaj. He determinedly asked, "Why did Kabji wait at the outskirts? This palace is not unknown to him. He should come here, and we can have the talks at length here."

Kulesh's secretary felt hopeful. He said, "Let me go back and bring him here." As he was about to leave, Ganoji arrived in the court room. As he entered the court room, silence prevailed in the room.

"Aaba, what is he talking about? Who is he going to bring here?" Ganoji raised his eyebrow and asked Pilaji while observing Kulesh' secretary. The Shirke secretary gave him detailed information. "What? That Kabji wants to enter Shringarpur? Aaba, why are you inviting him to our residence? Or has he charmed you, too?" Ganoji glanced at Kulesh's secretary furiously and said, "Go and tell your Dhani, this is the kingdom of the Shirkes and not Sangameshwar."

"The Chhandogamatya has come on behalf of Raje. He has brought the king's message for you. Please listen to it." Kulesh's secretary said courteously. As soon as Ganoji heard his words, he thundered, "Which king are you talking about? This is Shirkan, we Shirkes are the kings here. We don't accept anyone else's authority. Tell that Kabji to go back quietly, or else…!"

His own employees in the court room were stunned. Kulesh's secretary also wondered how to handle the situation. He somehow managed to say, "How can you think like this?"

"What do you mean? The emperor who overturned the Adil Shahi and Qutub Shahi, has himself appointed us. Soon everyone will come to know whether the Bhosale will survive against him. Kabji too is the emperor's spy! He is here to test our loyalty!"

Kulesh's secretary was shocked to hear that. He said, "Farewell" and left from there with a lowered head. Pilaji tried to stop him, "Please wait…"

"Aaba, have you forgotten how we were humiliated at Raigad? You may have forgotten the response of the Bhosale about Shirkan, but I haven't." Ganoji exclaimed and stopped him.

As the head of the family, Pilaji exclaimed, "What the Bhosale said is not important. I have given my daughter into that family. How can I forget that?"

"She is not your 'daughter'. She is the 'Rani Saheb' of the kingdom! You think of her as your daughter, but she doesn't consider you as her father." Ganoji silenced Pilaji with his response. He gave a strict warning to Kulesh's secretary and said, "Go and tell your Kabji, that Shirke's don't arrest the people who come to visit Shirkan."

Stunned, Kulesh's secretary turned around and left. Pilaji helplessly exclaimed, "As you wish, Goddess Waghjai!' and left the court room. Enraged, Ganoji kept pacing in the court room. Kanhoji, who had gone out to survey the fields, came inside. He had no idea what had happened here. Ganoji was worried that after Kulesh got his message from the secretary, he might launch an attack on Shringarpur. As soon as he saw Kanhoji, he instructed him to go out again and said, "Take the cavalry with you; Kabji is waiting at the border, attack him and chase him away." Ganoji himself led the infantry and joined Kanhoji.

Kulesh was waiting at the outskirts with the army; the Shirke brothers chased his army away from Shringarpur and out of Shirkan. Kulesh returned to Khelana. He immediately summoned his Chitnis and instructed him to send a message to Raje about the events in Shirkan. Furious and restless Kulesh started dictating the letter –

"To His Highness Swami – from your loyal servant, Chhandogamatya – "

Meanwhile, at Raigad, in the sanctum of the palace, the Maharani of the kingdom was taking darshan of her family deity, Waghjai, and praying to her, "Take care of everyone in Shringarpur! Aaba has become old now. I would like to meet him sometime!"

And there from Azam Shah's encampment in Kolhapur, Sheikh Nizam Dakkhani and his son, Ikhalas were marching to attack Panhala as they had received news that 'The King of the Marathas, Sambha is in Panhala.'

Chapter 16

Khandoji started reading Kulesh's letter aloud – "An altercation with Ganoji Shirke took place during the negotiations in Shirkan. He attacked my military camp with his army. I have withdrawn the forces, and taken shelter at Khelana. This matter of the Shirkes will not be resolved unless Swami comes in person with additional forces. I would like to share many things with you, but I have not got an opportunity to talk to you. Looking forward to meeting you."

Aurangzeb had vanquished Adil Shahi and Qutub Shahi, integrated their armies into his own, and their combined forces had infiltrated the Maratha kingdom from all sides. 'What should I do? Should I leave Raigad in such trying times? What Kulesh says is also right. Even if anybody other than he went there, he wouldn't dare to challenge Shirke. I need to go to Shirkan myself, to solve this family matter.' The Chhatrapati observed Khandoji, who had risked his own life in the Goa campaign, to save the Chhatrapati and his horse drifting in the creek and wondered, 'Should I dispatch Khandoji to Shirkan? No…' He left the court hall with Raya and Anta and started walking towards his private chamber.

As they came to his chamber, Raya and Anta waited outside. Raje entered the chamber and saw young Shivajiraje riding on Bhavanibai's back. Maharaj watched the scene intently. Yesubai saw him and, quickly moving forward, she picked up Balraje and put him on the floor. Maharaj saw it and asked her, "Why did you do that? He looked so handsome on the high seat!" The Chhatrapati pulled Balraje close and wondered how to share the news about Shirke with Yesubai. He hesitated for a moment. Yesubai noticed it and said, "I have come to know that a letter has arrived from Khelana! What has Swari decided to do?"

"I am thinking of sending Khandoji there." Maharaj responded.

"I think...Swari should go to Shirkan himself. This is a family matter. Khandoji would be hesitant to deal with my family!" Yesubai spoke Maharaj's mind.

At daybreak, Maharaj was ready to leave Raigad and start his journey to Shirkan. Five thousand cavalries and infantries were at the ready in the stable of Pachad. The Chhatrapati had decided to fight with the Shirkes only if required. With Peshwe Nilopant, Ramchandrapant, Khandoji, Changoji, Raya and Anta, he came in front of the royal throne. Maharaj's mind was crowded with thoughts; he touched his hand to the base of the royal throne and to his forehead. He started walking to Yesubai's chamber to bid farewell. Others waited in the central chowk, in front of the royal throne.

Yesubai had just returned to her chamber with Balraje and Bhavanibai after worshipping and imploring Goddess Jagadamba to ensure that nothing went wrong. Raje approached her and said, "Keep a close eye on the fort in my absence".

Yesubai had heard many times from Jijau that family feuds debilitate the head of the family considerably. She exclaimed, "Take care of yourself"; bowed down and touched her Swari's feet three times. Maharaj also became solemn as he heard her words.

"You be vigilant on the fort. Aurangzeb's forces have spread all over the kingdom. Farewell now." Maharaj patted Balraje's back. Yesubai offered him the tirtha of Goddess Bhavani; he consumed it and said to Bhavanibai with a smile, "I am drinking your tirtha!" Bhavanibai blushed. Yesubai held Balraje and Bhavanibai on her sides. Maharaj descended Raigad with the people waiting for him in the central chowk in front of the royal throne.

In the Balekilla of Khelana, Kulesh was reporting to Maharaj, "Swami, Shirke doesn't recognize your authority!"

"What is he up to Kaviji?" Maharaj asked Kulesh.

"Ji. He considers himself as the 'King' of Shirkan, appointed by Aurangzeb. Word is, that he intends to stoke a rebellion in collaboration with Ramraje."

"What...?" Eight years back, Maharaj had to go through a series of undesirable events and now something similar had come up again.

"Kaviji, I will charge upon Shirkan. I have left Raigad for that very purpose. You personally supervise my forces." Raje said determinedly.

Maharaj camped at Khelana for two days. Shirke had also got intimation about his arrival. Ganoji, Kanhoji... all the Shirke brothers were prepared for battle. Maharaj's mind was filled with memories of Pilaji.

On the third day, Maharaj had to charge upon Shringarpur; where he should have been honourably invited as the son-in-law. The Shirkes who had joined hands with Aurangzeb, were prepared for battle. A fierce battle took place in Shirkan; Shirkes lost the battle. Ganoji and Kanhoji abandoned their army and fled in the direction of Kolhapur. Pilaji's whereabouts were unknown too. When the same Pilaji was serving under the Surves, Aabasaheb had noticed his loyalty and bravery; he had taken Pilaji into his service and appointed him as an assistant administrator of Shringarpur region. When Maharaj himself went from Panhala to Raigad after Aabasaheb's demise, Pilaji had assisted him in taking control of Raigad. More than anything else, the fact that he was Yesubai's father, left Raje heartbroken. He made arrangements for the governance of Shirkan and left for Khelana.

As he had surveyed Khelana with Kulesh, he realized that the fort which was convenient to keep watch on the Shirkan region, was badly in need of repairs.

"Kulesh, get the entire fort repaired." He commanded Kulesh. But…he wondered, 'A fort can be repaired… but how can I repair the relationship with family members like Ganoji?'

"Kaviji, you stay put here and keep a keen eye on Shirkan. I will travel via Panhala, Battis Shirala, Satara, Wai and Mahad ghat, to go back to Raigad." Maharaj told Kulesh, and, after spending a night on Khelana, he travelled to Panhala.

After taking the darshan of the Shivlinga, the Chhatrapati came to the court hall of the Balekilla. Lost in memories, he was pacing back and forth. He remembered the recent battle with the Shirkes.

"Krishnaji Kanhere is here to see you." The Sarnoubat of the fort, Mhalojibaba said. Raje gave him a startled look. Mhaloji's young brothers, Santaji and Bahiroji Ghorapade were standing by his side. Nyayadhish Prahladpant, who Raje had sent to Panhala, to keep Azam Shah in check was also present. He said, "Krishnaji has some trade-related complaint."

Raje raised his hand and granted permission. He listened to Krishnaji Kanhere's complaint in detail. "Nyayadhish, you deal with Krishnaji's case. Discuss the matter with the officer-in-charge of the Pargana, and other concerned officers, before delivering the verdict." Raje handed the responsibility of Kanhere's case to Prahladpant.

"Prahladpant, let's go to the Sajjakothi." He deliberately took the Nyayadhish with him. From the court room he came to the Sajjakothi along with everyone.

"Pant, I am anxious about the issue with the Shirkes. You have spent quite some time in this region. What are they up to?"

Pant was startled. When he heard the question…his mouth

went dry. "It's a family matter Swami… How can I interfere?" He barely managed to answer. It was true. No one could do much in this matter.

Everyone started climbing the stairs leading to the terrace of the Sajjakothi. Mhaloji followed Raje and climbed the stairs briskly.

Raje glanced over the region of Kolhapur, Jotiba that was visible from the terrace and asked, "Which Mughal sardar is posted in Kolhapur?"

"Sheikh – Nizam of Qutub Shahi! After the fall of Bijapur, the emperor honoured him with the title of 'Mukarrab Khan'. He is keeping a keen eye on Panhala." Mhaloji's replied.

"Has he ever launched an attack on the fort?"

"Ji. He tries from time to time, but I keep a hawk-like watch." Mhaloji said.

Obviously, neither Raje nor Mhaloji knew that Ganoji and Kanhoji who had fled from Shringapur, had visited the same Mukarrab Khan in his encampment. The cold evening wind started blowing. The evening round of kettle drums resounded. Paach Darwaja, Teen Darwaja… all gates of Panhala were being closed. At the foothills of the fort, dim lamps were lit up in every house. Raje savoured the tranquil, serene evening on Panhala and turned around to leave the terrace. Just then the custodian of Panhala rushed from the staircase to the terrace of the Sajjakothi. Gasping for air, he exclaimed, "…Raigad…has been…besieged by… Etikad Khan… Dhani!" He barely managed to utter the words and had forgotten to pay obeisance to Raje. Countless thoughts swirled in Raje's mind. The faces of Yesubai, Balraje, Ramraje, Changoji, Jotyaji… flashed in front of his wide-open eyes. Raigad! Besieged!

He went down the stairs briskly, without even looking at anyone.

Within half an hour, one unit of the army was ready to march. Raje dispatched the unit towards Raigad and as he was leaving Panhala with select men, he said to Mhaloji, "Don't lose hope, Mhalojibaba. Hold your courage. If I need your assistance, I will send a messenger. Come immediately when you get my message."

Mhaloji, Santaji and Prahladpant made an obeisance. Thinking about Raigad, Raje prodded Chandravat, and left the serene evening at Panhlala behind him. Aurangzeb's military camps were stationed on the Battis Shirala, Wai-Mahad route. Except for the Khelana-Sangameshwar route, there was no other way to reach Raigad. Raje's army started galloping in that direction.

In the Balekilla of Khelana, the Chhatrapati was restlessly pacing back and forth. He said to Kulesh, "Kaviji, I am going to march to Raigad right away. I will take as many of your soldiers with me as possible. There is no time to waste now." Kulesh, the custodian of the fort, Raya and Anta were standing around him in the court room; everyone was anxious. They knew very well the purpose of the attack on Raigad.

"Swami, whatever the problem is, just give me the order, and I will deal with it!" Kulesh said firmly.

But he had something else on his mind that he wanted to share with Raje.

"Kulesh, send intimation of my arrival to Sangameshwar."

"Ji." Kulesh exclaimed habitually. But he was lost in thought.

As it was unavoidable, Raje spent the night at Khelana. At daybreak, he left for Sangameshwar with select men. Kulesh was riding by his side and the entourage followed them. None of them had a clue that Ganoji, Kanhoji Shirke and Nagoji Mane had spent the night at Mukarrab Khan's military camp in Kolhapur, and provided him with the details of the Chhatrapati's whereabouts, and the number of men accompanying him. Then they had taken darshan of the Goddess Ambabai of Kolhapur in the wee hours, and had returned to their camp as the festival of Shivaratri was approaching.

The border of Sangameshwar, which was located at the confluence of two rivers came into sight. Some stablemen had brought horses to the confluence to quench their thirst. While returning to the stable, they came across Maharaj who had entered the town. They quickly dismounted to make an obeisance to Maharaj. Maharaj didn't even notice it. As he saw the horses passing in front of him, he pulled Chandravat's reins and stopped in his tracks. Those horses were 'defective'! The front hooves of the dark black horses had white spots on them.

As Maharaj noticed it, an apprehension rattled his heart, 'Has something bad happened in Raigad…."

Raje went to the temple near the confluence and took darshan of Lord Shiva. He prayed to the Shivlinga in front of him, 'No harm should fall upon Aabasaheb's beloved Raigad. To keep it safe, I would sacrifice my life.'

Raje stayed at the Sardesai residence in Sangameshwar with his entourage and Arjoji–Girjoji Yadav who had come from Karhad joined him there. Ranganath Swami Gosavi who had come from Sajjangad, came to meet Raje at the Sardesai residence and left for Waghapuri after meeting him.

Maharaj was pondering Etikad Khan's siege of Raigad. Kulesh was worried about Raigad too. He courageously said, "Before going to Raigad…"

"Yes Kaviji." Maharaj was lost in thought.

"If we perform Lord Shiva's puja, our problems might alleviate. Shivaratri is approaching so…." Shiva devotee Kulesh said.

"Kaviji, I have been so preoccupied, that I forgot Shivaratri is approaching. Aabasaheb raised a Shiva temple at every fort. Why? So that he could take the darshan of Lord Shiva, as soon as he climbed up the fort. Today his own Raigad is in trouble. Pray to Lord Shiva on our behalf for resolution. The cavalry at Pachad will not surrender to the attacks until I reach there." For the first time ever in life, he was going to break the siege of

Raigad. His heart was seeking some kind of support. It was essential to break the siege of Raigad. Backing out now would be heart breaking.

"Send letters to Khelana, Panhala and Vishalgad to dispatch the additional infantry to Raigad. You make preparation for Lord Shiva's puja in person. I have heard that Aurangzeb performs his Namaz in the morning, afternoon and evening without fail." Raje looked calm outwardly, but no one could unravel the mysteries of his deep thought.

The Sardesai residence in Sangameshwar got engaged in the preparations for Lord Shivas's puja. The rivers merging at the confluence were flowing smoothly. The towering mountains stood firm. They were surrounded by the green flora of Konkan.

Kulesh invited erudite Brahmins of the Malakapur, Khelana and Sangameshwar regions to Sangameshwar. In the central chowk of the Sardesai residence a yajna pit was raised for Lord Shiva's puja. In the family sanctum of the Sardesai residence, the Shivlinga was continuously getting drenched under the stream flowing from the vessel of Abhishek. As if every drop of water was whispering, "Raigad-Raigad". The Sardesai residence was getting enveloped by the smoke of the yajna offerings. Raje used to come to the court hall after performing the religious rituals. After two days of rituals, when the Chhatrapati came to the court hall, Kulesh said to him, "We have to leave for Raigad now. I will take the responsibility of Malakapur, Panhala and Sangameshwar. Therefore…." Kulesh who had been wanting to share some news with Maharaj since their meeting on Khelana, hesitated.

"You are coming with me for sure. Now think about Raigad only. The situation here will continue to pose challenges." Maharaj said.

"I must say that in the case of Raigad, the goddess of Justice has betrayed us. The Nyayadhish…himself…" Kulesh hesitated again.

"What did he do?" Maharaj's forehead puckered.

"The Nyayadhish has conspired against Maharaj!"

"Kaviji!" Maharaj stood up at once. It was as if somebody had poured boiling oil all over his body. His entire body trembled. He shook with anger, loneliness and a strange suffocation. "Chhandogamatya, don't accuse anyone! You must have made a mistake. The Nyayadhish…and conspiracy? The news of a mother pushing her own child off a cliff is indeed unbearable. Any evidence of it?" The Chhatrapati remembered that he had honourably discharged Nyayadhish Prahladpant during the first conspiracy. He also remembered that he had warned the Chief Justice at that time, "Please don't commit such a mistake again. I won't be able to tolerate it." He fixed his gaze on Kulesh. Kulesh, a strong person himself, was terrified to look into his eyes.

"Kulekhtyar, you had better present some evidence."

"Ji." Petrified, Kulesh pulled out a roll of a letter from the scarf tied around his waist with trembling hands, and held it in front of Maharaj. The Nyayadhish, Prahladpant, had written a letter to the Mughal mansabdar, Ganoji Shirke. Maharaj opened it and started reading it. Each word scalded his heart like molten lead. The Nyayadhish, who travelled all over the kingdom for various missions, who represented Swaraj as an envoy in the British durbar, had written to Ganoji, "Ramraje is alone. If he is enthroned, you will obtain the post of Kulekhtyar for sure. Kulesh came out of nowhere and now has become more powerful than all of us. Raje doesn't listen to anyone except him." As soon as the Chhatrapati finished reading the letter, he instantly closed his eyes. Many memories of Prahladpant flashed in front of his closed, distressed eyes.

With his eyes still closed, trembling with rage, he ordered Kulesh, "Send this letter to Panhala. Inform Mhaloji to let the Nyayadhish read this charge sheet against him written with his own hands. Detain him whenever and wherever he is found!

And… and you immediately stop worshipping Shiva for Raigad's safety!" Kulesh' head was hanging. Maharaj hurled the roll of the letter towards Kulesh and briskly walked towards his chamber. He was deeply hurt and wanted to be left alone.

Kulesh implored Maharaj and barely managed to convince him to leave after the concluding ceremony of Lord Shiva's puja. The day of the concluding ceremony dawned in Sangameshwar. Today, the townspeople presented themselves at the Sardesai residence and offered oblations in the yajna pit. The entire town felt jubilant to relish the delicious food prepared for the concluding ceremony.

In the late afternoon, Arjoji Yadav who had come from Karhad, came to visit Maharaj. He put forth a matter that he had wanted to share with Maharaj since his arrival in Sangameshwar. Arjoji was the designated in-charge of the construction department. His brother, Girjoji had travelled on foot to Burhanpur, Khuldabad to pursue the whereabouts of Durgabai Rani Saheb. The Yadav brothers had faithfully served the kingdom. Thorale Maharaj had promised the vatan of Karhad and Aundh to the Yadav brothers. But soon after that, he had breathed his last. The matter was still pending, after eight years.

"Dhani, please pursue the matter of our vatan of Karhad and Aundh, and provide us with the official documents. The Mughal prince is camped in the Miraj region with his army. We would like to return there." Arjoji put forth the proposal to his Dhani. Maharaj intently observed Arjoji, who had raised the temple in Pachad at the foothills of Raigad as per Yesubai's wish.

"Arjoji, your family has been very closely associated with our family since Aabasaheb's time. But I couldn't pay you enough attention. You must be disappointed."

Maharaj summoned the chitnis of the Sardesai family and instructed him to prepare the documents of Karhad and Aundh vatan in the name of the Yadav brothers. After the documents were prepared, he signed them and said to the chitnis, "Stamp these documents with the royal seal, and hand them to Arjoji. And Arjoji, once you receive the documents stamped with the official seal, travel to Karhad with your retinue.

The Brahmins who had come to perform the concluding ceremony accepted the Dakshina from Kulesh, blessed Raje, and returned to their hometowns. This was the last night to be spent in Sangameshwar.

Meanwhile, Ganoji whispered in Mukarrab Khan's ears, "Only five hundred horses are stationed in Sangameshwar. It is surrounded by high mountains. There is no military post nearby that can rush to their aid. We just need to keep in check Sardar Ghorpade on Panhala. This is a great opportunity to capture the enemy. But Khan Saab, after the success of this mission, please do not forget to propose the subject of the vatan of Shirkan to the emperor."

In the Mahalakshmi temple of Kolhapur, the evening prayers were in session. Ganoji's loyal words were scattered in the sound of the bells tolling in the temple. Mukarrab Khan left immediately, with a troop of fifteen hundred staunch soldiers. He was going to travel from Kolhapur to Sangameshwar via Amba ghat.

Fifteen hundred armed cavalry led by Mukarrab Khan, and his son Ikhalas Khan galloped from Kolhapur. Ganoji and Kanhoji riding on the right, and Nagoji Mane on the left, accompanied them to show the fastest way to Sangameshwar.

Mukarrab Khan was galloping frantically. Streams and brooks on the way kept passing by quickly. At dusk, the troops took a quick break.

Torches were ignited. The torchbearers, astride their horses, holding the torches in one hand went to the forefront. Some of them dispersed in the army. Like a burning flame leaping forward, the determined army galloped ahead.

The sentry guarding the Konkan Darwaja of Panhalgad noticed the moving line of torches and rushed to the Balekilla.

Gasping for air, he told Sarnoubat Mhaloji Ghorpade, "Ghorpade baba, we are undone. The enemy forces stationed at Kolhapur are riding in the direction of Sangameshwar. I couldn't estimate the number of the riders in the darkness of the night."

Immediately, quick commands were given in succession. Mhaloji approached the stable with his sons, Santaji and Dhanaji. Five hundred horses were saddled in a short time. With the five hundred riders, Mhaloji descended Panhala through Konkan Darwaja. He took the fastest way, in the direction of Vishalgad and started galloping towards Sangameshwar. The aged Ghorpade was riding desperately with his two young sons, to save the Maratha kingdom from the enemy's clutches.

"Aaba, will we be able to reach Sangameshwar on time?" The elder son, Santaji asked with uncertainty.

"Just reaching on time isn't going to be enough. We might have to sacrifice our lives to keep Shivajiraja's heir safe." Mhaloji's long white moustache fluttered in the wind.

Mhaloji on one side and Mukarrab Khan and his troops from the other, kept galloping desperately to reach Sangameshwar as soon as possible. In the Mahalakshmi and Jotiba temples of Kolhapur the bells resonated as usual. The dark night was ascending.

Meanwhile, Sangameshwar was in deep slumber. Armed guards were keeping watch on the Sardesai residence. The Chhatrapati was unable to sleep; he was tossing and turning in his bed. Aurangzeb, who had devoured Adil Shahi and Qutub Shahi and was stationed in Akalooj, many traitors of the kingdom, the Portuguese and the Siddis who were ready to seize control of the ocean – many images were flashing in front of his eyes. The faces of Yesubai, Aabasaheb, Thoralya Aau, Dharau, Samartha, Putalabai Saheb, Durgabai and Ranooakka who were detained in Khuldabad, were mingling with those images. In the stable of the Sardesais, the horses were snorting occasionally.

After midnight, Maharaj dozed off. The night was ascending

faster. A new day was striving to break through the womb of the night. In the late night, two riders entered the central chowk of the residence breaking the silence of the night and darted in like arrows. They told the attendant to quickly wake Kulesh quickly. The attendant entered Kulesh's chamber located next to Maharaj's sleeping chamber and woke him up. A bareheaded Kulesh came outside in anguish.

"What is it?" He suspiciously asked the riders who were making an obeisance to him.

"The enemy has taken the fastest way through the forests and is approaching Sangameshwar. Wake up Maharaj immediately. We need to deliver the news to him." One of the riders said, looking around, shaking in fear. Kulesh rushed to Maharaj's sleeping chamber. He went inside, stood by his bed and promptly called him out, "Swami, please get up."

"Who is it?" Maharaj asked and sat on his bed. Outside, the roosters in the households of Sangameshwar were crowing.

"We don't have time. An army is galloping through the forests. Maharaj should leave Sangameshwar without wasting a moment."

"The army has many more horses than we have here. We won't be able to face them." Both messengers exclaimed one after the other.

The riders were curiously watching the Chhatrapati who was pacing back and forth. Raje gazed at a torch burning in a corner, stopped in his tracks and said to Kulesh, "Shirke – those must be Shirke's men. There is no enemy camp nearby, except that of Kolhapur. They wouldn't dare to ride in the middle of the night through the thick forests to attack Sangameshwar. Kulesh, make arrangements for the messengers." Maharaj commanded. Preoccupied Kulesh and the messengers made an obeisance and left the chamber nervously. Maharaj continued pacing back and forth. After some time, he returned to his bed, but could not sleep. Thoughts of the Shirkes occupied his mind.

'After reaching Raigad, how am I going to tell Yesubai that I had to drive her brothers out of Shirkan? What kind of a bond do I have with the Shirkes? What did Yesubai gain by getting married to me?' Raje was lost in thought.

There, Mhalojibaba had entered the boundary of Sangameshwar, surrounded the town with his cavalry, and stood guard to defend it. As he had galloped speedily by a shortcut, he had reached in time. His troops shouted at the top of their lungs, "Har Har Mahadev!".

Before their slogans could fade, Mukarrab and Ikhalas pierced the borders of Sangameshwar with their frenzied, belligerent army behind them. The rising sun was overshadowed with clouds of dust. Sangameshwar echoed with the shouts of "Dheen.... Dheen..." Chaos ensued. Maharaj heard the commotion. He rose at once and leapt towards the door. Trembling, Kulesh rushed from outside and almost bumped into him. Raya and Anta were not in their right minds. Raya disregarded the usual royal protocol; he held the Chhatrapati's upper arms and shaking him vigorously he exclaimed, "Don't waste a single moment. We are undone. Just take your sword and get out of here – go... go..."

Raje swirled around, placed his Jiretop on his head, pulled his sword out of the scabbard and wielded a shield in his left hand. Kulesh also rushed to his chamber, wielded his sword and shield and came out. Everyone in the Sardesai residence picked any weapon they could grab and tried getting out while shouting, "Get out, we are surrounded by the enemy." Bedlam ensued in the Sardesai residence. Maharaj came out with Raya-Anta, Kulesh and Arjoji. The stablemen had already pulled the horses out of the stable and were staring (anxiously) at the door. They were first going to slay a few Mughal soldiers that had broken through the wall of Mhaloji's troops and entered the Sardesai residence, and then hand over the horses to Maharaj. Just then, wielding his sword, Ikhalas Khan approached the door with a few hundred belligerent soldiers who were shouting 'Dheen…Dheen'. Mhalojibaba, who was worried to death about Maharaj, desperately approached the door with Santaji and Bahirji while dodging the strikes of Mukarrab Khan's troops. A battle broke out right in front of the door. Raje, Kulesh, Arjoji, Raya and Anta had managed to mount the horses the stablemen had brought. Mhaloji had managed to bring his horse close to his Dhani. He was moving around his Dhani rapidly and while dodging the strikes coming his way and striking back, he was shouting and telling Raje, "Dhani, get out of here, and go to the Navadi river. Take a boat and escape. We will fight till our last breath." It was as if the Maratha kingdom was crying out loud through him. Fierce clashes between armed Mavalas and Mughal soldiers had broken out at many places. The clanging of the swords, the war cries, the tapping hooves, and the neighing of the horses… there was commotion everywhere.

Ferocious Chhatrapati Sambhajiraje astride Chandravat, brandished his sword and swiftly broke through the commotion wherever he could. Fierce, adept fighters like Mhaloji, Kulesh, Santaji, Bahirji, Arjoji surrounded him. They kept clearing the way for him towards Navadi river, like one carefully shelters a tiny lamp through a storm. Just as Maharaj's horse, Chandravat was moving forward, Ikhlas Khan was also moving forward dodging the Mavala soldiers engaged in fighting with his soldiers. Now, Maharaj had come quite close to Navadi river. Mhaloji – Kulesh and Mukarrab - Ikhalas were shouting war slogans at the top of their lungs to inspire their soldiers. Some of the Mavalas had broken away from the commotion and had the boats (with weapon) ready in the river. The boats anchored near the shore were swaying on the water; the soldiers standing in them were anxiously watching the tussle on the ground.

Ikhalas noticed that Mhaloji was preving the biggest obstacle in capturing the king of the infidels; he pointed towards Mhaloji and screamed, "Capture that old man." The infuriated Mughal soldiers surrounded Mhaloji, who was taking the lead in protecting Raje. Mhaloji was separated from others. Still, he kept shouting loudly in his aged voice, "Dhani… Navadi…. the boats…". No place on his body was left to bear any more strikes. And… and… finally, one Mughal soldier's sword struck him on the chest! Mhaloji collapsed from his horse. The second pugnacious Sarlashkar of the Maratha kingdom fell on the battleground.

In the meantime, Raje had reached the shores of Navadi river, fighting. "Mhalojibaba has fallen". The news singed his ears. For a split moment, the sword in his hand stopped. A Mughal soldier took that opportunity and tried to strike Raje, but Raje quickly tilted his neck and dodged the strike; his Jiretop fell on the ground. Stunned, Raje prodded Chandravat so hard with his mojaris that he sprinted wildly towards the riverbank.

But…he couldn't enter the river; it was already blocked by armed Mughal soldiers. As the Chhatrapati turned his horse around, he saw Santaji – Bahirji following him like his shadow. He shouted at them, "Don't wait here. Go to Raigad immediately and protect it with your life… go." Raje and the Ghorpade brothers, both were returning the blows of the Mughal soldiers around them. A devastated Santaji shouted at the top of his lungs, "Whatever is going to happen is going to happen. Aaba is no more. How can we leave Dhani alone at such a time?"

"In the name of Goddess Jagadamba, I command you to leave now…" In all the commotion on the battlefield, Santaji looked into his unfathomable eyes and shouted while striking with his sword, "Ji." He turned his horse around; Bahirji followed him.

The dead bodies of slain Mavala and Mughal soldiers lay askew along the banks of Navadi river. The white sideburns of Mhalojibaba's motionless body were fluttering on the wind. His open eyes were riveted on the banks of Navadi river with some kind of hope. Arjoji, Raya and Anta followed the Chhatrapati like his shadow. Kulesh, who had been derided as 'Kanoja' by all ministers throughout his life, fought on Raje's right. The clanging of clashing swords kept echoing everywhere; suddenly an arrow, shot from somewhere, pierced Kulesh's upper right arm. He clasped his right arm with his left hand and collapsed.

The Chhatrapati approached Kulesh while dodging the strikes made at him. He jumped down in a flash, put his arm under Kulesh' arm, and pulling him up, he exclaimed, "Arise, Chhandogamatya. Hold your courage. We will fight till our last breath." Kulesh had already pulled out the arrow and thrown it aside. His jama on the upper right arm was soaked in blood, but he was still holding his sword in his hand. Raya-Anta, Arjoji and many other swordsmen had dismounted with Raje and were staving off the Mughal soldiers who were trying to attack Raje and Kulesh. Ikhalas and Mukarrab had also dismounted. It was so crowded that many soldiers couldn't even wield their swords. Raje was encircled by the crowd. Many spear heads and sword blades grazed his wounded body from all sides. The Bhavani sword froze in his hand. Kulesh, Rayaji and Antaji were also trapped. Mukarrab's young son, Ikhalas made his way through the crowd and came in front of wretched Sambha, the scion of the Maratha kingdom; who had plundered Burhanpur and Aurangabad; who had harassed the Portuguese of Goa and terrified the Siddis of Janjira; who had forced his Aka-Hazrat to pull out his forces from the Maratha kingdom.

"Drop your weapon." Ikhalas roared. His words passed over Raje's ears like an ocean wave passing over a solid boulder. He did not move at all.

"Did you hear me, Kafir? Drop your weapon!" An enraged Ikhalas grabbed Raje's hair in his fist and roared while shaking it. This was the same hair that had been blessed by the pure water of holy rivers during the coronation ceremony. His arrogant action infuriated Raje and he stared at Khan with fiery eyes. Khan was terrified by the piercing gaze; he thought Raje was going to strike him with the sword. Just then, making his way through the crowd, Mukarrab Khan, with his thick red beard and moustache came there. Ikhalas made an obeisance to him and said, "He is not dropping his weapon. This kafir is too insolent."

"Have some patience, my son. True warriors don't give up their weapons easily." Mukarrab consoled his son and approached Raje. He looked at Raje and said to the Mughal soldiers around him, "Shackle him with ropes first and then pull his sword out of his hand. Take him away."

The battle was over. All living Mavala soldiers had been captured. Maharaj and Chhandogamatya Kavi Kulesh were shackled in front of the Lord Shiva of Sangameshwar!!

A new day was about to break. At that time, in the encampment of sixty thousand soldiers in Aklooj, Muhiuddin Mohammed Alamgir Gazi Aurangzeb was kneeling on a carpet in his shamiana and performing his Sabra-ki-Namaz.

After finishing his Namaz, he asked Wazir Asad Khan, "Is there any news of Mukarrab from Kollapur? Is he chasing Sambha at all, or just spending time in the company of women in Kollapur?"

Mukarrab Khan had no time to wait. He knew very well that if he waited there, the Mavala soldiers would attack them and leave no stone unturned to free their king from captivity.

He left a troop of armed soldiers behind to bury his dead soldiers and ordered Ikhalas, "Whoever is ready to convert to Islam, release them." Raya and Anta were among the captured soldiers, they were never going to agree to conversion. Their fate was sealed. Arjoji had managed to escape. But he knew he couldn't do anything alone, so he had travelled towards Karhad. Santaji and Bahirji, who had escaped safely were riding towards Raigad as per the command they had received from Raje.

After Raje dismounted Chandravat, the Mughal soldiers had

struck him repeatedly in their wrath; wounded Chandravat had collapsed to the ground, his chest was gently heaving up and down. He was in pain and tears were streaming from his eyes. To one side, among the Ghorpade troops that had lost their lives, lifeless Mhaloji's fist was still clamped around his sword's handle. His twisted red turban lay on the ground near his sword.

Ikhalas and Mukarrab had ordered the spearmen to surround Kulesh and Raje and trapped them together. Mukarrab moved around briskly, and gave quick orders to his soldiers, "Hurry up. We don't have time." His face betrayed excitement as he stroked his reddish beard from time to time.

Detained Maratha soldiers were being carried away for slaughter.

Mukarrab Khan's army was now ready for the return journey. Mukarrab Khan inspected everything in person to make sure it was okay and roared, "Dump the kafirs on the horses. Fasten them tightly with ropes and take this royal gift to our Hazrat. The Maratha king and his Brahmin poet. This is great. Allah has blessed us."

The spearmen poked Raje with the spears and the shackle-holders started pulling the shackles. Raje planted his feet firmly on the ground, clasped the chains in his own fists and staring at Mukarrab he exclaimed determinedly, "Khan, this is a battle. I want to see my Sarlashkar."

Baffled, Mukarrab looked at the soldiers around him and asked, "What is he saying? What does he mean?"

Raje kept his eyes fixed on Mukarrab and quickly said in the Hindustani language, "This is a battleground. I am a king. I want to see my commander who sacrificed his life."

"Certainly, certainly" Mukarrab threw his head back and laughed so hard that his eyes got misty. Raje rushed towards the place where Mhaloji lay dead; he almost dragged the shackle-holders with him. Raje touched dead Mhaloji's chest and touched the hand to his own forehead to pay his respects. Mhaloji had earned that honour from the king of the Maratha kingdom by sacrificing his life!

The shackle-holders pulled the shackles. The spearmen poked the spears. Raje and Kulesh were pushed forcibly onto the horses. Both their hands were tied tightly with ropes. Their bodies were tightly fastened to the horses with ropes. Ikhalas held the reins of Raje's horse in his fist. Two spearmen got ready to poke the horses with spears to keep them trotting. After the Chhatrapati and Chhandogamatya were fastened to the horses like sacks, Mukarrab Khan raised his sword high and roared loudly, "Dheen… dheen… march forward…"

The army of Mukarrab and Ikhalas rode in the direction of Miraj. In the regions around Sangameshwar, Khelana, Panhala, Malakapur…none of the military camps had any inkling of what had transpired in Sangameshwar. Santaji and Bahirji were galloping in the direction of Raigad with a few soldiers; their hearts still lingered in Sangameshwar. "We should rescue Maharaj, but how are we going to do it? Where could those scoundrels have taken him? In all that commotion, we couldn't even cremate our father's body. What to do and how to do it?" Their minds were racing way ahead of their horses.

The Sardesai residence was in tatters. Valiant soldiers had lost their lives. Detained prisoners were being gathered for slaughter. The ashes from the yajna pit in the central chowk of the residence scattered all over. The vessel of Abhishek above the Shivlinga in the sanctum had run out of water and was gaping at the Shivlinga. It was a grim and ominous scene.

Mukarrab's triumphant army passed by Panhalgad and was on its way to the secured ground fort in Miraj via Bhedasgaon and Battisashirala.

The sentinels guarding the bastion walls of Panhala also saw it from afar. But no one had a clue that it was carrying the scion of Swaraj with it. A few Mavala horse riders who had somehow managed to escape from Sangameshwar had taken a shortcut and were galloping back to Kolhapur thinking that Mukarrab will take Raje to his camp in Kolhapur.

Mukarrab's army crossed the Varana River near Malakapur and reached the ground fort of Battisashirala which had belonged to Adil Shashi previously but was now under the command of Aurangzeb. Four Mughal military camps were located on this side of the Varana River. Khan was now relieved and relaxed. During the last two days he had successfully managed to travel during the night, win the battle of Sangameshwar and start the return journey even at the cost of his own soldiers' lives.

Among the sixty thousand soldiers in the encampment of Aklooj there was a huge uproar. The messengers that Mukarrab had sent from Sangameshwar had reached Aklooj. Within moments, the news that "The devil Sambha has been captured" spread in the encampment. The Mughal soldiers in the encampment were embracing each other in joy and were exclaiming, "Did you hear that kafir Sambha has been caught? Allah is gracious!"

Wazir Asad Khan had shared the incredible news with Shahen Shah Alamgir in his royal shamiana while bowing to him frequently. Aurangzeb kept moving the beads of his rosary faster and, containing the joy in his heart with a lot of effort, he commanded the Wazir in a calm voice, "Prepare to move the army from Aklooj to Bahadurgad now. Send the royal Khilat to Mukarrab."

Meanwhile, Mukarrab had left from Battisashirala and reached the land fort of Miraj; he was making every possible effort to keep his precious prisoners alive. He believed that both prisoners would ultimately convert to Islam to save their lives. Valiant Raje may accept the Khilat and become the Subedar of Deccan. Sikandar Adil shah of Bijapur and Tana Shah of Golconda could not survive the onslaught of the Mughal sultanate; how could an ordinary king like Sambha survive it? That was why he was taking every precaution to prevent them from getting hold of a weapon, so that they could not take their own lives; and he was trying his best to ensure that they consumed enough food. But, since the meal they had eaten during the final puja ceremony, Raje and Kulesh had not touched a single morsel.

Aurangzeb had left Aklooj and gone ahead to Bahadurgad in Pedgaon with his personal troops. More than half of his encampment also moved from Aklooj. Mukarrab who was keen on presenting the prisoners in front of the emperor, reached from Miraj to Aklooj. The soldiers in the encampment started shouting in excitement and crowded to see the prisoners.

Raigad was rattled as if shaken by an earthquake. Santaji and Bahirji had reached Raigad. They had evaded Etikad Khan's siege around Raigad from the side of Pachad and arrived on the fort through a secret door. As they stood in front of Yesubai in her chamber, Santaji covered his face with the saddle he had brought, and, sobbing loudly he said, "Masaheb, Goddess Jagadamba has cursed us. I have no courage to share this, but Dhani was betrayed in Sangameshwar! He was besieged and captured by Mukarrab Khan who was stationed in Kolhapur!" His face still covered with the saddle, Santaji fell at Yesubai's feet and started crying; his whole body trembled. Yesubai instantly placed her hands on her ears; she was benumbed as if struck by lightning. She lost awareness that she was the Maharani, and she was in Raigad. "Oh, mother Waghjai!" she screamed silently in her heart, her entire body was on fire. She rushed to the sanctum and started weeping in front of Goddess Jagadamba; she was all alone, and her entire body was shaking. Neither Jijau nor Dharau were there to hold her close and console her. Only Goddess Jagadamba was there!

Countless thoughts swirled in her mind. I must leave no stone unturned to get Swari released. But how? Raigad was also besieged by Etikad Khan.

She remembered and missed Sarlashkar Hambir mama

strongly. She burst into tears. Rupaji and Manaji were engaged in the Tryambak-Ramsej campaign. Nilopant was in Kalyan-Bhivandi. All the prominent sardars were sparing no efforts to defend the region under their command.

Yesubai felt utterly lonely; she was trembling like a creeper of jasmine quivering in a storm. Her entire life flashed in front of her misty eyes. 'Her family was in Shringarpur, but it was now estranged due to aspirations of a vatan! Aabasaheb who loved her unconditionally and never made her feel like she was his 'daughter-in-law'. Thoralya Aau and Putalabai Masaheb, who committed Sati, who loved her affectionately like a daughter of the family. Ramraje's Masaheb due to her greed for the royal throne had always held a grudge against Swari and herself. Hambir mama, who despite being the Maharani's brother, supported them. Pure-hearted Swari, who bluntly spoke his mind whenever something wrong happened in front of him. The people of Faltan, despite being his relatives deprived Swari of sound sleep.

"Rani Saheb! Hold your courage. Not only on the fort, but in the entire kingdom,you are now the only one who can take the form of Goddess Jagadamba. Thoralya Aausaheb had faced a similar situation when Maharaj and young Raje were imprisoned in Agra by the same Aurangzeb! When Thorale Swami was confined in Siddi Jouhar's siege on Panhala, she had tied a sword around her waist and got ready to break the siege herself. Remember all that, and arise. Reassure the people on the fort. Khandoji had come to the sanctum; his words affectionately stroked Yesubai's back and comforted her. If it is true that a 'king' is an enjoyer of no privileges, then his queen also has no privileges; the only privilege she has, is to carry the onus of duties on her shoulders. She is a mere shadow; not only the king's shadow but also the shadow of all the people who readily sacrifice their lives for their king.

Yesubai dried her tears with the edge of her sari and got up.

She gazed at the murti of Goddess Jagadamba once and spoke in a firm voice, "Khandoji, send a message to Rupaji and Manaji to leave Ramsej, gather their forces and come to break the siege of Raigad. Tell Ramraje to come and live with me in my palace. Tell Yesaji Dabhade to summon Arjoji, Girjoji immediately to Raigad.

Don't leave the fort for any reason. I am sure that Swari might sacrifice his own life, but will never accept any deal for Raigad. Now all of us should consider Ramraje as our king and run the kingdom wisely!"

Khandoji felt as if Goddess Jagadamba Herself was speaking through her.

Mukarrab and Ikhalas had left the land fort of Miraj, and after taking a sojourn at the Aklooj camp they gathered necessary provisions for their journey ahead and were on their way to Bahadurgad with the dangerous prisoners. The rest of the imperial army that was left behind in Aklooj, also accompanied them. Mukarrab's army now looked like a river bulging with flood waters. Raje and Kulesh were firmly fastened to the necks of the horses they were mounted on. Under the burning sun, in the desolate, barren region, the entourage of thousands of horses was moving forward slowly. Among the thousands of people, only three people were lost in thought. Mukarrab Khan who was fortunate enough to get an opportunity to present a live gift to the emperor since coming to the Deccan, was thinking, 'The emperor acts as he pleases; what if he makes Samba the Subedar of Deccan? Then, I might have to bow down to him tomorrow!' Raje whose neck was tied to the neck of his horse was wondering, 'What fate awaits Yesubai if at all Raigad falls?'

Mile after mile passed by. Raje and Kulesh were perspiring in the scorching heat; Ikhalas would approach them and ask them mockingly, "Are you feeling thirsty, oh king and wazir of the Marathas?" And when the prisoners turned their heads away, he would sprinkle their faces with water from the pouch he held under his arms and, putting the pouch to his own mouth, he would guzzle it, laugh loudly and say, "Oh, it's so hot, and this water is so cool!"

When the heat got unbearable, the horses and soldiers would rest in sprawling mango orchards on their way, but the horses of Raje and Kulesh were purposely left under the scorching sun. The night was about to fall, and the army was not too far away from Bahadurgad. Mukarrab-Ikhalas were waiting for someone. Both were frequently taking their horses to the frontline and holding their palms to their foreheads, they kept looking in the direction of Bahadurgad.

After quite a while, a cavalry unit came into sight. There were also two camels with no riders on their backs. Their necks kept swaying up and down as they ran with the cavalry unit. Even they were suffering from heat exhaustion.

Aurangzeb had sent two loyal sardars – Sardar Khan and Hamid Uddin Khan to welcome triumphant Mukarrab Khan. They had brought with them, new Khilats for Mukarrab Khan. An attendant carried two 'takht-i-kulah' or Irani style wooden crosses on his horse. Mukarrab and Ikhalas dismounted when they saw Sardar and Hamid Uddin. They moved forward and embraced each other. Hamid Uddin said to Mukarrab, "Well done Khan – Alampanah has ordered that the prisoners should be shackled to the 'takht-i-kulah'. Remove their kafir garments and put the clown's costumes on them. Put them on camels and parade them to Bahadurgad with pomp.

Mukarrab Khan's attendants quickly pulled Raje and Kulesh down from the horses. The attendants forcibly removed their necklaces, golden earrings and other ornaments. Their jamas were ripped off from their bodies and they were forced to wear loose kurtas like the ones a clown wears. Chains of bells and thorny creepers were tied around their waists. Tall, wooden clown hats were placed on their heads. Their hands and necks were tightly fastened to the wooden 'takht-i-kulah'.

He was not 'Raje' anymore. He was a 'sacrificial offering' dressed in a clown's costume to be presented to the emperor. Only one ornament was still on his chest, that no one had considered worth removing from his body; it was the sixty-four-cowrie necklace that Aabasaheb always used to wear on his chest! Only one person was with him – Chhandogamatya – Kulekhtyar – Kavi Kulesh who had been born in the faraway place of Kanoj!

A cacophony of trumpets and kettle drums arose. The frenzied Mughal soldiers screamed at the top of their lungs – "Dheen… Dheen."

At last, the parade of the kafir prisoners surrounded by armed guards began. Aurangzeb had mercilessly killed his own brothers and enemies in his lifetime, but this was the first parade taken out by his order. Why did he take such a decision? With only one intention – like the wild wind, the news of this parade would spread in the Maratha kingdom and after hearing the news, the unnerved Maratha sardars would come to him pleading for mansabs and Khilats. Once the Maratha kingdom fell, the territory from Kanjiwaram to Kabul could be easily converted to Islam! And Delhi would become the capital of that vast kingdom.

The horsemen pulled the shackles of the prisoners. Raje and Kulesh were dragged by the jerk. The gathered crowds started hurling abuses – "wretched… evil… – pull the fiends harder."

During the last nine years this Sambha had ravaged many of their military camps such as Burhanpur and Aurangabad. He had pushed many of their valiant warriors into the jaws of death. The fakirs didn't dare to perform their Namaz on Fridays. They were not just infuriated – if possible, they would have attacked the prisoners brutally and reduced them both into a bundle of flesh.

With their heads hanging, the Chhatrapati of the Maratha kingdom and the Chhandogamtya Kulesh swayed in the direction in which the armed soldiers pulled them. Even in such conditions, many people who wished to see them, tried to break through the crowds. Chhatrapati's ruddy, stout feet that had stepped on lavish carpets and walked with confidence until today, were getting dragged in the desert of Pedgaon. He who had enjoyed the privilege of royal parades on Raigad, had to now suffer this mortifying parade.

Raje had closed his eyes to avoid watching the scene around him. Kulesh' eyes were open – though he could see everything, he couldn't feel anything. An arrow had pierced his upper right arm in Sangameshwar; now the blood running from that wound was clotted and had turned blackish. Thousands of Mughal soldiers around them were cheering in joy. Nobody could hear anybody properly. The soldiers were shouting, "Pull harder – pull. Well done – Mukarrab-Ikhalas – way to go."

The annoyed shackle-holder pulled the chain so hard that Raje tumbled, and fell face down on the ground! A wave of excitement arose in the crowd.

The camel-herders comforted the camels which were agitated by the crowds, and somehow made them sit. The shackle-holders of Raje and Kulesh started pulling their chains to dump them on the back of the camels, but they couldn't do it. The prisoners had firmly rooted their feet on the ground and were not ready to move an inch. Ikhalas noticed the tussle between the shackle-holders and the prisoners, and looking at the soldiers around them he roared, "What are you looking at, you fools? Pick them up and dump them on the camels." A few rugged soldiers among the crowd put their swords in the scabbards and came forward. They forcibly picked up Raje and Kulesh as if they were picking up sacks of booty and placed them on the backs of the camels. They tied both tightly to the camels. The camels moved their hooves awkwardly and stood up in fear as the crowd around them was shouting, "Dheen... Dheen". The camel-herders twisted their tails sharply. Raje and Kulesh's feet were fastened tightly around the camels' bellies. Mukarrab and Ikhalas were astride their horses up front, holding the reins in their hands. Amidst the ear-splitting cacophony of the musical instruments and clamour of the soldiers an unprecedented delirious parade commenced.

As the parade passed through the small towns on the way, the townspeople showered Mukarrab and Ikhalas with pieces of coconuts and dates and danced deliriously. The day was celebrated like the festival of Eid, the night was going to be celebrated like the festival of Shab-e-barat. In the entire encampment, there was not a single person who did not have the heavenly desire to feast their eyes on the evil prisoners. The armed sentinels of the army were pushing their own men, women and children back while saying, "Be patient, move back." The men, women and children kept eluding them and picking up the stones and pebbles on the ground, hurled them at the prisoners. They were unreservedly cursing the prisoners, "you dog, devil, fiend" and spitting spitefully on the ground.

Now, Sambhajiraje, the son of Shivajiraje, born in the Kshatriya clan had opened his eyes completely and they were filled with an invincible glow. Even amid all that commotion he looked at Kulesh and asked him in his usual royal tone, "Chhandogamatya, are you afraid?"

Kulesh immediately turned his head towards Raje, lowered it a little bit and said, "Not at all. I wish I had no eyes; then I couldn't have seen Swami in such a condition!"

Ikhalas turned around suddenly and snapped at them, "What are you two talking about? Just take the name of khuda."

The distance that usually would have been covered in a few minutes, was now being covered in two-three hours while letting the soldiers witness the parade to their hearts' content. It was the wish of Alamgir, the emperor of Hindustan, and he had given orders to that effect.

The parade reached the entrance gate of Bahadurgad. Prominent sardars such as Bahadur Khan, Ranamast Khan, Shabdi Khan, Hasan Ali Khan, and Ghazanfar Khan who were stationed at various places, stood near the gate. They had travelled to Bahadurgad under some pretext or the other. Bakshi Ruhulla Khan who had bought off many Maratha sardars with Khilats was moving excitedly among the crowd. He too desperately wanted to have a glimpse of the devil Samba who had been the biggest obstacle since coming to the Deccan. The cannons on the fort boomed in celebration of the joyous moment.

Raje and Kulesh were brought down from the camels. Their loose, clown costumes were torn off, they were drenched in sweat, and wounded in many places by the stones hurled at them. A few select ironsmiths dispatched from the smithy on the fort, quickly fastened iron chains around the shoulders and chests of the prisoners and fixed them around their feet tightly. Aurangzeb, who was suspicious by nature and always took disproportionate precautions, had given strict orders to shackle the prisoners in the metal chains first.

On Bahadurgad, the durbar of Diwan-e-Aam was overcrowded. The Mughal sardars who had arrived from all over the kingdom, Adil Shahi and Qutub Shahi sardars such as Sarja Khan and the Mughal princes stood up front as per the royal protocol of the durbar.

As soon as the honorifics were announced, the spear-holders pounded their spears on the floor three times to alert the courtiers. A dread silence spread in the durbar; even the buzzing of a fly could be heard. From the door behind the imperial throne, Wazir Asad Khan came out first and after him came the emperor of Hindustan, Mohiuddin Mohammed Alamgir Gazi Aurangzeb. His beard had now turned completely white. But despite his age, his lean figure was still upright. His eyes were inquisitive and sharp. As soon as he came, all courtiers bowed promptly to make an obeisance to him.

"Present those filthy, kafir prisoners in front of the durbar." Asad Khan conveyed the emperor's wish to Mukarrab Khan. Mukarrab signalled to Ikhalas with his eyes. Surrounded by a few armed soldiers, both prisoners, who had become a nuisance to Aurangzeb since arriving in the Deccan, were presented in front of the durbar. The prisoners stood upright.

The moment Aurangzeb saw Seva's son, Sambha who had escaped from the prison of Agra, with his Brahmin Ekhtyar, shackled to the takht-i-kulah, aged Aurangzeb's heart bubbled with joy; he had not felt such joy even when he had heard the news of the death of his own brothers Darah-Shukoh, Murad, Shuja and Abbajan Shahjahan. He had never broken the royal protocol even by mistake, but today he unwittingly did that. He arose at once from the throne. The prisoners, Sambhajiraje and Kulesh still held their heads high among the crowded durbar. Finally, it happened! So many years after they had met in the Agra durbar, the eyes of the Maratha king, Chhatrapati Sambhajiraje and the emperor of the imperial throne of Delhi, Mohammed Aurangzeb, met at this moment. As if all-consuming Death was gazing at strong willpower; merciless imperial vanity was testing a kafir's spirit!

Aurangzeb would have never thought of family matters at such a time, but at this moment a bizarre thought occurred in his mind, 'How could Allah produce such fearless, valiant men from the wombs of kafir women? And my own seditious, rebellious son on the other hand! I named him Akbar, in the memory of my great grandfather, in a grand ceremony!'

Aged Aurangzeb felt happy like a child who finds a royal toy, after spending a long time in the wilderness.

He looked calm and quiet outwardly, but irrepressible fountains of joy were gushing in his heart. The emperor of Hindustan was eager to display his delight; he climbed down the carpeted steps of the imperial throne and stood on the rug in front of the imperial throne. For a moment, he threw a glance around the durbar and facing in the direction of Mecca, looking at the sky he knelt on the rug. As per the decree of the Quran-e-Sharif, he used to perform his Namaz, five times a day, even during the military campaigns or hunting expeditions. Even Wazir Asad Khan did not dare go in whenever he performed his Namaz. And – and today, tears of joy filled his eyes, while performing the Namaz in front of the crowded durbar. His own durbar viewed the spectacle in wonder. Many courtiers knelt on the floor to escape the emperor's wrath afterwards.

Chhatrapati Sambhajiraje was also watching the spectacle along with the courtiers. Even after such abominable humiliation, the spirit of a poetry-loving Maratha king who had inherited the legacy of his Aabasaheb honouring Kavi Bhushan, and who was the composer of 'Budhabhushanam' emerged from his heart. He gazed at Chhandogamatya Kavi Kulesh and spoke slowly but in a loud and clear voice, leaving the entire durbar astonished, "Chhandogamatya, your whole life, you had so many discussions with me about poetics, now compose a few lines about what you feel when you see Aurangzeb at this moment. Right now! And don't tell me that you don't have a quill to write with!"

Kavi Kulesh who was utterly exhausted by all the parading was moved from the bottom of his heart by his words. He immediately raised his head high and kept gazing at the faded stripes of sandalwood paste on Raje's forehead. Words flowed spontaneously from his lips, - "As you wish – here it is –

"Oh, valiant king you fought the battle so bravely that even the Mughal emperor Aurangzeb is dazzled by your valour and has abandoned his imperial throne."

As Aurangzeb was far away from them, he could not hear it. But the durbar was abuzz after hearing those words, "Inshalla, what he says is true! What is that dog saying, slash the tongue of that despicable man… he is a true poet… how apt is his poetry! Beware… slow down… your tongue will be sliced… in this durbar!" The emperor did not even take cognizance of the buzz in the durbar; he concluded his Namaz, got up and said to Mukarrab, "Remove them from here! Take them away from me!"

As the courtiers heard the emperor speak, the whispers stopped at once. Aurangzeb climbed up the steps as gradually as he had descended them and left the durbar. The durbar was over. The shackled prisoners were being carried to the prison.

Aurangzeb detested the idea of keeping the dangerous, trouble-making prisoners in a royal prison such as Bahadurgad. The very next day, as per his order, both prisoners, dressed in the same clothes, were paraded in the same manner as before and were brought in tight security, to the village Vadhu near the military camp of Tulapur close to Koregaon.

Aurangzeb's army of sixty thousand had moved from Aklooj and was spread across the region of Bahadurgad, Koregaon, Tulapur and Vadhu. The holy confluence of the Indrayani and Bhima rivers was located here. Near the banks of the confluence, two poles were raised facing the west. Both prisoners were brought amid heavy security and were dragged from the backs of the camels. Already bound to the takht-i-kulah and shackled in chains, both prisoners were again securely fastened to the poles under the guidance of Mukarrab and Ikhalas. As the takht-i-kulahs were fastened around their necks, their hands were already spread like wings. Both had not eaten a single morsel since they left from Sangameshwar. Their faces were drawn due to the fast, but their eyes looked extremely tranquil and radiant despite the pain they were suffering.

Though it was not required, wielding their broad-bladed, bare swords Mukarrab, Ikhalas, other sardars and Hamid Uddin were pacing around, keeping an eye on the prisoners and the guards surrounding them. Their only fear was a sudden appearance of the Maratha army that was known for manifesting anywhere like ghosts. They were certain that if such a thing happened, and something unwarranted took place, Hazrat would fasten them to the same poles. They frequently glanced in the direction of Bahadurgad, expecting someone's arrival. Suddenly, there was a commotion among the thousands of armed soldiers, "Here they are! They have come! A troop of a few hundred Pathan soldiers galloped from the side of Bahadurgad. Bakshi Ruhulla Khan gestured the riders following him to stop and dismounted. His master, Alamgir Gazi had had a secret meeting with him and had dispatched him there. He did not bother to look at anyone around him; holding the hilt of his sword that was covered with the Khilat placed on his shoulder, he walked briskly and directly approached Raje and Kulesh.

As Mukarrab saw him, he came forward with courtesy stemming from helplessness and asked, "What has Alampanah ordered for the kafir prisoners?"

"Shut up..." Ruhulla threw a contemptuous glance at Mukarrab from head to toe and said condescendingly. After all, Mukarrab was a sardar from the Deccan. Ruhulla was Aurangzeb's loyal sardar from North Hindustan. As he had been assigned a special duty, he was clad in the lush green Khilat. He stood in front of the shackled Chhatrapati, placed his hands on his waist, arrogantly gazed at Raje with piercing eyes and exclaimed, "Subedar, if you want to save your life, answer my question carefully. Alampanah wants your statement, Khuda has given you this last chance – On which fort have you hidden your royal treasure?" It was the first time that Raje had heard someone call him 'Subedar'. "Hmm...!" Raje shook his neck and shrugged off the question.

"I am asking you, where is your royal treasure?" Khan vigorously shook the tall, wooden, clown's hat on Raje's head. Raje stared at Khan with fiery eyes, his nostrils flared in rage. His chest shackled in chains heaved up and down in fury. He had taken a firm decision after a great deal of thought – that of not uttering a word!

"Speak up. Have you gone dumb, you kafir? It's a very small

thing. Just give me the information and save your life, you fool."

Raje only kept staring at Khan. To make him speak, Ruhulla Khan asked him the same questions repeatedly, "Where is your royal treasure? Who were the traitors?" Ruhulla Khan spared no efforts and was exhausted in the end. Drops of sweat gathered on his forehead due to the heat and the continuous questioning. He wiped the sweat with his index finger and with exasperation he said in an abusive tone, "You dog, you don't know the consequences of revolting against Alampanah. Now, you will pay for keeping your mouth shut – you will receive the death sentence!"

Ruhulla Khan spared no efforts to make Raje open his mouth, but Raje did not budge. Likewise, Khan tried to entice Kulesh by his usual tactic of offering a mansab and said to the Chhandogamatya, "He is going to die anyway – you seem to be a wise person. You tell me where he has hidden the booty that he plundered from the Mughal cities of Burhanpur and Aurangabad. Which traitors of the Mughal army had joined hands with him? The emperor will grant you the mansab and make you rich. Tell me. Don't be afraid of him now. Just speak."

Kulesh shook the takht-i-kulah around his neck and the wooden hat on his head left and right and spoke in a clear, loud voice teaching Khan a lesson about the true spirit of a loyal servant – "Khan, if I would have gotten the same opportunity, I would have asked you the same question. Your emperor has robbed the treasury of entire Hindustan. You can never buy off a poet's allegiance by throwing a piece of mansab in front of him!"

"Shut up, you wretched kafir!" Khan screamed as if bitten by a snake. He quickly moved forward and slapped the Kulekhatyar, Chhandogamatya of the Maratha kingdom, very hard. His face contorted with anger.

As Raje saw it, he sprang forward in rage. His forceful efforts jolted the pole he was tied to!

So far, Raje had remained determinedly quiet due to the royal values inculcated in him since his childhood, but now he broke his silence. His words ignited a raging fire in the hearts of Ruhulla, Mukarrab, Ikhalas and the Mughal soldiers standing around them – "Khan, go and tell your master 'Subedar' that I am ready to embrace death. The Bhosala clan doesn't commit atrocious actions like your emperor who locked up his father in the Lal Killa. He even ensured that his aged father was massaged with toxic oil! In our family, brothers don't betray brothers to seize the royal throne!"

"Be quiet!" Trembling Ruhulla screamed. "Sever his head! Place him under the elephant's feet! Feed his flesh to the dogs!" Fuming Mughal soldiers started shouting from all sides; a big commotion arose. But still, fearless and furious Raje continued talking –

"If the dogs eat my flesh, even their puppies will be born loyal.

Tell your arrogant master, Khan – the way you finished your brothers, your father, Mirza Raja who served you faithfully throughout his life and Diler Khan, what more can you do to me? Even at this moment, I have prepared my mind for that! Tell him to mark my words, that even after my death, this kingdom will not crumble in front of him as easily as Adil Shahi and Qutub Shahi. Every household in this kingdom will give birth to Seva and Samba!!"

Ruhulla couldn't bear the fact that Raje had not stopped abusing his emperor; he rushed forward in a rage. He tried placing his hand on Raje's lips to catch them together in a clasp, to make him shut his mouth. Raje shook his head throwing his hand off and for the last time shouted out loud so everyone could hear it; his words left them stunned – "Your evil emperor will never escape the consequences of killing me! He is committing countless crimes for the royal throne of Delhi, but he will never find enough space for his own tomb in the same city! Our ferocious Mavalas who are ready to sacrifice their lives for their kingdom, will dig his grave in this land of Maval! Tell him that I refuse to answer any of his questions! Go...get lost!" Raje's entire body was still trembling in rage.

Ruhulla who had never heard such things in his life burst out in anger, "Shut up… you wicked dog…" He leapt forward and slapped hard the face that had been affectionately stroked by Dharau and Thoralya Aau. Khan was shaking in fury. Raje threw such a fiery glance at Khan's hand, that he unwittingly pulled his hand back. The soldiers were stunned. Kulesh struggled in frustration in the takht-i-kulah and ultimately dropped his neck helplessly.

Khan, who had been unsuccessful in the task assigned to him, spat on the ground and muttered to himself, "Both these kafirs are going to die a dog's death. Our Emperor, the follower of true Islam, will torture them more than he tortured Murad and Dara. These kafirs will be wiped out from the face of the earth.

Stamping his feet on the ground, Ruhulla Khan mounted his horse and left with his unit to report the impudence of the prisoner to the emperor. He did not dare convey Raje's precise words to his Hazrat. While galloping he wondered how to present his words mildly in the durbar.

Now, Aurangzeb left Bahadurgad and arrived at the Koregaon encampment. A royal shamiana was raised for him. When he left Delhi, his first and foremost aspiration was to convert 'Seva's' Maratha kingdom into an Islamic state. To that effect, he had launched the first military attack on this hilly region. Four years ago, he had had to withdraw his forces, accepting defeat from the son of Seva. The same 'Sambha' was his captive today. After torturing him brutally and killing him, he was easily going to wrap the feeble, half-naked soldiers of the hilly kingdom around his rosary. But for now, he was lost in a bizarre thought. He had not understood the purpose of his son Akbar and Diler's brother Mirbat Khan teaming up with Sambha.

He had noted the reckless responses that Sambha had given. He had lured many Maratha sardars to his side by bribing them. One thought continuously nagged him, 'I left Delhi and came here with great hope. I am getting old now. Will my dream of spreading Islam from Kanjiwaram to Kabul be fulfilled?'

The emperor's daughter, Zeenat-un-Nissa, had come with him to serve him. Every day, at mealtime she would taste every dish prepared in front of her father to assure him that the food had not been poisoned, and only after that she served it to him. One such time, when he was having a meal, a messenger of Mukarrab arrived with a message, "The stubborn kafirs haven't eaten anything yet."

Every day, Mukarrab and Ikhalas had tried to present delicious Mughal dishes and sweets such as Sheer Khurma to Raje and Kulesh to entice them into breaking their fast but had completely failed in their attempts. The zest that Mukarrab Khan possessed when he captured the prisoners was now replaced with worry – "What if the kafirs die soon?"

When Aurangzeb heard the news that the prisoners were not eating anything, he left his food untouched and started pacing restlessly. Zeenat-un-Nissa started covering the open platter with brass plates to ward off flies. Aurangzeb saw it; he stopped in his tracks and laughed in a bizarre way. Zeenat wondered if she had made any mistake in tasting the food, and asked him courageously, "Why are you laughing, Abbajan? Is anything wrong?"

Aurangzeb laughed loudly and said to her, "You covered the food to keep the flies away, but my dear daughter, sometimes flies eclipse the human heart too! How will you cover it? On the one hand, your brother Akbar is wandering from one place to another, in search of food, and on the other hand, Seva's son,

Sambha, is not even touching the food." He looked at his daughter's astonishment and commanded, "Take this food away. I don't want to eat."

The emperor summoned Wazir Asad Khan and ordered him, "I want to see the prisoner Samba in person! Make arrangements. Go!" For the first time in his life Aurangzeb wanted to meet a prisoner in person!

It had been three days since the prisoners had been fastened to the poles. Neither had given a satisfactory response to any of the emperor's queries. Neither had consumed a morsel. Some kind mussalman would plead with them and give them some water to frink from time to time. He would wipe his teary eyes and mutter to himself, "Oh Allah, you have given them such determination. Had they got a chance to grab hold of their swords, they would have slit their own throats. Some people are so doomed! Oh, Parvardigar, please make them see sense."

As the emperor heard about the defiant silence of the prisoners from Ruhulla, he convened an urgent meeting of his mullahs and maulvis. Whenever he wanted to make a final decision, he always got it sanctioned by them. He made sure that every time his rulings were approved by the religious decree of Islam. He followed the same protocol in the case of these prisoners. What is the punishment prescribed in the Quran-e-Sharif for an insurgent who had plundered and burnt an imperial city of the Mughal Empire, mercilessly killed many mussalmans and desecrated the masjids? The death sentence!" The maulvis handed a written decree with their signatures to the emperor.

The emperor of Hindustan left his imperial shamiana, in a silver howdah with a golden ceiling, on the back of an embellished elephant. He was casting his keen penetrating eyes, over the crowd around him, and he finally arrived. The elephants carrying the emperor's grandsons and princes, followed. Even the imperial zenana including Zeenat, sat on one elephant. Everyone was eager to see Seva's son Samba shackled, even more eager than they had been to see the rebel Seva in the Agra durbar. Many sardars, who were walking slowly, were wondering about the Alamgir's decision to come and see the prisoners in person.

Emperor Aurangzeb's entourage arrived at the town of Vadhu. The mahouts goaded the elephants to sit down. The emperor dismounted with his princes and grandsons.

On the plateau of the Indrayani and Bhima confluence at Vadhu near Tulapur, this was a peculiar meeting between Aurangzeb, the emperor of Delhi who had arrived in a grand procession, and prisoner Sambhajiraje, the Chhatrapati of Raigad's royal throne, who had been striving to defend his kingdom against four nemeses for the last eight years! The entire encampment was thronging with crowds, but a grim silence prevailed.

The emperor started walking towards the prisoners tied to the pole. Keeping a safe distance, surrounded by armed guards and accompanied by Wazir Asad Khan, Ruhulla Khan, Mukarrab Khan, Ikhalas Khan, Aurangzeb stood in front of Sambhajiraje who was fastened to the pole but with his head held high. He observed shackled Raje from the toes and in the end his imperial eyes met Raje's; his heart was in utter turmoil. He was shaken from the bottom of his heart and for the first time he realized, 'So many sons have been born to me in this dynasty of Taimur, but not a single one has eyes like this, as radiant as the sun!'

Aurangzeb glanced at Ruhulla and Asad and questioned Raje himself, "Tell me, where is our treasure that you plundered? Who are the traitors who teamed up with you?" Raje glared at Aurangzeb with his fiery eyes and kept staring at him in utter contempt. Even the ruthless Aurangzeb was scorched by those eyes and the utter contempt spewing out of them!

He was not used to people raising their head and staring at him directly; especially with a look filled with such contempt!

The grave silence between them terrified Ruhulla Khan to the core; he moved forward, bent down and whispered in his

Alampanah's ears, "Mercy, Akah Ali! This arrogant kafir will soon convert to Islam. After that, he will open his mouth and tell us everything." As he had been successful in buying off the Maratha sardars in large numbers, he had unrealistic hopes that his Hazrat would accept his advice.

"Shut up! Bakshi, you are such a fool!" The emperor threw a contemptuous, fiery glance at Bakshi Ruhulla Khan as he would at a puppet that danced to his tune. He did not move his eyes from Raje, even a bit, and said, "Take a closer look at his eyes carefully. When he came to meet me in the Agra durbar with his father, these eyes were so innocent. You think, he will convert to Islam? He will perform the Namaz? You are utterly mistaken. See, how he is staring at me with contempt. These are not eyes, but burning torches! Trying to convert him to Islam is akin to befriending a traitor!

"Ikhalas, pluck out these defiant eyes! Shove burning rods through them. Give this arrogant kafir a new sight!" The emperor completely neglected Ruhulla and gave orders to Ikhalas Khan.

Raje roared like a booming cannon, "You can only see these two eyes, that torment you, but these are not my only eyes. The hundreds and thousands of Mavala soldiers are also my eyes! Do you think that you can you pluck them out too as you are the emperor of Hindustan? Go ahead and pluck my eyes without wasting any time. I don't want to see your face anymore! I will lose my eyes, but it will give a new vision to my daredevil Mavalas!!"

Aurangzeb did not care to pay any attention to that 'rubbish' and moved towards shackled Kulesh for a moment. He observed that prisoner from head to toe. Even amidst all that commotion a fleeting thought agitated him, 'What if the rebellious prince Akbar would have been shackled to the takht-i-kulah? It would have been a great blessing of Allah!'

He looked at Kulesh and instantly ordered Ikhalas who was following him like a short and plump mutt, "Execute each punishment on this Brahmin poet first! I would like to see how the son of kafir Seva who calls himself a 'lionheart' watches his poet friend being tortured.

"Ji Huzur," Mukarrab and Ikhalas who were unnerved after hearing the sentence for both prisoners, bowed together and exclaimed at the same time.

The emperor shook his thick, white bearded face. He felt that he had wasted too much time on the worthless, kafir prisoners, and turned around to leave. The green emerald and the pearl strands studded in his kimosh sparkled in the sun.

Raje boiled in rage as he realized that after this moment, he was never going to see Aurangzeb again. Despite being a king, Raje had been publicly paraded like a goat being carried away for a sacrifice. To avenge the disgrace that had been heaped on him, an agitated Raje hurled profane abuse towards Aurangzeb, humiliating him in the presence of his own men, "You despicable swine! A lion's cub lives like a lion and dies like a lion too!"

Aurangzeb had never heard such profane language in his life; his entire body trembled with rage. A worthless prisoner calling the emperor of Hindustan a 'swine'! And that too, in front of his princes, Wazir, sardars and servants! His devious lean lips, curled inside, trembled in wrath; the vein on his forehead started throbbing. He clasped the rosary in his hand tightly. The tip of his pointed nose and his fleshy earlobes turned red. Throughout his life, he had never raised his calm voice while giving any harsh order; but today his tongue betrayed him. He roared in a loud voice that left even his Wazir, Asad Khan trembling, and gave an order that he had never given before –

"Ikhalas...Dakkhani..., before plucking his eyes out, chop off his defiant tongue from its root and throw it out for the dogs to eat!!"

"Hmm...you imbecile Aurang, spoken words do not get

wiped out by chopping off someone's tongue!" Raje licked his dry lips and exclaimed very calmly.

Aurangzeb disregarded everyone, and walking briskly, he climbed up his elephant and sat in the howdah.

As his Hazrat had expressed the wish to slash the prisoners' tongues before plucking their eyes out, Ikhalas selected a few unflinching executioners from the squad of executioners. To make sure that they wouldn't hesitate while executing the sentence, they were taken aside and made to drink a potful of liquor.

From the smithy in the camp, Ikhalas had assembled the ironsmiths, with burning stoves and pincers. The ironsmiths placed a couple of arm-long iron rods in the furnace. A piece of cloth was tightly wrapped around one end of the rods, to protect the hands of the person holding them. A few executioners held pincers in their hands to pull the prisoners' tongues out of their mouths. Some others readied their sharp bare swords to slash the tongues of the prisoners. All of them lined up, waiting for the command.

Alampanah's command was to "Slash the tongue before plucking out the eyes. Implement every sentence on the poet first and then on Samba!"

What was the intent of Aurangzeb's command to implement every sentence on Kavi Kulesh first? He wanted to see Raje shattered and demoralized while watching his dear friend being tortured. He should be crushed and dispirited and should plead for his own life at any cost. If that did not happen, at least his heart would bleed profusely to watch his friend's suffering.

Ikhalas approached Kulesh with four to five thick-lipped, bare-chested Siddi executioners, drenched in sweat and holding bare swords in their hands.

By this time, the news of the sentence had spread throughout the entire encampment. Soldiers thronged to watch and enjoy the execution of the sentence to their hearts' content. Rising on their heels, they were watching the unprecedented scene over each other's shoulders. The area was overcrowded but utter silence prevailed; one could even hear the insects buzzing over their heads.

"Open your mouth, you poet!" Ikhalas held Kulesh's face and shook it vigorously left and right. Kulesh was calm as if he had heard nothing at all.

It was such a stupid command by Ikhalas! Who would open their own mouth to get their tongue slashed?

Ikhalas went wild when he saw the composure of Kulesh, who was staring at him. He moved forward and tried to open Kulesh's mouth with his own hands. Kulesh was not a mere poet; he was a fine warrior who had fought many battles. Ikhalas tried his best, but he could not open Kulesh's mouth by himself. Kulesh had locked his jaws tightly! Exhausted Ikhalas got drenched in sweat; he got irritated and angry.

He looked at the executioners and raising his hand he fumed and roared, "All of you, open his jaw together, and pull his tongue out!" Four to five muscular executioners promptly stepped forward and tightly held the face of Kulesh, the Chhandogamatya of the Maratha kingdom.

Kulesh realized that he was indeed going to lose his tongue now; with all his might he shouted, "Swami, this ordinary poet from Kanoj bows down to you. I am so fortunate that today I could join you on the path of death! Jai Bhavani...Jai Chandi...!" The executioner shoved the pincer in Kulesh's mouth and grabbed his tongue with it tightly. With one jerk, he pulled it out forcefully. With that pain, the tongue wiggled in the clasp of the pincer. As Mukarrab signalled an executioner holding a sword, he struck a hard blow on Kulesh's tongue; it sliced through his tongue and, breaking a few teeth, it slit through his lower lip and chin. A loud scream was heard; it quickly got suppressed amidst the joyous uproar of the spectators. A stream of blood spurted out of Kulesh's slit jaw soaking the takht-i-kulah around his neck! It shrouded the Kanoj style tilak on his forehead. His clown's costume got soaked in streams of blood.

From his takht-i-kulah, Raje glanced at Kulesh's blood-soaked face. He called out to Kulesh as gently as he would call his own son – "Kaviraj!"

Despite the agonizing pain arising from the wound in his mouth, Chhandogamatya Kulesh opened his eyes and gazed at his Swami calmly.

Ikhalas went wild as he heard the soldiers around him cheering loudly. As he had had a tough experience with Kulesh, he astutely decided not to touch Raje's jaw. But he snapped at the executioners who implemented the punishment, "Are you scared, you cowards? Now, open his jaw too, and slash this kafir's nasty tongue that abused our Hazrat!"

Five to six executioners came forward to obey the command. A tussle took place between shackled Raje and the executioners, to open Raje's jaw. Raje wasn't letting them get hold of his jaw at all.

"He was a poet, still he gave us a hard time! This is a lion, he will never let us touch him, all of you must grab him with all your might." Mukarrab-Ikhalas started cheering to motivate the executioners. A few spectators moved forward to assist the executioners.

Finally, ten to twenty hairy hands grabbed Raje's head and held it tight so he couldn't move it at all. The Shivlinga was overshadowed by scorpions. They pressed Raje's jaw with sheer force; the agonizing pain forced his jaw open.

Sambahjiraje was the enthroned emperor of the Hindu kingdom. His royal tongue used to chant the name of his family deity, Goddess Jagadamba in moments of joy as well as sorrow. The same tongue was now caught tightly in the pincers.

"Lailaha…" The executioner wielding his sword roared loudly, inciting the spectators, and opening his eyes as wide as he could he struck a hard blow on Raje's tongue caught in the pincers and pulled out of his mouth. Streams of blood spurted out.

The spectators raucously screamed "Dheen…Dheen…". The executioner spitefully spit on the piece of the defiant, insolent tongue wiggling in the clasp of the pincers and exclaimed, "Let the dogs have it…" He threw the tongue with the pincers in the hot sand of Vadhu!

The body on which holy waters of sacred rivers had been sprinkled at the time of coronation, was soaked in its own blood. Excruciating pain arose from the wound, but he did not even let out a moan.

He firmly pressed his lips under his teeth, closed his eyes tightly and let the blood from the wound trickle down only because he couldn't stop it. He calmly opened his eyes after some time. As he saw his own tongue trembling in the sand in front of him, his heart bled with only one thought –

'Not a single word that this tongue uttered had ever been disobeyed, but…but today the tongue itself had fallen! It is saying to me, "Dhani, give me a command– I will obey it even now!"

Raje and Kulesh were gazing at each other with their blood-stained faces. They were not two separate individuals now but rather two cantos of a 'royal epic' composed in the Mavala tongue seemingly separate, but one in purpose. The Chhatrapati and Chhandogamatya were united by the streams of blood spurting from their wounds, trickling all over their bodies and merging at their feet. The blood that flowed from their wounds had united their hearts.

The first part of the sentence had been carried out. Both prisoners were now suffering excruciating pain due to their sliced tongues. Both of them hardly cared about their own pain, but rather they were anxious about only one thing – Aurangzeb's next move against the Maratha kingdom. But they had now lost the medium to share their thoughts with each other. Kulesh wanted to tell Raje, "We should erect more water forts – before the Mughals and the Siddis unite – it is quite possible that Shirke who revolted against Swami might seek the support of Aurangzeb and deprive the Maharani of her sleep. But… but he couldn't speak. His eyes reflected his plight and his pain.

Raje felt suffocated like an eagle caught in a cage. He also wanted to tell Kulesh – "Hambirarao, Mhalojibaba have already sacrificed their lives! Kank kaka has become quite old. Who can be the Sarlashkar now who would capably lead my armies all over the kingdom? Could that be Rupaji, Manaji, Vithoji or Santaji-Dhanaji? What a big blunder it would be if Maharani instates Balraje in my place!

Would Ramraje be courageous enough to face Aurangzeb's onslaught? And what will happen to Maharani after my death?"

The memory of Durgabai in the prison of Khuldabad wrenched his heart.

The sun was about to set now; it kept growing bigger and bigger.

"You can leave now and rest…" Ikhalas ordered the squad of executioners who were drenched in sweat while implementing the sentence of slashing the prisoners' tongues. He summoned a new squad of executioners to implement the second part of the sentence. Ikhalas was moving with such vigour today that he had not shown even on the battlefield. He was positive that fulfilling this difficult task would not go in vain. His Hazrat would take note of that.

Ikhalas selected two rugged Siddis from the new squad and took them aside. Ikhalas himself bent down, grabbed the cloth-wrapped ends of the iron rods heating in the furnace and pulled them out. He pointed them at the eyes of the executioners he had selected to test their guts. They did not move at all. Ikhalas happily handed the hot rods he was holding to one of them, and, looking at Kulesh he said, "Shove these hot rods in this bamman poet's eyes. Let his king see the blood flowing from his friend's eyes."

The Siddi executioner said, "Ji Huzur" and moved towards Kulesh with the hot rods – to pluck his eyes out.

Kulesh was a poet after all. He had feasted his eyes upon the natural beauty of the Mavala kingdom. He had left the towering Raigad, his family and above all, he had left his native place, Kanoj, for Sambhajiraje. He realized that he was going to lose his eyes and would not see his Swami again; therefore, he gazed at Raje's blood-soaked face for the last time. As the executioner started bringing the hot, red rods close to his eyes, Kulesh started turning his head quickly from side to side.

The executioner kept trying to shove the rods in his eyes; they kept brushing against the prisoner's cheeks and ears, searing them. Finally, the executioner shouted in frustration – "What are you looking at, you idiots! Hold his head tight!

Other executioners quickly moved forward and held Kulesh's head firmly; they were shocked as such assistance had never been needed before, to pluck out the eyes of prisoners shackled to the takht-i-kulah.

"Churr…churr…" Like a carpenter using his chisel to make holes in wooden logs, with his wide-open eyes, the executioner shoved the hot, red rods into Kulesh's eyes and rotated them quickly. The stench of burning eyeballs spread everywhere. Kulesh's body trembled, "Awww…awww..." A strange sound came from his tongue-less mouth.

As Raje smelled the stench of burning flesh and heard the strange sound from his mouth, Raje misunderstood his intent. He thought, Chhandogamatya was shouting in fear of death. As he couldn't bear the thought, similar sounds came out of his own mouth – "Awww…. awww….!" He wanted to ask Kulesh – "Since when is the Chhandogamatya of the Maratha kingdom scared of death?"

Kulesh, in fact, wanted to say, "You are a great king and you have given a really tough fight."

Though their minds were united, they had misunderstood

each other, because they had lost their tongues.

At this moment, the spectators went wild with joy and started clapping and shouting hysterically, "Well done by the grace of Allah. Hurry up, you brave man. Remove his eyes too!"

The executioner implementing the sentence, was still holding the hot rods blackened by the burnt blood. He exclaimed, "These rods are useless now" and tossed the rods at the bare feet of Kulesh who had already lost his tongue and eyes.

He turned around, and from another furnace he quickly picked up the second pair of red hot rods. He looked at them with his red eyes and to show the spectators how hot they were, he raised his hand and moved it around while chanting 'La…ilah". Before he could shout again, four to five soldiers had already come forward to assist him and had firmly held Shivaji's son, the Maratha king, Chhatrapati Sambhajiraje's head, for his convenience.

Raje's eyes that were soon going to be burnt were utterly calm and steady. They were not merely eyes, but two radiant orbs.

The executioner bit his usually protruding flabby lip between his teeth, and pointing the hot rods towards Raje, he came in front of him. The stress of implementing the harsh punishment caused him to sweat profusely.

Taking small steps, holding the hot rods in his hands, he kept coming forward while staring at Raje's eyes.

And…suddenly…for some reason, holding the rods in his hands, he stopped in his tracks like a statue. Looking at Raje's fearless and glowing eyes, he felt in his heart – 'I have burnt so many eyes in my life but…but…I have never seen eyes like these! No…no…these eyes do not deserve to be burnt; they actually deserve to be cherished!"

He was a stone-hearted executioner! But even he was taken aback; he looked at Raje and nodded his head and took a few steps back. Suddenly, a strong blow struck his back, drops of sweat splashed from his sweaty back. Ikhalas' berating words fell on his ears – "You traitor! Why did you stop? Pluck out his eyes!"

The pain forced the obedient executioner to suppress the compassion in his heart, and move forward. When he took the blazing red rods close to Raje's eyeballs, he tightly closed his own eyes with the stress of implementing the harsh punishment. At that moment, a strange image of his family deity, eight-armed Goddess Tulja Bhavani flashed in front of Raje's eyes. Her face resembled Thoralya Aau's face, instead of the crown on her head there was a Jiretop like Aabasaheb's Jiretop, her eight arms displayed the faces of the family members – Masaheb who committed Sati, Yesubai and yes – Ramraje's Masaheb too! Each finger of those arms revealed many faces that he had seen in his childhood and youth such as Prataprao, Malusare kaka, Murarbaji, Kondaji, Krishnaji Kank, Hambirarao, Mhalojibaba and others. Chants of "Jai Jai Raghuveer Samartha! – Ude ga Ambe ude! – Har Har Mahadeo!" echoed in his ears.

Churr… churr… The executioner shoved the blazing rods in the prisoner's eyes, rotated them. Once his job was done, exhausted, and with eyes closed, he fell on his knees.

The onlookers shouted deliriously, "Dheen… Dheen… Release him! Let him go to Aurangbad and Burhanpur now!"

Even in that condition, Raje regretted one thing – 'Why didn't any loyal executioner of Alamgir ram nails in my nose and ears? Then I wouldn't have smelled the burning flesh and wouldn't have heard this derisive tumultuous display of joy!'

Now Raje and Kulesh's faces looked so gruesome, that had any of Aurangzeb's young grandchildren seen them, it would have scared them to death! Tall wooden hats on their heads, their hands and necks shackled to the takht-i-kulah, the blood-stained, clown's clothes on their bodies, the thorny creepers tied around their waists and the chains of bells sprinkled with drops of blood, their burnt eye sockets, streaks of blood running through their sliced mouths and oozing onto their thick, curly beards!

The sun had set on the western horizon. The waves kept rising and falling at the confluence of Indrayani and Bhima.

The kettle drums in the encampment resounded to announce the time of the evening Namaz. Soon, the Azan could be heard all over the camp – "Alla ho Akbar"

Raje and Kulesh were now beyond any pain, beyond their bodies. Raje was having a dialogue with himself, like never before. As it was getting dark, torches had been lit all over the encampment. But a bigger fire was raging in Shambhooraje's royal heart.

A tumultuous storm of thoughts was whirling in Raje's mind, that surprised him too. He was observing himself like a stranger and remembering his journey from childhood upto now.

Unrestrained fountains of thoughts erupted in Raje's mind. Now, the territory of the Maratha kingdom that he had seen in all three seasons, flashed in front of his mind's eye – the rainy evenings descending on Raigad, the flooded shores of Kushavarta and Ganga Sagar lakes, the Jagadishwar temple, Balekilla, the market-place, Mantribadi, Hirkani machi, Bhavanitok, Takamaktok, the queen's palaces, the royal throne…and his beloved Raigad, that looked like a Shivlinga getting drenched under the stream of Abhishek water. Thoralya Aau's palace in Pachad, the sentinels braving the rains while patrolling back and forth, and the inundated Kal and Gandhar rivers meandering like a slithering serpent.

The dense fog shrouding the forts throughout the kingdom in winter. The informers of Bahirji, Vishwas and Karmaji's surveillance troops, who travelled all over the kingdom, gathered important news and delivered it shivering with cold, but making an obeisance courteously. The hundreds and thousands of cavalry and infantry who galloped all over the kingdom in the cold weather, from Varhad, Khandesh, Konkan, Marathwada, Baglan to Goa.

The bowl of steaming hot porridge that Yesubai herself had served him when he was at Raigad!

The bonfires, that the peasants had lit in the sunny season in their fields by gathering heaps of fallen leaves at the foothills of the fort. The weary, parched cattle ruminating under the sprawling trees of mango, banyan, pipal and tamarind.

Mother Earth! She feeds milk in childhood, provides food and water in the young age, and shapes the character of a person! Not as a king, or a commander, or even as a soldier, but as a 'human being' What is my bond with Mother Earth? Can there be a bond between man and the earth? Indeed, man shares a bond with the earth. Most people die an ordinary death, but very few die fighting for the honour of Mother Earth! Will I be fortunate enough to die such a death?

"Jagadamb...Jagadamb" as his throat was parched, he muttered to himself. Instead of drops of water, drops of his own blood dripped into his parched mouth.

Meanwhile, Ikhalas was giving a detailed report to Aurangzeb, who had just returned to his royal shamiana after performing Namaz. Despite his age, Aurangzeb was rapidly pacing back and forth in the shamiana. Ikhalas was nervous to see his unrest and agitation. What if Hazrat gets angry for any reason?

But Aurangzeb was agitated for a different reason. He was stopped in his tracks every so often and lost in thought, kept staring at the roof of the shamiana now and then.

"That kafir did not scream at all even after suffering such harsh punishment?" He asked Ikhalas as if he was questioning himself.

"Ji. Not at all." Ikhalas bowed down and responded for the sake of responding.

As he heard it, the emperor of Hindustan wondered about only one thing – 'What if my rebellious prince Akbar would have been here in his place? What if he had to go through the same painful punishment?'

He did not realize that Ikhalas was still waiting for his permission to leave. His entire life flashed in front of his eyes – since the time he imprisoned his own father in Agra and spent the rest of his life marching through the territories of Rajasthan, Bengal, Bijapur, Golconda and the Maratha kingdom. He was agitated by the feeling that he had lost something invaluable. He felt utterly lost. He saw Ikhalas still standing in front of him and shouted at him – "Leave!"

The day broke on the encampment. The warm rays of the rising sun caressed Raje's body. He felt the warmth intensely. Memories of Thoralya Aau, Putala masaheb, Yesubai, Dharau, Durgabai, Bhavanibai…all ladies in the family sprang up in his mind. Especially Thoralya Aau! And Aabasaheb, who was precious to me and Thoralya Aau, what would he have done, had he been in my place?

An unknown rush surged through Raje's spine. Just the thought of Aabasaheb raised his head high. In his mind, he touched his forehead to Aabasaheb's holy feet and to the samadhis in Pachad. Our own relatives and people around me turned traitors. Give me strength that my flesh and my mind nurtured under your care, will not betray me at this final moment!

He tried hard to remember the face of his birth mother. Instead, he kept seeing Dharau's face over and over again. Dharau – a peasant woman with a pure heart full of affection. She showered unconditional love on me, even more than on her own sons, Raya and Anta.

Raigad witnessed the demise of many women but Putala masaheb was the first to receive the honour of going 'Sati'. She placed Aabasaheb's mojaris in front of her when she sat on the funeral pyre. What must have she felt while burning to ashes in the rising flames of fire! Even today her courageous last words echo in my ears – "Remember me in the difficult times! You are my son!"

As Raje remembered her words, his heart was stirred from the bottom. Masaheb, Masaheb, I didn't just remember your final moments, but I am living them at this moment. You went Sati for Aabasaheb. I am going Sati too – as a man – for the land of Maval! I was there to light your funeral pyre as a family member but here, I am surrounded by Aurangzeb's wretched lackeys. After your death, I raised the 'Sati Vrindavan' in Raigad, in your memory. Will my kingdom and my people remember me after my death?

I never regretted anything I did in my life consciously; never felt any remorse for it at all. But Durga, whenever I remember you, my heart shatters into pieces. Despite being the queen of the Chhatrapati, you spent your life in a prison, with our sons, and Ranooakka who came to her parental home, to support her young brother! Though she was Aabasaheb's daughter she suffered the fate of being a detainee in Aurangzeb's prison. Aabasaheb and I escaped from the Agra prison, but I couldn't free you despite trying so many times. Ugh… ugh…! What kind of life is this?

And… and innocent Godavari who threw herself off Lingana's cliff! I never regretted my decision of putting Annaji under the elephant's feet, but Godavari's needless death still pricks at my heart, like the rods that just pricked my eyes. The pain of her death still burns my heart!

And Yesubai's face reminds me of a garland of sparkling stars. Apart from being my wife, she was just like a daughter to Aabasaheb! For some reason, I always remembered Thoralya Aau whenever she was around. She must be in so much trouble at this time. She always used to say to me, "I have been married to the wild wind!"

Indeed, what would she do and how would she behave after my death? What a great gift Ganoji and Kanhoji have given to their younger sister! Whenever I remember Durgabai, in the prison of Khuldabad, my heart fills with guilt! But Yesubai's memory fills my heart with sheer gratitude.

"Hmm..." He shook his head to chase away the memories of his family. In front of him, Indrayani and Bhima merged into each other and continued flowing in the scorching heat. The sun had ascended and was shining overhead!

The memories of the ministers and the soldiers who had lost their lives in various skirmishes with Aurangzeb's army, throbbed in Raje's heart.

Delusional Moropant, who in the last moments of his life pulled out the casket of the earrings and the Peshwas' royal seal from under his pillow and handed it to his son Nilopant! How did he get trapped in the clutches of Annaji and Masaheb?

I remember Aabasaheb every now and then; wouldn't Peshwe Nilopant remember his own father occasionally? Why did he never mention Moropant to me? Or does one have to sever familial ties when entrusted with any responsibility? Pant, as a human being, my heart is yearning to seek forgiveness from you, Aabasaheb and Godavari, but all of you are waving your hands in refusal. Why? Why?

Annaji's face stood in front of his blood-soaked, empty eye sockets! Annaji! Annaji who faithfully performed his duty of tax collection during Aabasaheb's reign; how did he dare to suppress me?

I think of apologizing to Godavari occasionally; then why did I never feel like apologizing to Annaji and Masaheb? Not even at this moment!

Khandoji saved my life in the Mandavi creek of Goa when my horse was drifting away in the creek! And his father Balaji, the most loyal scribe of Aabasaheb! The quill – a weapon much more powerful than actual weapons! How could he yield to Masaheb's pressure and use his quill against me? Despite being his sons, Niloji and Khandoji also never mentioned his name while talking to me. Suppose, Balaji, Annaji and Masaheb's plan of poisoning me had succeeded?! Would my last moments be any less painful then? But why does the pain not seem as painful at this moment?

What must have Annaji, Balaji, Shamaji, Hiroji felt while being trampled under the elephant's feet? Regret? Pain? Torture?

Raje shook his entire body and tried to raise both his hands. The takht-i-kulah cut into his wrists again!

In frustration, Raje remained calm outwardly; but in his mind many voices kept flapping their wings – "Nyayadhish Prahladpant!" I pardoned his first mistake and reappointed him as the Nyayadhish. At that time, I had told him, "I consider the Nyayadhish of a kingdom as the unwavering mountain of the domain. I can understand if the trees and bushes swing back and forth with gusts of wind. But what will happen if the mountains start quivering?" How could the Nyayadhish team up with the Shirkes when Aurangzeb launched his fierce final attack to destroy Swaraj? That is why I had to give the final order of his arrest. And today...Aurangzeb had got the opportunity to pass judgement on me! Time and destiny are the ultimate judges of man. Isn't it so?

A bizarre mesh of varied thoughts had spread all over the encampment. Both prisoners who had lost their tongues and eyes were thinking about each other. The only other thought bothering them was – 'Maharani is left all alone. How will she summon the courage to comfort and rejuvenate the ryots of the vast kingdom? Who will help her?'

Aurangzeb was pacing back and forth in his shamiana, pondering both prisoners and how to conquer 'Seva's' rebellious kingdom while counting the beads in his rosary and looking at the roof from time to time.

He was also worried about who was going to shoulder the responsibility of Hindustan's royal throne after him! It is indeed easy to raise kingdoms by means of conciliation, bribery, punishment and treachery, but very difficult to maintain them.

The next day broke. As if the prisoners had not suffered enough torture, Ikhalas brought a new squad of executioners in front of them.

The squad ripped the clothes off the prisoners' bodies. Only a few pieces stuck between the chains and the takht-i-kulah that could not be torn, remained.

"What are you looking at? Splash that saltwater on those scoundrels after peeling their skin off!" Ikhalas shouted at the baffled and bewildered executioners.

A few executioners stepped forward with cleavers. They started scraping the skin off the prisoners' bodies with the sharp cleavers as if they were grating a coconut. They were stunned that both prisoners were not whimpering at all. Until today, the executioners had scraped off the skin of many insolent prisoners. At that time, they had felt quite motivated by their screams and their suffering. But today? They were experiencing something very peculiar! Their own hands trembled while using the cleavers.

Raje and Kulesh no longer looked like human beings. They looked like murtis of Lord Hanuman smeared with red lead paste.

The executioners using the cleavers stepped back, and the executioners holding copper pots in their hands stepped forward. Those pots were filled with saltwater. Like an ironsmith splashing water on heated bellows, the executioners started splashing the saltwater all over Raje and Kulesh's bleeding bodies. The hissing sound of water falling on hot bellows can be heard, but no one could hear the hissing sound of the saltwater. Only Raje and Kulesh felt as if hundreds of needles were piercing all over their bodies. Their bodies had turned into pits of burning fire. They had no eyes to close tightly and bear the pain.

Even the spectators felt that the prisoners looked like the 'Satan' and fell silent in fear. Had Aurangzeb been present to watch the punishment, he would have surely ordered all his sardars to remove their Khilats and wrap them around the prisoners' bodies as a royal honour. He had never in his life sentenced anyone to such excruciatingly painful death.

The fearful spectators were now returning to their tents one by one. The executioners' squad tossed aside the cleaver and the saltwater pots and left. Only Ikhalas stayed behind. He still had to carry out the last part of the punishment. Once the prisoners breathed their last, he was supposed to bring two hefty executioners and chop their heads off. Then he was supposed to hang them on two spearheads and take out a procession in the entire encampment to show them off to the soldiers. Finally, he was going to toss their torsos shackled in chains and the chopped off heads along with the spears, somewhere outside the encampment, to feed the dogs and wolves. But there was still some time before he did that.

The execution of the punishment was so nerve-racking for Ikhalas that for a moment he felt like he himself was also shackled to an invisible pole. He kept staring at both prisoners. Only a few of his own attendants were with him now. An unknown urge drew him towards Raje; he walked steadily and approached Raje. He observed the hideous looking rebel subedar of the Marathas from bottom to the wooden hat on his head. Ikhalas' eyes that usually appeared merciless and haughty, had a strange look in them now. His eyes moved all over Raje's body and fixed on the cowrie necklace on Raje's chest. He muttered in a low voice audible to Raje only, "Give me this, subedar." He clasped the cowrie necklace smeared with blood, salt water and sweat.

"Awww…aww…aww…" Raje started shaking his entire body, resisting vehemently with his last breath. While shaking his body, he kept shaking his head in refusal. The pole started wobbling.

Ikhalas stepped back instantly; he let go off the cowrie necklace. Why did he want the necklace? Ikhalas wanted it as a souvenir of the valiant warrior! He had realized after observing Raje from top to bottom, that the necklace was the only thing that he could take. He understood Raje's hint, "No – don't take it."

He yelled at his attendants standing around him, "Everyone watching the punishment has already left! Why are you still here? Go away." Ikhalas himself mounted his horse and left.

What remained were the cerulean skies, the ancient land of Vadhu budruk, the Indrayani and Bhima rivers flowing hand in hand nearby and the Chhatrapati of the Marathas, Sambhajiraje and Chhandogamatya Kavi Kulesh, left alone on the bank.

Now, Raje's argument with himself stopped and then began the final calm and peaceful dialogue between the individual soul and the almighty universal spirit.

'Who is a king; a king undergoing severe punishment?' Sambhajiraje Bhosale was seeking answers to such questions while reviewing his entire life dispassionately.

"Who gave birth to me? Why can't I remember her face? Aabasaheb too must have remembered Thoralya Aau during his last moments. And…and…even the heartless and greedy Aurangzeb will certainly remember his own mother during his last moments!

Who was Aabasaheb? Who is Aurangzeb? Aabasaheb was the warm breath of the rugged land of Maval! He motivated the weak people to live honourably while performing their duties. Had that not happened, Aurangzeb wouldn't even have had to charge upon the Deccan.

He had spoken so prudently in our last meeting on Panhala – 'Even though the eyelashes are small, they don't easily allow the chaff to enter the eyes. And you are the heir of the kingdom today – the king of tomorrow. Keep in mind that a person's heart dies first, and physical death comes much later! Don't just be the king; be a Mavala soldier first." The memory of Aabasaheb saddened him.

Aurangzeb is so old now yet so cold-hearted; he punished me severely to break my spirit. He wants to convert the entire Hindustan to Islam; he wants to extinguish humanity in one blow. No. There is no comparison between Aabasaheb and Aurangzeb.

Neither me nor any of my Masahebs…none of us could understand Aabasaheb. Only three people could understand him – Thoralya Aausaheb, Samartha and…Aurangzeb!

Who am I to these three? To Thoralya Aau and Samartha, I was just Aabasaheb's shadow; and what am I to Aurangzeb? To him, I am a mere mirror to examine Aabasaheb's character! Could it be possible that the emperor of Hindustan saw Aabasaheb's real character in that mirror?

When Kondaji, Sarlashkar, Mhalojibaba died, why did I feel like I had lost a part of my own body? Why did Nilopant, Khandoji, Ramachandrapant, Harajiraje, Rupaji, Vithoji Chavan, Manaji More and – Kulesh from the faraway kingdom of Kanoj, staunchly support me? Was it only because I was a king? No – no.

It is not easy to sacrifice one's life for a cause. At this moment, I feel proud of all the people who supported me in defending this kingdom of Aabasaheb, raised in the name of God to uphold the rights of destitute people. I don't care about those who betrayed me and turned their backs on me.

The evening descended on Vadhu. But both prisoners had no clue whether it was evening, morning or afternoon? They had realized now that the last stop of their life's journey was coming closer. They were completely exhausted and didn't feel the need to prod their bodies any further.

The twelfth day since the plucking of Raje and Kulesh's eyes and tongues, dawned. Chhandogamtya Kulesh had succumbed to the brutal torture sometime during the night. Before his last breath, he loudly screamed "Aww… aww" to say "my obeisance to you Swami!" That bizarre noise had startled the sentries patrolling the area.

Raje responded to Kulesh with "Aww... aww...". Chhandogamtya could no longer respond to Chhatrapati's call. Raje realized that he was no more.

Kavi Kulesh's soul had merged into the divine spirit.

The twelfth day! What is happening to me today? From my toes to my head, my whole body is heating up.

The father did his best to teach people how to live. The son was going to show people how to die if the situation demanded.

Raje could now sense that the unison of his soul with the Universal spirit was fast approaching.

He remembered Samartha's letter advising him after Aabasaheb's demise, word by word – Remember how your father looked, how determined he was. Remember his valiant feats, the legacy he left behind in the world. Remember the way he walked, the way he talked and how he inspired people. He renounced all pleasures of life and lived his life like a Yogi. Examine his life and learn how to run the kingdom. If you can achieve more than what he achieved in his life, only then will you be considered his true scion. Consider your own life as trivial, and be humble.

Samartha promoted governance through Dharma and Aabasaheb nurtured Dharma even amidst political turmoil! They both had understood each other so well!

"Consider your own life as trivial and be humble! – "Samartha's advice echoed in Raje's ears – it circulated through his entire body.

He visualized the Maratha kingdom as a grand display of the Gondhal dance. Hambirarao, Khandoji, Nilopant, Bahirji, Kondaji Farzand, Mhalojibaba, Krishnaji Kank, Ramchandrapant, Kulesh – many people who had died and who were still alive were playing the Sambal drums and the Tuntune, and chanting with closed eyes, "Ude ga Ambe Ude". Oh, what a grand Gondhal dance of Mother Jagadamba! I have never seen such a dance before! I can vividly see that everyone has their foreheads smeared with the haldi powder! But I can't see Goddess Tulja Bhavani! Where is she? Oh, it is so strange. Is this a dream? I can see Goddess Jagadamba's murti, but her face looks like Thoralya Aau.

Aabasaheb and Samartha's faces are visible in both her eyes. Between the two horizontal stripes of kumkum on Goddess Jagadamba's forehead, I can see Yesubai and Ramraje's Tarau. Ramraje's whole face is visible in the background. But – but how come I don't see myself in this grand murti of Goddess Jagadamba? Why so?

At that moment, Raje saw the flame of his own soul. The limbs of Shambhooraje's sightless body transformed into eyes and started gazing at the flame–

That flame was not of an accused Sambhajiraje, the son of Shivajiraje.

It was not the spirit of the wild, delusional young boy, who couldn't be controlled even by his conscience, who had gone astray and teamed up with Diler and had exclaimed, "I will come back to conquer the Sahyadri!"

It was not the Chhatrapati, Swami or Dhani to anyone; not a husband, a father or a brother to anyone.

That flame had gone beyond the bonds of any relationship, with people or with the land.

"The sovereign king of the Hindus, from the lineage of the Kshatriyas; the possessor of many virtues; the owner of immense wealth; the crowned king and the saviour of the cows and the Brahmins, Shriman Chhatrapati Sambhaji Maharaj!" ... He had already washed off with his own blood the appellations that he had carried for so many years.

He felt that his entire body had transformed into a grand, sky-high, blazing flame.

"How do I look?" The flame questioned itself.

"How? How?" The sound of bells tolling in the temple intensified, the rhythm of the Sambal drums escalated. The sky was overcast by the haldi tossed around –

"How does this flame look?" The flame had merged the five senses within it and had transformed into a blazing torch in the grand Gondhal of Goddess Jagadamba!

As the torch flared up, it discarded the three gunas, Satva, Raja and Tama. The torch couldn't see anything now, except for the holy confluence of the Indrayani and Bhima. On the banks of the same Indrayani, Dnyanoba had given a discourse to the Varkaris in Marathi – *Dnyaneshwari*! Tukoba composed his grand verses. The blood that has drained from my body is now composing a royal saga, a saga of Shambhoo, a 'Shambhoobhushanam!'

The torch magnified and flickered. It was leaving the body of Shambhoo, destroyed by Ikhalas, at the hands of the executioners, at the order of Aurangzeb.

It was now getting immersed in the holy confluence of Indrayani and Bhima! Even while sinking, it flickered – "Jagadamb… Jagadamb…!"

"Churr…" the sizzling sound echoed.

Indrayani and Bhima absorbed the torch of Jagadamba in their bosom, turned their necks around for the first time, gazed at the poles where the execution had taken place, and kept flowing gently.

The only thing they could still see was the blood-soaked, invincible cowrie necklace resting on Shambhooraje's lifeless chest, glowing in the rays of the setting sun!

◆

Acknowledgements

Translating this historical novel penned by my father has been an incredible experience. Publishing this book has been a team effort. I would like to acknowledge the people who selflessly assisted and encouraged me throughout the process.

First and foremost, I would like to express my gratitude to Akhil Mehta of Mehta Publishing House for launching this book.

Heartfelt thanks to Sonia Khare for her professional services in editing this book and my school friend, Sukanya Kulkarni for recommending historical reference books.

I am deeply grateful to my mother, Mrinalini Sawant, for her monumental throughout the course of the translation process. Heartfelt thanks to my brother, Amitabh Sawant and Vahini, Soha Sawant, for their emotional support. And of course, my husband, Parag Dharap's genuine encouragement means a great deal to me.

Lastly, I would like to thank the readers worldwide for reading this book. You motivate us writers to pursue writing.

GLOSSARY

Aafrin – Bravo!

Asababkhana – A storage room for garments and upholstery

Abbajan - Father

Abhishek – a religious ritual where a liquid is poured on the murti of a deity as an offering.

Alahamd Allillah – Hail Allah!

Alampanah – protector of the universe

Aukshan – a process of waving a platter containing lighted lamps around a murti or the head of guests

Baksheesh – a reward, a prize

Batu – a young boy, a person who practices celibacy

Bhutya – a devotee of goddess of Bhavani

Buruj – crenelation, a wall built at the top of a fort or castle with holes or spaces in it thorough which the inside people can shoot the outside enemy

Chitnis - secretary

Daftar Khana – an office

Dakshina – a remuneration given to brahmins for performing religious rituals or offered to a guru as appreciation.

Diwan – a minister

Faujdar – a sheriff

Feel Khana – a place where elephants are kept

Hamam khana – a Mughal structure combined with a dressing room, cold room and hot room (a place for taking a bath)

Hawaladar – a constable -

Homa – a fire ritual performed in Hindu households on special occasions

Hons – gold coins used during 17th century

Inam – a reward, a prize

Inamdar – a person who has received land in grants as a reward for their service to the king

Jahagir – a piece of land rewarded to a person for their service to the king

Jamindar - a person who has received land as a reward for their service to the king

Jiretop – a special kind of head gear that the Maratha Chhatrapati used to wear

Khilat – a ceremonial robe given to a person by the Mughal emperor as a mark of honour

Kimosh – a Mughal headgear

Kulekhtyar – a person of high authority

Machee – flat area or land around a fort

Majumdar – a record keeper

Mallakhamba – a pole on which a person performs various exercises

Mama – mother's brother

Mangalsutra – a special necklace a bkack beads that married Hindu women wear

Mansab – a post of an office in the cavalry

Mansabdar – a person who holds a mansab

Marahabba - Grace of Allah

Mashalla – as Allah willed

Maval – a region of the Maratha empire

Mavala – soldiers of the Maratha empire

Meghadambari – a special canopy

Mirasdar – a person who has inherited land from ancestors

Mojari – a special kind of footwear

Mokasa – land received as reward for military service

Nagar Khana – a place where kettle drums are kept

Nyayadhish – a judge

Paduka – a special kind of wooden footwear

Peshwa – the Prime Minister of the Maratha empire

Pinda daan – a ritual performed to unite a recently departed soul with its ancestors

Sarlashkar – a commander in the army

Sarnoubat – a commander in the army

Shahenshah – the Mugahl emperor

Shalu – a designer sari

Shikke-Katyar – the royal seal and the royal dagger

Shraddha – a ceremony performed to honor the dead ancestors

Subhan Allah – Glory to Allah

Subah – a region

Surnis – an officer who looked after all correspondence and land revenue

Suvasini – a married woman

Swari – a respectful way to address a husband

Thanedar – station house officer

Tuntune – a single string instrument

Vaan – gifts given to married women on special occasions

Vaknis – officer who oversees the private affairs of the king

Vatan – land inherited from ancestors

Vatandar – person who holds a vatan

Vaidya – a physician

Yaa ali meherbaan – By the grace of Allah

Yuvraj – the designated prince, the next heir

Yuvaradnyi – the wife of the Yuvaraj